The Clewiston Te~~st~~

She was consumed by two passions – her husban~~d~~ ____ical research. Or was it first her work and then her husband?

At twenty-eight Anne had made a scientific breakthrough that would be a financial miracle for her employers. But was it safe yet to use the serum on humans? Anne found the answer – after her perfect marriage and her courage had been tested by inward conflict and the politics of power.

The Infinity Box

Suppose you could enter the mind of a beautiful woman; see what she sees, feel what she feels, and control her completely. Suppose you could turn back the hands of your watch, and relive your life. Suppose the stories you wrote kept coming true.

Welcome, Chaos

The more man learns, the more dangerous he becomes. The greater the civilization, the greater the chaos it eventually unleashes ...

If you discovered the secret of immortality, to whom would you give it? To the scientists, the politicians, the military? To the Americans? The Russians? The Chinese?

If you weren't after power or money or fame but really wanted to increase human happiness, what would you do with your secret? Go underground? Run away? Pray that you might outlive civilization and be given the chance to start it all over again?

And if the authorities found you, what would they do?

Here is a chilling, provocative and unforgettable novel about the present and the future of mankind.

Also By Kate Wilhelm

Novels

The Clone (1965) (with Theodore L Thomas)*
The Nevermore Affair (1966)
The Killer Thing (1967) (aka The Killing Thing)
Let the Fire Fall (1969)
The Year of the Cloud (1970) (with Theodore L Thomas)*
Margaret and I (1971)
City of Cain (1974)
The Clewiston Test (1976)
Where Late the Sweet Birds Sang (1976)
Juniper Time (1979)
A Sense of Shadow (1981)
The Winter Beach (1981)
Oh, Susannah! (1982)
Welcome, Chaos (1983)
Huysman's Pets (1985)
Crazy Time (1988)
Moongate (2000)

Collections

The Mile-Long Spaceship (1963)
The Downstairs Room (1968)
Abyss: Two Novellas (1971)
The Infinity Box (1975)
Somerset Dreams: and other fictions (1978)
Better than One (1980) (with Damon Knight)
Listen, Listen (1981)
Children of the Wind (1989)
And the Angels Sing (1992)

*Not available as SF Gateway eBooks

Kate Wilhelm

SF GATEWAY OMNIBUS

THE CLEWISTON TEST
THE INFINITY BOX
WELCOME, CHAOS

GOLLANCZ

LONDON

First published in Great Britain in 2013 by
Gollancz
An imprint of the Orion Publishing Group
Orion House, 5 Upper St Martin's Lane,
London WC2H 9EA

An Hachette UK Company

A CIP catalogue record for this book is available
from the British Library

ISBN 978 0 575 11995 6

1 3 5 7 9 10 8 6 4 2

Typeset by Input Data Services Ltd, Bridgwater, Somerset

Printed and bound by CPI Group (UK) Ltd, Croydon, CR0 4YY

The Orion Publishing Group's policy is to use papers
that are natural, renewable and recyclable products and
made from wood grown in sustainable forests. The logging
and manufacturing processes are expected to conform to
the environmental regulations of the country of origin.

www.orionbooks.co.uk
www.gollancz.co.uk

CONTENTS

ENTER THE SF GATEWAY . . .

Towards the end of 2011, in conjunction with the celebration of fifty years of coherent, continuous science fiction and fantasy publishing, Gollancz launched the SF Gateway.

Over a decade after launching the landmark SF Masterworks series, we realised that the realities of commercial publishing are such that even the Masterworks could only ever scratch the surface of an author's career. Vast troves of classic SF & Fantasy were almost certainly destined never again to see print. Until very recently, this meant that anyone interested in reading any of those books would have been confined to scouring second-hand bookshops. The advent of digital publishing changed that paradigm for ever.

Embracing the future even as we honour the past, Gollancz launched the SF Gateway with a view to utilising the technology that now exists to make available, for the first time, the entire backlists of an incredibly wide range of classic and modern SF and fantasy authors. Our plan, at its simplest, was – and still is! – to use this technology to build on the success of the SF and Fantasy Masterworks series and to go even further.

The SF Gateway was designed to be the new home of classic Science Fiction & Fantasy – the most comprehensive electronic library of classic SFF titles ever assembled. The programme has been extremely well received and we've been very happy with the results. So happy, in fact, that we've decided to complete the circle and return a selection of our titles to print, in these omnibus editions.

We hope you enjoy this selection. And we hope that you'll want to explore more of the classic SF and fantasy we have available. These are wonderful books you're holding in your hand, but you'll find much, much more . . . through the SF Gateway.

www.sfgateway.com

INTRODUCTION

from The Encyclopedia of Science Fiction

Kate Wilhelm (1928–) is the working name of US author Katie Gertrude Meredith Wilhelm Knight, married to Damon Knight until his death in 2002; beyond her writing, she was long influential, as co-director from 1963 with her husband of the Milford Science Fiction Writers' Conference, which he founded in 1958; and in its offshoot, the Clarion Science Fiction Writers' Workshop, with which she was associated from 1968. She edited one of the anthologies of stories from the latter, *Clarion SF* (anth **1977**); and in the nonfiction *Storyteller: Writing Lessons and More from 27 Years of the Clarion Writers' Workshop* (**2005**) she argued in favour of the hothouse intensity of the experience, and the prescriptive simplicities she enforces upon beginning authors of short fiction.

From the first, however, Wilhelm was best known for her own writing, and by the 1980s was a ranking figure in the field, though her first work would eventually be seen as atypical, and by the 1990s she was concentrating on crime fiction, sometimes with fantasy elements incorporated. She started publishing sf in October 1956 with 'The Pint-Sized Genie' for *Fantastic,* and continued for some time with the relatively straightforward GENRE SF stories of the sort to be found in her first book, *The Mile-Long Spaceship* (**1963**); it was not until 1967 that she began to release the atmospheric, character- and landscape-driven mature stories which seem likely to remain her finest work, beginning with 'Baby You Were Great' (**1967**), and which have made her career an object lesson in the costs and benefits of the market: for it has seemed clear from as early as 1970 that Wilhelm is most happy at the commercially unpopular novella length, and only intermittently happy as a novelist. Her strategy for many years was to publish her most powerful work – longer stories and novellas brought together in book form as 'speculative fiction' – while at the same time producing intermittently capable and variously ambitious full-length novels.

Wilhelm's shorter fictions have been assembled in *The Downstairs Room and Other Speculative Fiction* (**1968**), which includes the NEBULA-winning 'The Planners'; *Abyss: Two Novellas* (**1971**); *The Infinity Box: A Collection of Speculative Fiction* (**1975**) (see below), the title story of which – also republished as *The Infinity Box* – is a darkly complex depiction of a Near-Future USA as refracted through the slow destruction of the conscience of a man gifted with a Psi Power; *Somerset Dreams and Other Fictions* (**1978**); *Listen, Listen* (**1981**); *Children of the Wind: Five Novellas* (**1989**), which includes the Nebula-winning *The Girl who Fell into the Sky; State of Grace* (**1991**) and *And the Angels Sing* (**1992**), which includes 'Forever Yours, Anna', also a Nebula-winner; although she has published at least twenty stories since 1992, she has released no further collections. Time and again, in the strongest of these tales, the narrative will begin within the mundane but shaky domesticity of a sometimes glaringly dysfunctional family, and move suddenly to an sf or fantasy perspective from which, chillingly, the fragility of our social worlds can be discerned. At this point, at the point of maximum realization, her best stories generally close in a Slingshot Ending, usually ominous.

With novels this pattern has not been followed; her early novels were in fact modestly traditional in form and subject. After *More Bitter than Death* (**1963**), a mystery, her first sf tale was *The Clone* (**1965**) with Theodore L. Thomas, one of the rare sf books to use clones in the strict biological sense, through the description of a formidable, voracious and ever-growing blob, and a competent demonstration of her workmanlike capacity to cope with genre content. *The Killer Thing* (**1967**), set almost uniquely for Wilhelm on another planet, also shows some facility in telling conventional sf tales. Her first tentative attempts at deepening her range by attempting to investigate character within novel-length plots, *The Nevermore Affair* (**1966**) and *Let the Fire Fall* (**1969**), fail in the first through over-explication, and in the second through an uneasiness of diction, so that the Near-Future religious revival at its heart is depicted with a diffuse sarcastic loquacity. This sense of drift – this sense that her novels continue past the point at which her interest in further unpacking of material has begun to flag – is avoided in some instances, though not in *Margaret and I* (**1971**) or *City of Cain* (**1974**). But *Where Late the Sweet Birds Sang* – which won Hugo and Jupiter Awards for Best Novel – successfully translates her interest in clones (this time in the sf sense of 'people-copies') to a Ruined Earth venue in the Appalachians, where an isolated community of clones has been formed to weather the interregnum until civilization can spread again, but develops in its own, perilously narrow fashion; significantly, the book is made up of three novella-length sequences, each superb.

After *The Clewiston Test* (**1976**), which deals with similar insecurities (see below), *Fault Lines* (**1977**), not sf, uses a displaced and edgy diction to present a woman's broken remembrances, the fault lines of the title representing her own life, her future, her unhappy marriages, the earthquake that traps her, and a powerful sense that civilization itself is cracking at the seams. These two novels stand out from the rest. More normally, even Wilhelm's later tales of the fantastic – like *A Sense of Shadow* (**1981**), *Welcome, Chaos* (**1983**) (but see below) and *Huysman's Pets* (**1986**) – can sometimes dissipate powerful beginnings in generic toings and froings. Her **Leidl and Meiklejohn** sequence of sf/horror/fantasy detective tales – beginning with *The Hamlet Trap* (**1987**) and ending with *A Flush of Shadows: Five Short Novels Featuring Constance Leidl and Charlie Meiklejohn* (**1995**) – seem in their compulsive genre-switching almost to parody this tendency to become digressive after the first 100 pages or so; but *Crazy Time* (**1988**), a late singleton, more successfully embraces the insecurity of the novel form as Wilhelm conceives it, and the ricochets of the plot aptly mirror the discourse it embodies upon the nature of institutionalized definitions of sanity and insanity. Most successfully of all, *Death Qualified: A Mystery of Chaos* (**1991**) – which initiates the mostly non-fantastic **Barbara Holloway** sequence ending with *Cold Case* (**2008**) – combines detection and sf in a long, sustained, morally complex tale whose central story-telling hook – solving a murder in order to free the innocent protagonist of suspicion – leads smoothly into an sf denouement involving chaos theory, new perceptions and a hint of Superman. It is the longest of her novels, yet the one which most resembles her successful short fiction. Kate Wilhelm was inducted into the Science Fiction Hall Of Fame in 2003; in 2009 she won a Solstice Award for her impact on speculative fiction.

The Clewiston Test (**1976**) is the first novel presented here, and is perhaps her most shapely full-length tale. The internal disarray felt by the female protagonist, an experimental biologist researching potentially dangerous drugs, is adroitly balanced against a portrayer of America in general, where moral convictions can dissipate under the stress of time and ambition. As Doctor Clewiston's marriage disintegrates, so do the convictions underpinning her work, for the world of science – in which Wilhelm has always been interested – cannot be divorced from the lives it affects, a truism rarely brought to bear with such sharpness, even though her tongue is kind

The Infinity Box: A Collection of Speculative Fiction (**1975**) is the second title presented here; the title story is a darkly complex depiction of a Near-Future America as refracted through the slow destruction of the conscience of a man gifted with a Psi Power. Among several other strong tales, the most distinguished may be 'April Fools' Day Forever', where a woman told she has lost her children in childbirth discovers that the unfeelingness that surrounds her has a reason: the village where she has moved is inhabited by immortals, who do not welcome intrusions of the human condition.

Welcome Chaos (**1983**), the final tale presented here, builds on the specific intuition – earlier expressed in *Where Late the Sweet Birds Sang* (**1976**) and *Fault Lines* (**1977**) – that the world and individual lives both exhibit essential fractures. Like 'April Fools' Day Forever', the plot subjects an already fragile world – and a disturbed woman in retreat from her experiences of sexual discrimination – to the manipulations of a secret cadre of immortals. Wilhelm never seems angry (not exactly), but her supple, savvy tales tell us, in a very calm voice, that we need to pay attention to the issues she evokes. We need to pay attention if we want to do right by ourselves, and for our children.

For a more detailed version of the above, see Kate Wilhelm's author entry in *The Encyclopedia of Science Fiction:* http://sf-encyclopedia.corn/entry/ wilhelm_kate

Some terms above are capitalised when they would not normally be so rendered; this indicates that the terms represent discrete entries in *The Encyclopedia of Science Fiction.*

THE CLEWISTON TEST

*This is for Ed, Eula,
Ken, Russ, and David
With much love always*

CHAPTER ONE

The watchman made his last round at six in the morning. He left his station at the back entrance of the company and slowly walked the wide corridor to his first checkpoint. The only sound was that of his foam-soled shoes as they made contact with, then pulled away from, the waxed vinyl floor. The sound was a faint, regular squeak. He had been making this round for twenty-nine years, and he no longer heard his own footsteps consciously. He no longer had to consider anything; his feet took him, his hands punched the clocks, and if ever anything was wrong, he trusted his nose to sniff it out, his eyes to focus again to spot the trouble. Like a sleepwalker he made his rounds, not aware of any discomfort, not especially tired, not even bored.

His first check was the animal division. Unhurriedly he selected the right key, opened the door, and entered. The room was dimly lighted in such a way that the walls seemed to recede into distance, and with no personnel cluttering up the aisles between the cages, the room took on proportions that were on an inhuman scale, as if somehow this room had grown larger than the building that housed it.

The squeak, squeak of his shoes as he walked among the cages was part of the routine; no animal stirred. He checked the great double doors at the back wall and then shone his flashlight over the high, useless windows on the same wall. He started up the far side of the room toward the front again, and, midway, he paused.

Something was wrong. Mentally he ticked off the sections of the room: the guinea pigs, all sleeping, curled up, invisible almost. Some of the cats were awake, were always awake no matter when he looked in. The dogs had been quiet, although he knew their sleep was deceptive, that their ears, like antennae, followed his progress through the room. The chimps were quiet, each in its separate cage, sound asleep.

He shook his head and turned back and walked down the aisle, this time looking through each row of cages he passed. Then he saw the chimp, a large one, made gargantuan by the feeble glow of the night lights cast up from below. The chimp was standing up grasping the bars of its cage. It was watching him.

The watchman exhaled softly. He took several steps toward the cage, played his light over the lock to make certain it was secure. 'Ugly bastard,' he muttered. The feeling of wrongness persisted as he made his rounds, and only gradually faded.

The chimp continued to stand holding the bars. Presently his lips stretched back over his teeth and the hair on the back of his neck began to rise. He gripped the bars tighter and tested them, tried to shake them. After a few more minutes, he left the front of the cage, withdrew to the shadows under the shelf, and sat down on his haunches to stare straight ahead unblinkingly. No other chimp stirred.

Miles away, across from Cherokee Park, a smudge of light appeared on the ground floor of one of the solid old three-story buildings. Drapes were opened and a three-sectioned bay window revealed, with greenery in it, and a warm light streaming from it.

The room behind the windows was large, with space enough for the oversized bed, two comfortable chairs covered with rust-colored velvet, a chaise, a card table with two straight chairs. Pushed to the side, leaving four feet between it and the bed, was an exerciser, parallel metal bars with a green rubber walkway. The house had been built when ten-foot ceilings were not an unacceptable expense, and the high ceiling had been followed by the bay window that made up the southern wall. The doors in the north wall were solid maple, the floor dark and light oak parquet.

The door to the bathroom opened and slowly Anne pushed it wider to give clearance for the wheelchair. Clark had been in to open the drapes. She wondered if he waited until he knew she was in the bathroom to do it every morning. He knew it pained her to be seen heaving herself out of the chair clumsily, fearfully; as graceful as a hippopotamus, she thought, eyeing the bed that sometimes seemed an impossible goal. That morning she felt stronger, she decided determinedly, setting the brake; she began to arrange herself for the pull up from the chair, the shift to the side of the bed. She winced when she lowered her body, and sternly she told herself it had not hurt, and it really had not. It was the thought of pain, the memory of pain that she feared. Then she lay back on her pillow and relaxed again. She was trembling slightly.

It was too early to tell if today the sun would shine. Beyond the bay window the world was dull and gray. She reached for a cigarette and drew back. Not before breakfast. Instead, she studied the bay window. She imagined she could hear Clark moving about in the kitchen getting coffee made, doing eggs and toast. He approached his cooking chores exactly the same way he did his lab experiments, with precision, working to an interior timetable that saw everything finished together with little wasted effort. She wished he would hurry with the coffee. Again she concentrated on the window.

It was made up of six small panes of glass in each section, bordered by smaller irregular bits of stained glass, not in a fruit or flower motif, but simply odd geometrical shapes leaded together randomly. The colors in the stained glass were rich, and when it was sunny, vibrant reds, blues, greens, yellows fixed first here, then there, changing, not always subtly, those objects so lighted. The bay window was ten feet wide, with a window seat painted soft white. There were no curtains, only opaque beige drapes that, when closed, followed the curve of the window, leaving the wide ledge clear. There were cushions on it, hot colors – bright yellows, oranges, crimson – and a terrarium, a five-gallon carboy that housed a little world of tropical lush growth – purple leaves, velvety greens, whites. The earth in the terrarium was jet black with flecks of white vermiculite that looked like snow. There were other plants on the window seat, but they had been neglected. Leaves had fallen from the African violets, there were brown-tipped leaves on the philodendron, and the dieffenbachia had grown toward the light without being turned, so that it seemed to have rejected the room, and showed the backs of heavily veined leaves – plant architecture that was stark and functional.

For two weeks Anne had been watching the leaves twist more each day, until now they were vertical, all looking out together. No one else had noticed them. How queer it would be to live in that time frame, she thought, where that gradual movement would seem natural and perhaps even swift. Once, as a child, she had sprouted beans in a glass with a piece of blotter that reached down into an inch of water on the bottom and held the beans against the clear side so their every change could be observed. But the changes had been impossible to watch, only the difference could be measured each day.

On either side of the bed were night tables, one of them a hospital stand with a plastic top and with doors that concealed a washbasin and bedpan. She no longer needed the equipment, but the stand was still there, and a pitcher of water on it sweated and made puddles. On the other table, books were stacked, along with an ashtray, a notebook and pencils, magazines – scientific journals and a chess magazine – and a calendar in an elaborate silver frame, deeply carved, rococo, a gift from Clark's mother. She drew the calendar to her and with heavy, firm strokes made a red cross through the date, Monday, February 6. She had started the crosses in November.

'Hi, honey. Coffee.' Clark came into the room with a tray and put it down on the card table before the bay window. They had been having their meals in the room at that table for the past months. He had poached an egg for her, had made bacon and fried eggs for himself, and a pot of coffee. In the mornings she didn't get up to sit at the table. Later, after Ronnie arrived, she would get up again. Clark was unwilling to go to work unless she was safe in bed. He was afraid she might fall. Because, she thought, she had fallen once, and it hurt like hell, but more than that, it had frightened them both terribly.

'The tibia is delicate,' the doctor had said. 'We don't know just why, but often there is trouble getting it to heal properly. You're not unique there, Annie.'

Clark propped her up with the chair pillow and then went to the window. A fine rain had started. In January there had been three days when the sun shone all day long. In February, still young, still hopeful, there had been one such day. Anne sighed and started to eat her egg.

'Might be late,' Clark said, chewing. 'Board-meeting day again.'

She nodded. After the board meeting the different departments had their own meetings. 'Klugman will manage to remind you gently that I'm still on payroll and my brain belongs to Prather,' she said.

Clark grinned at her and said, 'That's okay as long as the rest belongs to me.' He drank his coffee. He had plenty of time. Clark always woke up before the alarm clock sounded; it was as if the action of setting the clock also set one in his head and it went off first, soundlessly, with greater urgency than the mechanical one. He poured more coffee for both of them.

'And Klugman will also remind me that March 30 is creeping up on us. He'll want reassurance that you'll be there, all well and glowing and smiling.'

'But I won't. I'll scowl and look like a mad genius,' Anne said, scowling to demonstrate.

Clark laughed and sat on the side of the bed with his cup in his hand, and smoothed her hair back with the other hand. 'You don't know how to scowl, and you don't look mad, and you aren't anyone's stereotypical genius. What you look like is a damn sexy blonde in a pretty frilly thing, and if I don't rape you outright in the next few weeks, I'll be a candidate for sainthood.' He spoke lightly, but his hand on her hair became too still and when he moved it away his motion was brusque. He returned to the table and lighted a cigarette.

Anne, looking at him, thought how broad he was. What thick arms and legs, deep chest. She always thought of him as a very large man when he wasn't there, but actually it was simply his massive build; he was not tall. She was an inch taller than he, but still he gave the impression, left the impression, of a very large man. He always liked sex in the morning, while she, as she once had whispered, liked to go to sleep wet between the legs. It was because he woke up so thoroughly so suddenly. He awakened in a room that was lighted, heated, everything ready to be used, needing only for the occupant to step inside to start functioning perfectly. And her room was dark when she awakened; she groped around for hours finding the light switches and the furniture, waiting for the heat to spread throughout. But, even if it never would occur to her to initiate sex in the morning, it didn't take much to make her as horny as he was, and looking at his broad back, she wanted him as much as he wanted and needed her.

'Deena will be here in ten minutes,' Anne said softly.

'Yeah. Be right back.' He moved fast, almost jerkily. His movements were those of a thin nervous person, not one built as solidly as he. In a moment he was back with his corduroy coat and rubbers. No particular dress was required in the lab, although it was understood that all other downstairs departments observed the coat and tie rule. Clark wore faded slacks that were fraying slightly at the bottoms, a short-sleeved shirt with ink stains at the pocket. His pockets all bulged with notes and trivia that he forgot to sort through for weeks at a time, simply transferring the mass from pocket to pocket each morning. His muscular arms were dark with hair; his shirt, unbuttoned at the neck, revealed thick hair on his chest. His belly was hairy, his back; if he let his beard grow, as he had done three years ago, it was bushy and wild-looking. Now and then, when he remembered, he cut his hair, and usually he kept it above his collar, but that Monday morning it was long, and it curled about his ears and over his shirt collar. It was very black and shiny.

A bear person, Anne thought, watching him pat his pockets, feeling for what she didn't know. He carried a pocketknife with a can opener and a corkscrew and a spoon and a screwdriver all built in. He had fingernail clippers, and a comb, cigarettes and a cigarette lighter that didn't work, but that he meant to leave off to be repaired when he thought of it. There were pens and pencils. At least two notebooks, small spiral ones with the pages loose and ragged. There were match folders, receipts, trading stamps, paper money, and coins. Once she had cleaned out his pockets and counted over eight dollars in change. There were keys. The house and car keys, lab keys, keys for his desk and his locker, and her desk and locker at the lab, keys to a car he no longer owned, keys to the suitcases in the apartment basement storage room, and keys to his parents' home. When she had said once how stupid it was to carry every damn key he owned, he had agreed, as he stuffed them back into various pockets.

He left again to get his briefcase, and now he was ready. 'I'll call you,' he said, pulling on his rubbers.

She nodded, smiling. He would call three or four times.

'Anything I can pick up on the way home?'

She shook her head, still smiling. He left their car for the practical nurse, Ronnie, to use to take Anne for therapy, or shopping, or whatever, and it never would occur to him to ask Deena to stop for an errand.

'Look, why don't you have Harry stay for dinner with you. I'll have a bite when I get home.'

Anne laughed. 'You always say the same things, did you know that? And I always answer the same. I'll wait. If Harry can stay, he'll wait too. Ronnie will fix us a casserole or something that will hold for however long it has to.'

He came back to the bed then and leaned over to kiss her chastely on the forehead. 'Right. Look, ask your doctor about that other little matter. Okay?

See you tonight.' The horn sounded outside, and he left, waving at the bedroom door. It seemed very still in the apartment as soon as the hallway door opened and closed.

Anne considered the day stretching out before her. Therapy on Mondays at ten. Back home exhausted, lunch, nap. Fifteen minutes with the exerciser at two. She looked at it distastefully. It was only fifteen feet long, but it seemed to her, standing at one end, looking at the other, an impossible distance. Rest after that. At four or so, Harry, her uncle, would come to keep her company, play chess, talk about his students. He taught eighth-grade classes in social science, history, and, it seemed, any other subject where there was a shortage of teachers. One year, he had a girls' gym class.

Leaning on one elbow, she began to work a thick notebook out from under the stack of magazines. Usually the stack started an inexorable slide to the floor at this point; she pulled the notebook free and leaned back with her eyes closed, the notebook in her hand, and listened to the noise the magazines made as they hit the floor. Her pen was clipped to the cover of the notebook; presently she began to write.

Deena talked disconsolately about the weather as she drove, and Clark listened without paying attention. He didn't understand people who gave thought to the weather. He never knew if it would snow or rain before the day was over. He wore his rubbers when it was raining and didn't think about them if the sun was shining. It wasn't that he was surprised by the elements, it was simply that he accepted whatever there was. His gaze was straight ahead, but instead of the rain-obscured traffic, in his mind there was an image of Anne in the bed, her pale wavy hair tight against her head, no makeup, and to him beautiful. It had surprised him once to overhear two of their friends discussing her coolly. One had said she was not very pretty, and the other had agreed, but both had said something about attractiveness. He hadn't understood that either. To him she was beautiful. Her hair was pale brown; she had been a towhead as a child and over the years it had darkened; her skin was warm and glowing without a blemish, her eyes deep blue. She was tall and slender, with broad shoulders, perhaps too broad for a woman, and lovely, long legs that she sometimes said just went on and on without knowing when to stop. She was comfortable in jeans, slung low on her slender hips, but when she dressed up and used makeup, she was model-lovely, and he knew most men envied him. She was quiet with strangers and few people ever realized how intelligent she was. Growing up in a family of mediocrities, she had learned very young that her own brilliance was the oddity, and she had learned not to voice her quips and judgments, not to demonstrate her intelligence in any way.

'I said, Emory wants to see you before the board meeting,' Deena said.

There was an exasperated tone in her voice, as if she had been talking for a while.

'Sorry.' Clark shook himself and looked about to see if they were there yet. They were a few blocks from the plant. 'I'll do it first thing. Anything in particular on his mind?'

'The usual thing. How long are we going to have to keep cluttering up our department with your monkeys? He knows as well as I, and you, that we'll keep them until Anne says she's through with them, but he has to ask, so his latest dope is the latest dope. You know.'

'Sure.' Deena was a psychologist, in the animal lab. Nearly forty, divorced, with a daughter in her early teens, Deena had to prove her own intelligence over and over, he thought. She had become a militant feminist in the past year and consequently most of the people in both departments tried to avoid her whenever possible, which made her still more aggressive. She had no illusions about whose work the Clewiston-Symons experiments were, really. Her reports to Anne each week were meticulously detailed and at least once a week she dropped by to talk with Anne about the work.

They turned in at the gate and followed a line of cars to the east lot behind the new research annex. Anne was the brains behind the idea; it had been hers from the start, and his name was attached only because she had insisted that without his encouragement, the long talks they had had, his role of devil's advocate, and then his meticulous follow-up work, nothing would be there to be called anything. All true, he reminded himself. Together they made a hell of a team. But it was her baby. And it was going to make her a big name in their field. Maybe even a prize. There was no resentment in the thought. He was very proud of his wife, very proud that she was his wife.

CHAPTER TWO

By nine o'clock the rain was steady and starting to freeze on the colder surfaces – wires, tree limbs, bridges. Bob Klugman stood at the window of Edward Helverson's office and watched the rain. Behind him, Jack Newell was leafing through pages of a report from the production department, muttering now and then, making notes. He had had the report all weekend, but hadn't found time to digest it. He was frightening, Bob Klugman thought, unable to watch the young man skim the meaning from the pages almost as fast as he could turn them. That speed-reading course had done it, of course. He should take a course like that. Wouldn't have to mention it, just do it quietly and let the results speak for themselves. He sipped black coffee and knew he wouldn't take any course ever again. The ship's clock on the wall chimed nine and he checked his watch. Helverson would be there within thirty seconds. Never be more than thirty seconds late, was his motto. Also, make the others be there ten minutes early. Bob sipped again. He hadn't had breakfast and there was a sour taste in his mouth; the coffee was bitter. Had to give up sugar, give up smoking, give up late hours, and what for? he wondered, watching the water run down the window. What the hell for? Sixty. Five more years, then out. And what for? Even knowing his thoughts were merely Monday-morning thoughts, he couldn't shake them. It was that damn Newell flipping pages, trying to prove some damn thing, making a big show out of it. If he was really efficient he would have done the homework at home, or in his office, not here.

The door opened and Edward Helverson entered. He was six feet tall, with prematurely silvered hair, and he looked like presidential material. He had the air of confidence, the openness, the friendliness mixed with reserve, the good health and lean, lithe figure that could endure the stress of being president of a company, or vice president of a corporation, with his eye on the chairman's seat in another ten years. At forty-four he was at the age to start the ascent to the very top.

Jack Newell stood aside while Helverson took Bob Klugman's plump hand and shook it warmly. Jack Newell was dark and slim, and unobtrusive, as an assistant should be. He and Helverson didn't shake hands. When Helverson turned to him, he nodded almost imperceptibly and Bob Klugman felt uncomfortable, aware a message had been passed.

'Bob, how's it going? What's new?'

Bob shrugged, never quite certain how to answer a question like that. Did he really want to know what was going on in R&D, or was he making conversation, warming up to the real subject that had summoned Bob to this pre-board meeting?

'Sit down, Bob. More coffee? Is it hot?' Helverson poured himself a cup of the steaming coffee and sat down with it, not going behind his large, empty desk, but choosing instead one of a pair of leather chairs with a table between them. Bob sat in the other chair, uncomfortable, wanting a cigarette. There was an ashtray on the table, but it was polished onyx and looked as if it never had been used.

'We've had a break, Bob,' Helverson said. 'A piece of incredible luck. How soon can you get things lined up for the pregnancy tests and the teratology studies on Clewiston's serum?'

Bob blinked rapidly. 'The end of March we're holding a meeting, have our plans ready to go as soon as the IND is approved.'

'We're getting the IND back this week, Bob,' Helverson said, and leaned back, smiling.

'This week?' Bob looked from him to Jack Newell in confusion.

'We'll be going ahead as soon as you can get the stuff ready. This afternoon I'm meeting with Dr. Grove to arrange subjects for the pregnancy studies. He'll have his data ready in a day or two and we'll have a full committee meeting then.'

'But our schedule ... There are problems with computer time. Collecting blood samples, making the analyses ...'

Helverson stood up and held out his hand. The interview was over. 'I know you can handle that end of it, Bob. First priority, all that. Arrange for overtime, whatever you need. This comes first. As it should,' he said, frowning slightly now. 'Think of the suffering, Bob, all that needless suffering. My God, if we can knock a week off for some poor soul out there, make life worth living again a day sooner, isn't it worth the extra effort it might take here? We can do it, Bob. At the meeting this morning I'm going to announce that we can go ahead by the fifteenth. And we can do it, Bob! We can!'

Bob Klugman was being propelled to the door. Momentarily, he resisted the gentle pressure. 'But Anne Clewiston, Mrs. Symons, she's not back yet.'

'And I'm counting on you to keep her informed every step of the way. My God, when I think of that brilliant young woman, a genius, Bob. One of God's gifted ones. I stand in awe of her ability, Bob! She's to be on the committee, just as planned from the beginning, and as soon as her recovery permits, she'll be there in person.'

Bob Klugman stood outside the door and blinked without understanding. He thought of the bottle in his desk, and he shuddered and started to walk. Nine o'clock and he was thinking of the bottle. Annie would kill him, he thought, work her way through him right up to Helverson and kill him, too. He felt sorry for Clark, who would have to tell her, and again the image of the bottle came to mind, and this time he hurried a bit.

Clark stood in the open doorway of Emory Durand's office and looked at the scene beyond while Emory talked of the lack of consideration everyone showed his department.

The animal laboratory was the biggest single room in the Prather Pharmaceuticals complex. Bigger even than the production departments on the second and third floors. This end of the lab was devoted to small animals, mice, guinea pigs, rats, even some snakes in glass cages. Beyond, out of sight from where Clark stood, were cat and dog cages. He could hear the excited yapping of the dogs as they were being fed, and the occasional howl of a cat. Farther still were the primates, spider monkeys, gibbons, and the chimps that he and Anne had used. At that time of day the lab was abuzz with activity as the animals were fed, specimens of stools and urine collected, blood taken for testing; animals were being taken from the night cages to various communal compounds for daytime study. White-coated figures moved among the animals, pushing carts of food, testing equipment, transport cages. The lab was spotless, and there was practically no odor.

Emory Durand was the supervisor of this department. He was a veterinarian, and it was rumored that he had taken this job only to escape having to sacrifice animals personally. He never attended the sacrificial slaughter or participated in autopsies. The lab people all called him Noah behind his back. The spotlessness of the lab was reflected in his office and his person. His shoes were polished, white. His trousers were creased, white. His lab coat never showed a smudge. They said Noah dusted his chair every time he used it. His hair was sandy, thin, kept short, and his skin was pale and looked unhealthy, although he never missed a day or complained of anything. He was a vegetarian with no vices. Altogether a despicable character whom everyone should automatically hate, Clark thought. But no one hated Emory Durand. He was one of the most popular men in the downstairs section. His own people feared and respected him, and brought him their troubles if necessary, and outside his department he was admired and liked. Anne had said once that it was because he treated people with the same grave courtesy and respect that he showed his animals. Clark had put it more bluntly. You could trust him. That summed up Emory Durand for him.

Emory's voice rose slightly and he knew Emory was trying to force him to pay attention, to be concerned. He listened.

'I fully expect a herd of elephants to show up any day. "Take care of them," someone will say and disappear. And I ask you, Clark, how many animals do they really think we can fit into a finite space? How many?'

Noah's Ark was packed, Clark admitted, silently. No one dared encourage him because they all felt some degree of guilt. Emory Durand was probably the most overworked person in the plant. 'Is the annex causing the trouble now?' he asked.

'The annex. Your goddamn monkeys. At least the control chimps. Can't we get rid of them?'

Clark shook his head. A white-coated girl passed, pushing a cart loaded with a stack of stainless-steel bowls, a scale, a bucket of malodorous mush that looked like shit. Feeding time for the guinea pigs. Clark wrinkled his nose and stepped backward into the office, closing the door.

'Soy beans and sawdust,' Emory said in disgust. The annex people were working on soy-protein products and their offerings seemed more noisome each day. Also, the guinea pigs were wasting away and showing a tendency to die in convulsions.

'Give us a couple more months,' Clark said, returning to the subject of the chimps. 'Probably three at the most. The IND should be in by then and we'll know if they've approved it.'

Emory sighed. 'So far, Henry Barrington's the only one to say heave them out. And he has a dozen white mice at stake. A lousy dozen white mice. Okay, Clark. I had to ask. So I'll go to the board and demand more money, an annex of my own, more assistants, more equipment ...' His voice was toneless now with resignation. 'And they'll pat me on the head and say what a fine job ...'

A hoarse scream followed immediately by the sound of breaking glass penetrated the office. Clark yanked the door open and moved out of the way as Emory dashed past him. They ran to the other end of the room.

One of the lab assistants was sitting on the floor, holding his arm close to his chest. The redness of blood against his white lab coat was shocking. A low moan started, rose, fell and repeated, over and over. A longhaired girl was standing rigidly, staring down the aisle of cages. She was pale, ready to go into hysterics. Clark grabbed her arm and shook her. 'What happened?'

Deena appeared, buttoning her lab coat. Emory was kneeling at the side of the injured man now, and others were gathering, getting in the way, asking questions. Above it all the animals were screeching, chattering, howling in excitement. Clark shook the rigid girl again. 'What happened?'

'The monkey bit him! It tried to kill him! I saw it! It tried to kill him!'

'Snap out of it!' Clark said, holding her arm too hard, ready to shake her again. 'Where is it now?'

She nodded toward the aisle and he released her. She staggered backward away from him, turned and ran.

Clark glanced toward the injured man. He seemed to be in shock. The moaning continued. Emory was telling someone to get a doctor, a stretcher, call an ambulance. Clark turned toward the aisle. Deena's voice sounded close by, calm, low, soothing.

'Duckmore, come here. Come on.' She came from between two cages, looking between the two opposite her. 'Come on, Duckmore.'

A large male chimp appeared and held out his hand. Deena took it and started to walk back toward the chimp cage with him, speaking in a low voice that somehow seemed to carry over the tumult of the lab. Clark watched while she put the chimp back inside the cage and locked the door. The chimp settled on his haunches and peered out calmly at the cluster of people around the man he had tried to kill.

Deena went to Emory then and knelt. 'Can he talk?'

Emory shook his head. He was holding the man's arm to his chest and was supporting his weight now. The assistant's eyes were open, but blind with shock. Even his lips were white.

Deena stood up. 'Did anyone see it? What happened?'

The girl who had been pushing the tray of guinea-pig food said, 'The chimp's been trying to get him for a week. He told me the chimp hated him. For nothing. No reason at all. He was good to the animals.'

Presently the doctor arrived and the first-aid crew, and the bystanders left. Clark stood by Deena's office as order gradually returned to the animal laboratory.

'Can you tell anything about Duckmore?' Clark asked, when Deena appeared.

'He's as normal as ever, as far as I can tell,' she said.

'Did the kid tease him? Hurt him over a period of time?'

She shook her head. 'You know we wouldn't tolerate anything like that. No, Pat was good with them. He likes animals. They respond.'

'Yeah,' Clark said moodily.

'Don't get in a panic,' Deena said. 'We'll observe Duckmore for a while, run some tests. Maybe he saw Pat fondle one of the young chimps, became jealous. God knows what's going on in their heads.'

'Yeah,' Clark said again. 'Look, can you get some blood tests right away? An EEG? Whatever else you can think of?'

'It's already started,' she said crisply. 'I'll send results over as soon as they start coming in.'

Scowling at the floor, Clark returned to his own office. The animal lab was the entire west portion of the sprawling complex. Separated from it by a wide corridor were the research laboratories: Petro-Chemicals, Dyes, Food Additives, Industrial Compounds, and Pharmaceuticals. The pharmaceutical division was the largest, the original lab space, with wide, high windows and ancient steel lockers, an uneven floor that tended to collect rollable objects in one spot under the water fountain. In Pharmaceuticals the walls had been painted yellow and green back in year one, and the color scheme never had been changed. This lab seemed abnormally quiet after the animal division. A dozen people were working at various pieces of equipment. The others were in their offices.

It was here that old man Prather had mixed up his first liniments, his first aspirins and cough syrups. He had compounded iron tablets as big as quarters and then worked to make them small enough for a gentlewoman to swallow. If ghosts walked, then Prather's must have wandered that lab, unchanged except for modern stainless-steel machines that surely would have puzzled him, and computer terminals that would have puzzled him even more. What would he make of cortisone doses so small that they had to be mixed with starch, just to make them visible? Of timed-release capsules that automatically regulated the doses of whatever was needed? Of radioactive materials in pretty blue and pink capsules that couldn't be handled by the people who filled them, but had to be manipulated through lead doors using waldoes?

Clark shook his head, bringing his thoughts back to now, back to the chimp that had gone berserk. He stared at the wall beyond his desk, almost close enough to reach from where he sat and thought. Duckmore had gone berserk, but maybe the assistant had teased him. Maybe he had a sadistic streak that he had managed to hide but indulged privately with the animals. Maybe inadvertently he had issued a challenge to the chimp. Maybe he had twisted Duckmore's arm unnecessarily in hurrying him from his cage to the compound. Maybe ... Maybe the *pa* factor they had given Duckmore almost a year ago had personality-altering characteristics that were just beginning to show up. Clark rubbed his eyes, tearing from staring so intently at the blank green wall. Maybe.

CHAPTER THREE

Bob Klugman looked at Clark obliquely and shook his head. 'You can't be serious,' he said, for the third time. 'We can't back up six months.'

'We can't go ahead,' Clark said impatiently. 'We can't start human testing in two weeks.'

'Deena, how's the monkey now?' Bob asked, turning from Clark. He felt a rumble in his stomach and knew that soon it would be burning and gas would be building, pressing against his heart, making him wheeze.

'It's a chimp, as you know,' Deena said, looking just above his shoulder as she spoke to him. She had smelled liquor on entering the office; her mouth was tight and hard, her gaze avoided his deliberately. 'Duckmore appears normal enough. We don't have any test results yet.'

'Well, give it your personal attention. Divert whatever else you can and follow it through.' Klugman looked at his watch; the board meeting had been in session for half an hour, too late to contact Helverson, to alert him to the possibility of trouble. He turned to Emory Durand. 'How are the other animals in that group? Any more trouble?'

Emory shook his head. 'I agree with Clark, however. It would be a mistake to ignore this incident. I'll talk with Pat as soon as he is out of sedation and find out what the hell happened, but even that won't be enough. We need weeks of close observation, followed by autopsy, brain examination, cellular-tissue study, the whole works. It's a setback, Bob. You have to face that and explain to Helverson what it means.'

'But chances are that it has nothing to do with the stuff. Isn't that right?'

'Hell, Bob, you know the scene. You were on this side of the desk for twenty years, damn it! Helverson's got a sudden itch to move, let him sweat out whatever's bugging him. You know and I know the FDA won't permit us to go ahead with this kind of situation hanging. We have to investigate it, and that means a setback. Even if nothing comes of the investigation.' Emory spoke calmly, but his words were too separate, too distinctly enunciated; they belied the calm.

For a moment Bob Klugman stared at Emory, then his gaze dropped and he watched his pudgy fingers trace circles on his desk top. 'Opinions,' he said. 'Do you believe this incident has anything to do with the *pa* factor? Emory?'

'I don't think so,' Emory said, after a pause. 'But I don't hold that as a belief. I would be unwilling to go ahead on that basis.'

'Deena?'

'No. It's been too long. The *poena albumin* dropped back down to normal in eight hours, and it's remained normal since. There has been no physiological change in the intervening months.' She didn't look at him; her voice was crisp and professional and very remote.

'Clark?'

'I don't know. My bias urges me to say no emphatically, but I don't know.'

Bob studied him. 'I wonder what Anne would say.' It wasn't a question. No one answered. 'How is Anne?'

'She's making fine progress.'

'You'll report this to her?'

Clark shook his head. 'Not just yet. It would upset her and we don't have enough facts yet. Let me wait for the lab reports on Duckmore. Let's hear what the kid has to say about the attack. Maybe he really did do something to stir up the chimp, maybe he'll admit to something.' Deena shook her head, and Emory frowned. Neither of them believed the lab assistant had been to blame. Clark turned back to Bob Klugman. 'I think we should wait for Gus to get back before we do anything. He's been following this from the start. Let's hear what he has to say about it. Besides, Emory is right. The IND won't be approved until we clear up any question about this incident.'

'The IND has already been approved,' Bob Klugman said then. 'Helverson wouldn't have told me to go ahead if he didn't know it had already been approved. He's seeing Grove today, and Wednesday we'll have a full committee meeting to finalize the testing procedures.'

There was silence in the office. Clark looked at the window streaming water under the steady rain. In the country the rain was still freezing, but in the city it was only rain. It coated the window, isolated them even more from the real world, changed the real world beyond the windows into a surreal, plastic place with shifting lines and unsteady surfaces. They were waiting for him to say something, he realized. On Anne's behalf he should protest, or comment, or belch, or do something. He continued to watch the water on the window. She would be wild with joy over the approval of the FDA of the investigational drug application, and furious that they were going ahead without her. She was to be one of the principals on the committee to oversee the human experiments; she had been looking forward to that for years. Sometimes he knew she was more knowledgeable about the procedure than he; she could see further ahead than he ever could. She had anticipated some of the problems of human testing along with the original conception of the *pa* factor, while he had been plotting their course on a day-to-day basis.

Deena spoke up suddenly, and she didn't attempt to hide the anger in her voice. 'Anne has been planning this part of the experiment for months, and everyone knows it. She's been working on the plans at home, flat on her back. You can't simple take this away from her just because Helverson is antsy.'

It wasn't fair, Bob Klugman thought, for them to treat him like this. He was their superior. They should treat him with the same deference he had to show his superiors. He stood up. 'We'll go ahead and plan for the tests to begin,' he said, trying to force the same firm decision into his voice that Helverson had used with him. 'Meanwhile, you'll be getting the lab reports on the monkey. We'll see if the IND comes through. Deena, you and Clark both know Anne's ideas for the human tests. You can represent her.' They all stood up and now Deena's gaze did stop on him; he turned away from it. As soon as they were gone, he thought, he'd call Gus, tell him they had an emergency, get him back on the job. It wasn't fair for him to have to decide this alone. Gus knew more about what was going on in the lab than he did. It really was Gus Weinbacher's job to make these decisions, not his.

Sometimes Bob Klugman almost recognized the truth that he didn't like being vice president in charge of research and development. He had wanted to be an organic chemist, had been a damn good chemist, had won top honors in his class, graduated *summa cum laude*. When this promotion had come, he and his wife had celebrated joyously. He was getting the recognition he deserved, he had thought then, and had made trips to several different libraries just to see his name in *Who's Who* and the regional biographies. And then what happened? he sometimes wondered, usually after his third drink and before his fifth. Something had happened, and he couldn't understand what it was. All the arguments he had to settle were petty; the scientists he had to handle were childish, demanding, selfish, each one convinced his work was of top importance, with no regard for anyone else's work. And they demanded Bob Klugman agree with them, each in turn. He didn't know how to stall them, how to soothe them when they were excited, how to encourage them when they were down, and over the years he had lost touch with the specific details of the various departments, so that he could hardly even follow their arguments now. Sometimes he dreamed of the time when he had had his own little office that no one could enter, when he would be engrossed in his own problems for weeks, months, even years at a time, bothering no one, demanding nothing except time to work, space to work in. Those were the days, he thought.

He had been easy to get along with, he knew. He hadn't made impossible demands on his superiors, had respected them, and they in turn respected him. His fellow workers had respected him then. And everything changed. The new breed, he thought bitterly, had only scorn for those who had been around a few years. They thought he was getting old, that he could be treated with contempt because he was getting old and was tired. Because he was ill sometimes. Even his wife was contemptuous of his illness, forcing him into one doctor's hands after another. She would be satisfied only when he could do nothing but sit and stare at a wall. Then she would be quiet. *Drinking won't help!* she'd scream at him. *If you're sick, see a doctor. If you're not sick, stop moaning and acting sick!* Just because there were still illnesses they couldn't diagnose, just because none of them could find his trouble, cure it, she pretended he didn't have a medical problem. *The only problem you have is the bottle!*

He shut his eyes. Not true. He was sick, and nothing helped. Nothing. His back ached and his head ached and there was the threat of a heart attack any time, and his stomach was bad, and he couldn't sleep ... He felt tears forming and he opened his desk drawer and took out the bottle and poured half a glass of Scotch. Now this, when Gus was gone, and no one was around to take care of it. And they treated him like dirt, less than dirt. He could feel his stomach churning and knew he was going to have another attack.

He lifted his phone and told his secretary to get Gus for him, and when she reported no one answered his room in the hotel on Antigua, he told her to keep trying until she did get him, to have him paged, to leave an urgent message with the desk. But get him.

Anne leaned back on the chaise and waited for Ronnie to bring lunch. She pulled the afghan higher and closed her eyes, going over the doctor's words once more. 'You have to get more exercise, young lady. You're getting lazy. We'll measure you for crutches today, and start you walking next week. How about that?'

And her reaction had been both excitement and reluctance. Crutches were ugly, she thought, and a person on crutches was ugly, his body hunched up grotesquely, dangling from the armpits while his legs flailed about in unco-ordination. Even as this thought had come to mind, over it she had recalled, from one of the early sessions with the therapist, his proposed treatments. After four to six weeks of the crutches, he had said, you'll be so sick and tired of them you'll heave them out and start walking again on your own. Six weeks! Possibly four weeks! She didn't believe the shorter time; she knew her own strength and didn't believe she could recover enough muscle tone in four weeks to permit her to walk unaided. But six weeks was nothing! Not after the months in bed, in the hated wheelchair. Six weeks!

The therapist had been full of surprises that morning. 'Can you swim?' he had asked. 'No matter. You'll learn if you can't.'

'I swim rather well.'

'I've scheduled you for four days a week at the health spa off Cherokee Drive. That's just a few blocks from where you live, isn't it?'

She stared at him. 'I don't understand.'

'You're getting flabby. Look at your arms. Flab. You'll start with ten minutes, and work up to forty-five to an hour in no time. It's a heated pool.'

She had stared, and he had laughed at her. Dr. Federicks was a comfortable man, easy to talk to, easy to confide in. Large, heavy-set, a tease in a pleasant way, like a grandfather, someone else's grandfather.

'Look, Anne, you're not a chronic invalid. You're making a very good recovery now and the rest will follow with an inevitable, even dull, routine. Just don't get pregnant for a while.'

'You mean ...?'

'Anne, you can do anything now. Have fun. I told you that weeks ago.'

'I didn't understand.'

'Oh, Lord! Go home and screw! Now you understand?' And he had laughed uproariously until she had been forced to laugh also.

Clark called before Ronnie appeared with the lunch tray. 'Tired?' he asked. His voice on the phone was mysterious, low, more seductive than in person; sometimes she felt that she was discussing intimate details of her life with a stranger when she talked by phone to her husband.

'Tired,' she admitted. 'But there's good news. I got measured for crutches. I'll get them next week.'

'Hey! I'll take you walking in the park!' They talked about crutches for a minute or so, and then, curiously reluctant to tell him the rest of her news, she said instead, 'Anything new down there?'

At once his voice changed. He knew she was holding back something, she thought, and closed her eyes hard, barely listening to his answer. And now it would sound silly, evasive, to say, oh, by the way, I'm going swimming tomorrow and the doctor said screw. She relaxed her grip on the phone and tried to find her place in his rambling talk. Something about a department meeting, he might not be able to call back later. She nodded. He knew.

Then they said goodbye and miserably she hung up and shivered under the afghan. Why hadn't she told him?

To punish him, she realized. To punish him for saying he'd take her for a walk. Show off his crippled wife in the park, hobbling along on crutches, feeling the stares follow her progress.

Suddenly she saw again the car out of control racing toward them on a rain-slicked street, on a day just like this one. Clark had been driving. Clark always drove. Having her drive made him feel superfluous. He swerved and they skidded and the oncoming car smashed into them, on her side. She remembered it remotely, as if it were a scene from a movie only partially recalled. There was no emotional overtone to her memory. Just the facts, she thought. Just the facts. She could remember the sounds of the crash clearer than any other details. The horrifying crash of metal on metal, of scream-ing wheels, of a human scream that she still didn't identify as hers. For a long time she had been pinned, and there were sounds connected with that. Someone sobbing, screaming with pain, and then again metal on metal as they tore the car apart to free her. Later she learned she had a crushed pelvis, and a compound fracture of the right tibia. Clark had been shaken up; he had suffered mild bruises, and contusions. The other driver, whose fault it all was, was uninjured.

She thought of Mr. Leonard Chelsea, seventy, drunk, careening about on slippery streets in his Cadillac, and she could almost sympathize with him. His lawyers were fighting hard to keep the old man out of jail. This was not the first accident he had caused.

Ronnie entered with the lunch tray and started to put it on the lap board. 'Bet he was happy about the swimming, wasn't he?' she said. Ronnie was thirty-eight; she had been married three times and was at present living with a man who already had a wife. She was cheerful and philosophical about it, and not a little obscene sometimes. 'Keep on trying to put a square peg in a round hole,' she would say with a wink, when talking about her marital adventures. 'No way it's going to fit.'

'I didn't tell him yet,' Anne said. Ronnie looked at her in surprise. 'I ... I thought I'd surprise him tonight.'

That day Anne worked out for twenty-five minutes on the exerciser. At the start of the session she cursed fluently, and toward the end, during the last ten minutes, she simply grunted, but she didn't stop until the alarm clock sounded. Flabby. He'd said she was getting flabby. Ronnie helped her back to the wheelchair and left her to draw the bath. Part of the routine – work, then bathe and soak in a hot tub for twenty minutes. And in six weeks, walk again.

Harry arrived before she was finished, and Ronnie ushered him to the living room to wait. When Anne was settled once more on the chaise, flushed from the hot water, fragrant from the back rub Ronnie had given her, Harry was finally admitted to the bedroom.

He was fifty-seven, her mother's only brother, and Anne never had known him, not really, until the accident, when he began visits that had now become as regular as everything else in her routine. He was tall, like all her maternal relatives, and like them, when he started to gain weight, it had all gone into his torso, leaving his arms and legs as thin as a boy's. His body was heavy, nearly barrel-shaped; his clothes fit poorly because he bought ready-mades that were not designed for anyone with his particular weight distribution. His trousers were too tight at the waist and through his hips, and hung too loosely on his thighs that, Anne imagined, were like broomsticks. She brooded about his figure, seeing in him and in her mother, who was shaped like him, a forecast of what she could become if she didn't exercise and stay fit and watch her diet.

Harry came in carrying his shoes and socks. 'Thought I'd better put them on the radiator,' he said apologetically. 'They're soaked.'

'You'd better get some of Clark's socks out,' Anne said, eyeing his long, narrow, elegant feet. Clark's feet were very short and broad, with high insteps; Harry would have to fold his feet in the middle to get them into Clark's slippers. But the socks were stretchable. 'The third drawer,' she said, pointing to the chest of drawers.

'You're looking pretty and fit,' he said, rummaging in the drawer, finally pulling out a pair of black socks. 'These?'

'Anything. What's new?'

'Nothing. Same old drudgery day after day, year in year out. Today I had a lively discussion with a twelve-year-old girl, in Civics.' He looked up at Anne and grinned. 'Shocked her into silence.'

'Did you give her a detailed account of the deflowering rites of some esoteric tribe that no one on earth except you has ever heard of?'

Ronnie came in with a tray loaded with coffee, cups, crackers, cheese, cookies. 'Hi, Harry! Hardly had a second to greet you before. Good Lord, you were one wet man! Better now? Dry? Warm?'

'Fine, Ronnie, thanks.' He turned back to Anne and said, 'Actually I told the child that there is no such thing as love. It's a habit, that's all. We try to glorify what is essentially a grotesque act by giving it a sublime name.'

Ronnie was arranging the tray, and now stood up, looking it over. She nodded to Harry. 'How old's the kid?'

'About twelve. They're all twelve or thirteen in that class.'

'Time she learned a thing or two. She won't buy it, though. Not at twelve. Too romantic.' She strode toward the door. 'Got things to do in the kitchen. You want anything, you just yell. Hear?'

'Right, Ronnie,' Harry said. He poured coffee for Anne and handed it to her. 'What a marvelous girl she is! She's smart, practical, capable, good-looking, not an illusion in her body, no hang-ups. How do you suppose that all happened?'

Anne sipped her coffee and put it down on the arm of the chaise. She felt pleasantly tired now, relaxed and cheerful. It was curious about Harry, she thought, how she had avoided him for years, until now. She had always assumed he was the male counterpart of her mother, but aside from appearances, they were as unlike as it was possible for two people to be. 'What *did* you tell that poor kid in your class?' she asked lazily.

'Well, look. You hate people from the time you're born. The doctor who gives you painful shots. Your mother for not feeding you when you're hungry, or not changing you when you're wet. Your father for being too rough, or not being there when you want him. Your brothers and sisters for teasing, for hurting, for being selfish. Then you get beyond the family circle and the hatred goes with you. Everywhere we turn there's someone new to hate for a real cause. Petty things to the big things that never stop hurting. We're all full of hate. So it's reasonable to assume because of our symmetrical selves, because of our love of balance, our trust in opposites of equal strength – black and white, hot and cold, high and low, and so on – we naturally assume there's a balancing emotion to offset the hatred. There really isn't, any more than there's an organ to balance the heart, or the liver. The symmetry is more apparent than real. But, in our need for balance and for equal opposites, and just to rationalize our ability to hate so fiercely, we invent love. At first, with the small child, it's a shield to protect him from the wrath of his parents. If he plays this role, they hurt him less often. Later, when the biological itch starts between the legs, again he rationalizes it as love. He knows the bull feels no love for the cow he mounts; the stallion feels no love for the mare; the dog humps and runs, and so on. But man is above nature, right? He has an immortal soul, and free will, and reason. If he mounts a female, it must be something more than a biological itch. *Violà!* Love!'

Anne laughed and caught her cup before it spilled over. 'You maniac! You'll get yourself fired!'

'Oh, I didn't go into all that. I merely said it was a habit. A man and woman live together and each fills a need for the other, and so long as that need is being filled, the habit is maintained. If the need no longer exists, this particular habit also dies.' He put cheese on two crackers and passed one to Anne, kept the other and said between bites, 'Any arguments with that?'

'Plenty. You're being cynical and cute because it's been raining for years and years, and you're bored with Civics classes. Maybe you're coming down with something. Clark and I love each other and have for seven years, and I don't see an end in sight yet. And it isn't just a biological itch, or filling some unspecified need that anyone else could fill.'

Harry nodded. 'I would expect anyone to defend, even to the death, the rationalization that permits him to continue an absurd activity that gives him pleasure, and relieves his anxiety.'

'Didn't you love Aunt Marya?'

'I thought I did, but now I wonder. I don't know any longer.'

With these words the air changed and the conversation was no longer light and amusing. Anne shivered and glanced at the window past the little-world terrarium. The rain was turning to sleet again. It was hitting everything with force that could be heard within the house.

'I don't know how much more of this weather I can take,' she said in a subdued voice. 'God, how I long for sunshine and heat. As soon as I'm well again, we're going on a vacation. To the Bahamas maybe.'

'When does the next stage of your work start?'

'Months and months from now. The government never hurries with the IND. Everything has to be checked and double-checked, and checked against the literature to make certain no one has done it already, with negative results. Things like that take time.'

'And someday, when the time's right, you're going to explain to me what it is you've done, remember?'

Anne looked at him steadily and said, 'Mother has a high pain threshold, did you know that? So does Hal, and Tres, too, although probably not quite as high as theirs. Wallace, however, has a very low threshold, and mine is probably even lower. When we were all kids they used to call Wallace baby a lot because he cried when he got hurt, the same kinds of hurts that Hal simply shrugged off without noticing. But things hurt me, too, more than they did Tres. I thought Hal and Tres were brave, Wallace and I were cowards. Mother certainly seemed to think we were cowardly. And Dad. But it wasn't that at all. We actually suffered more from pain than they did. Our threshold was lower. How do you think you'd rate yours?'

'Very low,' Harry said at once. 'I've marveled at your bravery with those multiple injuries, wondering if I'd be able to endure it. I don't think so.'

Anne made a waving-away gesture and said, 'I puzzled about this when I was very young, and then forgot it until I was a senior in high school. An article in the newspaper brought it all back, and seemed to give me an insight that I've been working on ever since. Eight years,' she said. 'Eight, long, fucking, hard years.'

'The article?'

'It was a human-interest story about a four-year-old child who was dying. One of those heart-wrenching sob stories. It seems that some people have such a high pain threshold they never feel any painful stimulus at all. They simply can't feel pain. And usually they don't survive childhood. You know, the pain of headache that goes with fever. The pain of a broken limb that sends a child screaming for help. The pain of a strep throat or an earache. Acute appendicitis. They don't feel any of those things, and often they die of undiagnosed disease before their parents realize how ill they really are. Or they die from accidental injuries that they never mention. And so on. And I thought to myself, they have something in them that's different from other people. Something that everyone has to a certain extent, but they have in excess. And I started looking for it in a high-school chemistry lab.'

She stopped speaking and stared at her coffee, and then quickly drank it down and held out the cup to her uncle.

'You found it then?' he asked, watching her intently, a little awed perhaps, she thought.

She nodded. 'I found it. And it works, without side effects. It will be cheap and safe. And no one ever need suffer again from pain. Never again.'

CHAPTER FOUR

'He won't be able to go through with it,' Deena said. 'Helverson can't be on that committee, and neither can Bob Klugman. Bad form. Against company policy. We'll outnumber them, won't we?'

Benny Bobson glanced at Clark and shrugged. Benny was a veterinarian, twenty-seven. He looked like a skinny kid, one of those late-maturing people who would look like an adolescent at forty. His head was oversized for his frail body, and he wore his hair fashionably long and full, adding to the bulk of his skull. He looked like a caricature scientist with his great head and stick figure. His hands were never still except when he was with his animals, and then he relaxed and all the superficialities vanished, leaving a competent, very intelligent doctor. In Deena's office he fidgeted and shifted his weight from foot to foot, unable to sit still long enough to take the chair she had offered him.

'We know Gus won't allow any short cuts,' Clark said. 'He'll carry the weight. Not us.'

'Do you know Grove?' Deena asked.

'I've met him, that's all. When Helverson first enlisted his help in setting up the pregnancy tests, I was called to his office; Anne, too; and we met long enough to shake hands and listen to him say what a marvelous thing it was we were doing. He's a politician first, doctor second.' He spoke bitterly.

Grove was the director of the State Board of Health. He had volunteered women in state prison hospitals.

Deena's nose wrinkled with distaste. 'So, there'll be Gus, you, Emory, me, Benny ...'

Benny cleared his throat and perched nervously on the edge of her desk. 'Don't be in such a hurry, Deena,' he said. His voice was high-pitched. 'Klugman's seen dozens of new drugs go through this. He knows what he's doing.'

'Klugman's an ass. And you can report that back to him if you choose,' Deena said. 'Are you on the fence, or have you jumped?'

'I just said don't rush things.' He moved away from the desk. 'The tests are coming in now and there's nothing wrong with Duckmore. If he checks out, there's no reason to wait. Clark can keep Anne informed, she'll still have a voice. God knows the tests will go on long enough. She'll be here long before they're through. It isn't as if she's being cut out altogether. No one even knows who'll be on the committee yet.'

'You pig!' Deena said. 'She's been on this for eight years! If it were Medgars's drug, no one would dream of moving without him. If it were yours, you'd have a screaming fit if anyone suggested a move was to be made when you were gone. But Anne? We can drop her a note from time to time. Is that it?'

Benny slouched to the door. 'Look, you're the one who's having a screaming fit. I'll talk to you later.' He left.

'That gutless wonder! Clark, don't you see what they're doing?'

'Yeah,' Clark said. 'I know. Let's go have coffee or something.'

'Well? What are you going to do about it?'

'Nothing today. I'm waiting for Gus to get back. It's his department. He won't let anything happen to destroy it, and if they try to go ahead, ignoring this incident, the department could be destroyed. He'll use that argument, not loyalty to Anne. It's the only argument that has any weight.'

Deena pulled her purse from a drawer and stood up. 'What if they do decide to go ahead, Clark? What will Anne do?'

Clark opened the door and, without looking back at her, said, 'Nothing. What could she do? She understood from the start that her discovery is company property. We all understand that. Theoretically she's in charge, but if she's incapacitated ... She won't do anything.'

Deena stared at his broad back and a shudder of rage passed through her, leaving her trembling. 'I won't let them do it to her. Not to her!' she whispered, too low for him to hear the words, but the vehemence reached him and he turned to regard her bitterly.

'Let's go for that coffee,' he said after a moment.

*

At four, Bob Klugman told the meeting of the R&D personnel they would be going ahead with the human tests in the middle of the month. 'You all understand what that means as far as the computer is concerned, the blood analyzer, everything else as far as equipment goes,' he said. 'Make your plans now to have completed your runs, or to postpone them. This takes first priority.'

Steve Ryman from the soybean annex stood up. 'What about our priority? Our tests are scheduled to run through June.'

'You'll have the facilities, but on a shared basis. I want schedules, projections for the next six months, you all know the sort of thing. Gus Weinbacher will be back tomorrow. Work it out with him.'

Clark watched him in silence. Bob Klugman had been drinking all day. His face was flushed and his words slurred just enough to be a giveaway. Six months, he thought, would be too long for Klugman. He'd bitch up something long before six months ended, and he'd get the can. Early retirement for health reasons. Then, if all went well, Gus would be promoted from supervisor of Pharmaceuticals to vice president in charge of research and development. But maybe not. Gus was a maverick. Prather, the old man, would have promoted him in a flash, before now even. Old man Prather would not have tolerated Bob Klugman. But old man Prather was out of the picture, and because young Master Prather didn't give a shit, it was Helverson's show. And Helverson was bucking for merger or incorporation, or submersion with one of the giants. For two years he had been working quietly behind the scenes to bring about the sell-out, and now he was working more openly, and even harder. And he was using Anne's discovery to help along the coming consolidation. Prather Pharmaceuticals was a medium-sized company with enormous prestige, and Anne's find was whipped cream on the cake for Helverson. He was a businessman, not a scientist. A setback at this particular time might make the cream appear curdled a bit. He'd have to push, not let a mere technicality slow anything down. Even if they went ahead today, it would be a year before the pregnancy tests and the following teratology tests could be completed. He would be able then to name his terms, if they had the *pa* factor secure, with the human tests behind them. Whatever he wanted that the parent company or corporation could furnish would be his. Chairman of the board? President of a giant corporation? Stock? Whatever.

He would take home the glory, Clark knew, but if there was no glory yet, if the incident with the chimp that morning was simply the first of a series of such incidents, or if something showed up in the blood, or in the brain or nervous system, then Helverson would be home free anyway. A drunken vice president who let the experiment proceed would be the goat. And the scientists who initiated the tests knowing there were possible hazards. Klugman and Anne, and probably Gus Weinbacher.

He realized with a start that people were milling about, talking in tones of frustration or anger or resignation. Everything changed in a flash, everything rescheduled. There would be lights burning late into the night as the various groups re-planned the spring.

In Pharmaceuticals, each scientist had a cubicle of an office, not big enough to pace, but offering privacy. When the office door was closed, no key was needed. No one ever interrupted another who had closed his door. Clark avoided the others from his section and went to his office and shut the door hard. Call Anne, he thought, and then ... He couldn't get beyond the 'call Anne' step, and he sat down and put the call through the board.

She had been laughing, he thought, when she answered. Harry was telling her funny stories about his students, or Ronnie was giving her the latest chapter of her sex life. He smiled at the wall and listened to her summarize Harry's argument against love. As she spoke, he realized there was an undercurrent in her voice that was not totally masked by the amusement. There was a tension she was trying to hide, play-acting for his sake, for Harry's, possibly for her own. He gripped the phone harder and visualized her on the chaise, dressed in a long, soft, brown robe of some sort, a drink or coffee in her hand, cigarette smoking itself away in the ashtray. She seldom smoked one all the way, but put it down and let it send its ribbon of smoke into the air until the filter burned, when she stubbed it out. She would be smiling. He wondered if she was grasping the telephone as hard as he was, and he relaxed his hand slightly.

When she finished her story, he told her he'd be home by seven or seven-thirty.

'Anything special going on?' she asked.

He couldn't tell if her voice had been too light, if there had been a hidden question. 'The usual,' he said. 'Klugman's hitting the bottle. He's unhappy about the scheduled computer time, and the analyzer being tied up by the soybean boys, stuff like that.'

'Ass,' she said cheerfully. 'Is it still raining there?' When he said yes, she said, 'I sent Ronnie home a while ago. Everything's getting coated with ice again. Who's going to bring you home?'

'D ... don't know yet,' he said. He closed his eyes. Deena never worked overtime. She refused to stay after five unless there was an emergency that involved her. Her daughter was not to be left alone after dark, she said emphatically. Tonight, Deena would be working overtime.

'Well, try to get away as early as you can. Driving will be bad. I'm going to talk Harry into staying the night.'

They chatted another minute or two and Clark hung up. He felt uneasy, resentful of the need to deceive her, and he knew she had sensed his deception.

It would be hard when the time came to justify it. He wondered if she ever would forgive him, in fact, if the plan did go on without her, without her knowledge that they were proceeding. What he ought to do, he thought, was saunter over to Klugman's office casually and hang around until Bob Klugman offered him a drink. Instead, he opened his door and almost immediately Wilmar Diedricks appeared, with Janet Stacey and Ernest James in tow.

'We've been assigned to you,' Wilmar said. 'Do with us what you will.' Janet Stacey giggled and Ernest James rolled his eyes in exasperation.

Janet and Ernest were laboratory assistants; Wilmar was a hematologist. Clark nodded. 'Okay, let's get to work. We'll start the separation process immediately, tomorrow, first thing. We'll need ...' He figured rapidly and said, 'Fourteen hundred milliliters by the fifteenth. Okay?'

Wilmar put his hands behind his head, sprawling out in the only visitor chair in the office. 'Not okay,' he said. 'At least two shifts. We'll have to process six liters of blood for every milliliter we extract. Might need three shifts.'

'Go to however many shifts you need,' Clark said. 'You heard Klugman. Helverson says go.'

'Can't run the processor and do the syringes, too,' Ernest said softly. 'Need an extra guy on each shift for that.'

'Get someone,' Clark said. 'Look, Wilmar, I know everyone has to drop what he's doing. I didn't order this. If we can stop it, we're going to, but meanwhile we have to assume the order's good. Now get to it.'

Wilmar stood up. 'I don't like having to run when a walk's good enough,' he said. 'It smells, Clark. Do you know why the sudden rush?'

'No. No one tells me anything.'

For a moment they stared at one another, then Wilmar shrugged. 'It still smells. Come on, children. Let's plan to get rich in the next two weeks. Hey, Ernest, your woman let you stay out past midnight? You want a night-owl shift?'

Ernest chuckled. 'Double time?'

'You betcha.'

'You're on.'

'Christ,' Clark said. 'Hold it a minute, Wilmar. You can't fill the syringes yet. Not until we get the blood analyses of the test subjects. It's a variable dose, remember?'

Wilmar paused at the door and shook his head. He motioned the two assistants to leave and closed the door after them. 'Clark,' he said again, 'it really smells. Doesn't it? When Gus gets back, I'm asking for a waiver of responsibility, or something.'

'Serious?' Clark asked, joining him at the door.

Wilmar nodded. 'Serious.'

'See if Gus can get you in that committee meeting, on the committee would be better.'

'Someone should bring out the thalidomide file and shove it under Helverson's nose,' Wilmar said.

'Be at the committee meeting,' Clark repeated.

Wilmar nodded and left, closing the door after him.

Harry was doing mysterious things in the kitchen; the heavy drapes were closed now, hiding the world that was being coated with ice, and with the closing of the drapes, the noise had faded, leaving the room as isolated as a space capsule in orbit. Anything might take place in such a room, Anne thought. The apartment was insulated, sound-proof almost, to the extent that no sounds from the kitchen or the living room penetrated this far. Restlessly she glanced about her space capsule: an Indian elephant, two feet high, adorned with blazing diamonds and rubies and emeralds (or possibly bits of colored glass); a shiny telescope on a stand, all black and silver and phallic as hell; everywhere books and bookcases; a small Sony television; a print of a Turner seascape; a woven wall hanging from Venezuela, geometric and garish and lovely; a radio-stereo combination with a plastic cover that from where she sat looked like a dome of smoky quartz. The control panel, she decided, where she could guide the ship, compute their course, decelerate to land, punch button *A* for food ...

She closed her eyes. Space capsule: prison. Lovely young woman held captive for seven years, chained to bed, her frail body covered with old scars, whip marks.

She should write in her diary now while Harry was busy. He was making dinner, probably. Something fancy, gourmet cook that he was, living on Campbell's soup and graham crackers and cheese spreads. And vitamins. Six a day of this, three of that, two of something else. And ice cream. He had a weakness for ice cream. Breyers all natural flavors only. Nothing artificial, except his vitamins and the additives in his soups and cheeses ...

She wrote in a scrawl that few others could read: *My sex drive is undiminished.* A biographer would play hell trying to piece together her inner life from her diaries, she thought, looking at the words. Only her professional notes were detailed and legible. Probably she deliberately reverted to the scrawl when she touched on her personal life, and then she wrote in cryptic one-liners. *My sex drive is undiminished.*

She was reluctant to write in the diary, she realized, because she didn't want to put down in black and white what she had withheld from Clark. Although sometimes she lied in the diary, and in person, she added, she was reluctant to write that, because if he saw it, he would be hurt and confused by her silence about what had to be a tremendous step forward. Or at least breaststroke forward. Of course he never looked in her diary. If he kept one, she knew she would sneak it out at every chance and read every word. And that was one of the great differences between them: he was willing to allow her to be her own person, separate from him, and she insisted on that; but she, on the other hand, could not bear for him to have a life apart from hers. What are you thinking? was her question, never his. What are you feeling, what's happening in your head, are you happy, unhappy, neutral? Check one. If only she could creep under his skin, just one time, and know.

'You should see this,' Harry said at the door; he crossed the room in a loose-jointed, almost awkward walk, as if his legs were as tricky under him, as unreliable, as hers. 'Watch,' he said, and opened the drapes again.

Anne slipped the diary back into the pocket of the wheelchair and pulled herself upright on the chaise. Laboriously she worked herself out of it and onto the chair. Harry didn't offer to help, and seemed almost impatient for her to finish and join him at the window seat. Beyond the window the street lights shone through the bare tree branches and were reflected in a million prisms of ice.

The building was fifteen feet above a winding road that skirted Cherokee Park, her apartment another ten feet above the terrace. A low-spreading wisteria tree, planted at street level, was outside the windows; its topmost branches came only to the windowsill. In summer it was the curve of a canopy of feathery leaves that moved when there was no discernible breeze, in winter a tracery of spiderweb twigs. It seemed too delicate to withstand weather of any sort. Now with the street light showing through the branches, each twig, each branch, every part of the tree sparkled and shone and gleamed in a sheath of ice that took on colors the source of which was not apparent. Surely not the drab yellow street light. A million prisms broke up the light and changed it – transcendent light of pure prismatic colors.

'Fairyland,' Harry said.

Anne nodded, gazing at the tree.

'Thought it a shame for you to miss it,' Harry said, and went back to the door. 'Busy. Be back in a couple of minutes.'

Ice sculpture. Ice pruning. Everything familiar became different and unreal, fairyland world. A face of reality that was mockery, as if taunting her that what she had thought real only moments earlier was subject to change without warning. The strangeness exists, she thought, and only by concentrating on what we need to have real can we keep the change from becoming visible. But it's there all the time. And now, as if freed by her acknowledgment of it, the strangeness seemed to flow through the tree limbs, along the twig ends that were invisible under the ice, and jump through the air to rest momentarily on the panes of glass, and then flow through, to the room, her prison, her space capsule, her sanctum, and the strangeness was all about her. For a moment she could sense the room changing behind her, changing to something she would not recognize, something alarming, threatening. She closed her eyes, refusing it, concentrating on the familiar. Elephant gleaming with colored glass, telescope, television, exerciser, bed ...

She opened her eyes wide and she felt for the first time, she understood. The strangeness was the reality; it was that which no one could face, and so they constructed and constructed and firmed everything and called it real. And it was ephemeral. All of it. Only the strangeness was real and would endure.

The slam of a car door roused her. She looked out and down across the narrow terrace of grass, down the stone steps to the street level, and there at the curb was a little yellow automobile, Deena's VW. Leaning over, speaking to Deena through the window, was Clark, oblivious of the freezing rain on his back.

Anne didn't know how long the car had been there. She hadn't heard it arrive, and she hadn't looked down before. It might have been there from the time Harry opened the drapes, from long before he opened them even.

Deena, she thought. Deena. It was almost eight. She turned from the window and when she looked about the room, it was familiar, known to the last detail, but the strangeness was still there, waiting to surge back in. Behind the facade of normalcy, she could sense the strangeness.

CHAPTER FIVE

'Anne, I'm home!' Clark called from the doorway to the bedroom. 'Anne!'

'In here,' she answered, her voice muffled by the heavy bathroom door.

'Hi. I'm dripping wet. I'll get a quick shower and be right back.'

He crossed the hallway to the guest room–study that had become his room during her convalescence. Harry appeared almost immediately with a drink in his hand.

'Bourbon on the rocks, right?'

'Couldn't be righter,' Clark said, taking it, stripping off his shoes and socks with one hand. 'Glad you could stay, Harry. How is she?'

'Fine, fine. She's really coming along now. Every week I can see great improvement. Couldn't for a long time.'

Clark finished undressing, upended the glass, and went into the shower. For several minutes he let the hot water sting him into feeling alive and human again. His feet and hands tingled from the cold. Twice on the way home he had had to get out of the tiny car and turn it right on icy roads. All the side streets and the county roads were getting impassable fast. Here in the city, the main streets were merely sloppy wet.

When he finished his shower, there was another drink on the desk. Gratefully he sipped at it, and dressed, feeling tired and hungry now.

Harry was in Anne's room when Clark got there. Anne was drinking a daiquiri, and Harry had coffee, he was an ex-alcoholic.

Clark kissed Anne. 'Sorry I'm so late. Took almost an hour and a half to get here.'

'I was afraid the streets would be completely closed by now.' She looked tense.

'They will be by morning.'

'Dinner in ten minutes,' Harry said. Anne looked at the card table, cluttered with magazines. 'Not in here,' Harry said happily. 'In a tiny, very romantic little restaurant I've found. Intimate, quiet. You'll like it.' He left them.

'Tell me what the doctor said.' Clark sat on the edge of the window seat, with the strange lights behind him.

'I'm getting flabby, need more exercise. I should stay out of the bed most of the time by now. There was a funny little man in the waiting room today …' She began to tell the story, making it up as she went.

'Dinner is served,' Harry announced from the doorway, a towel folded neatly over his arm.

Anne laughed and Clark pushed her chair across the room, through the doorway, and down the hall. At the end, where the hall turned left for the kitchen and dining room, Harry motioned them to go right, into the living room. Inside, Anne drew in her breath. The large cheerful room had been transformed. There was a fire burning in the fireplace. A table was set in front of it, with candles; the only other light in the room was a lamp at the far end, and Harry had thrown something red over the shade.

'It's beautiful,' Anne said. 'It's really beautiful.'

'Change of lighting works magic, doesn't it?' Harry said, nodding. 'Now, the soup.'

'You said you lived out of cans,' Anne exclaimed after her first taste of the thick, creamy soup.

'So I lied. More, Clark?'

Later Clark would remember that night with puzzlement, aware of something different about Anne, something different in the air perhaps. She tightened up too much when Harry said he lied, and her quick glance at Clark had been too revealing. From too tense to talkative back to a strained tautness when there was a pause in the conversation, she changed without any apparent awareness of her shifts. Several times he caught her looking about the room as if seeing it for the first time, or as if searching for something she had misplaced. Clark took little part in the conversation, content to eat the delicious food Harry had prepared, to let the waves of fatigue and tension flow from him like an outgoing tide, feeling a lassitude creep up his legs, into his body, so that by the time Harry suggested ice cream and cookies, he could only shake his head and sigh.

'You used to bring gallons of ice cream to our house when we were kids, remember?' Anne said, too gaily.

'Always chocolate, and something fancy for me. Pistachio nut–maple cream, or mint flake–raspberry. Something you dumb kids wouldn't touch with a ten-foot pole.'

'I was afraid of you, I think. You'd sit there and watch us like a gargoyle, brooding, analyzing. I didn't know what you were doing and it bothered me.'

'I can't remember that,' Harry said, frowning. His face lightened. 'I know one of the things that might have worried me. You see, your mother is a damn smart woman. You didn't know that?'

Anne shook her head, and looked at her plate.

'Anne, don't be ridiculous! Of course, she's very intelligent. She never used it, never trained herself, but it's there. I was looking for a trace of it in one of the kids from time to time. Never found it. I was looking in the wrong place. I thought it would pop up in one of the boys. A great physicist, or composer, or something.'

'What would you have done, if you had found what you were looking for?' Clark asked. He never had thought of Anne's mother as intelligent, rather dull in fact, with piercing eyes and a caustic tongue that he had attributed to malice. Anne's mother was clearly jealous of Anne, resentful of her successes.

'I don't know. I really don't know. At the time I thought I did. I'd take the kid in hand, try to infuse him with some sense of destiny, with ambition. That's been our curse, you see. We have the brains, but no ambition to go with them. Until Anne came along.'

Anne laughed, too quickly, too loudly. 'What nonsense we're talking tonight. Harry, speaking of nonsense, do you remember the upstairs of our house on Dewitt Street? There was a long, narrow closet that connected two of the upstairs bedrooms. I used to go in there and pretend it was my door to somewhere else. I wonder if all kids have a door to somewhere else.'

'Not just kids,' Harry said. 'I still do. At school in the teacher's lounge there's a door that's locked shut, always has been, far as I know. It goes to the broom closet or something that has another entry in the back of the building. I pass through that door like smoke through a screen.'

'To somewhere else,' Anne repeated. She thought of the little-world terrarium, where she could be the size of a microscopic spore, or where she
could swing through the tropical leaves Jane-like, fighting off dragons, or
ape men, or Martians. Like smoke through a screen, she thought.

Clark yawned and tried to stifle it. It was almost ten-thirty. He felt Anne's
gaze and turned to her, but she shifted and looked at the window at the
far end of the room. The wind was driving the sleet against the windows.
'Honey, I'll help Harry pick up and then get you tucked in. Okay? I'm really
beat.'

Harry refused help, shooed them both out of the way, and Clark pushed
Anne's chair back to her room. Later, in bed, aware that Anne was awake
still, not yet in her own bed, he tried to sort out impressions of the evening,
but they were jumbled and unorderly. She had avoided seeing him, he decided, at least directly. But how many times had he looked up only to find
her just then shifting her gaze? And her brightness and gaiety had been
faked, at least much of it had been faked, but he couldn't tell which half had
been real, which part had been acting. You don't usually think of people
with such mobile faces as being able to conceal themselves, but she could,
and did. He had watched her do it with others, a sudden change that he
couldn't identify, a change in direction when she had seemed immobile, a
change of attitude, something, and the new Anne would rise and take over.
But never, he thought, had he had the feeling that she was doing it with him,
as she certainly had done it that night.

Again Clark felt a rush of gratitude for Harry's presence. And he realized
he didn't really want to be alone with Anne until he could tell her what was
happening at the lab. He sighed and rolled over to his stomach and in a few
minutes he was asleep.

Anne had always known she would be famous by the time she was thirty.
When she first thought of a date, a deadline, it had been misty with tempo-
ral distance, twelve years. Anything could happen in twelve years. But now
thirty was coming at a rate that seemed to be accelerating. Two years, three
months. There was still time, but just barely, and no time to spare. She had
had the drive, the ambition, the vision, the talent. From that first day when
she had recognized what the problem was, and found a way to circumvent
it, she had wasted no time. No time at all.

She sat at the fairyland window and stared at the mystical tree, her diary
on her lap, alone for the night. Slowly she began to write:

> *Look at all the time*
> *I've saved—*
> *Bits and pieces, odds and ends—*

Crammed into boxes,
Put away neatly on shelves,
Saved for the day
I shall be old
And the only goal
Will be time.

What form, she wondered, would the interest take to be paid on saved time? Abruptly, angrily, she snapped the notebook shut and jammed it back into the chair pocket. Abstractions, she was worrying with abstractions. Harry's fault, talking about love as if it were something that could be destroyed by an act of reason.

She remembered one of her early teachers, also bored, misplaced in a high school where only one or two in each class of forty wanted to hear what he had to say, and of them, perhaps one would remember, perhaps neither. Custer, she thought. That had been his name. Mr. Custer. 'We attack reality on the fringes,' he had said. 'It's all we can do. The hard core of reality is impenetrable.' Abstractions again.

We tell ourselves stories, she thought, and the stories are real, even if they don't touch objective reality anywhere. The story she had told Clark about the old man was real; the story amused him, it had allowed her to talk about her visit to the doctor without having to lie. It had a function in reality, then; it served reality in a way that lying about the therapy would never serve. For a brief moment, she thought, I added something to the dimension of reality.

She visualized Clark sleeping, on his stomach, one arm under his pillow, the other at his side, not snoring. He slept like a child, totally still for a long period of time, then an abrupt change of position, back into the stillness that was almost absolute. Anne was a restless sleeper, awakened by any noise; thoughts, plans, details of work never far from the surface of her mind, ready to flood in, to rouse her to complete wakefulness off and on during the night.

She began to think again of the final human tests. Five hundred women in the first trimester of pregnancy, five hundred in the last trimester. She remembered reading that a woman in the last trimester should turn to her side, permit her husband to enter from behind in order to relieve his sexual needs. She had read the article through twice, trying to find a hint that the author had a clue about the woman's sexual needs. Cattle, she thought. They were treated like cattle. But not the women in her study. She and Deena had worked it out in detail. They would interview each and every woman. Not Africans, not South American Indians, not Mexican peons. American women who could understand what a double-blind experiment was, how it was conducted, what the injections were expected to do, what the possible consequences were. Only women with medical complications that would warrant their taking the *poena albumin* in the first place. Immaculate, impeccable work, that's what they would have to say.

Clark had argued that she personally didn't have to interview each applicant for the experiment, but she knew she did. And afterward, one of the big universities would make her an offer, a grant, facilities, everything. And the company would make a counteroffer. But she would go with the university, get out from under the machinery that let people like Klugman be over her. Clark would go, too. She would make them understand from the start: where she went, he went. They would consider her eccentric, but that was all right. Genius could afford eccentricity that would cripple a more ordinary being. She would flaunt her eccentricity, in fact.

She remembered one of the sex manuals she and Clark had read together, giggling at the sketches, trying them out, giggling even more, finding a few of them amazingly effective.

Her hands were clenching the arms of her chair too hard, hurting. Waking, dazed with sleep, to find his penis hard against her back, his hands caressing her with greater and greater urgency. His hand at her breast, hand gliding over her belly, down to her pubis, the hot, rising, painful need snapping her to full wakefulness ...

She bowed her head and waited for the moment to pass, and slowly she loosened her hands from the chair arms, but she was afraid now to let either hand touch her body; she let them dangle over the sides of the chair and raised her eyes finally to stare at the glistening wisteria tree beyond her window.

Harry, she would say, people can and do love each other terribly. It isn't just need, she would say, although that plays a very large part, of course. Naturally. It came as a surprise to me, too, she would say. In my family, she would say, if you were a boy you had to be big, muscular, and make the team, and nothing else mattered very much at all. If you were a girl, you had to be small, petite even, doll-like pretty, and nice. God, *nice*! And I grew up ungainly, with legs that just kept going on, and too smart-assed most of the time, and scornful of the things that mattered – things like making the team, and curling hair, and telling Daddy he was strong and brave and I loved him most of all, because he wasn't, and I didn't. And, of course, I lied, and this made my mother fear for my soul. As if she didn't have enough on her mind without that.

So, she would say, you see, I started at the point you have only now reached; that is, not believing in love. When the day came that I found myself thinking I would rather die than live without Clark, I realized how terribly a person can love another person. Because I truly meant it, even if I was very young at the time. And it is a terrible thing to love so passionately that the self is eclipsed. Whatever he wants me to do, she would say emphatically, *whatever* he wants, I do gladly, happy there is something above the call of duty that I can do.

Harry, she would say quite calmly, without shame or hesitancy, we, Clark and I, engage in all sorts of sexual perversions. Things that are quite against the law in most states, certainly against the law in this state. I welcome each new perversion as a new test of my love, she would say. And, she would say, when we do those things, they are no longer perversions, they become holy almost, and our love deepens.

But she wasn't ready yet, and she knew it. Not yet. In spite of her great love for her husband, and her great need of his love, she was not yet ready to be a receiver only, to be a passive container into which he could pour his fluids. That would only start resentments that had no place in a happy marriage. She hadn't told him, hadn't mentioned it to anyone. Thank God, she hadn't mentioned it to Ronnie, didn't have to face her knowing looks and winks. If only she had been able to withhold the swimming prescription from her, but Ronnie was necessary to get her there and back. There was no way for her not to know.

If she sent Ronnie home by five every afternoon, it would be possible to keep her from seeing Clark altogether. And she would tell Clark when the time was right, when she had tried it out for several days and knew it was working. Not now while there was a problem at the lab.

Poor Clark, she thought, so worried about schedules and computer time, and that ass Klugman and his mini-crisis of the month. There was simply no need to burden him with anything else right now. She thought of him tenderly, exhausted, inert until his body demanded a change in position, then a sudden burst of activity, back to inertness again. He didn't need anything new to worry about just now.

A snapping noise roused her and she started in confusion. The ice had broken a twig, she decided. It had grown thicker while she had been sitting before the window. There would be branches and limbs all over the streets by morning.

She wheeled herself to the side of the window and closed the drapes, and then got ready for bed. Throughout the night she heard the snapping of branches, punctuation marks for her dreams.

CHAPTER SIX

'What you need is confidence!' Miss Westchester said merrily. 'Dr. Federicks sends us a lot of patients. Broken backs, broken everything, and the swimming does wonders for them! Confidence!'

Anne had hated her on sight. Pretty, dimpled, compact, she looked like a smiling gymnast, all smooth muscles and hard high breasts, eighteen-inch waist, long golden braids down her back, like a transplanted Heidi. She glowed with health and the brainless gaiety of childhood.

'Now, can you walk at all?' Miss Westchester asked. 'Is your nurse going to go into the water? Can you swim?'

'I can swim,' Anne said. She looked at Ronnie, who shook her head emphatically.

'Water's for drinking if you've got nothing better. And for taking a bath with, and putting in with the beans. And that's about it,' Ronnie said. 'I'll watch.'

'Sorry,' Miss Westchester said, dimpling again. 'We don't allow spectators at all. There is a competent staff,' she added. 'We are trained, you understand, to handle crippled people.'

Anne felt her jaw tightening. 'Can we just get to it?'

'Oh, my, yes! I'll take you to the dressing room. Do you need a handler?' Anne looked at her until she said, 'Someone to lift you from your chair, dress you, things like that?'

'No.'

'Good! That's fine!'

'I'll stay with her until she's ready to get into the water,' Ronnie said then. 'You just lead the way.' She winked at Anne as she elbowed the pretty girl away from the chair.

The water was soft and lovely, and Anne could swim almost normally, in a lazy, effortless way, on her side, moving her legs only enough to keep them horizontal. She was sorry when the ten minutes were over.

'Now, wasn't that nice!' exclaimed Miss Westchester from the far side of the pool, beaming across at Anne. 'Time's up!'

For a moment Anne visualized that pretty face under her hands, below the water, mouth open, eyes bugging out with terror. It was such a real image it frightened her, and she turned away from the girl quickly and swam to the chair lift that would take her from the water.

There was a sauna bath and a sun-lamp treatment, and then she was in the car with Ronnie, heading home through the slushy streets. She felt relaxed, tired, content, the way she always felt after swimming. Ronnie's voice droned on without pause.

She had wanted to kill that girl, Anne thought, but distantly. Probably everyone wanted to kill her. Probably one day they would find her on the bottom of the pool, finger marks on her throat. She shook her head, not good enough. Not good enough just to have someone do it, she wanted to do it herself. Ronnie turned into the alley behind the apartment house and muddy water flew through the air, spattering the car's windows.

'Filthy weather,' Ronnie said. 'Your chair's a real mess. Soon's you get inside, I'll take it out to the porch and clean it.'

Anne nodded. She never had hated anyone like that before, she thought. Instant hatred that wanted an outlet, in violence. It disturbed her that she had reacted so harshly to the girl, who was, after all, simply stupid, not malicious. She was overreacting to situations that used to amuse her, if she had noticed them at all. A few months ago that girl wouldn't have been able to get anywhere near her, she thought with a sense of disquiet. Being locked up in her prison so long had done something to her armor; her insulation from the world had been pierced.

Ronnie parked under the canopy of the parking area and got the chair out of the back, and Anne began to work her way up from the car seat. Ronnie knew when to help, and when to stand clear and wait. Now she waited, always watchful, but not offensively so, not as if she didn't trust Anne to behave responsibly. She waited with the same good humor and patience that she always showed. Anne got into the chair and took a deep breath.

'Made it,' Ronnie said, and pushed her toward the back entrance and the ramp Clark had had installed at their back porch. 'I'll give that kid a shove into the pool next time. Okay?'

'If you don't, I will,' Anne said, and they both laughed.

Gus Weinbacher gazed moodily at the group assembled in his office. Gus was five feet five inches, deeply tanned from his week on Antigua, but ugly. His face was prematurely aged with a thousand etch marks, and his slender body was frail-looking, deceptively so, for he had good muscles, but his appearance was of frailty and old age, contradicted by his gleaming teeth, and his thick hair, dark brown, luxuriant, and his energy when he chose to use it. He could move faster than most people, get more done in a shorter time than anyone else in the pharmaceutical division, endure longer hours for longer periods. He had a knack for cutting straight through all the fluff to get to the core of a problem, and his sharp blue eyes seemed to deride those who hadn't already seen what he then could demonstrate.

Unwilling to believe Bob Klugman, who saw catastrophe every time the wind changed, he had called Emory Durand the previous night, and afterward had taken the first flight back. He had left his wife, Elaine, to rest for the next two weeks in the golden sun, with the promise to straighten things out as soon as possible and rejoin her. It had been a bad winter for them, he thought, what with Rickie getting married at twenty, and Jud dropping out of pre-med school, and Elaine's asthma and allergies triggered by a series of emotional blows. He didn't want to be in his office that bleak morning. He didn't want to confront a problem with Anne's discovery. Most of all, he didn't want Helverson pushing too hard too fast.

He understood Helverson, who was of the school that said it was better to make a decision, any decision, quickly than let matters drift. A gambler. For Helverson it had worked. As long as his decisions dealt with figures, with paperwork, probably it would continue to work, at least long enough to get him to where he wanted to be. When his decisions had to do with premature human experimentation, Gus knew, he had to be stopped. Bob Klugman was out of it. He never made a decision in his life that he could delegate to someone else. His present position was the result of longevity, and the fact that he had very good people under him. Today Bob was home nursing a sore throat, possibly flu, he had said by phone earlier. He would remain out until matters were settled.

That left him, Gus knew. He was afraid it couldn't be wrapped up in a day or two. Yesterday he had been scuba diving among coral reefs; today slush, icy spots on the roads, and now a hospital visit to pay.

'The four of us will go see Pat,' he said. 'Clark, you want to drive along with me?'

Clark nodded, and Gus went on: 'Deena, sometime, as soon as you can get to it, I'll want a summary of your behavior charts. Make a note of anything at all unusual, even if you tend to discount it. Okay? And, Emory, the same with a chart of the physical examinations. Just a summary for now. We might have to go back over it all day by day, but not yet. How are the other chimps? How's Duckmore this morning?'

'Normal, apparently,' Emory said. 'I decided not to vary their routine, but to use transport cages for them all, not allow a situation that might make another attack possible.'

Gus nodded. 'Right. Let's go.'

Gus drove, efficiently, a touch too fast, the way he did everything. 'If we have to check Helverson,' he said to Clark, 'I'll need you. I wish to God Anne were here. You haven't told her yet?'

'Not yet. No real point in it until we know something.'

'Right. Anyway, if I have to beard Helverson, I'll want you along. If you protest premature testing, with your name on the factor, he will have to accept it. Now you and I both know that, but I doubt if Helverson knows it. We'll have to convince him. He could make things uncomfortable.'

Clark nodded. 'I don't understand how he could consider going ahead with any doubt about its safety,' he said.

'He's a gambler. Probably he'd be right in this instance. This isn't the usual reaction – wrong timing, wrong kind of reaction. Everything so far says it's still okay to go on. Probably he'd be able in a year or two to point to a success and laugh at us for worrying.'

'Probably. What odds?'

'God knows. Hundred to one. I don't know. I think it's unrelated.'

'You know Grove's volunteered women prisoners?'

'I know. But first things first. Where is that goddamn hospital?'

He had passed the street he should have turned onto, and he made a U-turn and swerved, cutting into the slow-moving traffic in the right lane of the highway.

They arrived at the hospital before the others, and after Gus cleared their visit with the head nurse, he and Clark waited. 'No point in making the boy go through it twice,' Gus said, pacing the tiny, vinyl-furnished room. 'He's twenty, night student studying to be a vet. Next year he plans to go full-time and his brother will start nights, working days. There are three boys, mother with a bad heart. They've got it all planned to get them all educated, keep her, keep the youngest one in school, the works. Hired him myself, a surprise for Emory.'

Clark nodded. Gus knew everyone in the animal and pharmaceutical divisions personally, almost intimately. It was like him to have hired someone for two years, put in the time and money training him, knowing he'd be gone long before the investment paid off. Not business-like; human.

Deena and Emory joined them and they all went to Pat's room together. The boy was pale, he had the withdrawn look of one who is sedated, not sleeping, not fully conscious either.

'Pat, just tell us what happened. Okay?' Gus said after touching the boy's forehead in a way that was almost a caress. Pat had one arm in a cast, the other heavily bandaged from the shoulder to the tips of his fingers.

'I've gone over it,' he said, his voice faint. He cleared his throat and started over. 'I've gone over it so I'd be ready. I had already taken Soupy and Chum to the communal cage, and when I opened Duckmore's cage, he didn't come out. I thought he was playing with me. I called him again, and still he didn't move. So I reached my hand inside, not trying to yank him or anything like that. It's a gesture you make with them. I think they see you don't have a weapon, something like that, and usually they'll just take your hand and come along. Duckmore always walked with me to the communal cage like that. You know, hand in hand. But yesterday ...' He closed his eyes and swallowed, but his voice was unchanged when he spoke again. '... He grabbed my arm, at the wrist, and he jumped out of the cage and twisted my arm at the same time. It was too fast. There wasn't anything I could do. I yelled, I guess. And I saw him baring his teeth, coming at my face, or my throat. I'm not sure now. I put up my other arm to ward him off and he bit it. I think I fell down and broke something. I had a cut on my back from something. Not sure what. I can't remember anything else. I don't know if he left me then, or what he did. Nothing else.'

The sedation kept the horror out of his voice, made him calm enough to relate it in a matter-of-fact manner, but listening to him, Clark felt a chill that raised the hairs on his arms, at the back of his scalp.

'Good, good,' Gus said, and he stood up and began to move about the small room, stepping over feet, detouring around the chairs the others had drawn up. 'Now, Pat, someone said one of the girls mentioned that you'd noticed a change in Duckmore recently. Anything to that?'

'I'm not sure,' Pat said. 'It wasn't anything really noticeable. You know he's always been friendly, curious, calm. You know. Very stable, dependable. But recently I've had a feeling that he was watching me in a different way. I was going to tell Dr. Wells, but no one else noticed it, and I watched him from behind a cage, or out of sight, and he didn't act like that with anyone else, so I decided he had just turned against me for some reason. And not always. I can't really explain it better. Sometimes he seemed hostile and watchful with me, but usually not. Yesterday morning ... there was no warning. Nothing.'

'You're doing fine,' Gus said, and patted the boy's head again. 'You're not to worry about anything while you're in here. You know experimental workers who are injured during the course of the experiment are on full salary until they recover. So just take it easy.' He stood at the side of the bed, frowning into space. 'How about the other chimps? Anything out of the ordinary with any of them?'

'I don't think so, nothing definitely, anyway. After I began to watch Duckmore more closely, I began to think that maybe Fannie was behaving strangely too, but I'm not sure.' His eyes were starting to look glassy and his words were being spaced as if with effort. 'I don't know,' he said. 'Something ... I can't remember.'

'Okay. You rest now. We'll all be back to see you from time to time, see how you're doing. If anything comes to mind, have one of the nurses give me a call. Okay?'

'Yeah. Okay,' Pat said.

Gus realized it wasn't medication glazing his eyes, but pain: the medication, sedation, whatever they were giving him was wearing off and the pain was weakening his voice, intensifying his pallor. 'We'll get the hell out of here. I'll tell your nurse to stop in and see how you're doing, son,' he said. For a moment it seemed he was going to bend to kiss the boy, but he merely touched his hair again, and they all turned and left.

'He should have told me,' Deena fumed as they waited for the elevator. 'That idiot should have told me!'

'Should have,' Gus agreed. 'But I can see why he'd be reluctant. Too indefinite. You look for more overt behavior than Duckmore showed.'

'He should have told me,' Deena muttered again.

None of them mentioned Fannie, whose behavior also might be strange. None of them mentioned that if they had trouble with another of the test chimps, they had to assume trouble with the *poena albumin.*

Anne dozed after lunch. She was in the little world of the terrarium where the leaves were as large as roofs, the light under them a soft green, the air fragrant and rich with the scent of fertile earth and growing things. She ran along a mossy path and came to a place she never had seen before. A deep pool of water stretched before her, its surface unmarred, reflecting back the leaves, and pale orchids that clung to the trees that edged the pool. She stripped and slid into the water. She swam underwater, through swaths of jade, into midnight blue, from that to a pale, milky-blue stream, back into jade. With delight she saw that her body had changed; she was an iridescent mermaid, gleaming, glistening golden tail flicking the water easily, propelling her faster and faster through the magic water.

A sound vibrated through the water and she knew it was Clark, trying to catch her, clumsy, awkward Clark stirring up clouds of silt that blinded her. She swam faster, streaking away from him. The sound was felt noise that touched her again, and she woke up abruptly, all at once out of the dream, and disoriented. She reached for the telephone, then drew back her hand and put it under the blanket. The muted ringing stopped. Moments later, when Ronnie looked into the room, Anne kept her eyes closed, and Ronnie withdrew.

Anne tried to fall asleep again, to return to the dream, and could not. Later, if Clark said, 'Ronnie told me you were exhausted from swimming,' she would say, 'She was lying. Or teasing. You never can tell with Ronnie which it is.'

She should get rid of Ronnie, she thought. She had become too familiar, taking it on herself to act almost as mediator between Anne and Clark, passing messages back and forth, giving unwanted advice.

CHAPTER SEVEN

Deena sat with her notebook on her knees, eating a tuna sandwich mechanically, concentrating on the female chimp, Fannie. The communal cage was large, easily containing the twenty-three test animals and eight infants. There was an identical cage for the control chimps. Deena was hidden from view by a one-way glass partition that allowed her to see into the cage, through it to the rest of the lab, nearly empty now during lunchtime. Chimps were grouped on high ledges, on a bench along one wall; several were swinging lazily on tire swings; infants tumbled with one another on the floor. Fannie sat alone with her infant, a mischievous three-month-old male. Fannie was scrawny and ugly and a devoted mother. As the infant suckled, she kept a sharp watch on the other chimps. Nothing erratic here, Deena thought, and realized she had finished her sandwich. Her coffee was tepid, but she drank it, and began to nibble on a candy bar.

She was almost ready to return to her office and the charts spread across her desk, when she stiffened with interest and looked beyond Fannie into the lab. Fannie was baring her teeth, clutching the infant harder against her, so hard she made it squeal in protest. She was looking intently beyond the bars of the cage. Several of the assistants had returned from lunch – three women, one of the young men.

Fannie leaped to her feet and ran up the series of shelves to the highest one, where several other females perched, grooming one another. Fannie paid no more attention to the arriving workers.

Deena made a note of their names. Eddie and Helen never tended the chimps, she was certain. They worked with the annex people. Thelma Pendleton sometimes worked with the chimps, and Jane Lyndstrom was a regular with them. Deena left her high chair and walked around the rear of the cages, out of sight, and returned to her office.

The first name plate they had put on Deena's door had said: 'Edwina Wells.' She had sent it back and now it read: 'Dr. Edwina Wells.' She seldom saw it any longer, but it had been very important then, and still was, that the name plate be right. Her office was neat and impersonal. The only non-functional object in it was a picture of her daughter, taken the previous year at her graduation from elementary school. The child was sober, with large dark eyes, long straight hair, and her mouth tightly closed to conceal braces. She would be beautiful when the chubbiness left her face and the braces were a memory. Sometimes Deena found herself studying the picture, wondering about her child, her future. And she thought with a touch of fear how little she saw her own mother.

Her mother had been different, she knew. Her permissiveness had been so tangled with neglect and indifference that it had been like growing up without a mother at all. She would never be like that with Marcie. She knew every intimate detail of her daughter's life; she was always interested in hearing more and Marcie knew that, knew she could trust her mother. She withheld nothing. Deena would know what to watch for, the signs to be read as certainly as a book. And if Marcie ever showed the first indication of the kind of wildness that had marked Deena's late teen years, she would know what to do about that. She remembered her own adolescence with disgust now. The school advisor had called her a nymphomaniac, had warned her mother to have her counseled, or analyzed, or something.

Idiot, she thought. Completely ignorant. Tying her up in Freudian knots, driving her further from her mother, straight into Roger's arms. And when it failed with Roger, as it had failed with everyone else, she had gone into psychology herself, knowing there were answers to be found, certain she had enough brains to find them without help from stupid psychiatrists who believed Freud was God. Her father had died when she was twelve, and her mother had neglected her; naturally, she had sought reassurance elsewhere. She never had found it, until she had her own daughter, who loved her without question, wholly, selflessly. And Deena had been able to stop searching and for years had been content living with her daughter, having her work, the recognition of her peers. That she had a Ph.D. in psychology and chose to work with animals instead of people never puzzled her at all. She didn't like people very much.

She especially didn't like the oversexed girls who worked in the lab, twitching their hips at the male assistants. She had spoken of them in her own group, and the leader, Sheila Warren, had been sharp with her. It was her duty to educate them, not denigrate them. But they wouldn't listen to her. One had even complained to Emory about her, and she had stopped trying with them. They'd find out, the hard way as she had done, that no male could fulfill them. They had to fulfill themselves, alone, and then just maybe they would find a meaningful relationship with a man. Maybe. She didn't believe it, but she was fair-minded enough to admit the possibility existed, theoretically anyway. She had yet to see it in practice. Marcie at least would not grow up with any illusions.

Deena sat at her desk, and looked at Marcie's picture without seeing it. She began to make notes after a moment, and a few seconds later, without thinking about it at all, she reached out and turned the photograph slightly, so that the wide questioning eyes were not directed at her. There were scratch marks on the desk where the photograph rubbed it, for every time she noticed that someone had turned it away, she turned it right again, and throughout the day the picture faced the wall, then her, then the window, over and over.

When she finished her notes she called Jane Lyndstrom and Thelma Pendleton to her office.

At four, Gus and Clark went over the charts supplied by Emory Durand. 'No variation in enzyme induction,' Gus said, 'and no variation in red or white blood counts. Only this little wave on the *pa* count. What do you think, Clark?'

'Too insignificant to mean anything,' Clark said. 'It varies with the control animals, too.'

'I'll have Jay put it through the computer with the rest of the data, see if there is a significant difference.' Gus sighed and tilted his chair back. His office was a shambles, a file drawer partly opened, untidy files at angles; his desk was covered with reports and charts; his bulletin board held current work programs as well as those long out of date; in the center of the bulletin board was a target with darts sticking out, clustered about the bull's-eye. Gus had thrown paper airplanes for years, until his secretary had bought him the dart board for a Christmas present one year.

'If there is a correlation between those waves and the waves on the behavior charts, we'll have to go back to the start with the animal tests, won't we?' Clark asked. He had seen it happen to others.

'It'll be rough on Anne,' Gus said, looking at the ceiling, his chair at a dangerous angle. He'd break his back one day doing that.

'How long can we hold off the autopsies?'

'Don't know. I'll see Helverson in the morning. He wants a staff meeting with Bob and me, for openers. I'll call you if I can.'

'Bob will be sick.'

'I know.'

'If we can hold up the sacrifice just three weeks, Anne can be here. She'll have crutches next week. A couple more weeks to get used to them, get some strength back. She should be here, Gus.'

'I know. I don't think anyone else really has the feel for it. She'd know what to look for. She's good, Clark. You know that.'

'I know.'

'I'll do my best.'

Clark nodded and stood up. There was a tap on the door, and Jay Ullman came in. He was the computer specialist. Clark left while Gus was explaining what they wanted, what comparisons they needed.

Clark found Deena perched on the high chair behind the chimp communal cage. 'I don't know yet,' she said in reply to his unasked question. 'I'm trying something.'

They were putting the chimps back in their overnight cages. Clark watched as a lab assistant wheeled the transport cage to the door of the communal cage and opened both doors. The girl put a bunch of grapes inside the small-wheeled cage, and then called out, 'Soupy! Come on. Soupy!' One of the female chimps ambled over to the cage and shuffled inside, squatted, and began to pick the grapes and eat them. A second girl wheeled another cage into place and repeated the routine. She called Chum, who was as docile and willing as Soupy had been. Clark started to speak, but Deena shushed him. 'Wait.'

The first girl was back. This time she called Fannie. The chimp didn't move, but stared at the girl and clutched her infant to her chest. 'Come on, Fannie. Come on.' Fannie sat motionless. She might have been deaf. Only her unblinking stare betrayed her; she knew she was being called. Clark felt a stir of excitement as he watched the chimp, not openly hostile, but not normal either. The girl said, 'Okay, Fannie, you wait. Come on, Finch. Here, Finch.' A young male that had been hanging about the door scrambled inside the cage and ate the grapes greedily. The other girl called Fannie and she got up and went without a moment's hesitation.

'She's all right with everyone except Jane,' Deena said. 'You saw Jane, how well she handled them all. She's good with them.' She slipped from the chair and started toward her office with Clark following. 'I'll keep a close watch on her and Duckmore,' she said over her shoulder. 'It's like Pat said, not quite normal, but not enough out of line to make you want to yell cop.'

'Are you going to come over to see Anne tonight?'

'I don't know,' Deena said. 'When are you planning to tell her?' They entered her office, only fractionally larger than Clark's.

'Not until after tomorrow's staff meeting.' Clark sat down and lighted a cigarette. 'It's a hell of a mess, Deena. I think she suspects something. Maybe it would be best just to level with her.'

'Thinking of her, or yourself?' Deena asked sharply.

'I don't know.'

'Well, think of her then. There's not a damn thing she can do. Everything's being done that can be done. You and Gus will have to handle Helverson. You know how it would affect her to know it's all up in the air again, especially while she's helpless. If you think she suspects because of your glum face, lie about it. Tell her you've got a severe case of hemorrhoids or something. Tell her Bob's been drunk on the job for a week and fouled up everyone's records. Tell her anything, except the truth for this one time.'

'Treat her like a child for her own good, is that it?'

'Exactly. Look, Clark, I'm speaking to you now as a professional psychologist. I know Anne. I know her impatience. I know her scorn for nearly everyone else in the lab. It's okay, she's better than most, she can afford a certain degree of egocentricity. But right now, helpless as she is, that egocentricity could become something else again. Don't you see how she would be certain you were all screwing up her work? The germ of every new idea, every great idea, is intuitive. She knows that. And she would know that no two people can have the same intuitive flashes. They are as individual as fingerprints. All anyone can do is the tedious, plodding, follow-through work now, and it would worry her back to the hospital if she thought there was any danger of lousing it up because she was absent during an emergency. Let's do that plodding follow-up work, and then, when she's able to contribute again, when there's no danger of another relapse, then tell her what happened. She'll blow, you'd better believe! But better then than now. Now, if she blows, it could damage her. Later it will be a relief valve. In either case, you're going to be the goat. Do you understand that?'

'Yeah,' Clark said. 'You're not coming out then?'

'No. It's bad enough that she's suspicious of you. If I show up and fudge it, she'll know something's up. I'll call her and tell her Marcie's got the flu or something. Maybe after tomorrow's meeting I'll come over. I'll call her right away.'

Anne hung up thoughtfully after Deena's call. Clark had said he would be late again, probably all this week they'd be working late. Deena and Clark? She shook her head. Not that. Clark might, he was certainly desperate enough, but Deena never. Anne didn't bother going over all the reasons for knowing this. Not an affair then. Something at work. She had known last night, she realized, and had refused to think about it. Deena working late? A real emergency, then. Something to do with her work, obviously, or they would have told her what the emergency was.

'Are you all right?'

Ronnie was standing a few feet from her; she looked alarmed. Anne nodded. 'Why?'

'I spoke a couple of times and you just sat there.'

'Sorry. Look, Ronnie, all week Clark's going to be tied up. How about just fixing me something light, a sandwich or something and coffee, and then you can leave at five. Okay?'

'I don't mind staying, honey. You know that.'

'I know, Ronnie. You've been a doll. But there's no need. And I have work to do anyway.'

Ronnie was reluctant, but in the end agreed, and shortly before five she brought a tray and plugged in the automatic coffee maker. 'Milk in the thermos,' she said. 'Are you sure?'

Anne smiled at her, all thoughts of the animosity she had felt earlier vanished now. 'Go on home to that horny man of yours.' She glanced at the table and said, 'Oh, just one thing. Can you clear all that stuff out of here and bring those notebooks from the night table?'

It took Ronnie a minute or so, then she was gone, and silence filled the apartment. Anne sat in the chaise for a long time seeing nothing, going over her notes in her mind. For now it didn't matter that she couldn't observe the chimps. The records were better than direct observation. Hormonal levels. Blood counts. Basal-metabolism records. Enzyme induction records. The fluctuation in the *pa* levels. She could almost visualize her own words, written a month ago, sometime in January: *Check: stress decreases* pa *in blood. Is it suppressed, or present somewhere else?* Somewhere else would be the brain, she thought. The theory was that the albumin clumped in the brain, attaching itself to various receptors so that pain stimuli failed to register. During stress, pain symptoms were decreased, suggesting an increase in the clumping.

There had been variation in the albumin levels, she knew, but there had been in the control chimps also, and it was assumed that variation was the norm. She blinked and rubbed her eyes hard. No good. She had to know exactly what had happened. Maybe the FDA had asked for more data. Maybe there was a conflict with another researcher somewhere, working on the same process. Maybe Bob Klugman had burned down the lab with all the records in it. Maybe …

Maybe it had nothing to do with her work. Maybe it was the soybean annex causing trouble. Everyone had predicted trouble from them. Each department thought its own was the only one worth financing, understandably, but the annex had demanded ever increasing amounts of money, computer time, equipment, personnel. Maybe they had given a party and poisoned everyone.

She worked her way out of the chaise, onto the wheelchair, and went to the table. Her records were complete, her graphs and charts exactly as she would have done them had she been at the office these past few months. She had every bit as much data here as she could have there – copies of everything from Deena's department of behavior, Emory's department of physical data, and there was nothing wrong. Up to a week ago, nothing had been wrong. Nothing!

She picked at the sandwich Ronnie had made, and ate the salad, and the cake. She still hadn't opened the many notebooks, and she realized she was too tired to want to get into any of it then. Swimming had done it. Ten minutes of unaccustomed activity and she was sitting like a bump, unable to keep her mind on any one thing for more than a minute or two. And now they were messing up her work.

The thought frightened her. She rejected it. She poured coffee and wheeled herself around the table to where she could look out the window. The ice was gone, it was already dark, little traffic passed by the house. If she looked straight out, across the top of the wisteria tree, there was nothing at all to see, blackness of the park, deeper blackness of the dense evergreen trees that were thick at this end of the park. No stars in the sullen sky, a glow here and there from street lights that were invisible, casting lights that were swallowed almost completely, leaving only pale holes in the darkness, as if there were weak spots where one could penetrate, to emerge on the other side of the darkness into somewhere else.

Captain! We're heading toward a black hole, from which no man, or woman, has ever returned. – Have courage, have courage! There must be a way to turn a ship streaking at the speed of light toward certain doom. Have courage! Go back to your cryonic sleep while I, your Captain, struggle with the forces of blackness that irresistibly pull us forever on toward that final maelstrom.

She wondered if the men who walked the moon felt as naked as she imagined them, so much nearer those black holes that drew everything in to themselves, or were they too preoccupied with their hardware, their records, the mechanics of staying alive to worry about them?

Resolutely she turned from the window back to the burdened table and opened her notebook. She wrote: 'I have been thinking strange thoughts for days, but that is a symptom of my accelerating recovery. I am impatient to return to work. My brain is stimulated while my body is still weak and unable to perform. I predict the strangeness of my thoughts will increase until I am able to go to the lab every day.'

And soon, she thought, she would have to have a real talk with Clark, find out how and why he had changed so much during the past weeks. She felt she could almost see the changes happening. He was getting heavier somehow, more clumsy, with a tendency toward sluggishness. Things he should have grasped instantly he fumbled with and didn't understand until she explained them, step by step. He hadn't been like that when they met, hadn't been like that a year ago. She was afraid some sort of middle-age decline in his mental abilities was already taking place, and he was only thirty-one.

Maybe Clark was in trouble at work, she thought. And she could believe it. They must have noticed the change in him also. Gus was perceptive enough to recognize even a slight decrease in his abilities. They would realize she had supplied the real initiative, the drive, the direction, that Clark had merely been a follower, her follower. He couldn't expect her to drag him along forever. He had to be able to keep up, or be left behind. The rule of the jungle, or the desert, or something. The rule of the little world anyway.

She remembered the clear pool of changing colors in the little world and regretted not being able to recapture that particular dream. But her life was full of dreams, of events never to be recaptured. The year she and Clark had decided to marry, they had taken a motorcycle tour of the Southwest, sleeping in a tent by night, the wind strong and wild in their faces by day. Sometimes they had sought out wild places by strange rock formations, or by springs, or streams, just to be able to make love in a new wilderness. Gone. Down one of the black holes, leaving only trace memories that stirred something in the pit of her stomach, in her vagina, something that was wholly sexual and had nothing to do with the reality of here and now. Here and now Clark seemed undesirable; it was only the memory of their love-making that could arouse her.

She thought of his thick hands on her body and could understand how some people equated sex with bestiality. Suddenly she began to weep and couldn't think why she was weeping.

This room, she thought, when the storm passed. This room, this prison is driving me bananas! She wheeled herself to the bathroom and washed her face, and now she could think clearly of the experiment she wanted to describe to Clark. She went back to the table and began to write in a fine, neat script, detailing the work step by step, with her predictions at the end. Clark came in while she was working on it.

'Darling,' she said, 'you look awful. My God, it's nine o'clock! No wonder. Have you eaten?'

He had, at the cafeteria. Anne made a face. 'Ronnie left some awfully good roast beef for sandwiches, and a salad, with dressing in a jar. Shake it first. I have coffee in here.'

'Be right back,' Clark said. He kissed her, lingering a moment, and for that moment she clung to him. As soon as he came back, she thought, as soon as he had his drink, and something to eat, she would say, Let's go to bed. The doctor says I should. And I want you, Clark. My God, I want you.

When he came back with his plate, the moment had passed and she began to tell him about the experiment she wanted him to conduct for her.

CHAPTER EIGHT

'The difference this time will be stress,' Anne said. 'Give them the *pa* factor and elevate the blood pressure, and then induce stress. We know the drug and *pa* together are harmless, no interaction showed up at all, but adding stress might make a difference.'

Clark looked over her notes. 'I'd like to add just one bit to it,' he said. 'I'd like to include one of the chimps from the test group, not give it additional *pa*, simply elevate its blood pressure and subject it to stress.'

Anne thought about it a moment. 'That's good. I should have seen it. I think my brain was fractured too sometimes.'

'No one else thought of this particular experiment in the first place,' Clark said.

'Lola would be good,' Anne said. 'And in the control group, Hermione. They gave birth within days of each other, the *pa* levels are about the same. Which one for the other test chimp? Do you have time to work this in, Clark?'

He nodded. 'I'll get it going first thing in the morning.'

He looked over the records of the two chimps she had selected. Lola had been given the factor three times during the last weeks of her pregnancy; the control chimp, of course, had had none. The births were normal, seven months ago, two male infants. Everything to date with both chimps had appeared normal. He was glad she hadn't chosen Fannie. But seven-month-old infants weren't as likely to be damaged by the separation as a three-month-old. They didn't demand as much nursing time; they were feeding themselves by now, and they would be company to one another during the experiment.

'Lilith,' he said finally. 'Her infant's only six months, but she's the closest we have. If you're right about the results,' he said, 'you realize it might be a contraindication for people with stress diseases – high blood pressure, atherosclerosis, the like?'

'I know. I suspect that will be the case.'

'Okay.' He glanced up from the notes to find Anne studying him. She looked away and yawned. 'Honey, you're tired. You should get to bed.'

Not looking at him, Anne asked, 'What's Klugman up to? What's the problem this time?'

The trouble was, Clark knew, there was no way he could tell her only part of it. If he told her about the approval of the IND, she would link that with his late hours, and conclude they were going on. As for the human tests, that was the most important part of the work remaining to be done. And she had fought for and won the right to supervise that phase from start to finish. Deena was right; Anne couldn't stand knowing any of it until she was able to deal with it herself. He was glad she had thought up the stress experiment. He could use this to explain his long hours; they could discuss it. He wouldn't be compelled to live a total lie.

This passed through his mind as he lighted a cigarette and finished his coffee. Then he said, 'Oh, Bob's got the flu. Several others are out with sore throats, stuff like that. A couple of accidents, that sort of thing. Routine.'

He waved it away. 'The guinea pigs are dying at a faster rate, the soybean-sawdust diet is a real killer.'

Now she smiled. 'Still smelling up everything?'

'Worse than ever. They need the computer twenty-six hours a day, as usual.'

She laughed and said, 'You know what'll happen. Gradually they'll take over everything and the company will become a super-cereal factory.'

'They left a tray of gift cookies at the end of the cafeteria line Monday, and nobody touched them. Nobody.'

She wrinkled her nose. 'The great white hope of the world. Ugh.'

Clark stood and picked up the newspaper from the end table by the chaise. 'Be back in a minute,' he said.

He would be in the bathroom for fifteen to twenty minutes and it would be eleven by then. He would yawn a couple of times, and carry stuff back to the kitchen, and then go to bed, and she would sit there. Visiting hour over, everyone back to the cell block. March! Or roll!

She closed the notebooks and folded her charts. The coffee pot was still half full. She poured another cup and opened a book that she then ignored.

This was the life most women led, those who didn't work anyway. Wait at home for the man, be ready for whatever he proposed, then unprotestingly withdraw when he was finished. Even this prison term she was serving was better than what most women had, she thought. At least once in a while she and Clark could still communicate something to one another. Like tonight, taking an hour to detail her experiment. It had drawn them together briefly, let them touch in the way that was even more important than the physical touch she no longer wanted. He had listened with concentration, had studied her plans, for a short time their minds had been one, and then it ended and he was now sitting on the john reading the newspaper, thinking tired thoughts, wanting the release of love, probably resentful that she wouldn't or couldn't offer it.

How long, she wondered, before he found someone who would fuck? Another week? A month? Oh, good and faithful husband, find thyself a whore, she thought bitterly. Sooner or later it would happen, it might as well be sooner.

It took Clark a long time to fall asleep that night. He thought of her body, first cool and smooth under his hands, against his thighs, her cool firm breasts gradually becoming warmer, then hot, shiny with sweat, the bed wet under them. He dozed and dreamed she kept opening her legs for him, opening her arms to embrace him, opening her mouth ... Always before he could reach her, a door slammed, and he was on the outside in a cold wind, standing before a featureless wall. He awakened and tossed, and remembered how soft and smooth her inner thighs were, and the underside of her breasts. They were in a motel room, garish, plush, with a panel of controls for air-conditioning, service, lights, radio, everything they could think of. The bed had a machine to vibrate it. All night, at least for hours, they had fed it quarters and made love on the quivering bed. And in the shower. And under the stars in the desert where the air temperature had dropped five degrees every twenty minutes, and they hadn't noticed until later when their breaths were frosty.

He dreamed she was there in his room, gliding toward him like a cloud, making no sound, her eyes shiny with love, her arms widespread for his embrace. She stopped and this time no door slammed. He struggled to waken himself thoroughly, breathing in her faint scent, certain she was waiting for him this time, really there this time. When he opened his eyes, sitting up in the dark room, it was empty.

Clark explained the experiment to his two assistants. 'We'll keep the mothers in isolation today and once an hour play the tape of the infants' cries. After four hours, and again after eight hours we'll get blood samples and test the *pa* level. After the four-hour period the babies will be returned briefly, only long enough to nurse. The babies will be returned at the end of the day. Tomorrow we'll repeat it, but keep the infants separated from them overnight and throughout Friday. Okay?'

'And you'll want constant observation?'

'Yes. I'll take the blood samples myself. You two are to keep watch during the day. Take turns, spell each other.'

Virginia Sudsbury and Phil Rudolf were two of the brightest of the lab assistants. They had worked closely with Clark and Anne from the start of the primate tests. At the prospect of the tedious job before them, both looked resigned, but unprotesting. Phil had been a laboratory assistant for twenty-two years. He had worked with old man Prather and had been the best then, and was still the best for the detailed, laborious observations that most experiments relied on. He was fifty, infinitely patient, and had never been known to speak unless asked a direct question. Virginia was twenty-one, plump, with black hair that reached midway down her back. She kept it tied with a scarf, or ribbon, or even a string at work, but as soon as her day ended, the hair came down, and it was like a dark river alive with gleaming highlights. Anne had said once that she must wash it every night for it to shine like that. She had said also, mischievously, that if a poll were taken she would bet every man in the building had a longing to run his hands through that cascade of hair. Virginia wore gold-rimmed glasses, perfectly round, like her pleasant face. Her eyes were round, too, Clark noticed, round and very quick to show understanding of what was required.

'Tomorrow we'll put them in the compounds for a few hours,' Clark said. 'That might liven it up a little.'

*

The infants played and showed no signs of alarm at the separation. At first the female chimps accepted the separation also, without alarm, or apparent awareness even. But when the tape was played and they heard their infants' distress cries, all three became agitated. Lola, the test chimp that had received the *pa* factor that morning, tried to shake the bars down, then tried to reach the lock, and when all else failed, sat on her haunches and stared at the section of the lab she could see and bared her teeth from time to time. The other test chimp and the control chimp reacted much the same but tired of their vigil sooner and resumed feeding and explorations of their new cages.

Gus found Clark at the confinement cage and reported on his meeting with Helverson. 'We've got a week to prove something, or forget it and go ahead as planned,' Gus said. 'Anything here?'

'I don't know. Lola's more excited than Hermione and Lilith, but that could be natural temperament. I'll extract blood in an hour.'

'Does Anne know then?'

'I don't know. She suspects something. But she's been worrying with this for a month or more. I saw her notes. Something about the way the levels of *pa* fluctuate alerted her to the possibility the cause is stress-connected.'

'She's good,' Gus said, as he had the day before. 'Wish to God she were here.'

'How did it go with Helverson?'

'He wants to forge ahead, naturally. He can't believe we'd get a reaction after this length of time. Find it hard to believe myself. But ... I convinced him it could be dangerous without further exploration. I think I convinced him. Enough to give us a week, and then I'll try to convince him again.'

Clark shook his head. 'That's not the way,' he said moodily.

'In this, the best of all possible worlds, it is the way, though,' Gus said. He put his hand on Clark's shoulder for a moment, and then slouched away.

After the incident with Duckmore, they would take no chances with any of the chimps. The transport cages would be used to take the animals to the examination table, where restraints would hold them securely long enough to extract the blood samples, and they would be returned to the isolation cages. They would have to be treated exactly alike, each subjected to the same amounts of stress. Clark left the lab assistants and returned to his office, where preliminary reports on Duckmore and Fannie were starting to accumulate.

At one, Deena collected him for lunch. He had forgotten. By three, Lola was showing signs of great distress, and he went to observe her when the tape was played. She cringed and looked about desperately and rattled the bars, and now she couldn't be still even after the crying stopped. She ran about the small cage, pulled at the ledge, flung herself off the far wall. She hurled a banana, smashing it against the wall, and continued around and around. Lilith's anxiety was acute also, as was the control chimp's, but they merely sat at the bars, clutching them, looking out at the lab and now and again making plaintive mewing sounds.

There was a meeting in Gus's office at four-thirty. 'Can we learn enough in a week to know for certain?' Gus asked generally. All day he had been doing his job and Bob Klugman's. There had been a fight over computer time. Cosmetics had been scheduled for that afternoon and he had canceled that and had faced down Sarah Zeller over it. Twice the blood analyzer had stopped functioning and a service call had been delayed. He had fought with the treasurer and the payroll superintendent over keeping Pat on full pay during his sick leave. He had a headache, and more than ever he wanted to lie on a golden beach and listen to the waves murmur, and his wife murmur, and drink tall smooth drinks with fruit salad floating on them, and eat exotic food in exotic settings.

'I think there's a pattern,' Deena said crisply. 'I charted Duckmore's deviation from the norm from the first time it was noted by Pat. He kept very good notes, by the way. You can see how it grew, up here, then again here. And finally the attack.' She pointed to a line she had drawn – all steep climbs and plateaus, always upward. 'Now here is Fannie's chart. Almost identical,' she said, putting the stiff papers aside. 'None of the others show just that kind of behavior line. Some of them seem to have steeper climbs than others, but not just like that. If this is right, then Fannie will erupt into violent behavior after two more minor incidents.'

Emory nodded. He and Deena had worked together for eleven years. He had as much trust in her charts as she did. Gus frowned. 'How far have you carried the same kinds of charts for the other animals, the control animals?'

'Obviously I haven't had time to do it thoroughly for more than these two,' Deena said, almost snapping at him. 'I expect to work on it for the next week at least.'

'What do you label minor incidents?' Gus asked, ignoring her sharpness.

'The same sort of thing that happened today. Fannie showed hostility for no apparent reason. Completely unprovoked hostility toward a lab worker.'

'Okay. Stick with it. We're going ahead with the blood processing, as planned. If we don't get to use it in the coming weeks, we'll be up to our asses in the stuff. Clark, how long will it remain potent, under what conditions?'

'We think room temperature is fine, but we've kept it refrigerated until we run the temperature control tests. The frozen protein is stable for months, no outer limits were found, but the tests haven't been concluded.'

'We'll have to do them now.' Gus sighed. 'Damn all people in a hurry,' he said quietly. 'Who can start it?'

'I'll find someone,' Clark said, 'or start it myself.'

'Not you. Goddamn, you're needed for other things right now. How about Virginia? Is she good enough?'

'Yes. I have her observing Lola, but I can bring in someone else for that. I'll need two more people. This is an around-the-clock test, you know.'

'Take whoever you want,' Gus said.

Deena stood up. 'Gus, one more thing, and then I'm leaving. I can do my work at home as well as here for the time being. I don't like to leave Marcie any more than I have to.' She took a breath. 'If Fannie does continue to show the same line as Duckmore, she'll attack someone, and if no one is available, the violence will be directed at one of the other chimps.'

'You think she should be confined then?'

'No! Then she'll have to attack the infant. Don't you see? There's an inevitability about it that's frightening. If I'm right.'

'Okay,' Gus said. 'We all know there's really insufficient data yet to call anything inevitable, but let's say a strong possibility exists she'll attack one of the other chimps. She's small and comparatively weak, isn't she? She'll get her ears flattened. Then what?'

'That's what I don't know,' Deena said. 'That's what worries me. Duckmore attacked and vanquished his enemy. At least, he's not around any more as far as Duckmore is concerned. He seems completely normal now, except for that persistent drop in the *pa* factor. But what will Fannie do if she is defeated and the enemy is still there?'

'What do you think?'

'Either she'll assault one after another of the adults, or she'll turn on the infant then.'

There was silence in the office for several seconds as they considered it. Clark shook his head. 'I can't buy it,' he said finally. 'Why?'

'I don't know why. I only know that when behavior is predictable up to a point, then it's usually predictable past that point. There comes a time when it's safe enough to say because this happened, this will happen.'

'On a statistical basis, not an individual basis,' Clark said.

'Watch.'

'How soon?'

'Within two weeks, probably; perhaps a bit longer, but I doubt it.'

Clark stood up, but there was no place in the small office he could pace, and he sat down again. 'That's too long.'

'I can't help that. Now, Gus, if you don't need me, I'll go home. Clark, can you get home, or go now?'

'I'll get a ride,' he muttered, not looking at her.

'Okay. See you in the morning.' She left, taking her charts with her.

'That woman drives me up the wall,' Clark said. 'What makes her so sure of herself all the time?'

'Success helps,' Emory said mildly.

'You'd better speak to Virginia before she leaves,' Gus said. He went to the dart board and pulled out the darts, took them across the room.

Clark nodded. 'She's waiting for me to relieve her at Lola's cage. I'll tell her.' He heard the first dart hit as he closed the door.

Virginia was making notes when he approached Lola's cage. The girl looked up at him and smiled. 'More good news, Doctor?'

'Yeah.' He looked at Lola. She had changed again. Now she sat staring at the lab with her teeth bared, clutching, releasing, clutching again the bars of the cage. Behind her everything breakable had been broken, water had been splashed about, food strewn all over the cage. 'How long has she been like that?'

'About an hour now. I think she suspects I'm over here out of sight. She tried to reach around the corner just before she sat down there.'

Clark nodded. 'Have you ever run a quality deterioration temperature test?'

'Yes, sir. I've done several for Dr. Diedricks.'

'Can you set it up, the works?'

'Yes, sir.'

'Okay. We're going to need the tests on the *pa* factor. I'll pull you and Phil off this, and bring in whoever worked with you before on it.'

'That was Ernest James, but I think he's tied up with Dr. Diedricks right now.'

'Okay, let's bring in Brighton. You go work out the schedule. Use my office. I'll look it over before I leave.' He glanced at the clock over the far door and swore. 'First thing in the morning. It's after hours already.'

'I can do it now,' Virginia said. 'Will you be over here?'

'Here or somewhere.' He watched her walk away, pleased she had asked no unnecessary questions, that she had not protested the lateness of the hour, had not made any demands of any sort. A good girl, he thought, and turned to find the transport cage. Time for the chimps' blood tests, then return the infants to mothers, analyze the samples taken, write up the notes ...

CHAPTER NINE

Harry had called at four and asked if he could drop in later, and now at seven he was in the bedroom holding a gray, tiger-striped, half-grown cat.

'I can't keep it,' he said, stroking the animal.

'What do you intend to do with it?' Anne asked.

'Give it to you.'

'You're out of your mind! We can't have a cat here.'

'Yes you can. I called the landlord and asked. He's a very nice cat, Anne, about three months old, I guess. House-broken.'

'But where did you get it?'

'An anonymous student left it on my desk, in a box, with a note saying his or her father wouldn't keep it and it was going to the pound.'

Anne studied the cat. It was handsome, with almond-shaped green eyes and a bushy tail that seemed to stay erect no matter what.

'I've never seen a tiger-stripe with this much fur,' Harry said. 'Listen, it's purring.'

'Harry, no. We don't want a cat. It would be alone all day, cooped up in an apartment. That's no life for an animal.'

'Exactly what they like best,' Harry said. 'After a few days, I'll install a cat window so he can get in and out, and you'll never know he's on the grounds, except when he wants to play or be petted.'

He put the cat in Anne's lap, and the little purring machine stopped momentarily, then resumed as her hands began to stroke it automatically. It was a very soft cat.

'I've brought a cat box and kitty litter, food, a feeding dish, water bowl – everything he'll need.'

'You're the cat freak,' Anne said, stroking the purring animal. 'Why don't you keep it?'

'We've got a cat poisoner in our block.'

The cat began to paw at the tie on Anne's blouse. She moved the tie end slightly and the cat pounced on it. 'For a few days,' she said. 'But you'll have to look around for a permanent home for it. What's his name?'

'Doesn't have one, far as I know.'

'There's coffee in the pot,' Anne said, watching the cat, who was exploring her chair. He reached for the wheel and slid down to the floor, leaped straight up in the air, all four feet and legs rigid, landed, and ran as if he had come down on live wires.

'He's a maniac,' Anne said, laughing.

'Crazy kitty time,' Harry said. He poured coffee and sat down opposite her. 'You like him, don't you?'

'How could anyone not like a kitten?' She looked at him sternly. 'But only for a few days.'

'Clark tied up at work?'

'Yes. There's an emergency. He'll be late every day this week.'

'I've been thinking about your experiment, Anne, and I've come to the conclusion there is no way you can do it and remain ethically pure.'

'Harry! For God's sake!'

He peered at her for a moment, confused by the sharpness of her tone. 'Oh, not you personally. I was thinking of it as a problem in ethics. A philosophical point.'

'I should have kept my mouth shut.'

'Don't feel that way about it,' Harry said. 'I'm very glad you told me. I never really gave this much thought before, but there is a real dilemma here, isn't there? If a person is terminal and everything's been done that can be, then to offer him an experimental drug, serum, or whatever, poses no problem. You throw a drowning man whatever you can, even a rotten rope, hoping it'll hold long enough. No fault can be found. But a relatively well person? One whose suffering is known to be temporary? To carry the analogy perhaps too far, isn't it like offering that same uncertain rope to save one in a boat that is bouncing about on the waves, maybe causing some upchucking and discomfort, but a boat that is all the time drifting toward the shore, with the goal in sight? What really puzzles me is why would that person, in sight of shore, or with the smell of land in his nose, why would he accept a rotten rope, or at best an uncertain rope?'

'If you had any idea of the steps we've gone through,' Anne said, 'the tests, the debates, the delays waiting for results to become conclusive before we can go on to the next step ...' She pointed to the table with the notebooks. 'I'm still dreaming up new tests. And we're on the primatology tests now. Chimps. Their reactions to something like this are almost human, as human as you can get without going to men and women. And up to now everything's checked, tested out, been okayed. It's been eight years!'

'From a handful of chimps you can generalize to over a hundred, two hundred ... How many women will you use?'

'A thousand. Five hundred will get the stuff, the others won't. They won't know which ones are which; the doctors who administer it won't know. Only after phase one has been concluded will the records indicate which women got the factor.'

'So, from a handful of chimps, to a thousand women, or at least five hundred, you can generalize to over two hundred million people?'

'That's how it has to be. There are laws governing new drugs, serums, everything. After that phase, there is the usage test, where doctors prescribe it to certain patients and keep records of their reactions. Only after that has been successfully reported is the new drug or serum approved for general use. Another two to three years, at least.'

Harry shook his head. 'What woman would risk her infant's well-being with an experimental drug? I just don't understand.'

'The literature has studies on that,' Anne said, annoyed with his devil's-advocate role. 'Some people really do have altruistic reasons, strange as that may seem.'

'I bet less than one tenth of one percent.'

'But by then we're so sure of its safety we can assure them the risk is infinitesimal.'

'Women in prisons, in welfare clinics, state-run hospitals, the poorest, worst-educated women in society.'

Anne shook her head helplessly. 'Not my experiment,' she said. 'It isn't going to be like that.'

'Ah, then you do see the ethical point I'm making. You've seen it all along.'

'Harry, you know, you drive me crazy? Every week you come here to start an argument with me. Why do you feel you have to engage in some kind of Socratic dialogue with me all the time?'

'Because I want to keep you human, honey.' The cat was stalking the shadow of a table leg. They watched. Harry began to rummage about in his pockets and found a ball of yarn. It was red, much frayed at one end. He leaned over Anne's chair and tied the end to the arm. 'Next you'll tell me you intend to try the stuff out on yourself before you go on to phase one. Right?'

'Yes,' she snapped.

'Thought so.' He started to straighten up, leaned forward instead, and kissed her forehead. 'Ever tell you how proud of you I am, honey? Leaving you my little house and garden, and my books, everything. Thought you'd like to know.'

Anne blinked at sudden tears. 'You're as crazy as that cat is,' she said. 'Just plain crazy.'

'Yes, probably.'

'I'll call him Tyger,' she said. 'With a y.' She threw the little ball of yarn and she and Harry laughed when Tyger attacked it ferociously.

Harry didn't stay very long. Papers to grade, he said. He promised to come back in a few days to check on the cat, but really to check on her, Anne thought, because he hated for her to be alone so much. She turned the television on, then turned it off again. There never had been time enough to become addicted, and the few things she did want to watch always seemed to be clumped at awkward times. She looked at the table with her papers and notebooks, but didn't approach it. She had been making tentative plans for following up the stress experiments, but she didn't want to get too firmly set on any of them until she had some results. Later.

The kitten had been playing with the fringe of the bedspread, and now it raced to the door and ran out into the hallway in its crazy rocking-horse gait. Anne wheeled herself to the doorway and looked for it. She crossed the hall to the study, now Clark's room, and paused inside. The sofa bed was open; the matching desks on the far side of the room looked naked, hers especially, since the contents had been carried across the hall. The cat wasn't in the room. She returned to the hallway and looked up its length, and then, instead of returning to her room, she began to wheel herself through the hallway.

Anything was better than staying in there all the time, she thought. Even the hall was better, narrow as it was, bare as it was. She longed to be able to run and play, as the cat ran, freely, without any consciousness of self at all. Run like the wind. If she could only get to the kitchen, she thought, rummage in the refrigerator. Perhaps get a glass of milk, or juice. Give the cat some milk in a saucer, watch it lap it up. Just poke about in the cabinets. Anything except stay in that room any longer. The apartment was divided by a hallway from the entrance door, with the two bedrooms on either side of it, to a turn where the living room opened on the right, and a narrower passage went on to the kitchen and dining room. The turn had proven impassable before, not because there wasn't room enough, for Ronnie or Clark could work her chair through it without any real trouble, but because the thick pile carpeting was hard to navigate for Anne, and because she needed to grasp the wheels of her chair on the outside to manage a turn. And grasping them on the outside instead of the top caused her to scrape her knuckles at that particular corner. She wheeled herself to it and paused, considering. There was nothing in the living room that attracted her. They seldom used it even during the best of times. They preferred the study, or their own bedroom with its easy furniture. Besides, the shag carpeting in the living room was an impossible thicket for her.

If she could only stand long enough to get the chair turned, she thought, and slowly, holding to the corner of the wall, she lifted herself and stood unsteadily, keeping her weight on her left leg, but now she couldn't move at all.

She fumbled behind her for the chair. It was caught at the corner. Desperately she tugged it and managed to move it farther from her. She thought of her pelvic bones mashing together from the unaccustomed weight and she thought of the long scar on her thigh, pulling, pulling, reddening, seeping ... She shut her eyes hard. Not true. She couldn't damage herself now at this late stage. It was a question of strength and confidence, just as that stupid, pretty-faced imbecile had said. Confidence to lift her right leg and put it down again. She couldn't do it.

How rough the wall was against her hands. She had become baby-soft. If she could flow down the wall to the floor, flow back to the chair, haul herself into it again ... She was crumpling, she thought in wonder. Like a tired paper doll, just folding in on herself, and she couldn't stop. And what, she asked herself sternly, will you do with that stupid leg when it's time for it to bend? She didn't do anything, as it turned out; her leg simply bent itself at the knee and she was sprawled on the hallway floor. She hadn't fallen, she decided. She had melted. In the strangeness of the apartment in the past few days, or maybe weeks – she couldn't be certain now when the strangeness had first appeared, not the night of the ice storm, that was simply the night she had acknowledged it – but since then anything had been possible, including a melting woman. And it really was all right, she was more mobile this way. She could get to one knee and creep quite easily, in fact.

She could move now, but for a time she lay unmoving, her cheek on her arm on the floor. Tyger tried to leap over her in a single bound, and missed, landing on her stomach, digging in in alarm. Anne disengaged the cat and it came up to sniff her face, and then bounded away in pursuit of a prey only it could see. She had to get up, get back to the chair, press on to the kitchen, or back to her bedroom, something. She couldn't stay there, although it felt very comfortable now not to be trying to go anywhere at all. What if Clark came home now?

Tyger ran past her again, the other way this time. She smiled and considered what she should do next. She got herself turned, pointed once more at the wheelchair and the bedroom at the end of the hall, but when she tried to bring the chair closer to her, she realized she would not be able to reach the brake, and without it she could not climb back into it. Finally she began to inch her way down the hall, dragging her right leg, pushing the chair ahead of her, until she reached the end and the outside door, where the chair stopped and became stable enough for her to pull herself up.

For a time she didn't move, was content to sit in the chair against the front door of the apartment and regard the hall. Well, she had had her little adventure, she thought ruefully, and to show for it she had a scraped knee, and a sore leg where she had dragged it on the carpeting, whose softness was illusory.

Finally she sighed and pushed herself back into the bedroom; Tyger was sitting on the bed, his eyes round with alarm. She nodded to him. 'Don't tell,' she whispered. 'And don't laugh. I couldn't stand it if you laughed at me for crawling like a baby.'

She had tried, she thought, heading for the bathroom to clean herself up. She had been perspiring heavily, her hands felt gritty, and her legs were dirty, she was certain. She had tried. And would again, but not too soon, she added, when she inspected her red knee. Not too soon.

*

Gus stood in the doorway to Clark's office and watched him for a minute before speaking. Clark was engrossed in a computer-analysis print-out.

'It'll keep until tomorrow, Clark,' Gus said.

Clark looked up then. He seemed to have trouble recognizing Gus.

'Go on home,' Gus said. 'Your eyes are glassy.'

'I'm glassy everywhere. I'm afraid I think Deena's right. Fannie's going the way of Duckmore.'

'Yeah.' Gus lighted a cigarette. 'Come on, I'll buy you a drink, or a doughnut and coffee. Christ, I had a lousy turkey sandwich at the cafeteria. Heartburn ever since. Hungry?'

Clark began to stack the papers on his desk. 'Had that same kind of sandwich. Think the annex boys have got to the cooks?'

'I'll kill them if that happens.' He looked like an old, tired, brown gnome, his suit coat dirty and wrinkled, his trousers a bad match, clashing in color, blue against a dark green coat, his trousers were too short, showing his socks, yellow and brown, scuffed shoes. Clark looked just as disreputable with his frayed slacks and ancient corduroy coat with a button missing. A couple of lab bums, he thought, switching off his light, following Gus through the dimly lighted laboratory that looked like something out of a Grade B horror movie at this time of night.

They met the night watchman as they left the lab. He waved to them and continued his round. He looked better-dressed, neater, than either of them. Clark needed a shave. His beard was always dark by evening, and by this time, ten, it was obviously trying to become whiskers. If a strange night watchman caught them in the building, he'd yell cop, Clark thought, grinning.

'Let's look in on Fannie,' he said, almost apologetically.

The animal division at night was strangely peaceful, and although the cats in particular seemed wakeful, they made no sound as the two men strode down the aisle to the rear, where the individual night cages for the chimps were.

Duckmore looked at them as they passed his cage. He should have been sleeping, not waking up for anything as routine as a man strolling by. The watchman made this round periodically; he was instructed to report any undue activity, and undue activity included wakeful chimps. There had been no such report. Fannie, when they paused before her cage, moved from her perch to one higher and watched them. None of the other chimps stirred.

'Stress symptoms,' Clark said. 'Wakefulness, restlessness at night.'

'Right.' Gus touched his arm and started for the door again. 'Tomorrow,' he said once more.

They went, to Al's Place for steak sandwiches and beer, and Gus talked of his wife and their two sons. 'Funny,' he said. 'You expect so goddamn much out of them, you know? You see the potential when they're still in diapers and you watch it come along and know you're right about them, what they can do if they want to. And then they just plain don't seem to want to. Funny.'

'They'll snap out of it,' Clark said. 'Lot of kids their age don't know what they want yet.'

'Look at Virginia,' Gus went on, ignoring him. 'Brains, plenty on the ball. She should have gone on to school, be working on her Ph.D. right now instead of locked into a job like she has.'

'Maybe it's what she likes to do.'

Gus shook his head. 'Not that. Too impatient to serve the apprenticeship, that's it. Can't see studying four, six, eight more years. Can't see how open it is after that time.'

'It isn't very open, Gus. That's what they see. Look at us, aren't we just as locked in?'

'You're just tired now.'

'No. Look at you. Me. They're screwing up what should have been a beautiful piece of work and there's not a damn thing we can do about it. Not a goddamn thing.'

Gus sighed and raised his hand for another beer.

'Anne might escape,' Clark said. 'She senses the need to escape. God, I don't look forward to telling her what we're doing.'

'I'll do it,' Gus said. He put his hand on Clark's arm when Clark started to protest. 'It's my job, remember. I was going to be the one to tell her about Grove and his test subjects anyway. When the time comes, I'll level with her right down the line.'

'And break her beautiful dream world into a million bits,' Clark said. 'You know she and Deena have worked it out, how to recruit subjects, what they'll tell them, the educational program they've been developing for them. Deena shouldn't have encouraged her. Deena knows it doesn't work like that.'

'She really thought Anne could pull it off,' Gus said mildly a hand on Clark's arm. He patted the arm and moved aside for the waitress, who brought two more mugs of beer. 'Deena thinks Anne can move mountains, dry up rivers, make the Red Sea part, whatever she sets out to do. If she hadn't got hurt, she would have done it her way. Bob's scared to death of her, and Helverson's afraid she'll take her lovely brain and go somewhere else.'

Clark felt himself withdraw and couldn't keep the stiffness from his voice when he said, 'I know. And one day she's going to look at me and think to herself, If it hadn't been for you. And that day everything goes down the drain.'

'For Christ's sake, Clark! Don't be an idiot. That girl is wild about you.'

'Until I get in the way of her dream,' Clark said. 'Just that long.'

They were all afraid of her, Clark thought. The assistants, the management, everyone. Even he, her husband, was a little afraid of her. It was her single-minded pursuit of this one thing, he knew. Everyone recognized a drive like that, even encountering it for the first time. It was as if she had blazoned on her forehead a message: *I'm going here, and don't get in my way!* No one wanted to be the one who got in her way. His fear was both more and less than the others'. He knew he could never be the one to get in her way, but he also knew he was deeply afraid he might somehow lose her. And this fear was more terrible than the other one. That he even considered ever losing her struck him as terrible, as if he intuitively realized he might do or say something wrong, something so horrendous that, once done or said, it could never be undone. He didn't know the source of this insecurity he felt surface now and again; he never had been insecure in any way before, and this proof of a basic need didn't assert itself often, but when it did, he became almost paralyzed with dread.

Now someone would have to tell her there was a flaw, they might have to start over, they might use women prisoners after all ... He was startled by Gus's voice. He had forgotten him.

'... sleep. Going to be a hell of a week.' Gus had paid the bill already. They left and Gus drove him home.

CHAPTER TEN

All day Thursday the test chimp, Lola, sat on her haunches, staring at the laboratory through the cage bars. The other two chimps had accepted their condition, apparently; one sat swinging on a tire, the other groomed herself. When the infants were brought at five, the difference was even more pronounced. Hermione heard the baby's whimpers before it was in sight; she raced about her cage in excitement, caroming off the walls, pausing at the bars, then tearing about again. As soon as the infant was admitted to her cage, she clutched it to her breast and withdrew with it to the highest ledge to let it nurse. Lilith repeated this performance. Lola remained hunched down, watching the large room, apparently unaware her infant was being transferred to her cage, until it actually was inside, the small door secured once more. Then she grabbed it roughly and swung herself to a perch. The infant was trying to reach her teats, but first she examined him minutely, ignoring his cries. When he finally began to suckle, she turned her gaze once more on the laboratory room and continued her vigil.

'She gives me the creeps,' Deena said, hugging her arms about her. 'Just like Duckmore and Fannie, only accelerated.'

Clark could see no one individual in Lola's line of sight. There were other animal cages, people moving in and out of the aisles between cages; Emory, attendants, came and went, but still the animal stared straight ahead.

'It's going to be something else trying to get those babies away from them,' Deena said.

They would use tranquilizers only as a last resort. The cages were equipped with movable sides, and up to now they had been able to maneuver the animals into the corner where the door was, and then offer food to the baby, opening the door only enough to permit it to pass through to the transport cage, not enough for the mother to follow. The stratagem worked once more with Hermione and her infant, who scampered through the small doorway without a backward glance. Hermione reached for it, was distracted by a bunch of grapes, and by the moving bars as they rolled into their original place. She began to pick off grapes and eat them, glanced at the transport cage as it was taken away, and returned to the grapes. Lilith made whimpering noises and watched her baby depart, then she too began to eat.

Lola clung to her infant tightly, too tightly. It cried out with rage and pain and she tried to climb to a higher ledge with it. The wall of bars moved inexorably closer, forcing her from the shelves, toward the door. The baby screamed again. She tried to force it back to the nipple, but it was trying to climb out of her arms, trying to get free. The wall was touching her, forcing her to move inch by inch. She bared her teeth and made a low, growling sound. She grabbed a bar and tried to shake it, all the while moving back inch by inch. Finally she was in position and the transport cage was attached to the front of her cage, the small door slid up partially. She clung even tighter to the infant, and now it fought back until she cuffed it sharply on the side of its head. The baby stopped struggling, but continued to whimper.

Clark held the tranquilizer needle. He went quickly to the side of the cage where Lola's body was pressed tight against the bars. She twisted her head to glare at him, but she couldn't move, confined as she was by the two sets of bars. He injected her in the hip, and within seconds her grasp of the infant loosened and it scampered to the safety of the transport cage and cowered in the rear, watching its mother fearfully as her head lolled and only the bars supported her.

'I'll take the blood sample now,' Clark said, and at that moment Virginia appeared with the tray of equipment. The movable wall was rolled back, so Clark could enter through the large door. He extracted the blood and withdrew. Already Lola was twitching, and before the door was locked again, she was shaking with long heaving tremors as she fought back to wakefulness. An assistant wheeled the infant away, and now Lola was pulling herself up from the floor. Dazedly she looked about for a moment, and then she straightened and leaped at the door. When it didn't give, she howled with rage. Screaming maniacally, she streaked back and forth in her cage, crashing into the walls, leaping into the air to race along the ledge, then flung herself back into the bars again. As abruptly as her rampage had begun, it ended. She sat on her haunches, edged her way to the front of the cage, her breath heaving her entire body. There was froth on her mouth, her eyes were wild. Clark had remained in front of the cage, and now her gaze fastened on him, her eyes sought his and she stared at him, baring her teeth widely, the aggressive, straightforward challenge that usually only the males exhibited, and only to each other.

For a moment Clark shared a full measure of her impotent fury, her despair, her madness, her hatred. Beside him he heard Virginia take a deep, quick breath. 'You should get out of here,' she said.

He turned and left. Deena caught up with him before he was out of the animal division. 'I've never seen anything like that,' she said.

Clark stopped and looked at her. 'Will you decide I'm crazy if I tell you something?'

She shook her head.

'That damn chimp was telling me she's going to kill me the first chance she gets. I could feel it coming from her.'

'I believe,' Deena said. 'My God, I could feel it!'

Virginia joined them, carrying the tray. 'Are you going to run this through, Dr. Symons? Shall I find someone to do it?'

'You're still on the temperature test, aren't you?'

'Yes. I was between runs and had a minute. I wanted to see Lola for myself.' She shivered. Clark took the tray from her. 'If I were you,' she said, 'I wouldn't let myself be caught in a room with her for a single second.'

'Yeah, I know. Thanks, for thinking of the tray. I intend to put it through myself.'

At eight Virginia tapped on his door, and when he answered groggily, she looked in and said, 'Have you eaten yet? I'm going to the cafeteria now. I could bring you something.'

Clark stood up and stretched. 'Jesus Christ!' he moaned. 'I'm as stiff as a corpse.' He looked at his watch in disbelief. 'I'll come with you.'

On the way they talked about the temperature tests. Nothing unpredictable there anyway, Clark decided. They had assumed the *pa* factor would be unstable at temperatures over eighty degrees. The tests would continue until they could predict exactly how long it could be stored at eighty, at seventy, sixty, and so on, and then they would narrow it even further. So many hours at seventy-three, or sixty-two. It would take time. Everything took time. And suddenly their time had been eradicated. Just like that, no more time. Ladies and gentlemen, we have an announcement. Henceforth there shall be no more time ...

They met Deena leaving the cafeteria. She turned and went back in with them. 'I wouldn't advise the ham or the turkey tonight,' she said, and made a face. 'My God, if they're experimenting on us, I'll blow up that goddamn annex!'

Not many people were in the cafeteria, a few people from the skeleton crew working a second shift to fill a government order, and a handful of people from the PR department, who were readying a campaign to introduce a new line of hypoallergenic cosmetics. There were three of them lingering over pie and coffee, their table littered with sketches and photographs. One of the watchmen was taking his break. The cafeteria echoed dismally with so few people in the cavernous space.

'I sent Marcie off to stay with my mother,' Deena said when Clark and Virginia joined her with their trays. She was having more coffee.

'Anything new?' Clark asked, not even trying to conceal his fatigue.

'I'm not sure yet. Let you know later. How did that last blood analysis turn out?'

'Down, not sharply, but down. I called Anne and told her what happened, told her I'd stick around and run one more blood test at ten.'

Deena nodded and sipped her coffee. Anne wouldn't have been surprised, she suspected. Anne must have figured this out on paper; putting it to the test was simply to verify what she already had decided. She realized she had been wrong about Anne, they had all been wrong. She looked up from her cup to see Virginia gazing at Clark. At her look, Virginia blushed a deep red that extended down her throat. She stood up. 'I'd better be getting back,' she said, and left very fast.

Clark looked startled, glanced at her departing back, then shrugged and pushed his food around on his plate.

Deena watched the girl walk away, and the fiercely maintained neutrality with which she regarded Clark flared with the pale painful fire of hatred. He knew and relished the anguish Virginia suffered. You always know if you hurt someone like that. For him it was a roller-coaster ego trip: for Virginia, a long slow slide into the shadows of despair. Deena stirred her coffee until there was a whirlpool and watched it until the motion ceased and the surface was calm again. Only then did she look at Clark, and by then her face was masked, the fire again banked.

'Saturday night we're having dinner with my parents,' Clark said, 'and I'll be damned if I'll give it up for more of this junk. No matter what happens around here between now and then.'

'Atta boy!' Deena murmured. She lighted a cigarette and said deliberately, 'We should tell Anne everything.'

Clark sighed. 'I keep coming back to that,' he said. 'If there was anything she could do about this mess, I would. But there isn't. Helverson, Grove, the human tests … It would drive her nuts.'

'She should know,' Deena repeated. 'Let her intuition get to work on it, see what happens then. This stress experiment seems proof enough to me. She is working. Let her work on the real problems now.'

'Look, Deena, she has therapy of some sort every day. She is out for several hours for that. She comes home exhausted. After she rests she works out on the exerciser, then she's supposed to soak and get massaged. It's an all-day job, just trying to get her strength back, learn to walk again. What part of it should she give up?'

Deena didn't have an answer then. Only much later, at home, after working until two, lying awake in bed, too tense and tired to go to sleep, did the elusive answer come to her mind. Anne could be thinking while she worked her body, she realized. She could think and tell Clark what had to be done even if she couldn't do a bit of it herself. She would tell Clark tomorrow, today, Friday, she thought sleepily. But on Friday too many things erupted all at once and she forgot.

And at two Anne was sitting in her chair looking at the dieffenbachia that had turned its back on her, on the room. She didn't blame it, she thought. If she could, she would turn her back and never see that room again.

Her bed was mussed, the sheet twisted into a hopeless tangle, the ashtray by the bed was full, magazines were on the floor by the bed. Her notebook was also on the floor. She had looked at it a long time, wondering if she could retrieve it some way, had decided not, and had gone to the window instead.

How dark the park was every night. She thought of the small hill on the other side of the park, lovers' lane, where she had done a certain amount of necking and petting as a teenager. How innocent it had been, she thought, and remembered her fear of being caught by the patrolling police, of having the bright light turned on in her face, hearing the scornful, hateful voice telling them to get the fuck somewhere else.

But all she had done was neck and pet a little. Not even enough to arouse her still-sleeping libido. That had come later, in college.

She should thank Clark, she thought soberly, for giving her this opportunity to discover she was hollow. Take away her work and what was left? 'Nothing,' she said. Hollow casing stuffed with work. She was tempted to pinch her arm, to see if her fingers would meet since there was nothing between to stop them.

The rubber treads of her wheels left faint marks on the hardwood floor of her bedroom. The marks didn't persist very long, and this was the first time she had seen them. It must be the lighting, she thought. Only a night light was on, low on the wall next to her bed; it cast a pale glow over the floor. She studied the tracks. How they crisscrossed. She tried to find a pattern. To the door, turn, to the window, turn, to the bed, to the bathroom door, turn, to the window ... In the center of the room the lines converged, like the center of a spider web.

Like a spider, unseen, unheard, she could roll about the apartment, into the hall, which looked dark and unfamiliar, with only a suggestion of light coming from her room. It was like a cave passage, she thought, and tried to see if the marks were visible. It was too dark. She went into Clark's room. Her eyes had adapted to the dim light and she could see his form on the bed, no more than that. A shape that her mind instantly identified as Clark. She watched him sleep.

'It's inconclusive, of course,' she said at breakfast with Clark. He looked very tired. 'It would take a full-scale test, but it's indicative of a trouble spot.'

'It's trouble, all right,' Clark said. 'I wish you had seen that chimp last night when she realized I was coming toward her. If she'd had a gun, she would have shot me.'

Anne nodded. 'Do chimps have high blood pressure naturally?'

'I don't know.'

'Will you ask Emory? We know we can't induce high blood pressure clinically without trouble, but what about animals with hypertension? Is there an adaptation process over a long period? We have to know.'

'I'll see if Emory can help. Anything else?'

'I don't know. Something is nagging, but I haven't been able to put my finger on it. You're sure Lilith is fine?'

'Yeah.'

'Are there other drugs that are used to elevate blood pressure? Some might produce different effects. We should try them all, same conditions otherwise. Drug, induce a state of stress, and wait. Clark,' she said, her gaze inward, 'it could mean a delay, couldn't it? We have to know.' She shook her head. 'After all this time.'

'Don't worry about it, honey. Okay? Just don't get in a sweat over it. If you think of anything else, give me a ring. I'll be late again.'

Anne swam again that day, and this time was less exhausted afterward. She could even turn off the smiling idiot, she realized on her way home. Miss Westchester had hardly bugged her at all. The sun was shining, and on the way home Ronnie drove through the park, stopping at the edge of the lake so they could watch a flock of eider ducks for a few minutes. Anne liked the way they upended and vanished under the water. The surface of the water was opaque; the ducks looked like toys being moved by magnets from underneath. When they finally returned to the apartment, she felt as if she might scream. She sat at the window, and could believe the end wall was moving closer, closer, pinning her in place, keeping her immobile while the experimenter prepared yet another test ...

CHAPTER ELEVEN

The holding cages were not very large, they could house two or even three adult chimps, but not comfortably, and not for long. One chimp had enough room to swing up and down from the shelf, take four steps to the front of the cage, four from one side to the other, back to the ledge. The bars were too close together to permit a chimp to get his hand through them.

In the rear of her cage that Friday morning, Fannie sat as the watchman made his check. Her lips were pulled back tightly, her eyes unblinking, unwavering, as she watched. He vanished. She continued to stare at the laboratory before her. Clinging tightly to her belly, her infant shifted position, awakened, hungry. He tried to get to a teat. Fannie growled. For a moment the infant hesitated, then began to mouth her again, groping. Fannie pulled him away, put him on the ledge beside her, not looking at him. The infant crept back to her, nearly slipped off the shelf, whimpered, and regained his balance. He had to crawl over her leg to get to her belly. Fannie continued to watch the laboratory. Again she growled, and again she pulled the infant away, and this time he fell to the floor.

He lay quietly for a minute, then began to whimper louder, and now he crept about, looking for a way back up to the shelf. A dog barked, and as if encouraged by this sound of activity, the infant chimp wailed and looked up at his mother. Fannie stared ahead, but as her baby crept back and forth crying, her gaze was drawn to its dark form and she transferred her stare to it. Her teeth remained bared, and she growled. The baby cried, tried to climb the bars of the side of the cage.

Suddenly Fannie leaped from the shelf and grabbed the infant by a leg and soundlessly began to tear about the cage, dragging it behind her. She raced up the bars, leaped to the shelf, back to the floor, to the side bars ... Around and around, leaping, climbing, dashing first one way, then another, she ran. Now the infant's head struck the shelf, now his back slammed into the bars, now he was thrown against the floor. He screamed and struggled briefly, then became limp, like a rag being swished over surfaces, leaving behind a trail of excrement and blood.

Other animals were excited by the frenzy; a cat howled, a dog barked and another growled continuously, another cat screamed. The chimps were all chattering in fear and excitement. The din rose and became tumultuous.

The watchman punched out at seven without returning to the animal division. The day man hung up his coat and lighted a cigarette, coughed long and hard, and started his first check. Outside the animal division he paused. He ground out his cigarette underfoot, something he had never done before in his fourteen years there, and ran into the room. Moments later he called Emory Durand.

*

'Okay,' Clark said. 'They go crazy. Now we have two psychotic animals. The only question I can see right now is, which one do we sacrifice?'

'Three,' Deena said. 'Lola's less than a step behind Fannie in her deterioration.'

'Not Lola,' Clark said quickly.

Emory nodded. 'I'd say Fannie,' he said. 'She's still showing symptoms, while Duckmore seems completely normal again.'

'Fannie,' Clark agreed. 'Immediately.' He looked at Emory, who kept averting his gaze. 'Will you help?'

Emory shrugged helplessly. 'Sure.'

'I want that brain sliced from one end to the other,' Clark said.

'Are you going to return Lola's baby this morning?' Deena asked.

'Yes. Right now. Someone else can extract the blood. I'll run it later.'

A tap on the door was followed by Gus entering the room. 'Can I come in?' He was already in. 'You fixed with enough people, Clark?'

'Hell no!'

'We'll get them,' Gus said, then added, 'This is first priority, remember?'

For ten minutes they talked about procedural matters, then they all went to observe Lola's behavior when her baby was brought to her. It was a repeat of the previous day. Clark breathed a sigh of relief when the baby was taken away again.

'We're ready for Fannie any time,' Emory said after consulting with one of the staff veterinarians.

Clark smoked a cigarette first, then he went to the operating room to cut up the brain of the newly killed chimp.

Sunlight coming from the stained glass cast pink and blue shadows in the little world of the terrarium. Anne looked at the broad leaves of an ivy that climbed up a twig, to cover it completely. The ivy was blue, green, and rose-colored.

They had played a game, she and Clark. A getting-acquainted game, they had called it. It had evolved from something one of them had said. Something like, I hate prunes. Gradually the rules had emerged and they had settled back warily to test it. The rules were simple – Clark had seen to that. He hated complexity when simplicity would do.

'We'll take turns,' he had said, 'naming things we hate. Personally hate, I mean. Not abstracts like war, or suffering. Okay?'

'Okay. But no Aha! reaction allowed.'

'Right. And after we've got ten each, we select one of the other's things and try to explain why. I try to tell you why you hate roses, you tell me why I hate canned vegetables.'

'And you have to confess if I hit it,' she had said. 'And if I miss, you have to explain it yourself.'

'If we can,' he had added.

'I'll start,' Anne said. 'I hate baseball.'

Clark nodded. 'Artichokes.'

Anne considered it, nodded reluctantly. 'We could use up all ten things by naming various foods.' She thought, then said, 'Dirty dishes left from the night before.'

'Musical comedies.'

'Being wrong.'

Clark looked startled, then said, 'Perfume.'

Anne looked at him quickly, decided he was serious, and said, 'Hairy soap.'

'Sweaty or dirty feet.'

Anne had gone on to name, in this order: Sharing a comb, hair brush, or most especially a toothbrush. Family reunions. Menstruation. Sentimental movies. Men over six feet tall. Hamburger in any form.

Clark's list had been: Gelatinous food. Writing compositions or papers of any sort. Situation comedies. Homosexuals. Mean drunks. Cheaters.

It had started in a light mood, with each of them intent on being honest, on keeping the other honest. By the time they finished, they were both subdued and serious.

'You want to drop it?' Clark asked.

'No! Why should I? Do you?'

He shook his head.

'You go first this time,' Anne said. 'Explain one of my things to me.'

'Men over six feet tall,' Clark said. 'You are tall for a girl. You feel superior until you get beside a man over six feet tall, and then you feel small again. Okay?'

'Wrong. Men over six feet tall have been conditioned to believe tallness is manliness, that to be big outside is somehow to be big inside, and it's been my experience that they are very little inside. Little and curled up like timid worms, always afraid someone will guess, so they develop big loud voices and their feet always trip anyone who gets near them. If they think you suspect the truth about them, they become bullies.'

Clark took a deep breath and said, 'Whew! A live wire there, isn't it?'

'Yes. My turn.' She closed her eyes, trying to remember what he had said. 'Perfume. Your first girlfriend wore perfume and she threw you over for a jock.'

Clark laughed. 'Wrong. I drank my mother's perfume when I was a kid. Made me sicker than a dog.'

'You drank your mother's perfume! Aha!' Anne cried, and clapped her hand over her mouth. They had struggled and he had kissed her and she had kissed back and later they both agreed it was that minute that they knew this was it.

She thought of her brothers and her father, all over six feet tall, all bullies. Come on and play with us, they'd yell at her, you're big enough and strong enough. She had been both, but they had hurt her anyway. They loved picnics and grilling hamburgers outside and going to ball games and friendly wrestling that always got something broken. They didn't hurt her sister, who had somehow missed the tall genes, and was small and dainty. They were always very careful with her, protective.

Clark's family was so different. He was the only child, dearly loved by mother and father, loving them in return. No hostility there, no remembrances of ugly things past, only good will and mutual respect. They had let him go without a struggle and he reciprocated by never really leaving them. Knowing you can removes the need to break away, she thought. They had accepted her with kindness, some reserve naturally, but nothing overtly unfriendly. They weren't sure how to treat her, she had realized early. She obviously was the equal of their son, whom they adored. They responded to her with uneasy kindness. His mother would have liked her better, she thought suddenly, if she had been a black militant. Then she could show her off to her friends. Anne would have become a cause for her.

Maggie Symons was a liberal who collected causes and antiques, and tried to sell both. Anne dreaded the day her parents, conservative Republicans, got into politics with Maggie Symons. Maggie would annihilate them. Mr. Symons was a mild man who was president of a bank, chairman of a hospital board, member of several other boards, and a founder of a youth camp. Anne supposed they were very rich. She supposed one day Clark would be very rich. If they had a child, it, he or she, would be very rich. That always seemed unimportant.

When they were not visiting them or not intending a visit in the near future, the Symonses seemed quite unreal to Anne. They were the sort of people who inhabited a world whose reality touched only briefly, sporadically, on the reality of the world Anne knew.

It was a wonder they hadn't spoiled Clark inordinately, she mused, and then realized she didn't know if Clark was spoiled or not. You only find out when you cross the person, she thought. And she never had crossed him. Their goals had been identical from the start. Neither of them had ever wanted anything the other hadn't wanted equally, or else had not cared enough about to oppose. And if I said no when he said yes, and if I made it stick, she wondered, what would he do? She didn't know.

When things went wrong, everyone in the department was affected, Gus thought. Francis Kirkpatrick and Ronald Medgars were feuding over sharing one lab assistant. Personnel was being funneled steadily away from everyone else to work under Clark now. Steve Ryman and Bert Cheezem had asked for an interview, and Gus had stalled them. More computer time for their soybean runs. He knew what they wanted, demanded. Damn Bob Klugman's eyes, he thought, but without heat. Bob on the job would be more trouble than Bob sick at home, or drunk at home. Here, he would tell everyone yes, take what you need, schedule time for the analyzer, or computer, or whatever, and he would let them fight it out at the site when three of them showed up at the same time. And the hell of it was, Gus knew, each one was involved in work that was vital, that had immediacy. All lab freaks are born equal, he thought, signaling his secretary to admit Walter Orne; only some are more equal because what they're doing will make zillions of dollars for the company.

'What's up, Walt?' he asked the stooped man who slouched into his office and looked at him with an oblique gaze that never seemed to center on his face, but held at his ear, or at the top of his head, or his Adam's apple.

'It's my capsule,' Walter Orne said. His gaze roamed the room, as if searching for something. 'I think I have the twenty-four-hour capsule ready for testing now.'

Anyone else would be celebrating, Gus thought, and at any other time he would have joined in the celebration. A twenty-four-hour capsule for aspirin, for decongestants, for whatever the hell they decided to put in them. And here Walter Orne was practically apologizing for bothering him with it. He pumped enthusiasm into his voice. 'Walt, that's swell! Good Lord, we're the first! Work out the test procedures and we'll start as soon as it's set up!'

Walter's eyes paused on his shirt collar, then resumed their scrutiny of the small office. He hadn't sat down. Now he turned and walked his shambling walk back to the door. 'Everything's ready.'

Gus sighed. 'Sit down, Walt. You have your notes with you?' In his mind he could visualize Clark slicing, slicing, preparing slides. They would photograph them with the electron microscope, feed them into the computer for analysis. Clark, of course, would ruin his eyes studying them personally. The problem was, he decided, taking the detailed notes from Walter Orne, he didn't give a damn if the world had to take a cold tablet every hour or once a day, or never. He was interested in that autopsy and its results. Gradually he began to make out the words, and the meaning of the words, and gradually Clark faded from his mind and he gave his full attention to Walter Orne and his twenty-four-hour capsule.

'What we think happens,' Clark muttered to Emory Durand, 'is that clumping occurs at the nerve endings. That's what I want most now.' Fannie had been dissected, her organs preserved for future study. Her frozen brain, exposed to the electric scalpel, was now being sliced neatly, spread out like so many leaves of a book to be read by the computer.

'Too bad you can't get a piece or two to study before the introduction of the *pa* factor,' Emory said. 'You know, a before-and-after examination.'

The dissection room was as modern as a hospital operating room, with shining stainless steel, pale green gowns for the attendants, and a look-through panel in the door for observers. Now Gus's face appeared in the opening. He was not gowned, did not enter the room. It was three-thirty.

'Enough,' Clark finally said, nearly an hour later. His legs ached, his back ached, his head ached. He knew his eyes would be bloodshot, and now that he had decided to stop, he was suddenly racked with pains in his stomach. 'Buy you some lunch,' he said to Emory as they stripped from the surgery gear and scrubbed.

'You're on.'

When they left for a restaurant, Emory was as immaculate as a camera-ready male model; Clark felt grimy beside him. 'What you said before, about a before-and-after comparison,' he said. 'Look, are you familiar with the divided hemispheres technique?'

'Not really. Read about it. Used in major epileptic cases, or massive brain-damage cases, isn't it?'

'Usually. But the relevant part to us is that a person can and does survive massive brain surgery. We could do a before-and-after examination. Take out a section of the left hemisphere; after recovery, inject the *pa* factor, and later do a study of the right hemisphere.'

They arrived at a small French restaurant, and over lunch made plans for the experiment. Their waitress viewed them from behind the serving screen and shuddered, wondering how they could eat and talk about the things they talked about.

'It's just like all the other variations in the body,' Clark said. 'Those born with high *pa* levels adapt to it at an early age. There's clumping in the brain, but they adapt. If the levels are too high, most often they don't survive childhood. When we artificially raise the level of *pa*, the same kind of clumping takes place in the brain, preventing the pain stimulus from registering. After six to eight hours the level has dropped back to normal, no more clumping, and pain is felt normally again. What Anne's been working on is the effect of the *pa* factor in conjunction with increases in chemical lactate in the blood, associated with anxiety, high blood pressure, hypertension, and so on. I don't know if there's any connection with the other effects we've been observing, but it's a lead. And we by God can use any leads we can get right now. I'll talk to Gus about a before-and-after examination as soon as we get back. Thanks, Emory. Great idea.'

Gus turned it down flat, however. 'Clark, who could do it? Do you realize we've got seventeen people tied up more or less full time on this now? Half of them acting as if we'll go ahead next week with human testing, the other half trying to find out what's gone wrong. I can't pull anyone else off other work for this.'

'I'll do it.'

'When? You're working double shifts as it is. It's a fine idea, and you'll do it, but not right now.'

'We need it now!'

'Clark, sit down.' Gus went to the dart board and pulled out the darts. He returned to his desk with them. 'This is your first setback, isn't it? Everything's been going great right along until now.' He threw the first dart, wide, almost off the target altogether. 'Damnation. Well, it isn't mine. I've seen dozens of experiments go sour after longer years than this of checking out right down the line. Relax. Go with it.' Another dart thudded into the board, this time a bull's-eye. 'There's nothing we can do now except what we're doing. If Helverson agrees to a postponement, we'll have more time available, but not until then.'

'What do you mean, if? There's no way we can go into human experiments now! Not with this new development.'

'Relax, Clark. Take it easy.' He threw again and again cursed. 'Lost it,' he said. 'It comes and goes. One day, all dead in the middle; next day, nothing.' He sighted the dart, looked at Clark, and said, 'I might succeed in making Helverson understand that, and I might not.' He sighted the dart again and this time threw it, but didn't watch where it landed. 'If I fail, Clark, I'm counting on you to make it as foolproof as you can with what we know now. No hypertension cases, things like that. Can do?'

Clark shook his head. 'I won't be a party to it, Gus. I can't.'

Gus leaned on his elbows and studied Clark. 'You can,' he said. 'So can I. We make it as safe as we know how, and go on that basis. It's all we can do, or get out of the game when it comes to the crunch. And it might come to the crunch next week. Either you'll do it, or someone else will. I prefer you.'

'An ultimatum, Gus?'

'I guess so. Whatever you choose to call it, Clark, there never will be a time when you'll know it's one hundred percent okay. Never. You do the best you can.'

'Even if you know it isn't safe?'

'Even so. There are categories of people who will have to be excluded. You exclude them for now. The testing goes on, you keep trying to improve it, find the reasons that necessitate the exclusions. Maybe you find them, maybe not. Meanwhile, you go ahead.'

'Or get out,' Clark added bitterly.

'Or get out,' Gus agreed. 'Sooner or later every new drug, every new serum, everything comes down to this, and you get scared, and should get scared, but you go ahead. I'm going to try like hell to get more time, but if I can't . . .'

'And if those women go the way of Fannie and Duckmore, what do we tell them, Gus?'

'Not a damn thing,' Gus said. He threw another dart, bull's-eye. 'Can't understand why it comes and goes like that,' he said, examining a dart.

Clark stood up, stared at him for a moment, then turned and left. Gus looked at the door for a long time, ignoring the darts now. He pulled the phone to him and placed a call to his wife, the third for the day, and while he waited for it to go through, he continued to stare at the closed door until his eyes hurt.

CHAPTER TWELVE

Anne watched Ronnie playing with the small cat and smiled. Ronnie loved animals, and children, and was very good with them. She was pulling a string tied to a strip of heavy plastic now. The cat's claws could not grasp the plastic, and time and again it watched in frustration as the captured strip moved out from under its paws. It crouched, its tail flicking out of control, and pounced again, and once more the plastic got away. Ronnie laughed heartily at it.

'He's a beauty, isn't he?' she said. 'Harry is a good sort to bring him over. Keep you a lot of company, he will.'

Tyger lost interest in the elusive plastic and began to clean his tail. It was a handsome tail, tall, full, white underneath, gray above. Ronnie laughed at him and tugged the string. Tyger pounced instantly.

'You can't fool an old cat hand like me,' Ronnie said. 'I know your tricks.' She tied the string to the arm of the chaise where Anne could watch the cat play with it. 'I'll just finish up your dinner and feed the crazy cat,' she said. 'Be back in a minute.'

At six, Ronnie was ready to leave. 'Honey, are you sure you don't want me to stay until Clark gets home? I wouldn't mind a bit. Really I wouldn't.'

'It's all right,' Anne said. 'He won't be very late. And I'll need you in the morning for swimming again. Is that a problem?'

'Nah! I've been wondering if they give swimming lessons at that place. I should take lessons. Scared to death of water. I've heard if you take lessons you get over being afraid. But I've always been afraid to take the lessons. That's how it goes, isn't it?' She pulled on her coat and tied a scarf over her hair. 'Going to rain cats and dogs again,' she said. 'Smell it in the air. God, I'm tired of this weather.' She glanced about the room, nodded, and waved. 'See you in the morning. Good God, Tyger! You're going to get stepped on and mashed flatter'n a pancake if you don't learn feet are dangerous.'

Anne could hear her good-natured scolding as she went down the hall-way to the back door. Presently Ronnie was back again.

'Honey, that damn cat ran out when I opened the door. I'll try to find him and bring him back, but he was running like a fire was on his tail last I saw him.'

'He's probably up in the top of one of those maples by now,' Anne said. 'Don't worry about him. If he can't find his way back, that's his tough luck. Just leave the dining room window open a little for him.'

'Damn cat. He ran out like greased lightning. His first big adventure. Just like a kid. Zip, gone!'

Anne waved her away. 'Don't forget the window.'

'Right. Can't get over how fast ...' Her voice faded out as she left once more.

Anne turned on the television, turned it off again after several minutes, and looked at the little world instead. She smiled dreamily. At the pool she had successfully eliminated everyone else, and had swum alone, just as she did in the little world, where the water was in distinct bands of color that didn't mix, didn't become diluted, but remained emerald, jade, pale blue, brilliant royal blue ... If she stretched out full length in the water, her fin-gertips were pale blue, her toes emerald, and her body a deep, almost black blue. Passing from one zone to another, she could feel the changes in the water. The emerald was best; it made her tingle with cool ripples of erotic pleasure. She could turn and follow the emerald, staying wholly inside that band, but she couldn't remain there long; it was too sensual, too arousing, and the pleasure became painful as eroticism grew and became a need. Then she dove into the midnight blue and all feeling left her and she was aware only of the satiny water on her skin.

Suddenly she jerked. She must have dozed, staring at the terrarium. It was eight o'clock. She heard again the noise that had roused her. A cat's scream. Tyger!

Somehow she got her chair down the hall to the corner which she could not turn. 'Tyger! Come here, Tyger!'

He was crying pitiably now. She called him again and again. She backed up her chair and tried to get around the corner, chipped plaster and paint off the corner, and got stuck. Working the chair loose, she scraped both hands, and hardly even aware of them, she gave one final tug on the wheels and got around the corner, heading toward the kitchen and dining room.

Tyger was on the floor, breathing in hard, racking gasps that sounded hollow. He was not crying now. His eyes were closed. She got closer to him and he pulled himself to his feet and staggered away from her chair.

'Tyger! Come here, Tyger!'

Blindly the little cat tried to run from her. He started to bleed. Anne eased herself from the chair to the floor and crept after him and finally caught him. He struggled to free himself and clawed her arm and she dropped him. He ran a few steps, stopped, fell down in a convulsion, and died.

Anne stared at the small cat in horror and disbelief, then she vomited and it seemed the room was spinning, faster and faster, and she felt she was falling a great distance.

It seemed a long time later that she began to pull herself back up to her chair and got down the hall to the corner again and stopped, knowing she could not turn from this side. This passage was narrower than the main hall. There was no way she could turn the chair from here. She sat still for several minutes and then left her chair and crept down the hall, dragging her right leg, to her room, to the bathroom. She didn't try to stand up, but washed her hands and face and rinsed her mouth at the bathtub. She was shivering uncontrollably and she felt hot as if she had a fever.

She had blood on her clothes. She undressed, leaving the things where they fell. The smell of vomit was heavy in the air. She felt the bathroom start to tilt, and she put her head down until everything was stable again. In her panties and bra she dragged herself to the side of the bed and pulled the telephone to the floor, not caring if it broke or not. She dialed the number for Clark's office. There was no answer. She was shivering too much to dial again and she pulled her robe from the foot of the bed and got it around her shoulders. She could hear a hard, pounding rain beating against the windows. It would break the windows, she thought. She should close the drapes so it couldn't get in all the way.

Her fingers trembled as she dialed again, this time the lab number. A woman's voice answered after half a dozen rings. Virginia Sudsbury.

'Dr. Symons isn't here right now,' she said. 'I think he's gone out for dinner. Probably to the cafeteria. I can find out for you.'

'Please do,' Anne said, fighting hysteria, fighting to keep her voice as calm as the girl's. 'Right away. Please.'

'I'll call back in a couple of minutes,' Virginia said. 'Are you all right?'

'Find him!' Anne cried, and bit her lip. 'Please just find him.'

Ten minutes later Virginia called back. 'I'm sorry, Dr. Clewiston. I can't find him. I think he went out to dinner with Dr. Wells and a couple of the others. As soon as they get back, I'll have him call you. Is there anything I can do?'

Tears were standing in Anne's eyes. She shook her head. 'No. NO! Just tell him!' Fumbling, she hung up the phone and the tears now ran down her cheeks.

This was the reality, she thought. The floor was cold and hard and she was too weak to climb up into the bed, too dizzy and sick to try to get to the chaise. She could only sit there on the cold hard floor and wait for her husband to come do something about it. Thunder rumbled distantly and the rain pounded as if frenzied. In a minute, she thought, she would try to get herself up to the bed, get under the covers, get warm. In a minute.

She thought of the wicked or cruel things she had done in the past. But she hadn't been evil, not really, not as evil is measured in the courts. She never had harmed anyone, not deliberately. She had lied a little, but not maliciously. She had not abandoned God. There never had been a God to abandon. She didn't deserve this, she thought, weeping. The agony of the accident, the operations, the months in this prison room, and now this solitary confinement and the destruction of the one thing that might have eased it for her.

The weeping stopped finally and she wiped her face on the sheet. 'Ah, well,' she said to herself, 'crying doesn't make the fire burn.' Her grandmother had said that, she remembered. Her grandmother had died when Anne was only six, how strange to remember her now. Very old and brown, with silver hair and merry blue eyes, and a quick tongue, that had been her grandmother. Even after she had become too frail to leave her bed, her mind had been sharp, her tongue sharper. 'Fretting doesn't make the train run faster,' she would say if the children fidgeted, in a hurry to do something or get something. Anne thought of her grandmother as she worked to get into the bed with the telephone beside her.

It was after nine when Clark called, and by then she was calm. She kept having to banish the image of the small gray heap of fur; over and over she was successful at banishing it.

'Clark, I need you,' she said, and was amazed at the steadiness of her voice.

'Are you all right?' His voice in contrast was almost shrill with apprehension.

'Yes. Please come home. I can't talk about it, not on the phone.' No more, she thought, no more talk now or I'll break and that will frighten him too much. No more.

'I'll leave now,' he said.

She closed her eyes, tried to recapture the lovely water, and saw instead the tiny animal blindly trying to escape its hurt. It would take him twenty minutes, maybe more in the rainstorm. Half an hour. The thunder was drawing closer, breaking with the sharp, close explosions of a summer storm. Probably there were tornado warnings out. May weather. Someone must have hit it in the parking lot, and it dragged itself back to the apartment, through the window, and died. Deena would drive Clark home, might come in with him. If there was nothing going on with Clark and Deena she would come in, they would have to pretend nothing was changed, all of them pretending, pretending. Deena looking at her from the corners of her eyes, wondering if she suspected. Clark uneasy with her, staying at the lab longer and longer hours ...

He arrived twenty-two minutes after her call. She told him what had happened. Under the covers her hands were clenched so tight that when she tried to open her fingers they felt paralyzed. Clark's face became set in the way it did when he received bad news. A stranger might think he was not reacting at all, but she knew he was shocked, more than just shocked, he was filled with the same horror she had felt.

'Oh, my God,' he said in a low voice. He left her, came back very quickly, and sat on the side of the bed and held her. 'It must have been awful for you. Are you all right? Do you need anything? Can I get you coffee, a drink?'

'Coffee,' she said.

He brought it and then left again to clean up the dining room. He was very pale when he returned the second time. He had her chair with him.

'I'll draw a bath for you,' he said. He went out and came back with a tall drink that appeared to be straight bourbon with a single ice cube floating in it. He drank deeply, then started her bath while she got into the chair.

Clark lifted her into the tub and washed her back. He examined the long scratches on her arm and when she was dry put Merthiolate on them, and a Band-Aid on her knuckles where she had scraped them on the corner wall. Neither spoke until he lifted her hand and kissed her fingers.

'Oh, Clark, don't or I'll cry again.'

He held her close for a minute, and then took her back to the bedroom, to the table by the bay window. He closed the drapes, and the storm became distant, not threatening, the room became the haven it should have been and she felt dry, warm, and safe once more. Clark's presence was too strong for the strangeness, she thought. When he was there, everything was normal.

He had almost finished his drink, and he showed its effects in a sleepiness that came over his face, softening his expression, slurring his words a bit when he spoke. 'Anne, this won't do,' he said, in his different, more Southern, voice. He had lost his accent, but it came back when he was very tired, or a little drunk, and he was both then.

'I don't know what you mean,' she said.

'You can't stay here alone again. I don't know how in hell you got back to this room from the hall, but what if you hadn't been able to? What if you got stuck somewhere and had to stay for hours and hours? Where the hell is Ronnie? I thought she could stay until I get home?'

'She needs some time off, too,' Anne said. 'She has to be here tomorrow, maybe Sunday. You can't expect her to stay day and night.'

Clark closed his eyes. 'We'll get someone else to relieve her,' he said. His accent was more pronounced. It was nearly twelve and he would fall asleep where he sat if he didn't get to bed soon, he knew. He shook himself and stood up. 'Tomorrow. Do you want to call the agency, or shall I?'

'Let's talk about it in the morning,' Anne said. 'You're so tired. Go on to bed. Should I call your parents and tell them we can't make it tomorrow night?'

He shook his head. 'I already told Gus I won't be staying late tomorrow.' He leaned over her to kiss her and for a moment rested his cheek against hers. He needed a shave. Then he sighed and pushed himself away. 'Can I help you get to bed?'

'Not yet. I'll go soon.' She watched to see if the strangeness returned with his absence. It didn't. Afraid he'll come back, she thought. He would be taking a shower, maybe getting another drink, fooling around. At one she knew he would be in bed, probably already sound asleep, and she could feel the other reality seeping in from the corners of her room where it lived now. The room became plastic that flowed into new shapes. Now it was a ship's prow, she the captain staring out at the storm that threatened to capsize them all. 'A female captain! By Thunder, no wonder we're sinking!' And she, the captain, fought the wheel and sensed the power of the waves and was one with the ship beneath her. She smiled and the room flowed again, back to her bedroom, with its elephant adorned with rare and costly jewels, and now she swayed with the rhythm of the elephant's measured tread, and on either side she could hear the excited murmuring of the boys as they neared the killer tiger. Only she, with her innate sense of danger, could be certain the tiger was near now, ready to spring, murder in its evil heart. She could feel it nearer, nearer. The elephant knew. He snorted. (Do elephants snort?

she wondered.) He snorted and tossed his trunk. (Scattering her clothes in every direction.) She sighed and willed the scene away, but the feeling persisted. The tiger at her back, ready to spring ... Springing. Leaping through the air ... She twisted in her chair and shot, and knew she had missed. She screamed and tried to smother the sound with both hands.

Trembling, she waited for Clark to appear, to demand to know what had happened. She could hear the scream bouncing off the walls, up from the floor, down from the ceiling, beating at her as the rain beat the windows, fading so slowly it seemed it would persist for hours, days even. Minutes passed and Clark didn't appear and gradually she relaxed again. He hadn't heard. She would be murdered here in her room and he wouldn't hear her screams for help.

She had been hallucinating, she thought in wonder, getting into bed. Really hallucinating. The feeling of a tiger had been real, the fear had been real. She almost laughed. In spite of herself, she had been able to reach a state of transcendental meditation. It was the isolation and the quiet, she thought. Sensory deprivation. Your mind will create its own diversions if none is provided by the outside world. And her mind was functioning perfectly in that regard.

She slept and dreamed that Tyger played on her bed, and every time she tried to pet him, he scratched her.

CHAPTER THIRTEEN

Maggie Symons stood in the doorway of her living room and looked back into the hall, then into the room. The entrance hall was a rather large room in itself, but it didn't seem so. Sixteen feet wide, twenty feet long, the room looked like a furniture storeroom, with narrow passages, one to the hall, another to the stairs, and this one that led to the living room. There was enough room for Anne's wheelchair, she hoped, but probably none at all to spare. She spread her arms and walked through the hall, stopped at a carved coat rack and frowned at it, drew in her hands an inch, then walked on to the door. She nodded.

Maggie Symons was only five feet two and over the years she had gained weight, one pound a year. She often thought with wonder at how they had accumulated. She had been petite for so long she still thought of herself as petite, until she looked in a mirror and saw a short, stout woman with a pretty face, naturally curly brown hair, who really should lose at least twenty pounds, and twenty-five would be even better. But she had kept her face and her hair, and her teeth. At that point she would always smile at herself, and she knew it didn't matter so very much about the weight. There were clever clothes, and she was fifty plus, after all. The smile would broaden and she would add, Joseph liked her plump.

There had been two bad times in their marriage. The first had been when Clark was a baby and she had come to realize her life was the house and the child, and a husband who was absent more frequently than necessary, who worked longer hours than he needed to, and who put in weekends on the golf course, or in traveling to meet with other businessmen, or something. The other young wives had the same complaints, but it hadn't mattered about them. She had suffered, and she had found relief. For three years the marriage had teetered. Then, with no explanation then or ever, he had started to court her again. He had sent her presents – flowers, candy, a mink stole, a trip for two to New York for a weekend. Neither of them ever mentioned those lost three years. And it had been good then until Clark went away to school.

Maggie knew who the girl had been, how long it lasted, where they went, what he bought her. This time she waited, and when the time was right, she sent him a present – an antique pocket watch, ornately carved gold, with a dent in the cover, said to have been made by a gambler in Summit, California, who had claimed it when a loser tried to welch.

She could remember, with some pain, and some amusement now, the look on his face when he had come home carrying the watch in his hand. He had stopped in the doorway of their bedroom and said something quite inane that she hadn't heard. Since then, everything had been fine, lovely in fact. And she believed him when he said she was prettier now than when they married. She knew he believed it.

Clark was like her, she thought. Clark was passionate, sensuous. She shied away from visualizing him with Anne, who always seemed very cool, too controlled, too cerebral. She shook herself and studied the cluttered entrance hall again.

'What do you think?' Maggie asked, reentering the living room. She sat on a rose velvet love seat, 1848, and addressed her husband, who was seated in a sturdier leather chair of Spanish origin.

'About what?' he asked, glancing at her. He was trying to read the paper, and he knew he would not be allowed to.

'Can Clark get her chair through the hall? I had Edgar clear it out a lot, but you know how he is. He means well, but you have to stand over him and point and explain in one-syllable words, over and over.'

'They'll get through.'

'But did you really notice when you came in?'

'I would have noticed if I hadn't been able to get through,' he said, turning again to the paper.

'Just go look, will you, dear? Just to make sure. It would be so embarrassing for Anne if we had to start moving anything after they got here. She's so sensitive.'

He didn't even sigh as he got up and walked to the front door, just as she had done. He was under six feet, but always felt and appeared much taller. His hair was white, fairly long. He looked like a successful banker. He sat down again. 'It's fine. Don't get in a stew.'

'I'm not in a stew. I don't think she thinks we like her much, that's all. I don't want to hurt her feelings. Clark would be annoyed. They might not come back for months and months. I really can't understand that girl. Can you?'

He shook his head. 'Nothing to understand. She's just like Clark. If you can understand him, you can understand her. Just alike.'

'That's the problem,' Maggie said with a soft sigh. 'I don't understand him a bit, and somehow it doesn't seem right for her to be so like him. I really think he would have been better off with someone altogether different. Like us. I don't have an inkling of your business and I don't want to. What would it be like if we got up and had breakfast and went to work together, had lunch with the same people every day, came home together? What would we have to talk about?' She paused and tried to imagine such a relationship. She said, 'She doesn't know a thing about art or music or anything except their work, I guess.'

'Neither does he,' her husband said, turning to the comics.

'That's the point. She should know something, be ready to coach him, or fill in for him, or, you know. The way I do for you if someone brings up opera.'

'Maggie, everybody doesn't have to be an opera fan.'

'Do you suppose they just talk about bugs and microscopes all the time?' He didn't answer, and presently she said, 'I bet they talk about sex a lot. They probably spend a lot of time in bed. They have sex books in the apartment. I saw them.'

Behind his newspaper Joseph Symons took in a deep, inaudible breath. Now she would say, I wonder if she intends to have a child …

'… With a woman like her, you never know. I wonder if she can have children. I think they turn to things like science when they know, even if only intuitively, that they won't have babies. Clark would be such a good father. I can just see him helping his son fly a kite. Like you did with him.'

Joseph Symons chuckled at *B.C.* He turned the newspaper to the local news section.

'Should I give her her present first, I wonder,' Maggie said after a pause.

'If I take Clark upstairs to show him the Chinese chest first, she might feel left out and be hurt. I should have told Edgar to bring her case in here. Then I could give it to her, and then take Clark ... Joseph, are you listening to me at all?'

'No, dear,' he murmured.

Maggie frowned in his direction, but not at him. She wasn't even seeing him. 'I think I'll have Estelle help me get them both in here now,' she said. She stood up, then sat down again. 'But then he couldn't get her chair in,' she sighed.

Joseph Symons liked the long-legged girl his son had married. He liked the way they looked at each other, and thought they probably did spend a lot of time in bed. He liked her reserve, the way her eyes twinkled just before she ducked her head when Maggie said anything especially ridiculous, like her method of attaining instant culture.

'You see,' Maggie said, 'it's so simple. Everyone is expected to know something about everything these days. And there's always someone to put you to the test. So you just have several things ready. Like you should know four different composers and specific compositions, and if music comes up, you can say your favorite is ... oh, something like Glière's *Red Poppy*. Or the Bernstein Mass. You see, not the usual things. Not Beethoven's Fifth Symphony, for instance.' She beamed at Clark, but she was directing her little lecture at Anne, who had ducked her head in order to concentrate on her salad.

Joseph grinned and said, 'I always tell 'em my favorite music is country fiddling.'

'And you lie about it,' Maggie said calmly. 'His favorite really is bawdy sea chanteys. No music to it, just dirty words.'

Joseph chuckled.

Clark said, 'And you should have a favorite moviemaker. Not Cecil B. De Mille. Someone obscure that only three other people in the room ever heard of.'

'And a favorite dish,' Joseph Symons said. 'Nothing as common as chili con carne – which really is, by the way – but exotic, like escargots stuffed with shallots and truffles, served in a champagne sauce, as made by Chef Jobert in some fancy hotel down in New Orleans.' He smacked his lips.

'And a favorite little ocean cruise,' Clark said laughing. 'Nothing like the Atlantic or even the Caribbean. A little out-of-the-way ocean, like the Caspian Sea, on this delightful little steamer that leaves promptly at ten every Tuesday.'

For a moment Maggie's lips tightened, but then she laughed, and after she caught her breath she said to Anne, 'My God, think how dishonest I would be without them!'

*

Going home, Anne said, 'I'm so glad we went. That was fun. I really am jealous of you for your parents, you know that.'

'I know. And it's so dumb. You're taken in like everyone else. Didn't you see how they treated me? As soon as I go in that door, I'm seventeen again. Mother lectures me, gently, and never directly, but she's still trying to turn out a proper son. Dad ... well, Dad is himself. I never did know what he was like, really.'

'But they love you so much. It's so obvious.'

'Not this me that I've become. They don't even see me. They see that awkward kid home from school, and they see a messy room with a microscope and an insect collection, and chemicals that scare them to death. They quit looking after I grew out of that phase.'

Anne was silent. He just didn't understand. It was easy at his parents' home. They wanted to please him. His mother and the presents she couldn't resist buying for Clark and Anne. It gave her pleasure to buy them, to give them.

'I go because every now and then it's nice to be that kid again,' Clark said softly. 'It's nice to feel even for a couple of hours someone else is being responsible. I don't have to do anything, be anything, except there, ready to kid them along, or be kidded.'

Anne laughed. 'And when you said you'd keep your opium and LSD and coke in that chest, I thought I would crack up. Did you see her face?'

Clark laughed. 'I know I shouldn't do it to them, but I can't seem to help it. What in God's name will I do with a fancy Chinese chest that cost five hundred dollars and is too fragile to hold booze?'

'Keep your fossils in it. You can't keep them in my jewelry case!' Anne laughed until she felt weak. 'That was an awful thing to tell her, by the way. She thinks we're barbarians as it is, and you tell her things like that.'

Watching Anne that night, being away from the gloom of the lab, laughing with her and his parents, Clark had felt a surge of confidence. He could tell her about the approval of the IND, he realized. It would never occur to her that anyone was considering going ahead, not in light of the trouble her own stress experiments had caused. She would think they were investigating that, being as cautious now as they had been from the beginning. He remembered their past successes and felt his heart lurch. It would be like old times, he thought, just like before. He had driven to the front of the apartment building without thinking. He turned off the motor and reached for her.

'Honey, I've been bursting with this all night. I couldn't tell you before them. We got the IND approval!'

She didn't move. She seemed to be holding her breath. Then she said, 'You're serious? It really came? This soon?'

'It came.'

'Clark! They approved? An approval?'

She laughed and wept and asked questions and didn't wait for answers before she asked other questions. And it seemed all the wine she had drunk at dinner, the brandy after dinner, all went to her head together and she was dizzy and floating and incoherent. Clark carried her chair to the apartment door, then returned for her. He kissed her when he picked her up, and again when he placed her in the chair.

'And my news,' she said. 'I thought you were so tired all week, working so late, it just didn't seem like the time to mention it. I've been swimming every day this week!'

'Good God!' Clark cried, swinging her chair around. He kissed her again. 'You just didn't mention it! You idiot!'

'My. Symons, is everything all right?' a voice asked from the stairwell. Anne, looking over Clark's shoulder, saw spidery little Mrs. Ochs peering down at them.

'Everything's beautiful!' Clark called back. He opened the apartment door and pushed Anne's chair inside. The apartment was dark; they had forgotten to leave a light on in the hall. Laughing, Clark pushed her chair through the bedroom doorway and groped for the switch.

She was drunk, Anne thought. Alcohol mixed with the adrenaline of excitement, release of tension, everything combined, and she was quite drunk. The room was unquiet. The space capsule tilted in a banked curve. 'Don't turn on the light,' she whispered, her eyes adjusting now. He was with her this time, they could share the strange room.

'I don't have much choice,' Clark said, still laughing. 'I can't find the bugger.'

Gradually the darkness gave way to a dimness, light through the wisteria tree softened the bedroom, made the walls recede into distance, made the bed appear very large. Clark carried Anne to the bed and she floated serenely. Free fall, she thought. Although the bed might waft gently from side to side, might even turn over all the way, she was safe there. No top, no up, no down. She felt the bed bobbing as Clark leaned over to kiss her. Now, she thought. Now she should tell him the other piece of good news. *The doctor said have fun, screw.*

She opened her eyes and saw him then. An intent look had come over him, and he was strangely exposed, as if a mask had vanished leaving his face almost twisted in pain and need. No hiding now, no pretense, only pain and need. And when he saw her, what would he see? Broken body, scarred, disfigured, crippled. She had a momentary vision of herself tied down by restraints, immobile while he fucked her, and when his lips touched hers, she jerked and tried to twist away from him.

Clark kissed her hard. He knew when the moment passed, when she withdrew in fear, and he could feel the tension in her body as his hands moved down her, taking off her skirt, unbuttoning her blouse. She was rigid with fear. He kissed her throat and whispered, 'It's all right, Anne. It's all right. Your doctor said it's all right. I won't hurt you. I'll be gentle.' He kissed her collarbone and then her breast and his hand moved down her stomach, rested a moment on the sharp hipbone and moved on to her thigh. She tried to hold his hand, tried to pull it away, and he kissed her palm, her fingertips, and then put her hand in his left hand and held it. He kept whispering to her, kissing her, and she was trembling now. 'You're so beautiful! I love you so much!'

'No!' she moaned. 'Clark, don't ...!'

'I won't hurt you,' he whispered at her ear, and then his mouth went to her nipple again, and his hand was at her pubis. 'Don't be afraid,' he whispered. 'It's all right.'

'No!' she cried, shaking her head. 'No! Don't!'

She pulled her hand out from under him and tried to push him away, and he whispered and kissed her and his hand found her clitoris and no words made contact.

She didn't know what he was saying, what she was saying, nor did he.

He knew she wanted him as much as he wanted her, her need was as great as his. He had felt it flowing from her, stronger every day. It was a palpable thing in the apartment. He knew he wouldn't hurt her, cause her pain now, and she would realize that, too, and they would be together again. 'Not just for me,' he said hoarsely. 'We have to. For you too.' And, over and over, 'I love you so much!' And, 'I'll be so careful. I'll be gentle. Please, don't be afraid. I won't hurt you. I promise I won't hurt you.'

She knew he would do it, and she struggled harder, then stopped. She couldn't move. A long shudder passed through her and she could hardly even feel him any longer. Tears of rage and self-pity and helplessness burned her eyes.

A new rhythm was beating in Clark's ears. *Now! Now! Now!* As carefully, as gently as he could, he rolled her to her side and lay down beside her.

She was dry, his penetration painful, and suddenly she began to weep convulsively, and he ejaculated. For several minutes neither spoke or moved, then he withdrew and left her.

She groped for Kleenex and wiped herself, then worked the bedspread down under her and got herself under the covers. She couldn't stop weeping.

When Clark returned, he had on his robe and slippers, carried a tray with coffee and cups. With his back to her, standing at the small table before the bay window, he said softly, 'Anne, forgive me. If I hurt you ...'

'You didn't hurt me.'

He came to the bedside and started to sit down. She turned her head away and he returned to the chair by the table.

'It's been driving me crazy,' he said after a moment. 'Seeing you in bed day after day, looking prettier all the time, wanting you so goddamn much. I dream about us, about sex. At the lab, it comes over me like a shock, the illusion of being with you. And tonight ... I've never seen you so beautiful as you were tonight. Anne, I swear to God I thought you wanted me! I thought you were afraid, that afterward you'd see it isn't going to hurt you now.'

'Once,' Anne said, looking straight ahead, 'we were making love and it was one of the good nights at the beginning, and then something happened, and later you said we never had been so out of rhythm. Do you remember?' Her voice was toneless, dead. She didn't wait for his reply. 'I know what happened. It was a year or so ago. I had my legs almost flat, and you were on me and it was building, building, to a slow beautiful climax. And you suddenly decided I would perform better with my legs up, and I resisted, not long, not hard, but I rebelled, and everything went away. It had to be your way. You always know what will be best for me, don't you, and I have to do it that way. If my legs ache, or I get a cramp in my thigh, or whatever, it has to be your way. For my sake, of course.'

Clark cleared his throat. 'All you ever had to do was give me a sign, say something ... Good God, Anne, if there's any one thing we have had together it's been sexual freedom.'

'No,' she said. 'I took it for granted we were equals in all ways. At work, here around the apartment. All ways. But I was kidding myself. All I have to do is say something. Tonight I said something and you went on anyway. Always your way. You know best. If there's something we do that you don't like, don't enjoy, it's simple, you just don't initiate that again, and if I start to, you ignore me. It has to be your way. If there's something I don't like, all I have to do is tell you, plead with you not to do it again, try to explain why, how I feel, explain I'm not rejecting you, but only a small act. And you'll stop, won't you? Just like you stopped tonight!'

'What don't you like that we do? Just tell me, for God's sake!'

'Don't you understand what I'm saying to you?' she cried. 'I won't be a supplicant! I won't plead with you, try to explain myself to you, beg you.'

'Jesus! I don't expect you to plead or beg. Just tell me.' Clark started to pace. He went to the bed, and when she continued to stare, dry-eyed now, past him at nothing at all, he reached down and turned her face, hurting her cheeks, knowing he was hurting her cheeks. 'Anne, you know tonight's the first time I've ever forced myself on you in any way, and I was wrong.

I thought that was the way it had to be, to show you it was all right now. I was wrong. We should have talked first. Anne, I swear to you I thought you wanted it too.'

Now she looked at him, and a tremor passed through her. He yanked his hand away as if it had been burned. He looked frightened.

'Anne, I've really upset you. I didn't realize it would do this to you. Anne, Christ, I'm sorry!'

She stared at him. 'It doesn't matter any more,' she said. 'It just doesn't matter.'

'Anne! Don't look like that. Don't talk like that. What's wrong with you?'

'I don't know,' she said, in that same lifeless voice she had used earlier. 'It doesn't matter.'

Clark dropped to the bed and tried to put his arms about her. She didn't protest, didn't resist, and after he had held her for a moment, she said once more, 'It doesn't matter at all. Please bring my chair over here.'

'Anne, I can't leave you like this. Something's terribly wrong. You're in shock or something. Lie down, try to relax. I'll get you a drink.'

'I don't want anything. Just my chair. And then go on to bed and leave me alone.'

Clark grabbed her by the shoulders and shook her. 'Stop it! Snap out of it!'

'Get your hands off me!' she cried in a low voice that was almost a sob. 'Don't touch me again! I want to go to the bathroom and clean myself. I feel filthy, used! I feel like a whore who let the slimiest prick in the world smear her up. I can feel it on my legs, on the sheet under me, and it makes me want to throw up! All at once here I am, a cunt for you to empty yourself into. Why didn't you go out and buy yourself a cunt? Why didn't you jerk off? You've killed it! Can't you see, it's dead, gone, and all I feel is dirty. If I thought you were coming at me again, I'd vomit. Now get out of here! Get out!'

CHAPTER FOURTEEN

Clark drove until almost three. He had gone out to put the car away, and instead had driven through the park, out the other side, and had kept going. He had stopped at red lights, at stop signs, and then, when he stopped in the middle of the street and a driver behind him had pressed his horn angrily, he had come to, as if out of a deep sleep, and had turned and gone back to the apartment. He couldn't recall what he had been thinking during the two and a half hours he had been out. He was cold and tired, the damp February night was in his clothes, his hair; he felt clammy all over.

Her light was still on. Her door was closed. It was the first time since they had been married that the door had been closed with one on the inside, one on the outside. Before he went to her, he had a hot bath, made two drinks, and entered her room.

'Are you all right?' he asked. She was sitting at the window, the drapes open now. The room was thick with smoke. She didn't look at him, didn't answer.

'Look, Anne, I said I'm sorry. I truly am. Will you talk to me?'

Still she didn't respond. He put her drink on the table where she could reach it, emptied the ashtray, and sat down opposite her. 'Anne, please don't do this. Try to see it as I saw it. We were happy, celebrating two pieces of incredibly good news. You said don't turn on the light. You lay there smiling, the way you do when you're inviting me, and my God, I wanted you.' She didn't move. He leaned toward her and said, 'Anne, I've known for a month you were ready to have sex again. I talked to your doctor and he told me. He said you were afraid but there was nothing to keep us from resuming our sex life. He said you'd regain your strength and lose your fear naturally. Nothing to worry about. I thought you were telling me you were ready.'

She looked at him then, and her eyes were very dark, almost black. She looked stricken, ill. 'You've been checking up on me behind my back?'

'No! It isn't like that,' he said. 'I've talked to Dr. Radimer a lot since the accident. In the beginning I called him every few days. Now maybe once a month. My God, Anne, I've been out of my mind, seeing you like this, hurt, helpless. If I'd been able to do something myself it wouldn't have been so bad, but knowing I could do nothing . . . I had to know how you were. I had to talk to him.'

She continued to look at him, and her gaze was that of a stranger who didn't like what she saw.

'Anne, he said you were ready! I wouldn't have touched you if I hadn't known that!'

'It wasn't his decision to make,' she said distantly. 'It wasn't yours, either.' She looked at the window again. 'You raped me. No amount of talk will change that. Go on to bed. Leave me alone.'

She felt only a great impatience with him for coming back, interrupting her thoughts, forcing her to pay attention now. She had managed to get a great distance away from the room, from everything, and he had brought her back; she wanted only to be alone again. She was hardly aware when he left her.

It always came to this, she thought. She was a woman, she belonged to him to be used or not, and all the rest of it was a sham. Just so long as their desires coincided she had been allowed to believe she was free, and she had believed wholly, harboring no doubt whatever. This is what happened. This is why women suddenly began to break up the crockery, smash up the house, this realization hit each and every one of them eventually, and while they might not articulate it, or think it through as she had been doing, the knowledge lay like a lump in their hearts. Or their wombs.

They can't talk about this, she thought, so they talk about everything else – jobs, being tied down to children, no money of their own. But at bottom it was this: if he wanted to do something, he did it; if he didn't want to, he didn't do it. If she wanted it, she had to ask, or explain; if she didn't, she had to struggle, beg, reject the act without rejecting the person, or he might lose his erection, or ejaculate prematurely.

All the little things she had overlooked, excused, because her sex drive had been satisfied. The times she had felt ridiculous with her long legs waving in the air, the times he had changed her position when she had been enjoying the act and hadn't wanted to change. Just tell him, she thought bitterly. When? When she was riding the crest of a coming orgasm? Afterward, when she was floating serenely? The next day? When she had tried to have her way, one time only, everything had gone, it had become awkward and unlovely and frustrating to both of them. What made him think he knew with a godlike certainty what she would enjoy most? What made that doctor think, with godlike certainty, she was ready to resume a sex life?

'There, there, now didn't that feel good?' That was their attitude after the fact. And after the fact she had felt good; unvoiced complaints became childish, selfish cries of a sated spoiled brat who would continue to eat even though he might become sick, or who would deny himself a goodie simply to hurt his parent.

She had gone inside her own brain to register a complaint, she thought, and she had found this tiny, almost invisible door to the right department. When she had opened the door she had discovered, to her amazement, the room stretched out in all directions; it was boundless, and there, waiting for her to recognize them, were all the minor complaints she had filed over the years. Each one had been belittled, its sharpness rubbed off by her easy acceptance of results, and her belief, unproven, untried, in her own freedom.

Now that belief was shattered and she felt strange, as if she had become someone else. A person she had to explore, that she needed time to accept. She didn't think she liked the person she had discovered. It seemed urgent for her to maintain as much distance as possible from that person until she understood her better, and she had succeeded in separating herself earlier while Clark had been out. He had forced her back, and the confusion had started again.

She realized she knew as little about Clark as she had known about herself, and this seemed a revelation as staggering as the first. She wheeled herself to the hall, across it to his room. She rolled close to the bed where he slept, and for a long time she sat motionless studying him in the dim light from the hallway. She shook her head. She didn't know him at all.

On Sunday, Clark went to the lab to observe the chimps on the stress experiment. Hermione and Lilith had accepted the new routine. They greeted their infants with delirious joy, nursed and groomed them, and when the babies were removed, resumed feeding themselves with no outward show of concern. Lola's baby was brought only after the others had been returned to the infant cage. Lola sat clutching the bars of her cage, staring at the laboratory. She transferred her unblinking gaze to Clark when he approached. A low moan seemed to issue involuntarily from her and she bared her teeth but otherwise didn't move. Clark felt the same prickles he had felt before under her stare. He motioned the attendant to bring the baby and stepped out of the way, around the side where he could get at Lola with his tranquilizer gun if he had to.

He glanced at the two assistants on duty, John Lincoln and Frank Egleston, both good enough, but not of the caliber of Virginia Sudsbury or Bob Brighton. Neither of them had been working with the chimps during the week. His tension mounted when Lola now fixed her gaze on the transport cage that was being maneuvered into position to release the infant. Something ... Something ... He didn't know what, but something was wrong, badly wrong, dangerously wrong. Then the cage door was being raised, and he knew what was wrong. Frank hadn't locked the transport cage into place. He raised his tranquilizer gun and at the same time Lola snatched her baby and threw it over her head and lunged at the opening; her long arm snaked out, shoved the wheeled cage away. Her hand fastened on Frank's lab coat and yanked. Clark's first shot only grazed the moving chimp. He fired again as she tore at the air to get at Frank. She slumped, half out of the cage, her arm dangling over the side. Frank was on his knees, his arm bleeding, his eyes large with shock and fright.

Moving very swiftly, Clark unlatched and pulled open the full-sized door and hurried inside the cage to retrieve the injured baby. He handed it to John Lincoln and tugged at Lola to get her fully inside so they could close the small door. She stirred and rolled over and lashed viciously at Clark. Her hand hit his thigh and he fell to his hands and knees. Lola tried to rise, was overcome with convulsive shaking, and before she could recover, Clark pushed himself to the door and rolled out. For a moment he thought she had broken his leg. John Lincoln slammed the door shut and locked it. He already had the small door closed and locked. Lola was shaking her head from side to side now. She stood up unsteadily, the effects of the tranquilizer fading, and she began to scream.

'You all right, sir?' John asked, helping Clark stand up.

'Yes. What about him?' He motioned toward Frank.

'He's okay. Pretty deep scratch down his arm, that's all.'

'Good. Get him to the infirmary, will you? Does he drive to work?'

John Lincoln shook his head. 'Bus.'

'Tell the infirmary to send him home in a cab, fill out an accident form for him. They'll know.'

'Sure,' John said. He led Frank from the animal division.

'You bitch,' Clark muttered, looking at the chimp, who had stopped howling and was again merely staring at him. 'You dirty bitch. You wanted to kill me, didn't you?'

He looked at the baby chimp in the transport cage and sighed. It was breathing. He started to push the cage toward the animal surgery room and winced. His leg would be good and sore for a while. He paused and glanced back at Lola once. She was still staring at him.

He had to get the blood samples, he thought, wheeling the injured baby to the veterinarian. Had to check out the temperature quality test. Had to check on the progress of the autopsy sections that were being photographed through the electron microscope. His head ached and his leg throbbed with each step.

Dr. Jerry Levy was on duty that day. He examined the baby chimp and shook his head. 'Broken neck, I think,' he said.

'Save it if you can,' Clark said, and left him. Another dead baby. Another crazy chimp.

He did the blood samples as quickly as he could, looked in on the other people working on this job, and then went home. He'd be back for the six o'clock feeding, he promised John Lincoln.

Anne still wasn't talking to him and he was too tired and preoccupied to care. He had stopped in a delicatessen for sandwiches, and when she didn't even look at hers, he shrugged and left it on the table where she could reach it later.

'I have to go back around six,' he said. 'I'll make us a steak after I get back. Is there plenty of coffee in the pot?'

She nodded.

'I'm going to see if I can sleep an hour.'

He dreamed they were flying kites in the park and it was fun with the sun hot on his face, the wind hard and fresh. Then his kite nose-dived and broke. He had another one, this time a yellow and red dragon that rippled sinuously. Anne's kite rose higher and higher, pure white, like a giant bird flying to the moon. His gaudy dragon began to climb, then it, too, nose-dived and fell. He looked at the ruins and sobbed like a child, and woke up, covered with sweat, as if he had been having a nightmare. He couldn't remember for a time where he was, or that it was Sunday afternoon, anything. He sat up and switched on the lamp and the light hurt his eyes. He had slept an hour and a half. For several moments he sat on the side of the bed, feeling the soreness in his leg, his aching head, stiffness in his back. Then he saw the lines on the rug. Parallel lines from the door to the bed. They stood out only because he was on the same side of them as the light; he could see the faint shadows cast in the depressions made by the wheels.

Images flashed before his eyes: the mangled kitten; the dead chimp infant; Fannie's stare that had become more and more malevolent; Lola's injured baby; the way Anne had looked at him with her stranger's eyes; the withdrawal of the chimps from normal contacts; Anne's withdrawal, her silences, and most of all the many times recently he had turned to her only to find her averting her gaze, as if she had been staring ...

He shook his head and the dull ache flared. She had rolled in, stopped, backed up, making an arc with the wheels, turned and left again, silently, not touching him, not making a sound to disturb his sleep. How long had she sat there staring at him? Why had she sat there staring at him?

She had wanted to talk, had found him sleeping and had left. He nodded. She wanted to make up. That stupid quarrel had upset them both and she wanted to make up. He stood up and grimaced at the soreness of his leg. He could no longer see the marks from her wheelchair. He stopped on his way to the bathroom and looked back. Not a sign of them. How many times had she done it? Did she come in every night and look at him as he slept?

Hurriedly he washed his face and brushed his hair. He needed a shave, but not yet. First they would talk, clear the air of the tension that was as poisonous as gas in the apartment.

Anne was on the chaise, a book in her lap. She didn't look up when he entered the bedroom. The sandwich was untouched. Clark poured coffee and sat down.

'Are you all right?'

'Yes.'

The coffee was thick and bitter. He put his cup down. He unplugged the pot, gathered the cups and sugar, cream, the sandwich. The table needed wiping. He'd remember to bring a dishcloth back and do that. When he looked again at Anne, he found her staring at him with an unreadable look on her face. She looked down at her book. Clark felt a chill.

CHAPTER FIFTEEN

Clark found himself on the ramp leading to the back door of the apartment. He had had the ramp installed the day before Anne's release from the hospital. The ramp led to a walk to the parking lot, covered for the occupants, open spaces for visitors.

The rain had washed it all clean. That goddamn, pounding, driving, relentless, scouring rain. He examined the windowsill again. Nothing. Nothing on the ramp. Nothing on the walk. Nothing in the parking shed. Nothing in the open lot. Nothing.

He leaned against the rail of the small porch. It could have been hit down there, dragged itself up the ramp, to the low window left open. It could have.

There had been blood under the window, on the carpet. None on the windowsill. It hadn't started to bleed yet. It coughed, cried out, then bled.

He went inside and searched every inch of the windowsill, the wall below it. Nothing. He sat at the dining-room table and stared at the wall.

He could ask the other people in the building if any of them hit a small cat or saw an injured cat. And skinny Mrs. Ochs would say, 'Oh, yes, come to think of it, I did.' He rubbed his eyes. The cat would have been invisible in the rain against the black pavement of the parking lot.

Images: Anne lying absolutely still, pale as death, her vital signs too low. The pain relievers they used, one after another, all depressed her too much, all were dangerous for her. Low blood pressure, respiration bad. Dr. Radimer: 'I think she will suffer less after you take her home. The psychological effects of being hospitalized, on top of her inability to tolerate the drugs, is impeding her progress. Take her home, Clark. See if that helps. We can put her back in if we have to.'

Home, around-the-clock nursing, and a nearly miraculous relief from pain, or from the expression of pain. After returning home she had never complained.

But how? One of the nurses? He'd check. If she had had the stuff in the apartment, she could have administered it herself, if she had a syringe.

The ifs were too big. He pushed himself away from the table and returned to her room. Anne was as he had left her, a book on her lap that she picked up when he appeared.

'You should eat something,' he said. 'I'll scramble eggs. Will you eat them?'

She shook her head.

'I'll call Harry, then. He can fix you something. I'll get a bite at the cafeteria.'

She made no response and he turned and left.

When Harry came in, Anne looked at him in surprise. She had forgotten Clark had said he would call him. 'The cat was killed,' she said.

Harry nodded. 'Clark told me. He said you weren't feeling well.'

'I'm all right. I don't want you to stay. Please.' She stopped and realized she was near tears. It was strange. Suddenly there was the constriction in her throat and her eyes were hot. She picked up the book.

'I won't stay. I'll just make you some dinner. Don't talk if you don't want to. I won't, either.'

She watched him leave, a nearly grotesque figure, with his too tight and too loose pants, straining the seams at his hips, flapping about his ankles. Scarecrow figure, she thought, and when he was out of sight, she forgot him.

They kept bringing her back, and it was so hard to get away again each time. She looked at the little world with longing. She had been unable to escape into it. The glass walls were infinitely high now, and unbreakable. She had circled it, had tried to rise over the glass walls, and each time she had failed. Her one refuge gone. She felt herself withdrawing again from that motionless figure in the wheelchair until she was distant enough to see that other person completely, and only then could she think.

She thought about freedom, not as abstraction, but her own freedom. Hollow word. That was how they fooled you. Pretending you were free to choose anything, everything, and you weren't. Everything fell into place and you walked among the pieces and believed you had put them there because you wanted them. Her thoughts changed and she was with Clark on his motorcycle, her arms tight about him as they roared down a glaring white concrete road, as straight as a rope stretched between two posts. The air had been so hot her skin had peeled later. Windburn, sunburn.

How casually his hand would find her breast, feel it, squeeze it. How casually her hand would pat his crotch. Sometimes he would gently remove her hand, as if to say not now. She never had removed his hand from her breast, or her buttocks. 'It's different,' he had said once. And she had accepted that. He could be aroused at her touch. She, because she didn't run a flag up the pole, obviously couldn't be, wasn't.

She was jolted once more when Harry appeared carrying a tray. She shook herself. 'I must have dozed,' she said faintly.

He nodded and prepared the table. 'Spanish omelette, salad. Okay?'

'Yes. Thank you.'

'Anne ... Nothing. Come on and eat.'

The omelette was good and she was hungry. Harry looked on approvingly as she finished it off. 'I'm thawing some raspberries, they'll be ready in a minute or so. Anything else?'

She shook her head. 'Harry, I keep thinking of Grandma, your mother. I was so small when she died. I keep wanting to cry for her.'

'You loved her very much. And she loved you. You were her favorite. When she died, everyone thought you were heartless because you pretended not to believe she was dead. I didn't understand either then.'

Anne looked at the small table top that was cluttered with dishes. She wanted to sweep them all off to the floor, to throw something through the window. 'My mother spanked me because I played the day of the funeral. I played hopscotch all afternoon and I sang.'

'You were about six,' Harry said, remembering. 'Six. A baby. Children don't know how to express grief of bereavement. They're not physiologically able to express it, there's no understanding possible to them. They think the person has gone away, that he'll return, or she will. Or they think they're being punished for something they did or said. It's abandonment they suffer from. Purely egotistical and purely normal. It's the nature of the little beast. Few people understand that, and the child carries it like a nickel sack of jelly beans all his life, guilt wrapped in layers of shame, ready to come undone at the most unexpected time. Anne, the only danger is in letting yourself substitute that ancient death and its feelings for whatever is going on in the present. If you're feeling the agonies of bereavement, it isn't for your grandmother, honey. You have to face that.' He stood up, an awkward, ungainly figure, too long in the arms and legs, and he said, 'I'll go get the raspberries, get rid of this stuff.'

He cleared the table and left. But she did want to cry for her grandmother, she thought. She hadn't cried then, now she wanted to.

They ate raspberries with thick cream and had coffee, and Harry said, 'The Sunday-night concert has already started. Mind if I turn it on?' She shook her head. He turned on the radio and sat down again with his eyes closed. 'Gluck,' he murmured. 'I've been looking forward to this.'

Anne felt herself drawn to the music and she found she could lose herself much easier with it on. She closed her eyes and there was only the music that filled the apartment.

Anne sent Harry home shortly after ten when the concert was over. 'You've helped,' she said. 'You're a good man, aren't you? I never thought about it before much, but there aren't many really good men. Thanks.'

'Now you're being maudlin,' Harry said, laughing. 'Are you sure you don't want me to stay awhile?'

'I have to think,' she said. 'It goes better alone.'

He nodded. 'See you in a day or two.'

She didn't blame Clark, she thought. It wasn't his fault. It was hers. It was everyone's fault, or no one's. She had accepted an attitude without question, and he had accepted her role also without thinking about it. Now they could think about it, talk about it. Maybe. Not just yet. But that it loomed as a possibility was hopeful. That she had thought of it was hopeful. It was like a bereavement; she wondered at Harry for knowing that. Like a painful bereavement, it could not be spoken of just yet. She was too near tears; she would weep and spoil everything by becoming incoherent when she needed to be reasonable, by becoming too emotional when she needed to make him understand, not with his reflexes that would want to love her into quietude again, but with his mind. He had to understand what she was discovering, had to look at her with different eyes, just as she was examining him with new eyes. If, through rediscovery of each other, they lost what they had once had, that too would have to be faced. If they could not build something else, then they would have to deal with it. But later. Not until she could finish thinking through her own attitudes, her acceptance, the reasons for her acceptance. Not until she could talk without crying.

When Clark came home at twelve, he was haggard. He needed a shave badly, and his clothes were rumpled and dirty-looking. Standing near the doorway, he stared at her intently, and asked, 'Anne, did you bring home some of the *pa* before the accident?'

'What's wrong?'

'Just tell me!' His voice was harsh. He was trembling.

'Yes. What's wrong?'

'Where is it?'

'I threw it out.'

Clark rubbed his eyes and came into the room in a lurching walk, as if he were drunk, not from liquor but fatigue. 'Anne, for God's sake don't lie about this. How could you have thrown it out? Where was it?'

Anne shook her head. 'No more. You tell me what this is all about first.'

Clark sat down and put his face in his hands. For a moment she thought he was weeping and during that moment, if she had been able to, she would have gone to him, would have taken him in her arms to comfort him. She started to move her chair, and he raised his face and stared at her. His eyes were bloodshot.

'There's something wrong with it. Three chimps have become psychotic. Two infants have been killed. Three out of twenty-three! And tonight Lilith began showing symptoms exactly like the others. It isn't just chimps on the stress experiment. Others too.'

'No!' she cried. 'No!' She moved without being aware of turning the wheels. 'You're lying to me! You want to pay me back! You're just tormenting me!'

'Anne, stop it! For God's sake, you know I wouldn't lie about it.'

'I don't believe you! What have you been doing down there? Who's been messing it up?'

'It just began happening Monday,' he said. 'Duckmore attacked a lab assistant, put him in the hospital. Then Fannie killed her baby. Lola injured her baby today, probably it will die before morning. It was just barely hanging on. It won't live.'

The wheel of her chair touched his foot and he jerked back. She stared at his foot, then raised her eyes to look at his face. 'And you think I ... Because I objected to being raped, you think I'm going crazy!' It ended high, too high. She wanted to scream. She turned her chair away from him. He caught it and swung it back. 'Let go! Don't you dare touch me!'

'You can't dismiss it like that,' Clark said desperately. 'Anne, if you took it, tell me!'

'I told you and you chose not to believe me!'

'Tell me how you got rid of it. Who helped you?'

'One of the night nurses. The first one. Ruth Gorman. I told her to bring me the package from the refrigerator. I looked at the stuff and wrapped it up and threw it in the waste can by the bed. I was afraid it wouldn't keep until I could test it on myself.'

Clark groaned and shook his head. 'As soon as you came home from the hospital, you stopped complaining of pain. In the hospital you were in constant pain.'

'I was in constant pain here,' she said furiously. 'How could I have complained! You would have taken me back!'

'Anne, that's not true! I didn't want you in the hospital!'

'You didn't want to see me suffer. It was easier on you if I did it somewhere else. I know you protested over bringing me home too soon. They told me.'

'Because I was afraid.'

'*No! Because you didn't want to know!* You put me in the hospital and you didn't want to see any of the rest of it.' He was still holding the wheel of her chair, preventing her from moving away. Brutally, she said, 'You knew it was your fault, all of it. You smashed us up, crippled me. You knew how I suffered, and now if you can ease your conscience by thinking I took the *poena albumin* to relieve that pain, you'll jump at the chance, won't you?'

Clark stood up and knocked over his chair. He took a step backward. When he let go, the wheelchair rolled slightly. 'You've thought all this time it was my fault?' He shook his head; his face was the color of putty. 'It was an accident! There was nothing I could do to prevent it.'

'If you had kept your head, it wouldn't have happened! You lost control of yourself and the car. You overbraked, overaccelerated, oversteered. You put us in a spin and let that other maniac hit us broadside. On my side. You know it. I know it. And I guess that poor slob we're suing knows it. And we'll all know it forever!'

Clark was shaking his head hard. 'It was an accident. The investigating police said there was nothing I could have done.'

Anne turned in disgust. 'It's late. Go to bed.' She was trembling and couldn't stop. She clenched her hands on the rims of the wheels and pressed her knees together to try to control her spasms.

'Anne, we have to talk about this tonight. I know you planned to try the stuff out first. I meant to do it too, when you did. I remember the day you ran our blood analyses to get our *pa* levels. Yours was about as low as it can get, remember? Is there a chance you could have used it and have forgotten doing it? You were on various things back then. One of them might have affected your memory.'

'Ask Dr. Radimer.'

'Is there a chance that happened?'

'No! I told you. I threw it out.' She didn't look at him again.

'Christ!' he muttered after a moment. 'Oh, Jesus Christ!'

She thought of the little cat, and jerked the chair around to stare at him with disbelief and fury. 'Get out of here!' she cried. 'For the love of God, just get out of here!'

Neither of them moved. Clark stared at her and she at him, and each was a stranger to the other. After a moment, Clark righted his chair again and sat down, his hands dangling between his knees.

'Anne, just let me tell you what's been going on since Monday.' He didn't wait for her response, but started with the announcement of the acceptance of the IND, and Helverson's orders for human testing. He didn't look at her as he spoke. His voice was almost singsong, he elaborated nothing and left out nothing.

He was doing it, too, she realized. He had put that part that could be hurt, that had been hurt, far back where it was safe, where it would not be trampled underfoot. The part that was left, that was detailing the long terrible week, was emotionless, toneless, a machine. And she, watching, listening, she was a machine. They could kill each other now, but neither of them would bleed, and if they touched, neither would be warmed by the touch of the other. Metal on metal. Her gaze slid past him to rest on the little world. Cool, misty world without pain, without torment, without accusations and guilt ...

'Anne, are you even listening to me?'

'Of course. Are you through?'

'I asked you why you thought of that stress experiment? What led you to suspect the results?'

'I don't know. A daydream. An article in a magazine.'

'Try to remember.'

'Why?'

'Anne, put yourself in my place. If I were the one here in this room acting as you've been acting, and you knew I'd had access to the *pa*, that I had desperately needed it, wouldn't you want to follow it through? Wouldn't you have to find out?'

'But I already told you.' She almost smiled at the reasonable tone they both used now. The return of sweet reason, she thought, how calming, how soothing, how phony.

Clark's face darkened and he looked away from her. Anne felt almost smug. He couldn't maintain the separation as long as she could.

'I'm very tired,' she said. 'I have a busy day tomorrow. If you don't mind ...'

When he walked to the door, his legs had lost their spring, his feet seemed almost to drag. He turned and regarded her with puzzled and unhappy eyes at the doorway; he didn't say anything else.

His thoughts were circling in tighter and tighter as he showered. Anne naked in his arms, laughing up at him. Anne in the hospital, her face gray with pain, tears standing in her eyes that were red-rimmed and sunken. Anne cool and distant, somehow superior, in her chair, staring past him with her lips not quite curled up in a smile. Anne at his bedside, staring down at him as he slept. The dead kitten. The dead chimp baby. Anne looking at him with an unreadable expression, a stranger's expression. Over and over, around and around they went, each forming and being chased by the next before the edges firmed. He sat on the side of the bed and knew he couldn't sleep. He went back to the bathroom and found sleeping capsules, for emergency, Anne had said, years ago, and now the emergency was there. He took two of them and went to the bed again, but again he paused, and then he went to the door and locked it. For a long time he stood with his forehead pressed hard against the frame, and his eyes were hot.

CHAPTER SIXTEEN

'How's Anne?' Deena asked when Clark got into her yellow VW.

'She's fi ... Deena, I have to talk to you and Gus as soon after I get those blood samples as possible. In his office.'

'Sure. About the *pa?*'

'About this whole fuckin' mess.' He looked out the window, seeing nothing, and Deena didn't ask anything else.

They sat in Gus's office with the door closed and locked. 'I think Anne used the stuff on herself before Christmas,' Clark said harshly. 'She denies it.'

Gus exhaled softly and picked up his darts. He didn't throw them, just held them, turning them over and over from one hand to the other.

'She knows better than that,' Deena said, frowning. 'I can't believe she'd do it under those circumstances.'

'I don't want to believe it, either,' Clark said, still too rough, too abrupt. He felt old and tired, and knew he looked old and tired. The sleeping pills had made his head ache even more than the day before, and he had a bad, fuzzy mouth. He glanced at Deena and said more quietly, 'I'm edgy. Sorry. I checked the records last night. She took enough out to last her two weeks. She had it all figured out long ago. For both of us,' he added.

'Bloody Christ!' Gus sighed. 'Start earlier, Clark. Why did you check the records?'

'Right. She's been acting strangely for weeks. Withdrawn, avoiding any personal talk, sending Ronnie home too early, staying alone too much. I don't know. Just not like her, not like she's been. Then Harry, her uncle, brought her a kitten, nearly full-grown. Friday night she called me home. Virginia said she was nearly hysterical on the phone. When I got there she was absolutely normal, very quiet, watchful. She said the cat was dead, out in the dining room. Her wheelchair was in the hall near the kitchen. She hadn't been able to get it around the corner again to get back to the bedroom. I didn't even know she had been leaving the bedroom.' He swallowed hard, then continued, speaking fast. 'I went in and found the cat. It was mangled, bleeding from the nose and mouth. She had vomited in the dining room near it. She said it must have been hit by a car in the parking lot, dragged itself through an open window to die in the apartment. I believed her.' He could hear the raspy quality in his voice without being able to do anything about it. He cleared his throat and lighted a cigarette. 'Saturday night we went to my parents' home for dinner and afterward she told me she's been taking swimming therapy for a week. I told her the IND had been approved. We were happy, laughing, both a little smashed. Then she went all to pieces, became hysterical, made accusations. She lost control completely. And since then she's been alternately wholly withdrawn or else in a fury. She sits and watches me. Just like Fannie. Just like Lola. I found the marks of her wheels on the bedroom carpet when I woke up. She had been sitting there watching me.'

Gus was shaking his head when Clark finished. 'For God's sake, she sounds normal to me,' he said. 'I can imagine myself cooped up like that for months. I'd really be in a rage most of the time.'

'Listen, Gus, don't you think I know how it sounds? Her pain-threshold index on the scale she worked out herself is two point four, on a scale of ten.

Mine is six point three, a little higher than normal. Gus, she suffers if she bumps her arm on a doorway. Her *pa* count is one half mil per liter, mine is fourteen. Point ten is the lowest we've ever found. And when she came home from the hospital she was in agony. You remember she couldn't tolerate anything they gave her. And within days she stopped complaining. She began to get interested in her notebooks again. She acted as if she had no pain.'

'Hold it right there, goddamn it!' Deena said. 'I was around her then, remember. She was scared out of her mind that she'd have to go back to the hospital, and she hated it with a passion. More than that, she has what amounts to a phobia about hospitals. She's afraid a stupid, or malicious, nurse will stick the wrong thing in her or something. She associates hospitals with people dying, not with people getting well. She told me if she continued to have so much pain they would put her back in. Under those conditions, she would have had to go into shock from pain before she would have admitted it.'

'Her index is two point four!' Clark said, nearly shouting. 'Two point four, Deena! How could she have concealed it?'

'Maybe you just didn't want to see it!'

Clark stared at her. *Déjà vu*, he thought. Again. He said, 'I could be wrong. God knows, I hope I'm wrong. But what if I'm not?'

'You've told her what's been going on, I take it?' Gus said.

Clark nodded. 'She thinks we're screwing up her work.'

Gus nodded. 'Can't blame her for that. You told her the symptoms the chimps showed before they went bananas?'

'I told her everything,' Clark said impatiently. 'Gus, what should I do?'

'Damned if I know,' Gus said, playing with the darts, examining the feathers. 'Is there anything else?'

'I keep seeing her hands and arms, scratched up, bleeding. One knee was bleeding. There was blood on her chair, on her robe ... Gus, she's alone every day with Ronnie for hours and hours. What if ...?'

'Who's Ronnie?'

'She's the practical nurse-companion we hired. She's supposed to stay until I get there, but Anne's been sending her home no later than five, but even so, from nine until five they're alone in that apartment.'

Deena stood up, her face very pink, her eyes glittering. 'I think this is a lot of bullshit. I'm going over to see Anne.'

'She's at the doctor's office getting crutches this morning,' Clark said. 'She'll be back around eleven. Wait until after lunch.'

Gus, looking at Clark, stood up then and motioned Deena to go away. She glanced at Clark, shrugged, and left.

'What am I going to do?' Clark said again, and this time his voice broke and he cradled his head in his arms and his body shook.

Gus took aim and threw the first dart. Ten, almost off the target. He threw again, and again, and presently gathered the darts and started over. His score was four hundred ten when the phone rang. 'No calls yet,' he said, then listened. 'Tell him you can't find me. I'll call back when I have the chance.' He threw another dart and said, not looking at Clark, who had grown quiet now, 'Helverson. He's got his wind up over possible trouble. Third time this morning he's wanted to talk to me. Poor bastard. Had his tongue out to lick the chocolate and they took the spoon away.'

Clark got up and went to the window and stood there with his back to Gus. 'I'm scared,' he said. 'Really scared. And I don't know what to do.'

'Either she did or she didn't,' Gus said. 'I can buy her actions as normal, the result of the accident, her inactivity, all the rest of it. It gets harder when you can see the end ahead somehow. That way with kids. Good as gold while they're really sick, but when they start to recuperate, then whammo, all hell breaks loose.'

Clark shook his head. 'And if she did use the stuff?'

'That's a tougher one. But you're right, we have to know. Think she'd tell Deena anything?'

'I don't know. She won't talk to me.'

'What set her off, Clark? Something must have started it all?'

'I made love to her. She's okay, the doctor told me. But she's calling it rape. Maybe it was. I don't know.'

Gus sighed and aimed another dart. He didn't throw it. He put it on his desk and asked, 'She's always liked me all right, hasn't she?'

'Yes, you know it.'

'I'll go see her.'

'Not Deena,' Clark said. 'She'd agree it was rape.'

Neither of them added to that.

'I'll go now. She should be home by the time I get there. If not, I'll wait.' He stopped at the door. 'You've got a hell of a lot of work to do, Clark. If anyone asks for me, just say I'm wandering about somewhere. Be back soon.'

Clark looked out the window at the back parking lot until his vision cleared and he was able to pick out individual cars, and then he went to the door, but he didn't leave just yet. He returned to the chair and sat down. Gus was right about the work, on both levels. It was there to be done, and Gus knew once Clark got caught up in it, he would be okay. But he wasn't ready yet. What no one, not even Anne, understood was how much he loved her. It was true he hadn't been able to bear her suffering. He had wept uncontrollably over it. He had haunted the doctor, urging him to do something, anything, to relieve her. And he had objected to having her sent home too soon, because he had recognized his own helplessness.

He loved her long smooth body, her sexuality. She was the most sexual woman he had known; before her, he hadn't realized a woman could be so responsive. He liked to contemplate how, even if their sex life diminished in time, they would still have everything else together. Their work, all their interests, their friends. He, never a romantic before, had come to believe that for each person there was one ideal mate, one other who was the perfect extension, the perfect complement. She was impatient with details, an innovator; he had infinite patience for details. It was as if she viewed the world through a wrap-around picture window that allowed her to see broad vistas at a glance, and he looked through a peephole that magnified one very small section at a time, so that when they combined their knowledge, and they always did, they saw the world in a way no one person ever could. The reality they shared had a breadth and depth few others could imagine. Once they had talked of their likenesses and their differences, and she had summed it all up: 'Where I go in, you go out.' And it had not been a facetious remark at all. It included everything.

They had become like two vines that intertwined to climb up into the sunlight, so that if you pulled off a leaf it would be impossible to say from which vine it came. And she had called it rape. He knew he could never forget that, never forgive her that. Nothing else she had said really mattered, he couldn't even remember what else she had said, but that had been too deliberately hurtful. That one word had ripped them apart, mutilating both of them, until now they stood with that barrier word between them, two separate beings, neither whole now, neither able to undo the damage one word had done.

But if she had used the *pa* factor, he thought, then she wasn't responsible, any more than Fannie was, or Lola. He saw again the look of shock and hatred on her face, heard her voice, 'If I thought you were coming at me again, I'd vomit.' And he knew she had used the *pa* factor. There was no doubt.

Gus was stunned by Anne's appearance. She was in bed, very pale, with deep dark lines under her eyes outlining them owlishly.

'My doctor is a brute,' she said with a faint smile before he could conceal his reaction to her condition. 'And we haven't had much sleep around here for several nights. Clark sent you, didn't he?'

Gus sat down on the side of the bed and held her hand for a moment. 'No one sent me. I came. Okay?' He got up and dragged a chair near enough to touch the bed. 'I'd fire a quack who sent me home looking like that.'

'We worked hard this morning. See?' She pointed to the new crutches. They were aluminum, with tripod ends capped with black rubber. 'More for balance than support, the doctor said. I believe. Who ever saw such hideous things?'

Her voice was strained. It must have been a bad session, Gus thought. 'And did you walk with them?'

'He wouldn't let me leave until I mastered them.' Her voice became more animated. 'You wouldn't believe how goddamn tired I am of being treated like a thing. Do this, don't do that, try again, you can't sit down, raise your foot, watch how you put it down ... Programming a computer or something, that's what it's like.'

'*Alles was nicht Pflicht ist, ist verboten,*' Gus said, grinning at her. She nodded and there was a hint of a smile. 'Can a guy get coffee around here?'

'You met Ronnie, didn't you? She's out making lunch. Tell her. I'd like some too.'

He nodded and went to the kitchen.

'You know who I am, Ronnie?'

'Sure. You're the boss, aren't you? She's talked about you from time to time.' Ronnie looked him over and then nodded. 'Okay, what can I do for you?'

'We'd both like coffee, if it isn't too much trouble.' Again she nodded. 'Ronnie, there may be a problem with Anne's medicine. Stuff she took months ago. It might begin to have an effect on her behavior. We're not sure, but there's a possibility. Have you noticed anything? Anything at all out of the ordinary?'

Ronnie's cheerful, open face closed, and she became very professional, very distant. 'Sorry, Dr. Weinbacher, but since when are you her doctor?'

'I'm a scientist, Ronnie, and a friend of them both. Did her physician recommend you?' She nodded. 'If you notice anything about her behavior, it's your duty to report it to him. You know that. I don't mean her physical condition, Ronnie. A change in her attitude, in her disposition, her appetite, anything. It could be dangerous to her.'

'I know my job.' Ronnie turned her back on him to stir something in a pan. 'I'll bring you some coffee in a minute.'

Gus hesitated, then shrugged and left. Whips wouldn't open her mouth, but he believed she would be alert to any change now, would report any change to Anne's doctor. They would have to get in touch with him right away, get a list of the medications she had taken.

'In a minute,' he announced to Anne, entering the room. Anne's eyes were closed. She opened them and motioned him to sit down again. 'You want to talk?' Gus asked.

'No. Not really. He thinks I'm crazy. Did he say I strangled the little cat, or ran over it with my wheelchair? I began to wonder how he thought I had done it.'

'He didn't say.'

'How will you resolve it, Gus? I say I didn't, he says I did. How do you resolve it?'

'Wish to Christ I knew.'

'A sanity test? I wouldn't submit to one. I believe I may be a little bit insane right now and I wouldn't like it officially confirmed. Bad news for an employment record.'

Gus grinned at her. 'You're a smart cookie, Anne. What else have you thought of?'

'Separation. I won't live with him now. He's afraid of me. Last night he locked his door.' She smiled, a chill, bitter smile. 'I checked just to see. I didn't believe it until then, what he was saying, I mean. Then I believed.'

'It's tearing him up, Anne,' Gus said. 'The scientist in him knows what he has to do, the man in love with you is unwilling to do it. Right down the middle.'

'It's the man who thinks I'm crazy,' Anne murmured. She raised herself on her elbow, and her face became tauter, harder. 'From now on, everything I do will have a double meaning. I've been thinking about it. If you don't want to find insanity, avoid all mirrors, Gus. You'll see it there first every time.' She reached for a cigarette. Gus held a match. Then she said, 'I want to go over all the records, everything that's happened since last week, since before then. Something like this doesn't just pop up overnight. There must have been clues, indications. No one was paying attention.'

'I'll send over everything this afternoon,' Gus said. 'Are you up to it?'

'Better that than lying here thinking about how not to appear crazy to someone who's looking for symptoms.' A slight change came over her, she looked at him with an expression at once sly and bashful. 'Do you believe, in the abstract, a man can rape his wife?'

Gus shifted in his chair. 'He told me. In the abstract, I'd say only under certain conditions. If they were separated. If she was trying to sell something he thought should be free. If it had become a weapon. All those things happen.'

Anne nodded and lay back down. She looked at the little world and yearned for the solitude there.

'Anne, that man worships you. You know that.' He had lost her, Gus knew. She was withdrawn, paying little attention to him. Her fingers were working with the fluff of her cover, rolling it up into small tight balls.

'Anne, look at me. I have to ask. You know I have to ask. Did you use it on yourself?'

She glanced at him, then away. 'No. Poor Gus. You should have listened to Bob Klugman. He didn't want to hire a man-and-wife team, did he? He predicted trouble from the start. You should have paid attention to him.'

Gus stood up and went to the window. He turned the dieffenbachia around. How beautiful its leaves had become, she thought, all streaked with white, pale greens, dark greens. Poor thing, it had worked so hard to escape, and with one careless motion it was captive again.

'Bob was wrong,' Gus said. 'You and Clark are the best people I have. As a team you're unbeatable, and you know it damn well.' He looked at her and said distinctly, 'I want a blood sample from you. I want to send in someone to talk to you, observe you, if you choose. You can take that with a damn female put-upon reaction, or you can accept it rationally and know it's necessary.'

She shook her head. 'You want too much. You send me the records, and we'll go on from there.'

'You won't cooperate?'

'You won't take my word?'

They stared at one another for what seemed a long time, until Gus shrugged. 'For the time being,' he said, and Ronnie appeared with a tray. Gus sat down again and patted Anne's hand. 'We'll work it out,' he said.

'You still pooped?' Ronnie asked. She winked at Gus. 'I thought she was going to hit the doctor the last time he said, "Just once more and then you're through."'

She was mocking him, Gus thought. Make something of that, she was saying. He grinned back at her. 'Aluminum's too light. She should carry a monkey wrench for things like that.'

Ronnie arranged the coffee things on the night stand. 'Lunch in twenty minutes. You staying, Doc?' She was already at the door.

'Can't,' he said.

'Dirty shame,' she called over her shoulder.

Anne laughed. 'You must have pinched her bottom or something out there in the kitchen. She likes you.'

'Just my irresistible charm. They fall down in droves before me.'

Anne refused to let the talk come back to her. She asked about his wife, their plans for another vacation, and he promised to send stuff over that afternoon, and presently he left, dissatisfied. She looked awful, not only tired, haunted almost. There had been a look about her, something different, remote, watchful, knowing. A look he was sure never had been there before. He had always thought of Anne as terribly young, so young, he had complained to his wife, he felt he had to watch his language around her. She had that look of innocence. And today he hadn't felt that at all.

CHAPTER SEVENTEEN

'I could ask her mother to come,' Clark said. He and Gus were having lunch in the cafeteria. 'They don't get along, though.'

Gus shook his head. 'I talked to her doctor. The list of medications is being sent over by a delivery boy. The nurse will call back as soon as she's off duty, around three. We've done all we can right now, Clark. Try to relax. If it's any help, I believe her. I don't think she used it.'

'She really said she wants a separation?' Clark's voice was dull. He had eaten nothing, was drinking his third cup of coffee.

'She said it,' Gus admitted. 'But you're both pretty upset right now. God, why is it no one can hurt you like the one you love, who loves you? Elaine can ice-pick me without even half trying, just off the cuff. She knows where to stick it in, how deep to stick it with a precision that's admirable.'

Clark grinned. 'You're a son of a bitch, Gus. Okay, it's our first real quarrel and we're both making a big deal of it. I could buy that, if this other thing wasn't hanging fire. And it scares me. This morning Duckmore is starting to withdraw again. He's moody, irritable, watchful. Is he working up to another outburst? And this time I know damn well there was nothing to stir him up. We've been handling him with kid gloves.'

Gus glanced at his watch. 'Got to see Helverson,' he said. 'I'll be in touch later.'

Gus had intended to return to his office for his coat and tie, but he forgot and didn't think of them again until he was inside Helverson's office. Bob Klugman was there already, in coat and tie, looking nervous and ill at ease. Helverson, as always, was elegantly dressed.

Helverson came around his desk to shake hands and propel Gus gently toward the small leather couch against the wall. He took one of the matching chairs, Bob Klugman the other.

'Gus, this problem, how's it coming?'

'It's a little soon to say.' Gus waited. Bob Klugman was twitching more than usual, and he avoided Gus's gaze.

Helverson nodded. 'Bob tells me it's confined to those chimps with high-blood-pressure symptoms, or those on a regimen to induce an increase in blood pressure. Seems a simple thing to list those conditions as contraindications.'

'We're getting the computer data now,' Gus said. 'The albumin tends to agglutinate at various nerve endings in the brain, and this in turn could be responsible for the psychoses, but we can't be certain yet. We don't know why it affected those chimps, not the others, or if it will affect the others also. None of the chimps had high blood pressure at the start.'

Helverson frowned and tapped his long slender fingers on the arm of his chair. 'Gus,' he said, 'I wonder if you realize the magnitude of this discovery. An end of needless pain, the dream of mankind since the beginning of time. It's our duty, Gus, to make this available to humanity just as quickly as we possibly can. I'm not a scientist, but I think I understand some of the caution a scientist feels. I've been around scientists for a good many years, and I respect that caution. But, Gus, there are times when the view from outside the lab just isn't the same as that from within. As I see this, there is really only one chimp whose case is in doubt, the male. Do you wonder at the females, with infants, in captivity, under conditions of induced stress? Of course they act strangely. It's such a normal, even human reaction, if I may say so. And the male. Can you say with no doubt in your mind that the lab assistant did not provoke an attack? Of course not. It's well known how animals in captivity harbor grudges against keepers. It's been documented time and again.'

He paused, his voice fading out to nothing, but his fingers kept tapping, tapping. Gus thought again of Anne's fingers balling up the fluff of her cover. Don't look in the mirror, he thought. Mr. Helverson, don't look into the mirror. He said, 'It isn't merely overcaution. If this had come up before we turned in the application for human testing, approval would have been denied until further work was carried out. We all know that.'

'But they didn't turn it down, Gus. That's the point. The work is brilliant, irrefutable. An end to pain, Gus! It's worth the risk of needing psychological counseling afterward! I've already spoken with Dr. Wells, who will be in charge of that department. Those women will receive the best medical care, physical and psychological, that any group of people has had since the first witch doctor shook a stick at a patient. We'll see to that.'

'Does Dr. Grove understand the complication that has arisen?' Gus asked.

'I've kept him informed,' Helverson said, and now his voice was cool and the interview was to be terminated. He glanced at his watch, discreetly, but not hiding the fact that he had other, equally pressing matters to attend to.

'Why did you want to tell me this now?' Gus asked.

'I understand there's been a good deal of discussion in the laboratories about this,' Helverson said, honey-smooth now. 'I rely on you, Gus, and Bob, of course, to keep in mind that once administrative decisions have been made, we're all united, like an army with a common battle to prepare for, a common enemy. Dissension after decisions have been made can ruin an army, a company, a family. When it's time to close ranks, Gus, I want every man and every woman to stand shoulder to shoulder, with no holdouts, no dissidents to cause confusion and delay the day we can make our glorious announcement to a suffering world. Think of the cancer patients, Gus ... the agonies of inoperable tumors ...'

Horse apples, Gus thought, and glanced at Bob Klugman, who was watching Helverson as if hypnotized.

Helverson stood up. 'I want you to make certain that every bit of new information is given to Bob immediately. And, Bob, you see it gets put into English I can understand and get it to me, day or night. When Dr. Grove gets here Wednesday afternoon for our meeting, I want to have a positive report ready for them. A positive report.' He escorted them to the door and held it for them. 'Do you need anything, more manpower? More money? Anything? Now's not the time to skimp, you understand. There are times for economy and times to expand and make use of all the resources of a great company. This is that time, gentlemen. Expand! Work! We're on the brink of a day that will revolutionize all humanity!'

Gus shuffled away, cursing under his breath, his head bowed, seeing nothing on either side. He knew Bob was trotting along, but he paid no attention to him.

Deena met him at his office door. 'He's going ahead with it,' she said. 'He told you?'

'In so many words. You're to be in charge of the psychological testing.'

She nodded. Bob Klugman joined them and they fell silent. Bob said, 'After all, we knew the albumin agglutinated at the brain nerve endings. That was the whole point.' His voice was a near whine.

Gus shrugged and opened his door. 'Not nine or ten months later,' he said. 'Did you want to see me, Deena?'

'Gus, wait a minute, damn it!' Bob said. 'Helverson had a point. Everything's been fine up to now. That damn experiment Anne wanted done just wasn't proper at this time. You can't include those reactions with the bulk of the experimental material. I could think of any number of experiments to distort the findings. So could you.' His voice was rising and he was breathing very fast, as if he had been running. 'Look, what Helverson didn't say, something we discussed before you got there. No more experiments that aren't cleared with me first. Not at this time. I'm the head of this department, damn it, and I must be consulted! We're at a crucial point here! All results, every experiment, must pass through my office from now on.' Neither Gus nor Deena replied, and he said, almost falsetto, 'Helverson's right! You can get results with humans! Results that aren't possible from animals. They can tell you if they're losing their grip. Or if they have headaches. We'll have them under close observation twenty-four hours a day for the next two to five years. They can't avoid telling us if anything's going wrong!'

Deena examined her fingernails and Gus looked at a point somewhere over Bob's head. Neither spoke. After a moment Bob Klugman said, 'Where's

Clark? I want him to understand, no new experiments that aren't okayed first.'

'I'll tell him,' Gus said.

'I'll tell him myself! I don't want any more foul-ups now!' Bob's face was red and he was sweating heavily.

'Leave him alone, Bob,' Gus said pleasantly. His ugly face looked uglier than ever as he smiled at his boss. 'He's been working twenty hours a day practically all week, and he's tired. You go in there yelling at him and he just might rip out your tongue and stuff it up your ass.' He looked at Deena. 'You wanted something? Come on in.'

They turned together and left Bob Klugman in the narrow hallway. The color drained from his face and he shook with rage, but he didn't go down the hall to Clark's office, didn't go back through the laboratory, but went out instead to the main hall and from there to his office.

'He won't fire you, or turn in a bad report, nothing like that,' Deena said, inside Gus's office. 'But he will begin a slow poison campaign. That's his style.'

'Been underway for months,' Gus said. 'He's running scared for his own ass. You're going along with Helverson?'

She shrugged. 'No choice. They're moving. We go with them or get out and let someone else go with them. I figure I know more about what to look for than an outsider would. I'll keep it cleaner than an outsider.'

'Sure. Sit down. I went to see Anne.'

'I meant to, but Helverson kept me tied up.'

Gus nodded. 'She wants to leave Clark. I'm worried she might have taken the stuff. If she did and recognizes the danger, that would explain her wanting a separation. Also, she wants everything we've got about the series of incidents last week, all the charts from the preceding weeks. She wants to make a general review of everything.' He sighed. 'Got a truck handy?'

'If you can get the material from your department, I'll get it from ours and take it all over myself,' Deena said. She looked at Gus, then averted her gaze. 'I can stay with her for a while. Marcie can stay with my mother for a while. She can go to school from there.'

'Clark thought he might ask her mother to come,' Gus said. He didn't like the way Deena avoided looking directly at him. He didn't like the idea of putting Deena in charge of Anne. She's not a lesbian, he thought, but close enough. And she admired Anne perhaps too much.

'When I met Anne's mother,' Deena said bitterly, 'she said to me' – her voice became falsetto – '"Isn't it too bad Anne didn't study just a little harder, get a better recommendation so that she could have gone to one of the really big companies?"' Her face was hard and set in an expression of disgust. 'Bitch. She's been giving Anne that crap from the day she was born.

If Anne killed her, it would be justifiable. I don't think she should be given the opportunity.'

'I had the same impression,' Gus said. 'Go get your stuff together and I'll talk to Clark about it. He may dig in his heels and stay in spite of what she said. We'll see.'

Clark was in the projection room. It was a tiny room, hardly big enough for two people, where the images could be projected manually or through a computer system. Clark had the slides on a table at his elbow.

'I need a brain man,' he said in greeting as Gus entered. 'Look at this. A massive clumping here, and here. Clumping, but not so much here.' He changed slides too rapidly for Gus to follow. 'And we'll need to sacrifice two more of the chimps, a control and a test animal. I'll do it this afternoon. I need comparative data.'

'You can use a man when? Wednesday, Thursday?'

'Better make it Friday,' Clark said. He had two slides side by side now and was going from one to the other, muttering under his breath. He cursed and put in a new set of two, and Gus withdrew.

Wilmar Diedricks was waiting for Gus at the end of the office hallway. 'We're going ahead, is that the word?'

'Looks like we might. What kind of shape are you in?'

'We'll be ready in ten days to two weeks. Is Grove going to furnish us with blood samples from his subjects? Do we have to collect them ourselves? It'll make a difference. And someone has to post a notice we'll have the super-centrifuge and the refrigerator room tied up until this is over.'

They talked as they went toward the office clerical pool, where Gus stopped and motioned his secretary. 'We'll need space and setups for two more autopsies this afternoon,' he said. 'Tell surgery to see to it. And don't take any arguments. I want it ready in an hour.'

Mary Johnston nodded and returned to her desk, picked up her phone.

'As soon as we get the subjects' samples, we'll be ready to move,' Wilmar Diedricks said. 'The program is set, the analyzer, everything. If I'm not allowed at the committee meeting, Gus, I want you to voice my protest though. I'll give it to you in writing. And I'll have to coordinate our matching symbols with Grove, make sure his people understand the system we'll have to use.' He paused near the door to his section. 'If you can put the brakes on it, Gus, for God's sake do it. I don't think we're ready yet. I can't document it, just a feeling, but I don't like the feeling.'

Gus nodded and went on to Virginia Sudsbury, who was monitoring the temperature quality test. 'Can you give me a copy of all your preliminary findings right away?' He smiled at her when she looked flustered. She relaxed and he patted her shoulder and turned. He paused and came back to her. 'How's it holding up at room temperature?'

'So far it's completely stable at 23 C.'

He nodded and left again. A brain man, he thought. Hutchinson, at Harvard. He probably couldn't come himself, although he might. But he could recommend someone else. He started toward the clerical pool again, swerved instead and went to his office, closed and locked the door, and got an outside line. He wasn't ready yet to tell Bob Klugman, or to have anyone else tell him, that he was bringing in an outsider.

An hour later Deena had gathered all the material ready to be taken to Anne. She stopped by Gus's office. 'I'll give you a call later, if I don't get back before you leave,' she said.

'Right. And, Deena, here's the list of medications Anne had while she was in the hospital, and afterward. Look at them carefully, Deena. Three of those damn things are to stimulate respiration, stimulate heart action.'

The crutches didn't fit under her arms at all. There was a strap that went around her wrist, and a leather-covered handgrip that was comfortable to hold, and the tripod at the bottom. They weren't designed to support her weight. Anne stood unsteadily and positioned them. A centipede, she thought, all those feet and she was still afraid she would fall. Left crutch forward. Left foot. Right crutch. Right foot ... It dragged. She swayed. Lift the foot! Damn it! Right foot, dummy! She had all the feet lined up again. Left crutch. Left foot. Right crutch. Right foot ... dragging. She made an effort and lifted her foot, too high. The tripods held her and she caught her breath.

'Honey, you're really dragging that foot,' Ronnie said.

'Don't you think I know that!' She got her feet aligned again, and only then looked up at Ronnie in the doorway. 'Don't watch me. You make me nervous.'

'Okay. But you don't have to do it all day, you know.'

'Leave me alone, can't you!'

Ronnie withdrew. Anne looked at her feet again. Left crutch forward. Left foot. Right crutch. Right ... Dragging. You goddamn stupid thing! she breathed at it. Get the fuck up off that goddamn floor!

She was in the middle of the room when Ronnie came back. 'Dr. Wells is here,' she said. 'She has a lot of stuff with her.'

'Not now! Tell her to wait a minute. I'll call you,' Anne said breathlessly. There were sweat beads on her upper lip. She didn't move until Ronnie was out of sight.

When Deena brought in the notebooks and record books, Anne was sitting on one of the straight chairs at the table by the bay windows. The table was cleared.

'Hi, honey,' Deena said. 'Santa with presents. There's more in the car.'

'Looks like plenty to start with,' Anne said. 'Tell me about it all first, will you?'

'Sure. I don't know how much Clark told you. I'll pretend nothing. First there was Duckmore ...'

At five, Ronnie looked in and backed out again without speaking. They were engrossed in the notebooks, Anne making notes as Deena talked. She went back to the kitchen. At six she looked in again and said, 'Anne, I've got dinner ready for you and Dr. Wells. Should I put it in the dining room?'

Anne looked up blankly. Ronnie repeated it.

'No!' Anne said.

'I thought this one was pretty well out of the question,' Ronnie said, motioning toward the cluttered table.

'Not in the dining room!' Anne said, and her voice was too high, too tight. 'In the living room. Where Harry set the table last week. We'll have a fire.'

Ronnie grinned. 'Okay. I'll get it ready. Five minutes.'

'And then you go on home,' Anne said. 'I didn't realize how late it was getting.'

'I don't mind ...'

'I know, and thank you. But we'll be working. You might as well go.' It was an order, not a request. Her voice was still hard and tight, her face closed.

'I'll clear up the stuff,' Deena said. 'Don't worry about it, Ronnie. I'll be with her for hours yet.'

Ronnie shrugged and went out to set the table in the living room.

'I'm sorry,' Anne said. 'She gets on my nerves sometimes.'

'I bet she does. Somehow the perpetually cheerful ones are the hardest ones to take. You want to go wash up or anything before we go in?'

Deena wheeled Anne to the living room. Ronnie had lighted a fire, but it was small and hissing, at the stage where it was as likely to go out as to burn. Deena blew on it and poked it, and then gave up. 'You're on your own, brother,' she said, gazing at the smoking flames. 'Don't burn, see if I care.'

Ronnie had made shrimp creole. There were biscuits and salad and string beans. Anne ate very little. She watched the fire become feebler. They were nearly finished when she said softly, 'He thinks I killed the little cat in the dining room.'

Deena poured coffee for them both and lighted a cigarette.

'He thinks I'm psychotic. I might be.'

'If you are, I'm Joan of Arc, and nobody's ever made that kind of accusation about me.'

Anne was sitting on the couch, Deena on a straight chair she had pulled up to the table. Now she moved to the couch to sit by Anne.

'What happened with you and Clark? Want to talk about it?'

'I don't guess so. He did something that made me realize I had to think everything through again. Us. Our relationship. Everything. And he thinks I'm crazy. That simple.'

Deena got up and started to pace. She moved out of Anne's line of sight. 'Is it true you're leaving him?' she asked from behind Anne.

Anne twisted to see her; Deena touched things as she moved. First her hand lingered on the carved Indian table, then went on to touch a Tiffany lamp, past that to the frame of a painting done by a school friend of Anne's. Anne turned to study the dead fire. With its unprotesting end, gone without even a sputter of sparks, the room had become chilled and unlovely. It needed more light, the furniture was wrong, the painting was wrong, all cool blues and whites and grays, not at all right.

'Is it true?' Deena repeated, and now she came back to the table and sat down in her chair once more.

Anne shrugged and didn't look at her. 'True.'

'Where will you go?'

'I haven't given it any thought yet.'

'Anne, come to my place. With Marcie and me. There's plenty of room. You can have your own room, and it's big enough for a study.'

'Thanks,' Anne said.

'But will you?'

'I don't know. I haven't given it any thought yet.'

'You'll remember? I mean, you won't go rent an apartment where you'll be alone or anything?'

Impatiently, Anne said, 'I'll remember. Let's go back to work. Okay?'

'Sure. I'll just move this table, bring your chair over.' Deena got the chair and took Anne to the hallway.

'You want to get the coffee? I can manage from here,' Anne said. She didn't wait for a reply, but pushed herself down the hall, and when Deena came to the bedroom several minutes later, she was frowning in concentration over the computer print-outs of the pa levels of the chimps.

'Let's find everything that relates in any way to this fluctuation,' she said, without looking up. 'Test chimps and controls.'

Hours later she pushed papers away from her side of the table and threw down her pencil. 'Damn, damn, damn. Has anyone made a real effort to explain this situation to Helverson?'

'Sure. He's convinced we're at the point where human reactions are necessary. I saw him this afternoon. He's adamant about going ahead. He thinks human subjects will report any changes as soon as they happen, changes in perception, headaches, anything.'

'He can't. It's this damn fluctuation. That's the key. I knew it was trouble! I knew it in my bones from the start, when it first showed up. We should have followed through on it back two years ago, last year. We have to stop Helverson.'

'We can't,' Deena said. 'Why didn't you follow through if you were bothered by it?'

'We finally decided it was normal. It shows up in every animal, everyone we've tested. We decided it was the norm.'

'We! You mean Clark, don't you?'

'Clark. Me. It was our decision.'

'Look, Anne, isn't it a fact that it was an intuitive urge that made you want to follow through on that? Just as it was an intuitive jump that led you to suspect something like the *poena albumin* existed in the first place? That's what it's all about. And someone like Clark, all rationality, all tests and proofs, hasn't he hung back when your intuition said go? I've seen it with you two a dozen times over!'

'That's not so. We always talked over every step and agreed before we did anything. It was mutual consent from the start.'

'Nuts! I know what I've seen happen again and again!'

'You don't know at all if that's what you think.'

'Don't defend him, for Christ's sake! Everyone knows this is your work, he's riding your coattails. And he's been a drag! You should have followed up on the fluctuation if you had even an iota of a suspicion something was wrong there! And you would have, if he hadn't urged you on. Wouldn't you?'

'I don't know. What have they been saying at the lab?'

Deena groped in her purse for a cigarette. 'You do the work, he gets the credit. He has half the girls watching him with bedroom eyes! And he knows it. He already has his name on this and he'll take it through the human tests, and when it's time for the bonus, and the glory, you know who'll be right there. You think it's yours, but it isn't. Who do you think will be invited to speak at seminars and conferences? Who'll get the promotion when Gus moves up? You? That's a laugh! They'll think of a million ways to keep you tied up, too busy to leave your hot little microscope, and let Mr. Big represent the firm! I've seen it happen before! Listen to me, Anne. Please believe me. I know.' Deena kneeled at the side of Anne's chair and took her hand. 'If you're serious about leaving him, do it now, before anything's announced, before there's a success with this stuff. It's your work, and yours alone. Get his name off it! You know he won't stay around if you simply tell them it's all yours. There'll be no reason for him to stay around, and then there won't be any doubt about whose work this is!'

Anne pulled away. 'You don't know what you're talking about. Of course it's his, too. He made it possible.'

'Any well-trained lab assistant could have done what he's done! You've told him every step of the way what had to be done next, and when you didn't force him to do it your way, it got off the tracks! You admitted that yourself!'

'Deena, you're talking crazy! You haven't an idea at all what went into this work before you even knew it existed! This phase, the phase you've been working on, is the result of seven years of hard work that we've done side by side!'

'It isn't crazy! It isn't crazy! You know what I am in that company? An assistant to Emory Durand! That's all I can ever hope to be! An assistant! And if he's promoted, and he will be, then I'll be Benny Bobson's assistant! And he'll be promoted and I'll be someone else's assistant! And you! You think you'll ever be anything more than what you are right now? Clark will take Gus's place one day, and eventually he'll be offered Klugman's job and he'll take that, and you know where you'll be? Exactly where you are right now! That's the way they play the game, baby! That's how it is and has been and will be!'

'And if you and I freeze Clark out and maybe put your name on the work, at least in this phase, we'll change that system?'

'You're damn right we'll change it!'

Anne felt her knees shaking, and her hands were sweaty. She wiped them on her pants legs. Deena was still kneeling at the side of her chair. Anne didn't look at her now. 'Why do you hate him so? What has he done to you?'

'I don't hate him! Not just Clark. Can't you understand what I'm telling you? I can see how they're working to take this away from you and me. It won't be ours at all! It will be his, and Klugman's and Helverson's, the company's!'

'And what makes you think it's yours now? Your work with the human experiments. Every idea we've worked on has been mine! *I* said we have to educate the women! *I* said we had to have personal interviews! *I* said no prisoners!'

Deena got up and went around the table. 'I didn't mean that the way it sounded. I know that. I misspoke myself. I just mean ours in that we've worked together to make it as good as we can.'

Watching her, Anne said, 'You said what you think. Ours. Freeze out Clark and add your name, isn't that it? Why do you hate him?'

'For the same reasons you do!' Deena cried. 'It's taken you longer to discover them, that's all!'

'Why did you become a psychologist? Why are you working with animals instead of people?'

'What are you driving at?'

'I don't know. But don't you see what you're doing? You're urging me to do the very thing you're accusing them of. You want me to take from Clark what is legitimately his, and you pretend it's what they are doing. Don't you see that?'

'That's not true!'

'Why aren't you urging me to make up with my husband? That's what a psychologist should do, isn't it? Try to reconcile differences? You're trying to drive a wedge even deeper. Take his name off, put yours on. Come to your place to live. Why?'

Deena paled and for a moment she seemed to sway, then color flared in her cheeks, and clutching the edge of the table, she leaned forward and whispered, 'That's a lie! That's what they say about me, isn't it? It's a lie! It's a damn lie!'

Anne watched her without speaking and Deena came around the table; her chin quivered and a twitch distorted her mouth, went away, and returned. She put her hand to her mouth, her finger shook. 'It's a lie!' she said hoarsely. 'You have no right to say something like that to me. I've been your friend! I've stood up for you over there all week! I've had faith in you and your work from the start. I've risked my professional life on this work. You have no right!'

'I didn't accuse you of anything,' Anne said. 'I think you'd better go home now. We're both tired.'

'It's what you think, isn't it?'

'I don't think anything.'

'You'd rather think that than face the truth about him, that's it. It's easier for you this way. And you don't have to think about how he betrays you …'

'Deena, for God's sake, don't try to psychoanalyze me! I don't need you to explain me to me!'

'But I do need psychoanalyzing, is that it? You think I need help?'

'I don't think anything! Deena, go home. I'm exhausted. I can't play this game with you! Just forget everything I've said. Everything you've said. We're both tired!' She heard the rising note in her voice and bit her lip.

'I'll go,' Deena said after a moment. 'But I won't forget. I'll never forget!'

CHAPTER EIGHTEEN

Lola's black leathery fingers plucked hairs from her flanks, first the left side, then the right. She pulled a few hairs, extended her hand, let them fall, then she pulled some more. Bald spots, larger than half dollars already, oozed blood, a spot here, another. She stared ahead fixedly.

'When did she start that?' Clark asked Bob Brighton.

'I don't know. I got here at ten-thirty, a little too early to relieve Virginia, and wandered over to have a quick look at the chimps before I started on the temperature quality work.'

'Christ!' Clark felt a rising nausea, and despair. 'I'll have to find someone to come in to keep her under observation. Will you stay put until someone comes? I'll tell Virginia you'll be a little late.'

Bob Brighton nodded, keeping his eyes on the chimp. He had a notebook, already one page was filled with notes. He sat down again, the notebook on his lap.

Clark's mind refused to supply a name and finally he called Emory Durand at home. Durand said he would take care of it and Clark went back to watch the chimp again. Lola stared ahead and her fingers plucked out hairs and dropped them. The bald spots were becoming elongated. Clark stood helplessly before the cage for another minute or two. Then, shoulders drooping, he returned to his own department.

In the pharmaceutical division half a dozen people were working; others were in the computer room, a technician was at the electron microscope. Diedricks's night staff was processing blood, extracing the *pa*. It was eleven-thirty.

'Dr. Symons?'

He turned to see Virginia Sudsbury approaching. 'I know Dr. Wells isn't here tonight,' she said. 'When Bob's relief comes ... I thought, if you wanted a ride ... I think we go the same way. I have my car.' She began to blush as she spoke, and looked about almost desperately, as if searching a way out of what she had started.

Clark nodded absently. 'It'll be twenty minutes or so.'

'I'll be by the back door,' she said.

Clark longed to go back to the electron microscope and try to speed up the man working there. He clenched his hands and went instead to his office. It was all going as fast as it could.

At twelve, Gus entered his office. Clark looked up bleary-eyed. 'What are you doing here?'

'What the hell are you doing here still is more like it,' Gus snapped. 'And did you know Virginia's waiting to take you home?' He had a paper bag, which he opened now, and flashed a bottle at Clark. 'Therapeutic dosage, one good jigger – and then off with you.' He produced two paper cups and poured. 'You must be seeing everything twice by now.'

Clark gulped his drink. 'What are you doing back?'

'Can't sleep with Elaine away,' Gus grumbled. 'What damn difference it makes I don't know, but there it is. I start itching. My legs actually start to itch. So I thought, what the hell, be better off down here than there scratching.' He sipped his bourbon and sighed. 'Good stuff. You know, I watch my hands start to scratch before I can stop them. Make sores, and I know damn well nothing's there. Not a bite, not a rash, nothing. But I scratch until I make sores. Thought Bierley would probably have some slides ready in another hour or two. Sneak preview.'

Clark finished his drink. 'You say Virginia's waiting? Christ, I forgot about her.'

'Yeah. I thought so. Go on home, get some rest.' Clark looked about vaguely, remembered his corduroy coat and pulled it on, and left. Virginia met him at the door. Her hair was loose on her back, lustrous, heavy, beautiful.

'My car's almost at the end of the lot,' she said. 'That's the worst part about coming in at three, no place to park closer than that. You want to wait while I go get it?'

'No. I'll come. The air feels good.' It was cold and still, the sky overcast. By the time they got to her car, he was shivering hard.

'My heater isn't too great,' Virginia said. 'But it'll help in a couple of minutes. You live on Cherokee Drive, don't you?'

He nodded, and it didn't occur to him to wonder how she knew. He didn't ask where she lived. He slumped down in the seat, huddled in his coat, and closed his eyes as she backed up from the parking space, drove slowly through the lot, and picked up speed on the highway, nearly deserted now.

From time to time Virginia looked at him, but she didn't speak; it made her glad that he slept in her car, that she was able to do this much for him. She knew where the apartment building was; she had looked up his address and had driven past a few times. She liked to think about him living in an elegant apartment overlooking the park. When they arrived, she slowed the car gently and came to an almost imperceptible stop. She shifted to neutral and twisted to look at him. He was sound asleep. She reached out to touch him, to awaken him, then moved her hand back and clutched both hands together. Not yet. In a minute. She watched him sleep.

Deena's little yellow car jerked away from the parking space, stalled, died, and jerked again as she drove through the alley, turned and entered the street without stopping. Halfway down the block she saw Virginia's car parked before the building, and without volition, she stopped at the curb. Her heater hadn't had time to warm the car and she shivered, but didn't start the engine again. She hugged herself and watched the old Ford. Its lights were off. Minutes passed and she was chilled through and through. Her fingers dug into her arms through the coat, released, dug in again. Finally the door opened and Clark got out. He swayed, leaned against the car, spoke to Virginia, then mounted the stairs, holding the rail, walking like an old man. Deena didn't start her VW until Virginia's car was gone, out of sight.

She'd tell Anne, she thought, tell her about Clark and that fat slut, open her eyes about him. She shook her head. Anne wouldn't believe her. She could never tell her anything ever again. Not after the vile, vicious things Anne had said to her.

She drove too fast, screeching to stops at red lights, behind slow-moving cars; she killed her engine several times, and by the time she reached her apartment she was furious with the automobile. She'd take it in for a checkup, make them fix whatever made it stop like that. And the brakes. Brakes shouldn't scream in agony. She made herself a Scotch and soda and sat down in her own living room and thought about Anne.

She was sick. If Deena had not reacted personally, had treated her more professionally, she would have seen that at once. It was hard to separate her professional self from the personal. That's why we don't treat friends and family, she thought. Of course, Anne needed professional help. Projecting like crazy. Like crazy, she repeated, and sipped her drink slowly. Sexual maladjustment of some sort, projecting to Deena what she was suffering. Anne felt a tug there, that was clear. Refused it, refused to acknowledge it even, and instead projected it. That much was clear.

Feelings of persecution there. *They* were ruining her work. *They* were trying to take it away from her. *They*, even Deena, probably the only real friend she had, were conspiring against her.

She probably had killed the cat, repressed it thoroughly. It fit the pattern. Deena had noticed the scratches. It was impossible not to notice them, and Anne had acted as if they didn't exist. Maybe she blanked them out, hysterical blindness.

It was almost a classic case, Deena thought. Interpreting a simple invitation as a homosexual threat. Classic. Anne was the type. Long legs, slender hips, boyish figure altogether. Hormones out of balance, obviously. Confused by her conflicting desires, repressing her urges ... Deena finished her drink and started to undress. Now she could pity Anne; with understanding came pity, not the fury she had felt earlier.

They had to know, of course. Anne had to have treatment. She had used the *pa* and it was having an effect on her. They had to know.

Clark hesitated outside Anne's door, his hand on the knob, but he didn't enter; he turned and went into his own room. The brief nap he had had in Virginia's car had cleared some of the fuzz from his brain, and he realized he had to get Anne's diary, and also that he could not ask her for it. She was too fine a scientist not to have kept scrupulous notes from the start. It would be there, dosage, times, reactions if any.

Across the hall Anne listened for him, and when it was apparent he was not coming in to her, she relaxed. After a time she became aware of the soreness in her arms and shoulders and she knew she wouldn't sleep soon. She thought longingly of a hot bath and wondered if she couldn't manage it alone; she was afraid to try. Getting out of the tub was hard. She turned off the light and sat in the dark room looking out the window and thought about the work being done at the lab, thought about Lola and Fannie and Duckmore. This long after being administered the serum. Why? A process of facilitation, obviously. The *pa* tended to migrate to the brain, and in normal subjects, accustomed to it from birth, it did no harm there. In subjects with high, artificially induced *pa* levels, the adaptation wasn't made. Why? There had to be another factor, she thought. Something they had overlooked, hadn't taken into account. The fluctuating *pa* level had to be the key.

They had to work with a brain specialist, after all. They had discussed it early and had decided not to bring in yet another person, but they needed that specialized knowledge. Gus would know someone. She remembered the early days after the accident, when Dr. Radimer had told her they would have to operate on her leg again. He had said, 'There's so damn much we don't understand, can't anticipate. Why the tibia is so hard to heal is a mystery.' Why the *pa* factor was agglutinating in the brain now was another mystery.

What would Clark say if she admitted she couldn't remember long stretches of her convalescence? The early days in the hospital were a blank, explainable because they had kept her doped all the time. Then there was a clear piece, hours of torment, days of torture. The trip home was a solid memory. Being brought into the house on a gurney, the transfer to bed. All that was clear. More days of torture, then another blank until the day she fell.

There were snatches, a piece here, another there. A visit by her mother, and her accusations, phrased as questions: Were you two drinking? Was he speeding? Were you arguing? Are you going to collect a lot of money? She remembered that visit perfectly.

She was evading what she had started to think through, she knew, and drew her thoughts back to the blanks. Traumas often brought their own amnesia, a simple protective mechanism, easily understood, usually easily overcome if the blank could be outlined. This period, starting with event A, lasting until event B. The fall was event B. Event A? She didn't know.

The fall. Sitting on the side of the bed, the chair within reach, knowing she could stand and draw the chair close enough to seat herself in it. A surprise for Clark, who was in the bathroom. He would return to find her in the chair, pouring coffee at the table by the bay window. She closed her eyes, visualizing what had happened. She had swung her legs over the bed, steadied herself with both hands on the edge. Then, still confident, she had stood up, unsteady to be sure, but she had stood and had reached out, and now the image she got became distorted. She could see her own hand reaching for the chair, her hand groping as the chair seemed to move away. She had lost balance and with a twisting motion of desperation had tried to grab the bed again, and she had fallen, dragging the blanket off with her. She might have screamed. She couldn't remember if she had screamed. Clark had come running; she must have screamed. And then she had felt pain and terror.

That had been months ago. Why had she been so certain she could do it? What had given her that false confidence? Most of all, why did she have those blanks?

If she had used the *pa* factor, she would remember, she knew she would remember. She saw again Ruth Gorman, a pleasant, middle-aged woman of medium height, tending to overweight. Ruth had knitted all night, night after night. Making an afghan with lovely orange and brown and gold yarns.

'There's a white plastic bag in the refrigerator,' Anne had said late one night. She had slept very little those nights. 'Will you bring it in here, please?'

Ruth asked no questions. Anne had been accumulating notebooks, magazines, boxes of slides, practically everything from her desk in the study that had become Clark's bedroom.

And later Anne had looked at the contents of the bag. There was a box with two dozen stoppered, one-dram sample bottles. Two dozen disposable syringes. Her passport to freedom, she had thought, looking at the bottle filled to the top with the colorless liquid.

The next day the doctor had come and they had done something new with the traction and the agonies had started over again. She had been in a hospital bed then, she remembered. She had forgotten that.

And, sometime, she had asked for the bedside table instead of the hospital stand on the right side of the bed. The table had a door that automatically locked when it closed. She had the key. She remembered opening it, putting the plastic-wrapped box inside the storage space, along with her original notes on the *pa* factor.

She had unlocked the door and put the package inside. It had hurt her to move that way, stretching down to reach. And sometime she had opened that door again, removed the package and wrapped it in newspaper and dropped it all into the waste can. She knew she had done that. She could remember wrapping it in newspaper.

Why had she wrapped it up? Why not just throw it away as it was?

She had wrapped it in newspaper. She had wrapped it carefully, as if it were something she wanted to preserve, not something to be discarded. She had tucked the ends in. So it wouldn't come open again. She had overwrapped it, tucking in opposite sides. She dropped it into the waste can, and then she folded newspapers and dropped them in. She dumped her ashtray out on top of them. She put a magazine in the waste can. And sheets of notebook paper, crumpled loosely. She had buried the package completely.

'I was afraid it wouldn't keep,' she whispered. 'There were so many strangers in and out of the apartment. I was afraid someone would take it, might even use it.' She heard the whispers and clamped her mouth shut. That wasn't the reason.

She had wrapped it in newspapers. Back, before that. She had opened it first, looked inside ... She unlocked the door and took the white plastic-wrapped package out. No one was in the room then. She always had to choose her moments carefully. They never left her alone. She wore the key on a charm bracelet on her wrist. She unlocked the door and opened it, leaning far down over the side of the bed. She groped for the plastic, it always felt cool, a little bit sticky. She put it on her stomach and lay back against the pillows. The plastic bag was ripped almost all the way down one side. She had the newspapers beside her on the bed. She opened the box ... She wrapped it in ...

Back, before that. She had opened it, had taken out one of the tiny bottles, held it up ... Why? She remembered holding it up, looking at the clear fluid. 'I discovered it! It has my name on it!'

Anne felt her heart thumping hard, and she closed her eyes and finally remembered that day. Her mother had been there. Weak with pain, dizzy from sleeplessness, she had tried to follow her mother's monologue, and had given up. Then her mother had said, 'He probably has a new girl to help him now. Have you seen her? Is she pretty?' Malicious bitch, Anne thought. How can you do this to me now? Her mother looked like Harry, tall, long arms and legs, thick through the middle. She looked unhappy also, but she had always looked unhappy.

'I am not his assistant,' Anne said, working to keep her voice firm.

'They'll let you back, won't they? But there must be lots of jobs for good laboratory people, even women.'

'I still am on full pay,' Anne said. 'I told you that.'

Her mother raised her eyebrows.

And Anne had twisted to reach the door of the cabinet, unlocked it with her key worn on her bracelet, and had taken out the white plastic-wrapped box, with the plastic ripped almost all the way down one side. The plastic had felt cold, clammy. Her hands shook when she lay down again, the box on her stomach. She opened it and withdrew one of the small, stoppered bottles.

'Look at it, Mother! I discovered it! It has my name on it! Mine! Anne Clewiston! Not Mrs. Clark Symons!'

'What is it for?'

'It will stop pain. Completely stop it.'

'Well, if it works, the way you look, you should be using it, I'd say. Why do you have it here if you don't intend to use it?'

Anne put the small bottle back carefully and kept her eyes on the box, not willing to see her mother, not willing to let her mother see her. She would use it, she realized. She had to. She couldn't bear it any longer. Her mother's voice went on and on, droning about how Anne had always complained so about the least little thing. A scratch would send her crying to her room. Desperately, Anne wrapped the box in newspapers, overwrapped it. A fall, you'd think she had broken every bone in her body. Tres had had a baby with natural childbirth, not a whimper had passed her lips. Anne stuffed the rest of the newspaper in the can on top of the box. And Hal! The day he broke his wrist playing football, he had finished the game! On and on and on and on.

The waste can was full, overflowing. She lay back against her pillow, shaking.

'Why are you throwing it away if it's any good?' Her mother reached for the waste can, and Anne rang the bell for the nurse. 'You can't just throw it away. Won't they need it at work? Won't Clark miss it and wonder what happened to it?'

Ruth Gorman entered and frowned at Anne's condition. 'Can I get you something?' she asked.

'Please, just empty the can.'

Ruth picked it up and carried it out. Anne's mother watched her and then turned to Anne. 'That's a sin, just throwing it away like that! Clark might have been able to do something with it! You always did do things like that. I remember when you threw away Hal's handmade fishing flies. Remember? You were mad at him or something ...'

'I didn't. Tres did it.'

'Now don't try to blame it on Tres. She and Hal were very close then, not like you and your brother at all ...'

'Mother, please go now. I have to rest. I'm tired. Please. Go! Don't come back!' Her voice was rising out of control. 'Don't come see me again. When I'm well, we'll visit you.'

'If you had something you could use and just threw it away, well, it's your decision. Stubborn, too stubborn for your own good ...'

Ruth Gorman had returned with the empty waste can and quite firmly had ushered Anne's mother from the room with no more delays.

Anne hadn't seen her mother since. There had been one very hurt letter, which she hadn't read all the way through. Someday, she thought, she would try to get to know her, to see the woman Harry talked about, a woman she never had seen. Someday. She left the window and got ready for bed.

She could tell Clark now, end it. And Helverson would go ahead with the human tests and her work would lie in ruins about her.

Her life. Her work. Everything. She thought how eagerly Clark had seized on this belief, that she had used the *pa*. How important it was for him to believe that. He had to believe it. Even if she told him now, right now, he would have to doubt until he called her mother, talked to the nurse. He might even think she coached her mother in what to say. No, Clark would never believe that. He knew her mother, knew their relationship. Others might believe it, but he never would. But he would call and confirm her story. And then what? He would have to face the same questions she was facing: Why did he have the need to believe she was psychotic?

She was too tired to think any longer. She lay still and tried not to think of the next day. Learning to walk again, swimming perhaps, more arguments... Who next? She was alienating everyone she knew. Poor Deena. She never had seen Deena so furious. Again she thought, poor Deena. And poor Marcie, Deena's daughter.

Her door opened and she stiffened but made no sound. She woke up completely. A shaft of light stretched into the bedroom from the hallway. The room had changed from dark to dim. It was possible to see Clark's outline when he came into the room. His face was a pale blur, his hands giant moths that made aimless movements. He stood over the bed a moment, and she closed her eyes at his approach. He didn't touch her. He moved away a step, stopped at her wheelchair, and the moths fluttered about it. He was searching the pockets of the wheelchair. He was looking for her diary. Presently he found it and he left and closed the door without a sound. He would be back to replace it, she knew. He would not find what he was looking for, and he would sneak back in and return it to the pocket, as puzzled as before, as certain as before. And he would reason that she, a fine scientist, would have kept notes, would have recorded dosage, times, dates, results, everything. He would come back to search again and again, certain of finding the notes sooner or later. He was so certain. So certain.

CHAPTER NINETEEN

Clark woke stiffly and made coffee, showered, and dressed before he went into Anne's room. She was already up, at the table by the windows. Clark's eyes rested a moment on the locked door of the bedside table. He resisted the temptation to try the door, see if it was locked.

'Breakfast?' he asked.

She shook her head. 'No, thanks. Just coffee.'

'Be right back.'

It was so normal, he thought, preparing the coffee for them both. Just like always, except he was no more than a servant now. Anne was studying the tree outside the window when he returned. Without turning to look at him, she asked, 'Can you make Helverson reconsider? Can you stop him?'

Clark put the tray down and poured the coffee, handed hers to her and sat down before he answered. 'I don't think so. Gus doesn't think so.'

'He won't believe the risks, is that it?'

'Partly. And he knows it will all be kept secret. Deena's working on it, you know. Prisoners. They'll be under observation for as long as it takes. Grove will see to that. All very hush-hush.'

Anne's hand was steady when she lifted her cup. She was facing Clark now, but was not seeing him. Her gaze was on a distant point, something not even in that room.

'There was a new development with Lola last night,' he said. He told her about it and she nodded.

'Is her *pa* increasing?'

'Yes. Not much, but steadily. I'll call and give you the exact figures if you want.' She nodded. 'You think she's manufacturing *pa* now. Is that it?'

'Looks like it, doesn't it?'

'And it's accumulating in her blood,' Clark said, narrowing his eyes. 'It could be the break, Anne.'

'And it could be disaster. If it continues to build to the level of her dosage, and then drops, especially if it drops very fast, she'll probably have a seizure. You should have close observation constantly from now on, for the next few days anyway.'

'We're doing that. What do you think?'

'I think we've taught them how to manufacture *pa* without at the same time knowing anything about the control of it. If Lola responds like I suspect she will, the stuff will begin to agglutinate at an accelerating rate, and since it seems non-selective, with this new assault on her brain, vital functions can as easily be affected as simple pain receptors. She's likely to die this time.'

Clark stared at her in horror. 'What can we do?' He wasn't asking about the chimps.

'Nothing, except wait.' Anne poured more coffee. 'You'd better call for a cab.'

She couldn't look at him now. She heard the horror in his voice and knew what he was thinking and couldn't look at him. You chose to believe, she thought, stirring her coffee. You chose this as the lesser of the evils, and now you have to accept all of it. And this is one of the parts. There are others, will be others. But she couldn't look at him. He had spoken.

'I'm sorry,' she said. 'I was thinking, I guess.'

'I asked why I need a cab. Did Deena say she wouldn't be here this morning?'

'She didn't say. We had a quarrel last night. She was pretty pissed off at me, and through me, you. I doubt she'll come by.'

'What did you fight about?'

'It doesn't matter. We were both tired, I think. It'll pass.'

Clark felt that things were happening he couldn't comprehend. Anne was different, cool, remote, abstracted, so deep in thought she hardly seemed aware of him until he spoke. Withdrawn, he thought, like Lola, and Fannie, and Duckmore. Gone into a world of her own where no one could follow her.

'Anne,' he said. 'Please don't turn me off, just listen to me.' She came back from wherever it was she went, and she looked at him, and for a moment he thought he saw pity on her face, something about the expression, something in her eyes. It was gone too quickly to be certain, and she was merely alert, listening, waiting. 'Anne,' he said, and now he was pleading, 'I want to call a doctor to come see you today.'

'A psychiatrist?'

'Yes. I can ask Dr. Radimer to recommend someone. We would confide in him, explain everything, what the stuff is, how the chimps have been reacting, how you ...'

'How I've been reacting? Is that the rest of it?'

'Anne, please. Just try to understand it from my side. Please.'

'And what if he found nothing? Then what? Another one? And another? Until you find someone who will say what you want to hear?'

'For God's sake, Anne, stop it! I don't want to hear anyone say you've taken the stuff and it's hurting you! But if you have used it, we have to know, someone has to be on hand to help you.'

'I told you I didn't.'

Clark shut his eyes and took a deep breath. 'You told me,' he said. 'It's late. I guess you're right about Deena. I'd better get a cab.'

At the door he stopped and said, 'Anne, at least think about it. I'll try to leave earlier today. We can talk about it tonight. Think about what I've said.'

'I think of little else these days,' she said. 'What else is there?'

Gus arrived late that morning. Before work he had gone to see Dr. Radimer, who didn't believe Anne had taken anything to relieve her pain. 'I would have known,' he had repeated several times, stiffly, as if being accused. 'Not necessarily,' Gus had explained. 'The stuff has no lasting effects. Within eight hours, the level of pain would be exactly what it had been before. If she knew she had an appointment with you, she might not have taken it that morning. How could you be sure?'

'I would have known,' Dr. Radimer insisted.

A washout, Gus thought. The nurse had been another washout. She didn't know if Anne had thrown away the package from the refrigerator. She didn't even remember getting it for Anne. There was the cleaning woman, and after that no one else they could ask. Only Anne, and Clark. Gus had no hopes the cleaning woman would remember that particular package, that one day in the middle of winter. Why should she? He scowled and, still scowling, entered the laboratory, where his secretary Mary Johnston was waiting for him.

'Mr. Helverson wants you right away,' she said. 'He came down personally to get you.'

'Shit,' Gus said, and his scowl deepened.

'He wants Dr. Symons at the same time,' Mary added. She glanced over her shoulder. 'He's been with Dr. Wells for almost an hour, and Dr. Klugman is with them now.'

'Is Clark here?'

'In the animal division.'

'Get him for me. Don't tell anyone I've come in yet. I'll wait for Clark in my office. Scat!'

He went inside his own office, to scowl even deeper at the dartboard.

Clark knocked and entered without waiting for an answer. Mary Johnston had alerted him, too, then. 'Do you know what's up?' Gus asked.

'Deena? And Bob? Why, unless Deena blew the whistle on Anne. What else?'

'Right. What happened?'

'Christ, I don't know. Anne said they had an argument. Anne wouldn't talk about it.'

Gus cursed fluently for several seconds, and then said, 'Okay, Deena's blown it. And she must have some ammunition. The question is, what will we do about it?'

Clark didn't answer.

'Goddamn it, Clark, snap out of it! Get on the outside for a quick look! You want a human subject and you find out someone took the stuff three months ago. You've got the subject! Then what?'

'Observation. Tests. Anne won't let them!'

'Can she stop them?'

Clark's eyes narrowed and he lighted a cigarette, thinking furiously. 'Is anyone else in on it?'

Gus snatched up the phone and told Mary Johnston to find out who else was in Helverson's office, and waited for her to call back with his hand on the receiver. The phone rang seconds later. He listened, grunted, and hung up. 'Grove,' he said. 'He got here ten minutes ago.'

'I won't let them touch her!' Clark said savagely.

'Not even for her own good?' Gus asked, and his voice was almost as savage as Clark's. 'You think she took the stuff. Deena must agree. Is she going psychotic? Will she become a psychopath tonight, tomorrow? Next week? Can you say she won't? Clark, she might not even know if she used it. I talked to a brain man, Hutchinson, described generally what we have, and he suggested the possibility that it might act as an amnesic, if it prevents certain synapses firing. She could have used it and have no memory at all about doing it.'

'They can't have her!' Clark stood up threateningly, his fists clenched. A muscle worked in his jaw, there was a pallor on his face that made him look ill, old.

'Can you say she'll be all right tonight? Tomorrow?' Gus stood up too and they faced each other across his desk, the little ugly man, as tight and hard now as Clark.

'I don't give a shit if she's all right tonight, or any time. They can't have her. I'm going home!'

Gus got to the door first. 'No, you're not! You're going up to Helverson's office with me and you're going to keep quiet and listen to them. You hear me! You're going to listen and keep your big mouth shut.'

Clark sagged. 'For now,' he said.

'Right. Now let's go.'

Dr. Lawrence Grove was almost bald, with a few pale hairs across the top of his skull, and a fringe that ran from ear to ear in such a way that a head-on view of him made it appear he had tufts of hair poking from behind his ears. His dome was very red, redder than his face, redder than he was anywhere else. His face was long and full, rectangular, with large features, a bony nose, full lips, large myopic eyes. Recently he had switched to glasses that darkened according to the available light, and now the glasses were violet-tinted, a hideous contrast to the redness of his scalp.

He tapped his fingertips together and shifted his feet, crossed his legs, automatically moving in such a way that the crease was not distorted. His shoes were highly polished. 'Dr. Wells,' he said, and his voice was surprisingly vibrant, alive. He would have been very good on radio. 'If this young woman is mentally ill, from whatever reason, it is our duty to care for her.'

'You don't listen to me,' Deena snapped. 'I admit that. What I am saying is that I'll have no part in trying to get her committed to any kind of institution. There are plenty of private hospitals. Even an experienced nurse in her apartment. Anything except one of the institutions.'

'I understand,' Dr. Grove said. 'And I heartily endorse what you say, but, my dear, this is an extraordinary case, and we must be absolutely certain that the doctor we select to handle her case is in sympathy with our cause. I can assure that in any of the hospitals under my jurisdiction, you see. However, if we go to a privately run hospital, a privately engaged physician, then …' He turned to Helverson, who was nodding. 'Yes. Now, naturally we will not take any precipitate action. This is understood. Nothing hasty, nothing to regret. Right?'

Edward Helverson listened to them without adding to any of it; he was planning the next move, the next few hours. That son of a bitch Symons might be a stumbling block. The fool took the stuff, that was certain, and she either was going mad or wasn't, and in either case they had to know. Perfect. Perfect. There was an estrangement, that too was clear from what Dr. Wells had said. Symons's name was on the project; he'd want to protect it at any cost, wouldn't he? He could handle Gus, had always been able to handle Gus. Klugman was nothing. Gus and Symons, then. Gus would play. He'd protest, but he'd come around. Symons had to play. He made a mental note to sic Jack on Symons and that idiot wife of his. Jack Newell would dig out anything there was. Good. There was always something. He realized he was staring at Deena Wells and he put her in the unknown column. He didn't know what was bugging her. A queer probably, that might be useful. Another note to Jack Newell. Trying to break up the Symonses' marriage? Why? No hint of perversion in Anne Clewiston. He underlined Deena Wells's name in the unknown column. Something about the way her eyes glittered, the way she kept moistening her lips. Jack would find out anything there was about her, too. He began to listen again to Grove.

'… her physician. A steady dosage of tranquilizers probably is all she'll need. You say the level of the *pa* fluctuates daily?' He was speaking to Bob Klugman.

Klugman could feel sweat trickling down his back, and he kept wiping his hands on his trousers. 'He, Gus, knows about the details more than I do,' he said. 'I was ill last week, you know.'

'What exactly do we need to commit her?' Helverson asked.

'No problem there,' Grove said. 'I'm qualified as a physician to sign the papers. Dr. Wells can be the second consultant. We'll need her husband's permission, also.' His voice rose in a near question.

Helverson nodded. 'No court order?'

'Not if we have her husband's permission. Or even hers. She can commit herself, you understand.'

Deena moistened her lips again. She was cold. 'What hospital?' she asked.

'State hospital down in Shepherdsville. Good man there. Avery Meindl. Know him?'

She shook her head.

'He'll understand. I'll brief him myself. We've worked together on other projects in the past. Good man.'

A state hospital, Deena thought, and visualized its grayness. Prison. Uniforms. Gatehouse and high fence and guards. She tried to moisten her lips, but now her tongue was also dry. 'I won't sign for that,' she said in a hoarse voice. 'Not a state hospital.'

Helverson looked at her and his eyes were very cold, very bright, as ice is bright under the sun. You will do exactly what we tell you, you stupid cunt, he thought. He said, 'This is merely a preliminary discussion, Dr. Wells. We must examine every aspect of this extraordinary situation, and keep in mind always that Anne Clewiston's well-being is our primary concern. We must protect her at all costs. Everything else is secondary.'

Deena's hands clenched and loosened, but she still couldn't moisten her dry lips.

Edward Helverson believed people were born to serve in different spheres. There were the natural military men, out of place anywhere else. There were the natural artists, who would produce art no matter what. There were the people like Gus, and Clark Symons, born to play with test tubes and microscopes. And there were the men born to move through the world of business. He knew his place had been ordained from the beginning. There had been no doubt in his mind at any time in his life about where he belonged. And even this mini-crisis was welcome to him, a new test of his skill; this victory would be another in a line of victories that would leave his mark on the world.

He had come to the company while old man Prather had been at the helm, his hand firm, his vision clear about where he was going and how to get there. It had been his goal to make the company the finest in the world, not in size, but in quality. Helverson had moved up the ranks as surely as a salmon moves upstream, incapable of resisting the inevitable, incapable of imagining such resistance. And now, with young Prather as president, suddenly there was no place to go. The boundaries had become visible, and as he approached them under steady acceleration, he knew he could not be contained within them. That was stasis, and stasis was death.

Six years ago the old man had died, and four years ago Helverson had understood what had to happen next. The company was good, but it could never be more than it was – a peanut concession at the World's Fair. Prather hadn't been interested when he first brought up the subject of a merger. There was some pride there, also laziness, and worst of all, lack of vision. Or perhaps he merely felt safe here and was afraid to compete in the real world. Helverson didn't know what held young Prather back, and he didn't care. When the ante became high enough, pride, and fear, and whatever else it was would fade from the scene, and the merger would go through. Prather might retire prematurely to spend his windfall, or invest it in a new peanut stand; Helverson didn't know what he would do, didn't care; he knew what he would do then.

He never entertained a worry that the *pa* factor was possibly dangerous. They would have found that out long ago. It was just the confounding pickiness of the scientific mind that insisted on one more test, one more run, one more delay. They acted as if they had all the time in the world, while he knew time was the everlasting enemy.

With Clewiston's find, the ante had shot up suddenly, and he knew that within a year he would deal himself a fistful of aces, and he wasn't going to let any sudden failure of nerve take that away from him. The IND made it legal; Grove would keep it clean professionally, add some prestige even, and they all knew anyone who stuck his pinkie in this would draw it out dripping honey. A bigger find than penicillin, bigger than the Salk vaccine, bigger than anything on the books. The story would be on the front pages of newspapers throughout the world – Clewiston's name, Symons's, Prather's, they all would be there – but the story that really mattered would be hidden away on the financial pages. In that story it would be his name that the people would read, the people who mattered.

Helverson had seen the power of the corporation when the IND approval had been rushed through. Nothing illegal, but they hadn't dragged their feet the way they would have done had it been only Prather Pharmaceuticals trying to get a decision. It wasn't merely another move up a ladder, he knew; it was a quantum leap, and he was going to make that jump. There was nothing shady, absolutely nothing illegal, in moving forward. If there were, he would not consider such a move. His record was unblemished, and would remain virgin-pure; that was important, he would guard it jealously.

He continued to listen to Grove and Deena Wells arguing about state institutions, and he knew Wells wouldn't be a problem. She was afraid, and he would find out why and use her fear. Subtly, of course, even sympathetically. There was no problem with her.

He was impatient for Clark Symons and Gus to arrive. They were the unknowns now. His impatience didn't show at all.

CHAPTER TWENTY

With the entrance of Gus and Clark, the office seemed to become very small. Helverson stood up and offered his hand; Clark apparently didn't see it, but went to the window and stood there, slightly behind Klugman, out of the line of sight of Dr. Grove. Gus shook Helverson's hand, nodded to the others in the room, and sat on the couch, next to Deena.

'You gentlemen all know each other,' Helverson said. 'Dr. Symons, I understand your wife might have used the *pa* factor on herself, and of course, that presents us with several problems. What I'd like is for you and Gus to consult with Dr. Grove, and Dr. Wells, of course, and answer any of his questions, explain exactly what has been happening in the animal division. Just a thorough briefing. Would you like to use the conference room?'

Helverson knew what he had to do. The decision had been there waiting for Clark's entrance to firm itself and make itself known to him; when he came to it, the plan was fully formed, ready to act upon. He trusted his decisions that came that way. They never had failed him in the past. The room had become small because of Clark Symons. Clark was radiating hostility and negativism. He would agree to nothing. Right. Helverson stood up and the others did also. Bob Klugman looked anxious, puzzled; Grove also looked puzzled. This wasn't what they had talked about at all.

'Bob,' Helverson said, 'you can show them all into the conference room. Order coffee. That always seems to help. Take your time, gentlemen, and Dr. Wells. There must be innumerable questions to be answered, points to be explicated.' Klugman bustled importantly now, led the way to the door. Helverson smiled at him.

'I have some rather pressing work to do,' Clark said brusquely. 'I'm sure there's nothing I can add to what Gus knows about the experiments.'

Helverson held the door, motioned him through. 'But only you know about your wife, Dr. Symons. You and Dr. Wells, that is.'

Clark looked at Deena and his face tightened even more. She flinched and looked away.

As soon as they were gone, Helverson called Jack Newell and told him what he wanted done. 'Bring me Anne Clewiston's file first, and then get to it. Very, very quietly, of course.'

'Of course,' Jack said.

'Where's Dr. Symons?' Emory Durand asked at the clerical-pool office door.

'A meeting,' Mary Johnston said. 'He and Dr. Weinbacher, Dr. Wells, Dr. Klugman, were all called to a meeting.'

'DND meeting?'

'Yes, sir.'

'Christ!' A 'Do Not Disturb' meeting now! Damnation! He returned to Lola's cage and shrugged at the question on Jane's face. 'She still out?'

'Yes, sir. No change.'

Lola lay in a fetal position. The assistant had called Emory Durand when she went into convulsions, and within seconds that phase had passed and she had curled up and was staying curled up.

'No medication, nothing,' Emory said. 'But don't take your eyes off her. If there's a change, call me.'

The image of the chimp in a tight ball stayed with him as he walked back toward his office and put in an emergency call for Clark, to be answered just as soon as the meeting ended.

'Why have you come here?' Anne demanded.

Edward Helverson was admiring the room. 'Very, very nice,' he said. 'These old houses are still the best, aren't they? I have a modern plastic-and-chrome apartment. Makes me feel like an exhibit sometimes.' He finished his survey and looked at Anne then. 'And you, my dear, are looking very lovely.' A mistake, he thought, the instant the words formed. He sat down opposite her at the small table covered with notebooks and charts. 'And working, in spite of everything.'

She continued to watch him. For a time there was silence as they regarded one another.

Arrogant, Helverson thought. Smart. Smarter than he was in many ways. And an idiot when it came to practical matters. How they detested him and his kind, and without him and his kind they'd all be blowing themselves up in basement labs. He had made a tactical error before; he wouldn't again.

'May I call you Anne?' he asked and waited for her nod before he went on. 'Anne, I learned this morning there is a possibility you have tested your *pa* factor on yourself, and in view of the trouble that has developed at the laboratory, it seemed imperative to call on you.'

She waited, suspicious and wary. Deena, she thought. Deena had done this. She didn't know why. She would have to think about the why later when she was alone, when there was time. She watched her tall elegant caller and waited for the rest of it.

Helverson wasn't perturbed by her silence. They were playing his game now, not hers; and in this game he was the expert. If she began to talk about experiments and *pa* levels and tests, he would take the back seat, but not now.

'If you used it, Anne, you have to submit to observation, testing procedures, you understand that. The only problem is where to do it. Not here, obviously. Competent people have to manage your case, and they are a scarcity. No one could ask them to abandon many patients to oversee the care of one, even if that one is as important as you to all of us.'

'No!' she said. 'You'd better leave now, Mr. Helverson. I am on a strict routine and it is time for my exercise.'

'Yes, Anne. The IND has been approved, the next step is the human testing and teratology studies. I am already committed to having those results by next spring, so we must take that step this month or next. Nothing that has happened in the lab is enough in itself to force a postponement. We simply have contraindications that we will observe in our testing program. No fault there.'

'I won't agree to go ahead until this problem is solved,' Anne said. 'I'll write to the FDA myself and outline what has happened.'

'I considered that,' Helverson said. 'I understand your idealism. Understand and sympathize with it. Your elaborate plans for educating the test subjects, for being absolutely certain they understood what was being done, your personal involvement with that phase. Very commendable. And we had agreed to permit you to do it your way. That's how highly we regard you, my dear.' He didn't reach over to pat her, but smiled gently and looked as if he might. Anne pulled back farther, hard against her chair. 'We will go ahead, Anne,' he said. 'We have to. This is too important to everyone to let it sit while you start over. Five more years? Eight more years? You know it works, don't you? It worked for you. If you write that letter, you'll be discredited, my dear. I have a signed and notarized statement from Dr. Wells that your mental condition is such that no letter of yours could be taken seriously. Hallucinations, delusions of persecution, sexual fantasies. You need treatment, my dear. If it is the *pa* causing your problems, it won't be a blemish on your future, don't you see? You sign the necessary papers, submit to treatment. You receive extraordinary care in a private room with the finest doctors available. If your illness isn't caused by the factor …' He spread his hands apart. 'The same care, of course, but there it will be. And you must be treated, my dear. Two highly qualified doctors agree on that.'

'Get out of here! Ronnie! RONNIE!'

Ronnie appeared so fast Anne suspected she had been standing at the door. Helverson stood up. 'He's leaving,' Anne said.

'We have scheduled a full committee meeting for 3 p.m. tomorrow,' Helverson said. 'I trust I'll hear from you before then.' He bowed and left, Ronnie at his heels.

*

Dr. Grove had asked his last question. He closed his notebook and put it in his breast pocket. 'I'll talk to Mr. Helverson,' he said. 'I'm sure we'll work out something that will be satisfactory to us all.'

Deena rushed out, not looking at Clark. Bob Klugman looked about for something else to delay him, found nothing, and he too left. Only then did Clark stand up.

'By the way, Doctor,' he said. 'I meant to ask Deena, but forgot. What did she report?' He shuffled his notebooks and stuffed them back inside various pockets, and didn't look at the doctor.

'The usual thing. Your wife is feeling persecuted, there are sexual fantasies concerning Dr. Wells. Feeling very threatened. I understand she made some accusations about you.' He patted his pocket, glanced at the table, and turned toward the door. 'I'll see you tomorrow at the meeting, if not before.'

Clark didn't move until Grove was out of the room. Then he sat down again hard. Gus went through the motions of pouring more coffee, which he didn't want, and sat down also, not looking at Clark.

'Deena's lying,' Clark said. His voice was strained. 'The filthy bitch! Why? Why would she?'

The phone rang. It was Emory Durand and he wanted Clark.

'... might try electroshock,' Durand said, and Clark couldn't remember what he had said before that, or after. Electroshock. Numbly, he turned to walk away from the cage where Lola lay barely breathing in catatonic withdrawal.

Durand started to call Clark back, and Gus's fingers hard on his arm stayed him. Gus shook his head and they turned to look at the chimp again.

Electroshock. Convulsions. Sometimes bone-breaking convulsions. Clark walked from the building and out through the parking lot to the street. He had not put his coat on, didn't feel the cold air. Presently he saw a taxi and hailed it and told the driver to take him home.

'Address, buddy?'

Clark told him and closed his eyes. He opened them again when the driver asked him a question. He hadn't heard the words, only the voice, the rising inflection.

'I said, I can't find that address. Isn't this Cherokee Drive?'

It was the wrong side of the park. Clark got out and started to walk through the winter park, desolate now, deserted, in shades of gray and brown and the deep holding greens of the firs and spruces. Mist blurred outlines and every depression was a pool. Now he was cold, the wind was starting to blow again. The sky was a rain sky; low, swollen clouds, shadows against the deeper shadows. He stopped to look down at a children's playground. The wind had started a swing in motion, and it squeaked, an eerie sound in the empty park.

Not Anne! he wanted to cry out, and there was no one to cry out to. Only naked trees, bare and black and uncaring. Somehow everything had got out of control. With Deena's damning confirmation of what he believed, it had been taken from his hands and there was nothing he could do. They knew. They would demand this and that and he would walk alone in the park and accept his impotence. He felt shocked and numbed by Deena's acceptance that Anne had used the *pa*. As long as he alone believed it, there had been the possibility he was mistaken, and that possibility now was gone. He could have been convinced eventually that Anne's behavior was the result of confinement, the result of his actions and her reactions, that somehow he had had a need to think she had used the *pa*, and the need had made the link appear inescapable. But that possibility was gone now. Deena's observations, her conclusion, echoing his own, killed the possibility of mistake.

He rubbed his eyes to rid himself of the image of Lola in a fetal position, catatonic, dying. The image persisted. The swing squealed, sending goose bumps up and down his arms, and he began to walk fast, faster, until he was running. He stopped to rest against a very old, very large spruce tree. The branches swept down head high and shielded him from the wind for the moment. The bark was rough and he welcomed it against his cheek as he panted and waited for his breathing to return to normal. He was in a sweat and the wind freezing cold. His feet were soaked; his trousers, wet halfway to his knees, clung to his legs. He began to shiver and his shivering increased until he couldn't stop his teeth from chattering.

He knew he had to get inside, or get a coat. He started to walk. He'd get his coat and go somewhere, some place where he could think and not have to look at psychotic chimps, not hear Helverson's cool voice, not see the accusations in Anne's eyes. A bar, he thought. A dark, quiet bar where no one knew him.

He made a turn at the next intersecting path and left the park, walked two blocks to a business district, and found a bar. He ordered a double bourbon and before he touched it he called his apartment. He didn't ask to speak to Anne, but said to Ronnie, 'Can you stay until I get there? It's important that she isn't left alone. And, Ronnie, don't let anyone at all in except me. No one. Do you understand?'

He hung up. There was nothing else he had to do, he thought, except get drunk. Nothing else at all.

Somewhere, Anne thought, way back in her head, or in her soul if it existed, she understood what Helverson had been saying, demanding of her, but she couldn't put it into words. She couldn't frame it in logical sequences so she could examine it and find its flaws. It hung over her like some ghastly repression that was responsible for flashes of terror that appeared inexplicably, just came and went at will. She shuddered and felt chilled and knew no cause for the mounting fear.

Ronnie brought lunch and Anne pushed it around on her plate until Ronnie took it away again. Shortly after that, Ronnie came back and said Gus was there, would she see him, should Ronnie let him in?

Anne looked at Ronnie questioningly. Not see him? It wouldn't have occurred to her not to see him. Gus was brought in.

'Anne, is Clark here?'

'No.'

'Goddamn it! Did he call, anything?'

'Edward Helverson came to see me,' she said slowly. 'He wants to put me in a hospital, doesn't he?'

Gus nodded. 'Son of a bitch,' he muttered. 'That's why he locked us up in the conference room.'

'Can he do it, Gus?'

'I don't know. Do you have a lawyer?'

Anne swallowed hard. The flood of terror washed over her again. She waited for it to subside, and said, 'You think he can, don't you?'

'Anne, I tell you I don't know. I'll write down a couple of names, good men, both of them. One will be able to see you today, I'm sure. Say it's an emergency, that I sent you. Okay?'

She took the slip of notepaper and put it in her pocket without looking at it. 'What did Deena say?'

'Nothing to me directly. I couldn't find her after our meeting. But I made Bob tell me. She said you, you accused her of an assault. A sexual assault. She said you were irrational, hysterical, completely out of control.'

Anne felt tears scalding her eyes. Furiously she blinked them back. 'And they believe her. The clincher. I didn't accuse her of anything, Gus. I didn't.'

He sighed. 'It's a real mess, Anne. Helverson hopes you took it, of course. You'd better call one of those lawyers.' He stood up and walked jerkily to the window. 'All this because Clark broke down one time and acted human!'

'It wasn't what he did,' Anne said almost inaudibly. 'It was what I had done. I wanted to be whole again, but on my terms. And that night ... I hadn't realized until then that I blamed him for everything, and I hated him like I've never hated anyone in my life. Terrible thoughts came and went. Things like how much he had hurt me. I'm crippled, you know. He knows it. I'll have a limp the rest of my life. His mark. That's what I thought. And I thought of how much pain I owed him. How I wanted to see him hurt. I understood all at once how much I had been hiding from myself, and I felt like a child who screams and cries and says, "I won't!" and all the while knows she is powerless.'

She lighted a cigarette and watched the smoke. 'After that kind of self-revelation, what can you do? You can yield, pretend it away, bury it again and be that child, forever hating, showing it in a thousand little ways every day. Or you can leave it. And if you've gone this far, you know burying it simply means it will ooze out when you least expect it. The hatred waits and strikes when the other is most vulnerable. It's a destroying kind of thing that will kill the hater and the hated.'

Gus turned and yelled at her, 'You can't hate him for loving you! You need him now! Can't you see that? He gave in to intolerable pressure. He couldn't keep up a superman role. Because he's mad with love! How can you hate him for that?'

She bowed her head. 'You really don't understand, do you? I don't hate him now. I can almost understand him, I think. Gus, he would rather believe I used the *pa*, that I am going crazy, that I'll become a psychopathic killer, than face the truth. That isn't love. That's the wail of a child who'd rather see the end of the world than give up his grubby teddy bear.'

'What goddamn fucking truth?'

'It doesn't matter. Let's leave it alone.'

Gus pulled his chair close to hers and took her hand. 'Anne, maybe you and Clark have a real problem. I don't know. I don't want to know. But put it aside now, for God's sake! Anne, you need him now. You need him to support you and hold them off! Let him off the hook so he can get his head straightened out again. He's in a daze, doesn't know his ass from a tea kettle. And you need him, Anne. Take him back. Tell him you don't want a separation. Let him help you.'

She shook her head. 'It would be a lie. He'd know.'

'He wouldn't know! You idiot! If you told him you were the Queen of Sheba he'd believe it!'

Again she shook her head. 'It isn't that simple. All the strands come together here, don't they, Gus? The human tests, what Clark believes, what Deena told them. This is the spot marked X, isn't it?'

'Do you know what it will be to go in the hospital with them thinking you've used the stuff? Daily blood tests! Maybe two, three times a day. Tests of everything. Metabolism. Enzymes. Tubes down your stomach, up your ass. Hours with psychiatrists, perception tests, eye tests. Drugs. The stuff you had to take before to raise your blood pressure. Stress experiments. Your own goddamn stress experiments! Twenty-four-hour observation! Have you thought it through, Anne?'

When the color drained from her face, she could feel it. Like drawing a blind, she thought. It was just like drawing a blind.

Gus was rubbing her hand and now his voice was low and hoarse. 'Anne, listen to me. I didn't want to do that to you, but you have to understand. If you didn't take the stuff, there has to be a way to prove it. Let Clark say he was mistaken. Your notebooks. Something. There has to be a way. A diary?'

'I've thought,' she said. 'There isn't. During the really bad times I didn't write in the diary. Too dreary. Too repetitive. They can't start the human tests, Gus. You can't let them. Something's wrong with it and we all know it. Helverson must know it. Why does he say he'll go ahead?'

'Ambition. He thinks human testing will let us find the flaw in the coming months instead of having to wait years. And probably he's right about that. Besides, no one will ever know. The women will get the best of care, his conscience will be clear, and the rest of the world, when they get the stuff, will bless you and the company, and indirectly him. He'll get what he's after. It's a small enough risk for those gains.'

'We don't even know if that percentage is right,' Anne said. 'Three out of twenty-three. Thirteen percent. That might mean sixty-five women, Gus! Sixty-five. What kind of facilities would they need to have the kind of care, the kind of observation you were talking about? What if that percentage isn't right? It could be twenty percent, or fifty. We don't know.' She closed her eyes. 'It could be all of them eventually.'

'And even if it is all of them, if we find the cause or a way to control the effects, it would be a small price.'

'You don't believe that.'

'No, I don't believe it. We need time. You need Clark on your side, and between the three of us we might be able to get that time.' He studied her for a moment, then took a deep breath. 'I'd better get back. Maybe he's there now.'

*

She hadn't been trained for success, Anne thought, after he had left, only for failure. Even her minor victories had been turned into failures. 'Only second place? If you'd worked harder, it would have been first.' 'You made up your own bed? Look how lumpy it is! I'll have to do it over.' 'You won the scholarship? Tres has a new job! Nine thousand a year.' 'You're getting married? Tres has a baby son.' 'You got the job at Prather's? Your sister's husband won't let her work. They have a house-cleaning woman.'

She knew how to handle failure. Work harder. But how would she have handled success? There was no way. It was inconceivable that anyone could be successful and cope with it.

She thought of her mother, only a housewife, she always said. Suspicious of Clark, of their work, of Anne's education. She believed the stones in the elephant were real. She still believed Anne was Clark's assistant at work. 'He probably has a new girl to help him now. Have you seen her?' She could almost understand her mother, she thought. If Anne succeeded, it meant her mother had failed. At life. At everything. As if the two life styles were so incompatible that the one had to exclude the other.

And she could almost understand Clark. He hadn't been responsible for the accident; they both knew that. But he had welcomed it in some never acknowledged way. He had become more loving, more solicitous, more everything. He would love her more than ever if she were marred, he seemed to be saying, and she had rejected that because she had sensed under it another statement. He was safer now, that was what he felt. His mother knew, Anne thought. Intuitively she knew she had to handle him as the small boy, not the man, because he demanded it. He had needed it from Anne even more as success drew closer, and the accident had provided him the added assurance of her need for him. And then she had rejected him that night. He had said she was in shock, but that was wrong. He had been in shock. And he hadn't been able to face it but had leaped at the chance she had used the *pa*. If she was mentally unstable, her rejection was meaningless, not real, not a threat. He had no choice but to believe she had used the *pa*. And once more he was safe. Damned but safe.

Crying in the dark won't turn on the sun. Her grandmother had said that, she remembered. All right, Clark had to believe. Helverson had to believe. Deena, for God alone knew what reason, had to believe. And between them they would put her in a hospital. She held the arms of her chair hard to prevent her hands from shaking.

'No!' she said aloud. 'I won't let them!'

CHAPTER TWENTY-ONE

At seven, Clark woke up with a hangover. He was on his bed, still dressed as he had been the day before. He had dim, disconnected memories of the afternoon and night. The bar, a movie, because he had been so cold, another bar, a girl. Her room sometime after that. She had thrown him out with two dollars clenched in his fist. She had also called him a cab. 'Good girl,' he had said, over and over to the driver. 'Heart of gold.' His watch was missing. Heart of gold, watch of gold. Good girl.

Anne's door was closed and locked. If his head didn't ache so goddamn much, he'd kick it in, Clark thought. He made coffee, tried the door again, and sat down in the dining room. 'You know the trouble with my wife?' he had said to the girl last night. 'Yeah, she doesn't understand you.' – 'Wrong. She understands me too fucking much.' He winced. He didn't think they had made it. He hadn't been able to get his clothes off. 'You know what I'm going to do to her?' he had said. – 'Walk out.' – 'Wrong. I'm going home and show her who's boss. That's what she needs. Uppity. She's uppity. She wants it, but she pretends.' – 'Some women are like that.' – 'Wants to be dominated, that's it. What she wants, to be dominated. Overwhelmed.'

Clark groaned and stood up. 'Keerist!' he muttered.

Another memory: 'Tell you about my wife?' – 'Yes, you did.' – 'Smart. She's smart. Smarter'n me.' – 'You told me.' – 'Smart as hell.' – 'But you're still boss. Right?' – 'Right. That's exactly right. Exactly right.'

Anne heard Clark at her door that morning. She had heard him come home, and after he had fallen across his bed, she had gone into his room to see if he was all right. She should stick a note to his pillow with a dagger, she had thought, and resisted the impulse. 'Kilroy was here!' affixed with a dagger. She had smiled and returned to her room and locked the door behind her.

After she was certain he was out of the apartment she got up, and using her crutches awkwardly, but better than the day before, she walked to the kitchen and poured coffee. She looked at the crutches with a gleam of triumph in her eyes. She had coffee and toast and then went back to her room. She timed herself going back. Five minutes. The triumph faded and she regarded the crutches with loathing.

There was a typewriter on the small table now, and many pages of typescript. She had worked on notes for hours, had written letters, more work notes. She wasn't finished, but she knew she would be in another hour at the most. When Ronnie arrived at nine, Anne was at work.

'Still?' Ronnie asked at the doorway. Her face reflected deep concern as she looked at Anne. Yesterday she had called Dr. Radimer only to learn he was due at the apartment that morning at nine. The news had not lessened her concern.

'More coffee,' Anne said, then looked up and smiled. 'Morning, Ronnie. Raining?'

'What else does it ever do around here?' She glanced at the other door, Clark's door, but he was gone. 'Be back in a minute with coffee.'

'Oh, Ronnie, no swimming this morning. Dr. Radimer's coming over.'

'Anne, is there something wrong?' Ronnie asked then, entering the room, her umbrella dripping on the floor.

'Yes. You know it. After I talk to the doctor, I'll tell you, Ronnie.' She turned again to the typewriter and began to type.

When Dr. Radimer arrived, Anne had Ronnie bring him coffee, and starting very slowly, speaking faster as she went, she told him everything. 'I can't prove I didn't take it,' she said. 'But I'm afraid of the state institution. Mr. Helverson is right in saying I must be under observation, however, until there is no longer any doubt one way or the other.'

'Bullshit!' Radimer said, explosively. 'The biggest crock I've seen in a long time. Of course you can't go to one of the state hospitals! If you weren't crazy when you went in, you would be within a month!'

'You'll find some place for me?' Anne asked. 'Get the papers for me to sign?'

'Yes! Take an hour, no more. Bloody Jesus! Goddamn chickenshit executives! You know what's ruining this country? Those goddamn chickenshit company men! *Ronnie!*'

Ronnie hurried in, examined Anne anxiously, and waited.

'Anne's going to a hospital. Mount Holly. Can you go, be with her?'

'Hospital? Anne?' Again Ronnie's eyes made a swift appraisal and she looked mystified. 'I can go,' she said.

'I'm leaving, be back in an hour. Ronnie, don't let anyone in here. No one, you hear? If you do, I'll skin you.' Muttering obscenities, he left.

Ronnie went with him to lock the door and returned to stand with hands on hips before Anne. 'Now,' she said. 'Now, you just unload. Mount Holly!'

Clark had haunted the hallway outside Helverson's office all morning, but Helverson didn't show up. His secretary said repeatedly he would be late; if Clark would return to his office, she'd call ... The son of a bitch used the private outside door, but sooner or later he would show, and Clark would be there. Gus found him and pulled him back to the lab.

'You're acting like an adolescent waiting for your girl's new boyfriend to show so you can punch him in the nose,' he said.

Clark yanked free of his hand. 'They can't have her! They can't have her!' He could think of nothing else.

Gus jerked him into his office and closed the door behind them. 'Sit down! Time for melodrama is over, Clark. They've got the votes in the committee to do whatever they want. The best we can hope for is to get Anne into a private hospital somewhere.'

'Sold out, Gus? What was the price?' Clark's voice was savage with hatred.

'I'm being realistic. If she used it, she belongs in a hospital. You want her to roll around on the floor in convulsions like Lola?'

'You son of a bitch! Company policy?'

Gus slapped him hard, then slapped him again. For a moment Clark swayed.

'You want to pull yourself together, or go out and hang on another one so you won't have to know what's happening?'

Clark shut his eyes, his fists slowly relaxed, and he sat down. Dully he said, 'I owe you for that, Gus. What do you want me to do?'

'You have to tell them you're putting Anne in a private hospital, and make it stick, no matter what they say. Can you?'

'I'll keep her home. Hire a special nurse. Stay with her myself.'

'That won't satisfy anyone. It has to be a hospital. Damn it, Clark! It has to be a hospital! You have to do it!'

'I can't.'

'If you don't, you're turning her over to Grove and his gang. It's that simple, Clark. You do it or they will.'

Clark's face was gray, eyes red-rimmed. Gus remembered what Anne had said. She had wanted to see him hurt. He turned to look out the window.

'You remember what Deena said about her fear of hospitals, Gus? It's true. A pathological fear of hospitals. She thought they took her grandmother to the hospital to kill her. Even knowing she thought that once, knowing why she's afraid, she has that kind of fear. They had to send her home too soon because she was making such a bad recovery there. And they'll hurt her. Every needle, each time they take blood, everything. How can I send her back, Gus? How?'

'You pick the lesser evil. It's all you can do.'

Clark shook his head. 'But I can't do it,' he whispered. 'She'd never forgive me. I'd lose her completely.'

'And I'm telling you if you don't, you'll deserve whatever hell you find yourself frying in!'

Anne waited for Edward Helverson and wished her hands would not perspire so much. She wiped them again and lighted a cigarette and stubbed it out. Her mouth felt parched from smoking so much. Dr. Radimer paced, not talking now, not even cursing under his breath. Finally Ronnie came to say Helverson was there.

'I'll wait in the other room,' Dr. Radimer said. 'Call me when you want me.' He left and Ronnie went to bring Helverson in.

'My dear, you didn't have to see me personally,' Helverson said. 'A phone call would have done. I can't stay more than a minute. A luncheon appointment, I'm afraid.'

'I am ready to tell you my plans,' Anne said, and her voice was crisp and steady. 'I have signed myself in as a patient in Mount Holly Hospital, under the care of my physicians, Dr. Horace Radimer, and Dr. Samuel Erikson. It is already done. I have only to report in person for treatment to begin.'

Helverson sat down and smiled gently at her. 'I'm afraid that won't do, my dear. We discussed this, you see. We feel we must have some control over the treatment, not possible in a private hospital, you understand. And the sympathies of the doctors? Altogether different, you see.'

'You don't understand, Mr. Helverson,' Anne said. 'I am not asking permission. I am telling you what I have done.' Her hands were steady as she lighted a cigarette. 'I have made out a statement for you in which I swear I am doing this of my own free will, that I understand there is a possibility I might have used the *pa* factor, and that I have no memory of having taken it. I believe it is sufficient. Also, I have given permission for certain experiments to be carried out, with the consent of my attending physician, and with the consent of Clark and Gus. If there is any dissent about the experiments or tests, Gus is to be the arbiter, the final choice his. My doctor has agreed this is necessary under the circumstances.'

Helverson had stood up and now he sat down once more, a watchful, wary look on his lean face. Like a silver fox, she thought, watching a rabbit.

'I must say,' Helverson said softly, 'this is most reasonable. I believe we can all live with this agreement.'

'The rest of it,' Anne said, 'is that you will not proceed with any human tests until a brain specialist, to be selected by Gus, is brought in and given time to assess our work and make his recommendations. However long he takes, you'll agree to wait. And if his report is negative, you will then withdraw the approved IND and wait for the solution of this problem before we submit it again.'

Helverson leaned back and studied her. He didn't reply for several minutes, then he shook his head. 'I don't think so, Anne. Legally we are free to take that next step. No fault could be found, because we do have the approved IND. No, I think you have stepped too far.'

'If you don't agree,' Anne said, and she could hear a new tightness in her voice, and didn't care: his renewed wariness meant he heard it too, 'I'll go public with the work. I have written a dozen letters with sufficient details to permit anyone in this line to pick it up and carry on with it. The letters will be mailed to newspapers, to other companies, to universities, to journals, and to the FDA, if you go ahead without the explicit recommendation of the brain specialist Gus brings in.' She could feel a pulse in her throat now, and she knew her hands were wet again. She didn't dry them.

Helverson got up and walked to the wall, where he studied the hanging from Venezuela. He touched the telescope. He went to the window and looked out over the wisteria tree to the park. 'You're threatening me with blackmail,' he said. 'That's a crime, you know.'

'So have me arrested.'

'It's also a breach of contract. You'd be blackballed. You'd never work again, or teach. Back to the kitchen scrubbing pots and pans, my dear. And your husband, I'm afraid, would be tarred with the same brush.'

'And that isn't a threat, I guess.'

'No. That's the reality.'

'Mr. Helverson, I didn't ask you here to bargain with you, or discuss this or anything else. I asked you here so I could tell you what I plan to do, what I have already done. Now you may leave.'

For a moment his face became rigid, then he turned away. Presently he asked, 'Have you discussed this with your husband, or Gus, anyone?'

'No. Only my doctor, and the attorney who is holding the letters.' She paused, then added, 'And I never will unless you force it.'

'I see.' Again he was silent, and when he turned to her again, he was smiling. 'My dear Anne, I confess I've been absolutely wrong about you from the beginning. I didn't believe you thought the problem was so serious. Of course, it is your work and if you feel this strongly there is a flaw in it, the company wouldn't condone exposing others to such danger. Naturally we will take no chances on premature testing. My dear, you have my word, my solemn word, that we will not go into the next phase until a brain specialist agrees it is safe to do so. I rely on the expertise of others in these highly specialized areas, as you know, and I was made to understand by Dr. Klugman that we were ready to go to the next step.'

There was fire in his eyes, and pools of ice, and admiration and hatred, Anne thought, and in his voice there was honey, and the ring of Carborundum on Carborundum. She watched him as he buttoned his coat.

'Now I really must leave. I'm afraid I shall be late, but I am glad we had this talk. You will enter the hospital when?'

'This evening.'

'I see. Mount Holly. And you will be ready to commence the tests tonight? In the morning?'

'Whenever it is convenient.'

'Good. At our committee meeting this afternoon I shall explain your decision and authorize Gus to bring in as many specialists as he feels necessary to expedite this research. And now may I wish you a speedy recovery, my dear.' He paused a moment as if considering if he should approach her, decided against it, bowed and left the room.

Anne sat without moving until Ronnie and Dr. Radimer joined her. She was afraid she would start shaking if she moved.

'That silver-plated bastard!' Ronnie said. 'He wanted to know if we were alone here. I think he meant to send a goon squad here to snatch you or something. I introduced him to Dr. Radimer and said he was staying with you this afternoon. Should have seen his face. Looked like a kid who swallowed castor oil thinking it was honey.'

Anne laughed and couldn't stop. Finally she gasped, 'He wouldn't have tried anything like that.'

Dr. Radimer scowled and muttered, 'Goddamn chickenshit company men think they own the country, do what they want to with the people in it ...' He looked at his watch. 'Shit, I'll have patients sitting on patients. Clark coming in at noon?'

Anne nodded. 'I asked Gus to bring him over. I'll tell them then.'

'Okay. Helverson won't try anything. He'll find out he can't have you legally committed since you've already signed yourself in Mount Holly. Nothing he can do but bear down and take it. I'll see you every day or so at Mount Holly. I'll keep in close touch with Sam Erikson. What a crock of shit!' He stamped out angrily.

CHAPTER TWENTY-TWO

Gus and Clark arrived before twelve. Clark glanced at the bed, covered with folded clothes, an open suitcase. Ronnie had been packing.

'It can't be true! I don't believe it. What did he say to make you do this?'

'Sit down, Clark. You look awful. He didn't do anything. I did it. I want to tell you about a dream I had last night. Or maybe the night before. I don't remember when.

'I was walking on a street in a city none of us has ever seen. Trees everywhere, blooming flowers, bushes, each building white, like the Parthenon, set in its own green frame. Beautiful. There were women everywhere, all pregnant. They crowded around me, smiling, happy, pressing bouquets on me, so many bunches of flowers I couldn't hold them all and they began to slip through my fingers. When they hit the sidewalk, they shattered, like wineglasses, into tiny, colored shards. I was afraid and started to run, dripping flowers as I went, cutting my feet on the pieces. There was a trail of blood behind me, and the women were running after me. I couldn't lose them or gain ground, and they couldn't catch me. And we all cut up our feet on those pieces of flowers.' She was shaking. Gus pulled a chair close to her and took her hand.

'Finally I came to the edge of the city and there was a high wall, so high it went out of sight. I turned and ran along the wall, trailing my hand along it, searching for a gate, a doorway, any way out. There wasn't any way out. Not for me. Not for them. I gave up. I just stopped and waited for them to catch me and I became more frightened than ever, more than I could bear. So I woke up.'

'For Christ's sake, Anne! A dream! A lousy dream and you come around to this?' Clark yelled.

'I have to. There's no choice left now. I'm fighting to protect my work with everything I can use! That's all! It's good work and they shall not ruin it! If this is the only way I can save it, this is the way it has to be done.'

'You don't have to go into any goddamn hospital! You're not crazy! They can't force you into a hospital!'

'Will you tell them and make them believe I didn't use the *pa*? Can you make them believe it? Do you believe it?'

The room became preternaturally quiet, as if they were in the void Anne had imagined so often. Accept it, she thought at him. Accept that there can be no guarantees, that we have problems, that we might not want each other when and if we ever face those problems. You can't bind me down, she cried silently. You can't tuck me on a shelf and lock the door and know I'll be there later.

Clark couldn't sort out the images that raced through his mind. The dead kitten, the baby chimps, Anne's stranger's eyes that examined him as if they never had seen him before. All he could coherently think was that he was losing her, and he didn't know why. Because he loved her, had forced love on her. Even as he thought that, he knew it was false, and there was no truth he could insert instead. 'Anne,' he cried, 'the accident was my fault. A better driver might have avoided it. God knows I'll live with that the rest of my life!'

She was shaking her head impatiently. And he knew this was another falsehood. And again there was no truth to replace it. 'I'll take you away!' he yelled. 'You don't have to do it this way. I'll take you some place where we can get a good doctor for you. Where we can relax and rest and you can be treated ...'

Gus held Anne's hand, and when it started to tremble again, he said, 'Clark, why don't you get us all a drink. I think we can all use one about now.'

Clark hurried from the room, relieved to be doing something. Give her a chance to reconsider, understand what he was offering. He would devote the rest of his life to caring for her, protecting her, loving her ...

'There isn't any other way, is there, Gus?' Anne asked, almost pleading with him.

He squeezed her hand and stood up, slouched across the room to the hallway door and closed it. 'No,' he said. 'What nails did you use to drive it into Helverson's hide?'

She shook her head. 'He has his test subject, we have what we need – time. You'll see me each week, and if he goes ahead with the human tests, you'll tell me, won't you?'

He nodded. Then he nodded again and the questioning look left his face. 'Honey, if I didn't have a perfectly good, usable wife, I'd propose right now.'

She smiled, a fleeting expression that was replaced by a look of haunting fear. In a whisper she said, 'Gus, I'm so afraid.'

'Yeah,' he said. 'I know.' He kissed her forehead, crossed the room, and opened the door again. 'I'll take you and Ronnie over there. What time?'

'Four.'

He nodded. Clark returned with a tray of drinks, and after sipping hers, Anne said, 'Clark, don't come to see me. It … it would be painful for both of us.'

Clark put his glass down and looked at her bitterly for a moment, then turned and left. They heard the front door close hard.

'It's a hell of a life,' Gus said and finished his own drink. He stood up. 'Be back before four.' He waved carelessly and ambled out after Clark.

Ronnie had gone on ahead, in order to have her own car available. The county road Gus was driving on now was winding through gentle hills and small farms. The road followed a stream, swollen with flood rains, brown with silt. The water lapped the edge of the road in many spots.

'You'll be all right,' Gus said. 'Of course, if you had taken the stuff it would be a different story. Not a nice one.'

'How long have you known?'

'I don't know. I didn't think so, then thought maybe, then definitely no. Put myself in your place,' he said, turning to grin slightly at her. 'Easy enough to do, actually. That's funny, you know. You and me. I'd have done the same thing. It'll be painful, humiliating, offensive, disgusting … You know all that. But it will end.'

'I know that, too,' she said. She was looking straight ahead. 'He'll probably get another job. Maybe teaching. He said once he'd like that. He'd be good.'

'Yeah.'

'We turn here.'

He turned and very soon they turned again to a small private road that ended at a gate with a guardhouse. A uniformed man came to the side of the car.

'Dr. Clewiston?' he asked, looking at a notebook.

'I'm Anne Clewiston.'

'And this gentleman?' He closed his notebook.

'Dr. Weinbacher,' Gus said.

'I'll have to call for permission to let you enter, sir,' the guard said. He looked again at Anne. 'Your nurse is here already. She didn't mention someone else would be bringing you.'

He started for the guardhouse and Anne opened the door. 'I'll walk,' she said. 'Don't call.'

'Anne, we'll wait,' Gus said. 'How far is the place?'

'Couple hundred yards,' the guard said. 'Can't see it from here, through that next gate, around those trees there. That gate isn't locked or anything. Just around the trees.'

'I need the exercise,' Anne said. 'I haven't practiced yet today.'

Gus got out and helped her out, handed her the crutches.

'How long will your brain specialist take, Gus?' she asked then.

'He'll get here in ten days to two weeks, another two or three weeks after that, give or take a week.'

She nodded. Six weeks. In six weeks she would be walking without the crutches. 'See you, Gus,' she said, and began to walk toward the gate. She didn't look back when the gate clanged behind her, but maintained her slow, deliberate progress. Gus watched as she opened the second gate and passed through it, closed it behind herself, and then continued toward the trees.

And in six weeks, he thought, he'd come back and take her away from here, back to the world. Eventually she'd go back to work, down at the bottom of the heap now. Maybe in ten years, or fifteen, or maybe never, they'd have answers, prove her right or wrong, and until then ... No husband, a dream turned into nightmare, and still, he thought watching her halting walk, still, he'd say to her, 'You've won, Anne. You've won.' And they'd both know it was true.

She had reached the trees now. She didn't look back at him, didn't pause, and she turned the corner and vanished behind the mist-softened trees already swollen with the promise of spring.

THE INFINITY BOX

For Vicky, with love and appreciation

speculative fiction seldom fits neatly into the confines of those predetermined boundaries. Moreover, each writer who calls what he does speculative fiction, no doubt has his own definition of what his or her fiction is.

INTRODUCTION

Some of my happiest memories of growing up involve wandering between the stacks at the public library. I evolved a number of systems of selecting books, but the most successful was dividing the eight books (the limit then) between fiction and nonfiction in an orderly way. I picked two nonfiction books each trip, starting with A – anthropology – and working through; one book of short stories, and when they ran out, all too fast, I moved on to plays; and five novels. Again I started with A, and went through the alphabet. When I found an author I particularly liked, I read everything by him or her. If that wasn't enough, I selected by association, and in that way I read all the other Russian writers when I had finished with Tolstoi.

Meanwhile, changes were being made in the library. A new stack was added in one of the back corners to shelve the mysteries. I didn't care; I had my system, and I stuck to it, only now I added a mystery from time to time. Then another stack was tucked away back there, and it was for westerns. I recall the romantic, mythical world of Zane Grey with great affection, and I am glad that when I was twelve he had not yet been categorized, or I might have missed him. A new stack appeared much later – science fiction.

I think with sadness sometimes of the people who now go directly to one of those stacks and take their limit; and of the others who avoid them altogether because they *know* they don't like those categories.

The problem with labels is that they all too quickly become eroded; they cannot cope with borderline cases at all. The books each label includes and excludes finally distort the label and render it meaningless. Science fiction came to mean almost everything that was not mundane, realistic fiction: aliens, galactic wars, robots, social satires, heroic fantasy ... No matter how expanded the label came to be, it was not comprehensive enough, and presently a new label was trundled out: speculative fiction. Quite likely most readers have their own ideas about what science fiction is or should be, and speculative fiction seldom fits neatly into the confines of those predetermined boundaries. Moreover, each writer who calls what he does speculative fiction, no doubt has his own definition of what his or her fiction actually is.

Speculative fiction as I define and use it involves the exploration of worlds that probably never will exist, that I don't believe in as real, that I don't expect the reader to accept as real, but that are realistically handled in order to investigate them, because for one reason or another they are the worlds we most dread or yearn for.

Who doesn't want to go back and change the past at certain vital points? Who doesn't want to write the script of his own daily life? In 'The Time Piece' and 'Man of Letters' I do both. In these two stories, in all my stories, I tried to be as honest as possible and answer What would it *really* be like?

What would it be like to live in the dream world, or the nightmare? What would it be like to be there when the wrong village and the wrong war meet? If you don't believe, you haven't been reading the papers for the past ten years.

The forms of corruption are many and varied; we are very skilled at recognizing it at the national level, but how corruptible is your neighbor, your spouse? You? Power and corruption, a pair of gloves that slide on so easily, that feel warm and comforting, until it is time to remove them. This was the genesis of the title story, 'The Infinity Box.' What kind of inner resources would a man need to resist a perversion that seemed irresistible and undiscoverable? I kept getting so many disparate images, scenes, actions that demanded to be part of this story that for a time I despaired of ever weaving them together, but then I discovered when I put them side by side, in an order of sorts, the edges of all those pieces seemed to flow together to make a whole. As soon as I knew I had the shape of a story I began to work on it, and no longer worried about too many parts. They were like pieces of a jigsaw puzzle that fill an entire table until they are put together.

The paranoia of pregnancy is caused by: (1) glandular secretions; (2) hormonal changes; (3) changes in the metabolism; (4) the presence of another person within one's body; (5) a latent instability; (6) the dehumanization of the patient by modern technology; ... (N) Unknown. Choose one and only one, or all, or none. No matter which you chose, you are in good company. It has a ring, doesn't it? The paranoia of pregnancy. This phrase objectified, made concrete, rationalized, became 'April Fools' Day Forever.'

Some dreamers yearn for a return to an agrarian society, a return to a natural state where there are no polluting factories, where energy is something one's ancestors were obsessed with. I find this both tiresome and alarming, and I wonder if they have realized what the intermediate steps would be like. The breakdown of a civilization is not pretty, cannot be made pretty. If civilization crumbles, my story 'The Red Canary' might be a prelude to an accelerating slide down the magic glass mountain.

Can a cataclysmic upheaval result in Utopia? Suppose you know exactly the society you wish to create; you have the methods to achieve it, and absolute control over the children and their education. Isn't this the ideal situation? When I thought about it at length, I knew that when the means are unworthy of the end, the end becomes ashes. Then I wrote 'The Funeral.'

If one could see into the future, would one be able to take that first step toward it? I mused about this, forgot it, and when it came back to me again, I saw that there wasn't one future, not for the protagonist in my story 'Where Have You Been, Billy Boy, Billy Boy?', but rather several. Perhaps this is why we can see only backward in time.

This is how I work. I don't go out looking for story ideas, but now and then an article, sometimes no more than a phrase, will catch on something in my mind, a rough spot maybe, and it will stay there undergoing metamorphosis; accretions collect, and when the idea surfaces again, there may or may not be enough for a story, but at that time I always know a story is happening. If it is still more space than content, I try to forget it again, send it back where it can grow undisturbed, gather other bits that have also been examined, however briefly, and put away until later. Sooner or later the idea serves up images, scenes, a character. When that happens, I know I am ready to work with the material, mold it, add whatever I can to give it depth, other dimensions, actual people. The finished stories are often not realistic in the sense of the materialists – you won't find my worlds in your road atlases – but they are always very real psychically. And the psychic landscape has a more enduring reality than suburbia U.S.A. can ever achieve.

K. W.

THE INFINITY BOX

It was a bad day from beginning to end. Late in the afternoon, just when I was ready to light the fuse to blow up the lab, with Lenny in it, Janet called from the hospital.

'Honey, it's the little Bronson boy. We can't do anything with him, and he has his mother and father in a panic. He's sure that we're trying to electrocute him, and they half believe it. They're demanding that we take the cast off and remove the suit.'

Lenny sat watching my face. He began to move things out of reach: the glass of pencils, coffee mugs, ashtray...

'Can't Groppi do anything?' He was the staff psychologist.

'Not this time. He doesn't really understand the suit either. I think he's afraid of it. Can you come over here and talk to them?'

'Sure. Sure. We just blew up about five thousand dollars' worth of equipment with a faulty transformer. Lenny's quitting again. Some son of a bitch mislaid our order for wafer resisters ... I'll be over in half an hour.'

'What?' Lenny asked. He looked like a dope, thick build, the biggest pair of hands you'd ever see outside a football field, shoulders that didn't need padding to look padded. Probably he was one of the best electronics men in the world. He was forty-six, and had brought up three sons alone. He never mentioned their mother and I didn't know if she was dead, or just gone. He was my partner in the firm of Laslow and Leonard Electronics.

'The Bronson kid's scared to death of the suit we put on him yesterday. First time they turned it on, he panicked. I'll run over and see. Where's that sleeve?' I rummaged futilely and Lenny moved stolidly toward a cabinet and pulled out the muslin sleeve and small control box. Once in a while he'd smile, but that was the only emotion that I'd ever seen on his face, a quiet smile, usually when something worked against the odds, or when his sons did something exceptionally nice – like get a full paid scholarship to MIT, or Harvard, as the third one had done that fall.

'Go on home after you see the kid,' Lenny said. 'I'll clean up in here and try to run down the wafers.'

'Okay. See you tomorrow.'

Children's Hospital was fifteen miles away, traffic was light at that time of day, and I made it under the half hour I'd promised. Janet met me in the downstairs foyer.

'Eddie, did you bring the sleeve? I thought maybe if you let Mr. Bronson feel it ...'

I held it up and she grinned. Janet, suntanned, with red, sun-streaked hair, freckles, and lean to the point of thinness, was my idea of a beautiful woman. We had been married for twelve years.

'Where are the parents?'

'In Dr. Reisman's office. They were just upsetting Mike more than he was already.'

'Okay, first Mike. Come on.'

Mike Bronson was eight. Three months ago, the first day of school vacation, he had been run over and killed by a diesel truck. He had been listed DOA; someone had detected an echo of life, but they said he couldn't survive the night. They operated, and gave him a week, then a month, and six weeks ago they had done more surgery and said probably he'd make it. Crushed spine, crushed pelvis, multiple fractures in both legs. One of the problems was that the boy was eight, and growing. His hormonal system didn't seem to get the message that he was critically injured, and that things should stop for a year or so, and that meant that his body cast had to be changed frequently and it meant that while his bones grew together again, and lengthened, his muscles would slowly atrophy, and when he was removed from the cast finally, there'd be a bundle of bones held together by pale skin and not much else.

At Mike's door I motioned for Janet to stay outside. One more white uniform, I thought, he didn't need right now. They had him in a private room, temporarily, I assumed, because of his reaction to the suit. He couldn't move his head, but he heard me come in, and when I got near enough so he could see me, his eyes were wide with fear. He was a good-looking boy with big brown eyes that knew too much of pain and fear.

'You a cub scout?' I asked.

He could talk some, a throaty whisper, when he wanted to. He didn't seem to want to then. I waited a second or two, then said, 'You know what a ham radio set is, I suppose. If you could learn the Morse code, I could fix a wire so that you could use the key.' I was looking around his bed, as if to see if it could be done, talking to myself. 'Put a screen with the code up there, where you could see it. Sort of a learning machine. Work the wire with your tongue at first, until they uncover your hands anyway. Course not everybody wants to talk to Australia or Russia or Brazil or ships at sea. All done with wires, some people are afraid of wires and things like that.'

He was watching me intently now, his eyes following my gaze as I studied the space above his head. He was ready to deal in five minutes. 'You stop bitching about the suit, and I start on the ham set. Right?' His eyes sparkled at that kind of language and he whispered, 'Right.'

'Now the parents,' I told Janet in the hall. 'He's okay.'

Bronson was apelike, with great muscular, hairy forearms. I never did say who I was, or why I was there, anything at all. 'Hold out your arm,' I ordered. He looked from me to Dr. Reisman, who was in a sweat by then. The doctor nodded. I put the sleeve on his arm, then put an inflatable splint on it, inflating it slightly more than was necessary, but I was mad. 'Move your fingers,' I ordered. He tried. I attached the jack to the sleeve wire and plugged it in, and then I played his arm and hand muscles like a piano. He gaped. 'That's what we're doing to your son. If we don't do it, when he comes out of that cast he'll be like a stick doll. His muscles will waste away to nothing. He'll weigh twenty-five pounds, maybe.' That was a guess, but it made the point. 'Every time they change the cast, we change the program, so that every muscle in his body will be stimulated under computer control, slightly at first, then stronger and stronger as he gets better.' I started to undo the splint. The air came out with a teakettle hiss. 'You wouldn't dream of telling Dr. Thorne how to operate on your boy. Don't tell me my business, unless you know it better than I do.'

'But ... Did it hurt?' Mrs. Bronson asked.

'No,' Bronson said, flexing his fingers. 'It just tingled a little bit. Felt sort of good.'

I removed the sleeve and folded it carefully, and at the door I heard Mrs. Bronson's whisper, 'Who is he?' and Janet's haughty answer, 'That's Edward Laslow, the inventor of the Laslow Suit.'

Enrico Groppi met me in the corridor. 'I just came from Mike's room. Thanks. Want a drink?' Groppi was an eclectic – he took from here, there, anything that worked he was willing to incorporate into his system.

'That's an idea.' I followed him to his office, left word for Janet to meet me there, and tried not to think about the possibility that the suit wouldn't work, that I'd built up false hopes, that Mike would come to hate me and everything I symbolized ...

I drove Janet home, leaving her car in the hospital lot overnight. That meant that I'd have to drive her to work in the morning, but it seemed too silly to play follow the leader back the county roads. To get home we took the interstate highway first, then a four-lane state road, then a two-lane county road, then a right turn off onto a dirt road, and that was ours. Sweet Brier Lane. Five one-acre lots, with woods all around, and a hill behind us, and a brook. If any of us prayed at all, it was only that the county engineers wouldn't discover the existence of Sweet Brier Lane and come in with their bulldozers and road-building equipment and turn us into a real development.

Our house was the third one on the narrow road. First on the left was Bill Glaser, a contractor, nice fellow if you didn't have to do more than wave and say hi from time to time. Then on the right came the Donlevy house that had been empty for almost three years while Peter Donlevy was engaged in an exchange program with teachers from England. He was at Cambridge, and from the Christmas cards that we got from them, they might never return. Then, again on the right, our house, set far back behind oak trees that made grass-growing almost impossible. Farther down and across the lane was Earl Klinger's house. He was with the math department of the university. And finally the lane dead-ended at the driveway of Lucas Malek and his wife. He was in his sixties, retired from the insurance business, and to be avoided if possible. An immigrant from East Europe, Hungary or some place like that, he was bored and talked endlessly if encouraged. We were on polite, speaking terms with everyone on the lane, but the Donlevys had been our friends; with them gone, we had drawn inward, and had very little to do with the neighbors. We could have borrowed sugar from any of them, or got a lift to town, or counted on them to call the fire department if our house started to burn down, but there was no close camaraderie there.

It was our fault. If we had wanted friends we certainly could have found them in that small group of talented and intelligent people. But we were busy. Janet with her work at the hospital where she was a physical therapist, and I at my laboratory that was just now after fourteen years starting to show a bit of profit. It could have got out of the red earlier, but Lenny and I both believed in updating the equipment whenever possible, so it had taken time.

It was a warm day, early in September, without a hint yet that summer had had it. I had the windows open, making talk impossible. Janet and I could talk or not. There were still times when we stayed up until morning, just talking, and then again weeks went by with nothing more than the sort of thing that has to take place between husband and wife. No strain either way, nothing but ease lay between us. We had a good thing, and we knew it.

We were both startled, and a little upset, when we saw a moving van and a dilapidated station wagon in the driveway of the Donlevy house.

"They wouldn't come back without letting us know,' Janet said.

'Not a chance. Maybe they sold it.'

'But without a sign, or any real-estate people coming around?'

'They could have been here day after day without our knowing.'

'But not without Ruth Klinger knowing about it. She would have told us.'

I drove past the house slowly, craning to see something that would give a hint. Only the station wagon, with a Connecticut plate. It was an eight-year-old model, in need of a paint job. It didn't look too hopeful.

Every afternoon a woman from a nearby subdivision came to stay with the children and to straighten up generally until we got home. Mrs. Durrell was as mystified as we about the van and the newcomer.

'Haven't seen a sign of anyone poking about over there. Rusty says that they're just moving boxes in, heavy boxes.' Rusty, eleven, probably knew exactly how many boxes, and their approximate weight. 'The kids are down at the brook watching them unload,' Mrs. Durrell went on. 'They're hoping for more kids, I guess. Rusty keeps coming up to report, and so far, only one woman, and a lot of boxes.' She talked herself out of the kitchen, across the terrace, and down the drive to her car, her voice fading out gradually.

Neither Pete Donlevy nor I had any inclination for gardening, and our yards, separated by the brook, were heavily wooded, so that his house was not visible from ours, but down at the brook there was a clear view between the trees. While Janet changed into shorts and sandals, I wandered down to have a look along with Rusty and Laura. They were both Janet's kids. Red-heads, with freckles, and vivid blue-green eyes, skinny arms and legs; sometimes I found myself studying one or the other of them intently for a hint of my genes there, without success. Laura was eight. I spotted her first, sitting on the bridge made of two fallen trees. We had lopped the branches off and the root mass and just left them there. Pete Donlevy and I had worked three weekends on those trees, cutting up the branches for our fireplaces, rolling the two trunks close together to make a footbridge. We had consumed approximately ten gallons of beer during those weekends.

'Hi, Dad,' Rusty called from above me. I located him high on the right-angled branch of an oak tree. 'We have a new neighbor.'

I nodded and sat down next to Laura. 'Any kids?'

'No. Just a lady so far.'

'Young? Old? Fat?'

'Tiny. I don't know if young or old, can't tell. She runs around like young.'

'With lots of books,' Rusty said from his better vantage point. 'No furniture?'

'Nope. Just suitcases and a trunk full of clothes, and boxes of books. And cameras, and tripods.'

'And a black-and-white dog,' Laura added.

I tossed bits of bark into the brook and watched them bob and whirl their way downstream. Presently we went back to the house, and later we grilled hamburgers on the terrace, and had watermelon for dessert. I didn't get a glimpse of the tiny lady.

Sometime during the night I was brought straight up in bed by a wail that was animal-like, thin, high-pitched, inhuman. 'Laura!'

Janet was already out of bed; in the pale light from the hall, she was a flash of white gown darting out the doorway. The wail was repeated, and by then I was on my way to Laura's room too. She was standing in the middle of the floor, her short pajamas white, her eyes wide open, showing mostly white also. Her hands were partially extended before her, fingers widespread, stiff.

'Laura!' Janet said. It was a command, low-voiced, but imperative. The child didn't move. I put my arm about her shoulders, not wanting to frighten her more than she was by the nightmare. She was rigid and unmoving, as stiff as a catatonic.

'Pull back the sheet,' I told Janet. 'I'll carry her back to bed.' It was like lifting a wooden dummy. No response, no flexibility, no life. My skin crawled, and fear made a sour taste in my mouth. Back in her bed, Laura suddenly sighed, and her eyelids fluttered once or twice, then closed and she was in a normal sleep. I lifted her hand, her wrist was limp, her fingers dangled loosely.

Janet stayed with her for a few minutes, but she didn't wake up, and finally Janet joined me in the kitchen, where I had poured a glass of milk and was sipping it.

'I never saw anything like that,' Janet said. She was pale, and shaking.

'A nightmare, honey. Too much watermelon, or something. More than likely she won't remember anything about it. Just as well.'

We didn't discuss it. There wasn't anything to say. Who knows anything about nightmares? But I had trouble getting back to sleep again, and when I did, I dreamed off and on the rest of the night, waking up time after time with the memory of a dream real enough to distort my thinking so that I couldn't know if I was sleeping in bed, or floating somewhere else and dreaming of the bed.

Laura didn't remember any of the dream, but she was fascinated, and wanted to talk about it: what had she been doing when we found her? how had she sounded when she shrieked? and so on. After about five minutes it got to be a bore and I refused to say another word. Mornings were always bad anyway; usually I was the last to leave the house, but that morning I had to drive Janet to work, so we all left at the same time, the kids to catch the schoolbus at the end of the lane, Janet to go to the hospital, and me to go to the lab eventually. At the end of the lane when I stopped to let the kids hop out, we saw our new neighbor. She was walking a Dalmatian, and she smiled and nodded. But Laura surprised us all by calling out to her, greeting her like a real friend. When I drove away I could see them standing there, the dog sniffing the kids interestedly, the woman and Laura talking.

'Well,' was all I could think to say. Laura usually was the shy one, the last to make friends with people, the last to speak to company, the first to break away from a group of strangers.

'She seems all right,' Janet said.

'Let's introduce ourselves tonight. Maybe she's someone from around here, someone from school.' And I wondered where else Laura could have met her without our meeting her also.

We didn't meet her that day.

I got tied up, and it was after eight when I got home, tired and disgusted by a series of mishaps again at the lab. Janet didn't help by saying that maybe we had too many things going at once for just the two of us to keep track of. Knowing she was right didn't make the comment any easier to take. Lenny and I were jealous of our shop and lab. We didn't want to bring in an outsider, and secretly I knew that I didn't want to be bothered with the kind of bookkeeping that would be involved.

'You can't have it both ways,' Janet said. Sometimes she didn't know when to drop it. 'Either you remain at the level you were at a couple of years ago, patenting little things every so often, and leave the big jobs to the companies that have the manpower, or else you let your staff grow along with your ideas.'

I ate warmed-over roast beef without tasting it, and drank two gin-and-tonics. The television sound was bad and that annoyed me, even though it was three rooms away with the doors between closed.

'Did you get started on Mike's ham set yet?' Janet asked, clearing the table.

'Christ!' I had forgotten. I took my coffee and headed for the basement. 'I'll get at it. I've got what I need. Don't wait up. If I don't do it tonight, I won't get to it for days.' I had suits being tested at three different hospitals, Mike's, one at a geriatric clinic where an eighty-year-old man was recovering from a broken hip, and one in a veterans' hospital where a young man in a coma was guinea pig. I was certain the suit would be more effective than the daily massage that such patients usually received, when there was sufficient help to administer such massage to begin with. The suits were experimental and needed constant checking, the programs needed constant supervision for this first application. And it was my baby. So I worked that night on the slides for Mike Bronson, and it was nearly two when I returned to the kitchen, keyed up and tense from too much coffee and too many cigarettes.

I wandered outside and walked for several minutes back through the woods, ending up at the bridge, staring at the Donlevy house where there was a light on in Pete Donlevy's study. I wondered again about the little woman who had moved in, wondered if others had joined her, or if they would join her. It didn't seem practical for one woman to rent such a big house. I was leaning against the same tree that Rusty had perched in watching the unloading of boxes. I wasn't thinking of anything in particular, images were flitting through my mind, snaps, scraps of talk, bits and pieces of unfinished projects, disconnected words. I must have closed my eyes. It was dark under the giant oak and there was nothing to see anyway, except the light in Pete's study, and that was only a small oblong of yellow.

The meandering thoughts kept passing by my mind's eye, but very clearly there was also Pete's study. I was there, looking over the bookshelves, wishing I dared remove his books in order to put my own away neatly. Thinking of Laura and her nightmare. Wondering where Caesar was, had I left the basement light on, going to the door to whistle, imagining Janet asleep with her arm up over her head, if I slept like that my hands would go to sleep, whistling again for Caesar. Aware of the dog, although he was across the yard staring intently up a tree bole where a possum clung motionlessly. Everything a jumble, the bookshelves, the basement workshop, Janet, Caesar, driving down from Connecticut, pawing through drawers in the lab shop, looking for the sleeve controls, dots and dashes on slides ...

I whistled once more and stepped down the first of the three steps to the yard, and fell ...

Falling forever, ice cold, tumbling over and over, with the knowledge that the fall would never end, would never change, stretching out for something, anything to grasp, to stop the tumbling. Nothing. Then a scream, and opening my eyes, or finding my eyes open. The light was no longer on.

Who screamed?

Everything was quiet, the gentle sound of the water on rocks, a rustling of a small creature in the grasses at the edge of the brook, an owl far back on the hill. There was a September chill in the air suddenly and I was shivering as I hurried back to my house.

I knew that I hadn't fallen asleep. Even if I had dozed momentarily, I couldn't have been so deeply asleep that I could have had a nightmare. Like Laura's, I thought, and froze. Is that what she had dreamed? Falling forever? There had been no time. During the fall I knew that I had been doing it for an eternity, that I would continue to fall for all the time to come.

Janet's body was warm as she snuggled up to me, and I clung to her almost like a child, grateful for this long-limbed, practical woman.

We met our new neighbor on Saturday. Janet made a point of going over to introduce herself and give her an invitation for a drink, or coffee. 'She's so small,' Janet said. 'About thirty, or a little under. And handsome in a strange way. In spite of herself almost. You can see that she hasn't bothered to do anything much about her appearance, I mean she has gorgeous hair, or could have, but she keeps it cut about shoulder length and lets it go at that. I bet she hasn't set it in years. Same for her clothes. It's as if she never glanced in a mirror, or a fashion magazine, or store window. Anyway, you'll see for yourself. She'll be over at about four.'

There was always work that needed doing immediately in the yard, and on the house or the car, and generally I tried to keep Saturday open to get some of it done. That day I had already torn up the television, looking for the source of the fuzzy sound, and I had replaced a tube and a speaker condenser, but it still wasn't the greatest. Rusty wanted us to be hooked up to the cable, and I was resisting. From stubbornness, I knew. I resented having to pay seventy-five dollars in order to bring in a picture that only three years ago had been clear and sharp. A new runway at the airport had changed all that. Their radar and the flight paths of rerouted planes distorted our reception. But I kept trying to fix it myself.

Janet was painting window shades for Laura's room. She had copied the design from some material that she was using for a bedspread and drapes. She had baked two pies, and a cake, and a loaf of whole-wheat bread. The house was clean and smelled good and we were busy. And happy. It always sounds hokey to say that you're a happy man. Why aren't you tearing out your hair over the foreign mess, or the tax problem, or some damn thing? But I was a happy man. We had a good thing, and knew it. Janet always baked on Saturday, froze the stuff and got it out during the week, so the kids hardly even knew that she was a working mother. They were happy kids.

Then Christine came along. That's the only way to put it. That afternoon she came up through the woods, dressed in brown jeans, with a sloppy plaid shirt that came down below her hips and was not terribly clean. Laura ran down to meet her, and she was almost as big as Christine.

'Hi,' Janet said, coming out to the terrace. 'Mrs. Rudeman, this is Eddie. And Rusty.'

'Please, call me Christine,' she said, and held out her hand.

But I knew her. It was like seeing your first lover again after years, the same shock low in the belly, the same tightening up of muscles, the fear that what's left of the affair will show, and there is always something left over. Hate, love, lust. Something. Virtually instantaneous with the shock of recognition came the denial. I had never seen her before in my life, except that one morning on the way to work, and certainly I hadn't felt any familiarity then. It would have been impossible to have known her without remembering, if only because of her size. You remember those who aren't in the range of normality. She was possibly five feet tall, and couldn't have weighed more than ninety pounds. It was impossible to tell what kind of a figure she had, but what was visible seemed perfectly normal, just scaled down, except her eyes, and they looked extraordinarily large in so tiny a face. Her eyes were very dark, black or so close to it as to make no difference, and her hair, as Janet had said, was beautiful, or could have been with just a little attention. It was glossy, lustrous black, thick and to her shoulders. But she shouldn't have worn it tied back with a ribbon as she had it then. Her face was too round, her eyebrows too straight. It gave her a childlike appearance.

All of that and more passed through my mind as she crossed the terrace smiling, with her hand outstretched. And I didn't want to touch her hand. I knew that Janet was speaking, but I didn't hear what she said. In the same distant way I knew that Laura and Rusty were there, Laura waiting impatiently for the introductions to be over so she could say something or other. I braced myself for the touch, and when our fingers met, I knew there had been no way I could have prepared myself for the electricity of that quick bringing together of flesh to flesh. For God's sake, I wanted to say, turn around and say something to Rusty, don't just stand there staring at me. Act normal. You've never seen me before in your life and you know it.

She turned quickly, withdrawing her hand abruptly, but I couldn't tell if she had felt anything, or suspected my agitation. Janet was oblivious of any currents.

'But you and Rusty and Laura have all met,' she said. 'I keep forgetting how great kids are at insinuating themselves into any scene.'

'Where's Caesar?' Laura finally got to ask.

I had another shock with the name. My nightmare, my waking nightmare. Or had I heard her calling to the dog?

'I never take him with me unless he's been invited,' Christine said. 'You never know where you'll run into a dog-hater, or a pet cat, or another dog that's a bit jealous.'

They talked about the dog we had had until late in the spring, a red setter that had been born all heart and no brain. He had been killed out on the county road. Again I was distantly aware of what they were saying, almost as if I were half asleep in a different room, with voices droning on and on beyond the walls. I was simply waiting for a chance to leave without being too rude.

The kids wandered away after a little while, and Janet and Christine talked easily. I began to listen when she mentioned Pete's name.

'Pete and Grace had been my husband's friends for a long time. Pete studied under him, and Grace and I were in classes together. So they invited me to stay in their house this year. Karl suggested Pete for the exchange program three years ago. He didn't believe there was a coherent American school of philosophy, and he thought that it would be good for Pete to study under the Cambridge system of Logical Positivism.' She shrugged. 'I take it that Pete didn't write to you and warn you that I'd be moving in. He said he would, but I guess I didn't really think he'd get around to it.'

Karl Rudeman. Karl Rudeman. It was one of those vaguely familiar names that you feel you must know and can't associate with anything.

Janet had made a pitcher of gin and bitter lemon, and I refilled our glasses while I tried to find a tag to go with the name. Christine murmured thanks, then said, 'It isn't fair that I should know so much about you both – from Pete – and that you know nothing about me. Karl was a psychologist at Harvard. He worked with Leary for several years, then they separated, violently, over the drugs. He died last May.'

I felt like a fool then, and from the look on her face, I assumed that Janet did too. Karl Rudeman had won the Nobel for his work in physiological psychology, in the field of visual perception. There was something else nagging me about the name, some elusive memory that went with it, but it refused to come.

Christine stayed for another half hour, refused Janet's invitation to have dinner with us, and then went back home. Back through the woods, the way she had come.

'She's nice,' Janet said. 'I like her.'

'You warn her about Glaser?'

'She's not interested. And it does take two. Anyway she said that Pete gave her the rundown on everyone on the lane. You heard her.'

'Yeah,' I lied. I hadn't heard much of anything anyone had said. 'He must have been thirty years older than she is.'

'I suppose. I always wonder how it is with a couple like that. I mean, was he losing interest? Or just one time a month? Did it bother her?' Since Janet and I always wondered about everyone's sex life, that wasn't a strange line for our talk to have taken, but I felt uncomfortable about it, felt as if this time we were peeking in bedroom-door keyholes.

'Well, since you seem so sure she wouldn't be interested in Bill Glaser, maybe she's as asexual as she looked in that outfit.'

'Hah!' That's all, just one Hah! And I agreed. We let it drop then.

We had planned a movie for that night. 'Get some hamburgers out for the kids and I'll take you around to Cunningham's for dinner,' I said to Janet as she started in with the tray. She looked pleased.

We always had stuffed crab at Cunningham's, and Asti Spumante. It's a way of life. Our first date cost me almost a week's pay, and that's what we did, so I don't suggest it too often, just a couple of times a year when things have suddenly clicked, or when we've had a fight and made up to find everything a little better than it used to be. I don't know why I suggested it that night, but she liked the idea, and she got dressed up in her new green dress that she had been saving for a party.

When I made love to her late that night, she burst into tears, and I stroked her hair until she fell asleep. I remembered the first time she had done that, how frightened I'd been, and her convulsive clutching when I had tried to get up to bring her a drink of water or something. She hadn't been able to talk, she just sobbed and held me, and slowly I had come to realize that I had a very sexy wife whose response was so total that it overwhelmed her, and me. She sighed when I eased my numb arm out from under her. Pins-and-needles circulation began again and I rubbed my wrist trying to hurry it along.

Christine Warnecke Rudeman, I thought suddenly. Christine Warnecke. Of course. The photographer. There had been a display of her pictures at the library a year or two ago. She had an uncanny way of looking at things, as if she were at some point that you couldn't imagine, getting an angle that no one ever had seen before. I couldn't remember the details of the show, or any of the individual pieces, only the general impression of great art, or even greater fakery. I could almost visualize the item I had read about the death of her husband, but it kept sliding out of focus. Something about his death, though. Something never explained.

Tuesday I went home for lunch. I often did, the lab was less than a mile from the house. Sometimes I took Lenny with me, but that day he was too busy with a printed circuit that he had to finish by six and he nodded without speaking when I asked if he wanted a sandwich. The air felt crisp and cool after the hot smell of solder as I walked home.

I was thinking of the computer cutting tool that we were finishing up, wondering if Mike had mastered the Morse code yet, anticipating the look on his face when I installed the ham set. I was not thinking of Christine, had, in fact, forgotten about her, until I got even with the house and suddenly there she was, carrying a tripod out toward a small toolhouse at the rear of the lot.

I turned in the Donlevy drive. If it had been Ruth Klinger, or Grace Donlevy, or any of the other women who lived there, I would have offered a hand. But as soon as I got near her, I knew I'd made a mistake. It hit me again, not so violently, but still enough to shake me up. I know this woman, came the thought.

'Hi, Eddie.' She put the tripod down and looked hot and slightly out of breath. 'I always forget how heavy it can get. I had it made heavy purposely, so it could stay in place for months at a time, and then I forget.'

I picked it up and it was heavy, but worse, awkward. The legs didn't lock closed, and no matter how I shifted it, one of them kept opening. 'Where to?' I asked.

'Inside the toolshed. I left the door open ...'

I positioned it for her and she was as fussy as Lenny got over his circuits, or as I got over wiring one of the suits. It pleased me that she was that fussy about its position at an open window. I watched her mount a camera on the tripod and again she made adjustments that were too fine for me to see that anything was changed. Finally she was satisfied. All there was in front of the lens was a maple tree. 'Want to take a look?' she asked.

The tree, framed by sky. I must have looked blank.

'I have a timer,' she said. 'A time-lapse study of the tree from now until spring, I hope. If nothing goes wrong.'

'Oh.' My disappointment must have shown.

'I won't show them side by side,' she said, almost too quickly. 'Sort of superimposed, so that you'll see the tree through time ...' She looked away suddenly and wiped her hands on her jeans. 'Well, thanks again.'

'What in hell do you mean, through time?'

'Oh … Sometime when you and Janet are free I'll show you some of the sort of thing I mean.' She looked up, apologetically, and shrugged as she had that first time I met her. It was a strange gesture from one so small. It seemed that almost everything was too much for her, that when she felt cornered she might always simply shrug off everything with that abrupt movement.

'Well, I have to get,' I said then, and turned toward the drive. 'Do you have anything else to lug out here, before I leave?'

'No. The timer and film. But that's nothing. Thanks again.' She took a step away, stopped and said, with that same shy apologetic tone, 'I wish I could explain what I want to do, in words. But I can't.'

I hurried away from her, to my own house, but I didn't want anything to eat after all. I paced the living room, into the kitchen, where the coffee I had poured was now cold, back to the living room, out to the terrace. I told myself asinine things like: I love Janet. We have a good life, good sex, good kids. I have a good business that I am completely involved in. I'm too young for the male climacteric. She isn't even pretty.

And I kept pacing until I was an hour later than I'd planned on. I still hadn't eaten, and couldn't, and I forgot to make the sandwich for Lenny and take it back to him.

I avoided Christine. I put in long hours at the lab, and stayed in the basement workshop almost every evening, and turned down invitations to join the girls for coffee, or talk. They were together a lot. Janet was charmed by her, and a strong friendship grew between them rapidly. Janet commented on it thoughtfully one night. 'I've never had many woman friends at all. I can't stand most women after a few minutes. Talking about kids sends me right up the wall, and you know how I am about PTA and clubs and that sort of thing. But she's different. She's a person first, then a woman, and as a person she's one of the most interesting I've ever run into. And she has so much empathy and understanding. She's very shy, too. You never have to worry about her camping on your doorstep or anything like that.'

She'd been there almost two months when Pete's letter finally arrived telling us about her. Janet read it aloud to me while I shaved.

'"She's a good kid and probably will need a friend or two by the time she gets out of that madhouse in Connecticut. Rudeman was a genius, but not quite human. Cold, calculating, never did a thing by accident in his life. He wound her up every morning and gave her instructions for the day. God knows why she married him, why they stayed together, but they did. In his own way I think Rudeman was very much in love with her. He said once that if he could understand this one woman he'd understand the entire universe. May he rest in peace, he never made it. So be good to her.

'"Grace sends love. She's been redoing our apartment …"' I stopped listening. The letter went on for three pages of single-spaced typing. The letter had left as many questions as it had answered. More in fact, since we already had found out the basic information he had supplied. I decided to go to the library and look up Rudeman and his death and get rid of that nagging feeling that had never gone away.

'Eddie, for heaven's sake!' Janet was staring at me, flushed, and angry.

'What? Sorry, honey. My mind was wandering.'

'I noticed. What in the world is bothering you? You hear me maybe half the time, though I doubt it.'

'I said I'm sorry, Janet. God damn it!' I blotted a nick and turned to look at her, but she was gone.

She snapped at Rusty and Laura, and ignored me when I asked if there was any more mail. Rusty looked at me with a What's-eating-her? expression.

I tried to bring up the subject again that night, and got nowhere. 'Nothing,' she said. 'Just forget it.'

'Sure. That suits me fine.' I didn't know what I was supposed to forget. I tried to remember if it was time for her period, but I never knew until it hit, so I just left her in the kitchen and went downstairs to the workroom and messed around for an hour. When I went back up, she was in bed, pretending to be asleep. Usually I'd keep at it until we had it out in the open, whatever it was, and we'd both explain our sides, maybe not convincing each other, but at least demonstrating that each thought he had a position to maintain. That time I simply left the bedroom and wandered about in the living room, picked up a book to read, put it down again. I found Pete's letter and saw that we'd been invited to visit them over Christmas. I seemed to remember that Janet had gone on about that, but I couldn't recall her words. Finally I pulled on a jacket and walked out to the terrace. I looked toward the Donlevy house, Christine's house now. Enough leaves had fallen by then so I could see the lights.

It's your fault, I thought at her. Why don't you beat it? Go somewhere else. Go home. Anywhere else. Just get out.

I was falling. Suddenly there was nothing beneath my feet, nothing at all, and I was falling straight down in a featureless grey vacuum. I groped wildly for something to hold on to, and I remembered the last time it had happened, and that it had happened to Laura. Falling straight down, now starting to tumble, my stomach lurching, nausea welling up inside me. Everything was gone, the house, terrace, the lights ... I thought hard of the lights that had been the last thing I had seen. Eyes open or closed, the field of vision didn't change, nothing was there. 'Janet!' I tried to call, and had no way of knowing if I had been able to make the sound or not. I couldn't hear myself. A second sweep of nausea rose in me, and this time I tasted the bitterness. I knew that I would start crying. I couldn't help it; nausea, fear, the uncontrollable tumbling, unable to call anyone. Fury then displaced the helplessness that had overcome me, and I yelled, again without being able to hear anything, 'You did this, didn't you, you bitch!'

Donlevy's study was warm, the colors were dull gold, russet, deep, dark green. There was a fire in the fireplace. The room was out of focus somehow, not exactly as I remembered it, the furniture too large and awkward-looking, the shelves built to the ceiling were too high, the titles on the topmost shelf a blur because of the strange angle from which I saw them. Before me was Donlevy's desk, cleaner than I'd ever seen it, bare with gleaming wood, a stand with pens, and several sheets of paper. No stacks of reports, journals, overflowing ashtrays ... I looked at the papers curiously, a letter, in a neat legible handwriting. Two pages were turned face down, and the third was barely begun: '... nothing to do with you in any way. When I have finished going through the papers, then I'll box up those that you have a right to and mail them to you. It will take many weeks, however, so unti ...' The last word ended with a streak of ink that slashed downward and across the page, and ran off onto the desktop.

Where was she, Christine? How had I got ... I realized that I wasn't actually there. Even as the thought formed, I knew precisely where I was, on my own terrace, leaning against a post, staring at the lights through the bare trees.

I looked at the letter, and slowly raised my hand and stared at it, both on the terrace and in the study. And the one in the study was tiny, tanned, with oval nails, and a wide wedding band ...

'Eddie?'

Janet's voice jolted me, and for a moment the study dimmed, but I concentrated on it, and held it. 'Yes.'

'Are you all right?'

'Sure. I thought you were sleeping.'

In the study ... who the devil was in the study? Where was *she*? Then suddenly she screamed, and it was both inside my head and outside filling the night.

'My God!' Janet cried. 'It's Christine! Someone must have ...'

I started to run toward her house, the Donlevy house, and Janet was close behind me in her robe and slippers. In the split second before that scream had exploded into the night, I had been overcome by a wave of terror such as I had never known before. I fully expected to find Christine dead, with her throat cut, or a bullet in her brain, or something. Caesar met us and loped with us to the house, yelping excitedly. Why hadn't he barked at a stranger? I wanted to kick the beast. The back door was unlocked. We rushed in, and while Janet hesitated, I dashed toward the study.

Christine was on the floor near the desk, but she wasn't dead, or even injured as far as I could tell from a hurried examination. Janet had dropped to her knees also, and was feeling the pulse in Christine's wrist, and I saw again the small tanned hand that I had seen only a few minutes ago, even the wedding band. The terror that had flooded through me minutes ago surged again. How could I have dreamed of seeing that hand move as if it were my own hand? I looked about the study frantically, but it was back to normal, nothing distorted now. I had been dreaming, I thought, dreaming. I had dreamed of being this woman, of seeing through her eyes; feeling through her. A dream, no more complicated than any other dream, just strange to me. Maybe people dreamed of being other people all the time, and simply never mentioned it. Maybe everyone walked around terrified most of the time because of inexplicable dreams. Christine's eyelids fluttered, and I knew that I couldn't look at her yet, couldn't let her look at me. Not yet. I stood up abruptly. 'I'll have a look around. Something scared her.'

I whistled for Caesar to come with me, and we made a tour of the house, all quiet, with no signs of an intruder. The dog sniffed doors, and the floor, but in a disinterested manner, as if going through the motions because that was expected of him. The same was true of the yard about the house; he just couldn't find anything to get excited about. I cursed him for being a stupid brute, and returned to the study. Christine was seated on one of the dark green chairs, and Janet on one facing her. I moved casually toward the desk, enough to see the letter, to see the top lines, the long streak where the pen had gone out of control.

Janet said, 'Something must have happened, but she can't remember a thing.'

'Fall asleep? A nightmare?' I suggested, trying not to look at her.

'No. I'm sure not. I was writing a letter, in fact. Then suddenly there was something else in the room with me. I know it. It's happened before, the same kind of feeling, and I thought it was the farmhouse, the associations there. But maybe I am going crazy. Maybe Victor's right, I need care and treatment.' She was very pale, her eyes so large that she looked almost doll-like, an idealized doll-like face.

'Who is Victor?' Janet asked.

'Eugenia's husband. She's ... she was my husband's daughter.' Christine sighed and stood up, a bit unsteadily. 'If it starts again ... I thought if I just got away from them all, and the house ... But if it starts again here ...'

'Eddie, we can't leave her like this,' Janet said in a low voice. 'And we can't leave the kids alone. Let's take her home for the night.'

Christine objected, but in the end came along through the woods with Janet and me. At our house Janet went to get some clothes on. Her gown and robe had been soaked with dew. While Janet was dressing, I poked up a fire in the fireplace, and then made some hot toddies. Christine didn't speak until Janet came back.

'I'm sorry this happened,' she said then. 'I mean involving you two in something as ... as messy as this is.'

Janet looked at me, waiting, and I said, 'Christine, we heard from Pete and he seemed to think you might need friends. He seemed to think we might do. Is any of this something that you could talk to Pete about?'

She nodded. 'Yes. I could tell Pete.'

'Okay, then let us be the friends that he would be if he was here.'

Again she nodded. 'Lord knows I have to talk to someone, or I'll go as batty as Victor wants to believe I am.'

'Why do you keep referring to him?' Janet asked. Then she shook her head firmly. 'No. No questions. You just tell us what you want to for now.'

'I met Karl when I was a student at Northwestern. He had a class in physiological psychology and I was one of his students and experimental subjects. He was doing his basic research then on perception. Three afternoons a week we would meet in his lab for tests that he had devised, visual-perception tests. He narrowed his subjects down to two others and me, and we are the ones he based much of his theory on. Anyway, as I got to know him and admire him more and more, he seemed to take a greater interest in me. He was a widower, with a child, Eugenia. She was twelve then.' Her voice had grown fainter, and now stopped, and she looked at the drink in her hand that she had hardly touched. She took a sip, and another. We waited.

'The reason he was interested in me, particularly, at least in the beginning,' she said haltingly, 'was that I had been in and out of institutions for years.' She didn't look up and her words were almost too low to catch. 'He had developed the theory that the same mechanism that produces sight also produces images that are entirely mental constructs, and that the end results are the same. In fact, he believed and worked out the theory that all vision, whether or not there is an external object, is a construct. Vision doesn't copy anything in the real world, but instead involves the construction of a schematic, and so does visual imagination, or hallucination.'

I refilled our glasses and added a log to the fire, and she talked on and on. Rudeman didn't believe in a psychological cause to explain schizophrenia, but believed it was a chemical imbalance with an organic cause that produced aberrated perception. This before the current wave of research that seemed to indicate that he had been right. His interest in Christine had started because she could furnish information on image projection, and because in some areas she had an eidetic memory, and this, too, was a theory that he was intensely interested in. *Eidetikers* had been discounted for almost a century in the serious literature, and he had reestablished the authenticity of the phenomena.

'During the year,' she said, 'he found out that there were certain anomalies in my vision that made my value to him questionable. Gradually he had to phase me out, but he became so fascinated in those other areas that he couldn't stand not starting another line of research immediately, using me extensively. That was to be his last year at Northwestern. He had an offer from Harvard, and he was eager to go there. Anyway, late in April that year I . . . I guess I flipped out. And he picked up the pieces and wouldn't let me go to a psychiatrist, but insisted on caring for me himself. Three months later we were married.'

Janet's hand found mine, and we listened to Christine like that, hand in hand.

'He was very kind to me,' Christine said slowly sometime during that long night. 'I don't know if he loved me, but I think I would have died without him. I think – or thought – that he cured me. I was well and happy, and busy. I wanted to take up photography and he encouraged it and made it possible. All those years he pursued a line of research that he never explained to me, that he hadn't published up to the time of his death. I'm going through his work now, trying to decode it, separating personal material from the professional data.'

She was leaving out most of it, I believed. Everything interesting, or pertinent, or less than flattering to her she was skipping over. Janet's hand squeezed mine; take it easy, she seemed to be saying. Christine was obviously exhausted, her enormous eyes were shadowed, and she was very pale. But, damn it, I argued with myself, why had she screamed and fainted? How had her husband died?

'Okay,' Janet said then, cheerfully, and too briskly. 'Time's up for now. We'll talk again tomorrow, or the next day, or whenever you're ready to, Christine. Let me show you your room.' She was right, of course. We were all dead tired, and it was nearly three, but I resented stopping it then. How had her husband died?

She and Janet left and I kicked at the feeble fire and finished my last drink, gathered up glasses and emptied ashtrays. It was half an hour before Janet came back. She looked at the clock and groaned.

'Anything else?'

She went past me toward the bedroom, not speaking until we were behind the closed door. 'It must have been gruesome,' she said then, starting to undress. 'Victor and Eugenia moved in with her. Karl's daughter and son-in-law. And Karl's parents live there, too. And right away Victor began to press for Karl's papers. They worked together at the university. Then he began to make passes, and that was too much. She packed up and left.'

I had finished undressing first, and sat on the side of the bed watching her. The scattering of freckles across her shoulders was fading now, her deep red tan was turning softly golden. I especially loved the way her hip bones showed when she moved, and the taut skin over her ribs when she raised her arms to pull her jersey over her head. She caught my look and glanced at her watch pointedly. I sighed. 'What happened to her tonight?'

'She said that before she finally had to leave the farm up in Connecticut, the last night there, Victor came into her third-floor room and began to make advances – her word, by the way. She backed away from him, across the room and out onto a balcony. She has acrophobia, and never usually goes out on that balcony. But she kept backing up, thinking of the scandal if she screamed. Her stepdaughter's husband, after all. In the house were Karl's mother and father, Eugenia … Victor knew she would avoid a scene if possible. Then suddenly she was against the rail and he forced her backward, leaning out over it, and when she twisted away from him, she looked straight down, and then fainted. She said that tonight she somehow got that same feeling, she thinks that that memory flooded back in and that she lived that scene over again, although she can't remember anything except the feeling of looking down and falling. She screamed and fainted, just like that other night.' Janet slipped into bed. 'I think I reassured her a little bit anyway. If that's what happened, it certainly doesn't mean she's heading for another break. That's the sort of thing that can happen to anyone at any time, especially where one of those very strong phobias is concerned.'

I turned off the light, and we lay together, her cheek on my shoulder, her left arm across my chest, her left leg over my leg. And I thought of Christine in the other room under the same roof. And I knew that I was afraid of her.

The next morning was worse than usual. Thank God it's Friday, we both said a number of times. I had no desire to see Christine that morning, and was relieved that she seemed to be sleeping late. I told Janet I'd leave a note and ask her to go out by the side door, which would latch after her. But when the kids left to catch their bus, she came out.

'I wasn't sure if you'd told them that I was here. I thought it would complicate things to put in an appearance before they were gone,' she said apologetically. 'I'll go home now. Thanks for last night. More than I can say.'

'Coffee?'

She shook her head, but I was pouring it already and she sat down at the kitchen table and waited. 'I must look like hell,' she said. She hadn't brought her purse with her, her long hair was tangled, she had no makeup on, and her eyes were deeply shadowed with violet. I realized that she was prettier than I had thought at first. It was the appeal of a little girl, however, not the attraction of a grown woman.

She sipped the coffee and then put the cup down and said again, 'I'll go home now. Thanks again.'

'Want a lift to your house? I have to leave too.'

'Oh, no. That would be silly. I'll just go back through the woods.'

I watched her as far as I could make out the small figure, and then I turned off lights and unplugged the coffee pot and left. But I kept seeing that slight unkempt figure walking from me, toward the woods, tangled black hair, a knit shirt that was too big, jeans that clung to her buttocks like skin. Her buttocks were rounded, and moved ever so slightly when she walked, almost like a boy, but not quite; there was a telltale sway. And suddenly I wondered how she would be. Eager, actively seeking the contact, the thrust? Passive? I swerved the car, and tried to put the image out of mind, but by the time I had parked and greeted Lenny, I was in a foul mood.

Lenny always left the mail to me, including anything addressed to him that came in through the lab. In his name I had dictated three refusals of offers to join three separate very good firms. That morning there was the usual assortment of junk, several queries on prices and information, and an invitation to display our computer cutting tool and anything else of interest in the Chicago Exposition of Building Trades. Lenny smiled. We talked for an hour about what to show, how best to display it, and so on, and finally came down to the question we'd both been avoiding. Who would go? Neither of us wanted to. We finally flipped a coin and I lost.

I called Janet at the hospital and told her, and she suggested that we have some literature printed up, ready to hand out, or to leave stacked for prospective buyers to pick up.

'We should have literature,' I called to Lenny, who nodded. 'We can have a sketch of the machine, I guess,' I said to Janet.

'Don't be silly. Let Christine take some pictures for you.'

'Our neighbor, Christine Warnecke, would probably take pictures for us,' I told Lenny. He nodded a bit more enthusiastically.

We scheduled the next two weeks as tightly as possible, planning for eighteen-hour days, trying to keep in mind the commitments we already had. We had to get a machine ready to take to Chicago, get it polished for photographs, get an assortment of programs for the computer, keep the running check on the wired suits in the hospital cases, finish installing a closed-circuit TV in a private school, and so on.

I was late for dinner, and when I got there Janet simply smiled when I muttered, 'Sorry.'

'I know,' she said, putting a platter of fried chicken down. 'I know exactly what it will be like for the next few weeks. I'll see you again for Thanksgiving, or thereabouts.'

I kissed her. While I was eating, the telephone rang. Christine, wondering if we'd like to see some of the work she'd done in the past few years. I remembered her offer to show us, but I shook my head at Janet. 'Can't. I've got to write up the fact sheet tonight and be ready for the printers. They can take it Thursday. Did you mention the picture to her?' I motioned to the phone. Janet shook her head. 'I will.'

'Hi, Christine. Sorry, but I've got things that I have to do tonight. Maybe Janet can. Listen, would you be willing to take a picture of a machine for us, Lenny and me? He's my partner.' She said of course, and I told her that Janet would fill in the details and hung up. I shooed Janet out, and went downstairs. Hours later I heard her come back, heard the basement door open slightly as she listened to see if I was still there. I clicked my pen on my beer glass, and the door closed. For a couple of seconds I considered my wife, decided she was a good sort, and then forgot her as I made another stab at the information sheet.

By twelve thirty I had a workable draft. It would need some polish, and possibly some further condensation, but it seemed to be adequate. I went upstairs for a drink before going to bed. I didn't turn on the living-room lights, but sat in the darkened room and went over and over the plans we had made. Tomorrow I'd get Christine over to take the pictures ...

I suddenly saw her buttocks as she moved away from me, and her enormous eyes as she sat at the table and sipped coffee, and the very small hand with its wide band of gold. I closed my eyes. And saw the hand again, this time it opened and closed before my face, turning over and over as I examined it. I saw the other hand, and it was as if it were my own hand. I could raise and lower it. I could touch the right one to the left one, lift one to ... my face. I stared at the room, the guest room in the Donlevy house. I had slept there before. Janet and I had stayed there years ago while paint dried in our house. I knew I was seated in the darkened living room, with a rum collins in my hand, knew Janet was sleeping just down the hall, but still I was also in that other room, seeing with eyes that weren't my eyes.

I started to feel dizzy, but this time I rejected the thought of falling. *No!* The feeling passed. I lifted the hands again, and got up. I had been in a deep chair, with a book on my lap. It slipped off to the floor. I tried to look down, but my eyes were riveted, fixed in a straight-ahead stare. I ordered the head to move, and with a combination of orders and just doing it, I forced movement. I forced her-me to make a complete turn, so that I could examine the whole room. Outside, I ordered, and walked down the hall to the living room, to the study. There were other thoughts, and fear. The fear was like a distant surf, rising and falling, but not close enough to feel, or to hear actually. It grew stronger as the walk continued. Dizziness returned, and nausea. I rejected it also.

The nausea had to do with the way my eyes were focusing. Nothing looked normal, or familiar, if my gaze lingered on it. And there was movement where I expected none. I made her stop and looked at the study from the doorway. The desk was not the straight lines and straight edges that I had come to know, but rather a blur that suggested desk, that I knew meant desk, and that did mean desk if I closed my eyes, or turned from it. But while

I looked at it, it was strange. It was as if I could look through the desk to another image, the same piece of furniture, but without the polish, without casters, the same desk at an earlier stage. And beyond that, a rough suggestion of the same desk. And further, wood not yet assembled. Logs. A tree on a forest floor. A tree in full leaf. As I looked at the tree, it dwindled and went through changes: leaves turned color and fell and grew again, but fewer; branches shortened and vanished and the tree shrank and vanished ...

I jerked away, and in the living room my heart was pounding and I couldn't catch my breath. I waited for the next few minutes, wondering if I were having a heart attack, if I had fallen asleep, wondering if I were going mad. When I could trust my hands to move without jerking, I lifted the drink and swallowed most of it before I put it down again. Then I paced the living room for several minutes. Nothing had happened, I knew. Overtired, imaginative, half asleep, with vivid near-dreams. I refused to believe it was anything more than that. And I was afraid to try it again to prove to myself that that was all there was to it. I finished the drink, brushed my teeth, and went to bed.

Christine turned up at the shop at four the next afternoon. She shook Lenny's hand, businesslike and brisk, and thoroughly professional. He could have eaten her for breakfast without making a bulge. Her greeting to me was friendly and open. She looked very tired, as if she wasn't sleeping well.

'If you don't mind, Eddie, maybe Mr. Leonard can help me with the machine. I find that I work better with strangers than with people I know.'

That suited me fine and I left them alone in the far end of the lab. Now and again I could hear Lenny's rumbling voice protesting something or other, and her very quiet answers. I couldn't make out her words, but from his I knew that she insisted on positioning the machine on a black velvet hanging for a series of shots. I groaned. Glamour yet.

'It's the contrast that I was after,' she said when she was through. 'The cold and beautifully functional machine, all shiny metal and angles and copper and plastic, all so pragmatic and wholesome, and open. Contrasted by the mystery of black velvet. Like a sky away from the city lights. Or the bowels of a cave with the lights turned off. Or the deepest reaches of the mind where the machine was really born.'

Right until the last I was ready to veto the velvet for background without even seeing it, but she got to me. It had been born in such a black bottomless void, by God. 'Let's wait for proofs and then decide,' I said. I wondered, had she looked at the machine, through it to the components, through them back to the idea as it emerged from the black? I tightened my hand on my mug and took a deep drink of the hot murky coffee. We probably had the world's worst coffee in the lab because Lenny insisted on making it and he never measured anything, or washed the pot. On the other hand, he seemed to think the stuff he turned out was good.

'I'll develop them later today and have proofs ready to show you tonight, if you want,' Christine said to us.

'You want to pick them up and bring them in with you in the morning?' Lenny asked. I said sure, and Christine left. I didn't watch her walk away this time.

After dinner Janet and I both went over to her house to see the proofs. While I studied the pictures, Christine and Janet went to the kitchen to talk and make coffee. I finished and leaned back in my chair waiting for their return. Without any perceptible difference in my thoughts, my position, anything, I was seeing Janet through Christine's eyes. Janet looked shocked and unbelieving.

I stared at her and began to see other faces there, too. Younger, clearer eyes, and smoother-skinned, emptier-looking. I turned my head abruptly as something else started to emerge. I knew that if I had tried, I would have seen all the personality traits, including the ugliness, the pettiness, every-thing there was that went into her.

'What is it?' Janet asked, alarm in her voice.

I shook my head, *her* head. She tried to speak and I wouldn't let her. With-out any warning I had crossed the threshold of belief. I knew I could enter her, could use her, could examine whatever was in her mind without her being able to do anything about it. I knew in that same flash that she didn't realize what was happening, that she felt haunted, or crazy, but that she had no idea that another personality was inside her. I pulled away so suddenly that I almost let her fall down.

From the other room I heard Janet's cry, followed by the sound of break-ing glass. I hurried to the kitchen to find her standing over Christine, who was sitting on a stool looking dazed and bewildered and very frightened.

'What's wrong?' I asked.

Janet shook her head. 'I dropped a glass,' she said, daring me not to believe.

I wondered why she lied to me, but leaving them alone again, I knew why. I had always been the rationalist in the family. I refused to grant the existence of ghosts, souls, spirits, unseen influences, astrology, palmistry, ESP, anything that couldn't be controlled and explained. I marveled at my absolute acceptance of what had happened. It was like seeing a puzzle sud-denly take form and have meaning, like a child's puzzle where animals are hidden in line drawings; once you locate them, you can't lose them again. You know. I knew now. It happens once, you don't believe it; twice, you still don't believe. Three times, it's something you've known all your life. I knew. My hands were shaking when I lighted a cigarette, but inwardly I felt calmer than I had felt before as I considered Christine. I wasn't afraid of her any longer, for one thing. It was something I was doing, not something being done to me. I could control it. And she didn't know.

I stubbed out the cigarette and sat down abruptly. Rudeman? Had he lived in her mind throughout their marriage? Is that what drew him to her, made him marry a girl twenty-five years younger than he'd been. Had he managed to keep her by this – control? I couldn't use the word possession then. I wasn't thinking of it as possession. It was more like having someone else's mind open for inspection, a tour for the curious, nothing more.

If I talked to her now, made her see what had happened, quite inadvertently, she could probably get help, learn how to control it so that future intrusion would be impossible. If Rudeman had cared for her at all, hadn't wanted to use her, he would have cured her, or had it done somehow. Maybe he had known, maybe that's what those boxes of books were about, the years of experimentation. A little human guinea pig, I thought. Large-eyed, frightened, trusting. Completely ignorant of what was being done to it. And over the image of the frightened woman came the image of her slight figure as she walked away from me toward the woods, with her little fanny swinging gracefully, the rest of her body a mystery under concealing clothes.

The way she saw things, there wouldn't be any mystery about anything. Into and through and out the other side. No wonder Rudeman had been fascinated. How did she manage to live with so many conflicting images? Did that explain her schizophrenia? Just a name they applied to a condition that was abnormal, without knowing anything about what it was actually? The questions were coming faster and faster, and the thought of her, sitting out there in the kitchen, with answers locked up under that skull, was too much. I began to pace. Not again. Not now especially, with Janet there. She'd begin to suspect me of being responsible, just as I had suspected her of being responsible long before I had an inkling of what was happening. I thought of Christine as *her*, with special emphasis on it, separating *her* from all other hers in the world, but not able or willing to think of her by name.

I wondered what they were doing in the kitchen. What was she telling Janet? I started through the hall toward the kitchen, then stopped, and hurriedly returned to the living room. I couldn't look at her yet. I had to think, to try to understand. I needed time to accept all the way through what had happened between us. And I suddenly wondered what she saw when she looked at me, through me to all the things that I had always believed were invisible.

I couldn't stand being in that house any longer. I grabbed the proofs and stuffed them back into the envelope. In the hallway I yelled out to Janet, 'I'm going back through the woods. I'll leave the car for you. Take your time.'

She stuck her head out from the kitchen. I thought she looked at me with suspicion and coldness, but her words were innocuous, and I decided that

I had imagined the expression. 'I won't be much longer, honey. Be careful.'

It was dark under the oak trees, with the tenacious leaves still clinging to the twigs, rustling in the wind. The ground was spongy and water came through my shoes quickly, ice cold, squishing with each step. A fine film of ice covered the two logs. I cursed as I slipped and slid across, thinking of the black frigid water below. At our side of the brook I paused and looked back at the glowing windows, and for just an instant I entered her. No transition now, just the sudden awareness of what she was seeing, what she was hearing, feeling, thinking. She moaned and fear throbbed in her temples. She shut her eyes hard. I got out as fast as I had entered, as shaken as she had been. I hadn't meant to do it. The thought and the act, if it could be called that, had been simultaneous. I rushed home, stumbling through the familiar woods, bumping into obstacles that seemed ominous: a log where yesterday the path had been clear, a hole covered with leaves, a trap to break an ankle in, a low branch that was meant to blind me, but only cut my cheek, a root that snaked out to lasso my foot, throwing me down face first into the ice-glazed leaves and dirt. I lay quietly for a minute. Finally I stood up and went on, making no attempt to brush off the muck. Muck and filth. It seemed fitting.

I still had a couple of hours of work to do that night. The following day Mike's body cast was being changed, and I had to be on hand. He had his ham operator's license, and Janet had said that the only problem now was that he didn't want to stop to sleep or eat or anything else. He was doing remarkably well in every way. She had kissed me with tears in her eyes when she reported. In the morning I had to drop the pictures off for Lenny, scoot over to the hospital, return for the pictures, take them back to her ... I changed my mind. I'd let Lenny deliver the proofs. In fact, I wouldn't see *her* at all again. Ever.

I got in the tub and soaked for fifteen minutes, then put on pajamas and robe and went down to the basement to check out the program for Mike's computer. I didn't hear Janet come in, but when I went up at twelve thirty, she was in the living room waiting for me.

'I'm really concerned for her,' she said. 'I don't think she ought to be alone. And I don't think she's crazy, either.'

'Okay. Tell.' I headed for the kitchen and she followed. Janet had made coffee and it smelled good. I poured a cup and sat down.

'I don't know if I can or not,' she said. 'Christine has a gift of vision that I'm sure no one ever had before. She can see, or sense, the process of growth and change in things.' I knew that I was supposed to register skepticism at that point, and I looked up at her with what I hoped was a prove-it expression. She became defensive. 'Well, she can. She's trying to duplicate it with the camera, but she's very frustrated and disappointed in the results she's been able to get so far. She's got a new technique for developing time-lapse photographs. Whether or not it's what she is after, it's really remarkable. She prints a picture on a transparency, and shoots her next one through it, I think. When she prints that on another transparency, it gives the effect of being in layers, with each layer discernible, if you look hard enough. But she claims that for it to be successful, you should be able to see each stage, with all the others a blur, each one coming into focus with the change in attention you give to it. And that's how she sees.'

I finished the coffee and got up to pour a second cup, without comment- ing. Standing at the stove, with my back to her, I said, 'I'm willing to believe that she's some kind of a genius. But, this other thing, the fainting, screams, whatever happened tonight. She needs a doctor.'

'Yes. I know. I talked her into seeing Dr. Lessing. Lessing will be good to her.' She made a short laughing sound, a snort of quickly killed mirth. 'And he'll tell her to pick up a man somewhere and take him to bed. He thinks that widows and widowers shouldn't try to break the sex habit cold turkey.' Again the tone of her voice suggested amusement when she added, 'Know- ing that she's coming to him through us, he'll probably recommend that she cultivate Lenny's company, two birds with one stone.'

My hand was painfully tight on the cup handle. I remembered one night with Janet, saying, 'Jesus, I wish I could be you just for once, just to see what happens to you when you cry like that, when you pass out, why that little smile finally comes through ...'

I knew my voice was too harsh then. I couldn't help it. I said, 'I think she's a spook. I don't like being around her. I get the same feeling that I got when I was a kid around a great-uncle who had gone off the deep end. I was scared shitless of him, and I get the same feeling in the pit of my stomach when I'm near her.'

'Eddie!' Janet moved toward me, but didn't make it all the way. She re- turned to her chair instead and sat down, and when she spoke again, her voice was resigned. Way back in Year One, we'd had an understanding that if ever either of us disliked someone, his feelings were to be respected with- out argument. It needed no rationalization: people liked or disliked other people without reason sometimes. And by throwing in a non-existent uncle I had made doubly sure that she wouldn't argue with me. Finis. 'Well,' Janet said, 'she certainly isn't pushy. If you don't want to be around her, you won't find her in your path.'

'Yeah. And maybe later, after I get out from under all this other stuff, maybe I'll feel different. Maybe I'm just afraid right now of entanglement, because I'm too pressed for time as it is.'

'Sure,' Janet said. I liked her a lot right then, for the way she was will- ing to let me drop Christine, whom she had grown very fond of, and was intrigued by. She was disappointed that she had been cut off at the water, that she wouldn't be able now to talk about Christine, speculate about her. God knows, I didn't want to think about her any more than I had to from then on.

The next few days blurred together. I knew that things got done, simply because they didn't need doing later, but the memory of seeing to them, of getting them done, was gone. The geriatric patient came out of his cast on Saturday practically as good as new. He was walking again the same day they removed it, with crutches, but for balance, and to give him reassurance. His leg and hip muscles were fine. Lenny and I laughed and pounded each other over the back, and hugged each other, and split a bottle of Scotch, starting at one in the morning and staying with it until it was gone. He had to walk me home because neither of us could find a car key. Lenny spent the night, what was left of it. On Sunday I slept off a hangover and Lenny, Janet, the kids, and Christine all went for a long ride in the country and came back with baskets of apples, cider, black walnuts, and butternuts. And Janet said that Christine had invited all of us over for a celebration supper later on.

'I didn't say we'd come,' Janet said. 'I can call and say you still are hung-over. I sort of hinted that you might be.'

'Honey, forget it. How's Lenny? You should have seen him last night. He laughed!'

'And today he smiled a couple of times,' she said, grinning. 'He's over at Christine's house now, helping with firewood, or something.'

'Tell her that we'll be over,' I said.

The kids grumbled a little, but we got Mrs. Durrell in to sit and we went over to Christine's. Lenny was in the living room mixing something red and steaming in a large bowl. 'Oh, God,' I prayed aloud, 'please, not one of his concoctions.' But it was, and it was very good. Hot cider, applejack, brandy, and a dry red wine. With cinnamon sticks in individual cups.

Steaks, salad, baked potatoes, spicy hot apple pie. 'If I knew you was coming,' Christine had murmured, serving us, but she hadn't belabored the point, and it was a happy party. She proposed a toast after pouring brandy for us. 'To the good men of the earth. Eddie and Lenny, and others like them wherever they are.'

I knew that I flushed, and Lenny looked embarrassed and frowned, but Janet said, 'Hear, hear,' and the girls touched the glasses to their lips. In a few moments we were back to the gaiety that was interrupted by the toast that lingered in my head for the rest of the evening.

Lenny was more talkative than I'd seen him in years. He even mentioned that he had been a physicist, something that not more than a dozen people knew. The girls were both looking pretty after a day in the cold air; their cheeks were flushed, and they looked happy. Janet's bright blue-green eyes sparkled and she laughed easily and often. Christine laughed too, more quietly, and never at anything she said herself. She still was shy, but at ease with us. And it seemed that her shyness and Lenny's introspective quiet were well matched, as if there had been a meeting of the selves there that few others ever got to know. I caught Lenny's contemplative gaze on her once, and when she noticed also, she seemed to consider his question gravely, then she turned away, and the flush on her cheeks was a bit deeper. The air had changed somehow, had become more charged, and Janet's touch on my hand to ask for a cigarette was a caress. I looked at her, acknowledging the invitation. Our hands lingered over the cigarette in the non-verbal communication that made living with her so nice.

I was very glad we had that evening together. Janet and I left at about twelve. Lenny was sitting in a deep chair before the fire when we said goodnight, and he made no motion to get up and leave then too. In our car Janet sighed and put her head on my shoulder.

Images flashed before my eyes: Christine's buttocks as she moved away from me; the tight skin across Janet's ribs when she raised her arms over her head; Christine's tiny, tiny waist, dressed as she had been that night, in a tailored shirt and black skirt, tightly belted with a wide leather belt; the pink nipples that puckered and stiffened at a touch; and darker nipples that I had never seen, but knew had to be like that, dark and large. And how black, would her pubic hair be, and how hungry would she be after so long a time? Her head back, listening to a record, her eyes narrowed in concentration, her mouth open slightly. And the thought kept coming back: What would it be like to be her? What did Janet feel? What would *she* feel when Lenny entered her body? How different was it for a woman who was sexually responsive? She wouldn't even know, if I waited until she was thoroughly aroused. Sex had been in the air in the living room, we'd all felt it. After such a long period of deprivation, she'd crumble at Lenny's first touch. She'd never know, I repeated to myself.

When we got out of the car I said to Janet, 'Get rid of Mrs. Durrell as fast as you can. Okay?' She pressed her body against mine and laughed a low, throaty laugh.

I was in a fever of anxiety then, trying to keep from going out into *her* too soon. Not yet. Not yet. Not until I had Janet in bed, not until I thought that *she* and Lenny had had time to be at ease with each other again after being left alone. Maybe even in bed. My excitement was contagious. Janet was in bed as soon as she could decently get rid of the sitter, and when my hand roamed down her body, she shivered. Very deliberately I played with her and when I was certain that she wouldn't notice a shift in my attention, I went out to the other one, and found her alone. My disappointment was so great that momentarily I forgot about Janet, until her sudden scream made me realize that I had hurt her. She muffled her face against my chest and gasped, and whether from pleasure or pain I couldn't tell, she didn't pull away.

She was fighting eroticism as hard as she could. Drawing up thoughts of plans, of work not yet finished, of the notebooks that were so much harder to decipher than she had suspected they would be, the time-lapse photos that were coming along. Trying to push out of her mind the ache that kept coming back deep in her belly, the awful awareness of her stimulation from too much wine, the nearness of Lenny and his maleness. She was hardly aware of the intrusion this time, and when I directed her thoughts toward the sensual and sexual, there was no way she could resist. I cursed her for allowing Lenny to leave, I threatened her, I forced her to unfold when she doubled up like a foetus, hugging herself into a tight bail. For an hour, more than an hour, I made love to Janet and tormented that other girl, and forced her to do those things that I had to experience for myself. And when Janet moaned and cried out, I knew the cause, and knew when to stop and when to continue, and when she finally went limp, I knew the total, final surrender that she knew. And I stared at the mirror image of the girl: large dark nipples, beautifully formed breasts, erect and rounded, deep navel, black shiny hair. And mad eyes, haunted, panic-stricken eyes in a face as white as milk, with two red spots on her cheeks. Her breath was coming in quick gasps. My control was too tight. Nothing that she thought was coming through to me, only what she felt with her body that had become so sensitive that when she lay back on the bed, she shuddered at the touch of the sheet on her back. I relaxed control without leaving and there was a chaotic blur of memories, of nights in Karl's arms, of giving up totally to him, being the complete houri that he demanded of her.

'Bitch!' I thought at her. 'Slut.' I went on and on, calling her names, despising her for letting me do it to her, for being so manipulable, for letting me do this to myself. And I brought her to orgasm again, this time not letting her stop, or ease up, but on and on, until suddenly she arched her back and screamed, and I knew. I don't know if she screamed alone, or if I screamed with her. She blacked out, and I was falling, spinning around and around, plummeting downward. I yanked away from her. Janet stirred lazily against me, not awake, hardly even aware of me. I didn't move, but stared at the ceiling and waited for the blood to stop pounding in my head, and for my heart to stop the wild fibrillation that her final convulsion had started.

Janet was bright-eyed and pink the next morning, but when she saw the full ashtrays in the living room and kitchen, she looked at me closely. 'You couldn't sleep?'

'Too much to think of,' I said, cursing the coffee pot for its slowness. 'And just four days to do it.'

'Oh, honey.' She was always regretful when I was awake while she slept. She felt it was selfish of her.

I could hardly bring myself to look at Lenny, but he took my moods in stride, and he made himself inconspicuous. The machine was gleaming and beautiful, ready to crate up and put in the station wagon. We wouldn't trust it to anyone but one of us, and I would drive to Chicago on Friday, install it myself Saturday morning, hours before the doors of the exposition opened at four in the afternoon. Lenny, like Janet, took my jittery state to be nerves from the coming show. It was like having a show at the Metropolitan, or a recital at Carnegie Hall, or a Broadway opening. And I wasn't even able to concentrate on it for a period of two consecutive minutes. I went round and round with the problem I had forced on myself by not leaving Christine Warnecke Rudeman strictly alone, and I couldn't find a solution. I couldn't speak out now, not after last night. I couldn't advise her to seek help, or in any way suggest that I knew anything about her that she hadn't told us. And although the thoughts of the night before were a torture, I couldn't stop going over it all again and again, and feeling again the echo of the unbearable excitement and pleasures I had known. When Lenny left for lunch, I didn't even look up. And when he returned, I was still at the bench, pretending to be going over the installation plan we had agreed on for our space at the exposition. Lenny didn't go back to his own desk, or his work in progress on the bench. He dragged a stool across from me and sat down.

'Why don't you like Chris?' he asked bluntly. 'I like her fine,' I said.

He shook his head. 'No. You won't look at her, and you don't want her to look directly at you. I noticed last night. You find a place to sit where you're not in her line of sight. When she turns to speak to you, or in your direction, you get busy lighting a cigarette, or shift your position. Not consciously, Eddie. I'm not saying you do anything like that on purpose, but I was noticing.' He leaned forward with both great hands flat on the bench. 'Why, Eddie?'

I shrugged and caught myself reaching for my pack of cigarettes. 'I don't know. I didn't realize I was doing any of those things. I haven't tried to put anything into words. I'm just not comfortable with her. Why? Are you interested?'

'Yes,' he said. 'She thinks she's going crazy. She is certain that you sense it and that's why you're uncomfortable around her. Your actions reinforce her feelings, giving you cause to be even more uncomfortable, and it goes on from there.'

'I can keep the hell away from her. Is that what you're driving at?'

'I think so.'

'Lenny,' I said when he remained quiet, and seemed lost in his speculations, 'is she? Going crazy again? You know she was once?'

'No. I doubt it. She is different, and difference is treated like mental illness. That's what I know. No more. From demonic possession to witchcraft to mental illness. We do make progress.' His hands, that had been flat and unmoving on the benchtop, bunched up into fists.

'Okay, Lenny,' I said. 'I believe you. And I won't see her any more for the next couple of weeks, whatever happens. And, Lenny, if I'd known – I mean, I didn't realize that anything of my attitude was coming through. I didn't really think about it one way or the other. I wouldn't do anything to hurt her ... or you.'

He looked at me gravely and nodded. 'I know that,' he said. He stood up and his face softened a bit. 'It's always people like you, the rationalists, that are most afraid of any kind of mental disorders, even benign ones. It shows.'

I shook my head. 'A contradiction in terms, isn't that? Mental disorders and benign?'

'Not necessarily.' Then he moved his stool back down the bench and went back to work. And I stared at the sketches before me for a long time before they came back into focus. The rest of the afternoon I fought against going back to her and punishing her for complaining about me. I thought of the ways I could inflict punishment on her, and knew that the real ace that I would keep for an emergency was her fear of heights. I visualized strolling along the lip of the Grand Canyon with her, or taking her up the Empire State Building, the Eiffel Tower, or forcing her up the face of a cliff. And I kept a rigid control of my own thoughts so that I didn't go out to her at all. I didn't give in all week, but I had her nightmares.

On Wednesday Janet suggested that I should let Lenny go to Chicago and I snapped at her and called her a fool. On Thursday Lenny made the same suggestion, and I stalked from the lab and drove off in a white fury. When Janet came home I accused them of getting together and talking about me.

'Eddie, you know better than that. But look at you. You aren't sleeping well, and you've been as nervous as a cat. What's the matter with you?'

'Just leave me alone, okay? Tired, that's all. Just plain tired. And tired of cross-examinations and dark hints and suspicions.'

They were getting together, the three of them, all the time. I knew that Lenny was spending his evenings with Christine, and that Janet was with them much of the time when I was busy down in the basement workshop or out at the hospital. They said, Janet and Lenny, that they were trying to decipher the code that Karl Rudeman had used in making his notes. I didn't believe them.

They were talking about me, speculating on whether or not I was the one driving *her* crazy. I imagined the same conversation over and over, with Lenny insisting that I could have done *that* to her, and Janet, white-faced and frantic with indecision, denying it. Not while I had been with her, she would think. Not at a time like that.

Then I would snap awake, and either curse myself for being a fool, or become frightened by the paranoid drift of my thoughts. And I would know that none of it was true. Of course Janet wouldn't discuss what went on over there; I had practically forbidden her to do so. And Lenny wouldn't talk about it under the happiest circumstances, much less now.

Friday, driving to Chicago I began to relax, and after three hours on the road I was whistling and could almost forget the mess, could almost convince myself that I'd been having delusions, which was easier to take than the truth.

I slept deeply Friday night, and Saturday I was busy, getting our exhibit set up and getting acquainted with others who were also showing tools and machinery. From four until the doors closed at eleven, the hall got fuller and fuller, the noise level became excruciating, the smoke-laden air unbreathable. Our cutting tool drew a good, interested response, and I was busy. And too tired for the late dinner I had agreed to with two other exhibitors. We settled for hamburgers and beer in the hotel dining room, and soon afterward I tumbled into bed and again slept like a child. The crowds were just as thick on Sunday, but by Monday the idle curiosity-seekers were back at their jobs, and the ones who came through were businesslike and fewer in number. I had hired a business student to spell me, and I left him in charge from four until seven, the slack hours, so I could have an early dinner and get some rest. But I found myself wandering the streets instead, and finally I stopped in front of a library.

Karl Rudeman, I thought. How did he die? And I went in and looked up the clippings about him, and read the last three with absorption. When I went to dinner afterward, I was still trying to puzzle it out. He had had dinner with his family: his wife, parents, daughter, and son-in-law. After dinner they had played bridge for an hour or two. Sometime after that, after everyone else had gone to bed, he had left the house to roam through the fields that stretched out for a quarter of a mile, down to the river. He had collapsed and died of a heart attack at the edge of a field. Christine, awakening later and finding him gone, had first searched the house, then, when she realized that Karl was in his pajamas and barefooted, she had awakened her stepson-in-law and started a search of the grounds. Karl wasn't found until daylight, and then the tenant farmer had been the one to spot the figure in orange-and-black striped pajamas. There was no sign of violence, and it was assumed that he had been walking in his sleep when the fatal attack occurred.

Back to the exhibit, and the flow of evening viewers. Invitations, given and accepted, for drinks later, and a beaver flick. Lunch with a couple of other men the following day. A long talk with a manufacturer who was interested in procuring the order for the cutting tool, should there be enough interest to warrant it.

The obscene movie had been a mistake, I knew as soon as the girl jerked off her slip and opened her legs. Suddenly I was seeing *her*, open-legged on the edge of the bed before a mirror.

I pushed my way through a cluster of men at the back of the theater to get out into the cold November air again. I walked back to the hotel. A freezing mist was hanging head high, not falling, but just hanging there, and I gulped it in, thankful for the pain of the cold air in my throat. A prowl car slowed down as it passed me, it picked up speed again and moved on down the street. I had bought a stack of magazines and some paperbacks to read, but nothing in the room looked interesting when I took off my damp clothes and tried to persuade myself that I could fall asleep now.

I had room service send up a bottle of bourbon and ice, and tried to read a Nero Wolfe mystery. My attention kept wandering, and finally I lay back on the bed, balancing my drink on my stomach, and thought about *her*.

It was so easy, and gentle even. She didn't suspect this time, not at all. She was saying, '... because they're abstractions, you see. Emotions like fear, love, anger. First the physiological change in the brain, the electrochemical changes that take place stimulating those abstractions, and then the experience of the emotion.'

'You mean to say he really believed that the feeling of anger comes after the chemical changes that take place?'

'Of course. That's how it is with a physiological psychologist. And you can see it operate; tranquilizers permit you to know intellectually but they don't let you react, so you don't experience the anger or fear, or whatever.'

Lenny was sitting back in the green chair in the study, and she was behind the desk that was spread with snapshots and proofs.

'Okay. What triggers those changes in the first place?'

'Well, his specialty was sight, or vision, as he preferred to call it. Light entering the eye brings about a change in the chromophore in the first thousandth of a second, and after that the rest of the changes are automatic, a causal chain that results in the experiencing of a vision of some sort.'

'I know,' Lenny said gently. 'But what about the vision that doesn't have an object in real space? The imaginary image? No light there to start the chain of events.'

'A change brought about by electrochemical energy? The leakage of energy from cellular functioning? The first step is on a molecular level, not much energy is involved, after all. Lenny, it's happening ...'

I got a jolt of fear then, along with the words spoken softly. Her hands clenched and a proof under her right hand buckled up and cracked. Before Lenny could respond, I pulled out and away.

I didn't know how she had found out, what I had done to give my presence away. But her knowledge had been as certain as mine, and the fear was named now, not the fear of insanity. It was a directed fear and hatred that I had felt, directed at me, not the aimless, directionless, more-powerful fear that my presence had stimulated before. She knew that something from outside had entered her. I sat up and finished my drink, then turned off the light. And I wondered what they had been finding in those notes ... Half a bottle and hours later I fell asleep.

I dreamed that I was being chased, that I kept calling back over my shoulder, 'Stop, it's me! Look at me! It's me!' But it didn't stop, and steadily it gained ground, until I knew that I was going to be caught, and the thought paralyzed me. All I could do then was wait in rigid, motionless, soundless terror for it to reach out and get me.

The nightmare woke me up, and it was minutes before I could move. It was nearly daylight; I didn't try to sleep any more. I was too afraid of having *her* dreams again. At seven thirty I called Janet.

'Hey,' she said happily. 'I thought we'd never hear from you.'

'I sent some cards.'

'But you'll be here before they will. How's it going?'

'Fine. Boring after the first day. I went to a dirty movie last night.'

'I hope you had bad dreams. Serve you right.' Her voice was teasing and cheerful and happy, and I could see her smile and the light in her eyes.

'How's everything there?' I couldn't ask about Lenny and Christine. If they had found out anything, they hadn't told her. I'd know, if they had. We chatted for several minutes, then she had to run, and I kissed her over the wire and we both hung up at the same time, the way we always did. I was being stupid. Naturally they wouldn't tell her. Hey, did you know that your husband's been torturing this woman psychologically, that he raped her repeatedly, that he's contemplating killing her? I jerked from the bed, shaking.

I had a dull pain behind my right eye when I went down to breakfast. A wind was driving sleet through the streets like sheer white curtains, and I stopped at the doorway, shivering, and went back inside to the hotel dining room. I couldn't think, and I knew that I had to think now.

If Lenny deciphered the notebooks, and if Karl had known that she could be possessed – there, I thought with some satisfaction, I used the word. If he had known and put that in his notebooks, then Lenny was bright enough to know that the recurrence of her schizophrenia was more than likely due to a new invasion. I groaned. He wouldn't believe that. *I* couldn't even believe it. No one in his right mind would, unless he had done it and could prove it to himself ... I gripped my cup so hard that coffee splashed out and I had to use both hands to return the cup to the saucer. Had Lenny gone into her too?

The pain behind my eye was a knife blade now. Lenny! Of course. I tried to lift the coffee and couldn't. I flung down my napkin and got up and hurried back to my room, as fast as I could get out of there. I paced, but no matter how I came to it, I ended up thinking that the only way Lenny could have accepted the thing was through experience. First Rudeman, then me, and now Lenny.

He couldn't have her. She was mine now. And I would never give her up.

The pain was unbearable and I collapsed, sprawled across the bed, clutching my head. I hadn't had a migraine in years. It was not knowing. Not knowing how much they had found out, not knowing what they were doing, what they were planning, not knowing if there was a way they could learn about me.

I went to her abruptly, roughly. She dropped a pan of developer and moaned, and caught the sink in a dark room. 'No!' she cried. 'Please. No!'

I tried to make her remember everything Lenny had said to her, tried to bring back his voice, but there was too much, it came too fast. She was too frightened, and intermixed were the revived thoughts of insanity, of Karl's voice, Lenny's words. Too much. She had to relax. I took her to the couch and made her lie down and stop thinking. I felt her fear, and hatred, and abhorrence, like a pulse beating erratically, with each beat the pressure increased, and then ebbed. She tried to break away, and we struggled, and I hurt her. I didn't know what I had done, how I had managed it, but she groaned and wept and fell down again, and now my pain was also her pain. 'Karl,' she whispered soundlessly, 'please go. Please leave me alone. I'm sorry. I didn't know. Please.'

I stayed with her for more than an hour, and then I tried to force her to forget. To know nothing about my presence. She struggled again, and this time she screamed piercingly, and for a moment the feeling of a plunge straight down was almost overwhelming, but everything stopped, and I could find nothing there to communicate with, nothing to probe. It was like being swallowed by a sea of feathers that stretched out in all directions, shifting when I touched them, but settling again immediately. She had fainted.

I fell asleep almost immediately and when I awakened it was nearly two, and my headache was gone. I went to the exposition.

That afternoon a man returned who had been at the stall for almost an hour on Saturday. He had a companion this time. 'Hi, Mr. Laslow. Hendrickson, remember? Like you to meet Norbert Weill.'

Of course, I knew who Norbert Weill was. If you had a home workshop, you had something of his in it. If you had a small commercial shop, you probably had something of his. If you had a hundred-man operation, you'd have something of his. He was about sixty, small and square, with muscles like a boxer's. He grunted at the introduction, his handshake was a no-nonsense test of strength. 'Hendrickson says, it'll cut through plastic, glass, aluminum, steel. Without changing nothing but the program. That right?'

'Yes. Would you like a demonstration?'

'Not here. In my shop. How much?'

'I can't discuss that without my partner, Mr. Weill.'

'Get him, then. When can he make it?'

So it went. In the end I agreed to call Lenny, then get in touch with Weill again at his Chicago office. Lenny didn't sound very enthusiastic. 'Let him have the machine in his own shop for a couple of weeks after you close down there. Then let him make an offer.'

'I think he'll make the offer without all that, if we're both on hand to discuss it. Outright sale of this machine, an advance against royalties. Could come to quite a bundle.'

'Christ! I just don't ... Eddie, can you get away from that place for a couple of hours? I've got to have a talk with you. Not about this goddam machine, something else.'

'Sure. Look, plan to fly up on Friday. It'll take an hour, no more. A couple of hours for the talk with Weill. A couple more with me, then fly back. Six hours is all. Or less maybe. You can afford to take one lousy day off.'

'Okay. I'll call your hotel and let you know what time I'll get in.' He sounded relieved.

'Hey, wait a minute. What the hell is going on? Is it one of the suits? The closed-circuit TV giving trouble? What?'

'Oh. Sorry, Eddie. I thought I said personal. Nothing at the shop. Everything's fine. It's ... it's something with Chris. Anyway, see you Friday.'

I didn't go back to the booth, but instead found a small coffee shop in the exposition building and sat there smoking and thinking about Lenny and Christine, and Janet and me, and Mr. Weill, and God knows what else. This was it, I thought, the break we'd been waiting for. I didn't doubt that. Money, enough for once to do the things we'd been wanting to do. A bigger shop, more equipment, maybe some help, even a secretary to run herd on books. And neither Lenny nor I cared. Neither of us gave a damn.

Sitting there, with coffee in front of me, a cigarette in my fingers, I probed Christine to see what was happening. She was talking in a low voice. Her eyes were closed. Going into her was like putting on distortion lenses, putting scrambling devices in my ears. Nothing was in clear focus, no thoughts were coherent all the way through. She was on something, I realized. Something that had toned down everything, taken off all the edges, all the sharpness.

'I used to walk on that same path, after ... I saw the fields sown, the tractors like spiders, back and forth, back and forth, stringing a web of seeds. And the green shoots – they really do shoot out, like being released, a rubber band that is suddenly let go, but they do it in slow motion. It was a wheat-field. Pale green, then as high as my shoulders so that I was a head floating over the field, only a head. Magician's best trick. Float a head. Then the har-vesters came and the snow fell. And it was the same walk. You see? And I couldn't tell which was the real one. They were all real. Are real. All of them are. The tranquilizers. He said I shouldn't take them. Have to learn how to find which one is now and concentrate on it. No tranquilizers.'

She sighed, and the images blurred, fused, separated again. She turned off a tape recorder, but continued to lie still, with her eyes closed. Her thoughts were a chaotic jumble. If she suspected that I was there, she gave no indi-cation. She was afraid to open her eyes. Trying to remember why she had walked along that path so many times after Karl died out there. In the be-ginning, the hours of training, hours and hours of testing. Then the exper-iments. Afraid of him. Terribly afraid. He had cleared the world for her, but he might scramble it again. So afraid of him. If she took the capsules and went to bed, it didn't matter, but now. Afraid to open her eyes. Lenny? Isn't it time yet? It's been so long – days, weeks. Snow has fallen, and the summer heat has come and gone. I know the couch is under me, and the room around me, and my finger on the switch to the recorder. I know that. I have to repeat it sometimes, but then I know it. Mustn't open my eyes now. Not yet. Not until Lenny comes back.

I smelled burning filter and put out the cigarette and drank coffee. What would she see if she opened her eyes now? Was that her madness? A visual distortion, a constant hallucination, a mixture of reality and fantasy that she couldn't tell apart? She turned her head, faced the back of the couch.

Very slowly I forced her to sit up, and then to open her eyes. It was much harder than making her respond had been before. She kept slipping away from me. It was as if there were so many other impulses that mine was just one of a number, no more powerful than any of the illusory ones that kept holding up images for her to scan and accept, or reject. Finally she opened her eyes, and the room began to move. There was no sequence, no before and after, or cause and effect. Everything was. Winter, with a fire in the fire-place, summer with fans in the windows, company talking gaily, the room empty, children playing with puzzles, a couple copulating on the couch, a man pacing talking angrily ... They were all real. I knew we – I had to get out of there, and there was no place to go. I was afraid of the outside world even more than the inside one. I was afraid to move. The couch van-ished from behind me. The room was moving again. And I knew it would vanish, and that I would fall, like I had fallen a thousand times, a million times.

'Help me!' I cried to the pacing man, and he continued to pace although the room was certainly fading. And the children played. And the couple made love. And the fans whirred. And the fire burned. And I fell and fell and fell and fell …

I sat in the coffee shop and shook. I was in a sweat, and I couldn't stop the shaking in my hands. I didn't dare try to walk out yet. No more! No more. I shook my head and swore, no more. I'd kill her. She had learned what to do, what not to do, and through my stupidity and blundering, I'd kill her.

'Sir? Is anything wrong? Are you all right?'

The waitress. She touched my arm warily, ready to jump back. 'Sir?'

'I … I'm sorry, Miss. Sleeping with my eyes open, I guess. I'm sorry.' She didn't believe me. Behind her I saw another woman watching. She must have sent the waitress over. I picked up the check, but I was afraid to try to stand up. I waited until the girl turned and walked away, and then I held the top of the table until I knew my legs would hold me.

I had the boy I'd hired relieve me for the rest of the day, and I walked back to my hotel, slowly, feeling like an old man. I started the hour-long walk making myself promises. I would never touch her again, I'd help Lenny find out the truth about her and do whatever could be done to cure her, and to get her and Lenny together. They needed each other, and I had Janet and the children, and the shop. Everything I had driven for was either mine, or within sight by now. Everything. She was a danger to me, nothing else. By the time I got to the hotel I knew the promises were lies. That as long as I could get inside that woman's head, I would keep right on doing it. And now the thought had hit me that I wanted to be with her physically, just her and me, when I did it next time. It was a relief finally to admit to myself that I wanted to seize her body and mind. And I knew that I wanted everyone else out of her life altogether. Especially Lenny. Everyone who might be a threat, everyone who suspected that there was a mystery to be unraveled. The notebooks would have to be destroyed. If Karl had known, the knowledge must be destroyed. All of it. No one to know but me.

I looked on her then as a gift from God or the Devil, but my gift. From the instant of our first meeting, when the shock of seeing her had rattled me, right through that moment, everything had been driving me toward this realization. I hadn't wanted to see it before. I had ducked and avoided it. Pretending that she was abhorrent to me, making Janet and Lenny shield me from her, shield her from me. I walked faster and with more purpose. I had too much to do now to waste time. I had to learn exactly how to enter her without the panic she always felt as soon as she knew. And I had to find a way to make her rid herself of Lenny.

I bought a bottle of bourbon, and some cheese and crackers. I had to stay in to plan my campaign, make certain of all the details this time before I touched her. I knew I would have to be more careful than I had been in the past. I didn't want to destroy her, or to damage her in any way. I might have to hurt her at first, just to show her that she had to obey. That's what always hurt her, having to fight with her. And no more tranquilizers. Karl had been right. She shouldn't have drugs, not she. What else had he learned about her? How deep had his control been? The line from Pete's letter came back to me: 'He wound her up each morning ...'

The bastard, I thought with hatred. Goddamned bastard.

It was almost five when I got to my room. There was a message from Lenny, to call him at *her* number. I crumpled up the note and flung it across the room. How much of the notebooks had he been able to get through? How much had he told her about what he had found there? I poured a generous drink and tried to think about Lenny and Karl, and all the time I kept seeing her, a tiny, perfectly formed figure, amazingly large dark eyes, doll-like hands ...

She would have called Lenny after my ... visit. I cursed myself for clumsiness. I'd have her in an institution if I wasn't more careful. Had she been able to get back to present after I ran out this time? I realized that that's how I had always left her, in a panic, or in a faint. What if she, in desperation, jumped out a window, or took an overdose of something? I took a long drink and then placed the call. I was shaking again, this time with fear that she was hurt, really hurt.

Lenny answered. 'Oh, Eddie. Can you get Weill tonight? I can get in by ten fifteen in the morning. Can you find out if he can see us then?'

I swallowed hard before I could answer. 'Sure. He said to call anytime. Someone will be there. Is that all? I mean when I got the message to call you at ... her house, I was afraid something had happened.'

'No. It's all right. Chris has decided to feed me, that's all.' There was a false note in his voice. Probably she was nearby, listening. I fought the impulse to go out to her to find out.

'Okay. If I don't call back, assume that it's set up.'

'What's wrong with you? You sound hoarse.'

'Out in the rain. A bug. I'm catching that mysterious "it" that's always going around. See you tomorrow.'

'Yeah. Take care of yourself. Get a bottle and go to bed.'

'Sure, Lenny.'

I stared at the phone after hanging up. He was suspicious. I could tell from his voice, from the way he hedged when I asked a direct question. Maybe not simply suspicious. Maybe they actually knew by now. Not that he could prove anything. To whom? Janet? A jury? I laughed and poured another drink, this time mixing it with water. 'This man, ladies and gentlemen, entered the mind of this woman at will ...'

At breakfast the next morning I realized that I hadn't eaten anything for a couple of days, and still didn't want to then. I had coffee and toast, and left most of the soggy bread on the dish, Lenny met me at the hotel.

'God, Eddie, you'd better get home and go to bed. We can close up the display. You look like hell.'

'A bug. I'll be all right. Maybe you could stay if I do decide to take off?'

'Let's close the whole thing. It's just three more days.'

'I'll stay,' I said. What an ideal set-up that would have been. Him here, me back home, Janet working.

I let Lenny do the talking at Weill's office, and we got a good offer, not as much as we had hoped, but probably more than Weill had planned to make. We ended up saying that our lawyer would go over the contract and be in touch.

'Let's go to your room where we can talk without interruption,' Lenny said then, and neither of us mentioned Weill again. A few months ago, B.C., Before Christine, we'd have been arrested for disturbing the peace if we'd had this offer from someone like Weill, and now, we didn't even mention it again.

I lay down on my bed and let Lenny have the only chair in the room. My head was ringing and aching mildly, and my back and legs were stiff and sore. I didn't give a damn about Lenny's problems then.

Lenny paced. 'God, I don't even know where or how to begin this,' he said finally. 'Back at the beginning of Christine and Karl. She was such a good subject for his experiments that he based much of his research on her alone, using the other two for controls mostly. Then he found out that she was too good, that what she could do was so abnormal that he couldn't base any conclusions on his findings on her. For instance, he trained her to see objects so small that they were too small to fall on the cones and rods in the retina. And he trained her to spot a deviation in a straight line so minute that it needs special equipment to measure. Same with a circle. She can tell the exact place that a circle deviates from sphericity, and again it needs sophisticated instruments to measure it. Stereo acuity. We lose it if the peripheral vision is flattened out, if we don't have the cues. She doesn't lose it. She can see things where there isn't enough light to see them. She can see things that are too far away to see. Same with her color perception. You need a spectrometer and a spectrophotometer to make the same differentiation she can do with a glance.'

He stopped and threw himself down in the chair and lighted a cigarette before he continued. 'I'm getting pretty well into the notebooks. It's tough going, very technical, in a field I know nothing about. And he knew nothing about physics, and used layman's language, and a sort of shade-tree mechanic's approach with some of the equipment he had to learn to use. Anyway, after a few years, he switched to a second code. He was paranoid about his secrets. A developing psychosis is written down there plain enough even for me to see. He was afraid of her.' Lenny put out the cigarette and looked at me. I was watching him, and now I shook my head.

'What do you mean afraid? Her schizophrenia? Was she showing signs of it again?'

'Will you forget that! She's not a schizo! Pretend you look at this room and you see it as it's been all through its history, with everyone who was ever here still here. Suppose you can't stop yourself from straying in time, just the way you stray in space. If you were lost in a hotel like this one and had to knock on doors, or ask people the way to your room, that's being lost in space. Lost in time is worse because no one answers until you find your own time. But those who are in your time see the search, hear your end of it, and wham, you're in a hospital.'

I swung my legs over the side of the bed and sat up, but the room was unsteady. I had to support my head on my hands, propped up on my knees. 'So why isn't she locked up?'

'Because she learned how to control it most of the time. Maybe a lot of people are born able to see through time and learn as infants to control it, how to tell this present from all the other images that they see. Maybe only a few do it, and most of them never learn control. God knows something drives some children into autism that they never leave. She learned. But in periods of high stress she backslid. If she became overtired, or sick, or under a strain, she couldn't hold the present in sharp enough focus. So they had her in and out of hospitals. And Rudeman became fascinated by her, and began to do his own line of research, using her, and he realized that she was seeing layers of time. Can't you just see it? Him the famous physiological psychologist denying mind from the start, being forced finally to concede that there's something there besides the brain. He struggled. It's all there. He couldn't accept, then he looked for a reasonable cause for her aberrations, finally he knew that she was somehow existing partly in another dimension that opened time just as space is opened to the rest of us.' Lenny's sudden laugh was bitter and harsh. 'He preferred to think he was going mad, that she was mad. But the scientist in him wouldn't let it rest there. He devised one experiment after another to disprove her abilities, and only got in deeper and deeper. First understanding, then control. He taught her how to look at *now*. He forced her into photography as part of her therapy, a continuing practice in seeing what is now.'

He couldn't see my face. If he had found out that much, he must have learned the rest, I kept thinking. I couldn't tell if he suspected me or not, but if he knew that someone was driving her back into that condition, he would go down the list of names, and sooner or later he would get to me. I knew he would stop there. Too many signs. Too much evidence of my guilt. He'd know. Janet would know. I remembered the toast that *she* had made that night in her house: to the good men. I wanted to laugh, or cry.

'Christ, Eddie, I'm sorry. Here you are as sick as a dog, and I'm going on like a hysterical grandmother.'

'I'm not that sick,' I said and raised my head to prove it. 'It just seemed like as good a way as any to listen. It's a pretty incredible story, you have to admit.'

'Yeah, but you ain't heard nothing yet. Chris thinks that Rudeman is haunting her. And why not? If you know you can see the past, where do you draw the line at what is or isn't possible? She's certain that he found a way to come back and enter her mind, and she's having a harder and harder time holding on to the present. She thinks he's having revenge. He always threatened her with a relapse if she didn't cooperate wholly with him in his research.'

Lenny's big face registered despair and hopelessness. He spread his hands and said, 'After you swallow half a dozen unbelievable details, why stop at one more? But, damn it, I can't take that, and I know something has driven her back to the wall.'

I stood up then and looked through the drawer where I had put the bourbon. Then I remembered that it was in the bathroom. When I came back with it, Lenny took the bottle and said, 'When did you eat last?'

'I don't remember. Yesterday maybe.'

'Yeah, I thought so. I'll have something sent up, then a drink, or you'll pass out.'

While we waited I said, 'Look at it this way. She sees things that no one else sees. Most people would call that hallucinating. A psychiatrist would call it hallucinating. She thinks her dead husband is haunting her somehow. What in hell are you proposing to do, old buddy?'

Lenny nodded. 'I know all that. Did you know that Eric is color blind?' I shook my head. Eric was his middle son. 'I didn't know it either until he was tested for it at school. A very sophisticated test that's been devised in the past twenty-five years. Without that test no one would have suspected it ever. You see? I always assumed that he saw things pretty much the way I did. I assume that you see what I see. And there's no way on this earth to demonstrate one way or the other that you do or don't. The mental image you construct and call sight might duplicate mine, or it might not, and it doesn't matter as long as we agree that that thing you're sitting on is a bed. But do you see that as the same bed that I see? I don't know. Let me show you a couple of the easy tests that Karl Rudeman used.' He held up a card and flashed it at me. 'What color was it?'

I grinned. I had expected to be asked which one it was. 'Red,' I said. 'Red Queen of Hearts.'

He turned the card over and I looked at it and nodded, then looked at him. He simply pointed again to the card. It was black. A black Queen of Hearts. I picked it up and studied it. 'I see what you mean,' I said. I had 'seen' it as red.

'Another one,' he said. 'How many windows are in your house?'

I thought a moment, then said, 'Twenty-one.'

'How do you know?'

'I just counted them.' I was grinning at him and his simple-minded games. But then I started to think, how had I known, how had I counted them? I had visualized room after room, had counted the windows on the walls that I had drawn up before that inner eye. The bellboy rang and came in with a cart. I tipped him and we sat down to eat sandwiches and drink coffee. 'So?' I asked, with my mouth full. 'So I visualized the windows. So what does that mean?'

'It means that that's how you remember things. If you had an eidetic memory, you would have seen the walls exactly as they were when you memorized them, and you could have counted the books in your line of vision, read off the titles even. The question is: are you looking into the past? No answer yet. That's what Chris can do. And that's how she sees the past. That clearly. And she sees the anomalies. You see what you expect – a red Queen of Hearts. She sees what is. But, as you say, no psychiatrist would believe it. Rudeman didn't for years, not until he did a lot of checking.'

I was wolfing down the sandwiches, while he was still working on the first one. I felt jubilant. He didn't know. She didn't know. Karl haunting her! That was as good a thing for her to think as anything else.

'Okay,' I said, pouring more coffee. 'I see that she'd have a problem with a psychiatrist. But what's the alternative, if she's as – sick – or bothered as she seems to be?'

'The answer's in the notebooks,' Lenny said. 'She knows it. She tried to find it at the farmhouse, but it was impossible to work there. And now she's afraid of Rudeman all over again. She believes that somehow she caused his death. Now she has to pay.'

The strong waves of guilt I had got from her. But why had he wandered out in the fields barefoot and in pajamas?

'What scares me,' Lenny said, 'is the slowness of getting through those notes. Bad enough while he was sane, but immeasurably harder as his psychosis developed, for the last seven or eight years. It's like trying to swim in a tar pit. By the end it was bad enough that he was certifiable, I guess. He knew the contents of those notebooks would invalidate all the work he had done in the past. Chris doesn't want to talk about it, and all I know for sure is What I've been able to dig out of that code he used.'

'Psychotic how?'

'Oh, God! I don't know what name they'd put on it. In the beginning he thought she was a puppet that he could manipulate as he chose. Then gradually he became afraid of her, Chris. Insanely jealous, mad with fear that she'd leave him, terrified that someone would find out about her capabilities and begin to suspect that there was more. Just batty.'

'So what do you intend to do?'

'That's what I came up here to talk to you about. I'm going to marry her.' I jerked my head around to stare at him in disbelief. He smiled fleetingly. 'Yeah, it's like that. Not until next year sometime. But I'm taking her on a long, long trip, starting as soon as we can get the books we'll need ready. That's why I want to wrap up a deal with Weill as fast as we can. I'll need my share. We can handle the shop however you want – keep my bench waiting, or buy me out. Whatever.'

I kept on staring at him, feeling very stupid. 'What books?' I asked finally, not wanting to know, but to keep him talking long enough for me to try to understand what it would mean to me.

'Rudeman used his library shelves as keys throughout. Things like one – eleven – two ninety-eight – three – six. Top row, eleventh book, page two ninety-eight, line three, word six. First three letters correspond to ABC and so on. He'd use that for a while, then switch to another book. Chris memorized those shelves, so she can find the key books. Stumbled onto it a couple of years ago. That's why she dragged all of his books with her when she ducked out of that house. She just didn't have time to go through the notebooks to sort out the ones he had used.'

'Lenny, are you sure? Isn't it just the sick-bird syndrome? I mean, my God, maybe she really *is* crazy! A lot of beautiful, charming, talented people are.'

'No. She isn't. Rudeman would have known after all those years. He wanted her to be, but he couldn't convince himself in the slightest that she was.' He stood up. 'I didn't expect you to believe me. I would have been disappointed in you if you had. But I had to get it out, get some of this stuff said. Let you know you'll have the shop to yourself for a year or so.'

'What are you going to do now?'

'Go home. Move in the Donlevy house. She's on tranquilizers, and they make it awfully hard to hold on to the present. She keeps wandering back and forth. It'll take a week to get things ready to leave.' He mock-cuffed me and said, 'Don't look so worried. I know what I'm doing.'

When he was gone I wished that he had a real inkling of what he was doing, and I knew that he would never know. I thought about that line that everyone has that he can't cross, no matter what the evidence, unless there is an inner revelatory experience. Rudeman couldn't believe she looked into the past, until he experienced it through her. Then he drew the line at possession, until it was proven again, and with its proof he had come to doubt his own sanity. Lenny could accept the research that proved she could see the past, but no farther. Whatever Rudeman had said about possession he had written off as insanity. And I had blundered in and swallowed the whole thing without reservation, through experience, firsthand experience. I tried to think in what ways I was like Rudeman, making it possible for me to do what he had done, wondering why Lenny couldn't do it, why others hadn't. My gift. Like my fingerprints were mine alone. I gave Lenny ten minutes to make sure that he really was gone, then I looked in on her. I said it to myself that way, Think I'll look in on her now.

Met by a wave of hatred stronger than anything I'd ever experienced. Resistance. Determination not to be taken again. Thoughts: not going crazy. You're real and evil. Die! Damn you, die! I killed you once! How many times! *Die!*

I drew back, but not all the way. She thought she was winning. She conjured a vision of a man in pajamas, orange and black stripes, walking, a pain in the chest, harder and harder, gasping for air ... I clutched the arms of the chair and said, 'No! Stop thinking. No more!' The pain returned, and this time I was falling, falling ... I had to get out. Get away from her. The witch, bitch, which witch bitch. Falling. Pain. I couldn't get loose. Falling. Out the window, over the rail, backward, seeing the ground ... She screamed and let go.

I lay back in the chair, trying to catch my breath, trying to forget the pain in my chest, my shoulder, my left arm. I didn't have a heart condition. Perfectly all right. Medical exam just last year. Perfectly all right. I flexed the fingers in my hand, and slowly raised the arm, afraid the pain would return with movement.

Bitch, I thought. The goddam bitch. She hadn't taken the tranquilizer, she had been waiting, steeled against me, ready to attack. Treacherous bitch. I pushed myself from the chair and stood up, and saw myself in the mirror. Grey. Aged. Terrified. I closed my eyes and said again, 'Bitch!'

Was she panting also, like a fighter between rounds? If I went again now, would she be able to attack again so soon? I knew I wouldn't try. The pain had been too real.

I looked at my watch then and nearly fell down again. An hour and a half? I held it to my ear, and shook it hard. An hour and a half! Shakily I called Weill's office and told Hendrickson that he could have the machine tool picked up any time. I was going home.

There wasn't much else there, nothing that I couldn't get to the car alone. And by five I was on the highway. An hour and a half, I kept thinking. Where? Doing what?

She would kill me, I thought over and over. Just like she killed her husband. The notebooks, I had to get them myself. I couldn't let Lenny take them away. Rudeman must have discovered too late that she had power too.

But he must have suspected before the end. His psychosis. The new code, afraid she had learned the old one. He must have learned about this. He had kept her ten years before she killed him. It would be in the notebooks. I drove too fast, and got home in six hours. And not until the car squealed to a stop in the driveway did I even think about what I would tell Lenny or Janet. But I didn't have to tell her anything. She took one look at my face and cried, 'Oh, my God!' And she pulled me from the car and got me inside and into bed somehow, without any help from me, but without hindrance either. And I fell asleep.

I woke up when Janet did to get the kids off to school, 'Are you better? I called Dr. Lessing last night, and he said to bring you in this morning.'

'I'm better,' I said wearily. I felt like I was coming out of a long drugged sleep, with memories hazy and incomplete. 'I need to sleep and have orange juice, and that's about it. No need for you to stay home.' She said she'd see about that, and she went out to get Rusty up, and to find Laura's red scarf. I hadn't seen them for almost a week, hadn't even thought of them. They would expect presents. They always expected presents. When Janet came back in fifteen minutes, I convinced her that I really was all right, and finally she agreed to go on to work. She'd call at noon.

I had breakfast. I showered and dressed. And smoked three cigarettes. And convinced myself that I wasn't sick at all. And then I walked over to Christine's house.

Lenny met me at the door. 'What the hell are you doing up and out? Janet said you came in sick as a dog last night.' He gave me more coffee. At the kitchen table.

'I kept thinking about what you were saying about her.' I indicated the rest of the house. 'And I was sick, feverish, and decided I couldn't do anything else in Chicago. So I came home. Anything I can do to help?'

Lenny looked like he wanted to hug me, but he said merely, 'Yeah, I can use some help.'

'Tell me what to do.'

'Just stick around until Chris wakes up. I gave her a sleeping pill last night. Should be wearing off soon. What I've been doing is going down the notebooks line by line and every time he used another book for his key, Chris visualizes the shelf and finds it there. Then we find that book in the boxes. And I go on to the next one. While she rests, or is busy with her work, I find the key words in the books and decode a line or two to make sure. Rather not lug that whole library with us if I can avoid it.'

I was watching him as if he were a stranger. I was thinking of him as a stranger. I had no definite plan worked out, just a direction. *She* had to get rid of him. Before he learned any more from the notebooks.

And her. What did she know? I knew I had to find out without any more delay. I tried to reach her and found a cottony foggy world. The sleeping pill. I tried to jar her awake, and got glimpses of a nightmare world of grey concrete expanses. A hall, the grey of the floor exactly matched the grey of the walls and ceiling. The joints lost their squareness ahead of me, and the hallway became a tube that grew narrower and narrower and finally was only a point. I was running toward the point at a breakneck speed.

You're not Karl! Who are you? I pulled out. What if she brought the pain again? The pseudo heart attack? I was shaking.

'Jesus, Eddie, you should be in bed.' Lenny put his hand on my forehead. 'Come on, I'll take you home.'

I shook my head. 'I'm okay. Just get a chill now and then. How about the couch here? At least I'll be handy when she gets up.'

He installed me in the study on the deep green couch, with an Indian throw over me. I drifted pleasantly for a while. Then, *Get out! Who are you? – I'll never get out again. Karl knew, didn't he? I'll finish what he started. You can't hurt me the way you hurt him. I'm too strong for you. We'll go away, you and me.* I laughed, and laughing pulled away. At the same instant I heard her scream.

I sat up and waited. Lenny brought her down in a few minutes. I didn't join them in the kitchen. I watched and listened through her, and she was so agitated now that she wasn't even aware of my presence. I was getting that good at it.

'Listen, Lenny, and then leave me alone. I thought it was Karl, but it isn't. I don't know who it is. He can get inside my mind. I don't know how. I know he's there, and he makes me do things, crazy things. He'll use me, just like Karl did all those years. I can't help myself. And night after night, day after day, whatever he wants me to do, wherever he wants me to go ...' She was weeping and her talk was beginning to break up into incoherent snatches of half-formed thoughts.

'Chris! Stop that! Your husband was crazy! He thought he could possess you. That's insane! And he half convinced you that he could do it. But God damn it, he's dead! No one else can touch you. I won't let anyone near you.'

'He doesn't have to be near me. All these weeks ... He's been in and out, watching, listening to us go over the notebooks. He knows what's in them now. I ... He won't stop now. And if he says I have to go with him, I'll have to.'

Her voice went curiously flat and lifeless. She was seeing again that tube that ended in a point, and suddenly she longed to be on it, heading toward that point. 'I'd rather die now,' she said.

Lenny's big face twisted with pain. 'Chris, please, trust me. I won't let anyone near you. I promise. Let me help you, Chris. Please. Don't force me out now.'

'It won't make any difference. You don't understand. If he makes me go with him, I can't fight it.'

But she could. I didn't know if my thoughts reminded her of the heart attack, or if she would have thought of it herself. Karl sitting in her room, watching her with a smile on his face. 'You will turn them down, of course, my dear. You can't travel to Africa alone.'

'No, I won't turn them down! I want to take this assignment ...' Slipping, blurring images, fear of being alone, of not being able to keep the world in focus. Fear of falling through the universe, to a time where there was nothing, falling forever ... Staring at the rejection of the offer in her own handwriting. Karl's face, sad, but determined.

'You really don't want to travel without me, my dear. It wouldn't be safe for you, you know.'

And later, waking up from dreamless sleep. Knowing she had to get up, to go down the hall to his room, where he was waiting for her. *No! It's over! Leave me alone.* Swinging her legs over the side of the bed, standing up, NO! I HATE YOU! *Your soft fat hands! You make me feel dirty! Why don't you die! Have a heart attack and die.*

Fighting it to the door, dragging herself unwillingly to the door, fighting against the impulse, despising him and even more herself. He was forcing her up flights of stairs, without rails, straight down for miles and miles, and he was at her side, forcing each step. She pushed him, and he screamed. Then he was there again, and she pushed again. And again. Then he was running, and she, clinging to the doorknob in her bedroom, she was running too, pushing him off the steps as fast as he managed to climb back on, and he stumbled and fell and now she knew he would fall forever, even as she fell sometimes. Swirling into darkness with pain and terror for company. She slipped to the floor, and awakened there much later knowing only that something was gone from her life. That she felt curiously free and empty and unafraid.

I lay back down and stared at the ceiling. I could hear her footsteps recede up the stairs, across the hall to her room. Lenny's heavy tread returned and there was the sound of measured pacing. Soon, I thought. Soon it would end. And after today, after she recovered from the next few hours ... She would have to remain nearby, here in this house as long as possible. Above me she was starting to dress. I was there. She didn't doubt a presence haunting her. Nor did she question that he could force her to go away with him if he chose.

'Who?' she whispered, standing still with her eyes closed. She imagined the suppressed fury on Lenny's big face, the pulse in his temple that beat like a primitive drum summoning him from this time back to a time when he would have killed without a thought anyone who threatened his woman. I laughed and forced his face to dissolve and run like a painting on fire.

Suddenly I was jerked from my concentration by the sound of Janet's voice. 'Where is he? How is he?'

'He's sleeping in the study. Feverish, but not bad.' Lenny's reassuring voice.

Janet came into the study and sat on the couch and felt my face. 'Honey, I was scared to death. I called and called and no answer. I was afraid you'd passed out or something. Let me take you over to Dr. Lessing.'

'Get out,' I said without opening my eyes. 'Just get out and leave me alone.' I tried to find *her*, and couldn't. I was afraid to give it too much attention with Janet right there.

'I can't just leave you like this. I've never seen you like this before. You need a doctor.'

'Get out of here! When I need you or want you I'll be in touch. Just get the hell away from me now.'

'Eddie!'

'For God's sake, Janet, can't you leave me alone? I've got a virus, a bug. I feel rotten, but not sick, not sick enough for a doctor. I just want to be left alone.'

'No. It's more serious than that. Don't you think I know you better than that? It's been coming on for weeks. Little things, then bigger things, now this. You have to see a doctor, Eddie. Please.'

Wearily I sat up and stared at her and wondered how I'd ever found her attractive or desirable. Freckled, thin, sharp features, razorlike bones ... I turned away and said, 'Get lost, Janet. Beat it. Yeah, it started a long time ago, but it takes a club over the head, doesn't it?'

'What do you mean?'

'Just what you think I mean. I'm sick. I'm tired. I want to be alone. For a long time. Tonight. Tomorrow night. Next week. Next month. Just get out of here and leave me alone. I'll pick up some things later on after you've gone to work.'

'I'm going to call Dr. Lessing.'

I looked at her and hoped I wouldn't have to hit her. I didn't want to hurt her, too. Her freckles stood out in relief against the dead white of her skin. I closed my eyes. 'I won't see him. Or anyone else. Not now. Maybe tomorrow. Just leave me alone for now. I have to sleep.'

She stood up and backed away. She had seen. She knew that I'd hit her if she didn't get out. At the door she stopped, and the helplessness in her voice made me want to throw something at her. 'Eddie? Will you stay here for the next hour?'

So she could bring in her men in white. I laughed and sat up. 'I had planned to, but I guess I'd better plan again. I'll be in touch.'

She left then. I could hear her voice and Lenny's from the kitchen, but I didn't try to make out their words. A clock chimed twelve. I wanted to go out there and throw Janet out. I didn't want her around for the next half hour or so. I heard the back door, then the sound of a motor, and I sighed in relief.

I went to the kitchen and got coffee and stood at the window watching snow fall.

Lenny joined me. 'Janet says you had a fight.'

'Yeah. I was rough on her. Sickness brings out her mother-hen instincts, and I can't stand being fussed at. What was wrong with Christine?'

'A dream.' He stared at the snow. 'Supposed to get a couple of inches by night, I think. Won't stick long. Ground isn't cold enough yet.'

'Lenny, for God's sake quit kidding yourself. She's sick. She needs professional help.'

'She thinks – she's certain that he learned enough about her to put an end to this so-called illness. She's desperately afraid of a relapse. Hospitalization, shock therapy ...'

'What if *you* are causing her present condition? Isn't it suggestive? Her husband, now you. It's a sexual fantasy. By making her reach a decision about you, you might push her off the deep end irreversibly.'

He looked shocked. 'That's crazy.'

'Exactly. Lenny, these things are too dangerous for a well-meaning but non-professional man to toy with. You might destroy her ...'

'If she was crazy you'd be making good points,' Lenny said distinctly. 'She isn't.'

I finished my coffee. *A doctor. Shots, pills, all yesterday and last years and decades ago. Questions. Lost forever and forever falling. Through all the yesterdays. Lenny wants to get a doctor for you. A psychiatrist. You have to get him out of here now. Immediately. Even if it kills him.*

She resisted the idea. She kept trying to visualize his face, and I wouldn't let it take shape. Instead I drew out of her memories of the institutions she'd been in.

Lenny's voice startled me, and I left her.

'I don't think it's such a good idea for you to be here when she comes down. She knows you think she's psycho.'

I put down my cup. 'Whatever you say.'

She came into the kitchen then. She was deathly pale. She had a gun in her hand. I stared at it. 'Where ...?'

She looked at it too, looked at it in a puzzled manner. 'I had it in my car when I came here,' she said. 'I found it when I was unpacking and I put it upstairs in my room. I just remembered.'

'Give it to me,' Lenny said. He held out his hand and she put the small automatic in it.

I sighed my relief. That was the last thing I wanted her to do. She'd be locked up the rest of her life. Now if I could make her drive him out, maybe he'd use it himself.

Lenny kept his hand in his pocket, over the gun. 'Why were you thinking of guns right now? Where was this?'

'In my train case. I told you …' She glanced at me and I turned my back to stare at the snow again. I was watching my own back then, and seeing Lenny's face and the kitchen that I was keeping in focus only through great effort. 'I told you,' she said again. 'If he makes me go back with him, I'll have no choice.' I made her add, 'The only way I escaped from Karl was through his death.'

She shuddered, and an image of Karl's face swam before her eyes. It was contorted with pain and fear. It was replaced by another face, Lenny's, also contorted by pain and fear. And the image of a hospital ward, and a doctor. And I watched his face change and become my own face. The image dimmed and blurred as I tried to force it away, and she fought to retain it. The concrete corridor was there. She forced the image of a man backward through the corridor, grey walls and ceiling and floor all one, no up and no down, just the cylinder that was growing smaller and smaller. I tried to pull away, and again there was a duel as she fought to keep the imagery. Cliffs, I thought. Crumbling edges, falling … Hospital, shots, electroshock …

'Chris, what is it?' Lenny's voice, as if from another world, faint, almost unrecognizable.

'I don't know. Just hold me. Please.'

Cliffs … Exploding pain in my chest suddenly. Burning pain in my shoulder, my arm. Darkness. Losing her, finding her again. Losing …

'You!' Her voice coarse, harsh with disbelief.

I turned from the window clutching my chest. The room was spinning and there was nothing to hold on to. *Let go. They'll lock you up.* Pain.

'Eddie!'

'You!' she said again, incredulously.

Get the gun back! Lenny. No more pretense now. My hand found something to hold, and the room steadied. Feeling of falling, but knowledge of standing perfectly still, fighting against the nausea, the pain. *Get the gun. Reach in his pocket and take it out.* We, she and I, were in that other place where the grey corridor stretched endlessly. We had time because there was no time. She backed a step away from Lenny, and I forced her to move closer again, seeing the beads of sweat on her forehead, the trembling in her hands. From somewhere else I could hear Lenny's voice, but I couldn't hear the words now. GET THE GUN!

'Lenny, get out! Leave. Go away fast. He'll kill you!' Her voice came from that other place, but the words were echoed up and down the corridor.

You and I. I'll take care of you. I won't let anyone hurt you.

Lenny's hands on me, trying to force me to a chair. Seeing myself sprawled across the table unconscious. '*No!*' I tried to make her fall down an elevator shaft, and saw even clearer my own figure across the table. I tried to remember how it felt to fall in an uncontrollable plunge, and nothing came. She had to faint. Something could be salvaged even now, if only she would faint, or have hysterics, or something, I couldn't break out, pull away. She was holding the back of a chair with both hands, holding so hard her muscles hurt. I saw her grasp tighten and felt the pain erupt again, this time blacking out everything momentarily. Lenny ... I couldn't make her move. I slipped my hand into his pocket then and my fingers felt the metal, warm from the close pocket. I pulled it out and aimed it at Lenny. I was seeing his face from a strange angle, her angle. A cross-section of his face. A Dali painting of fear and shock. She was beating on me and I closed my other hand over her wrist, a child's wrist. Laura's wrist. Back in that timeless corridor. *Why didn't you look into the future too? Why just the past?*

He said I did. I repressed it. Too frightening. The image of the man sprawled across the table, clearer, detailed. Real.

Absolute terror then. Hers. Everything shifting, spinning away, resolving into strange shapes, displaced items of furniture, strange people moving about. Intolerable pain as she lashed out in desperation to find her way through the maze of time. And I was outside again.

I tried to go into her and couldn't. I could see her, wide-eyed, catatonic, and couldn't reach her at all. It was as if the wall that had been breached had been mended now, and once again kept me and all others outside. I didn't know how I had gone through it before. I didn't even know if I had.

I heard the gun hit the floor before I realized that I had dropped it. I felt the table under my cheek before I realized that I had collapsed and was lying across it. I heard their voices, and I knew that she had found her way back, but I couldn't see them. For the moment I was free of the pain. Almost uninterested in the figure slumped across the table.

'You'd better get an ambulance,' she said. I marveled at the calm self-assurance in her voice. What had she seen while she had stood unmoving, rigid? She touched my forehead with fingers that were cool and steady.

'Was it real?' I whispered. 'Any of it?'

'You'll never know, will you?' I didn't know if she said the words aloud or not. I listened to their voices drifting in and out of consciousness while we waited for the ambulance. Was it real? I kept coming back to that.

Was what real?

Anything.

THE TIME PIECE

On a snowy December night in Manhattan, Richard Weiss was given a testimonial dinner, a solid gold watch, and told good-bye by his company. Following the official ceremonies there was a private party given jointly by the president of the company, Hanson Blakesley, and William Weiss, the firstborn son of the newly retired treasurer. William was the fastest-rising star of the company, the president said proudly with one arm about the younger Weiss's shoulders. A photographer duly snapped a shot, and the elder Weiss drank another glass of champagne.

'Rich, are you ready to go now?' his wife, Myrtle, asked later. 'These parties just wear me out. Never can find a chair. All these people ...'

'My last official party,' he said. 'Is my tie all right? Where'd the photographer go? We need pictures to go with the story in next month's magazine.'

Myrtle sighed.

Rich posed with the president, with his fast-rising star-son, with the new treasurer, and at two in the morning he was ready to leave. The snow measured four inches. There were no taxis, and he no longer had use of the official company car.

'Hey, Dad, wait a sec! We'll drop you!' Jerry Lister, his daughter's husband, yelled from the doorway, not risking a snowflake on his tarnished-varnished hair. Rich sighed, as Myrtle did, and their sighs were harmonious.

'How the mighty ... he said.

'It's a ride,' Myrtle said.

Kathleen was in a pout at being dragged from the party so early. Sulkily she said, 'So you are off tomorrow to the Bahamas, huh?'

'Forty-one years,' her mother said. 'Forty-one years in that company. And tonight, the last night, last official function. And we get no car.'

'And then Florida. Boy, that's some life. Cruises, winter in Florida.'

'Your father worked twelve hours a day, six days a week, in the beginning.'

'You hear that, Jerry? Just listen to her. Are you ever going to be able to take *me* on a Bahamas cruise? A winter in Florida?'

Jerry whistled and cut into fast-moving traffic, sliding on a layer of icy water over snow.

'Jerry, we've got time,' Myrtle said. 'Admire the snow. Like Christmas Eve.'

'He always drives too fast,' Kathleen said. 'Ever since I bought that insurance. Thinks if he wrecks us, I'll be the one to get it, not him. Thinks that lucky star is all his. All his.'

'Hey, let's see the watch,' Jerry said, reaching over his shoulder. 'How much is it worth?'

Rich clamped his right hand over the wrist watch as if afraid the groping fingers would somehow get it off his arm. 'Tomorrow you can see, Jerry. Now you drive, okay? With two hands.'

'Sure, Dad. Relax. Relax. Beats walking, doesn't it?'

'We'll let you know when, and if, we get there,' Myrtle said. 'The truck, Jerry. Watch the truck!'

'I don't know, Myrtle. I just don't know,' Rich said later, peeling off his formal clothes. 'William can't wait to usurp me. My only girl child married to a bum. Michael alienated, yes, alienated because his wife thinks we're poor white trash, or something. I can't figure out that girl. Never could. What does she expect? A strange woman Michael chose for his wife. Strange. And Eric. My poor little Eric. A hippie. What's it all about?' He turned to look at Myrtle but she was sleeping, with her mouth partly open.

'I just don't know,' he said again. 'My pretty little wife all blubber and open mouth and curlers,' he said, even louder. Then he turned off the light and climbed into his own bed.

Myrtle started to write postcards as soon as they were shown to their cabin on the cruise ship. She wrote her way down the coast, across the ocean, through the islands, and on to Miami. What impressions she carried away from the cruise were formed by the postcards and curio shops. They sent tons of souvenirs home. She gained seven pounds on the trip.

They bought a three-bedroom house on the ocean, and every day for the first week they swam. Myrtle stepped on something that slithered under her foot, and she never went into the water again. Rich took up fishing and golf. He called his former associates once every three or four days, but the last call he made to Mr. Blakesley, he was told that the president was in conference and would call him back. He never did. Rich didn't call north again.

Myrtle joined several clubs and was happy with their activities. She went on a diet and bought new clothes in anticipation of the day she would be able to wear them. Rich canceled his golf appointments and bought a snorkel. He bought a small boat and sold it again when he learned that it was more trouble to launch and keep in repair than the pleasure he gained from it seemed worth. Kathleen left her husband and visited them for three weeks crying almost continuously. Jerry came to collect her and there was a noisy reunion and a reconciliation. They left together. Michael and Phyllis, his strange wife, visited them with their three children. Phyllis sniffed the ocean air through her long, straight nose and promptly started to sneeze and didn't stop again until they got to the airport to return to

Denver, her home town. She pronounced the ocean too big and smelly.

'In New York she got claustrophobia, out here it's the sneezes. I think she should see a head-shrinker,' Rich said after seeing them off.

'Rich, what's the matter with you? You never used to brood and worry about the kids. Not when they were home and you could have been some help to me. Not when they were young and I was the one who sat up night after night, and you were always off somewhere, and they were out too late. Why didn't you worry then when it might have done some good?'

He paced. 'Four times I gave Jerry Lister a job. Four times. Why does she always go back with him? You tell me, Myrtle. You're a woman, you know your daughter. Tell me, why?'

'When Michael broke his arm, where were you? Cleveland! You were in Cleveland.'

'If I could only understand this one crazy girl. I think he even hits her.'

'I'm going to the Women's Auxiliary. We're discussing the increase of filthy literature on newsstands this week, and what to do about it. What's the matter with you, you don't go to any of your clubs any more? For thirty years you were out three, four nights a week, this club, that club, this emergency. Now nothing. What's the matter?'

'We could go on a longer cruise ... You'd get writer's cramp.' He lighted a cigar and said suddenly, 'I'm going to get a job.'

'Job? What do you mean get a job?'

'I mean work. Honest work.'

'At your age? You're crazy. Who'd hire you now? For what? You just want to embarrass me.'

'Got nothing to do with you. I need a job.'

'Rich, have you been playing the market? You promised ...'

'We are not in trouble. The only time I ever played the market we came out forty thousand dollars to the good.'

'But I was scared silly all the time.' She looked at her watch and picked up her purse and gloves. 'Anyway, what kind of a job? Bank trustee? Adviser to a firm here?'

'God, I don't know. Just a job. After all, forty-five years of experience ...'

A horn sounded from the driveway and Myrtle hurried to the door. 'There's Lucille. I have to go, dear. Have a good evening. Back early.'

'... shouldn't be allowed to go to waste,' he finished to the empty room. His watch told him that it was March 14, 1970, 8:03 P.M.

On television there was a situation comedy, an action western, a game of some sort with people jumping up and down and hugging each other over a refrigerator that one or another of them had won, or had not won, but might. He turned it off. His watch told him that it was March 14, 1970, 8:13 P.M.

He walked on the beach for half an hour, then went to his library and picked up the volume of Mann that he was reading: *Joseph and His Brothers*. He was catching up on some of the things he hadn't had time for in the past. He read, and when he put the book down, his eyes tired, his watch told him it was March 14, 1970, 10:30 P.M. 'Never did give Jerry a chance to examine it,' he said aloud. 'Never did tell him how much it was worth. Eight hundred thirty-nine dollars and ninety-eight cents. Retail. Cost four hundred fifty-nine dollars to manufacture.' He rubbed a finger over the crystal, smearing it. He polished it to a gleaming surface with his handkerchief and then opened the case to look at the jeweled insides. 'Preset at the factory,' the advertisements read, 'You need never do a thing but wear and admire it. Never wind, never set, never worry about the time again.'

'Let time take care of itself,' Rich said, repeating the first advertising slogan that had heralded the new watch. He found the screw that reset the watch during its annual cleaning, and he turned it.

He closed the case hurriedly when he heard Myrtle's voice from the other room. Finally. He got up and walked toward the door, and his steps faltered, then stopped.

'Rich, aren't you ready yet? Come on, it's getting late.'

Myrtle was in front of him, climbing steps. She stopped, silhouetted against a closed door. Tall, statuesque, wide hips and narrow waist, full breasts. 'For heaven's sake, Rich, come on. Let me look at you.'

He backed down a step; she followed and touched his shoulder, brushing something from it. 'You look fine, dear. Come on now. Don't be nervous. After all, Mr. Blakesley must like you or he wouldn't have invited us over, now would he?' She turned again toward the door saying, 'It must be a promotion. Why else would he have us to tea?'

Rich looked down at himself: dressing gown, slippers. He felt his face, the heaviness at his jawline, the bushy eyebrows, and he turned to the glass door, using it as a mirror. White hair, lines, heavy glasses. He hadn't changed, was still Rich. But Myrtle?

'Myrtle,' he said choking, 'Look at me. What's happened?'

'I hear someone coming now. Don't forget, Rich, no language and don't eat as if you didn't get anything at home ... Here they come.'

'Myrtle, look at me! I'm not who you think ...'

'Mr. and Mrs. Weiss? This way, please.'

He tried to hang back, but Myrtle's hand was firm on his arm. The maid closed the door and walked before them. Rich looked about desperately, searching for someplace to hide, someplace to run to. He remembered the old house. Blakesley's first house, a handsome brownstone that had long since been torn down to make room for high-rise apartments.

'Ah, Richard.' Hanson Blakesley met them and took Rich's hand, squeezing it, pumping it vigorously. He was young, his hair dark, untouched by grey. 'How pleasant this is, don't you think? Away from those musty offices. And the charming Mrs. Weiss. Come in, my dear. Here, this is a comfortable chair. You know Mrs. Blakesley, don't you.'

Dianne Blakesley smiled at them wearily. She was pale and thin with great luminous eyes. Her hand that she held for Rich to kiss was limp.

He didn't touch the hand. She acted as if he had kissed it, and her eyes gazed into his with embarrassing candor.

'I don't know how to explain any of this,' he said, pointing to his clothes. 'Frankly ...'

'I know you are surprised at this offer, but I've been watching you closely this past year that you've been with us ...'

'What I mean is that either I'm dreaming, or else something really wonky has happened ...'

'And now, no more business. You can let me know in a few days ... Mrs. Weiss, you are looking even more lovely than usual. It was a boy, wasn't it?'

'Yes. William.'

'How nice. Is he a fat baby? Is he good?' Dianne Blakesley poured tea and smiled pleasantly.

'Look, you don't have to pretend that you don't notice anything. I mean that makes it even worse than it is. Myrtle, put down that cup and look at me. William is a grown man, older than Blakesley here even.'

'Our two girls are in Newport with their grandparents. When they return we must let the children get together.'

'God damn it! Look at me! I'm an old man. I retired from the company last winter. I'm sixty-five years old.'

'I predict that we'll expand year after year. These are fine workmen who've come over as immigrants from Germany. Clock-makers, fine detail workers ...'

'Myrtle, let's get out of here. They're crazy. Both of them ...'

'Mrs. Blakesley, they are beautiful children, both of them. Five and three? How wonderful ...' Myrtle handed the photographs to Rich. He dropped them.

'... and we'll be planning for new plants on the west coast in the next five or ten years. Diversify. That's the new word, Weiss. Spread out, cover the fields, as many of them as you can ...'

'Myrtle, I'm going. Right now. You can do as you please. I'm leaving.' Backing toward the door, he waited for a sign of understanding. They continued to make small talk, to smile at each other.

Myrtle stood up. 'Thank you so much for having us. We must be going. The baby, you know ...'

'Of course, my dear.' Dianne Blakesley didn't rise. She looked too frail to lift herself. Her eyes met Rich's again, and this time her eyelids drooped ever so slightly.

'No,' he said. 'You did that to me once and I was too young and green to know any better, but not again. Not with you.'

She smiled at him gently. 'Good-bye, Richard. I may call you Richard? I do hope that we'll all become very good friends.'

'Oh, no, not this time. You'll not see me again, Mrs. Blakesley. I'm turning down the job. I know what'll happen to me. Stuck in that same office for the next forty years. Not this time.'

Outside the house, waiting for a taxi, supplied by Blakesley, Myrtle squeezed his arm. 'I can't stand it,' she said. 'I can't wait to get out of sight of the house and kiss you. What would they think if I kissed you here on the street? Treasurer's assistant at your age, with no more experience than you have. I knew you would be a success, Rich. I knew it. I told Papa that you would.'

'God damn it, Myrtle! *Look at me!*'

'We'll move, of course. No more walk-ups. A first-floor apartment for now, and in a year or two, a house. Like this one. With an upstairs, and a maid to open the door ...'

The watch. It was to blame. He fingered it, trying to shake her loose from his arm so he could open the back and get to the mechanism that would reset it.

'... and a nurse for William.'

'And grandparents in Newport?' He had it opened now.

'We'll have to buy new clothes. Did you notice the lace on her blouse? Handmade, of course ...'

He turned the screw as far as it would go.

'... and Lucille said that if I would be willing to serve on the board for the coming year, she is certain that we can clean up this whole area ...'

'Clean up?' He looked about quickly. The living room on the beach.

'Of course, I'm not at all certain that she's right. I mean, this has been going on for so many years that I'm afraid it will take more than just one year to drive them all out entirely, but ...'

'Did you just get in?'

'... at least we can make a stab at it. Did you watch the news? I heard that the blizzard has become worse.'

'What? No. No, I was reading.'

'Well. I guess there's always a blizzard somewhere or other. I hope Kathleen has enough sense not to get out in it.'

Rich looked at the watch: 11:26. He opened it and turned the screw, very slowly and carefully, watching the hand until it was at 11:15. He looked up to see Myrtle coming through the doorway.

'It was such a good meeting, Rich. You wouldn't believe the stuff that's available on the stands right now, to say nothing of the films.' She moved past him, taking off her gloves. She went into the bedroom and came out with her slippers on. 'But the refreshments. Yii! German chocolate cake, at this time of night. I need something to settle my stomach. You want tea?'

'Kathleen called. She's pregnant.'

'You'd think they'd take into consideration that some of us aren't as young as we used to be. You know. German chocolate cake at this time of night.' Her voice faded as the kitchen door swung shut. She was back in a moment. 'But the most exciting thing. Lucille is taking the bit in her own two hands. Forming a committee, a board of responsible women ...' She moved toward the kitchen again.

'Jerry was killed in an automobile accident.'

'... and Lucille said that if I would be willing to serve on the board for the coming year, she is certain that we can clean up this whole area ...'

He turned the screw as far to the right as it would go.

'You'd think a woman who's almost forty would have enough sense not to get caught out in a blizzard, but I worry about her.' The teakettle whistled and she left again.

Very cautiously he reset the watch for two minutes in the past.

'... this time of night.' Her voice faded as the kitchen door swung shut. She was back in a moment. 'But the most exciting thing. Lucille is taking the bit in her own two hands. Forming a committee, a board of responsible women ...' She moved toward the kitchen again. He followed her and caught the doorknob and held it. He felt the pressure from the other side as she tried to turn the knob '... and Lucille said that if I would be willing to serve on the board for the coming year, she is certain that we can clean up this whole area ...' Her voice faded out, then sounded behind him stronger than before. She had gone out the other door, through the hallway and back into the living room.

'Of course, I'm not at all certain that she's right ...'

He turned the screw as far as it would go.

Rich heard her coming toward the door, and he moved to the living room and sat down. She followed with a tea tray.

'I thought you might change your mind,' she said. 'Honestly, I don't like to even think it, but I really believe that young snippet, Harry Lowenstein's wife, you know, the freckled girl all elbows and knees always uncovered almost up to her bottom, had the cake on purpose. At that age they can eat glass at midnight and sleep like angels.' She sipped steaming tea, then belched.

'I can do it,' Rich said. 'I can do it! I can change the past.'

'The way she smokes. And drinks, too, I hear, she'll get hers soon enough. Won't take another forty years either ...'

'I can go back and turn things around, undo things, do other things ...'

'You didn't hear *her* voting to clean the bookstores and the news-stands. Bet she reads every piece of trash that comes along. Wait until you see some of the stuff that's available. Lucille's bringing some of it over tomorrow.'

'Myrtle, will you listen to me for just one minute? Please?'

'Oh, yes. I almost forgot. We had this film, too. I never believed in such things before. Never heard of such a thing. I always thought when they talked about blue films, that it had to do with color photography. But it doesn't, Rich. Did you know that?'

'Myrtle, just shut up a minute. Try to understand what I'm telling you. I can go back and change the past. Alter it. Make it different.'

'We'll change things. You bet your little old shaving mug we will.' She fin-ished her tea and patted her stomach. 'There. That's better. Are you coming now?'

'Myrtle! Look at me. Can't you hear what I'm saying to you? I can change things. I can change things for Eric, give him another chance ...'

'Oh, Eric's all right, Rich. He wouldn't be mixed up with anything like this stuff. I mean, all young people aren't, you know, even if they don't work, and drop out of school, and play the guitar. He wouldn't do anything like this.'

'Myrtle, not another word. Don't say another word. Just shut up and listen to me for one minute. Will you please?'

'Why, Rich, is something wrong?'

'Listen, Myrtle. I can make things different. I can change things. I made you go around through the hall, and the first time, two times, you came through the door to the living room. I made you do something different. The past can be changed.'

She belched again. 'I wish you would do something about that second piece of cake, then. She pressed it on me deliberately, I'm sure.'

'Not your past. Just mine. I have to have been there.'

'Oh, that's too bad.' She went around him into the bedroom. 'I almost forgot. Lucille's husband will talk to you about a position with the hospital. They need an advisor, or something ...'

He went back to the living room and her voice faded out. In a moment she looked through the open door and said, 'Did you hear what I said?'

'I did change something. It can be done.'

'I told her you'd give him a call ...' As she moved about getting ready for bed her voice rose and fell '... no salary, naturally ...'

'Naturally,' he said, fingering the watch.

He walked around the living room, trying to think of another test. He stopped before the rogues' gallery: twenty or more pictures of the four children that covered one of the walls. Eric at twenty-one, handsome, laughing, a guitar on his legs. Kathleen in her sweet-sixteen party gown. Pretty, slim. William, forty, too much like his father to be handsome, but rugged-looking, capable. Michael. His hand stopped fingering the watch and he studied Michael's picture. He remembered exactly when and how Michael had met that strange girl. If he could change that ... He turned away. None of his business. And besides they had three children, his grandchildren.

His gaze fell on snapshots on an end table. Jerry Lister and Kathleen had taken them after their boisterous reunion. Jerry Lister.

He sat down and closed his eyes, trying to remember. Finally he turned the watch hands backward.

He looked about the room and nodded. Okay so far. He was in his robe and slippers, and Jerry Lister was there, red-faced, almost frozen, no more than twenty. And Kathleen, a slip of a girl of seventeen.

She said, 'Can we borrow your car? You know nothing will go wrong ...'

He turned the screw to the right. He had gone into it just about three minutes too late. He reset the watch and this time found himself seated, with the *Times* on his lap. He heard the record player from upstairs, and the television from the study, and he waited for the doorbell to ring. When it did he opened the door, admitting a frigid wind, barring a red-faced young man.

'Hi, I'm Jerry Lister. Is Kathleen home?'

'No. She is at her aunt's house. Good-bye.' The boy pushed past him and was inside before he could brace himself. He turned the screw to the right. Again.

The doorbell rang. He answered it grimly. The wind rushed in and the boy tried to squeeze by Rich, who stood firmly in the way.

'Hi, I'm Jerry Lister. Is Kathleen home?'

'No. Get lost.' He braced himself, but the wind blew stronger, and with it added to the weight of the boy who was also pushing now, he found that he couldn't shut the door.

'My car broke down. Water in the gas line froze, I think. Five or six blocks from here.' The boy had won – he was stronger than he looked. He panted slightly and handed his coat to Rich and walked past him to the living room, where he held his hands out to the fire. 'I heard on the radio that it's going down to twenty below tonight. Man, it's cold ...'

Rich turned the watch screw to the far right.

Another way. Meet him outside, before he got to the door. He reset the watch. In his robe and slippers he went out on the porch and met Jerry Lister coming up the walk.

'Just hold it right there, young man.' Jerry kept walking. Rich grabbed his arm and Jerry tried to move toward the house, not looking at him. Rich pushed him from the sidewalk. The boy hesitated momentarily, then darted behind Rich and trotted through the frozen grass to the porch. 'Like a goddam salmon,' Rich muttered. He reached out toward the boy, running also now, and his hand closed on the doorknob. He looked about. He was in the hallway ready to open the door. He didn't turn the knob, but stood with it in his hand. It turned. Before he could shoot the bolt into place, the door was pushed open and Jerry Lister stood before him, half frozen, panting.

'Hi, I'm Jerry ...'

'Oh, shut up!' Rich turned the screw.

He looked at the picture of Kathleen and Jerry taken here in his living room. Jerry was smiling broadly, and Kathleen was laughing. He had just told an obscene joke. 'One more time,' Rich said. 'I'll try one more time.' He reset the watch.

The doorbell rang and he opened the door, and when the red-faced boy stepped inside, he swung at him with all his strength. The boy ducked.

'Hi, I'm Jerry Lister ...'

He swung again, and this time his fist glanced off Jerry's chin. Jerry hit Rich once, just above his robe belt. Rich staggered back and caught the wall to steady himself.

'... Is Kathleen home?' The boy was taking off his coat. He held it out to Rich and walked past him to the living room. 'My car broke down ...'

'You're a bum. You'll always be a bum. "Water in the gas line froze, I think."'

'... Water in the gas line froze, I think.'

Rich left him still talking and waited at the stairs. Kathleen came running down and past him into the living room. 'You should see your face!'

'Kathleen, get back upstairs. You can't go out with this bum and he can't stay here and listen to records or watch television '

'Dad, have you met Jerry? My father, Mr. Weiss.'

'I said, get back upstairs. And tell Eric to turn off that goddamned record player! Where is your mother?'

'Can we borrow your car? You know nothing will go wrong with it.' Kathleen smiled prettily at him and he grabbed her shoulders and shook her.

'Will you listen to me! Tell him to go away.'

'Hey, you got a television? Let's do that, Kathleen ...'

'All right! All right! I tried. So do whatever it is you do and next week tell me that you want to get married and see if I care. You'll be sorry. Both of you!' He turned the watch screw to the right.

'I tried,' he said. 'By God, I tried.' He picked up the snap shot of the pair twenty years later, laughing, smiling, going nowhere, doing nothing, just laughing away their lives. Laughing, fighting, separating, going back together. 'I just don't know,' he said, and went to bed. Myrtle stirred restlessly throughout the night and he wondered if it was the German chocolate cake, or the dirty movies she'd seen.

'Have some more honey, dear. The biscuits are very good this morning. I have to remember to tell Hannah. I think she forgets to put in the soda sometimes ...'

'Myrtle, when was Eric home last time?'

'She never makes them the same way two days ... What, dear?'

He repeated the question.

'Oh, two years ago, wasn't it? Right after the Chicago mess. Do you like this tupelo honey, or do you like the wild honey better? I can't make up my mind.'

'Did you talk to him then?'

'Who?'

'Did you talk to Eric?'

'Of course.' She opened another biscuit and considered the two pitchers of honey.

'I don't mean just polite conversation, or mother-son fussing. Did you really talk to him?'

'You know that Lucille is bringing over those pictures at eleven? I told you, didn't I?' She looked up from the biscuit and said then, 'I'm sure we talked, dear.'

'Don't you remember?'

'You know how upset I was with him. What do you want to know?'

'I can't remember really talking to him. I wondered if you did.'

She became thoughtful for five seconds, then shrugged and said, 'I'm sure we talked.'

'Do you remember exactly when he came home, the day?'

'Let me think. He still had stitches, or were they out by then? It was snowing. I remember that he was tracking snow on the Aubusson. It must have been a few days before Christmas. He wasn't there for Christmas, I know. But he drank a lot of eggnog. I remember that I told him he was drinking too much eggnog ...'

Rich stood up. 'Okay, I thought you might know the exact day.' He went to the study and closed the door. He had made a list earlier, a list of his children and what they talked about. He had written by William's name: business, inanities. Kathleen: Jerry. Michael: Denver real estate, or the grandchildren. And by Eric's name he had been able to write down nothing at all. When Myrtle had become pregnant at forty, people had predicted either a moron or a genius. Always one or the other, they had said, when the mother gets to that age. He'd been the other. But what did Eric talk about? How could he have forgotten? His fingers rested on the watch, but he didn't turn it yet. He wanted to remember first, then go back.

He thought a long time before he could remember when they'd had the very brief conversation. The night before Eric left again. He had given him a Christmas present, a check. Later it had come back endorsed over to ... it was gone. Well, he could find the canceled check if he really wanted to know who Eric had given it to. That wasn't important now. Some charity, orphans, something like that. He tried several times before he got the time set for that night, and then when he returned to the present, he couldn't remember what they had talked about. He tried again.

'I will remember,' he said. He had a notebook out and when Eric spoke, he made notes.

'Of course you're not bad, I didn't mean to imply that you were. Or the others like you.'

Rich wrote: 'I'm not bad.'

'Have it your way, evil. But, you see what you do? You say if we're not evil, then we must be good. And I don't buy that.'

Rich was busy writing and made no response. After a moment Eric continued.

'People have always done it. You hear what you want to hear, see what it pleases you to see, and let the rest go by the board. When America went pragmatic, it took most of the world with it, but now the excluded parts are pulling their way. Pragmatism just isn't good enough.' He was talking too fast for Rich now. All he could do was make notes of key words and trust his memory to fill in. Or replay it over and over until he got it all.

'Dad, cut it out. You know I'm not a communist, or an anarchist. Not the way you mean that.' Had he called his son a communist? He scribbled faster.

'... keep right on playing. And we're not willing to any longer. But it won't just change. You have to do it yourself, scrap the part, create a new one and be ready to scrap it when it doesn't work, or doesn't mean anything any longer. And not just once a year, but every day, every minute, every second.'

Myrtle entered, carrying a tray of eggnog and cookies. 'Make him stay home, Rich. Tell him you'll give him a good job. How much would you want, Eric?'

'So long, Mother. Dad.'

Rich turned the watch to the present. Most of the conversation was already gone. He looked at the notes and the scattered words meant nothing to him: communist ... anarchy ... roles, playing games ...

Roles? Games? He shook his head and put the notebook down. He didn't understand. He heard Myrtle's voice from the other room and the door opened. 'Rich, Lucille's here. Did you want to see any of this material she brought along?'

'What? What material?'

'I told you. The stuff the club members picked up at various newsstands and bookstores.'

'Not right now. Later maybe.'

Had she told him? He couldn't remember. He supposed she must have. It was part of her role as the wife of a retired executive to take part now in citizens' groups for this or that cause. She would duly report to him anything of interest, and he would forget it, recognizing at some level that it was unimportant. When it was brought up, he would have to search for it, then remember vaguely, only to let it slip from consciousness as soon as she stopped talking about it. Dirty pictures. He laughed suddenly and went to the door and listened. They were in the next room. He could hear Myrtle's gasp, and a smothered scream. 'They sell things like that?' He returned to his chair.

At lunchtime he went into the living room, where Myrtle and Lucille had the photographs and magazines opened on the coffee table and spread over the couch. Hurriedly they began to gather them together when he opened the door.

'Hannah says lunch is ready,' he said.

'Don't look,' Myrtle said, her face flame-colored. Lucille had turned her back, but her neck was scarlet.

'Why? If they're for sale they can't be all that bad.'

'Just don't look now. I'll leave them for you,' Lucille said.

He watched them scramble to pick up the offensive material. He said, 'I don't think you ladies should spend hours poring over stuff like that.'

'When you consider that children can just walk in and buy it ...'

'I read that most of it's bought by men between twenty-three and thirty-five.'

'Ten-year-olds, fourteen-year-olds. Getting their impression of the world from this ... this ... filth.'

'And then going out and raping, torturing ...'

'Ten-year-olds? Besides I read that these provide an outlet for repressed people. Psychiatrists say that it actually helps them.'

'Spending lunch money on this filth, waiting to attack some lonely old woman who is helpless ...'

Rich looked from his wife to her friend. Very slowly he said, 'One, two, three, testing.'

Myrtle looked up at him. 'What did you say?'

'Nothing. Lunch is ready.'

'Yes, we're coming.'

He backed out and closed the door again.

He tried to turn the watch screw, but it was already as far as it would go to the right. He waited for them in the dining room, looking through the *Times*. He didn't read anything there.

Hannah came in and placed vichyssoise on the plates. Water beads formed on the iced bowls. Suddenly Rich became aware that she was talking to him.

'... so I'll bring her on Friday, and then you can get acquainted and not have a complete stranger around.'

'Who, Hannah? Who are you going to bring in?'

'My cousin. I told you, remember? She'll do for you and Mrs. Weiss while I'm gone.'

'You're leaving?'

'Mr. Weiss, don't you remember? My daughter's getting married and I have to go to Arizona for the wedding, help her get ready and all. I told you last week.'

'I guess I forgot. I'm sorry, Hannah.'

Lucille swept into the room then, followed by Myrtle, who looked at Rich guiltily. When he met her gaze, she blushed. 'I was thinking,' he said, seating them, 'what a curious thing memory is. Kids have such a different set of memories than their parents. We forget the unconnected things that to them were very important. Things they remember. We remember other things that were important to us and meant nothing to them.'

There was an uneasy silence and the two women spooned soup. Rich tasted his and then put his spoon down. 'So there are all those different sets of memories floating around, and no one to say which set is right, if any of them are ... Maybe there is no one single past.'

'That's why we study history and keep diaries, records. I mean, you just can't trust your own memory even,' Lucille said. She had been a history teacher in the thirties.

'I don't mean only big things that can be checked in books. I mean little things that you might forget within minutes, or seconds even.'

'Like what?'

'Oh, like turning your back on someone and not knowing what he had on, or what color his eyes are. Little things. Like forgetting what someone said to you on a bus, or in an elevator; like forgetting who was in the elevator with you, although at the time you knew.'

'But they don't mean anything to you. Why should you remember anything that has no meaning in your life? You are busy with your own thoughts at those times. You just answer people automatically.'

'That's what I mean. And you live ninety percent of your life automatically, without remembering anything about it.'

'Rich, what's got into you?' Myrtle glanced nervously at Lucille, then back to her husband. She touched the bell for Hannah. 'Dear,' she said to Lucille, 'are you going to show those films to the Eastern Star committee on Friday night? Perhaps I could help you, if you need help ...'

'Fine. I really could use a hand. I'll pick you up ...'

Hannah brought in cheese soufflé and cleared away the soup bowls.

'I almost forgot,' Rich said. 'There's a call that I have to make. If you'll excuse me.'

'Rich? Who to? Why now?'

'I'll be right back,' he said and went into the study. He kicked at the door as he passed it, but he saw when he picked up the telephone that it hadn't closed. He shrugged.

'Operator, I want to call Eric Weiss at this number. If he isn't there, leave your operator's number for him to return the call, will you?'

'Rich, are you calling Eric? Why?' Myrtle stood in the open doorway.

'Go back to lunch, dear. I'll be with you in a minute.'

She left the door and sat down again.

He could hear her say to Lucille, 'Of course he isn't calling Eric. We haven't heard from him since he left the last time. Nothing in two years. You'd think he'd have a little more consideration for his mother, but not Eric ...'

'Hello. Eric? ... Yeah, it's me. I remembered that you said you could be reached here if there was an emergency. Listen, Eric, I think I have found out something. I have this watch, the company gave it to me, and I can turn to the past. But nothing changes. Is that what you were trying to tell me? Today, suddenly, it was like living in the past. No matter what I said, they heard something else, just like the time you said I couldn't hear you. Is that what you meant?'

Myrtle smiled toward the door and had more soufflé. He could see her clearly, could hear her voice and Lucille's, but not the words.

'Hello? Eric ... No. No, don't tell him. I'll call him back ... sometime.' He looked at the phone, puzzled, and slowly hung it up. 'Eric wasn't in,' he said, too low for the women to hear. 'That was his roommate.' He started to go back to his chair in the dining room.

'I think that's exactly right,' Myrtle was saying. 'Show all of it to as many organizations as we can, and then mobilize ...'

'I could have sworn it was Eric,' Rich said, picking up his napkin again.

'Probably a few PTAs at some point ...'

'But wouldn't that be a mixed group? I mean ...' Myrtle gulped some of her water.

'I just wanted to hear Eric's voice, so I did,' Rich said.

'Well, sooner or later we'll have to. After all, it is the children we're concerned about.'

'I know. I didn't mean … Yes, of course, PTA groups …'

Hannah brought in chocolate éclairs and coffee. Rich watched the women eating the pastries. 'Six hundred calories at least,' he said. They didn't hear him. Lucille was talking about the plans she had made for the coming weeks. He looked past them, not listening to their words at all. 'Ever since Eric was born,' he said softly. 'Twenty-seven years now. Never lost an ounce after he was born, just got fatter and fatter. Why?' Retaliation?

He left them still talking avidly, and he was certain that neither of them noticed when he left. He wandered to the yard and trimmed the roses. He talked to the bushes as he cut them back.

'We are making up our life stories as we go,' he said. 'That's why there's no future yet, why the watch turns to now and stops.' He touched a tight green bud. Black spot. He'd have to spray. He pruned and the women came out and left in Lucille's car. He didn't know where they were going, although probably Myrtle had told him. She never went anywhere without telling him. He finished the roses and went back inside. They had left the magazines and pictures for him in his study. He pushed the heap to one side of the couch and sat down at the other end. Two old women poring over dirty pictures. He sighed.

Hannah brought in the mail and he looked through it, stopping at a letter from Kathleen. The envelope looked as if she had wiped a breakfast table with it. He ripped it open and took off his glasses to read the tiny, almost illegible script.

'Hold on to your hats. We're going to France, and God only knows where else after that. Jerry heard this fellow talking in a bar about the ship needing a bartender, and he went right down and got the job and got one for me to boot, in the nursery, so we're off next Tuesday.' Rich put it down and lighted a cigar. 'That bum,' he said through the smoke. 'That rotten bum. Bartender! By God, Myrtle will have a heart attack.' He picked up the letter to finish reading it, but suddenly he started to laugh. 'Bartender! Nursery helper!'

'What do you mean, you envy them?' Myrtle screamed at him that night. 'Envy them! They're crazy, the both of them!'

'They're alive. They're keeping each other alive and conscious all the time.'

'You're as crazy as they are.'

'I'm waking up, after sixty-five years of dozing away my life. I'm waking up!'

'We just won't mention it to anyone. If anyone asks, we'll just say that they're abroad. That's all.'

'It's a good feeling, Myrtle. Good. Going back to the past like I've been doing made me see it for the first time. How we always did what seemed expected. Not what we wanted, or what we should have done, only what was expected. Who did we think we were pleasing by acting all the time?'

'Lucille will know something's wrong. That bitch. She'll pry and pry.'

'That's why we've hated him all these years. We knew he wasn't putting on an act. That scared us. We never knew what to expect out of him because he wasn't acting, wasn't even in the same play.'

'I just won't mention Kathleen. She won't think to bring it up unless I give her a clue.'

'Ninety percent of our lives gone. Just gone. Blanked out completely. High spots and low spots. Memories of high spots and low spots, and that's it.'

'And William. Have they told him yet? Of course. Jerry never would keep his mouth shut about any of his nonsense. William won't talk. He knows about these things ...'

'Of course, I can have it all back now that I've got the watch ...'

'You and that watch! That's all you think about. What about this mess? What are we going to do? William could become vice-president within the next five years, but now ... What a scandal for him to have to live down. His sister working in a nursery, his brother a bartender.'

'Myrtle, shut up. Just shut up.' She did, staring at him wide-eyed. 'Now, just try not to react like this. Try a different set of reactions. Laugh, dammit. It's funny.'

She shook her head and took a backward step. 'You're crazy!'

'No, not that. That's standard reaction. Dance! Or ... throw something. Break something nice, something that you like. The way Kathleen does when she gets mad. Try it ...'

She shook her head wordlessly. She looked frightened.

'Can you remember anything about yesterday? Say, at three in the afternoon, where were you, what were you doing?'

'I ...' She shook her head again. 'I don't know.'

'And don't you see that your whole life is like that? A blank?'

'I'm going to bed. I have a terrible headache.' She backed to the door and when he didn't try to stop her, she said, 'You just don't know how hard this day has been, how busy I've been, and then to get news like that ... You just don't understand. And tomorrow is going to be even busier, and then on Friday we have the films to show to the Eastern Star girls, and I have to help Lucille ...'

'And you will live in your world, and I'll live in mine, and now and then when something happens that rocks both of them we'll see each other, and maybe even hear each other, but most of the time we won't.'

'And, Lucille's husband wants to know if you can come to his office next Wednesday. For the interview for the trustee's position, or whatever it was that he said he had.'

'Someday, when Eric comes home for a visit, I'll talk to him about this. I think he might understand what I'm saying. Not about the watch. He'd say that it was a focus for my attention, that's all. A focal point to let me examine myself ...'

'You didn't tell Hannah anything about Kathleen and Jerry, did you?' He didn't answer, and she continued as if he had. 'That's good. I think Lucille's girl, Tully, pumps her without mercy. Nothing would be a secret long, once Hannah ...'

THE RED CANARY

Sometimes the baby played with old blocks that Tillich had found. The blocks were worn almost smooth, so that the letters and numbers were hard to read. You had to turn them this way and that, catch the light just right. The corners were rounded; there was no paint on them. Tillich remembered blocks like them. He thought the old worn ones were much nicer than the shiny sharp-cornered new ones had been. He never watched the baby play, actually. He would see it on the floor, with the blocks at hand, and he would busy himself somewhere else, because there was the possibility that the baby's movements with the blocks were completely random. In Tillich's mind was an image of the baby playing with blocks. He was afraid of shattering the image.

There had been another image. The baby sleeping peacefully, on its side after its morning bottle; its forefinger and index finger in its mouth. Tillich glanced at it each morning before leaving for work, in case it had wiggled out from its covers, or was under them completely. Always, in the dim dawn light the baby's sleep had been peaceful and Tillich had left quietly. One morning, for no reason, Tillich had entered the room, had gone to the other side of the bed to look at the infant. It wasn't asleep. It was staring, not moving, hardly even blinking, just staring at nothing at all, the two fingers in its mouth. It shifted its gaze to Tillich and stared up at him in an unfathomable look that was uncanny, eerie, inhuman, and somehow evil. Tillich backed away, out of its line of sight. At the partition that separated that end of the bedroom from the rest of it, he paused to look back. The baby looked asleep, unmoving, peacefully asleep.

'Tillich,' he said at the dispensary. 'Norma Tillich.' The dispensary nurse read the card he handed her. 'Any change? Does she need an appointment?'

'No. No change.'

'Two a day, morning and night. Fourteen capsules. Please verify fourteen and sign at the bottom.'

He hated the young woman on duty in the dispensary. If he could get there during his lunch break, she wouldn't be on duty. He never could make it until after work, however. She had a large, bony face. Her hands were large; strong fingers flicking out capsules, pills, moving deftly, sure of themselves. No need to verify the count when she was on duty. The computer card went back into the machine. He moved on. The line was always there, might always have been the same people in the same order. He hurried home. She would be hungry. The baby would be hungry and crying.

'Good morning, Mr. Rosenfeld.'

'Good morning, Mr. Tillich. You are well, I trust?'

'Quite well, thanks.' He poured boiling water over the soup powder, spread two large crackers with Pro-team and put them on the tray. He filled Mr. Rosenfeld's water pitcher and got some fresh cups out and put them on the bed stand. 'Anything else, Mr. Rosenfeld?'

'No. No. That'll do me. Thank you kindly.'

'You're welcome. I'll just drop in this evening.'

'Not if you're busy, my friend.'

'No trouble. Have a good day, Mr. Rosenfeld.'

The old man nodded. He was eyeing his tray, impatient for his breakfast, too polite to begin until Tillich was gone.

The baby was always wet and usually soiled as well when he got home. Tillich changed it and put it in its bed with its bottle propped by it. Its color was greyed yellow.

'Norma, did he eat anything today?'

She looked vague. Then her face folded in somehow and collapsed in tears. 'I don't know. I can't remember. You left the formula, didn't you? Did you forget its formula?'

'I didn't forget. The bottle's gone. You must have put it in the disposer. Did he take the milk?'

She wept for another minute or two, then jumped up, peeking at him between her ringers. She sang, '*I had a red canary. He couldn't sing. I left the window open and he flew away.* Would that be a bad thing to do? Let it fly away, I mean.'

'No, that wouldn't be bad.'

'Because I would. And I'd watch him fly away. Fly away. Fly away.'

Sometimes she brought him her brush. 'Would you like to do my hair?' It was long and silky when it was clean and brushed, alive with red-gold high-lights in the dark blond. Her eyes were blue, sometimes green, her skin very pale and translucent. Blue veins made ragged ray patterns on her breasts, which were rounded, firm, exciting to him. She had nursed the baby for months. One day she hadn't, then another and another. It took days and days for her milk to stop, and all the while it seemed to puzzle her. She would come and show him her wet clothes, or drying milk on the bedding, on her belly. When he tried to put the baby to her breast again, she recoiled as if terrified. He awakened one night to find her kneeling over him trying to force the nipple between his lips. There was a taste of sweet milk on his mouth.

Mrs. de Vries lived on the same floor; he met her often. She usually had a child by the hand when they met. She was very thin and tired-looking.

When he opened the door to an insistent knock, she was there.

'Mr. Tillich, will you please come? Please. I need someone.'

He glanced back inside, Norma hadn't even looked up. She was watching the TV with a rapt expression. He hesitated a second, then stepped out into the hall, closing the door behind him. 'What's wrong?'

'One of the kids. God, I don't know.' She hurried him down the hall to her apartment. A girl about ten stood in the doorway. He had seen her before in the hall, down in the lobby. She had always seemed normal enough. She held the door open and moved aside as they came near.

Mrs. de Vries pushed Tillich past the girl, through the living room to a bedroom that had mattresses all over the floor. Two more children stared at him, then he saw the other child, alone on a mattress that was against the wall. The child, a boy, four, five, was having a convulsion. His back was arched, his tongue protruded between clamped jaws, blood and foam on his chin. He was already cyanotic.

Tillich turned to the woman. 'Don't you have any medicine for him?'

'No. He never did this before. My God, what is it?'

'Call Pediatrics, Emergency.' She stared. 'Do you have a phone?'

'No.'

'I'll go. What's his name? Symptoms?'

'Roald de Vries. Fever a hundred and four, all day.'

He called Pediatrics, Emergency. 'I'm sorry. We are already over capacity. Please leave patient's identification number, name, and reason for calling. Take patient to nearest hospital facility at eight A.M. Thank you. This is a recording.'

He didn't have the number.

'I'll stay here,' he told Mrs. de Vries. 'Call them back and give his file number. Or they won't see him tomorrow.'

The oldest child was the girl he had seen before. Waiting for her mother to return, he saw the welts on her arms, her neck. She seemed to have conjunctivitis. The next two children, boys about six and five, were very thin, and the larger of the two peed on the floor. The girl cleaned it up soundlessly. There were two bedrooms. A man slept in the other one. He had the dry, colorless skin of long illness; his sleep was unnatural. He was heavily sedated. Tillich looked at the ill child. His body was limp now and dripping sweat. The woman came back and he left. He saw her again a week later. Neither of them mentioned the child.

Tillich brought in the trains in section 3B. He picked them up fifty miles from the city, each one a brilliant speck of white or green light. His fingers knew the keys that opened and closed switches, that stopped one of the lights, hurried another. It was like weaving a complex spider web with luminous spiders.

He worked three hours, had a twenty-minute break, worked three more hours, had forty minutes for lunch, then the last three hours. He worked six days a week. He compared his work with a friend, Frank Jorgens, and both agreed it was harder than the air-traffic control job that Jorgens had.

'I have to have a raise,' Tillich said to the union representative.

'You know better than that, Tillich. We don't ask for a raise for just one guy and his problems. Every sod has them.'

He tried to apply directly to the personnel department; his application was rejected, accompanied by a notice that he could appeal through his union representative. He threw the application and the notice away.

'Tillich, Norma Tillich.'

'Any change? Does she require an appointment?'

'Yes, we need to see her doctor.'

'Please take your card and this form to one of the tables and fill it out. When you have completed it, return it to one of the attendants in Section Four-N. Thank you.' The young woman looked at him directly, he frowned with disapproval.

Name. Age. Copy code from Line 3 of patient's identity card. Copy code from Lines 7, 8, 9 … Reasons for request to see physicians. Check one. If none apply, use back of application to state reason.

He rubbed his eyes. He should have written it out at home so he could simply copy it here. *She can't take care of the child. She neglects it. She doesn't eat or feed the baby, or keep it clean. It might injure itself. Or she might.* He read it dissatisfied. It was true, but not enough. He added only: *injure herself.*

'Thank you, Mr. Tillich. You will be notified next week when you come back. Report to this desk at that time. Fourteen capsules. Will you please verify the count and sign here.'

His request was turned down. There was a typed message attached to her card. Tillick (they had misspelled the name), Norma. Non-aggressive. A series of dates and numbers followed. The times she had seen doctors, their diagnoses and instructions, all unintelligible to Tillich. Request denied on grounds of insufficient symptomatic variation from prognosis of 6-19-87-A-D-P/S-4298-Mc.

'Fourteen capsules. Verify count, please, and sign here.'

The baby learned a new cry. It started high, wailed with increasing volume until it hit a note that made Tillich's head hurt. Then it cut it off abruptly and gasped a time or two and started over.

'You have to feed it while I'm gone,' he said. 'You can hold its bottle. Remember. Like this.'

She wasn't watching. She was looking beyond him, past the baby, smiling at what she saw between herself and the streaked blue wall. He looked at the child, who was taking formula greedily, staring at him in its non-blinking way. Tillich closed his eyes.

After the baby was through, Tillich made their dinner. Tastimeat, potatoes, soy-veg melange. She ate as greedily as the baby.

'Norma, while I'm at work you could eat some of the crackers I bought for you. The baby could chew on one. Remember them, Norma?'

She nodded brightly. The baby started to wail. She seemed not to hear it. While he cleaned up the dishes she watched TV. The baby wailed. Its next clinic appointment was in two months. He wondered if it would wail for the whole eight weeks, fifty-nine nights. He broke a plate, each hand gripping an edge painfully. He stared at the pieces. They were supposed to be unbreakable.

The baby wailed until twelve, when he fed it again. Gradually it quieted down after that, and by one it seemed to be sleeping. He didn't go past the partition to see.

Norma was waiting for him on their bed. Her cheeks were flushed, her nipples hard and dark red. He started to undress and she pulled at his clothes, laughing, stopping to nip his flesh on his stomach, his buttock when he turned around, his thigh. She crowed in delight at his erection, and he fell on her in savage coitus. She cried out, screamed, raked his back, bit his lip until it bled. She clung to him and tried to push him away. She called him names and cursed to him and whispered love words and gutter words. When it was over, she rolled from him, felt the edge of the bed and crept from it, staring at him in horror, or hatred. Or a combination. She backed to the door, crouching, ready to bolt. At the doorway she shrieked like a wild animal mortally wounded. Again and again she screamed. He buried his head in the bedding. Presently she became silent and he took a cover from the bed and put it over her on the couch, where she slept very deeply. He knew he could pick her up, carry her to bed, she wouldn't wake up. But all he did was cover her. He looked at the baby. It hadn't moved. He shivered and went to bed.

'Fourteen capsules. Verify fourteen, please, and sign ...'

'There are only thirteen.'

The long capable fingers stopped. Tillich looked up. She returned his glance with no expression, then looked again at the pale green capsules. Her fingers moved deliberately as she counted, '... twelve. Thirteen.' She pushed another one across the counter. 'Fourteen. Please verify fourteen, Mr. Tillich.' Again she met his gaze. Her eyes were grey, her eyelashes were very long and straight.

'Fourteen,' he said and signed, and moved on.

The baby hated the park. It wailed and wouldn't be propped up. Tillich picked it up and for a time it was silent, staring at the bushes. Children were swinging, shouting, laughing, screaming. The spring sun was warm although the air still had a bite. Forsythias were in bloom, yellow arms waving. The baby stared at the long yellow branches. Soon it grew bored and started to cry again.

'I'm cold.' Norma clung to his arm, her gaze shifting nervously, rapidly, very afraid. 'I want to go home.'

'You need some sun. So does the baby. Let's walk. You'll get warm.'

He put the screaming child back in the baby carriage. The carriage was older than Tillich was; it squeaked, one wheel wobbled, the metal parts were all rusty, the plastic brittle and cracked. He knew they were very lucky to have it.

He wheeled the yelling baby and Norma clung to his arm. No one paid any attention to them. 'I'm cold. I want to go home!' Soon, she would be crying too. He walked a little faster.

'We'll go home now. This is the way.' He didn't look at the people. The trees were leafing out, bushes in nearly full leaf, blooming. The grass was richly green. White clouds against the endless blue. He took a deep breath and closed his eyes a moment. For four weekends they hadn't been able to get out because of rain, or cold weather, or Norma's sniffles. Always something.

'I want to go home! I want to go home! I'm tired. I'm cold. *I want to go home.*' She was beginning to weep.

'We're going home now. See? There's the street. Just another block, then onto the street and a little more ...' She wasn't listening. The baby screamed.

He saw the girl from the dispensary. She was wheeling a chair-bed, with a very old, frail-looking man on it. His face was petulant, half turned, tilted toward her, talking. She was walking slowly, looking at the trees, the flowering shrubs, the grass. A serene look was on her face.

Tillich turned the carriage to a path that led out of the park. The baby screamed. Norma wept and begged to be taken home.

Mrs. de Vries was in the hall outside his apartment. He thought she had been waiting for him.

'Mr. Tillich, is your wife better? Such a pretty girl.'

'Yes, yes. She's coming along.'

'I heard her screaming. Couple nights ago. Poor child.'

He started to move on. She caught his arm. 'Mr. Tillich, I'm only thirty-three. Would you believe that? Thirty-three.' She looked fifty. Her fingers on his arm were red and coarse. 'I ... You need a woman, Mr. Tillich, I'm around. Wouldn't charge you much.'

'No. Mrs. de Vries, I have to go in. No. I'm not interested.'

'What am I to do, Mr. Tillich? What? They won't give us more money. I have two jobs and my kids are in rags. What'm I to do?'

'I don't know.' He moved forward a step.

She motioned and her daughter approached. 'She's a virgin, Mr. Tillich. Been having periods for six months now. All growed up inside. Five dollars, Mr. Tillich. Five dollars and you can keep her all night.' She motioned the child closer. The girl pulled up her shift. Pale fuzz covered the mound. She turned around to show her round buttocks. They were covered with hives.

Tillich pushed Mrs. de Vries aside. 'Bitch! Bitch! Your own daughter!'

'What'm I to do, you bastard? You tell me that. What'm I to do?' He saw her yank the child to her and slap her hard. 'Go get some pants on. Pull down your dress.'

Tillich got his door open and slid inside. He was breathing hard. Norma didn't look up. She was watching TV. The baby was on the floor with the smooth blocks.

'Mr. Rosenfeld, don't you have any relatives?'

'None able. Brother's been in a house for twenty years.'

'No children?'

'Son's dead. Cancer of the larynx. They didn't have a bed for him. He had to wait almost two years. By then it was Katie-bar-the-door.' He looked thoughtful. 'Two daughters, you know. Don't know where they are. Their husbands won't let them come around. First one shows up, state says I'm hers.' He chuckled.

'Mr. Rosenfeld, don't you read the newspapers?'

'Watch it on TV.'

'They miss some things, Mr. Rosenfeld. Starting next month there won't be any visiting-nurse service. Too expensive. Not enough nurses.'

Mr. Rosenfeld looked frightened. After a moment he said, 'Not the necessary visits.'

'All of them, Mr. Rosenfeld.'

'But ... Look, son, I've got a tube in me that has to be changed every last day. Y'know? Every day. Takes someone who knows how. Good clean tubes. Dressings. Who's going to do all that except a nurse?' He picked at his sheet. 'And change that? And give me a bath? Who?'

They stared at each other.

'Not you. Not you. I didn't mean that,' Mr. Rosenfeld said. 'You've been good to me. But you're not qualified for the tube job. Takes special training.' He was paralyzed from the waist down.

'You'd better apply for a home,' Tillich said finally.

'Did. Four years ago. I'm on the list.'

'Well,' Tillich said, 'I have to go. I'll be by in the morning.'

'Sure. Sure. Goodnight. Goodnight.' Before Tillich got out he asked, 'Your wife? I guess she wouldn't be able to have the training?'

'No. She's ill. Impossible.'

'Oh, yes. Of course.' He was staring fixedly at the ceiling when Tillich left.

'Do you walk here often?'

'When I can. That isn't very often.' She looked at him. 'How about you?'

'Not often enough. Not enough time.'

'I've seen you a few times. Your wife is very pretty.'

He didn't reply. There was nothing he could say. They were getting near the exit path that he would take. 'Do you suppose you'll have time tomorrow to take a walk?'

She was silent so long he thought she hadn't heard. Then: 'I think I will tomorrow.'

'Maybe we'll see each other. I always come in at path number one-oh-two.'

'That's near where I enter. Ninety-six.'

'I'll wait for you at ninety-six.'

She crouched in the doorway staring at him and shrieked. She didn't close her eyes while she screamed. He could see her stomach muscles tighten, her hands clench, then the shriek came. There was a glistening streak across her white thigh. Her legs were beautifully shaped. She shrieked. He pulled the cover over his head, pressing it against his ears. Twice or three times he had tried to comfort her, to quiet her, and it had been worse. He pressed harder on the covers. When she fell asleep on the couch, he covered her. She was thinner than she had been in the winter.

'Please verify fourteen ...'

'You weren't in the park all week.'

'Please sign. I was busy.'

'When do you get off? I'll wait for you.'

'Ten. Your wife and child. They need you. Who will make their dinner? Please, you must sign the forms and move on. Don't wait for me. I don't want to see you. I'm busy.'

He signed and moved on.

The waiting room of the pediatrics center was an auditorium with all the sections filled to capacity. Tillich had to stand with the baby for half an hour before there was a vacant seat. The din in the hall was constant, very much like the sound of a high-powered motor. The loudspeaker was on steadily: 'UN-3742-A-112.' – 'UN-2297-A / C-797.' – 'UN-1296-A / F-17.' – 'UN-3916-D-2000.'

The smells of formula, vomit, urine, feces hung in the air, combining and recombining to make smells unnamed as yet, but much more repellent than any of them singly. The baby's screams were hardly noticeable here.

'Please refresh your memory regarding your child's identification number. You will be admitted to the doctors' examination rooms by number. Please refresh your memory regarding your child's identification number.' – 'UN-694-A/D-4921.' – 'UN-7129-A/F-1968.'

He had to wait nine hours before he heard their number. He started; he had dozed; holding a screaming baby in the stinking auditorium amidst the bathroom and sickroom odors, he had dozed.

'Please strip the child and place it on the table. Keep on the far side of the table. Do not ask any questions, or give any medical details at this time. Thank you.' It was a recording, activated by the closing of the door.

Tillich had barely finished undressing the baby when the second door opened and a woman came in. She was stooped, white-haired, with a death's-head face. The baby was screaming more feebly now, exhaustion finally weakening him. He was revived by her approach.

She held him with one hand and did a rapid and thorough eye, ears, nose, and throat examination. She went to his genitals, studied his feet. She pushed his legs up to his chest, then spread them apart. She sat him up and felt his back, then tried unsuccessfully to stand him up. Finally she made notations on his card. Only then did she glance at Tillich.

'We must make other tests. You will wait outside, please.' She pressed a button. The door she had used was opened and an orderly motioned for Tillich to follow him.

'Why? What's wrong? What is it?'

The orderly touched his arm and wearily Tillich followed him. The baby wailed. This waiting room was even more crowded than the auditorium had been, but there was only a scattering of children; most of them were somewhere inside undergoing specialized diagnostic procedures. His head ached and he was very hungry. He didn't know how long he waited this time. Finally the orderly motioned for him to come.

'Please dress your child as quickly as possible and exit through the door marked B. An attendant on the other side will be happy to answer any questions. The time for your next appointment is indicated in the upper right-hand corner of your child's identification card. Thank you for your cooperation.'

He carried the baby into the other room. The baby was listless now, no longer crying. Overhead a light sign flashed on and off: 'If you have any questions, please be seated at one of the desks.' He sat down.

'Yes, Mr. Tillich?' It was a young man, an orderly, or nurse, not a doctor.

'Why has his classification been changed? What does the new number and designation mean? Why is his next appointment a year from now instead of six months?'

'Hm. Out of infant category, you see. There will be medication. You can pick it up at Pediatrics dispensary, a month's supply at a time, starting tomorrow. Twenty-three allergens identified in his blood. Anemic. Nothing to be alarmed about, Mr. Tillich.'

'What does the "R/M.D. 19427" stand for? He's retarded, isn't he? How much?'

'Mr. Tillich, you'll have to discuss that with his doctor.'

'Tell me this, would you expect a P/S 4298-MC to be able to care adequately for an R/M.D. 19427?'

'Of course not. But you're not ...'

'His mother is.'

'Why did you decide to come, after all?'

'I don't know. I guess because you look so miserable. Lonely, somehow.' She stopped, looking straight ahead. A young couple walked hand in hand. 'You do see people like that now and then,' she said. 'It gives me hope.'

'It shouldn't. Norma was twenty-two before she ... She was as normal as anyone at that age.'

She started to walk again.

'What's your name?'

'Louisa. Yours?'

'David,' he said. 'Louisa is pretty. It's like a soft wind in high grass.'

'You're a romantic.' She thought a moment. 'David goes back to the beginning of names, it seems. Bible name. Do you suppose people are still making new names?'

'Probably. Why?'

'I used to try to make up a name. They all sounded so ridiculous. So made up.' He laughed.

'You turn off here, don't you? Good-bye, David.'

'Tomorrow?'

'Yes.'

Norma slept. The baby lay quietly; he didn't know if it was asleep. He remembered laughing in the park. The sun shone. They walked not touching, talking fast, looking at each other often. And he had laughed out loud.

'No one came,' Mr. Rosenfeld said. His voice rose. 'No one came. They know I need a nurse. It's on my card. I signed over my pension so they'd take care of me. They agreed.'

'Can I do something?'

'No!' he said shrilly. 'Don't touch it. You know how long I'd last if an infection set in? Call them. Give them the numbers on my card. It's a mistake. A mistake.'

Tillich copied the numbers, then went out to make the call. The first phone was out of order. He walked five blocks to the next one. Traffic was light. It was getting lighter all the time. He could remember when the streets had been packed solid, curb to curb, with automobiles, trucks, buses, motorbikes. Now there were half a dozen vehicles of all kinds in sight. He waited for the call to be completed, staring toward the west. One day he'd make up a little back pack, not much, a blanket, a cup, a pan maybe, a coat. He'd start walking westward. Across Ohio, across the prairies, across the mountains.

To the sea. The Atlantic was less than five hundred miles east, but he never even considered starting in that direction.

'Please state patient's surname, given name, identification number, and purpose of this call.'

He did. There was a pause, then the same voice said, 'This data has been forwarded to the appropriate office. You will be notified. Thank you for your cooperation. This is a recording.' So no one would argue, he knew. He stood staring westward for a long time, and when he got back to his building, he went directly to his own rooms.

'And so he died.'

'He didn't just die. They killed him. *I* killed him. They were smart. They saw to it that he had a full week's supply of those pills. He took them all.'

'I guess most of them had saved enough pills or capsules, same thing.'

'So now they can claim truthfully that everyone who needs home nursing gets it.' He kicked a stone hard.

She walked with her head bowed. 'If they had known about you, your daily visits with the old man, probably they would have discontinued his nursing service sooner.'

'But I'm not trained to insert a drainage tube.'

'You learn or you lose whoever needs that kind of care.'

He looked at her. She sounded bitter, the first time he had heard that tone from her. 'You had something like that?'

'My husband. He needed constant attendance after surgery. On the sixth night I fell asleep and he hemorrhaged to death. I had learned how to change dressings, tubes, everything. And I fell asleep.'

He caught her hand and held it for a moment between both of his. When they started to walk again, he kept holding her hand.

'When I get well, we'll have a vacation, won't we? We'll go to the shore and find pretty shells. Just us. You and me. Won't we?'

'Yes. That would be nice.'

'Will they hurt me?'

'No. You remember. They'll look at your throat, listen to your heart. Weigh you. Take your blood pressure. It won't hurt.' He held the baby because he hadn't dared leave it. They might be there all day. The baby cried very little now. It slept a lot more than it used to and when it was awake it didn't do anything except suck its fingers and stare fixedly at whatever its gaze happened to focus on. Tillich thought he should cut down on the medicine for it, but he liked it better like this. He didn't know what the medicine was for, if this effect was the expected one or not.

'You'll stay with me! Promise!'

'If I can.'

'Let's go home now.' She jumped up, smiling brightly at him.

'Sit down, Norma. We have to wait.' The waiting room held over a hundred people. More were in the corridor. In this section few of the patients were alone. Many of them looked normal, able, healthy. Almost all had someone nearby who watched closely, who made an obvious effort to remain calm, tolerant, not to excite the patients.

'I'm hungry. I feel so sick. I really feel sick. We should go now.' She stood up again. 'I'll go alone.'

He sighed, but didn't reply. The baby stared at his shirt. He shifted it. One eye had crossed that way. She went a few feet, walking sideways, through the chairs. She stopped and looked to see if he was coming.

'Don't shriek,' he prayed silently. 'Please don't shriek.'

She took several more steps. Stopped. He could tell when the rush of panic hit her by the way she stiffened. She came back to him, terrified, her face a grey-white.

'I want to go. I want to ...'

Over and over and over. Not loud, hardly more than a whisper. Until her number was called. They didn't admit him with her. He had known they wouldn't. She could undress and dress herself.

The trains came in from Chicago; from N.Y.; from Atlanta. Fruit from the south. Meat from the west. Clothing from the east. A virulent strain of influenza from the southwest. Tillich had guided it in.

'Cleanliness and rest, nature's best protection.' The signs appeared overnight.

'If it gets worse,' the superintendent said, 'we'll have to quarantine our people here at work.'

'But my wife is sick. And my child.'

The superintendent nodded. 'Then you damn well better stay well, don't you think?' He stomped off.

He thought of Louisa at the dispensary, in constant face-to-face contact with people. After work he was shaking by the time he reached Gate 96 and saw her standing there. He began to run toward her. She came forward to meet him. She looked frightened.

'Are you ill?' she asked.

'No. No. I'm all right. I got it in my head that you ...' He took her face in his hands and examined her. Suddenly he pulled her to his chest and held her hard. Then he loosened his arms a bit, still without releasing her, and put his cheek on her hair, and they stayed that way for a long time, his cheek on her hair, her face against his chest, both with closed eyes.

He called the hospital about Norma. He told the recording about her shrieking fits after intercourse; about her sexuality that was as demanding as ever, about her neglect of self, of the baby. 'Thank you for your cooperation.

This is a recording.' He called back and told the recording to go fuck itself. It thanked him.

'You should have reported an adverse reaction immediately,' the nurse said. 'Decrease the dosage from twenty drops to ten drops daily.' She read the prescription from a computer printout.

'And if that doesn't help?'

'There are several procedures, Mr. Tillich. These are doctor's orders. Report back in two weeks. You will be given a two-week supply of the medication.'

'Can't someone just look at him?'

'I'm sorry, Mr. Tillich.'

The baby wasn't eating. He moved very little and slept sixteen hours or more a day.

'You're killing him,' he told the nurse. He got up. She would merely summon an orderly if he didn't leave. There was nothing she could do.

'Mr. Tillich, report to Room twelve-oh-nine before you leave the building.' She was already looking past him at a woman with red eyes.

'My baby, she's been vomiting ever since she took that new medicine. And her bowels, God, nothing but water!'

Tillich moved away, back to the dispensary for the baby's medicine. He had been there for three hours already. The line was still as long as before. He took his place at the end.

Ninety minutes later he received the medicine. The dispensary nurse said, 'Report to Room twelve-oh-nine, Mr. Tillich.'

In 1209 there was a short line of people. It was a fast-moving line. When Tillich entered the room, a nurse asked his name. She checked it against a list, nodded, and told him to get in line. When he came to the head of the line, he was given a shot.

'What is it?' he asked.

The doctor looked at him in surprise. 'Flu vaccine.'

He saw the nurse at the door motioning to him. She put her forefinger to her lips and shook her head.

As he went out she whispered, 'Louisa slipped your name in. For God's sake, keep your mouth shut.'

A fast-moving freight from Detroit derailed when the locomotive's wheels locked as it slowed for a curve. Sixty-four cars left the track, tearing up a section a quarter of a mile long. It happened during the night, the specks of light were still motionless in that section when Tillich arrived.

'No more direct connection with Detroit,' the superintendent said. 'We're working on alternate routing now.'

'Aren't they going to fix the tracks?'

'Can't. No steel's being allotted to any non-priority work. Just keep a hold on Sec. Seven until the computer gives us new routing. What a goddam mess.'

Detroit was out. Jacksonville was out. Memphis was out. Cleveland. St. Paul.

Tillich wondered what a high priority was. Syringes, he thought. Scalpels. Bone saws. He wondered if steel was still being produced.

'Can you get away at all?' he asked her desperately.

She shook her head. 'No more than you can.'

'I'll leave them. She isn't helpless. It's an act. If she got hungry enough, she'd get something.'

She continued to shake her head. 'I looked her up. She is very ill, David. She isn't malingering.'

'What's wrong with her?'

'Primary schizophrenia. Acute depressions. Severe anemia, low blood sugar, renal dysfunction. There was more. I forget.'

'Why don't they treat her? Try to cure her?' She was silent.

'They know they can't. Or it would take too long to be worthwhile. Is that it? *Is that it?*'

'I don't know. They don't put reasons on the cards.'

'Is there someplace we can go? Here, in the city?'

'I don't have any money. Do you?'

He laughed bitterly. 'Your apartment?'

'Father, Mother, my brother Jason. He has tuberculosis, one lung collapsed. We have two rooms.'

'I'll get some money. I'll get us a room somewhere.'

He heard the baby wailing halfway down the hall. It was making up for the weeks of drugged silence. As he got nearer he could hear the TV also. Norma was watching it, singing, '*I had a red canary. It wouldn't fly.*' She didn't look at him.

If it weren't for them, he thought clearly, he could take another job. Able-bodied men could work around the clock if they wanted to. All those hours in lines waiting for her medicine, waiting for the baby's medicine, waiting for her examination, the baby's examination. Shopping for them. Cleaning up after them. Cooking for them.

He shut his eyes, his back against the door. For a long time he didn't move. He felt a soft tug on his shirt and opened his eyes. She was there, holding out the hairbrush.

'Would you like to do my hair?'

He brushed her pale silky hair. 'After I'm well, we'll have a vacation, won't we? Just the two of us. We'll go to the seashore and find pretty shells.'

The baby wailed. The TV played. She sat with tears on her cheeks and he brushed her pale silky hair.

MAN OF LETTERS

When their father didn't die after all, but rallied on his eighth day in Intensive Care (Terminal Section, they had both been certain), Mildred and her brother Hank stared at the doctor with almost moronic incomprehension. Prepared for death, they didn't know how to react to the new prognosis. Not that they disliked him, or wanted him dead (after all, both had more money than he would leave, and he was a nice man), but they had expected his demise long enough to go through the stages of unaccepting disbelief, to numbed no-think, to making unvoiced plans about the afterward. After the final announcement, after the public sorrow, after the smell of flowers faded and Mildred's collapse and subsequent week under a southern sun amidst rich foliage that, dying, knew nothing of death, so fast did the new replace the old. Hank had even visualized new letterheads, without the 'Jr.,' just plain Henry Sillitoe. Period. He had visualized his father's desk in his own office. The desk had a writing area marked off with heavy, deeply carved inlaid leather. He had done pencil rubbings of the ornate design as a child.

Warner put out the stub of a cigarette, lighted another one, put it down on the ashtray, and skimmed what he had written. With his fingers poised over the keyboard, he hesitated, then reread the opening of the new story. Nellie knocked on the door and he said, 'Come on in.'

'I just wanted to remind you that I have to go shopping, and Mrs. Olson might drop in with the curtains while I'm out. Give her the check on the table, will you?'

'Sure. Got a minute?'

Nellie nodded. She was dressed in sky-blue slacks and a sweater, her long black hair tied back with a blue-and-red polka-dot scarf. She looked sixteen, possibly eighteen, and was thirty. 'I heard you clicking away,' she said.

'Yeah. I'd like for you to read something.' He handed her the page of typescript and she read it, then looked at him expectantly. 'Just like Janice and Eugene, isn't it? Then what?'

'Janice and Eugene?'

'Yes, you know, Janice Murphy and her brother. Their father had a stroke or something and had to live with one or the other of them. Oh, it was awful ... Poor Janice.'

'I don't know Janice Murphy.'

'Really? She lives over at Pine Acres, and last year, or the year before that,

I forget which, she was the chairman of the entertainment committee for the PTA. I told you. She's the one who planned that awful Halloween party where the parents had to dress up and you wouldn't go and Terry pretended that you had mumps or something. Anyway, she told me all about it when her father nearly died and they sold his house and everything because the doctors were so sure that he wouldn't live, and the house was jointly owned or something so that they could sell it, or else they got power of attorney because he was paralyzed or something like that, but then. Then, he got well. Just like that. And he had to move in with Janice …'

Warner turned her off and stared at the page he had written. Again, he thought. He'd done it again. For three weeks he had been writing beginnings that were real, beginnings of life stories of people he knew, or that Nellie knew, or that he subsequently read about in the papers.

'But I don't even know Janice Murphy,' he said again.

Nellie shrugged and returned the sheet of paper to him. 'I guess there must be a lot of cases like that. It could happen to almost anyone. Well, I'm leaving. Don't forget Mrs. Olson. The check is on the table, all ready for her. Be back in a couple of hours.'

At the door she said, 'If I didn't have so darn far to drive, I wouldn't bother you about the check, you know. But thirteen miles to the underpass.' She shrugged eloquently and left.

They lived five miles from Pine Acres, on the other side of the interstate highway. To get there they had to drive thirteen miles to the underpass, then twelve back down to the stores. Then twelve back up, and thirteen back down. 'We could still sell this house and move,' she said often, very often. But he wouldn't. He refused to live in a development. He couldn't stand the city any more. And they were within reach of New York, less than a two-hour drive. 'But fifty miles just to shop!' That's what she always said. Always.

He heard the car starting. A two-year-old model with an insatiable thirst, a tendency to spring out of alignment if it even grazed a pebble, it had more recently developed a peculiar growl when the key was turned. It growled, gasped, choked, then started the more reassuring, mildly uneven hum.

Warner got out the folder of starts that he had discarded during the past three weeks and added the new one to the stack. He fanned them out on his desk and studied them. He wondered how different, if at all, they were from the stories he'd been doing for thirteen years. He was afraid that he wouldn't be able to find much difference if he went back to check through the others, the published stories.

He heard the back door slam. Terry and his friends after a snack, young teenagers, as insatiable as the car. He strained, listening, but he couldn't hear the refrigerator from his study. Presently the door slammed again.

A clock chimed, muffled by closed doors.

The cat returned and the garage door clanged. It fell the last foot or so. He closed his eyes, concentrating. The radio came on. He was certain that the radio had come on, turned to low volume instantly. Nellie would be putting groceries away. And humming. He stood up, waiting for the squeak of leather, a spring rasping slightly with release. His shoes, leather-against-rug-scuffing sound, then leather on hardwood. At the door he tightened his lips, metal grated on metal from the hinge that he always forgot to oil. Down the hallway, carpeted, carpeting on stairs, the third and seventh steps loud, green wood that screamed when touched.

'Don't hum,' he said under his breath to Nellie, 'Don't be humming.' At the door to the kitchen he stopped, trying to hear her over the cheerful radio voice. He opened the door gently, touching it with his fingertips only.

'... drizzle and fog. Tomorrow, cloudy and cooler.'

Nellie was humming.

Warner drew his hand back. His mouth twitched and suddenly he was laughing. He laughed almost silently, eyes tearing, his entire body shaking. He laughed until he ached, and felt weak, and had to lean against the wall for support. Finally finished, he pushed himself upright and went through the dining room to the entrance foyer, then out the front door.

He should go to the library, he thought as he walked. He should check it out for himself. A month ago he had listened with a sardonic grin as Hal Vronsky told about the story he had read. Story about a writer and wife and kid, living five miles from the nearest town, but having to drive nearly fifty miles to get to it and back. How the wife kept them just a little bit in debt, enough so that the guy never could break out of the kind of thing he was doing, hackwork of some sort. Hal had looked embarrassed suddenly. 'Hell, not that part. But the rest of it – you know, the general situation – made me think of you right off.'

'And you read it in a dentist's office, I suppose?'

'Yeah, as a matter of fact, I did. How'd you know that?'

And Warner had laughed. And again today he had laughed, but now, walking through fields that had turned brown with autumn, that would cover his legs and socks with sticktights, and fill his shoes with seeds and dust from dead grasses, now he was not laughing. He should go check it out at the library, just to satisfy his curiosity.

'So I'm cliché,' he said. 'And Nellie is a cliché wife. And Terry is a cliché son.' He kicked a clump of mushrooms and watched the pieces scatter. And he finished the thought, 'And I write cliché fiction.'

He turned to his right, paralleling the highway that was half a mile away now. It was a river of many colors, with a swift current that now and then eddied ... Was that thought a cliché? He wondered. He was afraid that it was. There was old man Brunhild's barn ahead of him now, folding in on itself down to the ground practically. This quarter of his acreage had been cut off from the rest by the highway, and the old farmer was ignoring it. The barn had long needed repairs, but with the announcement four years ago of the highway's location, all thoughts of maintaining this part of the farm had vanished. On the roof of the barn, in letters that filled the available space, was the command: SEE ROCK CITY. Warner leaned against a fencepost and contemplated the sign moodily. He wondered if the paint that the old man had put in the barn was still there. As he drew nearer the decrepit building there was a scurrying sound. Rats, he thought with disgust, and hesitated, then started to whistle loudly, and scrape his feet breaking dead grasses with audible snaps and rustlings. He found the paint and broke the end off his pocket knife opening the can. There were two broad brushes in the barn, and a homemade ladder that looked like it had a fifty-percent chance of holding his weight. Still whistling, he leaned it against the building, moved it when the roof edge crumbled, and then started to climb up, carrying the paint with him, and the brush in his teeth. He worked until it got so dark that he couldn't be certain that he had obliterated the T and Y in CITY, and then he went home.

'For God's sake, Warner, where have you been? Look at you!' Nellie, sweet in a white organdy pants suit, stared aghast, and he glanced down at himself. He was smeared with red paint from head down, his clothes spattered, smeared, caked with it. Both hands looked like he had been engaged in butchery. When he grinned he could feel the drying paint pulling his mouth and cheeks. 'You've been painting!' Nellie exclaimed.

Warner shook his head hard. 'I'll clean up,' he said.

'You can't have a martini like that,' she said, as if puzzled.

At the door to the garage he paused, wondering if she would improvise, or just wait until everything got back on the tracks that she was familiar with. She chose to wait. He scrubbed, first with turpentine, then in the shower with hot water and a bar of pink, engraved soap that looked edible, and still when he dressed and went to the living room, he had red paint deep in the pores of his hands and wrists, and his eyebrows were tinged with it, and when he smiled, the creases in his face were exaggerated, as if outlined with a red pencil. Nellie stared at him hard, then turned away with a sigh of patience tried and found not wanting.

'What in the world were you painting?' she asked, pouring his martini for him.

'Brunhild's barn.'

She didn't know about Brunhild or his barn. She never had walked through the fields back that way. 'Henry called twice,' she said then, dismissing the paint. 'He has something for you. An emergency, or something.'

'Probably wants to know why the hell I haven't sent in a story for a month,'

Warner muttered. He sipped the martini, and shuddered. He looked at the drink and sniffed it cautiously, then tasted it again, more gingerly this time. Still bad. 'How long till dinner?' he asked. 'Do I have time to call him back first?'

Nellie nodded. 'Half an hour. What's wrong with the martini? It's the same mix that I always use.' She picked it up and sniffed it, then put her tongue in it and finally drank it down. 'What's wrong with it?' She sucked on the lemon slice. 'You've just got paint-and-turpentine taste in your mouth.'

Henry was his agent, and only once before had he wanted a call returned after office hours, and then it had been to talk Warner into doing a translation of an article a midwestern politician had written for one of the men's magazines. The trouble had been that it was in illiterate, phonetic, midwestern dialect, that it hadn't made any sense, that he had forgotten what his starting point was by the end of paragraph two and had rambled on for twenty pages. Warner was known to be reliable, with a readable style, and a knack for making sense out of incomprehensible sentences, even if he had to insert the sense.

He dialed Henry's number and he thought, The net will tighten now. I'm starting to wiggle a little bit, so they'll tighten the net, pull me back in. The thought was fleeting, and by the time Henry's voice was booming over the wires, he forgot it entirely.

'Warner, the ax has just fallen over at *The Woman's Home Advisor*. Adamski's out, and all the stuff he commissioned, right down to fillers. Stu Pryor is in, and he's desperate for material. He wants a four-parter, fifteen thousand words each installment, and he wants it by next Tuesday, the first part of it, anyway. I told him you'd do it for twelve thousand an installment.'

Warner stared at the wall and tried not to think of twelve thousand dollars times four. 'By Tuesday?' he said. 'That's less than a week ...'

'Yeah, I know. They offered five thousand, and when I pointed out that the only man I knew who could do it that fast wouldn't consider it for anything less than fifteen ...'

He went on at some length. By the time the conversation ended, Warner had agreed to start immediately and have the first installment ready to deliver by Tuesday. Over dinner he told Nellie about it. 'Nothing far out. No drugs, no youth rebellion, no alienation. Just good wholesome women's fiction. A mystery maybe, with a put-upon heroine.'

Nellie's eyes were shining and she leaned over the table to put her hand on his. 'Thank God,' she said. 'I was afraid you'd turn it down. You've been acting so funny lately.'

'Funny how?'

'Oh, not finishing anything. Sketching in incidents, then leaving them for new ones. Then today, going out to paint a barn, for heaven's sake! I mean, that's not your typical behavior, now, is it?'

They were alone, tall candles on the small table that she used when they dined together without Terry. Good heavy silver, crystal, china. Thick, thick carpet underfoot, ladderback chairs, a frostlike draperied wall for a background. Warner stared about with an air of discovery. They were a magazine illustration, he thought. Nellie, lovely in white, her husband, tall and distinguished-looking, even with a touch of red paint here and there. Wine on the table, a casserole in a silver stand ... He stood up abruptly and dropped his napkin on his plate, with chicken and pea pods and saffron rice. Out of a gourmet magazine.

'I ... excuse me, honey. I'll be in my study.' He almost ran from the dining room. Nellie, he knew, would put the dishes in the dishwasher, leave the pans for Mrs. Wasserman to do in the morning, and spend the rest of the evening in front of the television, spending forty-three thousand two hundred dollars, what he would get after the ten percent taken out by his agent. He corrected himself. Nellie would know exactly how much to deduct for taxes too, and she would go over what was left by a couple of hundred dollars. A new car. Redecorate the kitchen. She'd been talking about a cooking island, with a copper hood, and a new ultrasonic oven ... And a second car for Terry, who would be sixteen in three months.

He sat at his desk and saw the fan of stories started and not finished. He picked up the latest one and put the page by his typewriter, then replaced the rest of them in the folder and returned it to his file, under INCOMPLETE.

Okay, he told himself, fifteen thousand words by Tuesday, or Monday night, actually, with delivery on Tuesday. Six days. Six into fifteen. All the time that he was doing his arithmetic, his fingers were busy, putting new paper into the typewriter, whipping it down to the midway point, titling the story: *The Day God Laughed.* Twenty-five hundred a day, he thought, then stared at what he had written.

Slowly he pulled the paper out of the carriage and inserted another piece, this time working deliberately. Mildred, he thought, Mildred should get her father first. Not yet thirty, lawyer husband, two children ... He wrote, *Mildred is social climber, very eager for her husband to get into local politics, then work up through the ranks, and she feels that having her father on her hands will be a hindrance because there will be some traveling, and a good deal of entertaining to do. Janice can't bring herself to approach her brother Eugene outright, but she thinks that if she makes the old man so uncomfortable that he brings it up ...* Warner stopped and shook his head. He scanned the page and crossed out the name Janice, and filled in with pencil above it, Mildred. He crossed out Eugene and wrote in Hank.

That would be the first part, he decided, and pulled the page from the machine. Part two. *The old man is shipped off to the son, but he never shows up there. Janice, Mildred, whoever the hell she is, is off with her husband on a speaking tour* ... He was jotting down the ideas now, sketching in the story. *End part two with confrontation between brother and sister, each accusing other of negligence. Eugene wants to notify police, etc., initiate a search, Janice-Mildred* ... He couldn't remember which name he had chosen for her. It didn't matter. *She is afraid of what publicity will do to husband now at such a crucial stage in his career. End part two.*

Three. He stared at the paper filling up now with notes, and shook his head. No part three. He was tired, and sore from the unaccustomed painting, and his eyes were becoming blurry. He got up and went to the kitchen to make coffee, and while he waited for it, he checked on Terry, who was asleep, then looked in on ... his wife. He couldn't think of her name for a moment and his hand on the doorknob tightened until it was painful. Nellie. Nellie was asleep.

Quietly he withdrew, tiptoeing away from the door, down the stairs again, hearing the scream of the third and seventh steps, and back to the kitchen, still trying to make no sound, as if afraid even down there he might awaken her, or the boy. Part three would have to be the search, he thought. And part four, reunion, and a subsequent search for a Good Home for the old man, a happy old folks' home where he could be of some use to others who were older and more helpless than he ...

Add a few subplots: Nellie's husband could misunderstand her ... Warner shook his head until it hurt. Nellie. His wife. The woman in the story was ... What the hell difference did it make? He had given her the wrong name, so he couldn't remember it from one sentence to the next. He'd call her Gladys, or Mary. Good safe name. He sipped coffee, but the story wouldn't stay in focus now. He wondered how the real-life story of Janice and her brother ended. At two he went to bed.

The next morning he got up after Terry had gone to school. He had coffee and then went to find Nellie, who was sunning herself under the lamp in the bathroom, spread-eagled on a white fake-fur rug with nothing on but two cotton pads over her eyes. She looked exactly like a centerfold model.

'Honey, whatever happened to Janice? You know, the one the story reminded you of?'

She waved a greeting to him. 'Oh, the poor thing. They finally had to put her father in a home, you know, one of those very pretty places for older people who aren't really sick or anything, but can't be expected to live alone either, and anyway he didn't have a home any more, and I guess he was sicker than they thought, because he died after a couple of months, but he was really happy there until the end. And Paul, her husband, you know, we voted for him last election and he's in the legislature now, a Representative from this district, and next national election he's going to run for Congress, I think. He seemed to think Janice did something terrible, but he was just under such a strain, too. Poor Janice has been going to a psychiatrist for months and months. He told her she has an identity problem, or something like that. I don't understand exactly, but it seems that sometimes she isn't really sure just who she is, or what she's up to, or anything at all. It couldn't be too serious because no one has even suggested that she be hospitalized ...'

Warner left her, closing the door gently. He pulled on an old hunting jacket and went outside. He walked through the fields until he came to the tilted barn whose roof he had painted. Nothing of the previous sign showed through. He continued to walk toward the highway; at that time of morning the traffic was scant, with bursts of automobiles, then nothing, then another flurry. He waited until he could cross, then went on to Pine Acres Shopping Center. He bought up all the slick magazines, all the pulps with any fiction, half a dozen paperback books, and six cans of white spray paint, and then started to walk back home. When he got to the barn again, he stopped to spray-paint on his own slogan:

GOD IS NOT DEAD
HE'S JUST A CLICHÉ

The letters were ten feet high.

Nellie nodded approvingly when she saw him with the magazines. 'Research?'

'Something like that.'

'Good. I'm off, dear. Historical Society meeting.' She was bewitching in a pink cashmere suit, with a pink feathery thing on her head. Author's device, he thought, to get rid of wife in order to have protagonist alone for the next scene. He waved good-bye and went on into his study with his magazines.

He looked over the fiction quickly – three of the stories he had written, one under his own name, two with pseudonyms. They were all familiar, even the ones he hadn't done.

'Okay,' he said then, and moved with a purposeful stride to his desk. 'Now we negotiate.' He put in a page of his best twenty-four-pound white bond with an embossed sun symbol on it, and began to type.

I quit. I resign. I want a better contract. Also, I am through with hackwork. I want to produce Art.

A blinding radiance filled the room, emanating from behind him. He didn't turn around. Crap. Cliché. Too many people saw God, or something that appeared with a blinding light. He studied the lines he had written, finding it hard to force his eyes to remain wide enough open to see them in the painful glare. He thought that God must be laughing although there was no sound. He examined the thought and shrugged. He didn't believe in God, and especially not a god that laughed. He wondered suddenly if that was a new idea, finally. The light dimmed and he was left with the idea of a laughing god. He gnawed on his thumb and tried to recall if he had ever read of such a thing in the Bible, where he seldom really read, but often browsed, for a title, or an appropriate quote for one of his characters to use at an opportune moment. He felt certain that God of the Bible never had laughed.

With the radiance gone, the room seemed dull and gloomy. He flicked on the lights, the desk lamp, the ceiling light, a floor lamp near the window where his armchair and end table were. The room still was cold and uncomfortable. He walked out to the hall, and thought he heard the sound of his typewriter, but when he stopped to listen, there was nothing. Mrs. Wasserman was in the kitchen cleaning the refrigerator, and she made him a chicken sandwich and talked endlessly about the failure of the walnut crop that year. Halfway through the sandwich Warner suddenly had to go back to his study to see what the typewriter had answered.

The lines he had written had been Xed out.

Warner laughed harshly. Even to his ears the laugh was ugly. 'Okay,' he said. 'Proof. You need proof.' He pulled the phone to him and as he was about to lift the receiver, the bell rang.

'Yeah,' he said.

'Warner, Henry here. Listen, kid, relax. I got to thinking last night, and you know that long novella you sent me a couple of months back, the one about the blind girl who makes it with the pianist, turns out that she has perfect pitch or some damn thing. Well. What the hell, it's perfect for this four-parter. I got it out and reread it and it breaks up beautifully, suspense, pathos, everything ...'

Warner hung up. He drummed on the desktop, then looked up Hal Vronsky's number and dialed it. Mrs. Vronsky answered. 'Our dentist? Hal's dentist?' There was a pause. Warner filled it in. 'I've had this tooth bothering me off and on, and my dentist is sick ...'

With the name and address in his pocket he left the house again, after retyping his resignation and leaving it in the typewriter. In the driveway he hesitated, then returned to the house and gathered up all the magazines he had bought earlier.

He stopped again. Nellie was gone with the car. Angrily he yelled for Mrs. Wasserman.

'Leave that, will you?' he said brusquely. 'I've got to get to the dentist over in Pine Acres. Can you run me over?'

She nodded and closed the refrigerator door and untied her apron. 'I know what it's like to have a toothache, yessirree. I had one once that wouldn't give me no relief for weeks and weeks and this was when I was a little girl, you see, and we didn't have no dentist near at hand, not like today with a dentist on every corner, as you might say. And we had to wait until our regular day over to Middlebury, and then found out that the dentist was sick, and my ma had to end up pulling that tooth in spite of everything. Never grew back either.'

She drove the thirteen miles to the underpass in half an hour, then twelve miles back to the shopping center in another half hour. 'I'll wait if'n you want me to,' she said kindly, jerking the car to a halt outside the medical building.

'No. I'll take a cab home,' Warner said. 'Thanks a lot, you were a big help.'

'Yes,' she agreed. 'Always try to help. Now I'll just get me back and finish up that refrigerator.' Still talking, she jerked away from the curb and rolled up the street in slow motion.

'Borgman, Borgman,' he muttered, walking around the building examining the names on the brass door plates. Then he saw it, MELVIN S. BORGMAN, D.D.S. The office was closed. He shifted the slithery magazines, and considered. There had to be an office manager, or maintenance superintendent, someone in charge with a key. He made the circuit again and this time saw a small white placard that said simply SUPERINTENDENT. He knocked and after a wait of several minutes the door opened. A very old man eyed him suspiciously.

'Mr. uh ...'

'Carmichael.'

'Yes. Mr. Carmichael, I'm the new distributor's representative to service the office of Dr. Borgman. I'm supposed to collect the out-of-date magazines and leave him these new issues.'

The old man didn't budge. 'Never done that before.'

'I know. It's a new, complimentary service. A trial run. I was due to arrive yesterday, but there was trouble with the shipment ...'

'Don't know. Never said nothing to me about letting you in.'

'Mr. Carmichael, you can go with me. All I want to do is put these new magazines in the office and take out the old ones.'

'I just don't know,' he said stubbornly, but now he was moving as he muttered, and fishing on a long chain of keys for the right one.

Mr. Carmichael watched him closely as he selected the magazines that possibly could have fiction in them. Warner didn't dare examine tables of contents under the frankly unbelieving gaze of the old man. Warner picked up nine magazines and left fourteen in their place. He didn't bother with things like *Field and Stream*, or *Mechanics Illustrated*, or *Humpty Dumpty*.

'Whyn't you take them all?' the superintendent asked, his suspicions renewed.

'Dr. Borgman collects those. He told me himself that he collects them.'
Very slowly the old man nodded, as if his worst fears and doubts about the
dentist had been confirmed. He never took his eyes off Warner until they
were again outside the office and he had locked and tried the door three
times. Then he turned and walked away without looking back.

Warner took a taxi home and beat Mrs. Wasserman by twenty minutes.

He skimmed through all the stories without finding one even vaguely
reminiscent of himself and his life. Then he paused. You never recognize
yourself in fiction, he knew. He had used any number of friends and acquaintances without their ever knowing. He began to comb through them
again, and finally decided he had the one that Hal Vronsky must have meant.
An artist, not a writer. A hack artist, an illustrator of the cheapest magazines, a penny-postcard sort of artist. With a wife and three children. But
he did live in a location that suggested Warner's. He read the story carefully.
The artist rebelled at doing hackwork after years of making a rather good
living. His wife refused to believe he wanted to gamble on serious work, and
spent all of the money they had, and some over, on a new house! Warner
swallowed hard. She wouldn't dare.

That was the climactic scene. Her announcement of the purchase, con-
ditional, of course, of the new house, on the other side of the country-club
community that she wanted so touch to be part of. Warner blinked. Incredible that such junk could have been written in the first place, bought and
published in the second place, and read in the third place. He found the continuation. They fought, naturally, and she said that she'd buy the house with
the money the courts awarded her from a divorce settlement. Warner shook
his head. No motivation had been given to her, nothing but the scantiest
sketch of her appearance, and here she was the pivotal character suddenly.
Coming out of nowhere to change the course of his life ... the character's
life, that was.

He found the next continuation. She said that she'd be better off with
him dead, his insurance would be sufficient, and he was a has-been anyway,
hadn't done any real work for a month ...

The next continuation. The artist collapsed, and on awakening in a hospital realized that he had suffered from a temporary nervous disorder, that
he had made life hell for everyone about him, that he was probably the best
of his kind going, and looked forward with great anticipation to returning
to his life's work, illustrating fourth-rate magazines that brought a touch of
escapism to so many people, making their lives tolerable. End.

Warner flung the magazine from him and went to his desk, where his
second ultimatum had been obliterated with h's and a's. *Hahahahaha.* He
yanked it out and wrote.

Let x be the events of the world, all the events, all combinations and

permutations of possible actions, places, things. New events can be added ar-
ithmetically only. One at a time. In the beginning when there were few events
the addition of one was exciting and fun, but with the growing number, the
addition of one is adding boredom to boredom. Ten million plus one. One is
lost in the shuffle. Meaningless.

Let y equal the people of the world, growing geometrically, exponentially.
Because already y is greater than x, there can only be constant repetition, and
more boredom.

Let z equal processes, the combinations of x and y in all possible equations:
x/x, x/y, y/y, y/x, xxy, x+y, etc. Because x is, practically speaking, finite, the
processes are again repetitive and boring after a short time. What can be has
been, endlessly.

Let x', or y', or z', or any combination, be the goal and the endless search
makes sense. An evolutionary leap, or a scientific breakthrough to a new kind
of reality, or the disclosure of the ultimate secrets, whatever x' combined with
y' could produce. Someone has to keep on searching, whether under a com-
puter's guidance, or a god's, or a committee's. And the numbers make it im-
perative that the task be broken up into sections, and that there be people to
run those sections, to keep mixing up the ingredients available and noting the
results. And I quit!

I QUIT!

He felt better than he had in days when he left his study that afternoon.
Terry had been home and was gone again, to band practice, or something.
Nellie wasn't home yet. Dinner, she had said, would be late, and maybe they
could go out …

Echelons, he thought. There were regular echelons. The masses that acted
like gas, predictable as a unit, but unpredictable molecule by molecule. Then
slightly above them the ones who had escaped from the flask somehow,
still more or less predictable, but capable now of new combinations. Janice,
Nellie … all his characters in all his stories, he supposed. Then came those
like him, capable of watching that level, but still watched by a level a bit
higher. Henry? And so on. At the top? He stopped in the middle of mixing
his martini, and wondered who, or what, was at the top, keeping an eye on
the whole. He knew it was a fruitless speculation, but still he wondered.
Was it someone, or something, capable of bargaining or willing to bargain?
He put the shaker down and forgot about it. Suddenly he was thinking of
the pulp magazines he had bought. Murders. Science fiction. Supernatural
stories. If the scenarios were being written by real writers, why weren't those
coming true also?

Why could he manipulate Janice, why could another writer determine
his actions? Why didn't the Martians land? Or a tidal wave wipe out
Los Angeles? Or a mad murderer chop off the hands of all spinsters

over thirty and send them to lonelyhearts clubs? Or ...

Nellie came home and he tried to forget the ideas for a while. She was adorable in a ... No, actually, he thought, she looked a little tired, and she had a smudge on her chin, and a run in one stocking.

'Tired?' he asked.

'Um. We're getting ready for our annual dinner and dance.' She looked in the martini shaker and glanced in surprise at the two empty glasses still on the tray, then filled them both. 'Cheers,' she said, upending hers. She poured another one and put it down on a table by the couch, where she sat down and took off her shoes. 'All day I've been peeling apples. For dessert.' She lighted a cigarette, and added, 'Apple pies.'

'What are you going to do with the money you raise?'

'Add to the kitchen facilities, enlarge the dining room of the club.'

'So next year you can have a bigger dinner and dance?'

'Um.' She sighed. 'I saw Janice this afternoon. Funny, isn't it, when you bring up someone like that how often you see them in a day or two after not seeing them for months. Serendipity.'

'Synchronicity,' Warner said and she nodded.

'Something. Anyway, she's in such a bad way. I never did like her very much, such a shallow person, you know, nothing beneath the nice clothes and phony smile, but anyway, I hate to see her feeling so bad, and lost! You wouldn't believe how really lost she is. I never saw anything just like it. She was talking to Mrs. Loewenstein and when I joined them she just went right on, although I've never been close or anything. You'd think she wouldn't want to say such things in the presence of someone who's almost a stranger, but she doesn't seem to realize that I am. A stranger.'

Warner watched her without listening closely. He had heard it said of someone who was acclaimed as a public speaker that his formula for success was to get before an audience, turn on his mouth, and when the time was over, to turn it off again. That was Nellie, he thought.

He wondered who was writing her.

He wondered who was writing him now. Not the same author as before, surely. He had got away from that creep. That slob wouldn't know what to do if he said jump and Warner laughed at him. Just like he didn't know exactly what to do about the character who laughed at his ultimatums. Wordlessly he left the living room, leaving Nellie talking on and on, with her eyes closed, wiggling her toes, holding her martini in one hand, a cigarette in the other.

His last message was gone altogether. He looked on the desk for it, and an accompanying message, but it wasn't there. When he turned to leave, he noticed scraps of paper on the floor and he picked up several and pieced them together enough to see that they were his last attempt to communicate. Torn into shreds.

Warner let the pieces float from his fingers. He sat down at his desk and thought for a moment, then put a fresh piece of paper in the typewriter. He wrote:

Janice, driven to despair by the continual absence of her husband, and the waves of guilt that washed her of all joy and happiness, drove faster and faster, as if she knew that ahead lay her final release from pain, that to achieve it all she had to do was concentrate on that point of light that lay ahead, as if that one red point was the gate to whatever heaven or hell awaited her ultimately. She felt peace for the first time in the two years since her father's death as she saw the point grow until she was lost in it.

He found the folder in the INCOMPLETE file, withdrew the story that he had started and outlined, and added the final page. He replaced the file, keeping out the finished story now. It would have to be titled and filed in the regular file, but tomorrow. He left it on his desk.

He took Nellie to dinner at an Italian restaurant that they were both fond of, and they drank too much Chianti, and Nellie's eyes sparkled, and she looked younger and more desirable than she had for a long time, so that when they got home he wanted to take her right off to bed. But they had to wait for Terry's arrival, and by the time they actually got to bed, it was after eleven, and the glow had faded somewhat. But it was still good, as always with Nellie. Afterward, she lay in the crook of his arm and with her face pressed against his ribs, she said in a low voice,

'I saw a beautiful house today ...' He grunted and pretended to be asleep.

The next morning he got out the INCOMPLETE folder and began finishing stories. At noon Nellie told him with a shocked expression that Janice had been killed on her way home last night. Driving too fast, possibly drinking, she had run into a traffic sign and had died instantly. Over the next few days it seemed that many of the people they knew were killed in sudden accidents.

Warner typed out his resignation and demands for a new contract every night before he closed his office. Along with the resignation one night he wrote: *Escape fiction is actually stimulus fiction. The writer doesn't believe in it; the reader doesn't believe in it. But now and again, someone is stimulated into new action by it, into a course that he might not have followed without it.* Sometimes the sheet vanished, sometimes it was Xed out, sometimes torn up. After he had gone through his files, finished every start of every story, he started a new story:

New York shivered under the icy blast of Arctic air that streamed out of the north. The very soul of the city seemed frozen, and it was as if the city had life, as if it was a living organism suffering now, shaken with death throes as its links with the rest of the country faltered and died, like the veins of a body fouled with calcium and other deposits that closed the vital passages ...

Warner paused, suddenly remembering the name of the writer who had written his, Warner's, story. Stephen Ashe. He was Henry's client too. Warner remembered seeing a manila envelope on Henry's desk once with that name, asking about him. Another pulp hack. Reliable. Can turn them out to order, makes him valuable. He'll learn to write well enough someday. Nurse him along.

And another scene flashed before Warner's eyes. Henry's office, young Stephen Ashe in the leather chair across from Henry's cluttered desk, hardly room enough to move his legs. Eager, fresh-looking.

'I don't seem to be able to do much with this character, Henry. You know, the series I'm doing for Talbot.'

'Yeah. Look, kid, I'll tell you. When you get a character that doesn't seem to come alive for you, or that doesn't seem to want to do the things that he has to to make the plot move along, get rid of him. Find someone else. God, the world's full of characters. Pick out someone new.'

'Yeah,' young fresh-faced Stephen Ashe said, relieved. 'Yeah, that sounds right.'

Warner pushed his chair back hard and stood up gripping his desk. '*No!* I won't ...' The room blurred slightly, seemed hazy around the edges of things, chairs merging with walls, walls and floor running together. He closed his eyes and when he opened them the room was gone, his desk gone, his chair, typewriter gone. And when he tried to open his mouth to scream, 'No,' again, his mouth was gone. They wouldn't deal, he thought sadly. Then that was gone too.

APRIL FOOLS' DAY FOREVER

On the last day of March a blizzard swept across the lower Great Lakes, through western New York and Pennsylvania, and raced toward the city with winds of seventy miles an hour, and snow falling at the rate of one and a half inches an hour. Julia watched it from her wide windows overlooking the Hudson River forty miles from the edge of the city and she knew that Martie wouldn't be home that night. The blizzard turned the world white within minutes and the wind was so strong and so cold that the old house groaned under the impact. Julia patted the window sill, thinking, 'There, there,' at it. 'It'll be over soon, and tomorrow's April, and in three or four weeks I'll bring you daffodils.' The house groaned louder and the spot at the window became too cold for her to remain there without a sweater.

Julia checked the furnace by opening the basement door to listen. If she heard nothing, she was reassured. If she heard a wheezing and an occasional grunt, she would worry and call Mr. Lampert, and plead with him to come over before she was snowed in. She heard nothing. Next she looked over the supply of logs in the living room. Not enough by far. There were three good-sized oak logs, and two pine sticks. She struggled into her parka and boots and went to the woodpile by the old barn that had become a storage house, den, garage, studio. A sled was propped up against the grey stone-and-shingle building and she put it down and began to arrange logs on it. When she had as many as she could pull, she returned to the house, feeling her way with one hand along the barn wall, then along the basket-weave fence that she and Martie had built three summers ago, edging a small wild brook that divided the yard. The fence took her in a roundabout way, but it was safer than trying to go straight to the house in the blinding blizzard. By the time she had got back inside, she felt frozen. A sheltered thermometer would show no lower than thirty at that time, but with the wind blowing as it was, the chill degrees must be closer to ten or twenty below zero. She stood in the mud room and considered what else she should do. Her car was in the garage. Martie's was at the train station. Mail. Should she try to retrieve any mail that might be in the box? She decided not to. She didn't really think the mailman had been there yet, anyway. Usually Mr. Probst blew his whistle to let her know that he was leaving something and she hadn't heard it. She took off the heavy clothes then and went through the house checking windows, peering at the latches of the storm windows. There had been a false spring three weeks ago, and she had opened windows and even washed a few before the winds changed again. The house was secure.

What she wanted to do was call Martie, but she didn't. His boss didn't approve of personal phone calls during the working day. She breathed a curse at Hilary Boyle, and waited for Martie to call her. He would, as soon as he had a chance. When she was certain that there was nothing else she should do, she sat down in the living room, where one log was burning softly. There was no light on in the room and the storm had darkened the sky. The small fire glowed pleasingly in the enormous fireplace, and the radiance was picked up by pottery and brass mugs on a low table before the fireplace. The room was a long rectangle, wholly out of proportion, much too long for the width, and with an uncommonly high ceiling. Paneling the end walls had helped, as had making a separate room within the larger one, with its focal point the fireplace. A pair of chairs and a two-seater couch made a cozy grouping. The colors were autumn forest colors, brilliant and subdued at the same time: oranges and scarlets in the striped covering of the couch, picked up again by pillows; rust browns in the chairs; forest-green rug. The room would never make *House Beautiful*, Julia had thought when she brought in the last piece of brass for the table and surveyed the effect, but she loved it, and Martie loved it. And she'd seen people relax in that small room within a room who hadn't been able to relax for a long time. She heard it then.

When the wind blew in a particular way in the old house, it sounded like a baby crying in great pain. Only when the wind came from the northwest over thirty miles an hour. They had searched and searched for the minute crack that had to be responsible and they had calked and filled and patched until it seemed that there couldn't be any more holes, but it was still there, and now she could hear the baby cry.

Julia stared into the fire, trying to ignore the wail, willing herself not to think of it, not to remember the first time she had heard the baby. She gazed into the fire and couldn't stop the images that formed and became solid before her eyes. She awakened suddenly, as in the dreams she had had during the last month or so of pregnancy. Without thinking, she slipped from bed, feeling for her slippers in the dark, tossing her robe about her shoulders hurriedly. She ran down the hall to the baby's room, and at the door she stopped in confusion. She pressed one hand against her flat stomach, and the other fist against her mouth hard, biting her fingers until she tasted blood. The baby kept on crying. She shook her head and reached for the knob and turned it, easing the door open soundlessly. The room was dark. She stood at the doorway, afraid to enter. The baby cried again. Then she pushed the door wide open and the hall light flooded the empty room. She fainted.

When she woke up hours later, grey light shone coldly on the bare floor, from the yellow walls. She raised herself painfully, chilled and shivering. Sleepwalking? A vivid dream and sleepwalking? She listened; the house was quiet, except for its regular night noises. She went back to bed. Martie protested in his sleep when she snuggled against his warm body, but he turned to let her curve herself to fit, and he put his arm about her. She said nothing about the dream the next day.

Six months later she heard the baby again. Alone this time, in the late afternoon of a golden fall day that had been busy and almost happy. She had been gathering nuts with her friend Phyllis Govern. They'd had a late lunch, and then Phyllis had had to run because it was close to four. A wind had come up, threatening a storm before evening. Julia watched the clouds build for half an hour.

She was in her studio in the barn, on the second floor, where the odor of hay seemed to remain despite an absence of fifteen or twenty years. She knew it was her imagination, but she liked to think that she could smell the hay, could feel the warmth of the animals from below. She hadn't worked in her studio for almost a year, since late in her pregnancy, when it had become too hard to get up the narrow, steep ladder that led from the ground floor to the balcony that opened to the upstairs rooms. She didn't uncover anything in the large room, but it was nice to be there. She needed clay, she thought absently, watching clouds roll in from the northwest. It would be good to feel clay in her fingers again. She might make a few Christmas gifts. Little things, funny things, to let people know that she was all right, that she would be going back to work before long now. She glanced at the large blocks of granite that she had ordered before. Not yet. Nothing serious yet. Something funny and inconsequential to begin with.

Still thoughtful, she left the studio and went to the telephone in the kitchen and placed a call to her supplier in the city. While waiting for the call to be completed, she heard it. The baby was in pain, she thought, and hung up. Not until she had started for the hall door did she realize what she was doing. She stopped, very cold suddenly. Like before, only this time she was wide awake. She felt for the door and pushed it open an inch or two. The sound was still there, no louder, but no softer either. Very slowly she followed the sound up the stairs, through the hall, into the empty room. She had been so certain that it originated here, but now it seemed to be coming from her room. She backed out into the hall and tried the room she shared with Martie. Now the crying seemed to be coming from the other bedroom. She stood at the head of the stairs for another minute, then she ran down and tried to dial Martie's number. Her hands were shaking too hard and she botched it twice before she got him.

Afterward she didn't know what she had said to him. He arrived an hour later to find her sitting at the kitchen table, ashen-faced, terrified.

'I'm having a breakdown,' she said quietly. 'I knew it happened to some women when they lost a child, but I thought I was past the worst part by now. I've heard it before, months ago.' She stared straight ahead. 'They probably will want me in a hospital for observation for a while. I should have packed, but ... Martie, you will try to keep me out of an institution, won't you? What does it want, Martie?'

'Honey, shut up. Okay?' Martie was listening intently. His face was very pale. Slowly he opened the door and went into the hall, his face turned up toward the stairs.

'Do you hear it?'

'Yes. Stay there.' He went upstairs, and when he came back down, he was still pale, but satisfied now. 'Honey, I hear it, so that means there's something making the noise. You're not imagining it. It is a real noise, and by God it sounds like a baby crying.'

Julia built up the fire and put a stack of records on the stereo and turned it too loud. She switched on lights through the house, and set the alarm clock for six twenty to be certain she didn't let the hour pass without remembering Hilary Boyle's news show. Not that she ever forgot it, but there might be a first time, especially on this sort of night, when she wouldn't be expecting Martie until very late, if at all. She wished he'd call. It was four-thirty. If he could get home, he should leave the office in an hour, be on the train at twenty-three minutes before six and at home by six forty-five. She made coffee and lifted the phone to see if it was working. It seemed to be all right. The stereo music filled the house, shook the floor and rattled the windows, but over it now and then she could hear the baby.

She tried to see outside; the wind-driven snow was impenetrable. She flicked on outside lights, the drive entrance, the light over the garage, the door to the barn, the back porch, front porch, the spotlight on the four pieces of granite that she had completed and placed in the yard, waiting for the rest of the series. The granite blocks stood out briefly during a lull. They looked like squat sentinels.

She took her coffee back to the living room, where the stereo was loudest, and sat on the floor by the big cherry table that they had cut down to fourteen inches. Her sketch pad lay here. She glanced at the top page without seeing it, then opened the pad to the middle and began to doodle aimlessly. The record changed; the wind howled through the yard; the baby wailed. When she looked at what she had been doing on the pad, she felt a chill begin deep inside. She had written over and over, MURDERERS. *You killed my babies*, MURDERERS.

Martie Sayre called the operator for the third time within the hour. 'Are the lines still out?'

'I'll check again, Mr. Sayre.' Phone static, silence, she was back. 'Sorry, sir. Still out.'

'Okay. Thanks.' Martie chewed his pencil and spoke silently to the picture on his desk: Julia, blond, thin, intense eyes and a square chin. She was beautiful. Her thin body and face seemed to accentuate lovely delicate bones. He, thin also, was simply craggy and gaunt. 'Honey, don't listen to it. Turn on music loud. You know I'd be there if I could.' The phone rang and he answered.

'I have the material on blizzards for you, Mr. Sayre. Also, Mr. Boyle's interview with Dr. Hewlitt, A.M.S., and the one with Dr. Wycliffe, the NASA satellite weather expert. Anything else?'

'Not right now, Sandy. Keep close. Okay?'

'Sure thing.'

He turned to the monitor on his desk and pushed the ON button. For the next half hour he made notes and edited the interviews and shaped a fifteen-minute segment for a special to be aired at ten that night. Boyle called for him to bring what he had ready at seven.

There was a four-man consultation. Martie, in charge of the science-news department; Dennis Kolchak, political-news expert; David Wedekind, the art director. Hilary Boyle paced as they discussed the hour special on the extraordinary weather conditions that had racked the entire earth during the winter. Boyle was a large man, over six feet, with a massive frame that let him carry almost three hundred pounds without appearing fat. He was a chain smoker, and prone to nervous collapses. He timed the collapses admirably: he never missed a show. His daily half hour, 'Personalized News,' was the most popular network show that year, as it had been for the past three years. The balloon would burst eventually, and the name Hilary Boyle wouldn't sound like God, but now it did, and no one could explain the *X factor* that had catapulted the talentless man into the firmament of stars.

The continuity writers had blocked in the six segments of the show already, two from other points – Washington and Los Angeles – plus the commercial time, plus the copter pictures that would be live, if possible.

'Looking good,' Hilary Boyle said. 'Half an hour Eddie will have the first film ready ...'

Martie wasn't listening. He watched Boyle and wondered if Boyle would stumble over any of the words Martie had used in his segment. He hoped not. Boyle always blamed him personally if he, Boyle, didn't know the words he had to parrot. 'Look, Martie, I'm a reasonably intelligent man, and if I don't know it, you gotta figure that most of the viewers won't know it either. Get me? Keep it simple, but without sacrificing any of the facts. That's your job, kid. Now give me this in language I can understand.'

Martie's gaze wandered to the window wall. The room was on the sixty-third floor; there were few other lights to be seen on this level, and only those that were very close. The storm had visibility down to two hundred yards. What lights he could see appeared ghostly, haloed, diffused, toned down to beautiful pearly luminescences. He thought of Boyle trying to say that, and then had to bite his cheek to keep from grinning. Boyle couldn't stand it when someone grinned in his presence, unless he had made a funny.

Martie's part of the special was ready for taping by eight, and he went to the coffee shop on the fourteenth floor for a sandwich. He wished he could get through to Julia, but telephone service from Ohio to Washington to Maine was a disaster area that night.

He closed his eyes and saw her, huddled before the fire in the living room glowing with soft warm light. Her pale hair hiding her paler face, hands over her ears, tight. She got up and went to the steps, looking up them, then ran back to the fire. The house shaking with music and the wind. The image was so strong that he opened his eyes wide and shook his head too hard, starting a mild headache at the back of his skull. He drank his coffee fast, and got a second cup, and when he sat down again, he was almost smiling. Sometimes he was convinced that she was right when she said that they had something so special between them, they never were actually far apart. Sometimes he knew she was right.

He finished his sandwich and coffee and wandered back to his office. Everything was still firm, ready to tape in twenty minutes. His part was holding fine.

He checked over various items that had come through in the last several hours, and put three of them aside for elaboration. One of them was about a renewal of the influenza epidemic that had raked England earlier in the year. It was making a comeback, more virulent than ever. New travel restrictions had been imposed.

Julia: 'I don't care what they say, I don't believe it. Who ever heard of quarantine in the middle of the summer? I don't know why travel's being restricted all over the world, but I don't believe it's because of the flu.' Accusingly, 'You've got all that information at your fingertips. Why don't you look it up and see? They banned travel to France before the epidemic got so bad.'

Martie rubbed his head, searched his desk for aspirin and didn't find any. Slowly he reached for the phone, then dialed Sandy, his information girl. 'See what we have on tap about weather-related illnesses, honey. You know, flu, colds, pneumonia. Stuff like that. Hospital statistics, admittances, deaths. Closings of businesses, schools. Whatever you can find. Okay?' To the picture on his desk, he said, 'Satisfied?'

Julia watched the Hilary Boyle show at six thirty and afterward had scrambled eggs and a glass of milk. The weather special at ten explained Martie's delay, but even if there hadn't been the special to whip into being, transportation had ground to a stop. Well, nothing new there, either. She had tried to call Martie finally, and got the recording: *Sorry, your call cannot be completed at this time.* So much for that. The baby cried and cried.

She tried to read for an hour or longer and had no idea of what she had been reading when she finally tossed the book down and turned to look at the fire. She added a log and poked the ashes until the flames shot up high, sparking blue and green, snapping crisply. As soon as she stopped forcing her mind to remain blank, the thoughts came rushing in.

Was it crazy of her to think they had killed her two babies? Why would they? Who were they? Weren't autopsies performed on newborn babies? Wouldn't the doctors and nurses be liable to murder charges, just like anyone else? These were the practical aspects, she decided. There were more. The fear of a leak. Too many people would have to be involved. It would be too dangerous, unless it was also assumed that everyone in the delivery room, in the OB ward, in fact, was part of a gigantic conspiracy. If only she could remember more of what had happened.

Everything had been normal right up to delivery time. Dr. Wymann had been pleased with her pregnancy from the start. Absolutely nothing untoward had happened. Nothing. But when she woke up, Martie had been at her side, very pale, red-eyed. *The baby is dead,* he'd said. And, *Honey, I love you so much. I'm so sorry. There wasn't a thing they could do.* And on and on. They had wept together. Someone had come in with a tray that held a needle. Sleep.

Wrong end of it. Start at the other end. Arriving at the hospital, four-minute pains. Excited, but calm. Nothing unexpected. Dr. Wymann had briefed her on procedure. Nothing out of the ordinary. Blood sample, urine. Weight. Blood pressure. Allergy test. Dr. Wymann: *Won't be long now, Julia. You're doing fine.* Sleep. Waking to see Martie, pale and red-eyed at her side.

Dr. Wymann? He would have known. He wouldn't have let them do anything to her baby!

At the foot of the stairs she listened to the baby crying. Please don't, she thought at it. Please don't cry. Please.

The baby wailed on and on.

That was the first pregnancy, four years ago. Then last year, a repeat performance, by popular demand. She put her hands over her ears and ran back to the fireplace. She thought of the other girl in the double room, a younger girl, no more than eighteen. Her baby had died too in the staph outbreak. Sleeping, waking up, no reason, no sound in the room, but wide awake with pounding heart, the chill of fear all through her. Seeing the girl then, short gown, long lovely leg climbing over the guard rail at the window. Pale yellow light in the room, almost too faint to make out details, only the silhouettes of objects. Screaming suddenly, and at the same moment becoming aware of figures at the door. An intern and a nurse. Not arriving, but standing there quietly. Not moving at all until she screamed. The ubiquitous needle to quiet her hysterical sobbing.

'Honey, they woke you up when they opened the hall door. They didn't say anything for fear of startling her, making her fall before they could get to her.'

'Where is she?'

'Down the hall. I saw her myself. I looked through the observation window and saw her, sleeping now. She's a manic-depressive, and losing the baby put her in a tailspin. They're going to take care of her.'

Julia shook her head. She had let him convince her, but it was a lie. They hadn't been moving at all. They had stood there waiting for the girl to jump. Watching her quietly, just waiting for the end. If Julia hadn't awakened and screamed, the girl would be dead now. She shivered and went to the kitchen to make coffee. The baby was howling louder.

She lighted a cigarette. Martie would be smoking continuously during the taping. She had sat through several tapings and knew the routine. The staff members watching, making notes, the director making notes. Hilary Boyle walked from the blue velvet hangings, waved at the camera, took his seat behind a massive desk, taking his time, getting comfortable. She liked Hilary Boyle, in spite of all the things about his life, about him personally, that she usually didn't like in people. His self-assurance that bordered on egomania, his women. She felt that he had assigned her a number and when it came up he would come to claim her as innocently as a child demanding his lollipop. She wondered if he would kick and scream when she said no. The cameras moved in close, he picked up his clipboard and glanced at the first sheet of paper, then looked into the camera. And the magic would work again, as it always worked for him. The *X factor*. A TV personality, radiating over wires, through air, from emptiness, to people everywhere who saw him. How did it work? She didn't know, neither did anyone else. She stubbed out her cigarette.

She closed her eyes, seeing the scene, Hilary leaving the desk, turning to wave once, then going through the curtains. Another successful special. A huddle of three men, or four, comparing notes, a rough spot here, another there. They could be taken care of with scissors, Martie, his hands shoved deep into his pockets, mooching along to his desk.

'Martie, you going home tonight?' Boyle stood in his doorway, filling it.

'Doesn't look like it. Nothing's leaving the city now.'

'Buy you a steak.' An invitation or an order? Boyle grinned. Invitation. 'Fifteen minutes. Okay?'

'Sure. Thanks.'

Martie tried again to reach Julia. 'I'll be in and out for a couple of hours. Try it now and then, will you, doll?'

The operator purred at him. He was starting to get the material he had asked Sandy for: hospital statistics, epidemics of flu and flu-like diseases, incidence of pneumonia outbreaks, and so on. As she had said, there was a stack of the stuff. He riffled quickly through the print-outs. Something was not quite right, but he couldn't put his finger on what it was. Boyle's door opened then, and he stacked the material and put it inside his desk.

'Ready? I had Doris reserve a table for us down in the Blue Light. I could use a double Scotch about now. How about you?'

Martie nodded and they walked to the elevators together. The Blue Light was one of Boyle's favorite hangouts. They entered the dim, noisy room, and were led to a back table where the ceiling was noise-absorbing and partitions separated one table from another, creating small oases of privacy. The floor show was visible, but almost all the noise of the restaurant was blocked.

'Look,' Boyle said, motioning toward the blue spotlight. Three girls were dancing together. They wore midnight-blue body masks that covered them from crown to toe. Wigs that looked like green and blue threads of glass hung to their shoulders, flashing as they moved.

'I have a reputation,' Boyle said, lighting a cigarette from his old one. 'No one thinks anything of it if I show up in here three-four times a week.'

He was watching the squirming girls, grinning, but there was an undertone in his voice that Martie hadn't heard before. Martie looked at him, then at the girls again, and waited.

'The music bugs the piss right out of me, but the girls, now that's different,' Boyle said. A waitress moved into range. She wore a G-string, an apron whose straps miraculously covered both nipples and stayed in place somehow, and very high heels. 'Double Scotch for me, honeypot, and what for you, Martie?'

'Bourbon and water.'

'Double bourbon and water for Dr. Sayre.' He squinted, studying the gyrating girls. 'That one on the left. Bet she's a blonde. Watch the way she moves, you can almost see blondness in that wrist motion ...' Boyle glanced at the twitching hips of their waitress and said, in the same breath, same tone of voice, 'I'm being watched. You will be too after tonight. You might look out for them.'

'Who?'

'I don't know. Not government, I think. Private outfit maybe. Like FBI, same general type, same cool, but I'm almost positive not government.'

'Okay, why?'

'Because I'm a newsman. I really am, you know, always was, always will be. I'm on to something big.'

He stopped and the waitress appeared with their drinks. Boyle's gaze followed the twisting girls in the spotlight and he chuckled. He looked up at the waitress then. 'Menus, please.'

Martie watched him alternately with the floor show. They ordered, and when they were alone again Boyle said, 'I think that immortality theory that popped up eight or ten years ago isn't dead at all. I think it works, just like what's-his-name said it would, and I think that some people are getting the treatments they need, and the others are being killed off, or allowed to die without interference.'

Martie stared at him, then at his drink. He felt numb. As if to prove to himself that he could move, he made a whirlpool in the glass and it climbed higher and higher and finally spilled. Then he put it down. 'That's crazy. They couldn't keep something like that quiet.'

Boyle was continuing to watch the dancing girls. 'I'm an intuitive man,' Boyle said. 'I don't know why I know that next week people will be interested in volcanoes, but if I get a hunch that it will make for a good show, we do it, and the response is tremendous. You know how that goes. I hit right smack on the button again and again. I get the ideas, you fellows do the work, and I get the credit. That's like it should be. You're all diggers, I'm the locator. I'm an ignorant man, but not stupid. Know what I mean? I learned to listen to my hunches. I learned to trust them. I learned to trust myself in front of the camera and on the mike. I don't know exactly what I'll say, or how I'll look. I don't practice anything. Something I'm in tune with ... something. They know it, and I know it. You fellows call it the *X factor*. Let it go at that. We know what we mean when we talk about it even if we don't know what it is or how it works. Right. Couple of months ago, I woke up thinking that we should do a follow-up on the immortality thing. Don't look at me. Watch the show. I realized that I hadn't seen word one about it for three or four years. Nothing at all. What's his name, the guy that found the synthetic RNA?'

'Smithers. Aaron Smithers.'

'Yeah. He's dead. They worked him over so thoroughly, blasted him and his results so convincingly, that he never got over it. Finis. Nothing else said about it. I woke up wondering why not. How could he have been that wrong? Got the Nobel for the same kind of discovery, RNA as a cure for some kind of arthritis. Why was he so far off this time?' Boyle had filled the ashtray by then. He didn't look at Martie as he spoke, but continued to watch the girls, and now and then grinned, or even chuckled.

The waitress returned, brought them a clean ashtray, new drinks, took their orders, and left again. Boyle turned then to look at Martie. 'What, no comments yet? I thought by now you'd be telling me to see a head-shrinker.'

Martie shook his head. 'I don't believe it. There'd be a leak. They proved it wouldn't work years ago.'

'Maybe.' Boyle drank more slowly now. 'Anyway, I couldn't get rid of this notion, so I began to try to find out if anyone was doing anything with the synthetic RNA, and that's when the doors began to close on me. Nobody knows nothing. And someone went through my office, both here at the studio and at home. I got Kolchak to go through some of his sources to look for appropriations for RNA research. Security's clamped down on all appropriations for research. Lobbied for by the AMA, of all people.'

'That's something else. People were too loose with classified data,' Martie said. 'This isn't in the universities any more. They don't know any more than you do.'

Boyle's eyes gleamed. 'Yeah? So you had a bee, too?'

'No. But I know people. I left Harvard to take this job. I keep in touch. I know the people in the biochemical labs there. I'd know if they were going on with this. They're not. Are you going to try to develop this?' he asked, after a moment.

'Good Christ! What do you think!'

Julia woke up with a start. She was stiff from her position in the large chair, with her legs tucked under her, her head at an angle. She had fallen asleep over her sketch pad, and it lay undisturbed on her lap, so she couldn't have slept very long. The fire was still hot and bright. It was almost eleven thirty. Across the room the television flickered. The sound was turned off, music continued to play too loud in the house. She cocked her head, then nodded. It was still crying.

She looked at the faces she had drawn on her pad: nurses, interns, Dr. Wymann. All young. No one over thirty-five. She tried to recall others in the OB ward, but she was sure that she had them all. Night nurses, delivery nurses, nursery nurses, admittance nurse ... She stared at the drawing of Dr. Wymann. They were the same age. He had teased her about it once. 'I pulled out a grey hair this morning, and here you are as pretty and young as ever. How are you doing?'

But it had been a lie. He was the unchanged one. She had been going to him for six or seven years, and he hadn't changed at all in that time. They were both thirty-four now.

Sitting at the side of her bed, holding her hand, speaking earnestly. 'Julia, there's nothing wrong with you. You can still have babies, several of them if you want. We can send men to the moon, to the bottom of the ocean, but we can't fight off staph when it hits in epidemic proportions in a nursery. I know you feel bitter now, that it's hopeless, but believe me, there wasn't anything that could be done either time. I can almost guarantee you that the next time everything will go perfectly.'

'It was perfect this time. And the last time.'

'You'll go home tomorrow. I'll want to see you in six weeks. We'll talk about it again a bit later. All right?'

Sure. Talk about it. And talk and talk. And it didn't change the fact that she'd had two babies and had lost two babies that had been alive and kicking right up till the time of birth.

Why had she gone so blank afterward? For almost a year she hadn't thought of it, except in the middle of the night, when it hadn't been thought but emotion that had ridden her. Now it seemed that the emotional response had been used up and for the first time she could think about the births, about the staff, about her own reactions. She put her sketch pad down and stood up, listening.

Two boys. They'd both been boys. Eight pounds two ounces, eight pounds four ounces. Big, beautifully formed, bald. The crying was louder, more insistent. At the foot of the stairs she stopped again, her face lifted.

It was a small hospital, a small private hospital. One that Dr. Wymann recommended highly. Because the city hospitals had been having such rotten luck trying to get rid of staph. Infant mortality had doubled, tripled? She had heard a fantastic figure given out, but hadn't been able to remember it. It had brought too sharp pains, and she had rejected knowing. She started up the stairs.

'Why are they giving me an allergy test? I thought you had to test for specific allergies, not a general test.'

'If you test out positive, then they'll look for the specifics. They'll know they have to look. We're getting too many people with allergies that we knew nothing about, reacting to antibiotics, to sodium pentothal, to starch in sheets. You name it.'

The red scratch on her arm. But they hadn't tested her for specifics. They had tested her for the general allergy symptoms and had found them, and then let it drop. At the top of the stairs she paused again, closing her eyes briefly this time. 'I'm coming,' she said softly. She opened the door.

His was the third crib. Unerringly she went to him and picked him up; he was screaming lustily, furiously. 'There, there. It's all right, darling. I'm here.' She rocked him, pressing him tightly to her body. He nuzzled her neck, gulping in air now, the sobs diminishing into hiccups. His hair was damp with perspiration, and he smelled of powder and oil. His ear was tight against his head, a lovely ear.

'You! What are you doing in here? How did you get in?'

She put the sleeping infant back down in the crib, not waking him. For a moment she stood looking down at him, then she turned and walked out the door.

The three blue girls were gone, replaced by two zebra-striped girls against a black drop, so that only the white stripes showed, making an eerie effect.

'Why did you bring this up with me?' Martie asked. Their steaks were before them, two inches thick, red in the middle, charred on the outside. The Blue Light was famous for steaks.

'A hunch. I have a standing order to be informed of any research anyone does on my time. I got the message that you were looking into illnesses, deaths, all that.' Boyle waved aside the sudden flash of anger that swept through Martie. 'Okay. Cool it. I can't help it. I'm paranoid. Didn't they warn you? Didn't I warn you myself when we talked five years ago? I can't stand for you to use the telephone. Can't stand not knowing what you're up to. I can't help it.'

'But that's got nothing to do with your theory.'

'Don't play dumb with me, Martie. What you're after is just the other side of the same thing.'

'And what are you going to do now? Where from here?'

'That's the stinker. I'm not sure. I think we work on the angle of weather control, for openers. Senator Kern is pushing the bill to create an office of weather control. We can get all sorts of stuff under that general heading, I think, without raising this other issue at all. You gave me this idea yourself. Weather-connected sickness. Let's look at what we can dig out, see what they're hiding, what they're willing to tell, and go on from there.'

'Does Kolchak know? Does anyone else?'

'No. Kolchak will go along with the political angle. He'll think it's a natural for another special. He'll cooperate.'

Martie nodded. 'Okay,' he said. 'I'll dig away. I think there's a story. Not the one you're after, but a story. And I'm curious about the clampdown on news at a time when we seem to be at peace.'

Boyle grinned at him. 'You've come a long way from the history-of-science teacher that I talked to about working for me five years ago. Boy, were you green then.' He pushed his plate back. 'What made you take it? This job? I never did understand.'

'Money. What else? Julia was pregnant. We wanted a house in the country. She was working, but not making money yet. She was talking about taking a job teaching art, and I knew it would kill her. She's very talented, you know.'

'Yeah. So you gave up tenure, everything that goes with it.'

'There's nothing I wouldn't give up for her.'

'To each his own. Me? I'm going to wade through that goddam snow the six blocks to my place. Prettiest little piece you ever saw waiting for me. See you tomorrow, Martie.'

He waved to the waitress, who brought the check. He signed it without looking at it, pinched her bare bottom when she turned to leave, and stood up. He blew a kiss to the performing girls, stopped at three tables momentarily on his way out, and was gone. Martie finished his coffee slowly.

Everyone had left by the time he returned to his office. He sat down at his desk and looked at the material he had pushed into the drawer. He knew now what was wrong. Nothing more recent than four years ago was included in the material.

Julia slept deeply. She had the dream again. She wandered down hallways, into strange rooms, looking for Martie. She was curious about the building. It was so big. She thought it must be endless, that it wouldn't matter how long she had to search it, she would never finish. She would forever see another hall that she hadn't seen before, another series of rooms that she hadn't explored. It was strangely a happy dream, leaving her feeling contented and peaceful. She awakened at eight. The wind had died completely, and the sunlight coming through the sheer curtains was dazzling, brightened a hundredfold by the brilliant snow. Apparently it had continued to snow after the wind had stopped; branches, wires, bushes, everything was frosted with an inch of powder. She stared out the window, committing it to memory. At such times she almost wished that she was a painter instead of a sculptor. The thought passed. She would get it, the feeling of joy and serenity and purity, into a piece of stone, make it shine out for others to grasp, even though they'd never know why they felt just like that.

She heard the bell of the snowplow at work on the secondary road that skirted their property, and she knew that as soon as the road was open, Mr. Stopes would be by with his small plow and get their driveway. She hoped it all would be cleared by the time Martie left the office. She stared at the drifted snow in the back yard between the house and the barn and shook her head. Maybe Mr. Stopes could get that, too.

While she had breakfast she listened to the morning news. One disaster after another, she thought, turning it off after a few minutes. A nursing-home fire, eighty-two dead. A new outbreak of infantile diarrhea in half a dozen hospitals, leaving one hundred thirty-seven dead babies. The current flu-epidemic death rate increasing to one out of ten.

Martie called at nine. He'd be home by twelve. A few things to clear up for the evening show. Nothing much. She tried to ease his worries about her, but realized that the gaiety in her voice must seem forced to him, phony. He knew that when the wind howled as it had done the night before, the baby cried. She hung up regretfully, knowing she hadn't convinced him that she had slept well, that she was as gay as she sounded. She looked at the phone and knew that it would be even harder to convince him in person that she was all right, and, more important, that the baby was all right.

Martie shook her hard. 'Honey, listen to me. Please, just listen to me. You had a dream. Or a hallucination. You know that. You know how you were the first time you heard it. You told me you were having a breakdown. You knew then that it wasn't the baby you heard, no matter what your ears told you. What's changed now?'

'I can't explain it,' she said. She wished he'd let go. His hands were painful on her shoulders, and he wasn't aware of them. The fear in his eyes was real and desperate. 'Martie, I know that it couldn't happen like that, but it did. I opened the door to somewhere else where our baby is alive and well. He has grown, and he has hair now, black hair, like yours, but curly, like mine. A nurse came in. I scared the hell out of her, Martie. She looked at me just like you are looking now. It was real, all of it.'

'We're going to move. We'll go back to the city.'

'All right. If you want to. It won't matter. This house has nothing to do with it.'

'Christ!' Martie let her go suddenly, and she almost fell. He didn't notice. He paced back and forth a few minutes, rubbing his hand over his eyes, through his hair, over the stubble of his beard. She wished she could do something for him, but she didn't move. He turned to her again suddenly. 'You can't stay alone again!'

Julia laughed gently. She took his hand and held it against her cheek. It was very cold. 'Martie, look at me. Have I laughed spontaneously during this past year? I know how I've been, what I've been like. I knew all along, but I couldn't help myself. I was such a failure as a woman, don't you see? It didn't matter if I succeeded as an artist, or as a wife, anything. I couldn't bear a live child. That's all I could think about. It would come at the most awkward moments, with company here, during our lovemaking, when I had the mallet poised, or mixing a cake. Whammo, there it would be. And I'd just want to die. Now, after last night, I feel as if I'm alive again, after being awfully dead. It's all right, Martie. I had an experience that no one else could believe in. I don't care. It must be like conversion. You can't explain it to anyone who hasn't already experienced it, and you don't have to explain it to him. I shouldn't even have tried.'

'God, Julia, why didn't you say what you were going through? I didn't realize. I thought you were getting over it all.' Martie pulled her to him and held her too tightly.

'You couldn't do anything for me,' she said. Her voice was muffled. She sighed deeply.

'I know. That's what makes it such hell.' He pushed her back enough to see her face. 'And you think it's over now? You're okay now?' She nodded. 'I don't know what happened. I don't care. If you're okay, that's enough. Now let's put it behind us ...'

'But it isn't over, Martie. It's just beginning. I know he's alive now. I have to find him.'

'Can't get the tractor in the yard, Miz Sayre. Could have if you hadn't put them stones out there in the way.' Mr. Stopes mopped his forehead with a red kerchief, although he certainly hadn't worked up a sweat, not seated on the compact red tractor, running it back and forth through the drive.

Julia refilled his coffee cup and shrugged. 'All right. We'll get to it. The sun's warming it up so much. Maybe it'll just melt off.'

'Nope. It'll melt some, then freeze. Be harder'n ever to get it out then.'

Julia went to the door and called to Martie, 'Honey, can you write Mr. Stopes a check for clearing the drive?'

Martie came in from the living room, taking his checkbook from his pocket. 'Twenty?'

'Yep. Get yourself snowed in in town last night, Mr. Sayre?'

'Yep.'

Mr. Stopes grinned and finished his coffee. 'Some April Fools' Day, ain't it? Forsythia blooming in the snow. Don't know. Just don't know 'bout the weather any more. Remember my dad used to plant his ground crops on April Fools' Day, without fail.' He waved the check back and forth a minute, then stuffed it inside his sheepskin coat. 'Well, thanks for the coffee, Miz Sayre. You take care now that you don't work too hard and come down with something. You don't want to get taken sick now that Doc Hendricks is gone.'

'I thought that new doctor was working out fine?' Martie said.

'Yep. For some people. You don't want him to put you in the hospital, though. The treatment's worse than the sickness any more, it seems.' He stood up and pulled on a flap-eared hat that matched his coat. 'Not a gambling man myself, but even if I was, wouldn't want them odds. Half walks in gets taken out in a box. Not odds that I like at all.'

Julia and Martie avoided looking at one another until he was gone. Then Julia said incredulously, 'Half!'

'He must be jacking it way up.'

'I don't think so. He exaggerates about some things, not things like that. That must be what they're saying.'

'Have you met the doctor?'

'Yes, here and there. In the drugstore. At Dr. Saltzman's. He's young, but he seemed nice enough. Friendly. He asked me if we'd had our ... flu shots.' She finished very slowly, frowning slightly.

'And?'

'I don't know. I was just thinking that it was curious of him to ask. They were announcing at the time that there was such a shortage, that only vital people could get them. You know, teachers, doctors, hospital workers, that sort of thing. Why would he have asked if we'd had ours?'

'After the way they worked out, you should be glad that you didn't take him up on it.'

'I know.' She continued to look thoughtful, and puzzled. 'Have you met an old doctor recently? Or even a middle-aged one?'

'Honey!'

'I'm serious. Dr. Saltzman is the only doctor I've seen in years who's over forty. And he doesn't count. He's a dentist.'

'Oh, wow! Look, honey, I'm sorry I brought up any of this business with Boyle. I think something is going on, but not in such proportions, believe me. We're a community of what? – seven hundred in good weather? I don't think we've been infiltrated.'

She wasn't listening. 'Of course, they couldn't have got rid of all the doctors, probably just the ones who were too honest to go along with it. Well, that probably wasn't many. Old and crooked. Young and ... immortal. Boy!'

'Let's go shovel snow. You need to have your brain aired out.'

While he cleared the path to the barn, Julia cleaned off the granite sculptures. She studied them. They were rough-quarried blocks, four feet high, almost as wide. The first one seemed untouched, until the light fell on it in a certain way, the rays low, casting long shadows. There were tracings of fossils, broken, fragmented. Nothing else. The second piece had a few things emerging from the surface, clawing their way up and out, none of them freed from it, though. A snail, a trilobite-like crustacean, a winged insect. What could have been a bird's head was picking its way out. The third one had defined animals, warm-blooded animals, and the suggestion of forests. Next came man and his works. Still rising from stone, too closely identified with the stone to say for certain where he started and the stone ended, if there was a beginning and an end at all. The whole work was to be called *The Wheel*. These were the ends of the spokes, and at the hub of the wheel there was to be a solid granite seat, a pedestal-like seat. That would be the ideal place to sit and view the work, although she knew that few people would bother. But from the center, with the stones in a rough circle, the shadows should be right, the reliefs complementary to one another, suggesting heights that had been left out, suggesting depths that she hadn't shown. All suggestion. The wheel that would unlock the knowledge within the viewer, let him see what he usually was blind to ...

'Honey, move!' Martie nudged her arm. He was panting hard.

'Oh, dear. Look at you. You've been moving mountains!' Half the path was cleared. 'Let's make a snowman, right to the barn door.'

The snow was wet, and they cleared the rest of the path by rolling snowballs, laughing, throwing snowballs at each other, slipping and falling. Afterward they had soup and sandwiches, both of them too beat to think seriously about cooking.

'Nice day,' Julia said lazily, lying on the living-room floor, her chin propped up by cupped hands, watching Martie work on the fire.

'Yeah. Tired?'

'Um. Martie, after you talked with Hilary, what did you do the rest of the night?'

'I looked up Smithers' work, what there was in the computer anyway. It's been a long time ago, I'd forgotten a lot of the arguments.'

'And?'

'They refuted him thoroughly, with convincing data.'

'Are you certain? Did you cross-check?'

'Honey, they were men like ... like Whaite, and ... Never mind. They're just names to you. They were the leaders at that time. Many of them are still the authorities. Men like that tried to replicate his experiments and failed. They looked for reasons for the failures and found methodological bungling on his part, erroneous conclusions, faulty data, mistakes in his formulae.'

Julia rolled over, with her hands clasped under her head, and stared at the ceiling. 'I half remember it all. Wasn't it almost a religious denunciation that took place? I don't remember the scientific details. I wasn't terribly interested in the background then, but I remember the hysteria.'

'It got loud and nasty before it ended. Smithers was treated badly. Denounced from the pulpit, from the Vatican, from every scientific magazine ... It got nasty. He died after a year of it, and they let the whole business die too. As they should have done.'

'And his immortality serum will take its place along with the alchemist's stone, the universal solvent, a pinch of something in water to run the cars ...'

''Fraid so. There'll always be those who will think it was suppressed.' He turned to build up the fire that had died down completely.

'Martie, you know that room I told you about? The nursery? I would know it again if I saw it. How many nurseries do you suppose there are in the city?'

Martie stopped all motion, his back to her. 'I don't know.' His voice was too tight.

Julia laughed and tugged at his sweater. 'Look at me, Martie. Do I look like a kook?'

He didn't turn around. He broke a stick and laid the pieces across each other. He topped them with another stick, slightly larger, then another.

'Martie, don't you think it's strange that suddenly you got the idea to look up these statistics, and Hilary approached you with different questions about the same thing? And at the same time I had this ... this experience. Doesn't that strike you as too coincidental to dismiss? How many others do you suppose are asking questions too?'

'I had thought of it some, yes. But last night just seemed like a good time to get to things that have been bugging us. You know, for the first time in months no one was going anywhere in particular for hours.'

She shook her head. 'You can always rationalize coincidences if you are determined to. I was alone for the first time at night since I was in the hospital. I know. I've been over all that, too. But still ...' She traced a geometrical pattern at the edge of the carpet. 'Did you have a dream last night? Do you remember it?'

Martie nodded.

'Okay. Let's test this coincidence that stretches on and on. I did too. Let's both write down our dreams and compare them. For laughs,' she added hurriedly when he seemed to stiffen again. 'Relax, Martie. So you think I've spun out. Don't be frightened by it. I'm not. When I thought that was the case, six months ago, or whenever it was, I was petrified. Remember? This isn't like that. This is kooky in a different way. I feel that a door that's always been there has opened a crack. Before, I didn't know it was there, or wouldn't admit that it was anyway. And now it's there, and open. I won't let it close again.'

Martie laughed suddenly and stopped breaking sticks. He lighted the fire and then sat back with a notebook and pen. 'Okay.'

Martie wrote his dream simply with few descriptions. Alone, searching for her in an immense building. A hospital? An endless series of corridors and rooms. He had forgotten much of it, he realized, trying to fill in blanks. Finally he looked up to see Julia watching him with a faint smile. She handed him her pad and he stared at the line drawings that could have been made to order to illustrate his dream. Neither said anything for a long time.

'Martie, I want another baby. Now.'

'God! Honey, are you sure? You're so worked up right now. Let's not decide ...'

'But I have decided already. And it is in my hands, you know.'

'So why tell me at all? Why not just toss the bottle out the window and be done with it?'

'Oh, Martie. Not like that. I want us to be deliberate about it, to think during coitus that we are really making a baby, to love it then ...'

'Okay, honey. But why now? What made you say this now?'

'I don't know. Just a feeling.'

'Dr. Wymann, is there anything I should do, or shouldn't do? I mean ... I feel fine, but I felt fine the other times, too.'

'Julia, you are in excellent health. There's no reason in the world for you not to have a fine baby. I'll make the reservation for you ...'

'Not ... I don't want to go back to that same hospital. Someplace else.'

'But, it's ...'

'I won't!'

'I see. Well, I suppose I can understand that. Okay. There's a very good, rather small hospital in Queens, fully equipped ...'

'Dr. Wymann, this seems to be the only hang-up I have. I have to see the hospital first, before you make a reservation. I can't explain it ...' Julia got up and walked to the window high over Fifth Avenue. 'I blame the hospital, I guess. This time I want to pick it out myself. Can't you give me a list of the ones that you use, let me see them before I decide?' She laughed and shook her head. 'I'm amazed at myself. What could I tell by looking? But there it is.'

Dr. Wymann was watching her closely. 'No, Julia. You'll have to trust me. It would be too tiring for you to run all over town to inspect hospitals ...'

'No! I ... I'll just have to get another doctor,' she said miserably. 'I can't go in blind this time. Don't you understand?'

'Have you discussed this with your husband?'

'No. I didn't even know that I felt this way until right now. But I do.'

Dr. Wymann studied her for a minute or two. He glanced at her report spread out before him, and finally he shrugged. 'You'll just wear yourself out for nothing. But, on the other hand, walking's good for you. I'll have my nurse give you the list.' He spoke into the intercom briefly, then smiled again at Julia. 'Now sit down and relax. The only thing I want you to concentrate on is relaxing, throughout the nine months. Every pregnancy is totally unlike every other one ...'

She listened to him dreamily. So young-looking, smooth-faced, tanned, if overworked certainly not showing it at all. She nodded when he said to return in a month.

'And I hope you'll have decided at that time about the hospital. We do have to make reservations far in advance, you know.'

Again she nodded. 'I'll know by then.'

'Are you working now?'

'Yes. In fact, I'm having a small showing in two weeks. Would you like to come?'

'Why don't you give me the date and I'll check with my wife and let you know?'

Julia walked from the building a few minutes later feeling as though she would burst if she didn't find a private place where she could examine the list of hospitals the nurse had provided. She hailed a taxi and as soon as she was seated she looked over the names of hospitals she never had heard of before.

Over lunch with Martie she said, 'I'll be in town for the next few days, maybe we could come in together in the mornings and have lunch every day.'

'What are you up to now?'

'Things I need. I'm looking into the use of plastics. I have an idea ...'

He grinned at her and squeezed her hand. 'Okay, honey. I'm glad you went back to Wymann. I knew you were all right, but I'm glad you know it too.'

She smiled back at him. If she found the nursery, or the nurse she had startled so, then she would tell him. Otherwise she wouldn't. She felt guilty about the smiles they exchanged, and she wished momentarily that he wouldn't make it so easy for her to lie to him.

'Where are you headed after lunch?' he asked. 'Oh, the library ...' She ducked her head quickly and scraped her sherbet glass. 'Plastics?'

'Urn.' She smiled again, even more brightly. 'And what about you? Tonight's show ready?'

'Yeah. This afternoon, in ...' he glanced at his watch, '... exactly one hour and fifteen minutes I'm to sit in on a little talk between Senator George Kern and Hilary. Kern's backing out of his weather-control fight.'

'You keep hitting blank walls, don't you?'

'Yes. Good and blank, and very solid. Well, we'd better finish up. I'll drop you at the library.'

'Look at us,' she said over the dinner table. 'Two dismaler people you couldn't find. You first. And eat your hamburger. Awful, isn't it?'

'It's fine, honey.' He cut a piece, speared it with his fork, then put it down. 'Kern is out. Hilary thinks he got the treatment last month. And his wife too. They were both hospitalized for pneumonia at the same time.'

'Do you know which hospital? In New York?'

'Hell, I don't know. What difference does ... What are you getting at?'

'I ... Was it one of these?' She got the list from her purse and handed it to him. 'I got them from Dr. Wymann's nurse. I wouldn't go back to that one where ... I made them give me a list so I could look them over first.'

Martie reached for her hand and pressed it hard. 'No plastics?'

She shook her head.

'Honey, it's going to be all right this time. You can go anyplace you want to. I'll look these over. You'll just be ...'

'It's all right, Martie. I already checked out three of them. Two in Manhattan, one in Yonkers. I ... I'd rather do it myself. Did Senator Kern mention a hospital?'

'Someplace on Long Island. I don't remember ...'

'There's a Brent Park Memorial Hospital on Long Island. Was that it?'

'Yes. No. Honey, I don't remember. If he did mention it, it passed right over my head. I don't know.' He put the list down and took her other hand and pulled her down to his lap. 'Now *you* give. Why do you want to know? What did you see in those hospitals that you visited? Why did you go to the library?'

'I went to three hospitals, all small, all private, all run by terribly young people. Young doctors, young nurses, young everybody. I didn't learn anything else about them. But, in the library I tried to borrow a book on obstetrics, and there aren't any.'

'What do you mean, there aren't any? None on open shelves? None in at the time?'

'None. They looked, and they're all out, lost, not returned, gone. All of them. I tried midwifery, and the same thing. I had a young boy who was terribly embarrassed by it all searching for me, and he kept coming back with the same story. Nothing in. So I went to the branch library in Yonkers, since I wanted to see the hospital there anyway, and it was the same thing. They have open shelves there, and I did my own looking. Nothing.'

'What in God's name did you plan to do with a book on obstetrics?'

'Isn't that beside the point? Why aren't there any?'

'It is directly to the point. What's going through your mind, Julia? Exactly what are you thinking?'

'The baby is due the end of December. What if we have another blizzard? Or an ice storm? Do you know anything about delivering a baby? Oh, something, I grant you. Everyone knows something. But what about an emergency? Could you handle an emergency? I thought if we had a book ...'

'I must have wandered into a nut ward. I'm surrounded by maniacs. Do you hear what you're saying? Listen to me, sweetheart, and don't say a word until I'm finished. When that baby is due, I'll get you to a hospital. I don't care which one you choose, or where it is. You'll be there. If we have to take an apartment next door to it for three months to make certain, we'll do it. You have to have some trust and faith in me, in the doctor, in yourself. And if it eases your mind, I'll get you a book on obstetrics, but by God, I don't plan to deliver a baby!'

Meekly she said, 'You just get me a book and I'll behave. I promise.' She got up and began to gather up their dishes. 'Maybe later on we'll want some scrambled eggs or something. Let's have coffee now.'

They moved to the living room, where she sat on the floor with her cup on the low table. 'Is Kern satisfied that no biological warfare agent got loose to start all this?'

Martie looked at her sharply. 'You're a witch, aren't you? I never told you that's what I was afraid of.'

She shrugged. 'You must have.'

'Kern's satisfied. I am too. It isn't that. His committee decided to drop it, at his suggestion, because of the really dangerous condition of the world right now. It's like a powder keg, just waiting for the real statistics to be released. That would blow it. Everyone suspects that the death rate has risen fantastically, but without official figures, it remains speculation, and the fuse just sits there. He's right. If Hilary does go on, he's taking a terrible risk.' He sighed. 'It's a mutated virus that changes faster than the vaccines that we come up with. It won't be any better until it mutates into something that isn't viable, then it will vanish. Only then will the governments start opening books again, and hospitals give out figures for admittances and deaths. We know that the medical profession has been hit probably harder than any other. Over-exposure. And the shortage of personnel makes everything that used to be minor very serious now.'

Julia nodded, but her gaze didn't meet his. 'Sooner or later,' she said, 'you'll have to turn that coin over to see what's on the other side. Soon now, I think.'

Julia wore flowered pants and a short vest over a long-sleeved tailored blouse. With her pale hair about her shoulders, she looked like a very young girl, too young to be sipping champagne from the hollow-stemmed goblet that she held with both hands. Dwight Gregor was in the middle of the circle of stones, studying the effects from there. Gregor was the main critic, the one whose voice was heard if he whispered, although all others were shouting. Julia wished he'd come out of the circle and murmur something or other to her. She didn't expect him to let her off the hook that evening, but at least he could move, or something. She probably wouldn't know what his reactions had been until she read his column in the morning paper. She sipped again and turned despairingly to Martie.

'I think he fell asleep out there.'

'Honey, relax. He's trying to puzzle it out. He knows that you're cleverer than he is, and more talented, and that you worked with the dark materials of your unconscious. He feels it and can't grasp the meaning ...'

'Who are you quoting?'

'Boyle. He's fascinated by the circle. He'll be in and out of it all evening. Watch and see. Haven't you caught him looking at you with awe all over his face?'

'Is that awe? I was going to suggest that you tell him I'm good and pregnant.'

Martie laughed with her, and they separated to speak with the guests. It was a good show, impressive. The yard looked great, the lighting effects effective, the waterfall behind the basket-weave fence just right, the pool at the bottom of the cascading water just dark and mysterious enough ... Martie wandered about his yard proudly.

'Martie?' Boyle stopped by him. 'Want to talk to you. Half an hour over by the fence. Okay?'

Gregor left the circle finally and went straight to Julia. He raised her hand to his lips and kissed it lightly, keeping his gaze on her face. 'My dear. Very impressive. So nihilistic. Did you realize how nihilistic it is? But of course. And proud, also. Nihilistic but proud. Strange combination. You feel that man almost makes it, this time. Did you mean that? Only one toe restraining him. Sad, So sad.'

'Or you can imagine that the circle starts with the devastation, the ruins, and the death of man. From that beginning to the final surge of life that lifts him from the origins in the dirt ... Isn't that what you really meant to say, my dear?' Frances Lefever moved in too close to Julia, overwhelming her with the sweet, sickening scent of marijuana heavy on her breath. 'If that's where the circle begins, then it is a message of nothing but hope. Isn't that right, my dear?'

Gregor moved back a step, waving his hand in the air. 'Of course, one can always search out the most romantic explanation of anything ...'

'Romantic? Realistic, my dear Dwight. Yours is the typical male reaction. Look what I've done. I've destroyed all mankind, right back down to the primordial ooze. Mine says, Look, man is freeing himself, he is leaping from his feet-of-clay beginnings to achieve a higher existence. Did you really look at that one? There's no shadow, you know.'

Dwight and Frances forgot about Julia. They argued their way back to the circle, and she leaned weakly against the redwood fence and drank deeply.

'Hey. Are you all right, Julia?'

'Dr. Wymann. Yes. Fine. Great.'

'You looked as if you were ready to faint ...'

'Only with relief. They like it. They are fascinated by it. It's enigmatic enough to make them argue about meanings, so they'll both write up their own versions, different from each other's, and that will make other people curious enough to want to see for themselves ...'

Dr. Wymann laughed and watched the two critics as they moved about the large stones, pointing out to one another bits and pieces each was certain the other had missed.

'Congratulations, Julia.'

'What did *you* think of it?'

'Oh, no. Not after real critics have expressed opinions.'

'Really. I'd like to know.'

Dr. Wymann looked again at the circle of stones and shrugged. 'I'm a clod. An oaf. I had absolutely no art training whatever. I like things like Rodin. Things that are unequivocal. I guess I didn't know what you were up to with your work.'

Julia nodded. 'Fair enough.'

'I'm revealed as an ass.'

'Not at all, Dr. Wymann. I like Rodin too.'

'One thing. I couldn't help overhearing what they were saying. Are you the optimist that the woman believes, or the pessimist that Gregor assumes?'

Julia finished off her champagne, looking at the goblet instead of the doctor. She sighed when it was all gone. 'I do love Champagne,' She smiled at him then, 'The stones will give you the answer. But you'll have to find it yourself. I won't tell.'

He laughed and they moved apart. Julia drifted back inside the house to check the buffet and the bar. She spoke briefly with Margie Mellon, who was taking care of the food and drinks. Everything was holding up well. A good party. Successful unveiling. A flashbulb went off outside, then another and another.

'Honey! It's really great, isn't it? They love it! And you! And me because I'm married to you!'

She never had seen Martie so pleased. He held her close for a minute, then kissed each eyelid. 'Honey, I'm so proud of you I can't stand it. I want to strip you and take you to bed right now. That's how it's affected me.'

'Me too. I know.'

'Let's drive them all off early …'

'We'll try anyway.'

She was called to pose by the circle, and she left him. Martie watched her. 'She is so talented,' a woman said, close to his ear. He turned. He didn't know her.

'I'm Esther Wymann,' she said huskily. She was very drunk. 'I almost envy her. Even if it is for a short time. To know that you have that much talent, a genius, creative genius. I think it would be worth having, even if you knew that tomorrow you'd be gone. To have that for a short time. So creative and so pretty too.'

She drained a glass that smelled like straight Scotch. She ran the tip of her tongue around the rim and turned vaguely toward the bar. 'You too, sweetie? No drink? Where's our host? Why hasn't he taken care of you? That's all right. Esther will. Come on.'

She tilted when she moved and he steadied her. 'Thanks. Who're you, by the way?'

'I'm the host,' he said coldly. 'What did you mean by saying she has so little time? What's that supposed to mean?'

Esther staggered back from his hand. 'Nothing. Didn't mean anything.' She lurched away from him and almost ran the three steps that took her into a group of laughing guests. Martie saw Wymann put an arm about her to help hold her upright. She said something to him and the doctor looked up quickly to see Martie watching them. He turned around, still holding his wife, and they moved toward the door to the dining room. Martie started after them, but Boyle appeared at the doorway and motioned for him to go outside.

The doctor would keep, Martie decided. He couldn't talk to him with that drunken woman on his arm anyway. He looked once more toward the dining-room doorway, then followed Boyle outside.

A picture or two, someone said. He stood by Julia, holding her hand, and the flashbulbs exploded. Someone opened a new bottle of champagne close by, and that exploded. Someone else began shrieking with laughter; he moved away from the center of the party again and sat down at a small table, waiting for Boyle to join him.

'This is as safe as any place we're likely to find,' Boyle said. He was drinking beer, carrying a quart bottle with him. 'What have you dug out?'

The waterfall splashed noisily behind them, and the party played noisily before them. Martie watched the party. He said, 'The death rate, extrapolated only, you understand. Nothing's available on paper anywhere. But the figures we've come up with are: from one million eight hundred thousand five years ago, up to fourteen and a quarter million this year.'

Boyle choked and covered his face with his handkerchief. He poured more beer and took a long swallow.

Martie waited until he finished, then said, 'Birth rate down from three and a half million to one million two hundred thousand. That's live births. At these rates, with the figures we could find, we come up with a loss per thousand of sixty-three. A death rate of sixty-three per thousand.'

Boyle glared at him. He turned to watch the party again, saying nothing.

Martie watched Julia talking with guests. She never had looked more beautiful. Pregnancy had softened her thin face, had added a glow. What had that bitch meant by saying she had so little time? He could hear Julia's words inside his head: *You'll have to turn it over sooner or later.* She didn't understand. Boyle didn't understand. Men like Whaite wouldn't have repudiated a theory so thoroughly if there had been any merit whatsoever in it. It was myth only that said the science community was a real community. There were rivalries, but no corruption of that sort. The whole scientific world wouldn't unite behind a lie. He rubbed his eyes. But how many of the scientists knew enough about biochemistry to form independent judgments? They had to take the word of the men who were considered authorities, and if they, fewer than a dozen, passed judgment, then that judgment was what the rest of the community accepted as final. Only the amateurs on the outside would question them, no one on the inside would think of doing so.

Martie tapped his fingers on the table impatiently. Fringe thinking. Nut thinking. They'd take away his badge and his white coat if he expressed such thoughts. But, damn it, they could! Six or eight, ten men could suppress a theory, for whatever reason they decided was valid, if only they all agreed. Over fourteen million deaths in the States in the past-year. How many in the whole world? One hundred million, two hundred million? They'd probably never know.

'Hilary, I'm going up to Cambridge tomorrow, the next day, soon, I have to talk to Smithers' widow.'

Hilary nodded. 'At that death rate, how long to weed us out? Assuming Smithers was right, that forty percent can be treated.'

'About twelve and a half years, starting two years ago.' Martie spoke without stopping to consider his figures. He wasn't sure when he had done that figuring. He hadn't consciously thought of it.

He watched as Julia spoke with Dr. Wymann, holding his hand several seconds. She nodded, and the doctor turned and walked away. What had Wymann's wife meant? Why had she said what she had? If 'they' existed, she was one of them. As Wymann was. As Senator Kern was. Who else?

'I don't believe it!'

'I know.'

'They couldn't keep such figures quiet! What about France? England? Russia?'

'Nothing. No statistics for the last four years. Files burned, mislaid, not properly completed. Nothing.'

'Christ!' Boyle said.

Julia smoked too much, and paced until the phone rang. She snatched it up. 'Martie! Are you all right?'

'Sure. What's wrong, honey?' His voice sounded ragged, he was out of breath.

'Darling, I'm sorry. I didn't want to alarm you, but I didn't know how else to reach you. Don't say anything now. Just come home, Martie, straight home. Will you?'

'But ... Okay, honey. My flight is in fifteen minutes. I'll be home in a couple of hours. Sit tight. Are you all right?'

'Yes. Fine. I'm fine.' She listened to the click at the other end of the line, and felt very alone again. She picked up the brief note that she had written and looked at it again. 'Lester B. Hayes Memorial Hospital, ask for Dr. Conant.'

'It's one on my list,' she said to Martie when he read it. 'Hilary collapsed at his desk and they took him there. Martie, they'll kill him, won't they?'

Martie crumpled the note and let it drop. He realized that Julia was trembling and he held her for several minutes without speaking. 'I have to make some calls, honey. Will you be all right?'

'Yes. I'm fine now. Martie, you won't go, will you? You won't go to that hospital?'

'Sh. It's going to be all right, Julia. Sit down, honey. Try to relax.'

Doyle's secretary knew only that she had found him sprawled across his desk and in the next few minutes, Kolchak, or someone, had called the ambulance and he was taken away to the hospital. The report they had was that he was not in serious condition. It had happened before, no one was unduly alarmed, but it was awkward. It never had happened before a show. This time ... Her voice drifted away.

Martie slammed the receiver down. 'It really *has* happened before. The hospital could be a coincidence.'

Julia shook her head. 'I don't believe it.' She looked at her hands. 'How old is he?'

'Fifty, fifty-five. I don't know. Why?'

'He's too old for the treatment, then. They'll kill him. He'll die of complications from flu, or a sudden heart attack. They'll say he suffered a heart attack at his desk '

'Maybe he did have a heart attack. He's been driving himself ... Overweight, living too fast, too hard, too many women and too much booze ...'

'What about Smithers? Did you see Mrs. Smithers?'

'Yes. I saw her. I was with her all morning ...'

'And within an hour of your arrival there, Hilary collapses. You're getting too close, Martie. You're making them act now. Did you learn anything about Smithers, or his work?'

'It's a familiar kind of thing. He published prematurely, got clobbered, then tried to publish for over a year and had paper after paper returned. During that time he saw everything he'd done brought down around his ears. His wife believes he committed suicide, although she won't admit it even to herself. But it's there, in the way she talks about them, the ones who she says hounded him ...'

'And his papers?'

'Gone. Everything was gone when she was able to try to straighten things out. There wasn't anything left to straighten out. She thinks he destroyed them. I don't know. Maybe he did. Maybe they were stolen. It's too late now.'

The phone shrilled, startling both of them. Martie answered. 'Yes, speaking ...' He looked at Julia, then turned his back. His hand whitened on the phone. 'I see. Of course: An hour, maybe less.'

Julia was very pale when Martie hung up and turned toward her. 'I heard,' she said. 'The hospital ... it's one of theirs. Dr. Conant must be one of them.'

Martie sat down and said dully, 'Hilary's on the critical list. I didn't think they'd touch him. I didn't believe it. Not him.'

'You won't go, will you? You know it's a trap.'

'Yes, but for what? They can get to me any time they want. They don't have to do it this way. There's no place to hide.'

'I don't know for what. Please don't go.'

'You know what this is? The battle of the Cro-Magnon and the Neanderthal all over again. One has to eliminate the other. We can't both exist in the same ecological niche.'

'Why can't they just go on living as long as they want and leave us alone? Time is on their side.'

'They know they can't hide it much longer. In ten years it would be obvious, and they're outnumbered. They're fighting for survival, too. Hitting back first, that's all. A good strategy.'

He stood up. Julia caught his arm and tried to pull him to her. Martie was rigid and remote. 'If you go, they'll win. I know it. You're the only one now who knows anything about what is going on. Don't you see? You're more valuable than Boyle was. All he had was his own intuition and what you gave him. He didn't understand most of it even. But you ... They must have a scheme that will eliminate you, or force you to help them. Something.'

Martie kissed her. 'I have to. If they just want to get rid of me, they wouldn't be this open. They want something else. Remember, I have a lot to come back for. You, the baby. I have a lot to hate them for, too. I'll be back.'

Julia swayed and held on to the chair until he turned and left the house. She sat down slowly, staring straight ahead. Martie looked at Dr. Wymann without surprise. 'Hilary's dead?'

'Unfortunately. There was nothing that could be done. A fatal aneurism ...'

'How fortunate for you.'

'A matter of opinion. Sit down, Dr. Sayre. We want to talk with you quite seriously. It might take a while.' Wymann opened the door to an adjoining office and motioned. Two men in doctors' coats entered, nodded at Martie, and sat down. One carried a folder.

'Dr. Conant, and Dr. Fischer.' Wymann closed the door and sat down in an easy chair. 'Please do sit down, Sayre. You are free to leave at any time. Try the door if you doubt my word. You are not a prisoner.'

Martie opened the door. The hallway was empty, gleaming black and white tiles in a zigzag pattern, distant noise of an elevator, sound of a door opening and closing. A nurse emerged from one of the rooms, went into another.

Martie closed the door again. 'Okay, your show. I suppose you are in charge?'

'No. I'm not in charge. We thought that since you know me, and in light of certain circumstances, it might be easier if I talked to you. That's all. Either of these two ... half a dozen others who are available. If you prefer, it doesn't have to be me.'

Martie shook his head. 'You wanted me. Now what?'

Wymann leaned forward. 'We're not monsters, no more than any other human being, anyway. Smithers had exactly what he said he had. You know about that. He really died of a heart attack. So much for history. It works, Sayre. For forty percent of the people. What would you do with it? Should we have made it public? Held a lottery? It would have gone underground even more than it has now, but it would be different. We don't want to kill anyone. The others, the ones who couldn't use it, would search us out and exterminate us like vermin. You know that. In the beginning we needed time. We were too accessible, too vulnerable. A handful of people knew what it was, how to prepare it, how to test for results, how to administer it, what to watch for, all the rest. It's very complicated. We had to protect them and we had to add numbers.'

Martie watched him, thinking, Julia knew. The babies. Both of them. The new pregnancy. She was afraid time was running out. This man, or another like him. Had they done anything, or simply failed to do something for the first two? Was there any difference really? His skin felt clammy and he opened his hands when he realized that his fingers were getting stiff.

'It's going on everywhere, more or less like here. Have you read ...? No, of course not ... I'll be frank with you, Sayre. The world's on a powder keg, has been for over a year. Martial law in Spain, Portugal, Israel, most of the Mid-East. Nothing at all out of China. Japan ripped wide open by strikes and riots, tighter than a drum right now. Nothing's coming out of there. It's like that everywhere. Clampdown on all news. No travel that isn't high-priority. France has been closed down for six months. More restrictions than when they were occupied. Same with England. Canada has closed her borders for the first time in history, as has Mexico. UNESCO recommended all this, in an effort to stop the epidemics, ostensibly. But really to maintain secrecy regarding the climbing death rate. And everyone's panic-stricken, terrified of being hit next. It must have been like this during the Plague outbreaks. Walled cities, fear. Your story coming now would ignite the whole world. There'd be no way to maintain any sort of order. You know I'm right. We couldn't let you and Boyle go on with it.'

Martie stood up. 'If you try to sell yourselves as humanitarians, I might kill you right now.'

'It depends entirely on where you're standing. Most men with any kind of scientific training see almost immediately that what we've done, how we've done it, was the only way this could have been handled. Out in the open, with more than half the people simply not genetically equipped to tolerate the RNA, there would have been a global catastrophe that would have destroyed all of mankind. Governments are made up of old men, Sayre. Old men can't use it. Can you imagine the uprising against all the world governments that would have taken place! It would have been a holocaust that would have left nothing. We've prevented that.'

'You've set yourselves up as final judges, eliminating those who can't take it ...'

'Eliminating? We upset the entire Darwinian framework for evolution by our introduction of drugs, our transplants, life-saving machines. We were perpetuating a planet of mental and physical degenerates, with each generation less prepared to live than the last. I know you think we're murderers, but is it murder to fail to prescribe insulin and let a diabetic die rather than pass on the genes to yet another generation?' Wymann started to pace, after glancing at his watch, checking it against the wall clock.

'There have been hard decisions, there'll be more even harder ones. Every one of us has lost someone he cared for. Every one! Conant lost his first wife. My sister ... We aren't searching out people to kill, unless they threaten us. But if they come to us for treatment, and we know that they are terminal, we let them die.'

Martie moistened his lips. 'Terminal. You mean mortal, with a temporary sore throat, or a temporary appendix inflammation, things you could treat.'

'They are terminal now, Sayre. Dying in stages. Dying from the day they are born. We don't prolong their lives.'

'Newborn infants? Terminal?'

'Would you demand that newborn idiots be preserved in institutions for fifty or sixty years? If they are dying, we let them die.'

Martie looked at the other doctors, who hadn't spoken. Neither of them had moved since arriving and sitting down. He turned again to Wymann. 'You called me. What do you want?'

'Your help. We'll need people like you. Forty percent of the population, randomly chosen, means that there will be a shortage of qualified men to continue research, to translate that research into understandable language. The same sort of thing you're doing now. Or, if you prefer, a change of fields. But we will need you.'

'You mean I won't suffer a thrombosis, or have a fatal wreck for the next twenty years, if I play along?'

'More than that, Martie. Much more than that. During your last physical examination for insurance you were tested, a routine test by the way. Not conclusive, but indicative. You showed no gross reactions to the synthetic UNA. You would have to be tested more exhaustively, of course, but we are confident that you can tolerate the treatments ...'

'What about Julia? What do you plan for her?'

'Martie, have you thought at all about what immortality means? Not just another ten years tacked on at the end, or a hundred, or a thousand. As far as we know now, from all the laboratory data, there is no end, unless through an accident. And with our transplant techniques even that is lessening every week. Forever, Martie. No, you can't imagine it. No one can. Maybe in a few hundred years we'll begin to grasp what it means, but not yet ...'

'*What about Julia?*'

'We won't harm her.'

'You've tested her already. You know about her.'

'Yes. She cannot tolerate the RNA.'

'If anything goes wrong, you'll fold your hands and let her die. Won't you? *Won't you!'*

'Your wife is a terminal case! Can't you see that? If she were plugged into a kidney machine, a heart-and-lung machine, with brain damage, you'd want the plug pulled. You know you would. We could practice preventive medicine on her, others like her, for the next forty years or longer. But for what? For what, Dr. Sayre? As soon as they know, they'll turn on us. We can keep this secret only a few more years. We know we are pushing our luck even now. We took an oath that we would do nothing to prolong the lives of those who are dying. Do you think they would stop at that? If they knew today, we'd be hunted, killed, the process destroyed. Lepers would rather infect everyone with their disease than be eradicated. Your wife will be thirty-five when the child is born. A century ago she would have been doomed by such a late pregnancy. She would have been an old woman. Modern medicine has kept her youthful, but it's an artificial youthfulness. She is dying!'

Martie made a movement toward Wymann, who stepped behind his desk warily. Conant and Fischer were watching him very closely. He sank back down in the chair, covering his face. Later, he thought. Not now. Find out what you can now. Try to keep calm.

'Why did you tell me any of this?' he asked after a moment. 'With Boyle gone my job is gone. I couldn't have hurt you.'

'We don't want you to light that fuse. You're a scientist. You can divorce your emotions from your reason and grasp the implications. But aside from that, your baby, Martie. We want to save the baby. Julia has tried and tried to find a book on obstetrics, hasn't she? Has she been successful?'

Martie shook his head. The book. He had meant to ask about one at Harvard, and he'd forgotten. 'The baby. You think it will be able to ... The other two? Are they both ...?'

'The only concern we have now is for the successful delivery of the child that your wife is carrying. We suspect that it will be one of us. And we need it. That forty percent I mentioned runs through the population, young and old. Over forty, give or take a year or two, they can't stand the treatments. We don't know exactly why yet, but we will eventually. We just know that they die. So that brings us down to roughly twenty-five percent of the present population. We need the babies. We need a new generation of people who won't be afraid of death from the day they first grasp the meaning of the word. We don't know what they will be, how it will change them, but we need them.'

'And if it isn't able to take the RNA?'

'Martie, we abort a pregnancy when it is known that the mother had German measles, or if there is a high probability of idiocy. You know that. Unfortunately, our technique for testing the foetus is too imperfect to be certain, and we have to permit the pregnancy to come to term. But that's the only difference. It would still be a therapeutic abortion.'

Martie and Julia lay side by side, not touching, each wakeful, aware that the other was awake, pretending sleep. Julia had dried tears on her cheeks. Neither of them had moved for almost an hour.

'But goddam it, which one is Cro-Magnon and which Neanderthal?' Martie said, and sat upright.

Julia sat up too. 'What?'

'Nothing. I'm sorry. Go back to sleep, honey. I'm getting up for a while.'

Julia swung her legs off the bed. 'Can we talk now, Martie? Will you talk to me about it now?'

Martie muttered a curse and left the room.

This was part of the plan, he knew. Drive them apart first, make it easier for him to join them later. He sat down in the kitchen with a glass half filled with bourbon and a dash of water.

'Martie? Are you all right?' Julia stood in the doorway. She was barely showing her pregnancy now, a small bulge was all. He turned away. She sat down opposite him. 'Martie? Won't you tell me?'

'Christ, Julia, will you shove off! Get off my back for a while?'

She touched his arm. 'Martie, they offered you the treatment, didn't they? They think you could take it. Are you going to?'

He jerked out of the chair, knocking it over, knocking his glass over. 'What are you talking about?'

'That was the crudest thing they could have done right now, wasn't it? After I'm gone, it would have been easier, but now ...'

'Julia, cut it out. You're talking nonsense ...'

'I'll die this time, won't I? Isn't that what they're planning? Did they tell you that you could have the babies if you want them? Was that part of it too?'

'Has someone been here?' Martie grabbed her arm and pulled her from the chair.

She shook her head.

He stared at her for a long time, and suddenly he yanked her against him hard. 'I must be out of my mind. I believed them. Julia, we're getting out of here, now. Tomorrow.'

'Where?'

'I don't know. Somewhere. Anywhere. I don't know.'

'Martie, we have to stop running. There are physical limits to how much I can run now. But besides that, there's really no place to run to. It's the same everywhere. You haven't found anyone who will listen to you. One check with your personal data file and that's it. We may never know what they put on your record, but it's enough to make every official pat you on the head and say, "Don't worry, Dr. S. We'll take care of it." We can't get out of the country, passport requests turned down for medical reasons. But even if we could ... more of the same.'

Julia was pale, with circles under her eyes. It was early in November, cold in Chicago, where the apartment overlooked Lake Michigan. A flurry of powdery snow blew in a whirlwind across the street.

Martie nodded. 'They've covered everything, haven't they? Special maternity hospitals! For the safety and protection of the mother and child. To keep them from the filthy conditions that exist in most hospitals now. Keep them safe from pneumonia, flu, staph ... Oh, Christ!' He leaned his head against the glass and watched the dry dustlike snow.

'Martie ...'

'Damn. I'm out of cigarettes, honey. I'll just run out and get some.'

'Okay. Fine.'

'Want anything?'

'No. Nothing.' She watched him pull on his coat and leave, then stood at the window and watched until he emerged from the building and started to walk down the street. The baby kicked and she put her hand over her stomach. 'It's all right, little one. It's all right.'

Martie was only a speck among specks standing at the corner, waiting for the light to turn. She could no longer pick out his figure from those around him. 'Martie,' she whispered. Then she turned away from the window and sat down. She closed her eyes for a moment. They wanted her baby, this baby, not just another child who would become immortal. They were too aware of the population curve that rises slowly, slowly, then with abandon becomes an exponential curve. No, not just a child, but her particular child. She had to remember that always. The child would be safe. They wouldn't let it be harmed. But they wouldn't let her have it, and they knew that this time she wouldn't give it up. So she'd have to die. The child couldn't be tainted with her knowledge of death. Of course, if it too was unable to tolerate the RNA, there was no real problem. Mother and child. Too bad. No cures for ... whatever they'd say killed them. Or would they keep her, let her try again? She shook her head. They wouldn't. By then Martie would be one of them, or dead. This was the last child for her.

'So what can I do?' she asked.

Her hands opened and closed convulsively. She shut her eyes hard. 'What?' she whispered desperately. '*What?*'

She worked on the red sandstone on the ground floor of the barn. It was too big to get up to her studio, so she'd had her tools, bench, table, everything brought down. It was drafty, but she wore heavy wool slacks and a tentlike top, and was warm.

She whistled tunelessly as she worked ...

Julia stood up too fast, then clutched the chair for support. Have to remember, she told herself severely. Work. She had to go to work. She picked up her sketch pad, put it down again. Red sandstone, $10 \times 10 \times 8$. And red quartzite, $4 \times 3 \times 2$. She called her supplier on Long Island.

'Funny, Mrs. Sayre. Just got some in,' he said. 'Haven't had sandstone for ... oh, years, I guess.'

'Can you have it delivered tomorrow?'

'Mrs. Sayre, everyone who's ever touched rock is working. Had to put on an extra man. Still can't keep up.'

'I know. And the painters, and composers, and poets ...' They settled for the day after her arrival home.

She reserved seats on the six P.M. flight to New York, asked for their hotel bill within the hour, and started to pack. She paused once, a puzzled frown on her forehead. Every one of her friends in the arts was working furiously. They either didn't know or didn't care about the disastrous epidemics, the travel bans, any of it.

Martie walked slowly, his head bowed. He kept thinking of the bridge that he had stood on for an hour, watching filthy water move sluggishly with bits and pieces of junk floating on the surface: a piece of orange, a plastic bag, a child's doll with both arms gone, one eye gone. The doll had swirled in a circle for several minutes, caught in a branch, then moved on out of sight. Of no use to anyone, unwanted, unloved now. Imperfect, cast away.

The wind blew, whipping his coat open, and he shivered. On trial, before his judges. Martin Sayre, do you dare risk your immortal soul for this momentary fling? Confess, go to the flame willingly, with confession on your lips, accept the flame, that too is momentary, and rejoice forever in Paradise.

'Dr. Sayre, you're a reasonable man. You know that we can't do anything for your wife. She will be allowed to bear her child here. No other hospital would admit her, none of the city hospitals would dare. We won't harm her, Dr. Sayre. We won't do anything that is not for her own good ...'

Torquemada must have argued so.

And, somewhere else. He couldn't keep them apart, all the same, different faces, but the same. 'Of course, the child will have to be taken from her, no matter what happens. The fear of death is a disease as dangerous almost as death itself. It drives man mad. These new children must not be infected with it ...'

And somewhere else. 'Ah, yes, Dr. Sayre. Meant to call you back, but got tied up. Appropriations Committee sessions, don't you know. Well now, Dr. Sayre, this little theory of yours about the serum. I've been doing some thinking on that, Dr. Sayre, and don't you know, I can't come up with anything to corroborate what you say. Now if you can furnish some hard proof, don't you know, well now, that would make a difference. Yes, sir, make a big difference.'

And again, 'Hello, Martie, I just don't know. You may be absolutely right. But there's no way to get to anything to make sure. I can't risk everything here on a wild-goose chase. I checked your data file, as you suggested, and they have a diagnosis made by a Dr. Fischer of Lester B. Hayes Memorial Hospital, who examined you extensively in four examinations from March through August of this year. He recommended treatment for schizophrenia; you refused. Face it, Martie, I have to ask myself, isn't this just a schizophrenic construct?'

He should have jumped, he decided. He really should have jumped. He opened the door to the apartment to find Julia surrounded by their luggage, her coat over a chair, and sketch pads strewn about her on the floor.

'Honey, what's the matter?'

'I want to go home. Now. We have seats for six o'clock ...'

'But, Julia, you know ...'

'Martie, with you, or without you, I'm going home.'

'Are you giving up, then? Is that it? You go slinking back licked now, let them take away your baby, do whatever they mean to do to you ...'

'Martie, I can't explain anything. I never can, you know. But I have to go back. I have work to do before the baby comes. I just have to. It's like this with every artist I know. Jacques Remy, Jean Vance, Porter, Dee Richardson ... I've been in touch with different ones here and there, and they're all driven to work now. Some of my best friends simply didn't have time to see me. None of them can explain it. There's a creative explosion taking place and we're helpless. Oh, if I could drink, I could probably resist it by getting dead drunk and staying that way ...'

'What are you going to do?' He picked up several sheets of her drawing paper, but there were only meaningless scribbles on it.

'I don't know. I can't get it on paper. I need my tools, the sandstone. My hands know, will know when they start ...'

'Julia, you're feverish. Let me get you a sleeping pill. We'll go home in a day or two, if you still feel like this. Please ...'

She grabbed up her coat and swung it about her shoulders, jerking her arms through the sleeves, paying no attention to him. 'What time is it?'

'Four. Sit down, honey. You're as pale as a ghost ...'

'We'll have to wait at the airport, but if we don't leave now, traffic will get so bad. Let's start now, Martie. We can have a sandwich and coffee while we wait.'

At the airport she couldn't sit still. She walked the length of the corridors, rode the ramps to the upper levels, watched planes arriving and departing, walked to the lowest levels and prowled in and out of shops. Finally they boarded their plane and the strap forced her into a semblance of quietude.

'Martie, how do you, science, explain dreams? The content of dreams?

Wait, there's more. And the flashes of intuition that almost everyone experiences from time to time? The jumps into new fields that scientists make, proposing new theories explaining the universe in a way that no one had ever thought of before? *Déjà vu* feelings? Oh, what else? Flashes of what seems to be telepathy? Clairvoyance? Hilary's *X factor*? All those things that scientists don't usually want to talk about?'

'I don't. I don't try. I don't know the answer. And no one else does either.' The engines roared and they were silent until the mammoth jet was above the clouds. Clouds covered the earth from Chicago to Kennedy Airport.

Julia looked down sometime later and said, 'That's like it is with us. There are clouds hiding something from us, and once in a while a strong light probes through for a minute. The clouds thin out, or the light is strong for a short time, whatever. It doesn't last. The cloud layer thickens, or the power source can't keep up the strength of the beam, and there are only the clouds. No one who wasn't there or didn't see through them at that moment would believe they could be penetrated. And trying to make a whole out of such glimpses is a futile thing. Now a bit of blue sky, now a star, now pitch-black sky, now the lights of a passing plane ...'

'So we invent an infrared light that penetrates the clouds ...'

'What if there were something on the other side of the layer that was trying to get through to us, just as much as we were trying to get through from this side, and with as little success ...?'

She hadn't even heard him. Martie took her hand and held it, letting her talk on. Her hand was warm and relaxed now that they were actually heading for home.

'Suppose that it, whatever it is, gets through only now and then, but when it does it is effective because it knows what it's looking for, and we never do. Not infrared ...' She had heard. 'But the other direction. Inward. We send other kinds of probes. Psychoanalysis, EEG, drugs, hypnosis, dream analysis ... We are trying to get through, but we don't know how, or what we're trying to reach, or how to know when we have reached it.'

'God?' Martie turned to look at her. 'You're talking about reaching God?'

'No. I think that man has always thought of it as God, or some such thing, but only because man has always sensed its presence and didn't know what it was or how it worked, but he knew that it was more powerful than anything else when it did work. So, he called it God.'

'Honey, we've always been afraid of what we didn't understand. Magic, God, devils ...'

'Martie, until you can explain why it is that more comes out of some minds than goes in, you haven't a leg to stand on, and you know it.'

Like the new geometries, he thought. The sum can be greater than its parts. Or, parallel lines might meet in some remote distance. He was silent, considering it, and Julia dozed. 'But, dammit,' he breathed a few minutes later . . .

'You're a Hull, Watson, Skinner man,' Julia finished, not rousing from her light sleep. He stared at her. She hadn't studied psychology in her life. She didn't know Hull from Freud from Jung.

The polishing wheel screamed for hours each day as the carborundum paste cut into the quartzite. Martie dragged Julia from it for her meals, when it was time to rest, at bedtime.

'Honey, you'll hurt yourself. It might be hard on the baby . . .'

She laughed. 'Have I ever looked better or healthier?'

Thin, pale, but with a fiery intensity that made her more beautiful than he had seen her in their lives together. Her eyes were luminous. The tension that had racked her for months was gone. She carried the baby as if unaware of the extra burden, and when she slept, it was deep untroubled sleep that refreshed her wholly.

'You're the one who is suffering, darling,' she said softly, fairy-touching his cheek. Her hands were very rough now, fingernails split and broken jaggedly. He caught her rough hand and pressed it hard against his cheek.

'Wymann has been calling, hasn't he?' Julia asked after a moment. She didn't pull her hand from his face. He turned it over and kissed the palm. 'It's all right to talk about it, Martie. I know he's been calling. They want to see me as soon as possible, to make sure of the baby, to see if the delivery will be normal, or if a section is called for. It's all right.'

'Have you talked to him?'

'No. No. But I know what they're thinking now. They're afraid of me, of people like me. You see, people who have high creativity don't usually have the right sort of genes to take their RNA. A few, but not enough. It worries them.'

'Who've you been talking to?'

'Martie, you know where I've been spending my time.' She laughed. 'It is nice to be home, isn't it?' The fireplace half of the living room was cheerful and glowing, while shadows filled the rest of the long room. 'Of course, when you consider that only about twenty-five percent of the people are getting the RNA it isn't surprising that there aren't many with creative abilities that have been developed to any extent. But, what is sad is that those few who were writers or painters, or whatever, don't seem to continue their work once they know they are immortal. Will women want to continue bearing children if they know they're immortal already?'

'I don't know. You think that the maternal instinct is just a drive to achieve immortality, although vicariously?'

'Why not? Is a true instinct stilled with one or two satisfying meals, or sex acts, or whatever? Women seem to be satisfied as soon as they have a child or two.'

'If that's so, then, whatever happens, the race will be finished. If women don't want children, don't have to satisfy this drive, I should say, it's a matter of time. We have the means to prevent pregnancy, why would they keep on getting knocked up?'

'Because something else needs the children, the constantly shifting, renewing vision that is provided by children. Not us, not me. It. Something else. That thing that is behind us pushing, learning through us. You have the books. You've been reading everything you can find on psychology. The nearest we have been able to describe that something is by calling it the collective unconscious, I think.'

'Jung's collective unconscious,' Martie muttered. 'You know, some scientists, philosophers, artists work right down the middle of a brightly illuminated strip, never go off it. Darwin, for instance. Skinner. Others work so close to the edge that half the time they are in the grey areas where the light doesn't follow, where you never knew if madness guided the pen or genius. Jung spent most of his time on the border, sometimes in the light, sometimes in the shadows. His collective unconscious, the fantasy of a man who couldn't stand mysteries not solved during his own lifetime.'

Julia stood up and stretched. 'God, I'm tired. Bath time.' Martie wouldn't let her get into and out of the bathtub alone now. 'Martie, if there is such a thing – and there is, there is – it's been threatened. It has to have the constantly shifting viewpoint of mankind in order to learn the universe. A billion experiences, a trillion, who knows how many it will need before it is finished? It was born with mankind, it has grown with mankind, as it matures so does man, and if mankind dies now, so will it. We are its sensory receptors. And what Wymann and the others propose is death to it, death to them eventually. It feeds the unconscious, nourishes it, gives it its dreams and its flashes of genius. Without it, man is just another animal, clever with his hands perhaps, but without the dream to work toward. All our probes into space, into the oceans, so few inward. We are so niggardly in exploring the greatest mystery of all, potentially the most rewarding of all.'

She had her bath, and he helped her from the tub and dried her back and smoothed lotion over it. He tucked her into bed, and she smiled at him. 'Come to bed, Martie. Please.'

'Soon, honey. I'm ... restless right now.'

A few minutes later when he looked in on her, she was sound asleep. He smoked and drank and paced, as he did night after night. Julia was like one possessed. He grimaced at the choice of words. She worked from dawn until night, when he forced her to stop. He made their meals, or she wouldn't have eaten. He had to touch her before she knew he was there to collect her for a meal. He stood sometimes and watched her from the doorway, and he was frightened of her at those times. She was a stranger to him, her eyes almost closed, sometimes, he thought, and discarded the thought immediately, her eyes were all the way closed. Her hands held life of their own, strong, white knuckled, thin hands grasping mallet and chisel. She couldn't wear gloves while she worked. She dressed in heavy wool pants, and a heavy sweater, covered by a tentlike poncho that she had made from an army blanket. She wore fleece-lined boots, but her hands had to be bare. He would touch her arm, shake her, and slowly recognition would return to her eyes, she would smile at him and put down her tools; without looking at the thing she was making, she would go with him. He would rub her freezing hands for her, help her out of the heavy garments that were much too warm for the house.

Sometimes after she had gone to bed, usually by nine, he would turn on the barn lights and stand and stare at her work. He wanted, at those times, to pull it down and smash it to a million pieces. He hated it for possessing her when he would have her sit on a velvet cushion and spend her last months and weeks with ...

He threw his glass into the fireplace, then started to pick up the pieces and put them in an ashtray. Something wet sparkled on his hand, and he stared at it for a moment. Suddenly he put his head down on the floor and sobbed for her, for himself, for their child.

'Sayre, why haven't you brought her in for an examination?'

Martie watched Wymann prowl the living room. Wymann looked haggard, he thought suddenly. He laughed. Everyone was looking haggard except Julia.

Wymann turned toward him with a scowl. 'I'm warning you, Sayre. If the child is orphaned at birth, the state won't quibble a bit about our taking it. With you or without you ...'

Martie nodded. 'I've considered that.' He rubbed his hand over his face. A four- or five-day beard was heavy on his cheeks and chin. His hand was unsteady. 'I've thought of everything,' he said deliberately. 'All of it. I lose if I take you up, lose if I don't.'

'You won't lose with us. One woman. There are other women. If she died in childbirth, in an accident, you'd be married again in less than five years ...'

Martie nodded. 'I've been through all that, too. No such thing as the perfect love, lasting love. Why'd you come out here, Wymann? I thought you were too busy for just one patient to monopolize your time. Farthest damn housecall I've ever heard of. And not even called.' He laughed again. 'You're scared. What's going wrong?'

'Where's Julia?'

'Working. Out in the barn.'

'Are you both insane? Working now? She's due in two weeks at the most!'

'She seems to think this is important. Something she has to finish before she becomes a mother and stops for a year or two.'

Wymann looked at him sharply. 'Is she taking that attitude?'

'You first. Why are you out here? What's wrong with the master plan for the emerging superman?'

'He's here because people aren't dying any more. Are they, Dr. Wymann?' Julia stood in the doorway in her stocking feet, stripping off the poncho. 'You have to do things now, don't you, Doctor? Really do things, not just sit back and watch.'

'There is some sort of underground then, isn't there? That's why you two made the grand tour, organizing an underground.'

Julia laughed and pulled off her sweater. 'I'll make us all some coffee.'

Martie watched her. 'A final solution, Doctor. You have to come up with a new final solution, don't you? And you find it difficult.'

'Difficult, yes. But not impossible.'

Martie laughed. 'Excuse me while I shave. Make yourself comfortable. Won't take five minutes.'

He went through the kitchen and caught Julia from behind, holding her hard. 'They'll have to change everything if that's true. They won't all go along with murder, wholesale murder. This will bring it out into the open where we can decide ...'

Julia pulled away and turned to look at him squarely. 'This isn't the end. Not yet. There's something else to come ...'

'What?'

'I don't know. I just know that this isn't the end, not yet. Not like this. Martie, have you decided? It's killing you. You have to decide.'

He shrugged. 'Maybe it will be decided for me. I'm going up to shave now.'

She shook her head. 'You'll have to make the decision. Within a week, I think.'

'Dr. Wymann, why is it that proportionately more doctors than laymen are suicides?' Julia poured coffee and passed the sugar as she spoke. 'And why are there more alcoholics and drug-users among the medical profession?'

Wymann shrugged. 'I give up, why?'

'Oh, because doctors as a group are so much more afraid of death than anyone else. Don't you think?'

'Rather simplistic, isn't it?'

'Yes. Often the most unrelenting drives are very simplistic.'

'Julia, you have to come in to be examined. You know that. There could be unsuspected complications that might endanger the baby.'

'I'll come in, as soon as I finish what I'm doing. A few more days. I'll check in then if you like. But first I have to finish. It's Martie's Christmas present.'

Martie stared at her. Christmas. He'd forgotten.

She smiled. 'It's all right. The baby is my present. The sculpture is yours.'

'What are you doing? Can I see?' Wymann asked. 'Although, remember, I like understandable things. Nothing esoteric or ambiguous.'

'This one is as simple ... as a sunset. I'll go get my boots.' As soon as she had left them, Wymann stood up and paced back and forth in quick nervous strides. 'I bet it reeks of death. They're all doing it. A worldwide cultural explosion, that's what the Sunday *Times* called it. All reeking of death.'

'Ready? You'll need warm clothes, Doctor.'

Muffled in warm garments, they walked together to the barn. The work was ten feet high in places. The quartzite was gone, out of sight. Martie didn't know what she had done with it. What remained was rough sandstone, dull red, with yellow streaks. It looked very soft. She had chiseled and cut into it what looked like random lines. At first glance it seemed to be a medieval city, with steeples, flattened places, roofs. The illusion of a city faded, and it became a rough mountainous landscape, with stiletto-like peaks, unknowable chasms. Underwater mountains, maybe. Martie walked around it. He didn't know what it was supposed to be. He couldn't stop looking, and, strangely, there was a yearning deep within him. Dr. Wymann stood still, staring at it with a puzzled expression. He seemed to be asking silently, 'This is it? Why bother?'

'Martie, hold my hand. Let me explain ...' Her hand was cold and rough in his. She led him around it and stopped at the side that the west light hit. 'It has to be displayed outside. It should rest on a smooth black basalt base, gently curved, not polished, but naturally smooth. I know that they can be found like that, but I haven't been able to yet. And it should weather slowly. Rain, snow, sun, wind. It shouldn't be protected from anything. If people want to, they should be able to touch it. Sculpture should be touched, you know. It's a tactile art. Here, feel ...' Martie put his hand where she directed and ran his fingers up one of the sharply rising peaks. 'Close your eyes a minute,' she said. 'Just feel it.' She reached out for Wymann's hand. He was standing a foot or slightly more to her left. He resisted momentarily, but she smiled and guided his hand to the work.

'You can see that there's order,' she said, 'even if you can't quite grasp it. Order covering something else ...'

Martie didn't know when she stopped talking. He knew, his hand knew, what she meant. Order over something wild and unordered, ungraspable. Something unpredictable. Something that began to emerge, that overcame the order with disorder, distorting the lines. The feeling was not visual. His hand seemed to feel the subliminally skewed order. Rain. Snow. Wind. The imperfections became greater, a deliberate deterioration of order, exposing the inexplicable, almost fearful inside. A nightmare quality now, changing, always changing, faster now. Grosser changes. A peak too thin to support itself, falling sideways, striking another lesser peak, cracking off the needle end of it. Lying at the base, weathering into sand, running away in a stream of red-yellow water, leaving a clean basalt base. Deeper channels being cut into the thing, halving it, dividing it into smaller and smaller bits, each isolated from the rest, each yielding to the elements, faster, faster. A glimpse of something hard and smooth, a gleam of the same red and yellow, but firm, not giving, not yielding. A section exposed, the quartzite, polished and gleaming. Larger segments of it now, a corner, squared, perfect, sharp. Even more unknowable than the shifting sandstone, untouched by the erosion.

But it would go, too. Eventually. Slowly, imperceptibly it would give. And ultimately there would be only the basalt, until in some distant future it would be gone too.

Martie opened his eyes, feeling as if he had been standing there for a very long time. Julia was watching him serenely. He blinked at her. 'It's good,' he said. Not enough, but he couldn't say anything more then.

Wymann pulled his hand from the stone and thrust it deep inside his pocket: 'Why build something that you know will erode away? Isn't it like ice sculpture, only slower?'

'Exactly like it. But we will have a chance to look at it before it is gone. And feel it.' She turned toward the door and waited for them to finish looking. 'Next year, if you look at it, it will be different, and ten years from now, and twenty years from now. Each change means something, you know. Each change will tell you something about yourself, and your world, that you didn't know before.' She laughed. 'At least, I hope so.'

They were silent as they returned to the house and the dancing fire. Martie made drinks for Wymann and himself, and Julia had a glass of milk. Wymann drank his Scotch quickly. He had opened his coat but hadn't taken it off. 'It reeks of death,' he said suddenly. 'Death and decay and dissolution. All the things we are dedicated to eradicating.'

'And mystery and wonder and awe,' Martie said. 'If you also kill those things, what's left? Will man be an animal again, clever with his hands and the tools he's made, but an animal without a dream. Inward that's what it means. Isn't that right, Julia? Inward is the only direction that matters.'

'It itself is what it means,' she said, helplessly almost. 'I tried to explain what it means, but if I could say it, I wouldn't have had to do it. Inward. Yes. A particular way of looking, of experiencing the world, my life in it. When it doesn't apply any longer, it should be gone. Others will reinterpret the world, their lives. Always new interpretations, new ways of seeing. Letting new sensations pass into the unconscious, into the larger thing that uses these impressions and also learns.' She drained her glass. 'I'll see you in a week at the latest, Doctor. I promise. You personally will deliver my baby.'

Why? Why? Why? Martie paced and watched the fire burn itself out and paced some more in the darkened, cooling room. Snow was falling softly, lazily, turning the back yard into an alien world. Why did she promise to go to them? Why to Wymann? What had he felt out there in the barn? Martie flung himself down in an easy chair, and eventually, toward dawn, fell asleep.

The hospital. The same dream, over and over, the same dream. He tried to wake up from it, but while he was aware of himself dreaming, he couldn't alter anything, could only wander through corridors, searching for her. Calling her. Endless corridors, strange rooms, an eternity of rooms to search ...

'Julia is in good condition. Dilating already. Three or four days probably, but she could go into labor any time. I recommend that she stay here, Sayre. She is leaving it up to you.'

Martie nodded. 'I want to see her before we decide.' He pulled a folded section of newspaper from his pocket and tossed it down on Wymann's desk. 'Now you tell me something. Why did Dr. Fischer jump out of his window?'

'I don't know. There wasn't a note.'

'Fischer was the doctor who, quote, examined me, unquote, wasn't he? The one who added that charming little note to my personal data record, that I'm schizophrenic? A psychiatrist.'

'Yes. You met him here.'

'I remember, Wymann. And you can't tell me why he jumped. Maybe I can tell you. He dried up, didn't he? A psychiatrist without intuition, without dreams, without an unconscious working for and with him. When he reached in, he closed on emptiness, didn't he? Don't all of you!'

'I don't know what you're talking about. Conant has scheduled you for testing starting tomorrow morning. If positive ...'

'Go to hell, Wymann. You, Conant, the rest of you. Go to hell!'

'All right. Maybe that's rushing it. We'll wait until Julia has delivered. You'll want to be with your child. We'll wait. Julia's in room four-nineteen. You can go up whenever you want.'

He tapped lightly on the door. Julia pulled it open, laughing, with tears on her cheeks. 'I know. I know. You're going to be all right,' she cried.

'Me? I came to tell you that *you'd* be all right.'

'I've known that for a long time now. Martie, are you sure? Of course you are. You've seen. He, Wymann, doesn't realize yet. I don't think many of them do ...'

'Honey, stop. You're six jumps ahead of me. What are you talking about?'

'You'll catch up. It, the thing, the collective unconscious, whatever it is, has withdrawn from them. They're pariahs to it. Empty. They think that it's a reaction to the RNA, but it isn't. They want babies desperately, but already the reason for wanting the babies is getting dimmer ...' She stopped suddenly and pressed her hand against her stomach. A startled look crossed her face. 'You'd better see if he's still in the building.'

'She'll be all right. A few hours more.' Dr. Wymann sat down in the waiting room with Martie. 'Tell me something, Sayre. Why did she make that stone thing? Why do any of them make the things they do, write poetry, plays, paint? Why?'

Martie laughed.

'Funny,' Wymann said, rubbing his eyes, 'I feel that I should know. Maybe that I did know, once. Well, I should look in on her now and then.' He stood up. 'By the way, I found a memo on my desk, telling me to remind you of your appointment with Dr. Conant in the morning. Are you sick or something?'

'I'm fine, Doctor. Just fine.'

'Good. Good. See you in a little while.'

He walked down the hallways, glancing into rooms here and there, all equally strange. 'Martie, down here. I'm down here.' He turned toward the sound of her voice and followed it. 'It's a boy, darling. Big, husky boy.' He bowed his head and felt tears warm on his cheeks. When Wymann came out to tell him about his son, he found Martie sound asleep, smiling.

He stood over him for a minute, frowning. There was something else that he had to do. Something else. He couldn't remember what it was. Perfect delivery. No complications. Good baby. Good mother. No trouble at all. He shrugged and tiptoed from the room and went home, leaving Martie sleeping. The nurse would wake him as soon as Julia was ready to see him.

'Darling, you're beautiful. Very, very beautiful. I brought you a Christmas present after all.' He held it out for her to take. A stuffed dog, one eye closed in a wink, a ridiculous grin on its face. 'You knew how it would be just like I knew about our son, didn't you?'

'I just knew. It was threatened. Any other way of countering the threat would have endangered it even more. We have all those terrible things that we would have used on each other. No one would have survived the war that would have come. It left them. That awful vacuum in Wymann, in Conant, all of them. They do what they are trained to do, no more. They do it very well.' She patted her newly flat stomach.

'You did it. You, others like you. The ones who could open to it, accept, and be possessed wholly. A two-way communication must take place during such times. That cultural explosion, all over the world. You at the one end of the spectrum, Wymann, them, at the other, from total possession to total absence.'

'It will take some time to search the records, find our babies ...'

'They'll help us now. They need guidance. They'll have to be protected ...'

'Forever and ever.'

WHERE HAVE YOU BEEN
BILLY BOY, BILLY BOY?

His building had fifty-nine floors. The outer walls were dark green marble with black trim; they had slit windows, not to aid visibility, but for aesthetic purposes. The slits reflected the evening sun and gleamed gold, they were silver in the morning, they sparkled and shone at times, then again they were merely black. The marble went up to about the third floor. It was very difficult to tell from the outside just how much of the building was faced with the polished marble, but surely not more than three floors. So wasteful to have carried it farther. From that point, not yet determined, but about the third floor, to the top the build-ing was grey. They had done the slit windows all the way. Sometimes it looked like corduroy. Sometimes it looked like the building was dripping gold.

There were three very broad, shallow steps that led to the entrance of the building. Like the windows, the steps were ornamental. The building just as easily could have been level with the street. The step risers were less than six inches, possibly five, and were actually awkward, between steps and a level surface. There were brass planters in the steps, four feet wide, nine or ten feet long. One year the plants had been changed twenty-three times. They all died. Cigarette butts stuck out of the dirt, and gum wrappers, and drink cans, flattened or squashed into shapes that were topologically rather pleasing. They lay about the plants like fallen blossoms, colorful, not really hideous except that training said so.

The doors. Revolving doors, three. Two double doors with ten feet of air space between them. Four air walls. Bill never did understand how or why they worked; in the summer the air was cool, in the winter, hot. There was a definite line that separated the outside from the inside, even if it was invisi-ble. The inside was different.

He walked alone, toward the elevators. No elevators went to all floors. There were banks that went from ground zero to eight, others that stopped first at nine and went up to fifteen, and so on. His first stop was thirty-four. He assumed that it continued after he left it at thirty-eight. The button lights indicated that it was prepared to rise another four floors.

Every morning from the time he left his spacious and empty apartment, got through the subway, across town on the bus, up the three low steps, and the elevators that went from the thirty-fourth floor to at least the thirty-eighth floor, he was quite alone.

'Let's take it again, something's wrong with the tempo ...' Roily shook his long hair and fingered his beard.

'How about trying it with the drums?' Mole said. Lettered on the bass drum was: THE PICKLE DOOR.

Bill stood up, pushing his electric organ away from him. 'Look, guys, let me set the stage. A guy alone, walking the streets. *Alone.* Dig? His girl's gone. Left him flat. No reason. Nothing. And there's not another one in the world for him.' He shrugged at the skepticism. 'Look, you want to hit the old crowd or not? You want to eat for a change? You want to get out of this stinking basement (no offense, Mole) with its rats that've evolved into five-foot-ten pink-skinned brown-suited squinty-eyed blood-sucking saber-toothed rodents, for chrissakes? No more fires, no more busts, no more gas attacks, just one winter of being warm and dry.'

'No drums?'

'No drums! You asshole. Soft. Melancholic. Sad. Wistful. Now. *Go!*'

They took it from the top.

The apartment was clean. They had scraped the paint off down to bare wood and started over with it. Bill had had to put up wall-board here and there where the plaster crumbled when they had begun to scour the walls, but it had been worth it. He had divided the room with wallboard at the same time, and had not been forced to get a permit, with the pages of questions to be answered first. They called it a three-room apartment now. After the streets, in that section of the lower East Side, it was like entering another world. Clean walls, clean wood, bare, gleaming floors with small washable, and often washed, scatter tugs. And they had used their total debt limit for an air-conditioner so that they didn't have to worry about the daily pollution index, at least not after they got home from work. They both hated to leave their own rooms even to go down the hall to the bathroom. In the beginning they had tried to keep that clean, but they had given up.

She worked half days only. She would be eligible for a full-time job as soon as the baby was registered in a nursery at three. She met him at the door and kissed him, then drew back and said, 'A few minutes ago Susan was looking at television with me, and as plain as day she said, "NBC". Can you imagine? And only two.'

Susan started to cry and continued to cry through the newscast. She did it almost every night. It was her daily crying time, they agreed.

Billy was ten and his mother was thirty-five and didn't look it, his father was forty and did look it. He was a professor with Grave Responsibilities and Moral Convictions. It was almost Christmas. Every year Billy's mother took him to town to look at the windows and shop for Father and have a hot-fudge sundae and buy an early, not-secret gift for him. To ease the anticipation pains.

It was snowing lightly and the train was coming around the mountain in miniature America with flags on almost all the houses and an army standing at attention while a band of inches-high red-white-and-blue members played silent music. Tiny Christmas trees blinked and Santa Clauses swayed holding bulging stomachs. The train flashed around a hill out of sight and the skaters waltzed and the band played and the tree lights blinked and the snow fell gently. But now the store window's music was drowned by a roaring sound from the other end of the street and he felt his mother's hand tugging at him.

'Come on, Billy. Let's go inside. It looks like a demonstration.'

He stared at the window, then down, the street where the cars were suddenly obliterated by what looked like a black tidal wave.

Roily twanged a discord. He looked at Bill helplessly. 'I just don't dig it. I mean, it's going to put them to sleep. It's not like there's only one chick in the world.'

'It ain't that,' Mole said. 'You know what it is. Crap. Shit. So he moons over a bird. So what?'

Bill ran his thumb over the keys, and then spun around. 'Look, I listened to records at the library for three solid weeks, five-year-old records, ten-year-old records, twenty-year-old records. There hasn't been anything like this for ten years, fifteen years. So what's it going to cost to gamble on it now? We can do it under a moony name. Dreamers. Or, The Stardusters. Something corny. Or, The Sound. That's pretty good. Nostalgia, that's what we'll give them. For a time when a guy could just go out and walk up and down the streets if he wanted to.'

On Monday, Wednesday, and Friday mornings they had meetings. And on Tuesday and Thursday afternoons they had meetings. The table was round. This month Henry Moreno was chairman. They discussed and planned for the next five years, so that no matter what the date, Bill's thoughts were supposed to be geared to five years in the future. Because We Plan Your Tomorrow – his department's motto.

'Say, who was it who came up with the idea of a self-rolling toothpaste tube?' Henry asked, during a pause in the proceedings.

He glanced at Walter Neery, who shrugged and looked blank. The inquiring gaze went around the table and no one suggested an answer. When it was Bill's turn to look blank, he did. He could have said, 'Matt's idea.' That would have singled out Matt for criticism. And next time he might be the one so named. So he looked blank, and Henry sighed and murmured, 'Too bad. Wanted to put his name down for a bonus. But that's the way it goes. Joint efforts, joint decisions, joint benefits. Right, fellows?'

They nodded. Bill wondered if anyone else could turn off the world. He doubted it. They were all too preoccupied with Creating A Better World – the company's motto. 'Like a phoenix,' the small print went on, 'we will rise again to fulfill the dreams of past generations ...'

'Anyway,' Henry said, 'market research has finished the survey. There will be a definite demand for the self-rolling tube. R and D is kicking it around now. And this department has earned another bonus point.'

The eleven-o'clock newscast rehashed the same items that the baby had cried through earlier. Casualty figures remained stable. The Senate had finished all the legislation that the President had asked for in what was called the most efficient, most farsighted, most patriotic assembly ever gathered in Washington. The air inversion over London had claimed the ten-thousandth victim that morning. Washington announced the plans to recall the history books in all elementary and secondary schools to correct mistakes discovered by the Advisory Committee on Education.

'Are you certain that you won't mind if Dad comes here for a few weeks, just until he gets his bearings again?'

'You know I don't mind.' She was applying a contact patch to his coveralls, and didn't look up.

'I'm sure that it won't be for long. He'll apply for a permit to move right away. He's pretty independent.'

'Don't be so apologetic. I knew about him when we were married. It's all right. He made a mistake, and he's paid. I certainly don't hold that against him. Here, will this hold, do you think?'

He took the coveralls from her and put them down. 'Let's turn off that blasted set and go to bed. We'll have our room to ourselves just five more nights before he gets here.'

'With the curtain up we'll never know the baby's in there. Wait a minute. I'd better check the schedule. I forget if I turned it on when I first came home.' He watched her check off the public-interest programs that had been on the air. She frowned over the schedule and he knew that she had forgotten. Rumor said that you could alter the meter, but he didn't know how, and he didn't know anyone who did.

'It's all right,' he said. 'Leave it alone. I'll turn it off later. Come on.' So they made love in the bedroom, and in the other room the set talked on and on about the patience of the government and the intransigence of the enemy at the conference table, and about the rules and regulations regarding the recently passed Right to Inspect Bill.

Billy eavesdropped on his parents at every opportunity. It was a game with him, but a serious game. He had trouble imagining them without him, and was almost convinced that they discussed him exclusively when he was absent. They sat on the couch listening to a small tape recorder. And Billy became cramped and chilled from kneeling on the hall floor in his pajamas, also listening, thoroughly bored.

'Gentlemen, this is an executive session, you all understand. No word of what gets said in this room will be carried beyond those doors, nor will it appear in any report. Now, we have all heard the evidence of the experts. We have studied the charts, and the data. Gentlemen, unless we act immediately with every measure put forth by Dr. Gordon, our entire civilization is doomed.'

'Now, Roger. Jest take it easy, son. Doctuh, do I understand you to say that unless each of those measures is enacted almost immediately and with absolute thoroughness, then there's no hope at all to save mankind?'

'No, sir. What I said, Senator, is that unless these things are done now, today, we'll all die. Our children will die. Their children won't be born. No "almost," Senator. No qualifications at all.'

'I see, Doctuh. I see. You've heard of Malthews? Haven't you, suh?'

'Malthus? The Malthusian theory? Yes, sir, I have.'

'Yes. You see, son, I jest read a little bit about this Malthews and it seems to me that he was saying a hundred years ago almost exactly what you're saying again today. Now, you see, son, how confusing this can get to an old non-scientist like me.'

'Senator, I could recapitulate all the evidence you have heard and seen, but we have done that. We've been holding these meetings six months now. You know what the consensus of the participating scientists is. Not simply the population explosion, but the concomitant pollution, which was not foreseen by Malthus, sir. That is our concern. Not only here in the States, but around the world. The only real division we have had, sir, is in the timetable for the disaster that we all see. And about half of us think that even if we did initiate those steps immediately, it would still be too late. That the only way to save any part of mankind is through the decimation of our population now. Halve it. In order to save half. Not through war that would leave ruins and a weakened and irradiated billion people, but through a humane program that would leave the technology intact, and the survivors healthy and aware of the sacrifice of the dead. They would have to have leadership that would infuse them with a new sense of purpose.'

'Doctuh, for weeks now something has been pestering at me. Jest won't go way, no, suh. Now in this here executive session, without anyone in here taking notes, and no tape recorders going, no stenographers. Jest between us here now, suh, I want to get this off my chest. You, suh, Doctuh Gordon, are looney.'

One day they didn't come back when he entered the office. For the first time since discovery of the wondrous gift that he had, the gift was frightening. He stopped and stared at the empty office, the desks without girls, the files without clerks, the water fountains without two or three natty young men. Slowly, very carefully, he made his way past his secretary's empty chair, into his small office, where a memo reminded him that today the chairman from R&D would visit the regular Friday-morning conference. He went to the meeting and sat down in his customary chair, in an empty room. Once he felt compelled to speak, which he did, immediately forgetting what it was that he said. He left promptly at twelve and returned to his office, where he got his hat and coat. He stopped then. He was supposed to have lunch with Walter Neery and someone from Sales. He went through all the motions, arriving at the elevators where they were to meet at precisely twelve ten, taking the empty car down, walking alone around the corner to a French restaurant that they always used when it was on expense account.

He ate alone, but now and then made a comment to the air. He didn't know what happened to the bill. It came and went again, as food had done. Back in his office he clutched his head for a long time, and finally when he put his hands down again, he was smiling. It really was much better this way.

'Billy, don't let go of my hand! Whatever happens, don't let go!'

They weren't going to reach the door to the store. Too many people with the same idea, and the demonstrators were filling the street and the sidewalks, and the police were coming from the other direction with sirens blaring and there were popping noises not at all like guns or even windows breaking. And over it all the loudspeakers played 'Silent Night' and when that was finished 'The Twelve Days of Christmas' and the train was coming over the mountain again.

'Honey, is it true that they have a way of telling if you're in the room with the TV or not?'

'No. Where'd you hear such a crazy thing?'

'Oh, some of the girls at work. You know. I mean it wouldn't do much good to turn it on and leave it on all the time if they know whether or not you're watching it too.'

'Well, forget it. Another rumor.'

'I wonder who starts such rumors. Haven't you ever wondered just where they come from, Bill?'

'Washington. What's to wonder? Is the room ready for him?'

'Yes. Do you think he'll be bitter?'

'About what? He made the speeches. He advocated genocide, or something. He never denied it. And they found him guilty of sedition. What's he got to be bitter about?'

'That sounds good. Keep it like that. Now let's try it again from the top.

Exactly the same way. I'll get it on the recorder and then we'll decide if that's what we want to tape. Okay, guys.'

They played it again, then listened to it. The Mole, whose basement room they used for practice, held his nose and made retching motions. But Roily stared at Bill thoughtfully. 'Yeah,' he said. 'Yeah. A guy alone, not in a compound or nothing, just alone, walking in the city at nighttime. The dumb bastards will eat their hearts out. They'll think it's romantic. Okay, let's make the master tape tomorrow.' They broke up then.

Roily and Bill stayed close together, and the handmade pipe gun in Bill's pocket was cool against his hand as they walked down the street. Rhonda joined them at The Joint and they stayed there until the crowds thinned out after three and then went to Bill's room. They skirted a bunch of blacks, twenty or twenty-five of them, conscious of the watchful eyes until they turned the corner. At his street Bill stopped again, briefly. An unmarked tank, with a uniformed skinhead visible through the observation bubble, was moving slowly down the street, sweeping for mines. They ducked into a doorway and waited for it to finish and rumble away. From the other end of the street a lone car appeared, headed for the tank. Bill looked up for the copter that he could hear faintly over the din of the city noise. He couldn't find its lights in the murky sky that seemed supported by the tops of the buildings.

'Christ!' he said in disgust. 'Come on, let's go in the back way.' He grabbed Rhonda's arm and nearly pulled her off her feet when she resisted.

'I want to watch.'

'Come on. The copter will pick you off if you're on the street.'

'What in hell's wrong with you guys tonight?' Rhonda asked furiously, inside the building. 'Pussyfooting around like a couple of blows from Missouri or something.'

'Wanta stay in one piece for just a little while, doll,' Roily said, panting. 'Long enough to cash in and live it up for a change.'

She marched into Bill's room and tossed a gas grenade down on a chair. Bill winced. One day when she did that, it would go. She hooked her thumbs under the tabs on her high pants and opened the twin zippers that let the pants fall down in two pieces around her knees. She kicked them off. The sounds of a pitched battle from the far end of the street erupted, and they all listened, identifying the equipment being used: gas bombs, homemade mines, automatic hand weapons, the whine of gas launchers. They relaxed.

'I can see it now,' she said. 'The Pickle Door, high as clouds on green stuff, living it up in a compound, manning the guns, taking guided tours of the city in armored buses. Funneeeee. They'll let you in the day it rains diamonds.'

'You did what you could, darling. God knows you tried to make them understand.'

'And what good will that do in ten years, or fifteen years? Who's going to say, "Oh, yes, Doctuh Gordon tried to make them see that the catastrophe was already on the way, a tiny snowball high on the slope"?'

'Sh, darling. I don't think Billy's asleep yet. He's all excited about going to town tomorrow. Christmas. Your coming home. It's all been too much for him too fast.'

'You don't believe me, do you? Not even you.'

'It isn't that. But what can I do? Except go on living. Try to keep us all alive and healthy and reasonably happy? What else can I do? What else can *you* do?'

'Write another book. Make more speeches. Find something that'll kill fifty percent of the population, without harming the other fifty percent.'

'William!'

'Can you convince me that it's wrong? Isn't it better to lose half than to lose all? Isn't it?'

'And what about Billy?'

Billy, shivering on the floor outside the door, fell asleep waiting for the answer to the question.

They came back now and then. Not often, and they didn't stay. Someone would bob into his line of vision, then float out again before he could focus on the image. He realized that there was a mechanism working for him, something that warned him, or guided him, so that he never stumbled over any of them, or missed a cue, although he wasn't aware of them as they came. Occasionally he felt that he should say something or other, and when he did, the feeling of unease that had bothered him went away.

He hadn't seen a child for over a month. He walked through the park now without seeing the rows on rows of perambulators, the toddlers, the pre-schoolers, the elementary-school children, as numerous as ants. Breeding like cockroaches, they were trying to fill the gap with babies. No one stared at him wondering if he was William Gordon's son, wondering why he wasn't married yet, why he didn't have four, five, six children yet. He was certain that he was as hard for them to see as they were for him. He felt safe. He liked the silent world.

Bill stared at the ceiling and tried not to hear the television. He tried not to think about the evening, and could think of nothing else.

Her whisper: 'He's so old. I thought he was younger.'

'He always looked older than he was. He's only fifty-five.'

Their bed touched the curtain that separated this half of the room from the baby's half. He could hear every snuffle that the baby made, every change in her breathing, every whimper and wheeze. And on the other side of the wallboard, *he* was listening to the television, chuckling at it, talking back. Bill's lips tightened. *He* had laughed a bit louder at a statement attributed to the President. He would get them all in trouble. He was a crazy, senile, babbling old man. They would have to take that into account, if he went on like that in front of anyone. They must know what they had done to him ... Bill heard his teeth grinding before he was aware of the movement of his jaw. What had they done to him? He was a prattling moron.

But why had he cried? What had he meant?

'I couldn't do it. I knew we should, that we could. I had the stuff. A last chance, that's what I told them. Just listen and do something now. A last chance. And when the time came, I couldn't do anything. They came and took away Billy and then they found it. We had it all. It would have been simple. I knew what to do. We had the stuff, all we needed. And they still trusted us enough. And I couldn't do it!' Then he had cried.

Why?

'Billy! Billy!' He couldn't see her at all. He was being pushed and he knew that he didn't dare fall. They'd walk on him. Boots cowboy boots snow boots police boots. He couldn't make out any of their faces they were all too close and he was too short. He couldn't tell the police from the marchers. The spectators from the demonstrators. He couldn't hear her screams any longer. There was one long scream in his ears and one long smear of red before his eyes. And a burning pain sharp burning pain of a cut or a lump or something that made him feel strange and lightheaded and not able to think. He couldn't breathe and his eyes were on fire and he was afraid to touch them because he might rub it in and he couldn't stop himself rubbing his eyes hearing the piercing scream that wouldn't end choking coughing being sick adding the smell of vomit to the scream and the red smear. Her face kept swimming before his burning eyes. White wide-eyed with a cut that started somewhere in her hair and went down her check down into her neck and blood on her lips like lipstick on Halloween coming down the corner of her mouth down her skin.

He wondered how long before someone noticed that he was acting strangely, or noticed that he wasn't really there much of the time. Promising young executive missing, without a clue. Would someone else move into his nice, airy apartment overlooking the Hudson? Would they put someone else in his office? Would he wander in one day and sit down in the new man's lap and never even realize it?

That night he burned all his father's notes, his diary, the newspaper clippings. He added them one page at a time, playing the 'He loves me, loves me not' game. But he said, 'He was right. He was wrong.' Toward the end he dozed and lost track. And knew that there was no way he would ever know.

Billy couldn't tell which side was which. He was being swept along with people and when he tried to hold on to someone he was flung off and couldn't get his balance again and he fell and the boots did walk on him. And he couldn't tell whose boots they had been.

Bill found his father the next morning. He had hung himself from the water pipe in the kitchen half of his room. There was only an inch of space between his feet and the floor. If he had been an inch taller, he wouldn't have been able to do it.

Bill stared at him, hating him for doing it there, then. Before he touched the body he turned on the TV set. The meter would be waiting and there'd be enough questions without having them add any more about why they were avoiding the news. Then he went out to the corner phone and called the police, listening absently to the beep-beep that said the call was being recorded. A platoon of adolescents in grey uniforms marched by on their way to school. They didn't turn their heads to look at him in the booth.

Bill stiffened at the sound of a police tank starting the high-pitched wail of the tear-gas launcher. He relaxed again. It was at least a block away.

'Tell me how you got the scars, Bill,' Rhonda said, tracing the one that started at his forehead and ended in his eyebrow. 'Your old man?'

'No. I told you, he was killed during the Christmas riots. My old man and my mother, or so they said.' He fingered the scars, then shook his head hard. 'I told you I don't remember. An accident, or something. It doesn't signify.' He sat up in the bed. 'Listen, I've been thinking. We'd go out of our skulls in a compound. Right? How about a trailer, an armored trailer with a grenade launcher? We could take a trip. Maybe even make it out to the coast.'

'Yeah, baby,' Rhonda said, sitting up too, her eyes sparkling. 'I heard that there are some small compounds out in the boonies that one guy with a launcher could take all by himself.'

THE FUSION BOMB

At dusk the barrier islands were like a string of jewels gleaming in the placid bay. The sea wasn't reflecting now, the only lights that showed were those of the islands and the shore lights that were from two to four miles westward. The islands looked like an afterthought, as if someone had decided to outline the coast with a faulty pen that skipped as it wrote in sparkles. Here and there dotted lines tethered the jewels, kept them from floating away, and lines joined them one to another in a series, connective tissue too frail to endure the fury of the sea. Then came a break, a dark spot with only a sprinkling of lights at one end, the rest of the island swallowed in blackness of tropical growth.

The few lights at the southern end seemed inconsequential, the twinkling of hovering fireflies, to be swept away with a brush of the hand. No lines joined this dark speck with the other, clearly more civilized, links of the chain that stretched to the north and angled off to the south. No string of incandescence tied it to the mainland. It was as if this dark presence had come from elsewhere to shoulder itself into the chain where it stood unrecognized and unacknowledged by its neighbors.

It was shaped like a primitive arrowhead. If the shaft had been added, the feathers would have touched land hundreds of miles to the south, at St. Augustine, possibly. The island was covered with loblolly pines, live oaks dripping with Spanish moss, cypress and magnolia trees. The thickened end was white sand, stucco houses, and masses of hewn stones, some in orderly piles and rows, others tossed about, buried in sand so that only corners showed, tumbled down the beach, into the water where the sea and bay joined. Philodendron, gone wild, had claimed many of the blocks, climbing them with stems as thick as wrists, split leaves hiding the worked surface of the granite and sandstone, as if nature were working hard to efface what man had done to her island. Those blocks that had been lost to the sea had long since been naturalized by barnacles, oysters, seaweeds; generations of sergeant majors and wrasses and blue crabs and stonefish had lived among them.

At low tide, as it was now, the water whispered gently to the rocks, secrets of the sea murmured in an unintelligible tongue that evoked memories and suggested understanding. Eliot listened hard, then answered: 'So I'll tell the old bastard, take your effing island, and your effing job, and your effing money and stuff it all you know where.' The sea mocked him and he took another drink. He sat on one of the stones, his back against another one, and he put a motor on the rocky end of the island and wound it up. It was a rubber-band motor. The arrowhead pointed due north and cut a clean swath, its motion steady and sure, like a giant carrier. And when he had circled the world, when he had docked at all the strange ports and sampled all the strange customs and strange foods, then he didn't know what to do with his mobile island, and he sank it, deep into the Marianas Trench where it could never be raised again, where it would vanish without a sign that it had existed. He drank again, this time emptying the glass. For a moment he hefted it, then he put it down on the rock next to him.

'Eliot! Where are you?'

He didn't answer, but he could see the white shape moving among the rocks. She knew damn well where he was.

'Pit, old man, I'm through. I quit. I'll leave by the mail boat in the morning, or swim over, or fly on the back of a cormorant.'

'Eliot! For God's sake, don't be so childish! Stop playing games. Everyone's waiting for you.'

'Ah, Beatrice, the unattainable, forever pure, forever fleeing, and fleet.' But I had you once, twice, three times. Hot and sweaty in my arms.

'You're drunk! Why? Why tonight? Everyone's waiting for you.'

She was very near now, not so near that he could make out her features, but near enough to know what she wore a white party dress, that she wore pearls at her throat, near enough so that the elusive whisper of the sea now became water swishing among rocks. He stood up. She was carrying her sandals.

'You'll bruise your feet. Stay there, or, better, go back and tell them that I do not wish to attend another bloody party, not another one for years and years.'

'Eliot, the new girl's here. You'll want to meet her. And … it's a surprise, Eliot. Please come now. He'll be so disappointed.'

'Why? He already hired her, didn't he? Tomorrow's time enough for me to meet her. And the only surprise around here is that we don't all die of boredom.'

He picked up his glass and let a trickle of melted ice wet his lips. He should have brought the pitcher of gin and lemonade. Have to remember, he told himself sternly, no half measures from now on. Been too moderate around here. Moderation's no damn good for island living. He stood up. The sea tilted and the rock tried to slide him off into the water. He could hear vicious laughter, masked as waves rushed around stones.

Beatrice caught his hand and led him out of the jumbled rocks. 'Come on, let's take a walk,' she said.

But the drunkenness was passing, and he shook his head.

'I'm okay,' he said. 'Sitting too long, that's all. Let's go to the damn party and get it over with.'

She half led, half pushed him along the cypress boardwalk toward the main house.

'The new girl. What's she like?'

'I'm not sure. You know she got over on the pretext that I had recommended her. Turns out that we lived in the same town back when we were growing up. So I should know her, except that I'm ten years older than she is. I dated her brother when I was sixteen, but I can't remember much about her. Or her brother either, for that matter. She was Gina's age when I saw her last. She's twenty now, a student, looking for summer work, perfect to spell Marianne while she has her baby, and so on. But you'll see.'

Just what we need, he thought. A young single girl to liven things up around here. 'Is she pretty?'

'No. Very plain actually. But do you think that will make any difference?' Beatrice sounded amused.

How well we know each other. She can follow my thought processes, come to my conclusions for me, without even thinking about it. A simple temporary dislocation of the ego.

The boardwalk led them around the ruins, and they approached the house from the back. Curiously old-fashioned and unglamorous, one floor that rambled, deep porch; there was a lot of ironwork, grilles, rails, scrolls, and curlicues that should have been offensive but were pleasing. They skirted a swimming pool that had been converted to a sunken garden and walked along the ornate porch to the front entrance. Wide windows, uncovered, with massive shutters at their sides. View of a room the width of the house, fireplace on one wall, bar and stools, low, gold-gleaming cypress furniture, red Spanish-tile floors that didn't show the scars of the constant polishing of the sand. Beyond the room there was a terrace, shielded from the sea wind by a louvered wall of glass. Moving figures broken into sections by the partly opened glass slats, the hum of voices, echo of Spanish guitars. All substantial and real, all but the fragmented people.

Eliot took a deep breath and entered the terrace. Beatrice paused a moment to speak to Mr. Bonner, who would go over to her place to baby-sit. Eliot was aware of their low conversation, as he was aware of the new girl, who stood out because she was new and very pale. Not pretty. Homely, actually. He nodded at Mr. Pitcock, whose eyes always seemed to see more than was visible. He was seventy; why weren't his eyes starting to dim? Pitcock knew that he'd been drinking, knew that he'd tried to forget the party, knew that if Beatrice hadn't been sent after him, he would have passed it up. So fire me, he thought at the old man, and knew that the old man was aware of that thought also. They shook hands and Pitcock introduced the new girl.

'Donna, this is the project director, Dr. Kalin. Eliot, Donna Bensinger.'

'Hello, Eliot.'

Too fast. Should have called him Dr. Kalin. He didn't like her pasty skin, or the limpness of her hand when he touched it, or the pale, myopic eyes, or the thin dun-colored hair that looked as if it needed a shampoo.

'I hope you won't find it too dull here, Miss Bensinger,' he said, and looked past her at Ed Delizzio, who was standing at the bar. 'Excuse me.'

He thought he heard the dry chuckle of Thomas Pitcock as he left them, but he didn't turn back to see. 'Christ,' he said to Ed. 'Just – Christ!'

'Yeah, I know what you mean.' Ed poured a martini and put it in Eliot's hand. 'Drink. That's all that's left.' He refilled his own glass. 'After this breaks up we're going to play some poker over at Lee's house. Want to sit in?'

'Sure.'

'The buffet is ready in the dining room.' Mrs. Bonner's voice was eerie over the intercom.

'Come on, let's eat.' Pitcock led them across the patio, into the house, his hand on Donna's arm, talking cheerfully to her. He was tall, straight, bald, brown. Why didn't he stoop and falter?

Mary and Leland Moore beckoned to Eliot. Mary was small and tanned, hair sun-bleached almost white. She always seemed breathless. 'Can you come over later? The boys are playing poker.'

Eliot accepted again and they went into the dining room with the others. On the table was a glazed cold turkey, hot lobster in sherry sauce, biscuits, salads. There was an assortment of wines. He picked at the food and drank steadily, refusing to pretend an interest in the small talk and forced gaiety about him.

'I have no theory to forward as yet, sir,' he said distinctly.

'Damn it, a hypothesis then.'

'I don't have that much yet.'

'A hunch. A wild guess. Don't couch it in formal terms. You must be thinking something by now. What?'

'Nothing. Can't you get it through your head that I won't be forced into a generalization?'

'You're afraid to.'

He reached for the champagne and when he raised his gaze from the iced bottle, he caught the bright blue eyes on him. For a second he almost believed they had been speaking, but then he heard Marty's voice, and a giggle from Donna, and he knew that he had said nothing. The old man continued to watch him as he poured more champagne, spilling some of it, and replaced the bottle. 'Fuck off,' he said, raising his glass and returning the silent stare. Donna giggled louder and this time the others laughed also, and the old man's gaze shifted as he, too, chuckled at Marty's story.

After they ate, Mrs. Bonner appeared with a birthday cake, and they all sang to Eliot and toasted him with champagne. At eleven thirty Beatrice signaled that they should wrap it up. Eliot stood up and made his way to Pitcock.

'Thanks for the party,' he said. He was very unsteady.

'Wait a second, will you? I have something for you, didn't want to bring it out before.' The old man said good-bye to his guests and then left Eliot for a moment.

If he brings me a check, I'll rip it to shreds before his eyes. He thought longingly of another drink, but he didn't want to delay to mix it and drink it. The old man returned carrying a bulky package. He watched Eliot's face as he tore off the wrappings.

'I know how much you've admired my Escher works; thought you might like one.' It was a large, complicated drawing of builders who were destroying what they built, all in one process. Eliot stared at it: the figures seemed to be moving, toiling up stairs, stairs that flattened out and went down again somehow even as he watched. He blinked and the movement stopped. 'Thanks,' he said. 'Just thanks.'

Pitcock nodded. He turned to the window to look out at the beach. 'It's a strange night, isn't it? Don't you feel the strangeness? If it were August I'd say a hurricane was on its way, but not so soon. Just strange, I guess.'

Eliot waited a moment, wanting to force the talk to the futile project, the open-ended task that Pitcock had hired them to do, but he clamped his lips hard and remained silent.

'You accept the job then?' the old man had asked, in the plush office on the thirtieth floor of the glass-and-plastic building in New York. 'Without questioning its merits? Promise to see it through?'

'I'll sign the three-year contract,' Eliot said. 'Seems fair enough to give it that much of a try.'

'Good. And at the end of the three years we'll talk again, and between now and then, no matter how many doubts you raise, you'll carry on.'

Eliot shrugged. I will do my best to uphold the honor of the project. He said, 'I don't pretend to think that we'll be able to accomplish anything, except to add to the data, and to bring some order to a field that's in chaos. Maybe that's enough for now. I don't know.'

The old man turned toward him, away from the window. 'It's working out. I know you don't agree, but I can feel that it's taking shape. And now this feeling of strangeness. That's part of it. Undercurrents. Someone's projecting strong undercurrents, strong enough to affect others. You'll see. You'll see.'

The others were loitering near the sunken garden, all except Beatrice, who had gone ahead to relieve Bonner of his baby-sitting chores. Eliot fell into step beside Mary.

Soon she'll say, You've been awfully quiet, something to that effect. And I'll say, Thinking. Been here two years and two months, for what? Doing what? Indulging a crazy old man in his obsession. 'Eliot, are you going to stay?'

'What?' He looked at the small woman, but could see only the pale top of her head.

'You've been acting like a man trying to come to a decision. We wondered if you are considering leaving here.'

'I've been considering that for two years and two months,' he said. 'I'm no nearer a decision than I was when I first took it up.' He indicated the house behind them. 'He's crazy, you know.'

'I don't know if he is or not. This whole project seems crazy to me, but then, it always did.'

'Is Lee getting restless?'

'Isn't everyone?'

'Yeah, there is that.'

The trouble was that there were only ten people on the island and they all spent nine tenths of their time on it. They were all tired of each other, tired of the island paradise, tired of Mrs. Bonner's turkeys and champagne parties, tired of the endless statistics and endless data that went nowhere.

We go through the motions of having fun at the parties, and each of us is there in body only, our minds busy with the data, busy trying to find an out without cutting off our connections with the old man. Each one of us afraid the goose will suddenly stop production, wondering if we have enough of the golden eggs to live on the rest of our lives, wondering if any of this is worth it. If anything out there in the real world would be any better, make any more sense. Twenty-five thousand a year, almost all clear, living quarters and most of the food thrown in, no need for cars or servants. Company plane to take us away for vacations, bring us back. Travel expenses, hotel expenses, everything paid for. Looking for ways to spend money. Endless project at twenty-five thousand a year, a raise to thirty, or forty? Keen eyes that see too much, files with too much in them, birthdays, childhood friends, illnesses, mistakes almost forgotten, but in the files.

Mary was talking again. 'I almost wish we never had come here, you know? Lee would have been fine. He had a job at Berkeley all lined up. He would like to teach, I think. But probably not now. Not after this kind of freedom and so much money.'

'He can always quit,' Eliot said more brusquely than was called for. He liked Mary. Mary and Gina were the only ones that he did like. Neither was a threat to him in any way.

'At least we can always *say* that, can't we?'

They paused at his house and he remembered that he was supposed to bring some mixer. 'I'll be over in a few minutes,' he said, and left her as Lee and Ed drew near. He put the drawing down, but he didn't want to look at it again yet. Not until he was sober.

He stared at himself in the bathroom mirror and thought, Thirty. Good Christ! Back in April Beatrice had become thirty, and had cried. Then, furious with him for taking her, with herself for needing solace, she had run away from him, and since then had been cool and pleasant, and very distant. If he cried now, would she appear from nowhere to put her arm about his shoulders, to pat him awkwardly as she maneuvered him into bed and reassured him that he still had most of his life ahead? He laughed and turned away, not liking the mirror image. He was deeply suntanned, and his eyes were dark brown, his eyebrows straight and heavy, nearly touching, like a solid, permanent scowl.

'Just one thing more, Mr. Pitcock. Why me? Why did you select me for this project?' The contract was signed, the question made safe by the signatures.

'Because you're avaricious enough to do it. Because you're bright enough to see it through. Because you're cynical enough not to get involved personally, no matter what the data start to reveal.'

That's me, he thought, searching his kitchen for mixer. Avaricious. Bright. Cynical.

Donna was seated at the round table, across from an empty chair, his chair. He put the mixer down and looked at them. Ed Delizzio, twenty-five, a statistician from Pitcock Enterprises. Dark, Catholic, observed all the holy days, went to mass each Sunday, had a crucifix over his bed, a picture of Mary and Jesus on his wall. Marty Tiomkin, atheist, twenty-four. Slavic type, tall, broad, serious, with a slow grin, a slower laugh, thick long fingers. Probably could swim to England, if the spirit ever moved him. Very powerful. He was the computer expert. He could program it, repair it, make it go when it was sick, talk it into revealing correlations or synchronicities where none seemed possible. He treated it like a wife who might fly to a distant lover at any time unless she received unswerving loyalty and devotion. Marty and Ed had been hired at the same time, almost two years ago. At first they had had separate houses, like the rest of the staff, but after a month they had decided to share one house. Inseparable now, they went off on weekend trips, during which they picked up girls from one of the northern islands, or made a tour of the houses of Charleston. Now and then they brought girls back to the island with them.

Donna was next to Marty, and on the other side of her was Leland Moore. He was tall and intense, probably the most honest one there, tortured by the futility of what he was doing, but also by the memory of a fatherless childhood in a leaky fifteen-foot trailer that his mother kept filled with other people's ironing. He wanted land, a farm or a ranch, with hills on it, and water. Slowly, month by month, he came nearer that goal, and he wouldn't leave, but he would suffer. Sitting by him was Mary, who worried about her husband too much. Who couldn't understand poverty as a spur because she never had experienced it, and thought only black people and poor southern dirt farmers ever did. Beatrice wasn't there.

'I can't stay,' Eliot said. 'Sorry. Too much booze too early tonight, and the champagne didn't help. See you tomorrow.'

To sit across from Donna all night, to watch her peer at her cards, and watch those pale fat fingers fumble ... He waved to them and shook his head at their entreaties to stay at least for a while.

'Will you show me the offices tomorrow, Eliot?' Her voice was like the rest of her, just wrong, too high-pitched, little-girl cute, with the suggestion of a lisp.

He shrugged. 'Sure. Eleven?'

He walked up the beach. The tide was coming in fast now, the breakers were white-frosted and insistent. In the woods behind the dunes night life stirred, an owl beat the wind steadily, a deer snorted, the grasses rustled, reviving the legend of the Spaniards who walked by night, bemoaning the abandonment of the fort they had started and left. The air was pungent with the sea smells, and the life and death smells of the miniature jungle. He walked mechanically. Whatever thoughts he had were dreamlike in that he forgot them as quickly as they formed, so that by the time he turned at the end of the island and retraced his steps along the beach, it was as if he had spent the last hour or more sleepwalking. He stopped at the pier and then walked out on it to the end, where he was captain of a pirate ship braving the uncharted seas in search of unknown lands to conquer. It was flat and stupid and he let it go.

The pier was solid, a thousand feet out into the ocean; it seemed to move with the motion of the sea and the constant pressure of the wind. Eliot leaned against the end post where a brown pelican roosted every day to watch the sea and the land, alert for subversives, immorality, unseemly behavior, including littering of the beach ...

Lee Moore's house had a light; the others were all dark. Eliot wondered if they were still playing poker, if Donna Bensinger had won all their money, if Lee and Ed were singing dirty sea chanteys yet. He flicked his cigarette out into the water. Thirty, he thought, thirty. Forty thousand dollars in the bank, more every day, and no one to tell me to do this or that, to come in or stay out. Freedom and money. The dream of a sixteen-year-old washing dishes after school in a crummy diner. Buy a boat and go around the world after this is over. Or start traveling on tramps and never stop. Or – get a little place somewhere and let the money draw interest, live on the dividends forever. Or ... He heard voices. Two pale figures running along the sand toward the waves. The tide had turned again. The urgency was gone. Proof, he thought, right here before our eyes day in and day out. Never changing, eternal cycles; he didn't know if he meant the tide or the couple. He looked at the nude figures. It had to be Donna, pale hair, white body. The man could have been any of them, too far up the beach to see him clearly. They ran into the surf and she shrieked, but softly, not for the world to hear. The man caught up with her and they fell together into the shallow water.

Eliot watched the laughing figures, rolling, grappling, and he felt only disgust for the girl, and the man, whoever he happened to be. Too quick. Everything about her was too quick. He started to move from the post, but there were others now coming from the dunes, running together so that it was impossible to say if there were two or three or even four of them. The light from a crescent moon was too feeble, he couldn't make them out. Now there was a tight knot in his middle, and he felt cold. He looked down at the swells of the sea, black and hard-looking here, but alive and moving, always moving. When he looked again at the beach he knew that there were six people, dancing together, running, playing. All naked, all carefree and happy now. They paired off and each couple became one being, and he turned away. Without looking again at the figures, he left the pier and hurried home. He was shivering from the constant wind on the pier.

Strange, fragmented dreams troubled his sleep. The night witch came to him and tormented his flesh while he lay unable to move, unable to respond, or refrain from responding when that pleased her. Then he was crawling up a cliff, barren and rocky, windswept and cold. He was lost and the wind carried his voice down into crevices when he tried to call for help. His hands hurt, and he knew his toes were bleeding, leaving strange trails, like the spoor of an unidentified animal. He was on a level plain, with a walking stick in his hand, weary and chattering with cold. The wind was relentless, tearing his clothes from him; the rock-strewn field that he traversed was like dry ice. He kept his eyes cast down, so he wouldn't lose the nebulous trail that he had to follow, strange reddish wavery lines, like blood from an unknown animal. He tried to use the walking stick, but each time he struck it on the boulder, he felt it attach itself, knew that it rooted and sprouted instantly, and he had to wrench it loose again.

Eliot sat on his porch drinking black coffee, a newspaper on the table ignored as he stared over the blue-green waters. The sun was hot already, the day calm, the water unruffled. Another perfect day in paradise. He frowned at the sound of light tapping on the screen door. Donna Bensinger opened it, called, 'Hello, are you decent? Can I come in?'

'Sure. Around the corner on the porch.' He didn't stand up. She had on shorts, too short for her bulging pale legs, and a shirt that didn't conceal her stomach at all. Her hair was pulled back with a yellow ribbon; there were bright red spots on her cheeks, and her nose flamed, as did the tops of her bare feet and forearms. One morning and she was badly burned already. By the end of the day she'd be charred and by the next day probably in the hospital, or at least on her way home again. He motioned for her to sit down.

'Coffee?'

'Oh, no, thank you. This is all so fantastic, isn't it? I mean, the island, the houses for, all of us, people to bring you groceries and anything you need, boats we can use. I never dreamed of a job like this. It's right out of a movie, isn't it?'

He turned from her to resume his contemplation of the quiet ocean. She continued to talk. He finished his coffee and stood up. 'Let's go. I have a date at twelve. I can show you the offices and explain briefly what you're to do in half an hour or so.'

Eliot was six feet tall, his stride was long and quick, and he made no pretense of slowing it for the girl. She trotted at his side. 'Oh, I know that people have planted all this stuff, that it didn't just happen like this, I mean the orchids in the trees, and the jasmine and hibiscus and everything, but doesn't it look just like one of those dream islands where the heroine wears a grass skirt and sings and the hero dives for pearls, and there's a volcano that erupts in the end and they all get away in those funny boats with the things sticking out of the sides of them? Who started to build something here?'

'Spaniards. They brought in the rocks to build a fort, then abandoned it.'

'Spaniards! Pirates!' She stopped abruptly, then had to run to catch up. 'I can see the ships with all those sails, and slaves hauling the blocks all roped together, a Spaniard in black with a long whip ...'

The pink stucco building that they were approaching was lavishly landscaped with tropical and semi-tropical plants imported from around the world: travelers' palms, fifteen-foot-high yucca plants, Philippine mahogany trees, a grouping of live oaks hung with grey-green Spanish moss that turned the light silver. A small lake before the building mirrored the trees, swans gliding through the water hardly distorted the images.

'The office building used to be a guest house,' Eliot said. 'It has its own kitchen, a hurricane-proof basement. Come on.' There was another of the wide porches; then they were inside, in the cooled air of the lobby. This had been converted into a lounge, with a coffee maker, tables and chairs, a color television, a fireplace. Eliot showed her through the building quickly. Her office was small but well furnished, and she nodded approval. The old dining room had been equipped with a computer, several desks and chairs, a typewriter desk, drawing table lighted by a pair of fluorescent lamps. Next door was the file room, cabinet after cabinet, with library tables in the center of the room, all covered with folders and loose papers. 'Marianne usually kept it up to date, but these last weeks she really wasn't well enough.'

She sounded put-upon. 'I have to file all that stuff?'

'Beatrice will come over a couple of hours every day to show you the system, help you get caught up. She's Pitcock's private secretary, but she knows this work too.'

He showed her the rest of the first floor, then they went downstairs to the recreation room, where he sat down and lighted a cigarette. 'Any questions?'

'But you haven't told me anything about what I have to do, except the filing. And what you're doing here, all of you, I mean.'

'Okay. I didn't know how much Pitcock told you. You'll handle correspondence, type up reports, keep the files up to date. We are studying the effects of cycles. First we establish the fact of cycles, correlate synchronous cycles, check them back as far as you can find records for, and predict their future appearance. We collect data from all over the world, Marty feeds it into his computer, and the monster spits out answers. The snowshoe hare and the lynx have the same cycle. There are business cycles of highs and lows that persist in spite of wars, technological discoveries, anything that happens. Weather cycles, excitability cycles in man. War and peace cycles. There are cycles of marriages in St. Louis, and cycles of migrations of squirrels in Tennessee.' He stopped and stubbed out his cigarette hard, mashing it to shreds.

After the silence had lengthened long enough for him to light a new cigarette and for her to start fidgeting, she said, 'But – why? I mean, who cares and why?'

Eliot laughed and stubbed out the new cigarette. 'That's the best damn question anyone's asked around here for over two years.'

At noon he picked up Gina to take her to Charleston. Beatrice was dressed, as if she too would go if he only asked again. He didn't look directly at her, nor did he ask. The day was not a success, although usually he enjoyed taking the child to town. He kept wondering what Beatrice was doing, what the others were doing, if they were all together. He returned to the island with Gina at six thirty. Pitcock and Bonner were talking on the dock when he brought the small boat in.

Pitcock reached for Gina's hand. 'Have a good time, honey?'

'Eliot bought me a see-through raft. And a book about sea shells. And we went on rides at a carnival.'

Eliot handed the parcels to Bonner, checked the boat again, then climbed out. The motor launch was gone. Pitcock stood up, still holding Gina's hand. 'Come over to dinner later, Eliot? The others have gone out fishing. I'll see Gina home.'

'Beatrice?'

'She's here. She'll be over later too.'

'Okay. See you around eight?'

Donna was there. Eliot paused in the doorway when he saw her, shrugged, and entered. She smiled at him, dimpling both cheeks. Beatrice nodded, murmured thanks for Gina's gifts, then turned away. Pitcock handed him a martini, and Eliot sat down with it and studied an Escher drawing over the mantel. It reminded him of his dream, following his own trail that he was making so that he wouldn't get lost when he came along. He shook his head and tried to pick up the gist of the story Pitcock was telling. Donna was hanging on every word. She was no more burned than she had been that morning, must have spent the day inside somewhere. He wondered with whom, then concentrated on Pitcock.

'Selling you down the river was no idle threat, not just a little piece of slang that got started; what it was was a death sentence. It meant actually selling a slave to work in the bottom lands on the coast – downriver. Swamps, disease, floods, alligators, snakes. Sure death real quick. And the sands kept piling up on the islands, the rocks got buried deeper and deeper. In eighteen forty my great-granddaddy bought three of these islands, ten dollars an island, or some such amount. He was ashamed to put down the real figure he paid for them, just said they were cheap. Along about nineteen twenty-eight, twenty-nine, a hurricane came and stripped a lot of the sand away again, and by the time I got around to coming out to see the damage, hell, I found a pile of rocks and stones, the foundation of a fort, all that stuff. Decided to keep the island. But I sold off the other two. One island's enough for a man.'

'Fifteen fifty,' Donna said, her eyes wide. 'Wow! I wonder what happened to them, the Spaniards.'

Pitcock shrugged and glanced at the glasses the others were holding. He poured more martini into Eliot's, was waved away by Beatrice. Donna hadn't touched hers. 'Malaria. Possibly a hurricane. They went ahead with St. Augustine, but they never came back up here.'

'Well, I think they were crazy. It's the grooviest place I've ever seen. Last night the wind in the palm trees and the sound of the ocean, and the way the air smells here. I mean, I slept like a baby. I've never slept like that before in my life. And awake at dawn! I couldn't stand not going out right away! I just had to go out and jump into the water and swim.'

Eliot laughed harshly and choked. 'Nothing,' he said when he finally could speak again. 'Nothing. Just thinking how we all felt at first, then how the days began to melt into each other, and the weekends tended to blur and run together, and how you're always tearing off another page of the calendar, another month gone to hell.'

Beatrice swept him with a sharp look, and he returned her gaze coldly. She was always so cool, so self-possessed, she didn't like scenes or emotional outbursts, and his voice had been thick with emotion. 'Just don't go childish on me, okay? If you have something to say, say it, but don't pout or sulk or scream obscenities.' And he said, 'You can sweat and moan and cry, just like any other woman.'

'But not with you, not again. I don't like performing, even for an audience of only one.'

'Dinner's ready.' The goddam intercom.

'But the work's coming along,' Pitcock said to Donna. Pitcock was laughing at him, Eliot knew, not on his face where it would show, or in his voice where it could be heard, but somewhere inside him there was laughter.

Pitcock told Donna about the hotel suite he maintained in the Windward Hotel, and the car there available at all times. 'Bonner will run you over to the mainland or the other islands any time you want to go, pick you up again later, or you can just check in and spend the night. Nice shops, a movie or two. Don't want you getting lonesome, you know.'

Donna's eyes grew larger and she ate without glancing at her food.

And later: 'Supposing that you were an intelligent flea on a dog. Life's been pretty good, plenty to eat, no real drastic changes in your life, or that of your parents or grandparents. You can look forward to generations of the same existence for your children and theirs. But supposing that, because you are intelligent, you want to know more about this thing that is home to you, and when you start digging you find that it isn't the universe after all. What you thought was the whole world turns out to be a tiny bit of it, with masters ordering it, forces working on it that you never dreamed of. Things you thought were causes turn out to be effects, things that you thought were making you act in one way or another turn out not to be causing any such thing, they just happen to correspond to your actions. Take weather, for instance. Sunspots affect weather. Weather affects people, the way they feel, moody or elated. Right? Maybe. What if weather, sunspots, and moods are all the effects of something else that we haven't even begun to suspect yet? You see, they are synchronous, but not causal. What else has that same periodicity of eleven point three years? Some business cycles.' Pitcock was warming up now. Eliot had forgotten how long it had been since there had been someone new to explain things to. He scowled at his wineglass and wished the old fool would finish. 'A businessman was shown a chart of the ups and downs of his business, and he nodded and said yep, and he could explain each and every one of them. A strike, a lost shipment of parts, an unexpected government contract. Another man might compare the ups and downs to the excitability curve and claim that that explained it. Someone else might point to a weather chart and say that was the cause. Or the sunspot charts. Or God knows what else. But what if all those things are unrelated to each other, just happen to occur at the same time, all of them caused by something apart from any of them, something that happens that has all those effects? That's what we're after. Keep taking another step back-ward so you can get far enough away to see the whole pattern.'

Or until you step off the end of the gangplank, Eliot added silently.

Donna was staring at Pitcock. 'That's … that's kind of spooky, isn't it? Are you serious?'

'Let me tell you about one more cycle,' Pitcock said, smiling benignly. 'Ed will give you a chart tomorrow, your own personal information chart. Every day at the same time you will be required to X in a square that will roughly indicate your mental state for the day. Feeling very optimistic, happy. Moody, apprehensive. Actively worried. At the end of the month Ed will go over it with you and draw you a curve that will show you your high point and your low. It'll take about fifty days to finish it, probably. Most people seem to have a cycle of fifty to fifty-five days from one high to the next. Now, I'll warn you, nothing you do or don't do will change that chart. You're like a clock ticking away, when it's time to chime, there it is.'

Donna made dimples, shaking her head. 'I don't believe it. I mean, if I flunk a test, I feel low. Or if a boyfriend shows up with someone else. You know. And I feel good when I look nice and someone pays attention to me.'

'Furthermore,' Pitcock said, ignoring her, 'statistics show that although the low points occupy only ten percent of the subject's life, during these periods more than forty percent of his accidents occur. This is the time that suicides jump, or take an overdose. It's the time that wives leave husbands, and vice versa. During the high points, roughly twelve percent of the time, twenty percent of the accidents take place, suggesting that there might be over-optimism. That other forty percent of all the accidents are spaced out in the rest of the time, sixty-eight percent of your life. It's the high and the low periods that you have to watch for.'

'But why?' Donna said, looking from him to Beatrice to Eliot.

'That's one of the things we want to find out with this research,' Pitcock said. He glanced at his watch. 'May I suggest coffee on the terrace? It's always pleasant out there this time of the evening.'

'Do you mind if I beg off?' Beatrice asked, rising. 'I still have some pack-ing to do. I want to get an early start with Gina in the morning.' She added to Donna, 'She's going to spend a couple of weeks with her grandparents in the mountains.'

Donna nodded. 'Could I come with you, help you pack or something?'

There was a quick exchange of glances between Beatrice and Pitcock; then she smiled and said of course. Eliot stood up also, but Pitcock said, 'You won't rush off, too, will you? Something I wanted to bring up, if you aren't in a hurry.'

Progress report? A dressing down? A boost in morale? Eliot shrugged and they watched the girls vanish among the magnolia trees. 'Drambuie and coffee on the terrace. Right?' Pitcock moved ahead of him and sat down facing the sea. The breeze was warm and gentle, clouds drifted by the moon; a shift, and the moon was gliding among castles.

'What would you do if you left here tomorrow?' Pitcock asked after several minutes.

'I don't know. Hadn't thought about it. Not much, at least not very soon.'

'Nothing so fascinating to you that you'd dash right off instantly to do it?'

''Fraid not.'

'Listen.' Pitcock leaned forward slightly. A loon cried out three times, then stopped abruptly, and once more there was only the sound of the waves and the wind in the palm trees.

Pitcock's voice was lower. 'I have a suggestion then, Eliot. Not an order, merely a suggestion. How about starting a book on the data we've collected here?'

'Me? Write a book? About what?'

He listened to Pitcock's low voice, and his own articulated thoughts, and those stirrings that never found words, and later he couldn't separate them. 'If you knew you had to have surgery, would you permit it when your cycle is at its low point? You know you wouldn't. How about starting a business? You know the figures for failures and successes, the peaks and troughs. You'd be crazy to pick one of the low spots. An eagle doesn't have to understand updrafts and currents and jet streams in order to soar and ride the winds ...'

Something for everyone. Cycles on every side, ready to be used, causes unknown, but obviously there. Circadian cycles, menstrual cycles, creativity cycles, excitability cycles. War cycles, peace cycles. Constructive and destructive cycles. Determinism as conceived of in the past, so simplistic, like comparing checkers to chess. A reordering of life-styles, acceptance of the inevitable, using the inevitable instead of always bucking it, trying to circumvent it.

He walked on the beach and seemed to feel the earth stirring beneath his feet. Bits of the earth flowing down the river, into the bay, material to be used by the sea as it constructed the islands grain by grain, shaping them patiently, lovingly, as the very face of the earth was changed, subsiding here, growing there, swelling and ebbing. Eternal cycles of life and death.

He stumbled over the stones of the ruins and climbed the rough steps of the uncompleted tower, a sand-filled stone cylinder. There was lightning out over the ocean, a distant storm too far away to hear the thunder. He watched the flashing light move northward. I don't want to do your goddamned book, Pitcock. Hire yourself a nice obedient ghost writer and do it yourself. Where does it lead? What does it imply? Something I don't want to examine. Flea on the dog, ready to be scratched off, sprayed off, get swept off in the torrent of the river when the dog swims.

'Something happened last night. I don't know what it was, but it has everyone on the island uptight today. Do you know?'

'No.' I don't know. I won't know. I dreamed a crazy dream. Or else they had a bacchanal, and I don't know which, and won't know.

'I thought I had time, five years, even more. But now ... Don't tell me you won't do it, Eliot. Don't say anything about it for a while. Let it lie there. You'll come back to it now and again. See what happens if you don't worry it.'

But I won't. I don't want to do it. I want to finish my three years and get the hell out. Chess and checkers. Not with humans, Pit. Not a game, even on a macrocosmic scale. Not fleas on a dog. Free agents, within the limits set down by our capabilities and the government.

He slept and dreamed, and rejected the dream on awakening. Although unremembered, it left an uneasy feeling in his stomach, and he felt as though he hadn't slept at all. Later he found himself at the ruins and he stood gazing at a mammoth oak tree. The Spaniards had built around it. They had laid a terrazzo floor between the tower and the fort, connected by a walkway that was to have been covered. The pillars were there. And they had built around the oak tree. Crazy pagans, he muttered. Hypocrites with your beads and crucifixes and inquisitions. He walked on the top layer of the stones that made up the fort. They hadn't closed the square. One tenth of it done, then abandoned.

That week Marty fell in love with Donna. Marty had been friendly to Eliot in the past, but now avoided him, refused to look directly at him, and managed to be gone with Donna every day when Mrs. Bonner announced lunch from the basement intercom at the office building.

Eliot kept to himself all week. He worked alone in his office, had a solitary dinner, then prowled about the island until early morning when fatigue drove him to bed and fitful sleep beset by dreams that vanished when he tried to examine them. He knew that the others were together much of the time. Sometimes late at night when the wind eased he could hear their voices, laughing, but he didn't see them again. He caught himself watching one or the other of them for an overt sign of conspiracy.

Friday afternoon Marty and Donna went to the northern islands for the weekend. Beatrice was gone, to the mountains to visit Gina. Ed Delizzio and Eliot were invited to Lee's house for dinner on Friday night, and there was no graceful, or even possible, way for Eliot to refuse without hurting Mary's feelings.

'It's been a funny week, hasn't it?' Mary said. 'Eliot ...' She looked toward her husband, set her mouth, and continued quickly, 'Last week, the night that *she* came, did you have a peculiar dream?'

Lee put his knife down too hard, and she said, 'I have to find out. Has

Marty spoken to you all week?' She had turned back to Eliot almost instantly.

'No. Why? What about a dream?'

'All right. We all dreamed of ... an orgy. Either we dreamed it, or it happened. Lee and I talked about it right away, of course. We thought it was our dream, strange, but ours. Then something Marty said made me realize that he had dreamed it, too. Only he had the players mixed up. And Beatrice ... Well, you can ask her what she dreamed sometime. So I asked Ed, and he said almost the same thing. You?'

Eliot nodded. 'Yeah. Except I wasn't asleep. I saw it, down on the beach. I hadn't gone home yet.'

No one moved or spoke. Mary paled, then she flushed crimson, and finally broke the silence with a sound that was meant to be a laugh but sounded more like a sob. She picked up her wineglass and choked on a swallow. Without looking at Eliot she said, 'Well, if you saw what Lee and I dreamed, you must have had quite a show.'

'It wasn't on the beach,' Ed Delizzio said hoarsely. 'It was back by the ruins, between the fort and the tower. We had a fire, and a ceremony. Rites of some kind.' He stared ahead as if seeing it again. 'I searched for ashes, for a scorched place. I got down on my knees the next morning and searched for a sign ... Nothing.'

Eliot looked at him curiously, wondering how he had missed noting the haggard appearance of the younger man. Ed's eyes appeared sunken, haunted, as if there were only darkness before him that he was trying to pierce.

'It's her fault,' Mary said softly. 'I don't know how or why, what she has done, anything. But I know she's to blame. Night after night I wake up listening and I don't know what for.'

'Hey, knock off talk like that,' Lee said, and while his voice was light, his hand that closed over hers on the table made her wince.

Mary looked at Lee and there was certainty on her face.

Eliot stood up. 'Is there coffee, Mary? I have an appointment with Pitcock later on. Can't dawdle here all night.'

Lee looked relieved as Mary's face relaxed and she smiled a genuine smile and stood up. 'Sorry, Eliot. Pie? Cherry pie and coffee coming up.'

They all helped her clear the table and ate pie and drank coffee. Mary refilled the cups, then asked, 'Are you quitting, Eliot? Is that why you have to see Mr. Pitcock?'

'Mary!' Lee looked at Eliot and shrugged eloquently.

Eliot laughed. 'No, dear heart, I'm not quitting. In fact, I might write a book for the old goat.'

Mary looked disappointed.

'She thinks that if you'd just quit then the whole thing will fold and I won't have to actually do anything,' Lee said.

'You really want to go, don't you?' Eliot asked her.

'I was willing to stay, wasn't I, Lee? I never mentioned leaving, did I? But now, after this week, I'm afraid and I don't know why. I don't like that.'

'Mary, relax. We were all together at dinner. Maybe the lobster was a little off. Or the wrong kind of mushroom in something or other. I mean, I was a lot more worried when I thought it was just me than I am now knowing that everyone experienced something like that.'

She studied his face for a long time, then nodded. 'You could be right, Eliot. I guess it must have been something like that.'

Lee sighed, and even Ed seemed relieved. Soon after that Eliot left them and walked over to Pitcock's house.

'I decided to do the book,' he said without preamble.

Pitcock was on the terrace alone. There was a touch of daylight remaining, enough to make the water look like flowing silver. 'Would you mind telling me why you decided to do it?' Pitcock said after a moment.

'Mainly because I feel like there's something trying its damnedest to keep me from doing it.' Eliot was surprised at his own words. He hadn't meant to say that, hadn't thought it consciously.

'I should warn you, Eliot, that it could be dangerous. Especially if you really feel that way.'

'Dangerous how? Psychologically?'

'Sometimes I forget how bright you are. Sit down, Eliot. Sit down. Have you had dinner?'

Eliot refused another dinner and left the old man on his terrace. They would talk the next day. All my life, he thought, always drifting, everything too easy, too meaningless to become involved with any of it. Like a cork on the stream, this way and that, touching reality now and then, then bobbing away again. Never mattered if I got waterlogged and sank, or if I kept on floating along. Just didn't matter. Then that crazy old man pulled me into his madness, and now I don't feel like I'm floating with the current at all. I'm bucking it and I don't know why, or where I'm going, what I'll find when I get there. And I don't want to get out. I won't get out, and it, that mysterious it that I feel now, it will get in my way, and maybe even try to hurt me ... He laughed suddenly, but his laughter was not harsh, or cynical, but light with amusement and wonder.

Sunday afternoon. 'Some things I should tell you, Eliot. There's a trust already set up, to continue this research. It's your baby.'

'When did you do that?'

'Almost as soon as you came here I started making the arrangements. It doesn't have to be here, you understand. You can move the operations if you want to.'

'And if I decide to quit, then what?'

'I would ask that you personally supervise finding the right man to carry on. I won't issue directives, anything like that, if that's what you mean. At your own discretion.'

Eliot stared at him coldly. 'No ties, of any sort. What I want goes. If I change the direction, whatever.'

'Whatever.'

They stopped to listen. Loud voices from the next house, Ed's house that he shared with Marty. Pitcock was staring toward the sound intently, not surprised, not startled.

Eliot left him and trotted along the boardwalk to Ed's house. Marty was backing Ed up against the screened porch. There was a cut on Ed's cheek. Marty's fists were hanging at his sides and at that moment neither was speaking. Off to one side Donna was pressed against the door of the house, holding her hands over her mouth hard.

'Knock it off, you two. What in Christ's name is going on?'

Neither of them paid any attention to Eliot. From nowhere a knife had appeared in Ed's hand. 'Okay, Marty, baby. Come on in and get it. Come on, baby. Come on.' Ed's voice was low.

Marty hesitated, his eyes on the knife. Before he could move again Eliot jumped him, knocking him to the ground. He brought his knee up sharply under Marty's chin, snapping his head back, then hit him hard just under the ribs. Marty gagged, doubled up gasping.

'Ed! Oh, Ed, he might have killed you! I thought he was going to kill you!' Donna ran to Ed and held him, sobbing.

Eliot watched, mystified. He helped Marty up, keeping a firm grasp on his arm. Marty had no fight left in him. He looked at Ed and Donna and from them to Eliot, his face twisted with contempt and hatred. Furiously he jerked loose from Eliot and turned away to go around the house, not speaking. A second later the front door, slammed.

'Ed, come over to my house. You're hurt! You're bleeding. He was going to kill you!' Donna was tugging at Ed's arm.

'Is anyone going to fill me in? What was that all about?'

Donna looked blank. 'I don't know. He went out of his mind. He started to scream and yell at me and I made him bring me back. Then he went at Ed. Over nothing. Nothing at all.'

Ed shrugged. The knife was gone. Eliot wondered if he had even seen a knife. 'Damned if I know,' Ed said. He was breathing fast now, as if fighting off shock or fear. 'He came at me calling me names like I haven't heard since I left the Bronx.' Donna started to sob again and he put his arm about her shoulders. 'It wasn't your fault,' he said. 'Hey. Don't do that. It wasn't your fault.' He led her toward her house.

'So,' Eliot told Pitcock later, 'I tried to get something out of Marty. He was packing. He cursed me out and finished throwing his stuff into his suitcases, then left. Period.'

Beatrice had returned, was waiting with Pitcock. Neither seemed at all surprised. 'It was bound to happen,' she said. 'They were deadly rivals. That togetherness was too openly self-protective. Donna should have been twins.' She shivered. 'I didn't know Ed carried a knife out here. He's an expert, you know. It's in his file.'

Eliot walked home with her later; at her door he said, 'Something else, Beatrice. Something happened here last week, something inexplicable that has affected us all. A mass hallucination, a mass dream. That's all it was, a psychic event of some sort, not explained yet, but not real.'

They had been standing close together; she drew away. 'Are you certain, Eliot? Absolutely certain? Anything strong enough to touch every one of us, change us somehow, must have some reality of its own.' Then she went inside.

They reorganized and rescheduled work on Monday. Without Marty at the computer there was much that would have to be postponed until they got a replacement. Donna and Ed smiled softly at each other and wandered off down the beach when it was lunchtime. Eliot watched and tried to see her as Marty must have seen her, as Ed obviously saw her. All he saw was the bulgy figure, sagging breasts in too-tight dresses, or halters. The thick legs and arms. Indentable flesh, skin that didn't tan but looked mottled, with red highlights. Thursday night he had dinner with Beatrice on her porch. She lived next to Mary and Lee Moore. They had no lights on yet when they heard Mary calling to Beatrice in a muffled but urgent voice.

'Damn,' Beatrice said. She left Eliot. After a moment he followed her.

'... your friend. Just do something. I won't have her crying on Lee's shoulder. Take her home, or something.' Mary's voice was too controlled, too tight.

'For heaven's sake, Mary. Tell her to clear out. It's your house. Where's Ed?'

'He went for a walk, *she* said. I don't know. All I know is that she's in there crying on Lee's shoulder and they won't even hear me.'

She broke then, suddenly and completely. Eliot couldn't see them, they were hidden by a fence of yellow oleanders, but he could hear her weeping and Beatrice's voice trying to soothe her. He circled them and approached the house.

Donna was in Lee's arms. He was holding her tightly, smoothing her dull hair. His eyes were closed. Their voices were too low to hear any of the words.

'Lee!' They didn't move apart. Lee opened his eyes and stared at Eliot blankly. 'Lee! Snap out of it!'

'They used her,' Lee said dully. 'They both used her to get even with each other for some childish thing. They didn't care what happened to her at all.'

Eliot took a step toward them, stopped again. 'Lee, Mary's hurt. She needs you now. She's hurt, Lee.'

Lee's face changed; slowly the life returned, then suddenly he looked like a man waking up. He dropped his arms from Donna and stepped around her without seeing her at all. 'Mary? What's wrong with Mary?'

'She's out there, Beatrice found her. She needs you right now. By the oleanders.'

Lee ran out of the house. Donna stared after him, her face tear-streaked and ugly. She turned to Eliot. 'I was frightened. Ed had a knife, he began to talk crazy, saying if I would repent now and die before I sinned again, my soul would be saved. I was so frightened. He wants to kill me.'

Eliot saw her hopelessness and despair, the overwhelming fear that had driven her to Lee for help. She was so agonizingly young and inexperienced, so susceptible. Her large eyes awash with tears that made eddies and shadows and revealed depths that he hadn't suspected before, her body hidden now by adolescent fat that would dissolve and reveal a woman with a firm slim figure, protected until she was ready to find union with ... He blinked and laughed raucously. 'God, you're good, doll!' He laughed again and now the tears were gone and her eyes were flat and hard, like a reflecting metal polished to a high sheen. Wordlessly she left the house.

He found Mary and Lee. Beatrice was nearby, her back to them. 'All of you, come on in. I want to say something.' Inside again he didn't know what he could say. Nothing that would make any sense.

'Mary, you have to forget this.' Mary looked at the wall, her face composed and set. 'I mean it, Mary, or else she will have won. You're giving her exactly what she came here for. She doesn't want Lee any more than she wanted Marty or Ed. She wants to drive wedges. To come between people. We all watched it happen. This is the very same thing. You're intelligent enough to see this, Mary. You too, Lee.'

Lee had been watching him stonily. Now he said, 'Hasn't it occurred to you that you're butting in on something you don't know a damn thing about? That girl was frightened. Mary acted like a bitch. Period.'

Eliot sighed. 'Oh, Christ.'

'I'm leaving,' Mary said furiously. 'I won't stand by and see you make a fool of yourself. And when she throws you over, you'll know where to look for me.'

'And you,' Eliot said. 'Right on cue. That's the scenario, all right. For God's sake, you two idiots, open your eyes and see what you're doing and why!' He jammed his hands into his pockets. They continued to avoid looking at one another. Finally Eliot shrugged. 'Okay. If you really can't see it, then leave, Mary. It's the only thing to do. I'll take you over tonight.'

'What are you talking about?' Lee demanded coldly.

'I mean that if you two are so caught up in this that you believe it's real, she has to go away, or one of you will kill the other one. Either snap out of it and convince me that you're aware of what's happened, or I'll take Mary to Charleston. I won't leave you together.'

A new intentness came into Lee's face. Ignoring Mary, he took a step toward Eliot. 'All this crazy talk. You're the one who started all this.' His eyes narrowed and his hands clenched. 'That night, down on the beach, I saw her with you. I let her convince me that it was a dream, but I saw you. I know what I saw. And I'm going to kill you, Kalin. I'm going to choke your lies right back down in your throat.'

Suddenly the screen door was flung open and Ed Delizzio stepped into the room. Mary screamed. Ed had the same knife that he had threatened Marty with. This time he was holding it to throw. His quick look swept the room, stopped at Lee, and in the same instant that his arm rose, Mary moved toward Lee, her hands out. She pushed him hard; the knife flashed; she screamed again, this time in fear and pain. She staggered against Lee and fell. For a second Lee swayed, grey-faced; then he dropped to his knees at her side.

'It's nothing,' she said shakily. 'It touched my arm, that's all. Lee ... Darling, please, don't. Please, Lee.' He was rocking back and forth, holding her, weeping. When she tried to get up, he gathered her into his arms and lifted her and carried her into the bedroom. Beatrice followed them.

Eliot picked up the knife, closed it, and put it in his pocket.

'I guess we should call the police,' Ed said emotionlessly.

'We'll call nobody,' Eliot said. He studied Ed, who continued to stand in the doorway. Even his lips seemed bloodless. 'Are you all right?'

'Yes. Spent. Used up. Everything's gone. I'm okay now. It's over.' He looked like a shock victim: ashen-faced, blank, rigid.

They waited in silence until Beatrice returned. She was pale and avoided Ed's glance. 'They're in there crying like babies. She's all right. Hardly even scratched. Mostly scared.'

'Let's go,' Eliot said. He motioned for Ed to leave with them. 'We could use a drink.'

Beatrice hesitated. 'Can we leave them? You said ...'

'Everything changes from moment to moment, honey. Everything's the same and everything keeps changing. They'll be all right now. Ed's going to keel over and I'm damned if I want to carry him across the island. Give us a drink, Beatrice. We all deserve it.'

Beatrice kept close to him as they walked around the oleanders. 'No lights,' she said on her porch, then added quickly, 'It makes us so visible.' She left them. There was the sound of the refrigerator door, ice in glasses, liquor being poured. Then she was back and handed them both glasses, very strong bourbon and water. She pulled a chair closer to Eliot's. 'How can she do this to us?'

'She's a witch,' Ed said.

'No. She's not a witch. And she hasn't done a damn thing to any of us. Whatever we're doing, we're doing to ourselves.' Eliot finished his drink and went inside to refill his glass. When he returned, Beatrice was alone.

'You upset him more than anything up to now. Eliot, is he likely to do anything like that again?'

'I don't think so. He sinned. Now he'll repent, in the good traditional way. Prayers, good deeds, confession. Whatever he does to atone.'

'Is it all over now? Who else is there to go berserk? Are you safe?'

'Nobody is safe from himself. Nobody that I know, anyway. Maybe Pitcock. I'm gambling on Pitcock, but I don't know.' He drank deeply. The alcohol was numbing him now and he felt grateful.

The wind blew harder and the palm trees came to life. On the porch the silence deepened. Beatrice took Eliot's glass from his hand and went inside with it, bringing it back in a few moments without speaking. He put it down this time. There had been a need before, but the urgency was gone.

'I don't understand what's happening,' Beatrice said quietly, 'but whatever it is, it's changed you.'

'Nobody understands, least of all me. I'm just groping for the right thing to do from one moment to the next, no plans, no overall theory to account for anything.'

'It won't go on like this, will it? We couldn't stand this kind of turmoil day after day.'

'No. It's building up to something. Can't you feel that? Each step is farther, each thrust more nearly mortal.' Lassitude was creeping through his bones. Abruptly he stood up. 'I have to go or I'll fall asleep here.'

'Eliot ... Do you have to go?'

'I think so. Are you afraid?'

'No. It isn't that. Yes, go now. I'll see you in the morning.'

'No work tomorrow. I'm going by the office and post a sign, a declared holiday.' He held her hand for a minute. Soon, he thought, soon. Then he left her and walked through the darkness of the shadows cast by the oak trees and the pines, around the ruins that rose abruptly, smelling the night-blooming cereus, and the sea, and the constant odor of decay that was present wherever there were tropical plants. The scents mingled, the drive toward life stronger than death, blossoms in decay, greenery erupting from the black. He didn't turn on a light when he got to the building, but walked through the dark lobby that echoed hollowly.

He sat at his desk for several minutes before he flicked the light switch. Then he typed the notice quickly and found Scotch tape to attach it to the door. His head was starting to throb and his weariness returned, making his legs ache and his back hurt. Outside the building, he hesitated at the lake. It was spring-fed, cool, clean water, without a ripple on its surface. The moon rode there as sedately as if painted. A whippoorwill cried poignantly.

Very slowly Eliot began to take off his clothes. He walked out into the water, and when it was up to his thighs, he dove straight out into it, down, down. The moon shattered and fled, the resting swans screamed alarm, and half a dozen ducks took flight. Eliot let out his air slowly, measuring it, and when it was gone he began to rise again, but suddenly he doubled in pain. He sank, struggling to loosen the knot in his stomach. The water was luminous now, pale green and silver, and where the bottom had been there was nothing. He sank lower, drifting downward like a snowflake. The broken moon was falling with him, flecks of silver, a streak of a heavier piece flashing by; the minuscule particles of it that touched him adhered, turning him into a radiant being, floating downward in the bottomless pool. From somewhere a thought came to him unwanted and obtrusive: The lake is only eight feet deep in the very center. He tried to push the thought away, but his body had heard, and the struggle began again, and now he tumbled and one leg stretched out until his toes felt the sandy bottom and pushed hard. He exploded in pain, as the moon had exploded. The water rushed in to fill his emptiness and he gasped and choked and coughed and the fire in his lungs was all there was.

He lay on the sand, raw and sore from retching, and he knew he couldn't move. His legs wouldn't hold him yet. Another spasm shook him and he heaved again.

He had little memory of getting to his house and into bed. He dreamed that the Spaniards dragged themselves up from the shadows where they lived and toiled to complete the fort throughout the night. They were crude shadow figures themselves, silent, carrying impossibly heavy burdens on their backs, climbing the crude steps to lay the blocks, and the fort took shape and rose higher and higher. He woke to find it nearly noon.

There was a note on his table to see Pitcock as soon as convenient. He showered and made coffee, and after he had eaten he walked over to the main house. Pitcock was in his office.

'Ed came by to say he was leaving,' Pitcock said. 'He wouldn't tell me what happened. Will you?'

'Sure.' His account was very brief, and when he got to his adventure in the lake, he summed it up in one sentence. 'I went for a swim in the lake and nearly drowned.'

'Part of the same thing?'

'I believe so.'

'Yes. Well, we agreed that it would get dangerous.'

'Yes.'

'Have you seen Donna this morning?' Pitcock toyed with a pencil and when it fell, he jerked. He looked at his hands with curiosity. Before Eliot could answer his question, he said, 'Maybe we should disband the project now. God knows we have to start over with a new staff.'

'I haven't seen Donna. Do you really want to quit?'

'I feel like a man swimming the channel. I'm three quarters of the way there, but I want to turn around and go back. I feel like either way I'll lose something. I don't think I can make it all the way, Eliot.'

'That's because we don't know exactly what's in the water for the last quarter of the trip. We keep finding out there are things that we weren't ready for. Ed's knife. I put it in my pocket, but it's not there now. Swimming in a lake that suddenly became bottomless. You can walk across that lake in the dry season. What's ahead? That's the question, isn't it?'

'Is it? I keep wondering, and if we found out that the earth is an illusion dreamed by a god, what harm have we done? Why are we being stopped? Who's meddling?'

Eliot stared at him, then shook his head. 'I think you should go away for the weekend. Get away from here for a few days, see how you feel about it Monday. If you want to break it all up then, well, we can talk about it.'

'You can't leave now, can you? You'll see it through, no matter what happens?'

'I can't leave now.'

Pitcock looked shriveled and old, and for several minutes his bright blue eyes seemed clouded. Surprisingly, he laughed then. 'You asked once why I picked you. Because I could see myself in you. The self that I could have been forty years ago. But instead I took the other path, extended an empire. Pitcock Enterprises. I thought there was time for it all, and I was wrong. I thought it was a kind of knowledge, that if I bypassed it, I could have it just the same if I forced someone else to seek it and let me see the results. Non-transferable. Not knowledge, then. Not in the accepted sense. I pushed you and prodded you and goaded you into going some-where and I can't follow you. Leave me alone, Eliot. I have some work to do now.'

Eliot stood up and started to leave, but stopped at the door. 'Pit, I don't *know* anything. If I did, I would make you see it. But there's nothing.'

Pitcock didn't look at him. He had picked up the pencil again and held it poised over a notebook as if impatient to resume an interrupted task. Eliot went out.

'Eliot, are you all right?' Beatrice was waiting for him. She held out his watch. 'I found it by the lake.'

Eliot took her in his arms and held her quietly for a long time. 'I'm all right.'

'The lake shore is a mess, as if you were fighting there. I went to your house and saw that you'd had breakfast. I knew it was all right, but still ...'

They walked in the shade, toward the far end of the island. The trees, the dunes to the seaward side, all masked the sound of the ocean, and there were only bird songs and an occasional rustling in the undergrowth. There was a cool, mossy glen, where the air was tinted blue by a profusion of wild morning glories that never closed in the shadows. Very deliberately and gently Eliot made love to Beatrice in the glen.

She lay on her back with her eyes closed, a small smile on her face. 'I feel like a wood nymph, doing what I have to do, without a thought in the world. My brain's on vacation.'

He ran his finger over her cheek. She was humming. With a chill Eliot realized that she was humming 'Ten Little Indians.'

That afternoon Eliot made some preliminary notes:

Any eschatological system, whether religious, mathematical, physical, or simply theoretical for purposes of analogies, is counter to the world as it exists. Experimental bias, observer effect, by whatever name science would call it, the addition of life in a universe reverses the entropic nature of matter. Eschatology can validly be applied only to inert matter; the final dispersion of the atoms in a uniform, energyless universe is a reformulation of what others have called the death wish. Since man rose from the same inert matter, this pull or drive or simple tendency exerts its purpose in every cell of his being. But with the random chemical reaction that brought life to the lifeless, another, stronger drive was created. The double helix is the perfect symbol for this new, not-to-be-denied drive that manifests in rebirth, renewal, in an ever widening spiral of growth and change ...

'Eliot!' Lee's voice jolted him awake. 'Pitcock's missing. We can't find him anywhere.'

'Where have you looked?' Eliot hurried out to join Lee. 'Where's Bonner?'

'He went to check out the office building. We went through the house, then the ruins. He likes to prowl among them. I looked in on Beatrice. I thought he might be with you.'

'Okay. Check out the other houses. I'll take the beach, work back through the stones toward his house.'

Two hours until it would be dark, two hours, plenty of time to find him. Not in the woods, but among the dead rocks. A quarter of a mile of jumbled rocks, fan-shaped, narrowed at the ruins, spreading out at the water's edge, piled higher there with deeper cracks between them. Eliot zigzagged from the edge of the water to the ruins, back to the water. He called, and the whispering sea mocked him. From a distance he could hear Lee's voice calling. A catbird practiced Lee's shout, then gave it up and trilled sweetly. Eliot stopped abruptly. He strained to hear, then began working his way more slowly toward a high place where six of the massive stones had been piled up. 'I'm coming, Pit.' He couldn't be certain now if he had heard the old man or not. He searched frantically but carefully among the bases. Here the water lapped at the rocks with every third or fourth wave. The tide was turning.

'Eliot.'

This time he knew he had heard. He found the old man lying in an unnatural position, his shoulders and his hips not in line. Pitcock was very pale, but conscious. His voice was a faint whisper.

'Can't move, Eliot. Back's hurt.'

'Okay. Take it easy, Pit. We'll get you out of here.' Eliot clambered back up the rocks and yelled for Lee. An answer came back faintly, and he waited until Lee was closer. 'Bring a stretcher, a door, something to carry him on.' Lee appeared at the head of the rocks and waved. 'Tell Bonner to get the launch ready. Mrs. Bonner to call the hospital.' Lee waved again and ran toward Pitcock's house. Eliot returned to the old man.

There was nothing he could do now. He found his handkerchief and wiped Pitcock's face gently. He was perspiring hard.

'Heard someone crying. Couldn't find her. Slipped . . .'

'Don't talk now, Pit. Save it. Your pulse is good. It's not serious, I'm sure. Rest.'

'Eliot, don't send me over tonight. Isn't fair, not now. Get me back to the house. Help me up.' His face was grey, cold, and moist. His eyes were glazed.

Damn Lee! Where was Bonner? 'Take it easy, Pit. Soon now. Just take it easy.' He yanked his shirt off and covered the old man with it. He mopped his face again.

'I didn't do it, Eliot. I didn't want to fall.' He looked past Eliot and groaned. His eyes closed. Beads of sweat came together and a trickle ran across one eye, another down his temple. Eliot wiped his face again and the man shuddered. 'She's up there,' he mumbled. 'Watching us.'

Eliot looked over his shoulder, across the tumbled rocks. She was standing on the wall of the fort, not moving, a dark shape against the paling sky. 'Don't worry about her, Pit,' he said. 'I'll take care of her.' He caught a motion and turned to see Lee and Bonner picking their way among the blocks with a door. Beatrice darted before them, burdened with blankets and a beach mat.

'How bad?'

'I don't know. Shock.' He glanced quickly toward the fort. She was gone.

'For God's sake, be careful!' he said moments later as they started to move

Pitcock to the door, padded now with the beach mat. They covered him and fastened him down securely with the blankets, and then Lee and Eliot carried him to the motor launch. Mrs. Bonner met them at the dock.

'There'll be an ambulance waiting.' She looked at Pitcock and turned white. 'My God! Oh, my God!'

'Go with them,' Eliot said to her. 'You too,' he told Beatrice. 'Get out of here.'

'No. I couldn't help him.'

They got him on board and Lee worked with the mooring line. Eliot turned again to Beatrice. 'Please go on. Stay with him. He might want you.'

'Don't send me away, Eliot. Please don't send me away.'

He nodded and the three of them stood on the dock and watched until the launch started to pick up speed in the smooth water of the bay. As the roar diminished, the silence of the island settled preternaturally. 'Where's Mary?'

'In our house.'

'Let's get her. We have to stay together tonight.' They started across the island. Under the trees the light was a somber yellow, the air hot and still, thick and oppressive. Through the branches overhead the sky was dirty yellow, the color of Donna's hair. No bird stirred, no tree frogs sang, the palm fronds stood stiff and unmoving. Eliot set a fast pace and they hurried a bit more. When they came to the ruins, twilight had descended, and rounding the aborted building they involuntarily stopped. Before them was a concrete ocean, gray on gray, the sea and horizon an encapsulating solid that was closing the distance to them rapidly.

'Get Mary, fast. We'll go to the office building.' Eliot's hand closed hard on Beatrice's arm. She was gazing about in wonder. She reached out to touch the granite block, then her hand swept through the air, her fingers spread apart, as if trying to feel for something not there. 'It's an illusion, a trick of the light. A storm's coming fast.'

She looked at him, touched his cheek as she had touched the rock. 'But I can't tell the difference. This afternoon I dreamed, I thought, or hallucinated, something. Everything was like a flat illustration from a book. I ...' She shook herself and laughed self-consciously. 'I found your watch. Here.' She pulled it from her pocket and handed it to him. Eliot stared at it for a long time. Then Lee and Mary were with them and they turned to go to the office building.

Halfway there, the wind came. It came with a shriek that was too high-pitched, and it carried sand and dust that brought night. The island shook, and the trees ground their branches together. Eliot grasped Beatrice's hand and pulled her, blinded by flying matter and the driving wind that was tearing up rotted and rotting leaves and twigs and stripping leaves from the oaks and needles from the pines. It was a hot wind. When the noises ebbed they could hear the sea pounding. A tree shuddered and crashed down across the walk and they stopped, panting, then ran on, clambering over the trunk. Now they could see the office building and the lake dimly. The lake looked like a saucer of water rocking back and forth. There was no sign of the waterfowl. They began to run across the parklike setting and the water rocked higher on the far side of the lake.

'For the love of God, hurry!' Eliot cried, and nearly yanked Beatrice off her feet. The water was swinging back now, and at the same time the wind increased, pushing the water up and out of its banks. Lee and Mary had reached the building, but Beatrice stumbled. Eliot knocked her to the ground and wrapped his arms around her, and the water hit them.

They rolled with the wall of water, tumbled over and over, grinding against the walk, against the sand and bushes. Beatrice went limp and Eliot held her head tight against him and let himself roll. He closed his hand over her mouth and nose so she wouldn't breathe in the roiling water and dirt. When he knew he could hold his breath no longer, that Beatrice would die if she didn't get air, the water abruptly fell. Everything stopped, even the wind paused. There were hands on him, Lee, trying to help him up. Eliot resisted feebly, the hands persisted, and the weight that was Beatrice was removed.

'Can you get up, Eliot? Can you move? I'll carry her inside and come back for you.' Again the peace returned, but after an infinitely long time he opened his eyes and knew that he had to get up, had to get inside the shelter of the building. The wind was starting to build again and he struggled to his knees, then pulled himself upright and, staggering uncertainly, stumbled to the entrance as Lee was coming out for him.

He was hardly aware of being led inside, of anything that happened for the next few minutes. Beatrice smiled wanly at him, then lay back on the couch where Lee had put her. Outside, the storm built to a new intensity.

'How long has it been?' Mary asked much later. There was no light in the building, the electricity had long since failed. They could hear the howling wind, now and again punctuated by explosive noises as if a wrecking crew were hard at work destroying the island and everything on it.

Eliot looked at his watch; it had stopped. He shrugged. Something crashed into the building and the whole structure shuddered.

'What is it?' Lee asked later. 'A tornado would have gone long ago. There wasn't any report of a hurricane. What is it?'

Eliot stood up. The building shuddered again with a new blast of wind. 'I have to go find her,' he said.

'No!' Beatrice, pale and torn and cut and filthy, and very beautiful. He touched her cheek lightly. She backed away from him and sat down. Very frightened. Tears standing in her eyes. No one else said anything.

No matter which way he went, the wind was in his face. The rain drove against him horizontally, blinding him, and he was buffeted with debris of the storm. There were trees downed everywhere, and he stumbled and fell over them and crawled and dragged himself to his feet again and again. He lost his sandals and knew that his feet were bleeding. His bare chest was hatchmarked by cuts and scrapes. Then he felt the smooth terrazzo underfoot and he knew that soon he would find her. He fell again, hard against a roughly worked block that was cold and wet. The pounding rain dissolved him; he flowed through the rock where there was silence and peace and no more pain. He rested. Very slowly, after a long time, he found himself withdrawing from the nothingness of rest; the rock was cutting into his chest, and where it had scraped his cheek raw there was pain. He pulled away. Lightning burned the air, sizzling so close that he was blinded. The thunder that was almost simultaneous with it deepened and he vibrated with the roar. Blinded and deafened, he pushed himself away from the rock, reeled backward, and clung to the great oak tree until his vision cleared again. Then he lurched away from the place, toward the water's edge and the jumbled rocks there. Behind him lightning flashed again, the tree exploded, showering a geyser of splinters over him. He didn't look back. The tree crashed to the ground, one of the branch ends brushing him as it fell.

The thunder of the sea contested the thunder of the air, overcame it as he drew nearer until there was only the roar of the ocean. The waves were mountainous, crashing over the highest of the rocks now, grinding rocks against rocks, smashing all to a powdery sand that it would fling away to rest in a watery grave. Eliot saw her then.

I've come for you.

You can't touch me.

Yes. I can. I know you.

She laughed and was gone. He waited, bracing himself against the wind, and lightning illuminated her again, closer.

Don't run any more. I'll still be here, no matter how far you run. Always closer.

A wave broke over his feet, and again she laughed and the moment was over. He didn't move.

Eliot, go back to them. Or they'll all die. And death is real, Eliot. No matter what else isn't, death is real.

He had only to reach out to touch her now. Her flesh was as alive as his own, the arm that he caught twisted and pulled reassuringly.

You'll kill them all, Eliot. Beatrice. Lee. Mary. They'll die. Look at the water. It's going to cover the island.

Another wave broke, higher on his leg this time. The water was rushing among the blocks, reaching out for the fort now.

She struggled to free herself, she clawed his face and bit and tried to bring her knee up. Eliot twisted her around and they slipped and fell together, his grasp on her arm broken. He brought his hands up her body and fastened them on her throat, and the waves were over his head as he choked her and beat her head against the rocks and knew that he was drowning, being swept out to sea by the furious undertow, but still he held her. Her struggles became feebler. God! Help me!

He can't! He brings destruction and plagues and wars and death. No help.

She was hardly moving, and they were both swept up together and dashed against the piled-up blocks. Eliot blacked out, but his hands didn't let go, and when the pain released him, he knew that he still held her although he could no longer feel her.

God, please! Please.

He brings the floods and the winds and devastates the land and kills mankind. He is death and I'm sending you back to him.

You're crazy. You can't kill. They'll punish you. They'll hang you. Put you in an institution for the rest of your life.

And the spark of life that is stronger than all the powers of death commands the waters to be stilled, and they are quiet.

There was only silence now.

'Help me pull him out of there.' Lee's voice. 'Can you unlock his hands?'

'Is he dead? For God's sake, Lee, is he dead?'

'No. Beatrice, get out of the way. He's ...'

Eliot opened his eyes to a tranquil night. He was between two stone blocks, waves breaking over his legs. His hands and arms ached and he looked at them; his fingers were locked together. There was no sign of her. Beatrice reached down to touch him and he felt his muscles relax, and took her hand.

'It's over then?'

'Yes. How? What happened?' Beatrice shook her head violently. 'Never mind. Not now. Let's get you inside. You're hurt.'

They walked around the toppled oak tree, but in the wet black ground there were sprouts already, palely green, tenacious. There would be a grove there one day.

'The oak tree is the only casualty,' Lee said in wonder. 'You'd think with all that wind, the thunder and lightning, the whole island would be gone. One tree.'

Eliot felt Beatrice's hand tighten in his, but he didn't say anything. She knows. A temporary displacement of the ego and she comes up with what I'm thinking, just like that. He didn't find it at all curious that no one asked what had happened to Donna. They were on the spiral, safely now, and they would continue to search for patterns that would prove to be elusive, but maybe, now, not too elusive after all.

THE VILLAGE

Mildred Carey decided to walk to the post office early, before the sun turned the two blocks into a furnace. 'They've done something to the weather,' she said to her husband, packing his three sandwiches and thermos of lemonade. 'Never used to be this hot this early.'

'It'll get cooler again. Always does.'

She followed him to the door and waved as he backed out of the drive. The tomato plants she had set out the day before were wilted. She watered them, then started to walk slowly to town. With a feeling of satisfaction she noticed that Mrs. Mareno's roses had black spot. Forcing the blooms with too much fertilizer just wasn't good for them.

Mike Donatti dozed as he awaited orders to regroup and start the search-and-clear maneuver. Stilwell nudged him. 'Hey, Mike, you been over here before?'

'Nope. One fucken village is just like the others. Mud or dust. That's the only fucken difference.'

Stilwell was so new that he was sunburned red. Everyone else in the company was burned black. 'Man, could we pass,' they liked to say to Latimore, who couldn't.

Mr. Peters was sweeping the sidewalk before the market. 'Got some good fresh salami,' he said. 'Ed made it over the weekend.'

'You sure Ed made it, not Buz? When Buz makes it, he uses too much garlic. What's he covering up is what I want to know.'

'Now, Miz Carey, you know he's not covering up. Some folks like it hot and strong.'

'I'll stop back by after I get the mail.'

The four Henry children were already out in the street, filthy, chasing each other randomly. Their mother was not in sight. Mildred Carey pursed her lips. Her Mark never had played in the street in his life.

She dropped in the five-and-dime, not to buy anything but to look over the flats of annuals, petunias, marigolds, nasturtiums. 'They sure don't look healthy,' she said to Doris Offinger.

'They're fine, Miz Carey. Brother bought them fresh this morning from Connor's down at Midbury. You know Connor's has good stock.'

'How's Larry getting along? Still in the veterans' hospital at Lakeview?'

'Yes. He'll be out in a couple of weeks, I guess.' Doris' pretty face remained untroubled. 'They've got such good doctors down there, I hate to see him get so far from them all, but he wants to come home.'

'How can these people stand this heat all the time?' Stilwell said after a moment. The sun wasn't up yet, but it was eighty-six degrees, humidity near one hundred percent.

'People, he says. Boy, ain't you even been briefed? People can't stand it, that's the first clue.' Mike sighed and sat up. He lighted a cigarette. 'Boy, back home in August. You know the hills where I come from are cold, even in August?'

'Where's that?'

'Vermont. I can remember plenty of times it snowed in August. Nights under a blanket.'

'Well, he can help out here in the store. With his pension and the store and all, the two of you are set, aren't you? Isn't that Tessie Hetherton going in Peters' market?'

'I didn't notice her. Did you want one of those flats, Miz Carey?'

'No. They aren't healthy. Connor's must have culled the runts and set *them* out.' She stood in the doorway squinting to see across the way to Peters' market. 'I'm sure it was. And she told me she's too arthritic to do any more housework. I'll just go talk to her.'

'I don't think she will, though. Miz Avery wanted her on Wednesdays and she said no. You know Mr. Hetherton's got a job? With the paper mill.'

'Shit. That won't last. They'll pay off a few of last winter's bills and then he'll start to complain about his liver or something and she'll be hustling for work. I know that man.' She left the store without looking back, certain that Doris would be eyeing the price tags of the flats. 'You take care of yourself, Doris. You're looking peaked. You should get out in the sun.'

'Mrs. Hetherton, you're looking fit again,' Mildred Carey said, cornering the woman as she emerged from the store.

'Warm weather's helped some.'

'Look, can you possibly come over Thursday morning? You know the Garden Club meets this week, and I can't possibly get ready without some help.'

'Well, I just don't know ... Danny's dead set against my going out to work again.'

'But they're going to have to close down the mill. And then where will he be?'

'Close it down? Why? Who says?'

'It's been in the papers for weeks now. All those dead fish, and the stink. You know that committee came up and took samples and said they're the ones responsible. And they can't afford to change over the whole process. They're going to move instead.'

'Oh, that. Danny said don't hold your breath. They're making a study, and then they'll have to come up with a plan and have it studied, and all in all it's going to take five years or even more before it all comes to a head.'

'Hm. Another big kill and the Department of Health ...'

Mrs. Hetherton laughed and Mildred Carey had to smile too. 'Well, anyway, can you come over just this time? For this one meeting?'

'Sure, Miz Carey. Thursday morning? But only half a day.'

The schoolbus turned the corner and rolled noisily down the broad new street. The two women watched it out of sight. 'Have you seen the Tomkins boys lately?' Mildred Carey asked. 'Hair down to here.'

'Winona says they're having someone in to talk about drugs. I asked her point blank if there are drugs around here and she said no, but you never can tell. The kids won't tell you nothing.'

'Well, I just thank God that Mark is grown up and out of it all.'

'He's due home soon now, isn't he?'

'Seven weeks. Then off to college in the fall. I told him that he's probably safer over there than at one of the universities right now.' They laughed and moved apart. 'See you Thursday.'

'Listen, Mike, when you get back, you'll go through New York, won't you? Give my mother a call, will you? Just tell her ...'

'What? That you got jungle rot the first time out and it's gone to your brain?'

'Just call her. Say I'm fine. That's all. She'll want to have you over for dinner, or take you to a good restaurant, something. Say you don't have time. But it'd mean a lot to her to have you call.'

'Sure. Sure. Come on, we're moving.'

They walked for two hours without making contact. The men were straggling along in two uneven columns at the sides of the road. The dirt road was covered with recent growth, no mines. The temperature was going to hit one hundred any second. Sweat and dirt mixed on faces, arms, muddy sweat trickled down shirts.

The concrete street was a glare now. Heat rose in patterns that shifted and vanished and rose again. Mildred Carey wondered if it hadn't been a mistake to rebuild the street, take out the maples and make it wide enough for the traffic that they predicted would be here in another year or two. She shrugged and walked more briskly toward the post office. That wasn't her affair. Her husband, who should know, said it was necessary for the town to grow. After being in road construction for twenty-five years, he should know. Fran Marple and Dodie Wilson waved to her from outside the coffee shop. Fran looked overdue and miserable. Last thing she needed was to go in the coffee shop and have pastry. Mildred Carey smiled at them and went on.

Claud Emerson was weighing a box for Bill Stokes. Bill leaned against the counter smoking, flicking ashes on the floor. 'Don't like it here, get out, that's what I say. Goddam kids with their filthy clothes and dirty feet. Bet they had marijuana up there. Should have called the troopers, that's what I should have done.'

'They was on state land, Bill. You had no call to run them off.'

'They didn't know that. You think I'm going to let them plop themselves down right outside my front door? Let 'em find somewhere else to muck about.'

Claud Emerson stamped the box. 'One seventy-two.'

Stilwell and Mike were following Laski, Berat, and Humboldt. Berat was talking.

'You let it stick out, see, and come at them with your M16 and you know what they watch! Man, they never seen nothing like it! Scared shitless by it. Tight! Whooee! Tight and hot!'

Stilwell looked as if he saw a green monster. Mike laughed and lit another cigarette. The sun was almost straight up when the lieutenant called for a break. He and Sergeant Durkins consulted a map and Humboldt swore at great length. 'They've got us lost, the bastards. This fucken road ain't even on their fucken map.'

Mildred Carey looked through the bills and advertising in her box, saving the letter from Mark for last. She always read them twice, once very quickly to be sure that he was all right, then again, word for word, pausing to pronounce the strange syllables aloud. She scanned the scrawled page, then replaced it in its envelope to be reread at home with coffee.

Bill Stokes's jeep roared outside the door, down the street to screech to a halt outside the feed store.

Mildred shook her head. 'He's a mean man.'

'Yep,' Claud Emerson said. 'Always was, always will be, I reckon. Wonder where them kids spent the night after he chased them.'

Durkins sent out two scouts and the rest of them waited, cursing and sweating. A helicopter throbbed over them, drowned out their voices, vanished. The scouts returned.

Durkins stood up. 'Okay. About four miles. The gooks are there, all right. Or will be again tonight. It's a free-fire zone, and our orders are to clean it out. Let's go.'

Loud voices drifted across the street and they both looked toward the sound. 'Old Dave's at it again,' Claud Emerson said, frowning. 'He'll have himself another heart attack, that's what.'

'What good does arguing do anyway? Everybody around here knows what everybody else thinks and nobody ever changes. Just what good does it do?' She stuffed her mail into her purse. 'Just have to do the best you can. Do what's right and hope for the best.' She waved good-bye.

She still had to pick up cottage cheese and milk. 'Maybe I'll try that new salami,' she said to Peters. 'Just six slices. Don't like to keep it more than a day. Just look at those tomatoes! Sixty-nine a pound! Mr. Peters, that's a disgrace!'

'Field-grown, Miz Carey. Up from Georgia. Shipping costs go up and up, you know.' He sliced the salami carefully, medium thick.

A new tension was in them now and the minesweepers walked gingerly on the road carpeted with green sprouts. Stilwell coughed again and again, a meaningless bark of nervousness. Durkins sent him to the rear, then sent Mike back with him. 'Keep an eye on the fucken bastard,' he said. Mike nodded and waited for the rear to catch up with him. The two brothers from Alabama looked at him expressionlessly as they passed. They didn't mind the heat either, he thought, then spat. Stilwell looked sick.

'Is it a trap?' he asked later.

'Who the fuck knows?'

'Company C walked into an ambush, didn't they?'

'They fucked up.'

Mildred Carey put her milk on the checkout counter alongside the cottage cheese. Her blue housedress was wet with perspiration under her arms and she could feel a spot of wetness on her back when her dress touched her skin. That Janice Samuels, she thought, catching a glimpse of the girl across the street, with those shorts and no bra, pretending she was dressing to be comfortable. Always asking about Mark. And him, asking about her in his letters.

'That's a dollar five,' Peters said.

They halted again less than a mile from the village. The lieutenant called for the helicopters to give cover and to close off the area. Durkins sent men around the village to cover the road leading from it. There was no more they could do until the helicopters arrived. There were fields under cultivation off to the left.

'What if they're still there?' Stilwell asked, waiting.

'You heard Durkins. This is a free-fire zone. They'll be gone.'

'But what if they haven't?'

'We clear the area.'

Stilwell wasn't satisfied, but he didn't want to ask the questions. He didn't want to hear the answers. Mike looked at him with hatred. Stilwell turned away and stared into the bushes at the side of the road.

'Let's go.'

There was a deafening beating roar overhead and Mildred Carey and Peters went to the door to look. A green-and-brown helicopter hovered over the street, then moved down toward the post office, casting a grotesque shadow on the white concrete. Two more of the monstrous machines came over, making talk impossible. There was another helicopter to the north; their throb was everywhere, as if the clear blue sky had loosened a rain of them.

From the feed-store entrance Bill Stokes shouted something lost in the din. He raced to his jeep and fumbled for something under the seat. He straightened up holding binoculars and started to move to the center of the street, looking through them down the highway. One of the helicopters dipped, banked, and turned, and there was a spray of gunfire. Bill Stokes fell, jerked several times, then lay still. Now others began to run in the street, pointing and shouting and screaming. O'Neal and his hired hand ran to Bill Stokes and tried to lift him. Fran Marple and Dodie Wilson had left the coffee shop, were standing outside the door; they turned and ran back inside. A truck rounded the corner at the far end of the street and again the helicopter fired; the truck careened out of control into cars parked outside the bank. One of the cars was propelled through the bank windows. The thunder of the helicopters swallowed the sound of the crash and the breaking glass and the screams of the people who ran from the bank, some of them bleeding, clutching their heads or arms. Katharine Ormsby got to the side of the street, collapsed there. She crawled several more feet, then sprawled out and was still.

Mildred Carey backed into the store, her hands over her mouth. Suddenly she vomited. Peters was still on the sidewalk. She tried to close the door, but he flung it open, pushing her toward the rear of the store.

'Soldiers!' Peters yelled. 'Soldiers coming!'

They went in low, on the sides of the road, ready for the explosion of gunfire, or the sudden eruption of a claymore. The helicopters' noise filled the world as they took up positions. The village was small, a hamlet. It had not been evacuated. The word passed through the company: slopes. They were there. A man ran into the street holding what could have been a grenade, or a bomb, or anything. One of the helicopters fired on him. There was a second burst of fire down the road and a vehicle burned. Now the company was entering the village warily. Mike cursed the slopes for their stupidity in staying.

Home was all Mildred Carey could think of. She had to get home. She ran to the back of the store and out to the alley that the delivery trucks used. She ran all the way home and, panting, with a pain in her chest, she rushed frantically through the house pulling down shades, locking doors. Then she went upstairs where she could see the entire town. The soldiers were coming in crouched over, on both sides of the road, with their rifles out before them. She began to laugh suddenly; tears streaming, she ran downstairs again to fling open the door and shout.

'They're ours,' she screamed toward the townspeople, laughing and crying all at once. 'You fools, they're ours!'

Two of the khaki-clad GIs approached her, still pointing their guns at her. One of them said something, but she couldn't understand his words. 'What are you doing here?' she cried. 'You're American soldiers! What are you doing?'

The larger of the two grabbed her arm and twisted it behind her. She screamed and he pushed her toward the street. He spoke again, but the words were foreign to her. 'I'm an American! For God's sake, this is America! What are you doing?' He hit her in the back with the rifle and she staggered and caught the fence to keep her balance. All down the street the people were being herded to the center of the highway. The soldier who had entered her house came out carrying her husband's hunting rifle, the shotgun, Mark's old .22. 'Stop!' she shrieked at him. 'Those are legal!' She was knocked down by the soldier behind her. He shouted at her and she opened her eyes to see him aiming the rifle at her head.

She scrambled to her feet and lurched forward to join the others in the street. She could taste blood and there was a stabbing pain in her jaw where teeth had been broken by her fall. A sergeant with a notebook was standing to one side. He kept making notations in it as more of the townspeople were forced from their houses and stores into the street.

Mike Donatti and Stilwell herded a raving old woman to the street; when she tried to grab a gun, Mike Donatti knocked her down and would have killed her then, but she was crying, obviously praying, and he simply motioned for her to join the others being rounded up.

The sun was high now, the heat relentless as the people were crowded closer together by each new addition. Some of the small children could be heard screaming even over the noise of the helicopters. Dodie Wilson ran past the crowd, naked from the waist down, naked and bleeding. A soldier caught her and he and another one carried her jerking and fighting into O'Neal's feed store. Her mouth was wide open in one long unheard scream. Old Dave ran toward the lieutenant, clutching at him, yelling at him in a high-pitched voice that it was the wrong town, damn fools, and other things that were lost. A smooth-faced boy hit him in the mouth, then again in the stomach, and when he fell moaning, he kicked him several times about the head. Then he shot him. Mildred Carey saw Janice Samuels being dragged by her wrists and she threw herself at the soldiers, who fought with her, their bodies hiding her from sight. They moved on, and she lay in a shining red pool that spread and spread. They tied Janice Samuels to the porch rail of Gordon's real-estate office, spread her legs open, and half a dozen men alternately raped and beat her. The sergeant yelled in the gibberish they spoke and the soldiers started to move the people as a lump toward the end of town.

Mike Donatti took up a post at the growing heap of weapons and watched the terrorized people. When the order came to move them out, he prodded and nudged, and when he had to, he clubbed them to make sure they moved as a unit. Some of them stumbled and fell, and if they didn't move again, they were shot where they lay.

The filthy Henry children were screaming for their mother. The biggest one, a girl with blond hair stringing down her back, darted away and ran down the empty street. The lieutenant motioned to the troops behind the group and after an appreciable pause there was a volley of shots and the child was lifted and for a moment flew. She rolled when she hit the ground again. Marjory Loomis threw herself down on top of her baby, and shots stilled both figures.

The people were driven to the edge of town, where the highway department had dug the ditch for a culvert that hadn't been laid yet. The sergeant closed his notebook and turned away. The firing started.

The men counted the weapons then, and searched the buildings methodically. Someone cut down a girl who had been tied to a rail. She fell in a heap. Fires were started. The lieutenant called for the helicopters to return to take them back to base camp.

Berat walked with his arm about Stilwell's shoulders, and they laughed a lot. Smoke from the fires began to spread horizontally, head high. Mike lighted another cigarette and thought about the cool green hills of Vermont and they waited to be picked up.

THE FUNERAL

No one could say exactly how old Madam Westfall was when she finally died. At least one hundred twenty, it was estimated. At the very least. For twenty years Madam Westfall had been a shell containing the very latest products of advances made in gerontology, and now she was dead. What lay on the viewing dais was merely a painted, funereally garbed husk.

'She isn't real,' Carla said to herself. 'It's a doll, or something. It isn't really Madam Westfall.' She kept her head bowed, and didn't move her lips, but she said the words over and over. She was afraid to look at a dead person. *The second time they slaughtered all those who bore arms, unguided, mindless now, but lethal with the arms caches that they used indiscriminately.* Carla felt goose bumps along her arms and legs. She wondered if anyone else had been hearing the old Teacher's words.

The line moved slowly, all the girls in their long grey skirts had their heads bowed, their hands clasped. The only sound down the corridor was the sush-sush of slippers on plastic flooring, the occasional rustle of a skirt.

The viewing room had a pale green plastic floor, frosted-green plastic walls, and floor-to-ceiling windows that were now slits of brilliant light from a westering sun. All the furniture had been taken from the room, all the ornamentation. There were no flowers, nothing but the dais, and the bedlike box covered by a transparent shield. And the Teachers. Two at the dais, others between the light strips, at the doors. Their white hands clasped against black garb, heads bowed, hair slicked against each head, straight parts emphasizing bilateral symmetry. The Teachers didn't move, didn't look at the dais, at the girls parading past it.

Carla kept her head bowed, her chin tucked almost inside the V of her collarbone. The serpentine line moved steadily, very slowly. 'She isn't real,' Carla said to herself, desperately now.

She crossed the line that was the cue to raise her head; it felt too heavy to lift, her neck seemed paralyzed. When she did move, she heard a joint crack, and although her jaws suddenly ached, she couldn't relax.

The second green line. She turned her eyes to the right and looked at the incredibly shrunken, hardly human mummy. She felt her stomach lurch and for a moment she thought she was going to vomit. 'She isn't real. It's a doll. She isn't real!' The third line. She bowed her head, pressed her chin hard against her collarbone, making it hurt. She couldn't swallow now, could hardly breathe. The line proceeded to the South Door and through it into the corridor.

She turned left at the South Door and, with her eyes downcast, started the walk back to her genetics class. She looked neither right nor left, but she could hear others moving in the same direction, slippers on plastic, the swish of a skirt, and when she passed by the door to the garden she heard laughter of some Ladies who had come to observe the viewing. She slowed down.

She felt the late sun hot on her skin at the open door and with a sideways glance, not moving her head, she looked quickly into the glaring greenery, but could not see them. Their laughter sounded like music as she went past the opening.

'That one, the one with the blue eyes and straw-colored hair. Stand up, girl.'

Carla didn't move, didn't realize she was being addressed until a Teacher pulled her from her seat.

'Don't hurt her! Turn around, girl. Raise your skirts, higher. Look at me, child. Look up, let me see your face ...'

'She's too young for choosing,' said the Teacher, examining Carla's bracelet. 'Another year, Lady.'

'A pity. She'll coarsen in a year's time. The fuzz is so soft right now, the flesh so tender. Oh, well ...' She moved away, flicking a red skirt about her thighs, her red-clad legs narrowing to tiny ankles, flashing silver slippers with heels that were like icicles. She smelled ... Carla didn't know any words to describe how she smelled. She drank in the fragrance hungrily.

'Look at me, child. Look up, let me see your face ...' The words sang through her mind over and over. At night, falling asleep, she thought of the face, drawing it up from the deep black, trying to hold it in focus: white skin, pink cheek ridges, silver eyelids, black lashes longer than she had known lashes could be, silver-pink lips, three silver spots – one at the corner of her left eye, another at the corner of her mouth, the third like a dimple in the satiny cheek. Silver hair that was loose, in waves about her face, that rippled with life of its own when she moved. If only she had been allowed to touch the hair, to run her finger over that cheek ... The dream that began with the music of the Lady's laughter ended with the nightmare of her other words: 'She'll coarsen in a year's time ...'

After that Carla had watched the changes take place on and within her body, and she understood what the Lady had meant. Her once smooth legs began to develop hair; it grew under her arms, and, most shameful, it sprouted as a dark, coarse bush under her belly. She wept. She tried to pull the hairs out, but it hurt too much, and made her skin sore and raw. Then she started to bleed, and she lay down and waited to die, and was happy that she would die. Instead, she was ordered to the infirmary and was forced to attend a lecture on feminine hygiene. She watched in stony-faced silence while the Doctor added the new information to her bracelet. The Doctor's face was smooth and pink, her eyebrows pale, her lashes so colorless and stubby that they were almost invisible. On her chin was a brown mole with two long hairs. She wore a straight blue-grey gown that hung from her shoulders to the floor. Her drab hair was pulled back tightly from her face, fastened in a hard bun at the back of her neck. Carla hated her. She hated the Teachers. Most of all she hated herself. She yearned for maturity.

Madam Westfall had written: 'Maturity brings grace, beauty, wisdom, happiness. Immaturity means ugliness, unfinished beings with potential only, wholly dependent upon and subservient to the mature citizens.'

There was a True-False quiz on the master screen in front of the classroom. Carla took her place quickly and touch-typed her ID number on the small screen of her machine.

She scanned the questions, and saw that they were all simple declarative statements of truth. Her stylus ran down the True column of her answer screen and it was done. She wondered why they were killing time like this, what they were waiting for. Madam Westfall's death had thrown everything off schedule.

Paperlike brown skin, wrinkled and hard, with lines crossing lines, vertical, horizontal, diagonal, leaving little islands of flesh, hardly enough to coat the bones. Cracked voice, incomprehensible: *they took away the music from the air ... voices from the skies ... erased pictures that move ... boxes that sing and sob ...* Crazy talk. And ... *only one left that knows. Only one.*

Madam Trudeau entered the classroom and Carla understood why the class had been personalized that period. The Teacher had been waiting for Madam Trudeau's appearance. The girls rose hurriedly. Madam Trudeau motioned for them to be seated once more.

'The following girls attended Madam Westfall during the past five years.' She read a list. Carla's name was included on her list. On finishing it, she asked, 'Is there anyone who attended Madam Westfall whose name I did not read?'

There was a rustle from behind Carla. She kept her gaze fastened on Madam Trudeau. 'Name?' the Teacher asked.

'Luella, Madam.'

'You attended Madam Westfall? When?'

'Two years ago, Madam. I was a relief for Sonya, who became ill suddenly.'

'Very well.' Madam Trudeau added Luella's name to her list. 'You will all report to my office at eight A.M. tomorrow morning. You will be excused from classes and duties at that time. Dismissed.' With a bow she excused herself to the class Teacher and left the room.

Carla's legs twitched and ached. Her swim class was at eight each morning and she had missed it, had been sitting on the straight chair for almost two hours, when finally she was told to go into Madam Trudeau's office. None of the other waiting girls looked up when she rose and followed the attendant from the anteroom. Madam Trudeau was seated at an oversized desk that was completely bare, with a mirrorlike finish. Carla stood before it with her eyes downcast, and she could see Madam Trudeau's face reflected from the surface of the desk. Madam Trudeau was looking at a point over Carla's head, unaware that the girl was examining her features.

'You attended Madam Westfall altogether seven times during the past four years, is that correct?'

'I think it is, Madam.'

'You aren't certain?'

'I ... I don't remember, Madam.'

'I see. Do you recall if Madam Westfall spoke to you during any of those times?'

'Yes, Madam.'

'Carla, you are shaking. Are you frightened?'

'No, Madam.'

'Look at me, Carla.'

Carla's hands tightened, and she could feel her fingernails cutting into her hands. She thought of the pain, and stopped shaking. Madam Trudeau had pasty white skin, with peaked black eyebrows, sharp black eyes, black hair. Her mouth was wide and full, her nose long and narrow. As she studied the girl before her, it seemed to Carla that something changed in her expression, but she couldn't say what it was, or how it now differed from what it had been a moment earlier. A new intensity perhaps, a new interest.

'Carla, I've been looking over your records. Now that you are fourteen it is time to decide on your future. I shall propose your name for the Teachers' Academy on the completion of your current courses. As my protégée, you will quit the quarters you now occupy and attend me in my chambers ...' She narrowed her eyes, 'What is the matter with you, girl? Are you ill?'

'No, Madam. I ... I had hoped. I mean, I designated my choice last month. I thought ...'

Madam Trudeau looked to the side of her desk where a records screen was lighted. She scanned the report, and her lips curled derisively. 'A Lady. You would be a Lady!' Carla felt a blush fire her face, and suddenly her palms were wet with sweat. Madam Trudeau laughed, a sharp barking sound. She said, 'The girls who attended Madam Westfall in life shall attend her in death. You will be on duty in the Viewing Room for two hours each day, and when the procession starts for the burial services in Scranton, you will be part of the entourage. Meanwhile, each day for an additional two hours immediately following your attendance in the Viewing Room you will meditate on the words of wisdom you have heard from Madam Westfall, and you will write down every word she ever spoke in your presence. For this purpose there will be placed a notebook and a pen in your cubicle, which you will use for no other reason. You will discuss this with no one except me. You, Quia, will prepare to move to my quarters immediately, where a learning cubicle will be awaiting you. Dismissed.'

Her voice became sharper as she spoke, and when she finished the words were staccato. Carla bowed and turned to leave.

'Carla, you will find that there are certain rewards in being chosen as a Teacher.'

Carla didn't know if she should turn and bow again, or stop where she was, or continue. When she hesitated, the voice came again, shorter, raspish. 'Go. Return to your cubicle.'

The first time, they slaughtered only the leaders, the rousers, ... would be enough to defuse the bomb, leave the rest silent and powerless and malleable ...

Carla looked at the floor before her, trying to control the trembling in her legs. Madam Westfall hadn't moved, hadn't spoken. She was dead, gone. The only sound was the sush, sush of slippers. The green plastic floor was a glare that hurt her eyes. The air was heavy and smelled of death. Smelled the Lady, drank in the fragrance, longed to touch her. Pale, silvery-pink lips, soft, shiny, with two high peaks on the upper lip. The Lady stroked her face with fingers that were soft and cool and gentle ... *when their eyes become soft with unspeakable desires and their bodies show signs of womanhood, then let them have their duties chosen for them, some to bear the young for the society, some to become Teachers, some Nurses, Doctors, some to be taken as Lovers by the citizens, some to be ...*

Carla couldn't control the sudden start that turned her head to look at the mummy. The room seemed to waver, then steadied again. The tremor in her legs became stronger, harder to stop, She pressed her knees together hard, hurting them where bone dug into flesh and skin. Fingers plucking at the coverlet. Plucking bones, brown bones with horny nails.

Water. Girl, give me water. Pretty pretty. You would have been killed, you would have. Pretty. The last time they left no one over ten. No one at all. Ten to twenty-five.

Pretty. Carla said it to herself. Pretty. She visualized it as p-r-i-t-y. Pity with an r. Scanning the dictionary for p-r-i-t-y. Nothing. Pretty. *Afraid of shiny, pretty faces. Young, pretty faces.*

The trembling was all through Carla. Two hours. Eternity. She had stood here forever, would die here, unmoving, trembling, aching. A sigh and the sound of a body falling softly to the floor. Soft body crumbling so easily. Carla didn't turn her head. It must be Luella. So frightened of the mummy. She'd had nightmares every night since Madam Westfall's death. What made a body stay upright, when it fell so easily? Take it out, the thing that held it together, and down, down. Just to let go, to know what to take out and allow the body to fall like that into sleep. Teachers moved across her field of vision, two of them in their black gowns. Sush-sush. Returned with Luella, or someone, between them. No sound. Sush-sush.

The new learning cubicle was an exact duplicate of the old one. Cot, learning machine, chair, partitioned-off commode and washbasin. And new, the notebook and pen. Carla never had had a notebook and pen before. There was the stylus that was attached to the learning machine, and the lighted square in which to write, that then vanished into the machine. She turned the blank pages of the notebook, felt the paper between her fingers, tore a tiny corner off one of the back pages, examined it closely, the jagged edge, the texture of the fragment; she tasted it. She studied the pen just as minutely; it had a pointed, smooth end, and it wrote black. She made a line, stopped to admire it, and crossed it with another line. She wrote very slowly, 'Carla,' started to put down her number, the one on her bracelet, then stopped in confusion. She never had considered it before, but she had no last name, none that she knew. She drew three heavy lines over the two digits she had put down.

At the end of the two hours of meditation she had written her name a number of times, had filled three pages with it, in fact, and had written one of, the things that she could remember hearing from the grey lips of Madam Westfall: 'Non-citizens are the property of the state.'

The next day the citizens started to file past the dais. Carla breathed deeply, trying to sniff the fragrance of the passing Ladies, but they were too distant. She watched their feet, clad in shoes of rainbow colors: pointed toes, stiletto heels; rounded toes, carved heels; satin, sequined slippers ... And just before her duty ended for the day, the Males started to enter the room.

She heard a gasp, Luella again. She didn't faint this time, merely gasped once. Carla saw the feet and legs at the same time and she looked up to see a male citizen. He was very tall and thick, and was dressed in the blue-and-white clothing of a Doctor of Law. He moved into the sunlight and there was a glitter from gold at his wrists and his neck, and the gleam of a smooth polished head. He turned past the dais and his eyes met Carla's. She felt herself go lightheaded and hurriedly she ducked her head and clenched her hands. She thought he was standing still, looking at her, and she could feel her heart thumping hard. Her relief arrived then and she crossed the room as fast as she could without appearing indecorous.

Carla wrote: 'Why did he scare me so much? Why have I never seen a Male before? Why does everyone else wear colors while the girls and the Teachers wear black and grey?'

She drew a wavering line figure of a man, and stared at it, and then Xed it out. Then she looked at the sheet of paper with dismay. Now she had four ruined sheets of paper to dispose of.

Had she angered him by staring? Nervously she tapped on the paper and tried to remember what his face had been like. Had he been frowning? She couldn't remember. Why couldn't she think of anything to write for Madam Trudeau? She bit the end of the pen and then wrote slowly, very carefully: *'Society may dispose of its property as it chooses, following discussion with at least three members, and following permission which is not to be arbitrarily denied.'*

Had Madam Westfall ever said that? She didn't know, but she had to write something, and that was the sort of thing that Madam Westfall had quoted at great length. She threw herself down on the cot and stared at the ceiling. For three days she had kept hearing the Madam's dead voice, but now when she needed to hear her again, nothing.

Sitting in the straight chair, alert for any change in the position of the ancient one, watchful, afraid of the old Teacher. Cramped, tired and sleepy. Half listening to mutterings, murmurings of exhaled and inhaled breaths that sounded like words that made no sense ... *Mama said hide child, hide don't move and Stevie wanted a razor for his birthday and Mama said you're too young, you're only nine and he said no Mama I'm thirteen don't you remember and Mama said hide child hide don't move at all and they came in hating pretty faces ...*

Carla sat up and picked up the pen again, then stopped. When she heard the words, they were so clear in her head, but as soon as they ended, they faded away. She wrote: 'hating pretty faces ... hide child ... only nine.' She stared at the words and drew a line through them.

Pretty faces. Madam Westfall had called her pretty, pretty.

The chimes for social hour were repeated three times and finally Carla opened the door of her cubicle and took a step into the anteroom, where the other protégées already had gathered. There were five. Carla didn't know any of them, but she had seen all of them from time to time in and around the school grounds. Madam Trudeau was sitting on a high-backed chair that was covered with black. She blended into it, so that only her hands and her face seemed apart from the chair, dead-white hands and face. Carla bowed to her and stood uncertainly at her own door.

'Come in, Carla. It is social hour. Relax. This is Wanda, Louise, Stephanie, Mary, Dorothy.' Each girl inclined her head slightly as her name was mentioned. Carla couldn't tell afterward which name went with which girl.

Two of them wore the black-striped overskirt that meant they were in the Teachers' Academy. The other three still wore the grey of the lower school, as did Carla, with black bordering the hems.

'Carla doesn't want to be a Teacher,' Madam Trudeau said dryly. 'She prefers the paint box of a Lady.' She smiled with her mouth only. One of the academy girls laughed. 'Carla, you are not the first to envy the paint box and the bright clothes of the Ladies. I have something to show you. Wanda, the film.'

The girl who had laughed touched a button on a small table, and on one of the walls a picture was projected. Carla caught her breath. It was a Lady, all gold and white, gold hair, gold eyelids, filmy white gown that ended just above her knees. She turned and smiled, holding out both hands, flashing jeweled fingers, long, gleaming nails that came to points. Then she reached up and took off her hair.

Carla felt that she would faint when the golden hair came off in the Lady's hands, leaving short, straight brown hair. She placed the gold hair on a ball, and then, one by one, stripped off the long gleaming nails, leaving her hands just hands, bony and ugly. The Lady peeled off her eyelashes and brows, and then patted a brown, thick coating of something on her face, and, with its removal, revealed pale skin with wrinkles about her eyes, with hard, deep lines beside her nose down to her mouth that had also changed, had become small and mean. Carla wanted to shut her eyes, turn away, and go back to her cubicle, but she didn't dare move. She could feel Madam Trudeau's stare, and the gaze seemed to burn.

The Lady took off the swirling gown, and under it was a garment Carla never had seen before that covered her from her breasts to her thighs. The stubby fingers worked at fasteners, and finally got the garment off, and there was her stomach, bigger, bulging, with cruel red lines where the garment had pinched and squeezed her. Her breasts drooped almost to her waist. Carla couldn't stop her eyes, couldn't make them not see, couldn't make herself not look at the rest of the repulsive body.

Madam Trudeau stood up and went to her door. 'Show Carla the other two films.' She looked at Carla then and said, 'I order you to watch. I shall quiz you on the contents.' She left the room.

The other two films showed the same Lady at work. First with a protégée, then with a male citizen. When they were over Carla stumbled back to her cubicle and vomited repeatedly until she was exhausted. She had nightmares that night.

How many days, she wondered, have I been here now? She no longer trembled, but became detached almost as soon as she took her place between two of the tall windows. She didn't try to catch a whirl of the fragrance of the Ladies, or try to get a glimpse of the Males. She had chosen one particular spot in the floor on which to concentrate, and she didn't shift her gaze from it.

They were old and full of hate, and they said, let us remake them in our image, and they did.

Madam Trudeau hated her, despised her. Old and full of hate ...

'Why were you not chosen to become a Woman to bear young?'

'I am not fit, Madam. I am weak and timid.'

'Look at your hips, thin, like a Male's hips. And your breasts, small and hard.' Madam Trudeau turned away in disgust. 'Why were you not chosen to become a Professional, a Doctor, or a Technician?'

'I am not intelligent enough, Madam. I require many hours of study to grasp the mathematics.'

'So. Weak, frail, not too bright. Why do you weep?'

'I don't know, Madam. I am sorry.'

'Go to your cubicle. You disgust me.'

Staring at a flaw in the floor, a place where an indentation distorted the light, creating one very small oval shadow, wondering when the ordeal would end, wondering why she couldn't fill the notebook with the many things that Madam Westfall had said, things that she could remember here, and could not remember when she was in her cubicle with pen poised over the notebook.

Sometimes Carla forgot where she was, found herself in the chamber of Madam Westfall, watching the ancient one struggle to stay alive, forcing breaths in and out, refusing to admit death. Watching the incomprehensible dials and tubes and bottles of fluids with lowering levels, watching needles that vanished into flesh, tubes that disappeared under the bedclothes, that seemed to writhe now and again with a secret life, listening to the mumbling voice, the groans and sighs, the meaningless words.

Three times they rose against the children and three times slew them until there were none left none at all because the contagion had spread and all over ten were infected and carried radios ...

Radios? A disease? Infected with radios, spreading it among young people?

And Mama said hide child hide and don't move and put this in the cave too and don't touch it.

Carla's relief came and numbly she walked from the Viewing Room. She watched the movement of the black border of her skirt as she walked and it seemed that the blackness crept up her legs, enveloped her middle, climbed her front until it reached her neck, and then it strangled her. She clamped her jaws hard and continued to walk her measured pace.

The girls who had attended Madam Westfall in life were on duty throughout the school ceremonies after the viewing. They were required to stand in a line behind the dais. There were eulogies to the patience and firmness of the first Teacher. Eulogies to her wisdom in setting up the rules of the school. Carla tried to keep her attention on the speakers, but she was so tired and drowsy that she heard only snatches. Then she was jolted into awareness. Madam Trudeau was talking.

'... a book that will be the guide to all future Teachers, showing them the way through personal tribulations and trials to achieve the serenity that was Madam Westfall's. I am honored by this privilege, in choosing me and my apprentices to accomplish this end ...'

Carla thought of the gibberish that she had been putting down in her notebook and she blinked back tears of shame. Madam Trudeau should have told them why she wanted the information. She would have to go back over it and destroy all the nonsense that she had written down.

Late that afternoon the entourage formed that would accompany Madam Westfall to her final ceremony in Scranton, her native city, where her burial would return her to her family.

Madam Trudeau had an interview with Carla before departure. 'You will be in charge of the other girls,' she said. 'I expect you to maintain order. You will report any disturbance, or any infringement of rules, immediately, and if that is not possible, if I am occupied, you will personally impose order in my name.'

'Yes, Madam.'

'Very well. During the journey the girls will travel together in a compartment of the tube. Talking will be permitted, but no laughter, no childish play. When we arrive at the Scranton home, you will be given rooms with cots. Again you will all comport yourselves with the dignity of the office which you are ordered to fulfill at this time.'

Carla felt excitement mount within her as the girls lined up to take their places along the sides of the casket. They went with it to a closed limousine, where they sat knee to knee, unspeaking, hot, to be taken over smooth highways for an hour to the tube. Madam Westfall had refused to fly in life, and was granted the same rights in death, so her body was to be transported from Wilmington to Scranton by the rocket tube. As soon as the girls had accompanied the casket to its car, and were directed to their own compartment, their voices raised in a babble. It was the first time any of them had left the school grounds since entering them at the age of five.

Ruthie was going to work in the infants' wards, and she turned faintly pink and soft-looking when she talked about it. Luella was a music apprentice already, having shown skill on the piano at an early age. Lorette preened herself slightly and announced that she had been chosen as a Lover by a gentleman. She would become a Lady one day. Carla stared at her curiously, wondering at her pleased look, wondering if she had not been shown the films yet. Lorette was blue-eyed, with pale hair, much the same build as Carla. Looking at her, Carla could imagine her in soft dresses, with her mouth painted, her hair covered by the other hair that was cloud-soft and shiny ... She looked at the girl's cheeks flushed with excitement at the thought of her future, and she knew that with or without the paint box, Lorette would be a Lady whose skin would be smooth, whose mouth would be soft ...

'The fuzz is so soft now, the flesh so tender.' She remembered the scent, the softness of the Lady's hands, the way her skirt moved about her red-clad thighs.

She bit her lip. But she didn't want to be a Lady. She couldn't ever think of them again without loathing and disgust. She was chosen to be a Teacher.

They said it is the duty of society to prepare its non-citizens for citizenship but it is recognized that there are those who will not meet the requirements and society itself is not to be blamed for those occasional failures that must accrue.

She took out her notebook and wrote the words in it.

'Did you just remember something else she said?' Lisa asked. She was the youngest of the girls, only ten, and had attended Madam Westfall one time. She seemed to be very tired.

Carla looked over what she had written, and then read it aloud. 'It's from the school rules book,' she said. 'Maybe changed a little, but the same meaning. You'll study it in a year or two.'

Lisa nodded. 'You know what she said to me? She said I should go hide in the cave, and never lose my birth certificate. She said I should never tell anyone where the radio is.' She frowned. 'Do you know what a cave is? And a radio?'

'You wrote it down, didn't you? In the notebook?'

Lisa ducked her head. 'I forgot again. I remembered it once and then forgot again until now.' She searched through her cloth travel bag for her notebook and when she didn't find it, she dumped the contents on the floor to search more carefully. The notebook was not there.

'Lisa, when did you have it last?'

'I don't know. A few days ago. I don't remember.'

'When Madam Trudeau talked to you the last time, did you have it then?'

'No. I couldn't find it. She said if I didn't have it the next time I was called for an interview, she'd whip me. But I can't find it!' She broke into tears and threw herself down on her small heap of belongings. She beat her fists on them and sobbed. 'She's going to whip me and I can't find it. I can't. It's gone.'

Carla stared at her. She shook her head. 'Lisa, stop that crying. You couldn't have lost it. Where? There's no place to lose it. You didn't take it from your cubicle, did you?'

The girl sobbed louder. 'No, No. No. I don't know where it is.'

Carla knelt by her and pulled the child up from the floor to a squatting position. 'Lisa, what did you put in the notebook? Did you play with it?'

Lisa turned chalky white and her eyes became very large, then she closed them, no longer weeping.

'So you used it for other things? Is that it? What sort of things?'

Lisa shook her head. 'I don't know. Just things.'

'All of it? The whole notebook?'

'I couldn't help it. I didn't know what to write down. Madam Westfall said too much. I couldn't write it all. She wanted to touch me and I was afraid of her and I hid under the chair and she kept calling me, "Child, come here, don't hide, I'm not one of them. Go to the cave and take it with you." And she kept reaching for me with her hands. I ... They were like chicken claws. She would have ripped me apart with them. She hated me. She said she hated me. She said I should have been killed with the others, why wasn't I killed with the others.'

Carla, her hands hard on the child's shoulders, turned away from the fear and despair she saw on the girl's face.

Ruthie pushed past her and hugged the child. 'Hush, hush, Lisa. Don't cry now. Hush. There, there.'

Carla stood up and backed away. 'Lisa, what sort of things did you put in the notebook?'

'Just things that I like. Snowflakes and flowers and designs.'

'All right. Pick up your belongings and sit down. We must be nearly there. It seems like the tube is stopping.'

Again they were shown from a closed compartment to a closed limousine and whisked over countryside that remained invisible to them. There was a drizzly rain falling when they stopped and got out of the car.

The Westfall house was a three-storied, pseudo-Victorian wooden building, with balconies and cupolas, and many chimneys. There was scaffolding about it, and one of the three porches had been torn away and was being replaced as restoration of the house, turning it into a national monument, progressed. The girls accompanied the casket to a gloomy, large room where the air was chilly and damp, and scant lighting cast deep shadows. After the casket had been positioned on the dais which also had accompanied it, the girls followed Madam Trudeau through narrow corridors, up narrow steps, to the third floor where two large rooms had been prepared for them, each containing seven cots.

Madam Trudeau showed them the bathroom that would serve their needs, told them goodnight, and motioned Carla to follow her. They descended the stairs to a second-floor room that had black, massive furniture: a desk, two straight chairs, a bureau with a wavery mirror over it, and a large canopied bed.

Madam Trudeau paced the black floor silently for several minutes without speaking, then she swung around and said, 'Carla, I heard every word that silly little girl said this afternoon. She drew pictures in her notebook! This is the third time the word cave has come up in reports of Madam Westfall's mutterings. Did she speak to you of caves?'

Carla's mind was whirling. How had she heard what they had said? Did maturity also bestow magical abilities? She said, 'Yes, Madam, she spoke of hiding in a cave.'

'Where is the cave, Carla? Where is it?'

'I don't know, Madam. She didn't say.'

Madam Trudeau started to pace once more. Her pale face was drawn in lines of concentration that carved deeply into her flesh, two furrows straight up from the inner brows, other lines at the sides of her nose, straight to her chin, her mouth tight and hard. Suddenly she sat down and leaned back in the chair. 'Carla, in the last four or five years Madam Westfall became childishly senile; she was no longer living in the present most of the time, but was reliving incidents in her past. Do you understand what I mean?'

Carla nodded, then said hastily, 'Yes, Madam.'

'Yes. Well, it doesn't matter. You know that I have been commissioned to write the biography of Madam Westfall, to immortalize her writings and her utterances. But there is a gap, Carla. A large gap in our knowledge, and until recently it seemed that the gap never would be filled in. When Madam Westfall was found as a child, wandering in a dazed condition, undernourished, almost dead from exposure, she did not know who she was, where she was from, anything about her past at all. Someone had put an identification bracelet on her arm, a steel bracelet that she could not remove, and that was the only clue there was about her origins. For ten years she received the best medical care and education available, and her intellect sparkled brilliantly, but she never regained her memory.'

Madam Trudeau shifted to look at Carla. A trick of the lighting made her eyes glitter like jewels. 'You have studied how she started her first school with eight students, and over the next century developed her teaching methods to the point of perfection that we now employ throughout the nation, in the Males' school as well as the Females'. Through her efforts Teachers have become the most respected of all citizens and the schools the most powerful of all institutions.' A mirthless smile crossed her face, gone almost as quickly as it formed, leaving the deep shadows, lines, and the glittering eyes. 'I honored you more than you yet realize when I chose you for my protégée.'

The air in the room was too close and dank, smelled of moldering wood and unopened places. Carla continued to watch Madam Trudeau, but she was feeling lightheaded and exhausted and the words seemed interminable to her. The glittering eyes held her gaze and she said nothing. The thought occurred to her that Madam Trudeau would take Madam Westfall's place as head of the school now.

'Encourage the girls to talk, Carla. Let them go on as much as they want about what Madam Westfall said, lead them into it if they stray from the point. Written reports have been sadly deficient.' She stopped and looked questioningly at the girl. 'Yes? What is it?'

'Then ... I mean after they talk, are they to write ...? Or should I try to remember and write it all down?'

'There will be no need for that,' Madam Trudeau said. 'Simply let them talk as much as they want.'

'Yes, Madam.'

'Very well. Here is a schedule for the coming days. Two girls on duty in the Viewing Room at all times from dawn until dark, yard exercise in the enclosed garden behind the building if the weather permits, kitchen duty, and so on. Study it, and direct the girls to their duties. On Saturday afternoon everyone will attend the burial, and on Sunday we return to the school. Now go.'

Carla bowed, and turned to leave. Madam Trudeau's voice stopped her once more. 'Wait, Carla. Come here. You may brush my hair before you leave.'

Carla took the brush in numb fingers and walked obediently behind Madam Trudeau, who was loosening hair clasps that restrained her heavy black hair. It fell down her back like a dead snake, uncoiling slowly. Carla started to brush it.

'Harder, girl. Are you so weak that you can't brush hair?'

She plied the brush harder until her arm became heavy and then Madam Trudeau said, 'Enough. You are a clumsy girl, awkward and stupid. Must I teach you everything, even how to brush one's hair properly?' She yanked the brush from Carla's hand and now there were two spots of color on her cheeks and her eyes were flashing. 'Get out. Go! Leave me! On Saturday immediately following the funeral you will administer punishment to Lisa for scribbling in her notebook. Afterward report to me. And now get out of here!'

Carla snatched up the schedule and backed across the room, terrified of the Teacher who seemed demoniacal suddenly. She bumped into the other chair and nearly fell down. Madam Trudeau laughed shortly and cried, 'Clumsy, awkward! You would be a Lady! You?'

Carla groped behind her for the doorknob and finally escaped into the hallway, where she leaned against the wall, trembling too hard to move on. Something crashed into the door behind her and she stifled a scream and ran. The brush. Madam had thrown the brush against the door.

Madam Westfall's ghost roamed all night, chasing shadows in and out of rooms, making the floors creak with her passage, echoes of her voice drifting in and out of the dorm where Carla tossed restlessly. Twice she sat upright in fear, listening intently, not knowing why. Once Lisa cried out and she went to her and held her hand until the child quieted again. When dawn lighted the room Carla was awake and standing at the windows looking at the ring of mountains that encircled the city. Black shadows against the lesser black of the sky, they darkened, and suddenly caught fire from the sun striking their tips. The fire spread downward, went out, and became merely light on the leaves that were turning red and gold. Carla turned from the view, unable to explain the pain that filled her. She awakened the first two girls who were to be on duty with Madam Westfall and after their quiet departure, returned to the window. The sun was all the way up now, but its morning light was soft; there were no hard outlines anywhere. The trees were a blend of colors with no individual boundaries, and rocks and earth melted together and were one. Birds were singing with the desperation of summer's end and winter's approach.

'Carla?' Lisa touched her arm and looked up at her with wide, fearful eyes. 'Is she going to whip me?'

'You will be punished after the funeral,' Carla said, stiffly. 'And I should report you for touching me, you know.'

The child drew back, looking down at the black border on Carla's skirt. 'I forgot.' She hung her head. 'I'm ... I'm so scared.'

'It's time for breakfast, and after that we'll have a walk in the gardens. You'll feel better after you get out in the sunshine and fresh air.'

'Chrysanthemums, dahlias, marigolds. No, the small ones there, with the brown fringes ...' Luella pointed out the various flowers to the other girls. Carla walked in the rear, hardly listening, trying to keep her eye on Lisa, who also trailed behind. She was worried about the child. Lisa had not slept well, had eaten no breakfast, and was so pale and wan that she didn't look strong enough to take the short garden walk with them.

Eminent personages came and went in the gloomy old house and huddled together to speak in lowered voices. Carla paid little attention to them. 'I can change it after I have some authority,' she said to a still inner self who listened and made no reply. 'What can I do now? I'm property. I belong to the state, to Madam Trudeau and the school. What good if I disobey and am also whipped? Would that help any? I won't hit her hard.' The inner self said nothing, but she thought she could hear a mocking laugh come from the mummy that was being honored.

They had all those empty schools, miles and miles of school halls where

no feet walked, desks where no students sat, books that no students scrib-
bled up, and they put the children in them and they could see immediately
who couldn't keep up, couldn't learn the new ways, and they got rid of them.
Smart. Smart of them. They were smart and had the goods and the money
and the hatred. My God, they hated. That's who wins, who hates most. And is
more afraid. Every time.

Carla forced her arms not to move, her hands to remain locked before
her, forced her head to stay bowed. The voice now went on and on and she
couldn't get away from it.

... rained every day, cold freezing rain and Daddy didn't come back and
Mama said, hide child, hide in the cave where it's warm, and don't move no
matter what happens, don't move. Let me put it on your arm, don't take it
off, never take it off show it to them if they find you show them make them
look ...

Her relief came and Carla left. In the wide hallway that led to the back
steps she was stopped by a rough hand on her arm. 'Damme, here's a likely
one. Come here, girl. Let's have a look at you.' She was spun around and the
hand grasped her chin and lifted her head. 'Did I say it! I could spot her all
the way down the hall, now couldn't I? Can't hide what she's got with long
skirts and that skinny hairdo, now can you? Didn't I spot her!' He laughed
and turned Carla's head to the side and looked at her in profile, then laughed
even louder.

She could see only that he was red-faced, with bushy eyebrows and thick
grey hair. His hand holding her chin hurt, digging into her jaws at each side
of her neck.

'Victor, turn her loose,' the cool voice of a female said then. 'She's been
chosen already. An apprentice Teacher.'

He pushed Carla from him, still holding her chin, and he looked down at
the skirts with the broad black band at the bottom. He gave her a shove that
sent her into the opposite wall. She clutched at it for support.

'Whose pet is she?' he said darkly.

'Trudeau's.'

He turned and stamped away, not looking at Carla again. He wore the
blue and white of a Doctor of Law. The female was a Lady in pink and black.

'Carla. Go upstairs.' Madam Trudeau moved from an open doorway and
stood before Carla. She looked up and down the shaking girl. 'Now do you
understand why I apprenticed you before this trip? For your own protection.'

They walked to the cemetery on Saturday, a bright, warm day with golden
light and the odor of burning leaves. Speeches were made, Madam Westfall's favorite music was played, and the services ended. Carla dreaded returning to the dormitory. She kept a close watch on Lisa, who seemed but a
shadow of herself. Three times during the night she had held the girl until

her nightmares subsided, and each time she had stroked her fine hair and soft cheeks and murmured to her quieting words, and she knew it was only her own cowardice that prevented her saying that it was she who would administer the whipping. The first shovelful of earth was thrown on top of the casket and everyone turned to leave the place, when suddenly the air was filled with raucous laughter, obscene chants, and wild music. It ended almost as quickly as it started, but the group was frozen until the mountain air became unnaturally still. Not even the birds were making a sound following the maniacal outburst.

Carla had been unable to stop the involuntary look that she cast about her at the woods that circled the cemetery. Who? Who would dare? Only a leaf or two stirred, floating downward on the gentle air effortlessly. Far in the distance a bird began to sing again, as if the evil spirits that had flown past were now gone.

'Madam Trudeau sent this up for you,' Luella said nervously, handing Carla the rod. It was plastic, three feet long, thin, flexible. Carla looked at it and turned slowly to Lisa. The girl seemed to be swaying back and forth.

'I am to administer the whipping,' Carla said. 'You will undress now.'

Lisa stared at her in disbelief, and then suddenly she ran across the room and threw herself on Carla, hugging her hard, sobbing. 'Thank you, Carla. Thank you so much. I was so afraid, you don't know how afraid. Thank you. How did you make her let you do it? Will you be punished too? I love you so much, Carla.' She was incoherent in her relief and she flung off her gown and underwear and turned around.

Her skin was pale and soft, rounded buttocks, dimpled just above the fullness. She had no waist yet, no breasts, no hair on her baby body. Like a baby she had whimpered in the night, clinging tightly to Carla, burying her head in the curve of Carla's breasts.

Carla raised the rod and brought it down, as easily as she could. Anything was too hard. There was a red welt. The girl bowed her head lower, but didn't whimper. She was holding the back of a chair and it jerked when the rod struck.

It would be worse if Madam Trudeau was doing it, Carla thought. She would try to hurt, would draw blood. Why? Why? The rod was hanging limply, and she knew it would be harder on both of them if she didn't finish it quickly. She raised it and again felt the rod bite into flesh, sending the vibration into her arm, through her body.

Again. The girl cried out, and a spot of blood appeared on her back. Carla stared at it in fascination and despair. She couldn't help it. Her arm wielded the rod too hard, and she couldn't help it. She closed her eyes a moment, raised the rod and struck again. Better. But the vibrations that had begun with the first blow increased, and she felt dizzy, and couldn't keep her eyes off the spot of blood that was trailing down the girl's back. Lisa was weeping now, her body was shaking. Carla felt a responsive tremor start within her.

Eight, nine. The excitement that stirred her was unnameable, unknowable, never before felt like this. Suddenly she thought of the Lady who had chosen her once, and scenes of the film she had been forced to watch flashed through her mind ... *remake them in our image.* She looked about in that moment frozen in time, and she saw the excitement on some of the faces, on others fear, disgust and revulsion. Her gaze stopped on Helga, who had her eyes closed, whose body was moving rhythmically. She raised the rod and brought it down as hard as she could, hitting the chair with a noise that brought everyone out of his own kind of trance. A sharp, cracking noise that was a finish.

'Ten!' she cried and threw the rod across the room.

Lisa turned and through brimming eyes, red, swollen, ugly with crying, said, 'Thank you, Carla. It wasn't so bad.'

Looking at her, Carla knew hatred. It burned through her, distorted the image of what she saw. Inside her body the excitement found no outlet, and it flushed her face, made her hands numb, and filled her with hatred. She turned and fled.

Before Madam Trudeau's door, she stopped a moment, took a deep breath, and knocked. After several moments the door opened and Madam Trudeau came out. Her eyes were glittering more than ever, and there were two spots of color on her pasty cheeks.

'It is done? Let me look at you.' Her fingers were cold and moist when she lifted Carla's chin. 'Yes, I see. I see. I am busy now. Come back in half an hour. You will tell me all about it. Half an hour.' Carla never had seen a genuine smile on the Teacher's face before, and now when it came, it was more frightening than her frown was. Carla didn't move, but she felt as if every cell in her body had tried to pull back.

She bowed and turned to leave. Madam Trudeau followed her a step and said in a low vibrant voice, 'You felt it, didn't you? You know now, don't you?'

'Madam Trudeau, are you coming back?' The door behind her opened, and one of the Doctors of Law appeared there.

'Yes, of course.' She turned and went back to the room.

Carla let herself into the small enclosed area between the second and third floors, then stopped. She could hear the voices, of girls coming down the stairs, going on duty in the kitchen, or outside for evening exercises. She stopped to wait for them to pass, and she leaned against the wall tiredly. This space was two and a half feet square perhaps. It was very dank and hot. From here she could hear every sound made by the girls on the stairs. Probably that was why the second door had been added, to muffle the noise of those going up and down. The girls had stopped on the steps and were discussing the laughter and obscenities they had heard in the cemetery.

Carla knew that it was her duty to confront them, to order them to their duties, to impose proper silence on them in public places, but she closed her eyes and pressed her hand hard on the wood behind her for support and wished they would finish their childish prattle and go on. The wood behind her started to slide.

She jerked away. A sliding door? She felt it and ran her finger along the smooth paneling to the edge where there was now a six-inch opening as high as she could reach and down to the floor. She pushed the door again and it slid easily, going between the two walls. When the opening was wide enough she stepped through it. The cave! She knew it was the cave that Madam Westfall had talked about incessantly.

The space was no more than two feet wide, and very dark. She felt the inside door and there was a knob on it, low enough for children to reach. The door slid as smoothly from the inside as it had from the outside. She slid it almost closed and the voices were cut off, but she could hear other voices, from the room on the other side of the passage. They were not clear. She felt her way farther, and almost fell over a box. She held her breath as she realized that she was hearing Madam Trudeau's voice:

'... be there. Too many independent reports of the old fool's babbling about it for there not to be something to it. Your men are incompetent.'

'Trudeau, shut up. You scare the living hell out of the kids, but you don't scare me. Just shut up and accept the report. We've been over every inch of the hills for miles, and there's no cave. It was over a hundred years ago. Maybe there was one that the kids played in, but it's gone now. Probably collapsed.'

'We have to be certain, absolutely certain.'

'What's so important about it anyway? Maybe if you would give us more to go on we could make more progress.'

'The reports state that when the militia came here, they found only Martha Westfall. They executed her on the spot without questioning her first. Fools! When they searched the house, they discovered that it was stripped. No jewels, no silver, diaries, papers. Nothing. Steve Westfall was dead. Dr. Westfall dead. Martha. No one has ever found the articles that were hidden, and when the child again appeared, she had true amnesia that never yielded to attempts to penetrate it.'

'So, a few records, diaries. What are they to you?' There was silence, then he laughed. 'The money! He took all his money out of the bank, didn't he?'

'Don't be ridiculous. I want records, that's all. There's a complete ham radio, complete. Dr. Westfall was an electronics engineer as well as a teacher. No one could begin to guess how much equipment he hid before he was killed.'

Carla ran her hand over the box, felt behind it. More boxes.

'Yeah yeah. I read the reports, too. All the more reason to keep the search nearby. For a year before the end a close watch was kept on the house. They had to walk to wherever they hid the stuff. And I can just say again that there's no cave around here. It fell in.'

'I hope so,' Madam Trudeau said.

Someone knocked on the door, and Madam Trudeau called, 'Come in.'

'Yes, what is it? Speak up, girl.'

'It is my duty to report, Madam, that Carla did not administer the full punishment ordered by you.'

Carla's fists clenched hard. Helga.

'Explain,' Madam Trudeau said sharply.

'She only struck Lisa nine times, Madam. The last time she hit the chair.'

'I see. Return to your room.'

The man laughed when the girl closed the door once more. 'Carla is the golden one, Trudeau? The one who wears a single black band?'

'The one you manhandled earlier, yes.'

'Insubordination in the ranks, Trudeau? Tut, tut. And your reports all state that you never have any rebellion. Never.'

Very slowly Madam Trudeau said, 'I have never had a student who didn't abandon any thoughts of rebellion under my guidance. Carla will be obedient. And one day she will be an excellent Teacher. I know the signs.'

Carla stood before the Teacher with her head bowed and her hands clasped together. Madam Trudeau walked around her without touching her, then sat down and said, 'You will whip Lisa every day for a week, beginning tomorrow.'

Carla didn't reply.

'Don't stand mute before me, Carla. Signify your obedience immediately.'

'I ... I can't, Madam.'

'Carla, any day that you do not whip Lisa, I will. And I will also whip you double her allotment. Do you understand?'

'Yes, Madam.'

'You will inform Lisa that she is to be whipped every day, by one or the other of us. Immediately.'

'Madam, please ...'

'You speak out of turn, Carla!'

'I ... Madam, please don't do this. Don't make me do this. She is too weak ...'

'She will beg you to do it, won't she, Carla? Beg you with tears flowing to be the one, not me. And you will feel the excitement and the hate and every day you will feel it grow strong. You will want to hurt her, want to see blood spot her bare back. And your hate will grow until you won't be able to look at her without being blinded by your own hatred. You see, I know, Carla. I know all of it.'

Carla stared at her in horror. 'I won't do it. I won't.'

'I will.'

They were old and full of hatred for the shiny young faces, the bright hair, the straight backs and strong legs and arms. They said: let us remake them in our image and they did.

Carla repeated Madam Trudeau's words to the girls gathered in the two sleeping rooms on the third floor. Lisa swayed and was supported by Ruthie. Helga smiled.

That evening Ruthie tried to run away and was caught by two of the blue-clad Males. The girls were lined up and watched as Ruthie was stoned. They buried her without a service on the hill where she had been caught.

After dark, lying on the cot open-eyed, tense, Carla heard Lisa's whisper close to her ear. 'I don't care if you hit me, Carla. It won't hurt like it does when she hits me.'

'Go to bed, Lisa. Go to sleep.'

'I can't sleep. I keep seeing Ruthie. I should have gone with her. I wanted to, but she wouldn't let me. She was afraid there would be Males on the hill watching. She said if she didn't get caught, then I should try to follow her at night.' The child's voice was flat, as if shock had dulled her sensibilities.

Carla kept seeing Ruthie too. Over and over she repeated to herself: I should have tried it. I'm cleverer than she was. I might have escaped. I should have been the one. She knew it was too late now. They would be watching too closely.

An eternity later she crept from her bed and dressed quietly. Soundlessly she gathered her own belongings, and then collected the notebooks of the other girls, and the pens, and she left the room. There were dim lights on throughout the house as she made her way silently down stairs and through corridors. She left a pen by one of the outside doors, and very cautiously made her way back to the tiny space between the floors. She slid the door open and deposited everything else she carried inside the cave. She tried to get to the kitchen for food, but stopped when she saw one of the Officers of Law. She returned soundlessly to the attic rooms and tiptoed among the beds to Lisa's cot. She placed one hand over the girl's mouth and shook her awake with the other.

Lisa bolted upright, terrified, her body stiffened convulsively. With her mouth against the girl's ear Carla whispered, 'Don't make a sound. Come on.' She half led, half carried the girl to the doorway, down the stairs, and into the cave and closed the door.

'You can't talk here, either,' she whispered. 'They can hear.' She spread out the extra garments she had collected and they lay down together, her arms tight about the girl's shoulders. 'Try to sleep,' she whispered. 'I don't think they'll find us here. And after they leave, we'll creep out and live in the woods. We'll eat nuts and berries ...'

The first day they were jubilant at their success and they giggled and muffled the noise with their skirts. They could hear all the orders being issued by Madam Trudeau: guards in all the halls, on the stairs, at the door to the dorm to keep other girls from trying to escape also. They could hear all the interrogations, of the girls, the guards who had not seen the escapees. They heard the mocking voice of the Doctor of Law deriding Madam Trudeau's boasts of absolute control.

The second day Carla tried to steal food for them, and, more important, water. There were blue-clad Males everywhere. She returned emptyhanded. During the night Lisa whimpered in her sleep and Carla had to stay awake to quiet the child, who was slightly feverish.

'You won't let her get me, will you?' she begged over and over.

The third day Lisa became too quiet. She didn't want Carla to move from her side at all. She held Carla's hand in her hot, dry hand and now and then tried to raise it to her face, but she was too weak now. Carla stroked her forehead.

When the child slept Carla wrote in the notebooks, in the dark, not knowing if she wrote over other words or on blank pages. She wrote her life story, and then made up other things to say. She wrote her name over and over, and wept because she had no last name. She wrote nonsense words and rhymed them with other nonsense words. She wrote of the savages who had laughed at the funeral and she hoped they wouldn't all die over the winter months. She thought that probably they would. She wrote of the golden light through green-black pine trees and of birds' songs and moss underfoot. She wrote of Lisa lying peacefully now at the far end of the cave amidst riches that neither of them could ever have comprehended. When she could no longer write, she drifted in and out of the golden light in the forest, listening to the birds' songs, hearing the raucous laughter that now sounded so beautiful.

WELCOME, CHAOS

For
Mary Ann, Jean,
Maisie, and Kitty, with love.

1

Hugh Lasater stood with his back to the window, watching Lloyd Pierson squirm. They were in Pierson's office, a room furnished with university-issue desk and bookshelves, as devoid of personality as Pierson himself was. He was one of those men no one after the fact could ever identify, so neutral he could vanish into a mist, become one with a landscape, and never be seen again.

Lloyd Pierson stopped fidgeting with his pencil and took a deep breath. 'I can't do it,' he said primly, examining the pencil. 'It would be unethical, and besides she would appeal. She might even have a sex discrimination case.'

'She won't appeal. Believe me, she won't make a stink.'

Pierson shook his head. He glanced at his watch, then confirmed what he had learned by looking at the wall clock.

Lasater suppressed a laugh.

'You do it, or I go over your head,' he said mildly. 'It's a funny thing how people hate having this kind of decision shoved at them when it could have been handled on a lower level. You know?'

'You have no right!' Pierson snapped. He looked at Lasater, then quickly away again. 'This is insufferable.'

'Righto. Dean McCrory, isn't it? I just happen to have his number here somewhere. I suppose your secretary would place the call for me?' He searched his notebook, then stopped, holding it open.

'I want to talk to your supervisor, your boss, whoever that is.'

Lasater shrugged. 'Got a piece of paper? I'll write the number for you.' Pierson handed him a note pad and he jotted down a number. 'That's a Washington area code. Dial it yourself, if you don't mind. You have an out-side line, don't you? And his is a direct line, it'll be his private secretary who answers. Just tell him it's about the bird of prey business. He'll put you through.'

'Whose private secretary?'

'Secretary of Defense,' Lasater said, as if surprised that Pierson had not recognized the number.

'I don't believe you.' He dialed the number.

Lasater turned to look out the window. The campus was a collage of red brick buildings, dirty snow, and too many people of an age. God, how tired he would get of so many young people all the time with their mini-agonies and mini-crises and mini-triumphs. Unisex reigned here; in their dark winter garments they all looked alike. The scene was an exercise in perspective: same buildings, same snow, same vague figures repeated endlessly. He listened to Pierson parrot his message about bird of prey, and a moment later:

'Never mind. Sorry to bother you. I won't wait. It's all right.'

Lasater smiled at the bleak landscape, but when he turned to the room there was no trace of humor on his face. He retrieved the notepaper, put it in an ashtray, and set it afire. After it was burned he crushed the ashes thoroughly, then dumped them into the wastecan. He held the pad aslant and studied the next piece of paper, then slipped the pad into a pocket. He kept his amusement out of his voice when he said, 'You will never use that number again, or even remember that you saw such a number. In fact, this entire visit is classified, and everything about it. Right?'

Pierson nodded miserably.

Lasater felt only contempt for him now; he had not fought hard enough for anything else. 'So, you just tell her no dice on a leave of absence. You have about an hour before she'll get here; you'll think of a dozen good reasons why your department can't do without her services.'

He picked up his coat and hat from the chair where he had tossed them and left without looking back.

Lyle Taney would never know what happened, he thought with satisfaction, pausing at the stairs of the history department building to put his coat on. He went to the student union and had a malted milkshake, picked up a poetry review magazine, bought a pen, and then went to his car and waited. Most of the poetry was junk, but some of it was pretty good, better than he had expected. He reread one of the short pieces. Nice. Then he saw her getting out of her car. Lyle Taney was medium height, a bit heavy for his taste; he liked willowy women and she was curvy and dimply. Ten pounds, he estimated; she could lose ten pounds before she would start to look gaunt enough to suit him. He liked sharp cheekbones and the plane of a cheek without a suggestion of roundness. Her hair was short and almost frizzy it was so curly, dark brown with just a suggestion of gray, as if she had frosted it without enough bleach to do a thorough job. He knew so much about her that it would have given her a shock to realize anyone had recorded such information and that it could be retrieved. He knew her scars, her past illnesses, her college records, her income and expenses ... She was bouncy: he grinned at her tripping nimbly through the slush at the curb before the building. That was nice, not too many women were still bouncy at her age: thirty-seven years, four months, sixteen days.

She vanished inside the building. He glanced at his watch and made a bet with himself. Eighteen minutes. It would take eighteen minutes. Actually it took twenty-two. When she reappeared, the bounce was gone. She marched down the stairs looking straight ahead, plowed through the slush, crossed the street without checking for traffic, daring anyone to touch her. She got to her car and yanked the door open, slid in, and drove off too fast. He liked all that. No tears. No sentimental look around at the landscape. Just good old-fashioned determination. Hugh Lasater liked to know everything about the people he used. This was data about Lyle Taney that no one would have been able to tell him. He felt that he knew her a little better now than he had that morning. He was whistling tunelessly as he turned his key, started the rented car, and left the university grounds. She would do, he told himself contentedly. She would do just fine.

Lyle put on coffee and paced while she waited for it. On the table her book looked fragile suddenly, too nebulous to support her entire weight, and that was what it had to do. The book had a flying hawk on the cover; sunlight made the rufous tail look almost scarlet. The book was about hawks, about the word *hawk*, about hawklike people. It was not natural history, or ornithology, or anything in particular, but it had caught on, and last week it had made the best-seller lists. A fluke, of course, such a long shot it could never happen again. She was not a writer, and she really knew nothing about birds in general and hawks in particular, except what she had researched and observed over the five years it had taken her to do the book. The book was so far removed from her own field of history that it was not even counted as a publication by her department.

Her former department, she corrected herself, and poured coffee, then sat down at the table with it and stared at the book, and went over the luncheon one more time.

Bobby Conyers, her editor for the hawk book, and Mal Levinson from the magazine *Birds* had insisted that a follow-up book on eagles would be equally successful.

'Consider it, Lyle,' Mal had said earnestly, on first-name basis instantly. 'We want the article. I know ten thousand isn't a fortune, but we'll pick up your expenses, and it'll add up. And Bobby can guarantee fifteen thousand up front for the book. Don't say no before you think about it.'

'But I don't know anything at all about eagles, nothing. And Oregon? Why there? There are eagles in other places, surely.'

Mal pointed to the clipping he had brought with him: a letter to the editor of a rival magazine. It mentioned the bald eagles seen along a stretch of Oregon beach for two years in a row, suggesting they were nesting in the vicinity.

'That part of Oregon looks like the forest primeval,' he said. 'And eagles, bald eagles, are on the endangered list. That may be the last nesting site on the West Coast. It'll make a terrific article and book. Believe us, we both agree, it'll be even better than *Hawks*. I'd like to call it *Bird of Prey*.'

Bobby was nodding. 'I agree, Lyle. It'll go.'

She sipped her coffee, her gaze still on the book. In her briefcase were contracts, a map of Oregon, another one of that section of coast, and a photocopy of an article on eagles that Mal had dug out of a back issue of his magazine.

'What if I can't find the nest?' she had asked, and with the question she had realized she was going to do it.

'It's pretty hard to hide an eagle's nest,' Mal had said, grinning, knowing she had been persuaded. He began to talk about eagles then, and for the rest of the hour they spent together, it had been as if they all knew she would go to Oregon, search the jagged hills for the nest, set up a photography blind, start digging for facts, tidbits, myths, whatever else took her fancy to make up a full-length book.

And she did want to do it, she told herself again firmly, and tried not to think of what it would mean if the book failed, if she could not find the nest, if the eagles were not nesting there this year, if ... if ... if ... She would have to face Pierson and ask for her job back, or go somewhere else and start over. She thought briefly of filing a claim of discrimination against Pierson and the university, but she put it out of mind again. Not her style. No one had forced her to quit, and no one guaranteed a leave of absence for a job unrelated to her field. Pierson had pointed this out to her in his most reasonable tone, the voice that always made her want to hit him with a wet fish. The fleeting thought about the statistics of women her age getting work in their own fields went unheeded as she began to think seriously about the difficulties of finding an eagle's nest in the wooded, steep hills of the coast range of Oregon.

Presently, she put the book on a chair and spread out the coastal map and began to study it. The nest would be within a mile or two of the water and the exact places where the birds had been seen were clearly marked – an area roughly five to eight miles by two miles. It would be possible, with luck, and if the bird watcher had been right, and if the eagles came back this year ...

Lyle sat on the side of her bed talking on the phone. During the past week she had packed up most of the things she would take with her, and had moved into her study those things she did not want her sublessees to use. She would lock that door and keep the key. Almost magically the problems had been erased before her eyes. She was listening to her friend Jackie plead for her to reconsider her decision, and her mind was roaming over the things yet to be done. A cashier's check to open an account with in the village of Salmon Key, and more film and printing paper ...

'Jackie, it's not as if I were a child who never left home before,' she said, trying to keep the edge off her voice. 'And, I tell you, I am sick and tired of teaching. I hadn't realized how tired of it I was until I quit. My God! Those term papers!'

She was grateful a moment later when the doorbell cut the phone call short. 'Lunch? Sure. I'll be there,' she said and hung up, and then went to open the door.

The man was close to six feet, but stooped; he had a big face. She seldom had seen features spread out quite as much as his were: wide-spaced eyes with heavy, long lashes and thick sable brown brows, a nose that would dominate a smaller face and a mouth that would fit on a jack-o'-lantern. The mouth widened even more when he smiled.

'Mrs. Taney? Could I have a few minutes to talk to you? My name is Hugh Lasater, from the Drug Enforcement Administration.' He handed her his identification and she started to open the door; he held it to the few inches the chain allowed.

'Ma'am, if you don't mind. You study the I.D. and the picture, compare it to my pan, and then if it seems okay, you open the door.' He had a pained expression as he said this.

She did as he directed, then admitted him, thinking he must be looking for an informant or something. She thought of the half-dozen vacant-eyed students in her classes; the thought was swiftly followed by relief that it no longer concerned her.

'What can I do for you, Mr. Lasater?' She motioned to a chair in a half-hearted way, hoping he would not accept the quasi-invitation.

'No one's here with you?'

She shook her head.

'Good.' He took off his coat and hat and put them down on the sofa, then sank down into the chair she had indicated. 'You almost ready to go?'

She started, but then, glancing about the apartment, decided anyone with an eye could tell she was going somewhere. 'Yes. Next week I'm going on a trip.'

'I know. Oregon. Salmon Key. The Donleavy house on Little Salmon Creek.'

This time when she reacted with surprise, the chill was like a lump of ice deep within her. 'What do you want, Mr. Lasater?'

'How'd you learn that trick?' he asked with genuine curiosity. 'You never had any intelligence training.'

'I don't know what you're talking about. If you'll just state your business. As you can see, I'm quite busy.'

'It's a dandy thing to know. You just step back a little and watch from safety, in a manner of speaking. Useful. Damned off-putting to anyone not familiar with it. And you're damned good at it.'

She waited. He knew, she thought, that inside she was frozen: her way of handling anger, fear, indignation? Later she would analyze the different emotions. And Hugh Lasater, she realized, was also back a little, watching, calculating, appraising her all the way.

'Okay, I'll play it straight,' he said then. 'No games, no appeal to loyalty, or your sense of justice, or anything else. We, my department and I, request your help in a delicate matter. We want you to get fingerprints from a suspect for us.'

She laughed in relief. 'You aren't serious.'

'Oh yes, deadly serious. The Donleavy house is just a hop away from another place that sits on the next cliff overlooking the ocean. And in that other house is a man we're after quite seriously. But we have to make certain. We can't tip him that we're onto him. We need someone so innocent, so unlikely that he'll never give her a second thought. You pass him a picture to look at; he gives it back and you put it away carefully in an envelope we provide. Finis. That's all we want. If he's our man, we put a tail on him and let him lead us to others even more important and nab them all. They're smuggling in two thirds of all the coke and hash and opium being used in the States today.'

He knew he had scored because her face became so expressionless that it might have been carved from wax. It was the color of something that had died a long time ago.

'That's contemptible,' she said in a low voice.

'I'm sorry,' he replied. 'I truly am. But we are quite desperate.'

She shook her head. 'Please go,' she said in a low voice. In a flash the lump of ice had spread; her frozen body was a thing apart. She had learned to do this in analysis, to step out of the picture to observe herself doing crazy things – groping for pills in an alcoholic fog, driving eighty miles an hour after an evening in a bar ... It was a good trick, he was right. It had allowed her to survive then; it would get her through the next few minutes until he left.

'Mrs. Taney, your kid wasn't the only one, and every day there are more statistics to add to the mess. And they'll keep on being added day after day. Help us put a stop to it.'

'You have enough agents. You don't need to drag in someone from outside.'

'I told you, it has to be someone totally innocent, someone there with a reason beyond doubting. You'll get your pictures and your story, that's legitimate enough. The contracts are good. No one will ever know you helped us.' He stood up and went to his overcoat and took a large insulated envelope from the inside pocket. 'Mrs. Taney, we live in the best of times and the worst of times. We want to squash that ring of genteel importers. People like that are making these the worst of times. It's a dirty business; okay, I grant you that. But Mike's death was dirtier. Twelve years old, overdosed.

That's pretty damned filthy.' He put the envelope down on the end table by the sofa. 'Let them make the first move. Don't try to force yourself on them in any way. There's Saul Werther, about sixty-two or -three, cultured, kindly, probably lonesome as hell by now. And a kid he has with him, cook, driver, handyman, bodyguard, who knows? Twenty-one at the most, Chicano. They'll want to know who you are and why you're there. No secret about you, the magazine story, the eagles, it's all legitimate as hell. They'll buy it. You like music, so does Werther. You'll get the chance. Just wait for it and then take advantage of it. Don't make a big deal of not messing up his prints if he handles a picture, a glass, whatever. Don't handle it unnecessarily either. There's some wrapping in the envelope, put it around the object loosely first, then pop it in the envelope and put it away. We'll be in touch.'

Now he put the coat on. At the door, he looked back at her. 'You'll do fine, Lyle. You really will. And maybe you'll be able to accept that you're getting back at them just a little bit. It might even help.'

2

Brilliant green moss covered the tree trunks; ferns grew in every cranny, on the lower dead limbs, on the moss, every inch of space between the trees. Nowhere was any ground visible, or any rock; all was hidden by the mosses and ferns. Evergreen bushes made impenetrable thickets in spots where the trees had been cut in the past, or a fire had raged. Logging had stopped years ago and now the trees were marching again, overtaking the shrubs, defeating them, reclaiming the steep hills. Raindrops glistened on every surface, shimmered on the tips of the emerald fronds; the air was blurred with mist. The rain made no sound, was absorbed by the mosses, transferred to the ground below efficiently, silently.

Lyle sat on a log and listened to the silence of the woods on this particular hill. The silences varied, she had learned; almost always the surf made the background noise, but here it was inaudible. This was like a holding-your-breath silence, she decided. No wind moved the trees, nothing stirred in the undergrowth, no birds called or flew. It was impossible to tell if the rain had stopped; often it continued under the trees long after the skies had cleared. She got up, and for another half-hour, climbed to the top of the hill. It had been a steep climb, but a protected one; here on the crest the wind hit her. Sea wind, salt wind, fresh yet filled with strange odors. The rain had stopped. She braced herself against the trunk of a tree twisted out of shape, with sparse growth clinging to the tip ends of its branches. She was wearing a dark green poncho, rain pants of the same color over her woolen slacks, high boots, a woolen knit hat pulled low on her forehead and covered with the poncho hood. A pair of binoculars was clipped to her belt under the poncho. She took them out and began to study the surrounding trees, the other hilltops that now were visible, the rocks of a ledge with a drop of undetermined distance, because the gorge, or whatever it was, was bathed in mist. She did not spot the nest.

She turned the glasses toward the ocean and for a long time looked seaward. A new storm was building. A boat so distant that it remained a smudge, even with the full magnification, was stuck to the horizon. She hoped that, if it was a fishing boat, it made port before the storm hit. There had been two storms so far in the sixteen days she had been in Oregon. It still thrilled and frightened her to think of the power, the uncontrollable rage of the sea under storm winds. It would terrify her to be out there during such a storm. As she watched, the sea and sky became one and swallowed the boat. She knew the front would be racing toward shore, and she knew she would be caught if she returned to her house the way she had come. She stepped back under the trees and mentally studied the map of this day's search. She could go back along the western slope of the hill, skirt the gorge (it was a gorge cut by a tiny fierce stream), and follow it until it met Little Salmon Creek, which would lead her home. It was rough, but no rougher than any other trail in these jagged hills that went up and down as if they had been designed by a first-grader.

The wind blew harder, its cutting edge sharp and cold. Her face had been chapped ever since day one here, and she knew today would not improve matters. She started down the rugged hillside, heading toward the creek gorge. The elevation of this peak was one thousand feet; her cabin was one hundred feet above sea level. She began to slide on wet mosses, and finally stopped when she reached out to grasp a tree trunk. Going down would be faster than getting up had been, she thought grimly, clutching the tree until she got her breath back. The little creek plunged over a ledge to a pool fifteen or twenty feet below; she had to detour to find a place to get down the same distance. 'A person could get killed,' she muttered, inching down on her buttocks, digging in her heels as hard as she could, sliding a foot or so at a time.

The trees were fir, pine, an occasional alder, an even rarer oak, and at the margins of the woods, huckleberries, blueberries, blackberries, Oregon grapes, raspberries, salmonberries, elderberries ... She could no longer remember the long list of wild plants. They grew so luxuriantly that they appeared to be growing on top of and out of each other, ten feet high, twenty feet. She never had seen such a profusion of vines.

Down, down, slipping, sliding, lowering herself from tree trunk to tree trunk, clinging to moss-covered rocks, feeling for a toehold below, sometimes walking gingerly on the scree at the edge of the creek when the berry bushes were impenetrable. Always downward. At last she reached a flat spot, and stopped to rest. She had come down almost all the way. She no longer had any chance of beating the storm; she would be caught and drenched. Now all she hoped was that she could be off the steep hill before it struck with full force. She looked seaward; there were only trees that were being erased by mist and clouds, leaving suggestive shadows. Then she gasped. There was the nest!

As Mal Levinson had said, it was hard to hide an eagle's nest. It was some distance from her, down a ravine, up the other side, a quarter of a mile or perhaps a little more. The rolling mist was already blurring its outlines. Impossible to judge its size, but big. It had to be old, used year after year, added to each new season. Eight feet across? She knew any figures from this distance were meaningless, but she could not stop the calculations. Half as deep as it was wide, four by eight then. It crowned a dead pine tree. A gust of wind hit her, lifted her hood, and now she realized that for some time she had been hearing the roar of the surf. She got up and started to make the final descent. In a few moments she came to the place where the little creek joined the larger one, and together they crashed over a rocky outcropping. Now she knew exactly where she was. She stayed as close to the bank of the creek as she could, searching for a place where she could cross. Farther down, near her cabin, she knew it was possible, but difficult because in its final run to the sea the creek was cutting a deep channel through the cliffs.

How lucky, she was thinking, to find the nest this close to her own place. The two creeks came together at the two-hundred-foot altitude, child's play after scrambling up and down one-thousand-foot peaks. Less than a mile from the cabin, it would be nothing to go back and forth, pack in her gear … She stopped suddenly and now felt a chill that the wind had not induced in her. There was the other house. Werther's house. The nest was almost in his back yard.

The boy appeared, coming from the garage carrying a grocery bag. He waved and, after a brief hesitation, she waved back, then continued to follow the creek down to the bridge where tons of boulders and rocks of all sizes had been dumped to stabilize the banks for the bridge supports.

The rain started as she approached the bridge, and she made her way down the boulders with the rain blinding and savaging her all the way. The creek was no more than a foot deep here, but very swift, white water all the way to the beach. Normally she would have picked her way across it on the exposed rocks, but this time she plunged in, trusting her boots to be as waterproof as the manufacturer claimed.

She had forgotten, she kept thinking in disbelief. She had forgotten about

Werther and his young driver/cook/bodyguard. At first it had been all she had thought about, but then, with day after day spent in the wet woods, climbing, slipping, sliding, searching, it was as if she had developed amnesia, and for a week or longer she had not thought of them at all. It was the same feeling she had had only a few days ago, she realized, when she had come upon a bottle of sleeping pills and had looked at it without recognition. Then, as now, it had taken an effort to remember.

She made her way up her side of the boulders; five hundred feet away was her cabin dwarfed by rhododendrons. Wearily she dragged herself toward it, turning once to glance briefly at the other house, knowing it was not visible from here, but looking anyway. The boy had walked to the edge of the creek, was watching her; he waved again, and then ran through the rain back toward his own house, disappearing among the trees and bushes that screened it.

Spying on her? That openly? Maybe he had been afraid she would fall down in the treacherous shallow stream. Maybe he thought she had fallen many times already; she considered how she looked: muddy, bedraggled, dripping, red-faced from windburn and cold. She looked like a nut, she thought, a real nut.

She found the key under the planter box and let herself in. The cabin was cold and smelled of sea air and salt and decay. Before she undressed, she made up the fire in the wood stove and put water on to boil for coffee. She wished she had not seen the boy, that he had not spoiled this moment of triumph, that the nest was not in Werther's back yard almost, that Lasater had never ... She stopped herself. She wished for golden wings.

'Don't waste perfectly good wishes on mundane things,' her father had said to her once when she had still been young enough to sit on his lap.

She was smiling slightly then as she pulled off her boots; her feet were wet and cold. Ah well, she had expected that, she thought sourly. She made the coffee, then showered, and examined new bruises acquired that day. She had not lost weight, she thought, surveying herself, but she was shifting it around a lot. Her waist was slimming down, while, she felt certain, her legs were growing at an alarming rate. She would have legs like a sumo wrestler after a few more weeks of uphill, downhill work. Or like a mountain goat. She pulled on her warmest robe and rubbed her hair briskly, then started to make her dinner.

She sniffed leftover soup, shrugged, and put it on to heat, scraped mold off a piece of cheese, toasted stale bread, quartered an apple, and sat down without another thought of food. As she ate, she studied her topographic map, then drew in a circle around the spot where she knew the nest was. As she had suspected, it was less than half a mile from Werther's house, but not visible from it because of the way the land went up and down. There was a steep hill, then a ravine, then a steeper hill, and it was the flank of the second hill that the eagle had chosen for a building site.

She started in surprise when there was a knock on the door. No one had knocked on that door since her arrival. She looked down at herself. She was in a heavy flannel robe and fleece-lined moccasins. Her hair was still wet from the shower and out every which way from her toweling it. Her wet and muddy clothes were steaming on chairs drawn close to the stove. Everywhere there were books, maps, notebooks; her typewriter was on an end table, plugged into an extension cord that snaked across the room. Mail was stacked on another end table; it had been stacked, now it was in an untidy heap, with a letter or two on the floor where they had fallen when the stack had leaned too far.

'What the hell,' she muttered, stepping over the extension cord to open the door.

It was the boy from Werther's house. He grinned at her. He was a good-looking kid, she thought absently, trying to block his view of the room. It was no good, though, he was tall enough to see over her head. His grin deepened. He had black hair with a slight wave, deep brown eyes, beautiful young skin. A heart throb, she thought, remembering the phrase from her school years.

'I caught a lot of crabs today,' he said, and she saw the package he was carrying. 'Mr. Werther thought you might like some.' He held out the package.

She knew he had seen the remains of her dinner, her clothes, everything. No point in pretending now. She held the door open and stepped back. 'Would you like to come in? Have a cup of coffee?'

'Thanks,' he said, shaking his head. 'I have to go back and make our dinner.'

She took the package. 'Thank you very much. I appreciate this.'

He nodded and left in the rain. He had come through the creek, she realized, the same way she had come. Actually it was quicker than getting a car down the steep driveway, onto the road, up her equally steep driveway. Over a mile by road, less than half a mile on foot. She closed the door and took the package to the sink. The crabs, two of them, had been steamed and were still warm. Her mouth was watering suddenly, although she had eaten what she thought was enough at the time. She melted butter, then slowly ate again, savoring each bite of the succulent crab meat. Werther, or the boy, had cracked the legs just enough; she was able to get out every scrap. When she finished, she sat back sighing with contentment. She was exhausted, her room was a sty, but she had found the nest. It had been a good day.

And Lasater? She scowled, gathered up her garbage and cleared it away. Damn Lasater.

3

For the next three days she studied the area of the nest minutely. There was no good vantage point actually for her to stake out as her own. The pine spur was at the end of a ravine that was filled with trees and bushes. Nowhere could she see through the dense greenery for a clear view of the nest. She had to climb one hill after another, circling the ravine, keeping the nest in sight, looking for a likely place to put her lean-to, to set up her tripod, to wait. She finally found a site, about four feet higher than the nest, on a hillside about one hundred feet from it, with a deep chasm between her and the nest. She unslung her backpack and took out the tarpaulin and nylon cords, all dark green, and erected the lean-to, fastening it securely to trees from all four corners. It would have to do, she decided, even though it stood out like a beer can in a mountain brook. She had learned, in photographing hawks, that most birds would accept a lean-to, or wooden blind even, if it was in place before they took up residence. During the next week or so the lean-to would weather, moss would cover it, ferns grow along the ropes, a tree or two sprout to hide the flap ... She took a step back to survey her work, and nodded. Fine. It was fine and it would keep her dry, she decided, and then the rain started again.

Every three or four days a new front blew in from the Pacific bringing twenty-foot waves, thirty-foot waves or even higher, crashing into the cliffs, tearing out great chunks of beach, battling savagely with the pillars, needles, stacks of rock that stood in the water as if the land were trying to sneak out to sea. In the thick rain forests the jagged hills broke up the wind; the trees broke up the rain, cushioned its impact, so that by the time it reached the mosses, it was almost gentle. The mosses glowed and bulged with the bounty. The greens intensified. It was like being in an underwater garden. Lyle made her way down the hillside with the cold rain in her face, and she hardly felt it. The blind was ready; she was ready; now it would be a waiting game. Every day she would photograph the nest, and compare the pictures each night. If one new feather was added, she would know. The eagles could no more conceal their presence than they could conceal their nest.

When she reached her side of the bridge again, she crossed the road and went out to the edge of the bluff that overlooked the creek and the beach. The roar of surf was deafening; there was no beach to be seen. This storm had blown in at high tide and waves thundered against the cliffs. The bridge was seventy-five feet above the beach, but spray shot up and was blown across it again and again as the waves exploded below. Little Salmon Creek dropped seventy-five feet in its last mile to the beach, with most of the drop made in a waterfall below the bridge; now Little Salmon Creek was being driven backward and was rising. Lyle stood transfixed, watching the spectacular storm, until the light failed, and the sounds of crashing waves, of driftwood logs twenty feet long being hurled into bridge pilings, of wind howling through the trees, all became frightening and she turned and hurried toward her cabin. She caught a motion from the cliff on the other side of the bridge and she could make out the figure of a watcher there. He was as bundled up as she was, and the light was too feeble by then to be able to tell if it was the boy or Werther.

The phone was ringing when she got inside and pushed the door closed against the wind that rushed through with her. Papers stirred with the passage, then settled again. She had to extract the telephone from under a pile of her sweaters she had brought out to air because things left in the bedroom tended to smell musty. The wood stove and a small electric heater in her darkroom were the only heat in the cabin.

'Yes,' she said, certain it was a wrong number.

'Mrs. Taney, this is Saul Werther. I wonder if I can talk you into having dinner with me this evening. I'd be most happy if you will accept. Carmen will be glad to pick you up in an hour and take you home again later.'

She felt a rush of fear that drained her. *Please*, she prayed silently, *not again. Don't start again.* She closed her eyes hard.

'Mrs. Taney, forgive me. We haven't really met, I'm your neighbor across the brook,' he said, as if reminding her he was still on the line. 'We watched the storm together.'

'Yes, of course. I'd ... Thank you. I'll be ready in an hour.'

For several minutes she stood with her hand on the phone. It had happened again, the first time in nearly four years. It had been Werther on the phone, but she had heard Mr. Hendrickson's voice. 'Mrs. Taney, I'm afraid there's been an accident ...' And she had known. It had been as if she had known even before the telephone rang that evening; she had been waiting for confirmation, nothing more. Fear, grief, shock, guilt: she had been waiting for a cause, for a reason for the terrible emotions that had gripped her, that had been amorphously present for an hour and finally settled out only with the phone call. No one had believed her, not Gregory, not the psychiatrist, and she would have been willing to disbelieve, yearned to be able to disbelieve, but could not, because now and then, always with a meaningless call, that moment had swept over her again. She had come to recognize the rush of emotions that left her feeling hollowed out, as the event was repeated during the next year and a half after Mike's death. And then it had stopped, until now. 'Mrs. Taney, I'm afraid there's been an accident. Your son ...'

She began to shiver, and was able to move again. She had to get out of her wet clothes, build up the fire, shower … This was Lasater's doing. He had made the connection in her mind between Werther, drugs, Mike's death. He had reached inside her head with his words and revived the grief and guilt she had thought was banished. Clever Mr. Lasater, she thought grimly. He had known she would react, not precisely how, that was expecting too much even of him. He had known Werther would make the opening move. If Werther was involved with drug smuggling, she wanted him dead, just as dead as her child was, and she would do all she could to make him dead. Even as she thought it, she knew Lasater had counted on this too.

Hugh Lasater drove through the town of Salmon Key late that afternoon, before the storm hit. He and a companion, Milton Follett, had been driving since early morning, up from San Francisco in a comfortable, spacious motor home.

'It's the hills that slowed us down,' Hugh Lasater said. 'The freeway was great, and then we hit the coastal range. Should have been there by now.'

Milton Follett was slouched down low in his seat; he did not glance at the town as they went through. 'Could have called,' he grumbled, as he had done several times in the past hour or so. He was in his midthirties, a blond former linebacker whose muscles were turning to flab.

'Thought of that,' Hugh Lasater said. 'Decided against it. Little place like this, who knows how the lines are connected, who might be listening? Anyway I might have to apply a little pressure.'

'I think it's a bust. She's stringing you along.'

'I think you're right. That's the reason I might have to apply a little pressure.'

He drove slowly, collecting information: Standard Gas, attached gift shop; Salmon Key Restaurant and Post Office, a frame building painted red; Reichert's Groceries, having a canned food sale – corn 3/1.00, tomatoes, beans, peas 4/1.00; Tomseth Motel, closed; a sign for a lapidary shop; farmers' market and fish stand, closed … Tourist town, closed for the season. There were a few fishing boats docked behind the farmers' market, and space at the dock for four times as many, unused for a long time apparently. A dying fishing town, surviving now with tourist trade a few months out of the year. Lasater had seen numberless towns like this one; he touched the accelerator and left the dismal place behind and started up another hill.

'Sure could have used a road engineer and a few loads of dynamite,' he said cheerfully, shifting down for the second time on the steep incline. The hill rose five hundred feet above sea level, reached a crest and plunged down the other side. He did not shift into higher gear as he went down. The wind was starting to shake the monster, forcing him to hold the steering wheel around at an unnatural position for a straight road. The wind let up, and the vehicle rebounded. He slowed down more.

'Another mile's all,' he said. 'We'll be in camp in time to see the storm hit.'

'Terrific,' Milton growled.

Lasater made the turn off the highway onto a narrow gravel road that was steeper than anything he had driven that day. The trees had been shaped here by the nearly constant wind and sea spray; there were stunted pines and dense thickets of low, contorted spruces. The motor home was vibrating with the roar of the ocean and the explosive crashes of waves on cliffs. There were other people already in the state park; a couple of campers, a van, and even a tent. As they pulled into the camping area a sleek silver home-on-wheels pulled out. Lasater waved to the driver as they passed in the parking turnaround; he took the newly vacated spot.

Milton refused a walk with him, and he went alone to the ridge overlooking The Lagoon. That was its name, said so on the map, and there it was, a nearly perfect circle, a mile across, surrounded by cliffs, with a narrow stretch of beach that gave way to a basalt terrace which, at low tide, would be covered with tide pools. The lagoon was protected from the sea by a series of massive basalt rocks, like a coral reef barrier. Although they ranged from twenty to forty feet above water, the ocean was pouring over them now; the lagoon was flooded and was rising on the cliffs. Waves crashing into the barrier megaliths sent spray a hundred feet into the air.

He looked at the lagoon, then beyond it to the next hill. Over that one, down the other side was Werther's drive, then the bridge over Little Salmon Creek, and then her drive. Here we all are, he thought, hunching down in his coat as the wind intensity grew. Time to go to work, honey, he thought at Lyle Taney. You've had a nice vacation, now's time to knuckle down, make a buck, earn your keep.

He had no doubt that Lyle Taney would do as he ordered, eventually. She was at a time of life when she would be feeling insecure, he knew. She had chucked her job, and if he threatened to pull the rug from under her financially, she would stand on her head on any corner he pointed to. He knew how important security was to a woman like Lyle Taney. Even when she had a reason to take a leave of absence, she had held on grimly, afraid not to hold on because she had no tenure, no guarantees about tomorrow. He had imagined her going over the figures again and again, planning to the day when her savings would be gone, if she had to start using that stash, trying to estimate royalties to the penny, stretching that money into infinity. He understood women like Taney, approaching middle age, alone, supporting themselves all the way. It was fortunate that she was nearing middle age. The kid was too young to interest her, and Werther too old; no sexual intrigues to mess up the scenario. He liked to keep things neat and simple. Money, security, revenge, those were things that were manipulable. They were real things, not abstracts, not like loyalty or faith. He did not believe a woman could be manipulated through appeals to loyalty or faith. They were incapable of making moral or ethical decisions. They did not believe in abstracts. Maternal devotion, security, money, revenge, that was what they understood, and this time it had worked out in such a way that those were the very things he could dangle before her, or threaten. Oh, she would do the job for him. He knew she would. He began to hum and stopped in surprise when he realized it was a tune from his boyhood, back in the forties. He grinned. Who would have thought a song would hang out in a mind all those years to pop out at just the right moment? He sang it to himself on his way back to the motor home: 'They're either too young or too old/They're either too gray or too grassy green ...'

4

Werther's house was a surprise to Lyle. It was almost as messy as her own, and with the same kind of disorder: papers, books, notebooks, a typewriter. His was on a stand on wheels, not an end table, but that was a minor detail. Carmen was almost laughing at her reaction.

'I told Mr. Werther that I thought you would be very simpatico,' he said, taking her coat.

Then Werther came from another room, shook her hand warmly, and led her to the fireplace.

'It's for a book I've wanted to do for a long time,' he said, indicating the jumble of research materials. 'A history of a single idea from the first time it's mentioned in literature, down to its present-day use, if any. Not just one idea, but half a dozen, a dozen. I'm afraid I keep expanding the original concept as I come across new and intriguing lines of inquiry.' His face twisted in a wry expression. 'I'd like to get rid of some of this stuff, but there's nowhere to start. I need it all.'

He was five feet eight or nine and stocky; not fat or even plump, but well muscled and heavy boned. He gave the impression of strength. His hair was gray, a bit too long, as if he usually forgot to have it cut, not as if he had intended it to be modish. His eyes were dark blue, so dark that at first glance she had thought them black. He had led her to a chair by the fireplace; there was an end table by it with a pile of books. He lifted the stack, looked about helplessly, then put it on the floor by the side of the table. *A History of Technology*, Plato's *Republic*, a volume of Plato's dialogues, Herodotus, Kepler ... There was a mountainous stack of the *New York Times*.

Many of the books in the room were opened, some with rocks holding the pages down; others had strips of paper for bookmarks.

'My problem is that I'm not a writer,' Werther said. 'It's impossible to organize so much material. One wants to include it all. But you ...' He rummaged through a pile of books near his own chair and brought out her book on hawks. 'What a delightful book this is! I enjoyed it tremendously.'

'I'm not a writer either,' she said quickly. 'I teach – taught – history.'

'That's what the jacket says. Ancient history. But you used the past tense.'

Although there was no inflection, no question mark following the statement, she found herself answering as if he had asked. She told him about the magazine, and the book contract, the nest.

'And you simply quit when you couldn't get time off to do the next book. Doing the book on eagles was more important to you than remaining in your own field. I wonder that more historians don't lose faith.'

She started to deny that she had lost faith in history, but the words stalled; he had voiced what she had not wanted to know. She nodded. 'And you, Mr. Werther, what is your field? History also?'

'No. That's why my research is so pleasurable. I'm discovering the past. That's what makes your hawk book such a joy. It sings with discovery. It's buoyant because you were finding out things that gave you pleasure; you in turn invested that pleasure in your words and thoughts and shared it with your readers.'

She could feel her cheeks burn. Werther laughed gently.

'What capricious creatures we are. We are embarrassed by criticism, and no less embarrassed by praise. And you have found your eagle's nest after all those days of searching. Congratulations. At first, when you moved in next door, I thought you were a spy. But what a curious spy, spending every day getting drenched in a rain forest!'

'And I thought you were a smuggler,' she said, laughing with him, but also watching, suddenly wary again.

'The lagoon would make a perfect spot for landing contraband, wouldn't it? Ah, Carmen, that looks delightful!'

Camen carried two small trays; he put one down at Lyle's elbow on the end table, and the other one within Werther's reach, perched atop a stack of books. There was wheat-colored wine, a small bowl of pink Pacific shrimp, a dip, cheese, crackers ...

'I've never tasted such good shrimp as these,' Werther said, spearing one of the tidbits. 'I could live on the seafood here.'

'Me too,' Lyle agreed. The wine was a very dry sherry, so good it made her want to close her eyes and savor it. The fire burned quietly, and Carmen made cooking noises that were obscured by a door. Werther had become silent now, enjoying the food; outside, the wind howled and shook the trees, rattled rhododendrons against the windows, whistled in the chimney. It was distant, no longer menacing; through it all, behind it, now and then over-whelming the other sounds, was the constant roar of the surf. She thought of the pair of eagles: where were they now? Were they starting to feel twitches that eventually would draw them back to the nest?

Werther sighed. 'Each of us may well be exactly what the other thought at first, but that's really secondary, isn't it? How did you, a history professor, become involved with hawks?'

She brought herself back to the room, back to the problem Lasater had dumped in her lap. Slowly she said, 'Five years ago my son, he was twelve, took something one of the boys in his class had bought from a drug dealer. There were twenty boys involved, three of them died, several of them suf-fered serious brain damage. Mike died.'

Her voice had gone very flat in the manner of one reading a passage in a foreign language without comprehension. She watched him as she talked. She could talk about it now; that was what she had accomplished under Dr. Himbert. She had learned how to divide herself into pieces, and let one of the pieces talk about it, about anything at all, while the rest of her stayed far away hidden in impenetrable ice.

Werther was shocked, she thought, then angry. One of his hands made a movement toward her, as if to touch her – to silence her? or share her grief? She could not tell.

'If you're not with young people, children, you don't realize,' she said slowly. 'They've changed. They don't seem to value life the way my genera-tion did. I used to ask my class what they saw themselves doing in five years, ten years. They looked at me as if I had gone mad. They wouldn't be around that long, they said, again and again. The world was going to be blown up before then; if they were alive at all, they'd be scratching for a living, digging in the ruins …' She shook herself. 'Mike thought that. We talked about it. I tried to make him believe there was hope, a future. I don't think I ever got through to him. They had a game they played, Mike, his friends. It was called After the Bomb. An adventure game where they had to survive any way they could. It was horrible. I realized later that he hadn't believed a word I said. My students don't – didn't – believe me. They see a different world. Maybe a realer world. I don't know. It's a world of hatred and destruction and evil. A world where experimenting with drugs doesn't seem to be taking such a terrible chance. Today, or next year … It's all the same to them.'

'And you turned to the world of hawks where there is no good or evil, only necessity.'

She felt bathed in the warmth of his words suddenly, as if his compas-sion were a physical, material substance that he had wrapped around her securely. He knew, she thought. He understood. That was exactly what she had looked for, had needed desperately, something beyond good and evil. Abruptly she looked away from his penetrating and too understanding gaze. She wanted to tell him everything, she realized in wonder, and she could tell him everything. He would not condemn her. Quickly then she continued her story, trying to keep her voice indifferent.

'I found I couldn't stay in our apartment over weekends and holidays after that. My husband and I had little reason to stay together, and he left, went to California, where he's living now. I began to tramp through the woods, up and down the Appalachian Trail, things like that. One day I got a photograph of a hawk in flight, not the one on the cover, not that nice, but it made me want to get more. Over the next couple of years I spent all my spare time pursuing hawks. And I began to write the book.'

Werther was nodding. 'Therapy. And what good therapy it was for you. No doctor could have prescribed it. You are cured.'

Again it was not exactly a question; it demanded no answer. And again she felt inclined to respond as if it had been. 'I'm not sure,' she said. 'I had a breakdown, as you seem to have guessed. I hope I'm cured.'

'You're cured,' he said again. He got up and went to a sideboard where Carmen had left the decanter of wine. He refilled both their glasses, then said, 'If you'll excuse me a moment, I'll see how dinner's coming along. Carmen's a good cook, but sometimes he dawdles.'

She studied the living room; it was large, with a dining area, and beyond that a door to the kitchen. The west wall was heavily draped, but in daylight with the drapes open, it would overlook the sea, as her own living room did. Probably there was a deck; there was an outside door on that wall. One other door was closed, to the bedroom area, she guessed. The plan was very like the plan of her cabin, but the scale was bigger. Both were constructed of redwood, paneled inside, and broad plank floors with scatter rugs. She began to look through the piles of magazines on tables: science magazines, both general and specialized. Molecular biology, psychology, physics ... History journals – some probably had papers of hers. There was no clue here, or so many clues that they made no sense. It would be easy to pick up a digest magazine or two, slip them in her purse, put them in the envelope, and be done with it.

But he wasn't a smuggler, she thought clearly. Lasater had lied. She picked up a geology book dog-eared at a chapter about the coast range.

'Are you interested in geology?' Werther asked coming up behind her.

'I don't know a thing about it,' she admitted, replacing the book.

'According to the most recent theory, still accepted it's so recent, there are great tectonic plates underlying the rock masses on earth. These plates are in motion created by the thermal energy of the deeper layers. Here along the coast, they say, two plates come together, one moving in from the sea, the other moving northward. The one coming in from the west hits the other one and dives under it, and the lighter materials are scraped off and jumbled together to make the coast range. That accounts for the composition, they say. Andesite, basalt, garnetite, sandstone, and so on. Have you had a chance to do any beach combing yet?'

She shook her head. 'Not yet. I'll have more time now that I've located the nest.'

'Good. Let me take you to some of my favorite places. South of here. You have to be careful because some of those smaller beaches are cut off at high tide, and the cliffs are rather forbidding.'

Carmen appeared then. 'I thought you were going to sit down so I can serve the soup.'

Carmen dined with them and his cooking was superb. When she complimented him, he said, 'No, this is plain everyday family fare. I didn't know we were having company. Next time I'll know in advance. Just wait.'

There was a clear broth with slices of water chestnut and bits of clam and scallions; a baked salmon stuffed with crab; crisp snow peas and tiny mushrooms; salad with a dressing that suggested olive oil and lime juice and garlic, but so faintly that she could not have said for certain that any or all of those ingredients had been used.

'And take Anaxagoras,' Werther said sometime during that dinner, 'nearly five hundred years before Christ! And he had formulated the scientific method, maybe not as precisely as Bacon was to do two thousand years later, and without the same dissemination, but there it was. He wrote that the sun was a vast mass of incandescent metal, that moonlight was reflected sunlight, that heavenly bodies were made incandescent by their rotational friction. He explained, in scientific terms, meteors, eclipses, rainbows ...'

The ancient names rolled off his tongue freely, names, dates, places, ideas. 'Empedocles identified the four elements: air, earth, fire, and water, and even today we speak of a fiery temper, an airy disposition, blowing hot and cold, an earthy woman, the raging elements, battling the elements, elemental spirits ... An idea, twenty-five hundred years old, and it's still in the language, in our heads, in our genes maybe.'

Before dinner there had been the sherry, and with dinner there was a lovely Riesling, and then a sweet wine she did not know. She told herself that no one gets drunk on wine, especially along with excellent food, but, once again before the fire, she was having trouble following the conversation, and somewhere there was a soft guitar playing, and a savage wind blowing, and rain pounding the house rhythmically.

She realized she had been talking about Prometheus and Epimetheus, about herself, her lack of tenure and seeming inability to get tenure. 'I'm not a hotshot scholar,' she said, thinking carefully of the words, trying to avoid any that might twist her up too much. She thought: hotshot scholar, and knew she could never say it again. She knew also that if she repeated it to herself, she would start to giggle. The thought of breaking into giggles sobered her slightly.

'You're interested in what people thought,' she said almost primly, 'but we teach great movements, invasions, wars, successions of reign, and it's all irrelevant. The students don't care; they need the credit. It doesn't make any difference today, none of it.'

'Why don't you do it right?'

'I'd have to go back to Go and start over, relearn everything. Unlearn everything. I've always been afraid. I don't even know what I'm afraid of.'

'So you bailed out at the first chance. But now I think Carmen had better take you home. You can hardly keep your eyes open. It's the fresh air and wind and climbing these steep hills, I suspect.'

She nodded. It was true, she was falling asleep. Suddenly she felt awkward, as if she had overstayed a visit. She glanced at her watch and was startled to find that it was eleven-thirty.

'Ready?' Carmen asked. He had her coat over his arm, had already put on a long poncho.

Werther went to the door with them. 'Come back soon, my dear. It's been one of the nicest evenings I've had in a very long time.'

She mumbled something and hurried after Carmen to the car. The wind had died down now, but the rain was steady.

'He meant it,' Carmen said. 'It's been a good evening for both of us.'

'I enjoyed it too,' she said, staring ahead at the rain-blurred world. The drive was very curvy; it wound around trees, downward to the road, and only the last twenty-five feet or so straightened out. It would be very dangerous if the rain froze. Down this last straightaway, then onto the highway, across it and over the cliff to the rocks below. She shivered. Carmen had the car in low gear, and had no trouble at all coming to a stop at the highway.

'Is he a doctor?' she asked. 'Something he said tonight made me thing he might be, or has been, a doctor.' She shook her head in annoyance; she could not remember why she thought that.

'I think he studied medicine a while back, maybe even practiced. I don't know.'

Of course, Carmen probably knew as little about his employer as she did. They had an easy relationship, and Carmen certainly had shown no fear or anxiety of any sort, but he was a hired man, hired to drive, to cook, to do odd jobs. They had arrived at her door.

'I'll come in and fix your fire,' Carmen said, in exactly the same tone he had used to indicate that dinner was ready. There was nothing obsequious or subservient in him.

He added wood to the fire, brought in a few pieces from the porch, and then left, and she went to bed immediately and dreamed.

She was in a class, listening to a lecture. The professor was writing on the blackboard as he talked, and she was taking notes. She could not quite make out his diagrams, and she hitched her chair closer to the front of the room, but the other students hissed angrily at her and the teacher turned around to scowl. She squinted trying to see, but it was no use. And now she no longer could hear his words, the hissing still buzzed around her ears. The professor came to her chair and picked up her notebook; he looked at her notes, nodded, and patted her on the back. When he touched her, she screamed and fled.

She was on a narrow beach with a black shiny cliff behind her. She knew the tide had turned because the hissing had become a roar. She hurried toward a trail and stopped because Lasater was standing at the end of the beach where the rocks led upward like steps. She looked the opposite way and stopped again. Werther was there, dressed in tails and striped trousers, wearing a pale gray top hat. She heard a guitar and, looking up, she saw Carmen on a ledge playing. Help me, she cried to him. He smiled at her and continued to play. She raised her arms pleading for him to give her a hand, and the eagle swooped low and caught her wrists in its talons and lifted her just as the first wave crashed into the black cliff. The eagle carried her higher and higher until she no longer could see Werther or Lasater or the beach, the road, anything at all recognizable. Then the eagle let go and she fell.

5

Hugh Lasater waited until the Volvo came out of Werther's drive and turned north, heading for town, before he went up Lyle's driveway. There was heavy fog that morning, but the air was still and not very cold. The front of her house had a view of the ocean that must be magnificent when the weather was clear, and no doubt you had to be quick or you might miss it, he thought, gazing into the sea of fog, waiting for her to answer his knock.

Lyle was dressed to go out, boots, sweater, heavy slacks. She had cut her hair even shorter than it had been before. Now it was like a fuzzy cap on her head. He wondered if it was as soft as it looked. Silently she opened the door wider and moved aside for him to enter.

'How's it going?' he asked, surveying the room quickly, memorizing it in that one fast glance about. A real pig, he thought with a touch of satisfaction. It figured.

'Fine. I've found the nest.'

He laughed and pulled a chair out from the table and sat down. 'Got any coffee?'

She poured a cup for him; there was another cup on the table still half filled. She sat opposite him, pushed a map out of the way, closed a notebook. Her camera gear was on the table, as if she had been checking it out before leaving with it.

'Pretty lousy weather for someone who has to get out and work in it every day,' he said. 'Your face is really raw.'

She shrugged and began to put the lenses in pockets of the camera bag. Her hands were very steady. She could keep the tension way down where it couldn't interfere with appearances. Lasater admired that. But the tension was there, he could feel it; it was revealed in the way that she had not looked at him once since opening the door. She had looked at the coffee cup, at the pot, at her stuff on the table. Now she was concentrating on packing her camera bag.

'Met Werther yet?' he asked casually.

'Yes. Once.'

'And?'

'And nothing.'

'Tell me about him.' The coffee was surprisingly good. He got up and re-filled his cup.

'You know more about him than I do.'

'Not what he's like; how he talks, what he likes, what he's like inside. You know what I mean.'

'He's educated, cultured, a scholar. He's gentle and kind.'

'What did you talk about?'

He caught a momentary expression that flitted rapidly across her face. Something there, but what? He saved it for later.

'Ancient Greece.'

'Lyle, loosen up, baby. I'm not going to bite or do anything nasty. Open up a little. Tell me something about the time you spent with him.'

She shook her head. 'I'm not working for you, or with you. I'm here doing a job for a magazine, and for my publisher. That's all.'

'Uh-huh. It was the cover story, wasn't it? You don't buy it.' He sighed and finished the last of the coffee. 'Don't blame you. After seeing that state park I don't blame you a bit. Have to be an idiot to try to smuggle anything into that cove. Who'd of thought there'd be dopes camping out all winter. It's February for Christ's sake!'

'You admit you lied to me?' She knew he was playing with her, keeping her off guard, but she could not suppress the note of incredulity that entered her voice. She knew he was a master at this game, also, and she was so naive that she didn't even know when the play started, or what the goals were.

'What'd you talk about?'

She started again. There was more than a touch of confusion in her mind about what they had talked about for nearly five hours, and somehow she had revealed something to Hugh Lasater. Almost sullenly she said, 'Philosophy, cuisines, the coast, geology. Nothing. It was nothing of any importance.' She finished packing her camera case and stood up. 'I have to go out now. I'm sorry I can't help you.'

'Oh, you'll help,' he said almost absently, thinking about the changes in her voice, subtle as they were. Although she had learned to step back, her voice was revealing in the way it changed timbre, the quickness of her words. He had it now, the cue to watch for.

'Have you read your contracts for the article and the book?'

She became silent again, frozen, waiting.

'You should. If you didn't bring copies with you, I have some. I'll drop them off later today, or send someone else with them.'

'What are you threatening now?'

'You've got no job, kiddo, and the contracts have clauses in them that I doubt you'll be able to fulfill. I doubt seriously that you can get your story together within ninety days, starting nearly a month ago. And I doubt that you really meant you'd be willing to pay half your royalties to a ghostwriter. But you signed them, both of them. Honey, don't you ever read contracts before you sign them?'

'Get out of here,' she said. 'Just get out and leave me alone.'

'People like you,' he said, shaking his head sadly. 'You are so ignorant it's painful. You don't know what's going on in the world you live in. You feel safe and secure, but, honey, you can feel safe and secure only because people like me are doing their jobs.'

'Blackmailing others to do your jobs.'

'But sometimes that's part of the job,' he protested. 'Look, Lyle, you must guess that this is an important piece of work, no matter what else you think. I mean, would anyone invest the kind of effort we've already put into it if it weren't important? We're counting on your loyalty – '

'Don't,' she snapped. 'Loyalty to what, to whom? In the middle ages the nobility all across Europe was loyal to nobility. The guilds were loyal to guilds. Peasants to peasants. Where's the loyalty of a multinational-corporation executive? Or the Mafia? Loyal to what? What makes you think there's anything at all you can tell me that I'd believe?'

'I'm not telling you anything,' he said. 'I know you won't believe me. Except this. He's a killer, Lyle. I don't want to scare you off before ...'

She pressed her hands over her ears. 'So let the police arrest him and take him in for fingerprinting and questioning, the way they do other suspects.'

'Can't. He has something stashed away somewhere and we want it. We want him to lead us to it. If he's our man. First that. Is he our man? We can't go inside his house for prints. There are dozens of ways of booby-trapping a place to let you know if someone has entered. A hair in a door that falls when the door's opened. A bit of fluff that blows away if someone moves near it. An ash on a door handle. A spiderweb across a porch. He'd know. And he'd bolt, or kill himself. That's what we want to avoid. A dive off a cliff. A bullet through his brain. A lethal pill. We want him very badly. Alive, healthy, and in his own house where he keeps his stuff. We'll put a hundred agents on him, follow him ten years if it takes that long. If he's our man. And we expect you to furnish something that'll let us find out if he is our man. Soon, Lyle.' He paused, and when she did not respond, he said, 'So you like the old fart. So what? Even the devil has admirers. There's never been a monster who didn't have someone appear as a character witness. You see it every day, the neighbors describing a homicidal psychopath as a nice, quiet, charming man, so kind to the children. Balls! Your pal is a killer resting between jobs. Period. You're in no danger, unless you blow it all in front of him. But I'll tell you this, I wouldn't underwrite life insurance on the kid with him.'

She regarded him bitterly, not speaking.

He got up and went to the door. 'I know, you're thinking why you. You didn't ask to get mixed up in something like this. Hell, I don't know why you. You were there. And you are mixed up in it. And I tell you this, Lyle baby. When it gets as big as this is, there's no middle ground. You're for us or against us. That simple. Be seeing you.'

Hugh Lasater had known Werther/Rechetnik would turn up at the most recent molecular-biologists' conference in UCLA this past fall. He had counted on it the way he counted on Christmas, or income tax day. And Werther had not let him down any more than Santa had done when he was a kid. Werther had been there and left in his white Volvo with the kid driving him as if he were a president or something. Since that day in November he had been under surveillance constantly. Twice they had tried ploys designed to get positive identification, and each time they had failed. The kid paid the bills, did the shopping, drove the car. Werther wore gloves when he went out, and the house was booby-trapped. Turk had spotted a silk thread across the porch the first day Werther had left, and Turk had backed off exactly as he had been ordered.

The first time they tried to get his prints indirectly, it had been through the old dog of a routine telephone maintenance visit. The kid had refused the man admittance, said they didn't want the phone in the first place and didn't care if it was out. Period. No one insisted. The next time a young woman had literally run into Werther on the beach. She had been wearing a vinyl cape, pristine, spotless, ready to receive prints. Werther had caught her reflexively, steadied her, then had gone on his way, and Milton Follett had received the cape. Nothing. Smudges. Just as reflexive as his catching the girl had been, his act of smearing the prints must have been also.

There were two men in the Lagoon State Park at all times, one of them on high enough ground to keep the driveway under observation through daylight hours, and close enough at night to see a mouse scamper across the drive. Farther south there were two more men in the next state park. He was bottled up tight, and they still did not have a positive identification.

They could have picked him up on suspicion of murder, staging the arrest, mug shots, prints, interrogation, everything, but Mr. Forbisher had explained patiently that without his papers Werther was simply another lunatic killer. He would surely commit suicide if cornered. They wanted it all in a neat package undamaged by rough handling. They wanted his papers.

It irked Lasater that no one would lay it all out, explain exactly what it was that Werther had. But Christ, he thought, it had to be big. Bigger than a new headache capsule. He suspected it was a cancer cure; the Nazis had used Werther's/Rechetnik's mother for cancer experiments, and he was getting his revenge. It had to be that, he sometimes thought, because what could be bigger than that? The pharmaceutical company that owned that secret would move right into the castle and be top of the heap for a long time to come. When he thought of the money they were already spending to get this thing – money they were willing to keep spending – it made his palms sweat. He did not really blame them for not telling him all of it; that was not how the game was played. All he needed to know, Mr. Forbisher had said primly, was that they wanted Werther, if he was actually Rechetnik; they wanted him intact with his papers. And Hugh Lasater had gone off looking for exactly the right person to put inside the house next door. Step one. He had come up with Lyle Taney.

6

She sat with her knees drawn to her chin, staring moodily at the nest. She did not believe Lasater, and she knew it didn't matter if she did or not. She might never know the truth about him, she thought, still bitter and angry with Lasater, with herself for stepping into this affair.

She had read the contracts, and she had asked Bobby about the time, about other things Lasater hadn't brought up yet, but no doubt would if he felt he had to. Formalities, Bobby had said, don't worry about them. Basically, he had said, it was the same contract as her first one, with a few changes because the work was not even started yet. And she had signed. She had drawn out so much of her savings to pay for this trip, for the three-month's rental on the house, for the car she had leased. It takes a month to six weeks to get money loose from the company, Mal had said. You know how bureaucracies are. And she did know.

They must have investigated her thoroughly; they knew her financial situation, the bills she had accumulated during those wasted, lost years; they knew about Mike; they knew she would be willing and even eager to leave her job. She remembered one thing Werther had said, about historians losing faith in what they taught. He was perceptive, Lasater was perceptive, only she had been blind. She put her forehead down on her knees and pressed hard. She wanted to weep. Furiously, she lifted her head and stared at the nest again.

The sun had come out and the day was still and warm. Down on the beach there would be a breeze, but up here, sheltered by hills and trees, the air was calm and so clear she could see the bark on the pine spur that bore the eagles' nest.

'Mrs. Taney?' It was Carmen's voice in a hushed whisper.

She looked for him; he was standing near a tree as if ready to duck behind it quickly. 'It's all right,' she said. 'The nest is still empty.'

He climbed the rest of the way up and sat down by her, not all the way under the tarp. The sun lightened his hair, made it look almost russet. 'You said last night that I could join you, see the nest. I hope you meant now, today. I brought you some coffee.'

She thanked him as he took off a small pack and pulled a thermos from it. The coffee was steaming. He wore binoculars around his neck. She pointed and he aimed them at the nest and studied it for the next few minutes.

She had forgotten that he had asked if he could join her. She frowned at the coffee, trying to remember more of the conversation. Nothing more came.

'It's big, isn't it? How soon do you expect the eagles to come?'

'I'm not sure. They'll hang around, fixing up the nest, just fooling around for several weeks before they mate. Sometime in the next week or two, I should think.'

He nodded. 'Mr. Werther asked if you have to stay up here this afternoon. There's a place down the beach a few miles he'd like to show you. Beach combing's great after a storm, and there's gold dust on the beach there.'

She laughed. 'I don't have to stay at all. I took a few pictures, I was just ... thinking.' She started to check around her to make sure she had everything. 'Have you been with him long?'

'Sometimes it seems a lifetime, then again like no time at all. Why do you ask?'

'Curious. You seem to understand him rather well.'

'Yes. He's like a father. Someone you understand and accept and even love without questioning it or how you know so much about him. You know what I mean?'

'I think so. It's a package deal. You accept all or nothing.'

'He's very wise,' Carmen said, standing, reaching out to pull her to her feet. He was much stronger than his slender figure indicated. He looked at her and said, 'I would trust him with my life, my honor, my future, without any hesitation.' Then he turned and started down the hillside before her.

Just like Werther, she thought, following him down. He side-stepped questions just as Werther did, making it seem momentarily that he was answering, but giving nothing with any substance.

Lyle left her camera bag at Werther's house; they all got in the Volvo and Carmen drove down the coast a few miles. Here the road was nearly at sea level; water had covered it during the storm and there was still a mud slick on the surface. Carmen parked on a gravel turnoff, and they walked to the sandy beach. In some places the beach on this section of the coast was half a mile wide with pale, soft sand, then again it was covered with smooth, round, black rocks, or a sliver of sand gave way to the bony skeleton of ancient mountains; here the beach was wide and level, and it was littered with storm refuse.

'We'll make our way toward those rocks,' Werther said, pointing south. The outline of the rocks was softened by mist, making it hard to tell how far away they were.

It took them five hours to get to the rocks and back. All along the way the storm detritus invited investigation. There were strands of seaweed, eighteen feet long, as strong as ropes; there were anemones and starfish and crabs in tide pools, all of them colored pink or purple, blue, green, red; there was a swath of black sand where Werther said there was probably gold also. It was often found in the heavy black sand; washed from the same deposits, it made its way downstream along with the dense black grains. They found no gold, but they might have, Lyle thought happily. She spied a blue ball and retrieved it. It was a Japanese fishing float, Werther said, examining it and handing it back. He talked about the fishing fleets, their lights like will-o'-the-wisps at sea. They had not used glass floats for thirty years, he said; the one she had found could have been floating all that time, finally making it to shore.

At one point Carmen produced sandwiches and a bottle of wine from his backpack, along with three plastic glasses. They sat on rocks, protected from a freshening breeze, and gazed at the blue waters of the Pacific. A flock of seagulls drifted past and vanished around the outcropping of granite boulders.

'It's a beautiful world,' Werther said quietly. 'Such a beautiful world.'

Carmen stood up abruptly and stalked away, he picked up something white and brought it back, flung it down at Werther's feet. It was half a Styrofoam cup.

'For how long?' he said in a hard furious voice. He picked up the wine bottle and glasses and replaced them in his backpack, then turned and left.

'You could bury it, but the next high tide will just uncover it again,' Werther said, nudging the Styrofoam with his foot. He picked it up and put it in his pocket. 'Speaking of high tides, we have to start back. The tide's turning now, I think.'

They watched the sunset from the edge of the beach, near the car. The water covered their footprints, cleaning up the beach again of traces of human usage. It was dark by the time they got back to Werther's house.

'You must have dinner with us,' he insisted. 'You're too tired to go cook. You'll settle for a peanut butter sandwich and a glass of milk. I feel guilty just thinking about dinner while you snack. Sit by the fire and nurse your images of the perfect day and soon we'll eat.'

Lyle looked at Carmen, who nodded, smiling at her. It was he who knew what she would eat if she went home now. She thought of what he had said about understanding and accepting Werther, and she had the feeling that he understood and accepted her also, exactly as she was, nearing middle age, red-faced, with frizzy hair going gray. None of that mattered a damn bit to him, not the way it mattered to Lasater, whose eyes held scorn and contempt no matter how he tried to disguise it. She nodded, and Carmen reached out to take her coat; Werther said something about checking the wine supply, and needing more wood. She sank into the chair that she thought of as hers and sighed.

Perhaps she could say to Werther, please just give me a set of good fingerprints and let's be done with that. She could explain why she needed them, tell him about the hook Lasater had baited for her and her eagerness to snatch it. He would understand, even be sympathetic with her reasons. And if he was the man Lasater was after, he would forgive her. She snapped her eyes open as a shudder passed over her. Lasater was sure, and she was too. She felt only certainty that Werther lived under a fearsome shadow. She felt that he was a gentle man, whose gentleness arose from a terrible understanding of pain and fear; that underlying his open love of the ocean, the beach, the gulls, everything he had seen that day, there was a sadness with a depth she could not comprehend. She believed that his compassion, humanity, love, warmth, all observable qualities, overlay a core as rigid and unweathered and unassailable as the rocky skeletons of the mountains that endured over the eons while everything about them was worn away. He was a man whose convictions would lead him to action, had already led him to act, she thought, and admitted to herself that she believed he was wanted for something very important, not what Lasater said, because he was a congenital liar, but something that justified the manhunt that evidently was in progress. And she knew with the same certainty that she had been caught up in the middle of it, that already it was too late for her to exclude herself from whatever happened here on the coast. Unless she left immediately, she thought then.

'You're cold,' Carmen said, as if he had been standing behind her for some time. He was carrying wood. 'These places really get cold as soon as the sun goes down.' He added a log to the fire, tossed in a handful of chips, and in a moment it was blazing. 'You're in for a treat. He's going to make a famous old recipe for you. Fish soup, I call it. He says bouillabaisse.' He stood up, dusting his hands together. 'Be back instantly with wine. Do you want a blanket or something?'

She shook her head. The shiver had not been from any external chill. Presently, with Carmen on the floor before the fire, and her in her chair, they sipped the pale sherry in a companionable silence.

Carmen broke it: 'Let's play a game. Pretend you're suddenly supreme dictator with unlimited power and wealth, what would you do?'

'Dictator of what?'

'Everything, the entire earth.'

'You mean God.'

'Okay. You're God. What now?'

She laughed. Freshman games out of Philosophy 101. 'Oh, I'd give everyone enough money to live on comfortably, and I'd put a whammy on all weapons, make them inoperative, and I'd cure the sick, heal the wounded. Little things like that.'

He shook his head. 'Specifically. And seriously.' He looked up at her without a trace of a smile. 'I mean if everyone had X dollars, then it would take XY dollars to buy limited things, and it would simply be a regression of the value of money, wouldn't it?'

'Okay, I'd redistribute the money and the goods so that everyone had an equal amount, and if that wasn't enough, I'd add to both until it was enough.'

'How long before a handful of people would have enormous amounts again, and many people would be hungry again simply because human nature seems to drive some people to power through wealth.'

She regarded him sourly. He was at an age when his idealism should make it seem quite simple to adjust the world equitably. She said, 'God, with any sense at all, would wash Her hands of the whole thing and go somewhere else.'

'But you, as God, would not be that sensible?'

'No. I'd try. I would think for a very long time about the real problems – overpopulation, for instance – and I'd try to find a way to help. But without any real hope of success.'

He nodded, and a curious intensity seemed to leave him. She had not realized how tense he had become until he now relaxed again.

Very deliberately she said, 'Of course, solving the population problems doesn't mean it would be a peaceful world. Sometimes I think history was invented simply to record war, and before records, there were oral traditions. Even when the world was uninhabited except for a few fertile valleys, they fought over those valleys. There will always be people who want what others have, who have a need to control others, who have a need for power. Population control won't change that.'

'As God you could pick your population,' Carmen said carelessly. 'Select for nonaggressiveness.'

'How? With what test? But, as God, I would know, wouldn't I?'

'There would be problems,' he said, looking into the fire now. 'That's why I started this game saying dictator; you said God. Where does assertiveness end and aggressiveness start? There are real problems.'

She was tiring of the adolescent game that he wanted to treat too seriously. She finished her wine and went to the sideboard to refill her glass. There was a mirror over the cupboard. She stared at herself in dismay. Her hair was impossible, like dark dandelion fluff; her cheeks and nose were peeling; her lips were chapped. She thought with envy of Carmen's beautiful skin. At twenty you seemed immune to wind damage. Sunburn on Saturday became a lovely glow by Sunday. She thought of Werther's skin, also untouched by the elements, too tough to change anymore by now. Only she, in the middle, was ravaged looking. She hoped dinner would be early; she had to go back to her house, take a long soaking bath, cream her skin, then get out her checkbook and savings passbook and do some figuring. She could do the book somewhere else, but if Bobby didn't take it, would anyone else? She remembered her own doubts about a second one so closely following the first, and she was afraid of the question.

The real fear, she thought, was economic. Whoever controlled your economic life controlled you. Overnight she could become another nonperson to be manipulated along with the countless other statistics. Her dread was very real and pervasive, and not leavened at all by the thought that Hugh Lasater understood how to use this fear because he also harbored it. That simply increased his power because he too was driven by uncontrollable forces.

Carmen joined her at the sideboard, met her gaze in the mirror. 'You said you would heal the sick, cure the wounded. What if you had a perfect immunology method? Would you give it to the drug manufacturers? The government?'

Slowly she shook her head, dragged back from the real to the surreal. 'I don't know. Perfect? What does that mean?'

'Immune to disease, radiation, cellular breakdown, aging ...'

She was watching the two faces in the mirror, hers with its lines at her eyes, a deepening line down each side of her nose, the unmistakable signs of midlife accentuated by the windburn; his face was beautiful, like an idealized Greek statue, clear elastic skin, eyes so bright they seemed to be lighted from behind. She knew nothing changed in her expression, she was watching too closely to have missed a change, but inside her, ice formed and spread, and she was apart from that body, safely away from it. Is that what Werther had? she wanted to ask, wanted to scream. Is that why they wanted him so badly?

She started to move away and he put his hands on her shoulders, held her in place before the mirror. At his touch the ice shattered and she was yanked back from her safe distance. Startled, she met his gaze again.

'Would you?'

She shook her head. 'I don't know. No one person could make such a decision. It's too soul killing.' It came out as a whisper, almost too low to be audible.

He leaned over and kissed the top of her head. 'I'd better see if Saul needs any help.' He left her, shaken and defenseless. When she lifted her glass, her hand was trembling.

Saul? Saul Werther. He called him Saul so naturally and easily that it was evident that they were on first-name terms, had been for a long time. Had Saul Werther promised him that kind of immunity? Was that the bond? Slowly what little she had read of immunology came back to her, the problems, the reasons that, for example, there had not been a better flu vaccination developed. The viruses mutate, she thought, clearly, and although we are immune to one type, there are always dozens of new types. Each virus is different from others, each disease different, what works against one is ineffective against the rest. But Carmen believed. Saul Werther had convinced him, probably with no difficulty at all, considering his persuasiveness and his wide-ranging knowledge of what must seem like everything to someone as young and naive as Carmen was.

He was crazy then, with a paranoid delusional system that told him he could save the world from disease, if he chose to. He was God in his own eyes; Carmen his disciple.

She went to stand close to the fire, knowing that the warmth could not touch the chill that was in her.

She would leave very early the next day. There were other eagles in other places – Florida, or upper New York, or Maine. And she would start filling applications for a job, dig out her old résumé, update it ... If she stayed, Lasater would somehow find a way to use her to get inside this house, get to Saul Werther. And she knew that Saul and she were curiously allied in a way she could not at all understand. She could not be the one to betray him, no matter what he had done.

She hardly tasted dinner and when Saul expressed his concern, she said only that she was very tired. She found to her dismay that she was thinking of him as Saul, and now Carmen did not even pretend the master/servant roles any longer. Saul left his place at the table and came up behind her. She stiffened, caught Carmen's amused glance, and tried to relax again. Saul felt her shoulders, ran his hands up her neck.

'You're like a woman made of steel,' he said, and began to massage her shoulders and neck. 'Tension causes more fatigue than any muscular activity. Remember that blue float? Think of it bobbing up and down through the years. Nosed now and then by a dolphin, being avoided by a shark made wise by the traps of mankind. A white bird swoops low to investigate, then wheels away again. Rain pounding on it, currents dragging it this way and that. And bobbing along, bright in the sunlight, gleaming softly in moonlight, year after year ... Ah, that's better.' She opened her eyes wide. 'Let's just have a bite of cheese and a sip of wine while Carmen clears the table, and then he'll take you home. You've had a long day.'

He had relaxed her; his touch had been like magic, working out the stiffness, drawing out the unease that had come over her that night. His voice was the most soothing she had ever heard. Perhaps one day he would read aloud ... She sipped her sweet wine and refused the cheese. He talked about the great vineyards of Europe.

'They know each vine the way a parent knows each child – every wart, every freckle, every nuance of temperament. And the vines live to be hundreds of years old ...'

The flame was a transparent sheet of pale blue, like water flowing smoothly up and over the top of the log. Lyle looked through the flame; behind them was a pulsating red glow the entire length of the log. There was a knot, black against the sullen red. Her gaze followed the sheer blue flames upward, followed the red glow from side to side, and Saul's voice went on sonorously, easily ...

'My dear, would you like to sleep in the spare room?'

She started. The fire was a bed of coals. She blinked, then looked away from the dying embers. At her elbow was her glass of wine, she could hear rain on the roof, nothing was changed. She did not feel as if she had been sleeping, but rather as if she had been far away, and only now had come back to this room.

'We have a room that no one ever uses,' Saul said.

She shook her head and stood up. 'I want to go now,' she said carefully, and held the back of the chair until she knew her legs were steady. She looked at her watch. Two? Everything seemed distant, unimportant. She yearned to be in bed sleeping.

Carmen held her coat, then draped a raincoat over her. 'I'll bring the car to the porch,' he said. She heard the rain again, hard and pounding. She did not know if she swayed. Saul put his arm about her shoulders and held her firmly until the car arrived; she did not resist, but rather leaned against him a bit. She was having trouble keeping her eyes open. Then Saul was holding her by both shoulders, looking at her. He embraced her and kissed her cheek, then led her down the stairs and saw her into the car. He'll get awfully wet, she thought, and could not find the words to tell him to go back inside, or even to tell him goodnight.

'Good thing I know this driveway well,' Carmen said cheerfully, and she looked. The rain was so hard on the windshield the wipers could not keep it cleared, and beyond the headlights a wall of fog moved with them. She closed her eyes again.

Then the cold air was on her face, and Carmen's hand was firm on her arm as he led her up the stairs to her house, and inside. 'I'll pull those boots off for you,' he said, and obediently she sat down and let him. He built a fire and brought in more wood, then stood over her. 'You have to go to bed,' he said gently. 'You're really beat tonight, aren't you?'

She had closed her eyes again, she realized, and made an effort to keep them open, to stand up, to start walking toward the bedroom. She was surprised to find that her coat was off already, and the raincoat.

'Can you manage?' Carmen asked, standing in the bedroom doorway.

'Yes,' she said, keeping her face averted so he could not see that her eyes were closing again.

'Okay. I'll look in on you in the morning. Goodnight, Lyle.'

She got her sweater off, and the heavy wool slacks, but everything else was too much trouble. She rubbed her arm where Saul had given her the injection and remembered his words: 'It may start to itch in a couple of hours, but it won't bother you.' The itching stopped as she crawled into bed partially dressed; she fell asleep even before her head touched the pillow.

7

The cabin was dark when she came awake. She could not think where she was for several minutes. She was very thirsty, and so tired she felt she could not move the cover away from her in order to get up. Her head pounded; she had a temperature, she thought crossly. In the beginning, the first several times she had come home soaked and shaking with cold, she had been certain she would come down with a cold, or flu, or something, but she had managed to stay healthy. Now it was hitting. Sluggishly she dragged herself from bed, went to the bathroom, relieved herself, and only then turned on the light to look for aspirin. She took the bottle to the kitchen; it would burn her stomach if she took it without milk or something. But when she poured a little milk into a glass, she could not bear the sight of it, and she settled for water after all. It was six o'clock. Too early to get up, too dark …

The cabin was cold and damp. She remembered how she had been chilled the day before and thought, that was when it started. She should have recognized the signals, should not have spent the day on the beach in the wind … She had been walking back toward the bedroom, now she stopped. How had she got home?

There was no memory of coming home. She tried to remember the evening, and again there was nothing. They had gone to Saul's house, where she and Carmen had played a silly game, then dinner, then … Then nothing.

Like the night before, she thought distantly, the words spaced in time with the pounding of her head. Ah, she thought, that was it. And still distantly, she wondered why it was not frightening that she could not remember two evenings in a row. She knew she was not crazy, because being crazy was nothing like this. She could even say it now, when she had been crazy she had been frightened of the lapses, the gaps in her life. And suddenly she was frightened again, not of the loss of memory, but of her acceptance of it with such a calm detachment that she might have been thinking of a stranger. She turned abruptly away from the bedroom and sat down instead on a straight chair at the kitchen table.

What was happening to her? She forced herself to go over the previous day step by step. Carmen's hands on her shoulders, her realization that Saul was crazy, paranoid, and her own panicky decision to leave today. She nodded. Leave, now, immediately. But she had to wait for Carmen to come, she thought plaintively. Her hands tightened on the table, made fists. She saw herself walking toward Saul's open arms, felt the warmth of them about

417

her, the comfort of resting her cheek on his shoulder ... Unsteadily, she stood up and got another drink of water. Leave!

She sat down with the water, torn between two imperatives: she had to leave, and she had to wait for Carmen. If she stayed, she thought, sounding the words in her head, Lasater would use her somehow to get to Saul. Still, she sat unmoving, wishing Carmen would come now, take the decision away from her. She pulled an open notebook close and with block letters drawn shakily she wrote *Leave*. She nodded and pushed herself away from the table.

Packing was too hard; she decided not to take some of her things – the typewriter, some of the books, one of her suitcases. Dully she thought of the refrigerator, of food turning bad. She shoved things into a bag and carried it to the car and blinked at the trunk already full. She put the food on the floor of the back seat and decided she had enough. It was eight o'clock when she left the house and started down the driveway. At the bottom, a large blond man waved to her. She made the stop, prepared to turn, and rolled her window open a crack.

'Yes?'

'Lasater wants to see you. He's in a camper in the park.' He went around the car, keeping his hand on the hood; at the passenger side, he opened the door and got in.

She looked at him, feeling stupid. Her door was locked, she had thought of it, but not that side. Slowly she pulled out onto the highway, climbed the hill, went down the other side thinking of nothing at all.

'There's the turnoff,' the blond man said.

She turned and drove carefully down the steep gravel road to the campsite. She stopped when he told her to. They both got out and he motioned toward the motor home at the end of the campgrounds. She walked to it.

'Lyle, what an early bird! I thought it would be later than this. Come on in. I'm making breakfast, Mexican eggs. You want some?'

The interior was exactly like the ads she had seen in magazines. There was a tiny living room area with a narrow sofa and two swivel chairs. There was a counter separating that part from the even smaller kitchen, and beyond that another curtained-off part. All very neat.

'Why did you send that man after me?'

'Afraid you'd be up and out early, and I wanted to talk to you.' He was dicing a red pepper. 'Look, I can add another egg, no trouble at all. Pretty good dish.'

She shook her head.

He reached below the counter and brought out a coffee cup. 'At least coffee,' he said, pouring. He brought her the cup and put it on a swing-out table by the side of the sofa. 'Sit down, I'll be with you in a minute. You hung over?' His scrutiny was quick, but thorough. He grinned sympathetically. 'Have you told them anything about me?'

'No. I'm sick, I'm going to buy juice and aspirin and go to bed.'

He backed away. 'Christ! What a lousy break! You okay? If you don't feel like driving to the village, I can send for stuff for you.'

She shook her head again. 'I'll go.'

'Okay, but then in the sack, and stay until you're tiptop again, right? It's the rain. Jesus, I never saw so much rain. Has it ever stopped since you got here?'

He went on cheerfully as he added onions to the chili pepper, then a tomato. He tossed them all into a small pan and put it on one of the two burners of the stove. He poured himself more coffee as he stirred the sauce, and through it he kept talking.

'You know, it might be a good ploy, your getting sick now. You pile up in bed and he comes to visit, right? I mean, he digs you or would he have spent all day and most of the night with you? So he comes to visit and you ask him for a drink, a glass of water or juice, and later we come collect the glass, finis. Not bad actually.'

Wearily she leaned her head back and closed her eyes. 'You've been so smart,' she said. 'If I did what you asked and no more, I was safe enough. Hand over the prints, get my story on the eagles, forget the whole thing. If I poked around and learned anything more than that, you could always point to my medical record and say I'm just a nut.'

'A plum,' he said, correcting her. 'You're a plum. I reached in and pulled out a real plum. You know there aren't any plums in plum pudding? Boy, was I ever disillusioned when I found that out.' He had broken his eggs into a frying pan; he watched them closely, turned them and then flipped them onto a plate. He poured his sauce over them. 'No tortillas,' he said regretfully. 'Toast just isn't the same, but them's the breaks.' Toast popped up in the toaster and he buttered it quickly, then brought everything to the living area. He pulled out another table and put his breakfast down. 'Look, are you sure you don't want something, toast, a plain egg?'

'No.'

'Okay.' He reached under the table and flipped something and extended another section. 'Presto chango,' he said. Then he pulled a briefcase toward him, rummaged in it, and brought out an envelope, which he put on the table. 'While I eat, take a look at the stuff in there.'

There were photographs. Lyle glanced through them and stopped when she came to one that had Saul Werther along with several other men, all looking ahead, as if they were part of an audience.

'Start with the top one,' Hugh Lasater said, with his mouth full.

She looked at it more closely. It was an audience, mostly men, all with an attentive look. She studied it, searching for Saul, and finally found him, one tiny face among the others. Two other photographs were similar, different audiences, but with Saul among the others. There was a photograph of four men walking; one of them was Saul. And there were two blown-up pictures of sections of the larger audiences.

Lasater had finished eating by the time she pushed the photographs aside. 'You recognize him without any trouble?'

'Of course.'

'But in one his hair's almost white, and in another one it's dark brown. He has a mustache in one, didn't you notice it?'

'I assumed they're over a period of time. People change.'

'Two years,' Lasater said. He removed his plate and leaned back in his chair once more, holding coffee now. 'One of those conferences was in Cold Spring Harbor, one's Vanderbilt, the last one's Cal Tech. He gets around to the scientific meetings. And at some of those conferences there were incidents. Each time, a young scientist either vanished or died mysteriously.'

Lyle closed her eyes. Don't tell me, she wanted to plead, but no words came; she realized her head was pounding in time with the booming of the surf. The booms meant another storm was coming. When the waves changed from wind waves to the long swells that formed a thousand miles offshore, or at the distant Asian shores, and when the waves did not dash frantically at random intervals, but marched with a thunderous tread upon the land, there would be a gale or worse. Saul had told her about the difference, and her experience here had confirmed it, although she had not been aware of the difference before his mini-lecture.

'I'm leveling with you,' Lasater said now. 'I want to wrap this up and be done with it. You must want to be done with it too. Lyle, are you listening to me?'

'Yes. My eyes hurt, my head aches. I told you, I'm sick.'

'Okay, okay. I'll make it short. Picture Berlin back in the thirties. You see *Cabaret*?' She shook her head slightly. 'Oh. Well, Berlin's recovering from the worst economic slump in history, expanding in all directions under Hitler. At the university they're developing the first electron microscope. And at the university is Herr Professor Hermann Franck who is one of the pioneers in biochemistry. He's using the prototypes of the electron microscope fifteen years before anyone else has it. Right? Franck has a Jewish graduate student working under him and the work is frenzied because Franck is tired, he wants to quit, go back to his family estate and write his memoirs. Only he can't because the work they're doing is too important. He's on the verge of something as big in his field as Einstein's work was in his, maybe bigger.'

'How do you know any of this?' Lyle asked.

'There were Gestapo stooges throughout the university. One of them tried to keep up with Franck and his work, made weekly reports that are mostly garbage because he wasn't being cut in on any of the real secret stuff. But enough's there to know. And, of course, Franck was publishing regularly. Then, something happened, and, I admit, this part gets shady. His grad student was beaten and left for dead by a youth gang. The professor applied for permission to take the body home for burial, and that's the last anyone knows of either of them. Obviously the kid didn't die. He survived, maybe killed the professor, maybe just hung around long enough and the old guy died of natural causes. He had a bum heart. Anyway, the student ended up with the papers, the notes on the work, everything. We know that because it all vanished. Eventually, when Franck didn't show up at work, the Gestapo got interested enough to make a search, and found nothing. The war thickened, things settled, and Franck was forgotten, another casualty. Then twenty years ago the Gestapo reports came to light and a mild flurry of activity began, to see if there was anything worth going after. Nothing. About twelve years ago a bright young scientist working on his thesis dragged out Franck's articles, and there was an explosion that hasn't stopped sending out ripples yet. Bigger than Einstein, they're saying now.'

'What is it?'

'I don't know. Maybe three people do know. But for twelve years we've been looking for that student, now an elderly gentleman, who makes it to various scientific conferences and kills young researchers. We want him, Lyle, in the worst way.'

Lyle stood up. 'It's the best story yet. They keep getting better.'

'I know. I can't top this one, though. He's crazy, Lyle. Really crazy. His family was wiped out without a trace, it must have done something to him. Or the beating scrambled his brains. Whatever. But now he's crazy, he's systematically killing off anyone who comes near Franck's research. He's able to keep up with what's going on. He can pass at those conferences. Maybe some of the time he actually works in a university somewhere. But if we can get a set of prints, we'll know. The Gestapo had them on file; they fingered every Jew in the country. All we want to do is see if they match. Maybe they won't. We'll step out, go chase our tails somewhere else.'

'And if they do match?'

'Honey, we'll be as gentle as a May shower. Somewhere there are a lot of notebooks, working notes, models, God knows what all. He can't keep all that junk in his head, and besides, he was just a student. Franck had been on it for years. It's on paper somewhere. We want him to lead us to it, and then he'll be picked up ever so carefully. There's a real fear that he'll commit suicide if he suspects we're anywhere near him, and he's too important to let that happen. He'll be better treated than the Pea Princess, believe me.'

She went to the door. Her eyes were burning so much it hurt to keep them open; she was having trouble focusing. She still did not believe him, but she no longer knew which part of the story she could not accept. It was all too complicated and difficult. She wanted desperately to sleep.

Lasater moved to her side, his hand on the doorknob. 'Honey, we're not the only ones looking for him. And we are probably the nicest ones. Science is pretty damned public, you know.'

'Now you wave the Russian threat.'

'And others,' he said vaguely. 'But also, there are pharmaceutical corporations that know no nationality. It's a real race and everyone in it is playing to win. Even if by default.'

'What does that mean?'

'The ultimate sour grapes, Lyle. A really poor loser might decide if he can't have the prize neither can anyone else.'

He opened the door. 'Look, no rain. I must be in California. Go on, get your juice and aspirin, and then pile in the sack for a day or two. I'll be around; see you later.'

He knew he had frightened her at last. It had taken the big guns, but there was a trick to knowing when to show strength and when to play it cozy. She was shaken. She had to have time now to let it sink in that her own position was not the safest possible. But she was a smart cookie, he thought with satisfaction, and it would sink in. She would get the point soon enough that this was too big for her to obstruct. The next time he saw her, she would ask what assurance she had that once done, she would be truly out of it, and he would have to reassure her, pour a little oil on her conscience.

Hugh Lasater was fifty, and, he admitted once in a while to himself, he was tired. Watching Lyle walk to her car, he thought of what it would be like to have a woman like her, to sit by a fire when the wind blew, play gin, read, listen to music, cuddle up in bed. There had been three women along the years whom he had tried that scenario with, and each time what he got was not exactly what he had been after. The women he liked to cuddle in bed were not the sort who played gin by the fire, and, he said to himself, vicy vercy. Lyle drove up the gravel trail to the highway and he motioned to Milt Follett to come back inside.

Not Lyle, or anyone like her, he decided emphatically. Too old, too dumpy. He hoped she had not spread flu germs around.

'Get up there,' he told Follett, 'keep an eye on her place. Werther's sure to pay a sick call, and when he leaves, the house is yours. She won't get in the way.' He did not believe Follett would find the prints, either. In his mind was a scene where Taney handed them to him; he believed in that scene.

Follett scowled. 'It's going to rain again.'

'Take an umbrella. Rain's good cover. They'll be in a hurry to get inside, you won't have to stay so far back.'

Follett cursed and, almost absently, Hugh Lasater slapped him. 'Get your gear together. You'd better take some sandwiches, coffee. He might not show until after dark.'

Follett's fists were as large as sacks of potatoes, and as knobby. 'Relax,' Hugh Lasater said. 'Someone has to teach you manners.' He began to gather the photographs, dismissing Milton Follett, who was, after all, no more than a two-legged dog, trained in obedience and certain indispensable tricks, but inclined to yap too much.

Two days, he thought cheerfully. After all those years, two more days was not much. He had been in the Company when Cushman first made the connection between Werther (or David Rechetnik) and Loren Oley's cancer research after Oley had vanished. Hugh Lasater had winkled out the details over a fourteen-month period, the Berlin connection, the old professor, everything he had told Lyle. Cushman had not then or ever grasped the implications and had shelved the investigation, but Lasater had stayed with it, working on it when he had time, keeping his own file. And four years ago Lasater had had enough to take his walk. He retired, pleading battle fatigue, nerves. He knew he had covered his traces so well that no one would ever be able to backtrack him. You're not going to write a book? they had asked, and he had laughed at the idea. A year later he had a new job, and was still on it. And in two days, he would know. But he already knew. He had known for over a year.

David Rechetnik, or Saul Werther, was smart, but not smart enough. He had left a trail, and if Lasater could follow it, so could others. Any spook in the business could stumble across the same opening information that he had found, could follow it to the same conclusions, and if there were official teams put on it – ours or Russian, or *even* the British, for Christ's sake – he knew they would muscle him out fast. He knew he had been right in not going to his own agency with it. They couldn't keep a secret from Monday breakfast to lunch time. And, he thought grimly, it would not do at all to let anyone even suspect there was a secret to keep. Not today. Not with fingers hovering over buttons constantly. No, he thought, let this come out exactly as aspirin had, neatly packaged, for sale to anyone with the right change, free market and all. No secrets. And soon, he added. It had to be soon. Too many people knew there was something now. He knew no one on God's little green earth who could keep his mouth shut, except himself.

He sat with his long legs stretched across the motor home, scowling at the carpet, while Follett grumbled as he began to put together sandwiches. Outside, the surf was booming like a cannon.

8

Inside Lyle's head the surf was booming also. She flinched from time to time, and she was squinting against the light even though the sky was solidly overcast now. Her legs ached and her arms felt leaden. A gust of wind shook her car and she knew the rising wind would make the coast road hazardous to drive. It was not too bad where the hills were high on the west side of the road, but every gap, every low spot, every bridge, opened a wind channel, and it howled through, threatening to sweep anything on the road through with it. She came to the village and stopped at the supermarket. She had not had time to become very friendly with anyone in town, but they all accepted her by now with amiable good will. Most of the townspeople she dealt with seemed to know her name although she knew none of theirs. The woman at the checkout stand in the grocery nodded when Lyle entered.

'Morning. How're you, Mrs. Taney? That's a real storm blowing in this time. Got gale warnings up at Brookings already. We'll get it.'

'Worse than last week's?'

'Last week?' The woman had to stop to think. 'Oh, that wasn't much at all. This one's a Pacific gale. Better make sure you have kerosene for your lamp, and plenty of wood inside. Could lose the lights.'

Lyle thanked her and moved down the aisle and began selecting her groceries. Juice, ginger ale. She remembered being sick as a little girl and her mother bringing her iced ginger ale with a bent straw. For a moment she was overcome with yearning for her mother's comforting presence. She saw straws and picked them up. Her pump was electric, she remembered, and picked up more juice. If the electric lines went down, she would have no water until they were restored. She knew she had to drink a lot; she was parched right now in fact. When she got to the checkout she was surprised by the amount and variety of potables she had picked up. Irritably she regarded them; she should put some of the stuff back, but it was too much effort and she paid for them and wheeled the cart outside to put her bag in the back seat. The wind was stronger, the gusts took her breath away. And the pounding of the surf was like a physical blow to her head again and again and again.

Before she started her engine, she found the aspirin bottle and slipped it inside her pocket where she could get it easily. She put a can of Coke on the seat next to her and then turned on the ignition.

This part of Salmon Key was on a bluff a hundred feet above sea level. On the streets running parallel to the coastline the wind blew fitfully, not too strong, but at each intersection and on the cross streets it was a steady forty miles an hour with gusts much stronger. Lyle went through an intersection, fought the steering wheel to keep her car in her lane, and then in the middle of the next block parked at the curb. She knew she could not drive up the coast against that wind.

She put her head down on the steering wheel and tried to think of someplace to go. The motel was closed for the season. She knew no one in town well enough to ask for a room for the night. Back to her house? She was afraid to go back. Saul would give her something to make her sleep again.

She jerked upright with the thought and knew it was right. He had given her something both nights. Why? She had no answer, only the question that kept slipping away as if she was not supposed to ask it, as if she had touched on a taboo that sent her mind skittering each time she came too close.

She remembered a gravel road that led from town up into the hills, following Salmon Creek to a picnic spot, going on upward past that. A logging road, dirty and rough, no doubt, but protected from the wind, and unused now since logging had stopped. She drove again, turned at the next corner and headed back toward Salmon Creek. It churned under the wind, whitecaps slapped against the boats at anchor at the docks. No one was in sight as she turned onto the gravel road, and within seconds she was out of town with only the trees on both sides of the road. At the picnic grounds she stopped to take aspirin and drink the Coke. She was very feverish, she knew. This had been a good idea, she decided, waiting for the aspirin to dull her headache and ease the aches in her arms and legs. She would rest until the storm passed – they never lasted more than a few hours – and by the time it was quiet again, probably after dark, she would go on, drive to Portland, return the car to the agency, get a flight back home.

She had no home, she remembered. She had leased her apartment. But there were people she could go to, she argued. Jackie, Chloe, Mildred and Jake ... Neither Lasater nor Saul could find her here, and tomorrow she would be safe. The aspirin was not helping very much; reluctantly she turned the key and drove; the little park was too open, too accessible. Now the road deteriorated rapidly, from gravel to dirt, to little more than ruts. She should have stayed at the picnic area, she realized. No one would be there on a day like this, and she could not find a place to turn around, or to park, or ... The road forked. Both sides began to climb steeply after this junction. Maybe she could turn around here. It took her a long time, and she knew she was scratching up the car, and scraping the bottom on rocks, but finally she had it pointing back down the dirt road and, exhausted, she turned the key again and leaned back with her eyes closed.

The wind was distant, high in the trees, hardly noticeable at ground level. She could not hear the surf, and that surprised her because her head was still pounding with the same rhythm and urgency as before, when she had thought the thunderous waves were causing her headache. The rain was starting finally, a pattering at first that eased up; soon it was falling harder. She had to get some things from the trunk. Warm clothes, her poncho, her afghan. It would get cold in the car. Still she sat quietly wishing she did not have to move again for a long time. The rain let up and now she forced herself out. She was appalled by the mess in the trunk. She had tossed stuff in randomly. Her camera case was not there, she realized, and remembered she had left it at Saul's house when they had gone down the beach. She had no further memory of it. She found a long coat, her poncho, boots, the afghan, notebooks. She knew she would not want anything to read; her eyes were bothering her too much. There was a fire banked just behind them.

She arranged the car, put down both front seats all the way, made sure her bag of groceries was within reach, and the can opener she kept in the glove compartment, and only then allowed herself to lie down and pull the afghan over her and finally closed her eyes. The rain on the car roof was too loud, but presently she grew used to it and found it soothing. She slept.

Her sleep was fitful and restless, beset by dreams. When she wakened, she was very thirsty; her lips were parched, and her eyes felt swollen. Her headache had intensified and her body hurt all over. She swallowed more aspirin and drank orange juice with it. She slept and dreamed:

Saul was her lover and they ran down the beach like children, hand in hand, laughing, tumbling in the surf, which was as warm as blood. They started to make love in the gentle surf, and she woke up suddenly, aching with desire.

She should drink again, she thought, but it seemed too much effort; she was too tired. She was curled in a tight ball, chilled throughout, and burning with fever. She would die, she thought then, and they would find her here one day and wonder what had happened to her. She dreamed they were finding her, poking at her body with sticks because no one wanted to touch her, and she woke up again. This time she rolled until she could reach a can of juice and she drank it all, and only then remembered she should have taken aspirin. She pushed herself up enough to reach the bottle, and she opened a second large can of juice and took aspirin again. It was nearly dark, the rain was hard and steady. She could not tell if the wind was blowing.

She dreamed she was telling her mother she had to go to the bathroom and her mother said, Not now, dear, wait. She woke up squatting near the car; the shock of icy rain on her back, face, arms, thighs brought her out of delirium. She was shaking so hard she could hardly get the car door open again, and, inside, her hands seemed uncontrollable as she pulled on her clothes. She could not remember undressing. Her hair was wet, ice water ran down her back, down her face. She found a dishtowel she kept in the car to wipe the windshield with and she dried her hair with it as much as she could. It was too dark to see her watch. She was so cold that she turned on the car engine and let it run long enough for the heater to warm the car. Then she was so hot that she began to tear off her clothes again.

She heard Carmen's voice: 'Don't be scared. I'll come get you and take you home. We'll take care of you.' She looked for him, but he did not come. He lied, she thought dully. Just like Lasater. Saul and Carmen examined her carefully; they looked at her throat, her eyes, listened to her heart, took a blood sample, and took her blood pressure reading. She answered Saul's questions about her medical history, her parents, everything. It was reasonable and thorough, and he wrote everything down.

'I'm dying,' she said, and he nodded.

She woke up. She remembered hanging the dishtowel outside the window to get it wet and cold. She dragged it inside and wrapped it around her head. She could hardly move now because of weakness and pain. It was not the flu after all, she thought distantly, as if diagnosing someone else. He had poisoned her with the injection she had watched him administer, she thought clearly. He was paranoid and he had known from the start that she was a spy. He told her so. He poisoned her and now she was dying from it. And they would find her body and prod it with sticks. She wept softly, then slept.

At noon the wind was rising enough to shake the motor home from time to time. The trees around the campsite bowed even lower, and the air tasted of salt. The tent in the campsite collapsed, started to fly away. The kid who had been camping out rolled it up and stuffed it in the trunk of his car, and then he joined Lasater who was standing at the railing of the park, overlooking the lagoon. The normally placid, protected waters were churning around and around; the wind-driven waves were meeting the outgoing tide in a free-for-all.

'Follett says something's wrong at Taney's house,' the boy said, close to Lasater's ear.

'What?'

'Didn't say.'

'Tell Turk to get his ass up there and find out.'

The boy watched the water another second, then left, leaning against the wind. A few minutes later the rain started and Lasater went inside the motor home. Follett came in dripping a short time later.

'She never came back,' he said, stripping off his wet clothes. 'Werther's kid came over in the car at ten, carrying her camera gear. He went inside and came back out, still with the camera bag. He left. Been back twice on foot. Must wade the creek and come up the bank.'

Lasater watched him with loathing. Follett's flesh shook when he moved; he had fatty flaps on his chest, like a woman who had been sucked dry.

'After he left the second time, I went to the house and looked around. She's flown. Half her stuff's still there, as if she wanted to fool you into thinking she'd be back. She left the refrigerator on, but she stripped it, and her toothpaste, deodorant, stuff like that, all gone.'

Lasater could feel his fury grow and spread as if it were heartburn, and it scalded him just as heartburn did. He was getting his ulcer back, he thought, enraged. She had sat there looking stupid, pretending she was sick, and all the time she had her car packed, her plans to skip out all made, everything go. And they were back at the starting post.

Wordlessly, he got out a map and looked at the roads, the distances. She could be halfway to Portland by now. And he did not have a man in Portland. Or, if she was heading south, she would be in the Siskiyous approaching the California border.

'Okay, so we change plans,' he said brusquely. 'Take me up to her place and then you get down to the village and ask around, find out who saw her, which way she was going. Come back up to her place. And for God's sake, keep your mouth closed until we have a new play to run with. Let's go.'

She had taken out maybe a third of the stuff she had brought in, he guessed, judging from the condition of the living room, where there were still books, papers, and even mail. She had not bothered to open many of the letters. He did so and scanned them quickly. Nothing. He went through her drawers, and the darkroom, where there were many prints of the coast, trees, hills, and an empty nest. Nothing. She had started to make notes in a new large notebook, nothing. His search was very methodical and, when he finished, everything was as she had left it, and everything had been examined. Nothing.

He built a fire in the stove and made coffee. She had cleaned the refrigerator but had not taken the coffee or sugar, or anything from the shelves. It looked to him as if she had left in a dead run. Why? Something had scared her out of here, what? Not his doing; she was already running by the time he had talked to her that morning. Werther? He heard his teeth grinding together and made himself stop. His dentist had warned him that unless he quit doing that he would be in dentures within a few years. He even did it in his sleep, he thought disgustedly. The thought of wearing dentures made him uneasy and irritable. It made him want to work his dentist over.

While he sat facing the door waiting for Follett to come back, he prepared his story. By the time the soft tapping on the door stirred him, he had made a phone call, and he had the new play ready.

Carmen stood with the wind whipping his hair into his face. 'Is Mrs. Taney here yet?' he asked, and the wind swept his words away.

Lasater stepped back and motioned him inside. 'What? Are we going to have a hurricane or something?' He slammed the door as soon as Carmen was inside. 'My God! It must be a hurricane!'

'I don't think it's that bad. Is Mrs. Taney back?'

'Oh, you're a friend of hers? Do you know where she is?'

Carmen shook his head. 'Who are you?'

'Oh. But we do take turns, you understand. I'm Richard Vos, assistant editor at Rushman Publications. Your turn.'

'Carmen Magone, just a friend. I got worried that she's out in this weather. She's sick with flu or something.'

'When did you see her? Today?'

'Last night. How'd you get here?'

'I was just going to ask you that. I didn't see a car out there.'

'I walked over from next door. You walk in from New York?'

Lasater didn't like him, too young, too flip, too bright-eyed. Mostly, too young. He had found his dislike of young men increasing exponentially during the last few years, and while he was prepared intellectually to admit it was jealousy, that did not prevent the feeling nor did it help once he recognized his antipathy had been roused yet again.

'I'm with a friend,' he said. 'Milt Follett, you ever see him play? We're doing his book on college football. He's gone to the village to buy some things. We thought Lyle would be here, she said she would be here. I brought her contracts to her.' He indicated his briefcase which he had brought in with him. Aggrievedly he went on, 'I could have mailed them, but she said she'd be here, and Bobby, her editor, said it would be nice to visit and see how it's coming, since I had to be in Portland anyway to see why Follett's stalled. We'll end up with a ghostwriter,' he confided. 'I could have mailed them,' he said again then. 'You say you saw her last night? Did she say anything about going somewhere for a few days? Maybe she went somewhere to wait out the storm. Maybe she's scared of storms.'

Carmen shrugged. 'She didn't say, but she seemed pretty sick, running a fever. I've got to go. If she comes in will you ask her to give us a call?'

'Camping out with a buddy?'

'Not exactly. See you later, Mr. Vos.' Carmen had not moved more than a few inches inside the door, and now he slipped out before Lasater could ask anything else.

That was a real bust, he admitted to himself. Briefly he had considered sapping the kid and giving the old man a call, tell him the punk fell and broke his leg, wait for him to drive over to pick him up and then grab him. How easy it could be, he mused. Grab him, make him tell us where the paperwork is, be done with it. He took a deep breath and went back to his seat on the couch. Maybe later it would come to that, but not yet. Taney would stay out a day or two, simmer down, but she would come back for her stuff. Someone like her wouldn't abandon a thousand-dollar camera. He'd twist her arm just a little and get what he needed that way. No suspicions, no fuss. And then, he thought coldly, Mrs. Taney, you and I have a little party coming up, just the two of us. First work, then play, right? Besides, he added to himself, the old man made a habit of killing off kids Carmen's age or a little older. No way could he believe Werther would lift a hand for this one. He made a bet with himself that Follett would suggest they grab the kid and use him for bait.

All afternoon Carmen was out in the white Volvo during the height of the storm. There was a report that he had shown up at the park twenty miles down the road. He had checked it out, then had left, heading south. An hour later he had driven past again. He had checked out the Lagoon camp, and had gone north from there. Looking for Taney, Lasater knew. Why? It had to be something that had happened at their house. He was convinced the old man had said or done something that had scared her off. At dark the Volvo made its way back up the steep driveway next door, and stayed put the rest of the night. Early the next morning Carmen was at it again. The storm had blown itself out overnight.

At eleven Lasater could stand it no longer and he called Werther's house. After six rings the old man answered, and Lasater released the breath he had been holding. Belatedly, it had occurred to him to wonder if Werther might sneak out in the trunk of the Volvo. He told his story about being an assistant to Lyle's New York editor, expressed his concern about her, suggested calling the police.

'I have done so,' Werther said. 'They obviously were not very impressed. You however have a vested interest in her, and you had an appointment with her that she missed. They would have to pay more attention if you voiced your fears.'

Lasater had no intention of calling the police, and he was mildly surprised that Werther had been willing to bring them in, if he had. Hugh Lasater seldom expected the truth from anyone. Truth, he was convinced, was of such a nebulous nature that no one should expect it more than once or twice within a lifetime. You have to ferret out facts, data, scraps of information wherever you can find them and arrange them in a pattern that seems to make sense, always knowing that tomorrow you may have to rearrange the same bits and pieces to make a different pattern. That was sufficient, that was truth, always relative, always changeable, always manipulable.

Late in the afternoon the sun broke through the clouds and the air was spring-warm and fresh. The sea had turned a deep unwrinkled blue; it rose and fell slightly like a blanket over the chest of a sleeping woman moved by gentle breathing. Sunset was breathtakingly beautiful without a color left out. Carmen returned home an hour after sunset. He was alone in his Volvo.

He looked exhausted, the report said, and mud was so high on the car that he must have been up and down logging roads all day.

At dark they all settled in to wait yet another day. Lasater felt he was caught up in a preordained configuration like the constellations of the zodiac, where each star is going at its own rate of speed in its own direction as a result of actions started long ago, which today resulted in this particular arrangement of parts. Although their motion might be imperceptible, they were all on the move; some of the stars were as close as they would ever get to one another and their destiny now was to separate, draw farther and farther apart. Others, he knew, were on a collision course that was equally predetermined and unavoidable.

He was nervous, and was keeping in very close contact with the watchers up and down the coast road. He had a man in Portland now, and another one on I-5. If anyone moved, he would be ready, and eventually someone had to move. Until then he had to wait. He had ordered Follett out to the motor home when he felt he would have to kill him if he remained in sight another minute, yawning, scratching, foot-tapping, too dumb to read, too restless to sit still. He wanted to go over and peek inside Werther's house, see what they were up to, and he knew there was no way. Heavy drapes, window shades; they were well hidden.

By late afternoon the next day fog moved in after a morning brilliant with sunshine. Carmen had gone out at dawn, and was back by two, and Lasater began pulling his watchers closer to the driveway. Fog was the most treacherous enemy of a surveillance job. The white car could move through it like a ghost, appearing to a watcher to be no more than a thicker drift, if it was spotted at all. The walkie-talkie unit remained silent through the long afternoon; no one was moving yet.

That afternoon Lasater felt like a chrysallis tightly wrapped in a white cocoon. The way the fog pressed on the windows gave him the illusion that the windows were giving, bowing inward slightly but inexorably. He half expected to see tendrils of fog forced through small entrances here and there, writhing like snakes as they squeezed in, then flowing down to the floor where they would spread out like wide, shallow rivers, join, become a solid white layer, and then begin to rise.

He got out the book on hawks, which he had started then put aside. He did not like books on natural history, could not understand people who became rapturous over animals or scenery. From time to time he looked up swiftly from the book as if only by catching it unawares would he be able to detect the fog if it did start to penetrate the house.

He came to a chapter that dealt with Sir John Hawkwood, a fourteenth-century mercenary, and his interest quickened. Here was a man he could understand thoroughly. With no nonsense about loyalty to a state or church or any abstract principle, he had gone about his business of hiring himself out to the highest bidder, had done the job contracted for, then gone on to the next without looking back. He had used the weaknesses of others against them and in the end had been rich and honored. Taney was sharp, Lasater thought then; she had made her point that Hawkwood and those like him somehow had been bypassed by one aspect of the evolutionary growth of consciousness. They had not achieved the level of conscience that would necessarily act as a rein on their desires. Unlike the hawk, also without mercy, they were creatures whose needs were not immediate and inseparable from survival. Forever barred from the garden where the innocents still dwelled, and stalled on the ladder of evolution, they existed apart; symbol making, dissembling, unrecognized before they acted and often after they acted, they were capable of incalculable evil.

Lasater snapped the book shut. She was going too far, talking as if those people had some kind of deficiency like a diabetic. And she contradicted herself, he thought angrily, first talking about all the stuff hawks grabbed for lunch – baby birds, rabbits, chicks, whatever they could lift – and then saying they could do no wrong. If he took something, she would be on his case fast. He despised people who were that unaware of their own double standards.

'Taney,' he muttered, 'deserves whatever she gets.'

9

Sunshine on her face awakened Lyle. She stirred, turned her head fretfully, and slowly drifted to full consciousness. Almost resentfully she pulled the afghan over her face and tried to go back to sleep, but she was fully awake. She did not move again for several minutes. She had not expected to wake up. She remembered snatches of consciousness, pain, fever, thirst, and she remembered that she had gone through the stages she had read about. She had felt self-pity, then anger, fury actually that this was happening to her, alone in the wilderness. That had passed and she had felt only resignation, and finally anticipation. She had read about those stages preceding death, and when she realized she was looking forward to the end, she had thought with a start: it's true then. And now she was awake.

Her fever was gone, or at least way down, and she felt only a terrible weakness and thirst. Her mouth was parched, her throat felt raw, her lips were cracked. She raised herself to her elbow and looked for something to drink and saw a can of orange juice; she had not been able to open it the last time she had been awake. She reached for it and pulled it close to her but was too tired to find the opener and finish the task. She rested until her thirst drove her to renewed effort and this time she found the bottle opener and punctured the can with it only to find she could not lift it to her mouth. Straws were scattered over the car; she groped for one and finally got it in the can and sipped the drink. She rested, drank again, then once more. By then she could pull herself up to a sitting position. Even propped up against the door, she found sitting too strenuous, and lay down again. She dozed, not for long; the sun was still on her when she opened her eyes the next time.

For the next several hours she sipped juice, dozed, sat up for seconds at a time, then minutes. She tried to remember what she had done through her ordeal, tried to remember her dreams. In one of them Lasater's face had grown so large it took up her entire field of vision; it had said, 'Are you going to do it?' When the mouth opened, it became a terrible black pit.

'No.'

'Honey, why can't you lie just a little?'

'Why can't you not lie just a little?'

'You make categorical statements and then feel obligated to live up to them. Now I have to get you out of here so I can bring in someone else.' He shot her, and while he was dragging her down the beach for the tide to take, he kept complaining, 'You're nothing but a headache, you know? What would it have cost you?'

'Stop,' she said then. He released her and she stood up laughing.

He stared at her aghast, then furiously stalked away.

She thought of the dream and could make no sense of it. It was either straightforward and meant exactly what it said, or it was so deep it eluded her. What would it have cost? she thought. She was not certain. Maybe she would have done a good thing even, but it was dirty; she felt certain of that, although she would have been unable to defend it if it were ever proven that Saul was a killer, or a smuggler, or whatever else they might claim.

She remembered a silver rain when all the fir trees had been transformed into Christmas trees heavily decorated with tinsel. She had been delighted with it, and if she had been able to get up and go out into it, she would have done so. That must have been when she was at her most feverish, her most delirious, she decided.

In a dream she had agonized over having to choose between Saul and Carmen, and they had waited patiently while she vacillated. She smiled; the rest of the dream was gone, forgotten, and probably it was just as well. Resting now she thought of the meaning of that dream: although she was almost ashamed of her admission, she was attracted to both of them. It was because they both accepted her unquestioningly, with approval, and either they were blind to her flaws, or thought them so unimportant that they actually became insignificant. She could not remember being treated exactly like this before. When she had been younger there had been the standard boyfriends, a proposal or two before she and Gregory had decided to make their arrangement permanent. All that, she thought decisively, had been biological, a burning in the groin, an itch between her legs, nothing more. Even at the height of passion, she had always known that Gregory was fantasizing someone else, someone made up of bits and pieces of movie stars and pictures in magazines. She never had talked about this with anyone because she had accepted it the way she accepted hunger and thirst and growing old, everything that was part of being human. But Saul and Carmen had not looked at her as if they were comparing her to an ideal who existed only in their heads. They had looked at her, had seen her as she was, and had accepted her. And she loved them both for it.

They were not afraid, she thought; everyone else she knew was afraid, at least most of the time. She remembered telling Saul she had been afraid all her life without ever knowing of what or why. Gregory was afraid. Mike's death had terrified him, as it had terrified her. She, blaming herself, had lived in dread of the day he would also blame her, because that would have justified her guilt. He must have felt the same way, she realized, and felt a rush of sympathy for him that she had not known before. He had needed to run all the way across the country, just as she had needed to run to the woods, to the hills.

She thought of Hugh Lasater, whose fear made him try to manipulate reality by manipulating truth, but the reality was always there, just out of sight, out of hearing, with its infinite terror.

Thinking about Hugh Lasater, she sat up again, this time without the accompanying dizziness she had felt before. She knew she needed food, her weakness was at least partly attributable to no food for … How long? It had not occurred to her to wonder until now. She tried the radio, nothing but static up here in the hills. She began to think of bread in milk, and chicken broth steaming hot and fragrant. She settled for an overripe banana and ate almost half of it before she was too tired to bother with any more. She dozed, wakened, tried another banana, and later in the afternoon decided she had to try to get to the creek for water. She had stale bread, and wanted only some water to soften it in.

She was sticky from spilled juice; she felt grimier than she had been since childhood. The creek was no more than fifteen feet from her car but she had to stop to rest twice before she reached it. The dishtowel she had been using to cool herself with was muddy, filthy; she could imagine what her face looked like. The water was shockingly cold; she held the towel in it until some of the dirt was washed away, wrung it out slightly and washed her face and neck. She was seized with a chill then. Shaking so hard that she spilled almost as much water as she had been able to get in the juice can, she started back to the car, thinking of the heater, of the afghan, of going back to sleep wrapped snugly in her poncho, covered from toe to head, sleeping deeply without dreams ... And she knew she could not do that, not now. It was time to go home.

The heater took a long time to warm the car. She sat huddled in the afghan until then, leaning against the door, her eyes closed. She was afraid to lie down for fear she would fall asleep. She kept seeing her own bed, her covers, sheets, a hot bath, something hot to drink, coffee. She wanted to be home before dark, and she knew it would take her a long time to get there.

She ate a few bites of bread softened in water and marveled at how hungry she was and how little she could eat at any one time. Two bites of this, three of that. She imagined her body as a giant sponge, absorbing water, juice, whatever she could pour into it, sucking it up greedily, dividing it fairly among her parched tissues. Her tongue felt more normal, and her throat hardly hurt now; she imagined her blood as sluggish as molasses from the refrigerator, demanding more and more of the fluids, stirring, starting to flow again, scolding ...

She smiled at her nonsense and turned the key, and this time she started down the dirt road. Within ten minutes she had to stop. Her arms were quivering with fatigue; her feet were leaden. And when Hugh Lasater turned up with more threats, more demands, she thought, with her head resting on the steering wheel, she would tell him to get out and, if he did not go, she would call the police and complain.

And she would call Saul and tell him a man was asking strange questions about him. No more than that. If he knew he was guilty of something, it would be enough. And if he was guilty of murder, she asked herself, was she willing to be his accomplice? She couldn't judge him, she knew, and she turned the key and started her lurching drive down the hill, down into fog.

She could remember nothing of this road, which was so steep and curvy it seemed now a miracle that she had driven up it. It twisted and turned and plummeted down, faithfully following the white water creek. As she went down, the fog thickened until by the time she knew she had come far enough to have reached the picnic area, she could see no farther than a few feet in any direction. She knew she had missed the park when her wheels began to throw gravel. She stopped many times, sometimes turning off the motor, sometimes leaving it on while she rested.

Then, with her front wheels almost on the coast highway, she rested for the last time. She would not dare stop again on the highway. She closed her eyes visualizing the rest of her route. The steep climb straight up, over the crest, down again, straight all the way to the lagoon, then the sharp upward curve around the far side of the lagoon, down to the bridge and her own drive. She could leave the car in the driveway and walk the rest of the way. Not soon, but eventually. Reluctantly she started the last leg of her jouney.

One more day, Lasater told himself, he'd give her one more day to show, and if she didn't ... He had no other plan and his mind remained stubbornly blank when he tried to formulate one. He was certain she would be back before his self-imposed deadline.

He should have used a professional, he thought suddenly, as if stricken with terrible hindsight. If this fizzled, it would be used against him that he had gone with an amateur when there were people available who could have done the job the first week. He worried it the way a cat worries a mouse, playing it this way and that, looking at the possibilities, and then he left it, just as the well-fed cat leaves the corpse behind. He did not believe Werther would have let any professional inside his house. He had not stayed loose and on the prowl all these years, first eluding the Nazis, and then customs, whatever had come along, by being stupid. He had accepted Taney because she was an amateur, and Taney had to deliver. Lasater still held the image of Taney handing over the evidence he needed. It was a strong image, strong enough to keep him immobile in her house while he waited for her to return.

It was nearly five when he heard the car in the driveway. A minute passed, another, and finally he could wait no longer; he stamped out into the fog to see why she was stalling. He yanked open her car door to find her slumped forward against the steering wheel. He thought she was out, but at the sound of the door opening she stirred and raised her head. She looked like hell. He had not taken it seriously that she might be really sick; he had been convinced that she had run because her nerve had failed. But she was sick all right.

'Lyle, baby, you look like death warmed over. Come on, let's get you inside.' He helped her out, then steadied her as she walked to the house. 'Jesus, you had us all worried. Carmen's been all over the hills looking for you, they called the cops even.' They had entered the house by then and he deposited her on the couch. 'What can I get you? Are you okay sitting up like that?'

'Just get out,' she said. Her voice was hoarse as if she had a sore throat. 'I won't do anything for you. I don't care what you threaten. Get out.'

'Okay, okay. I'll give Werther a call. I told him I would when you showed up. He's been worried.' She started to get up and he pushed her back. She was too weak to resist his shove, which actually had been quite gentle. For the first time he wondered if she was going to get well, if she had pneumonia or something.

Carmen answered the first ring. 'Mrs. Taney's back,' Lasater said. 'She's really sick, she might even be dying. I think she should be taken to a hospital, except there's no way you could get there through that fog. Is there a doctor anywhere nearby?' He knew there was no doctor closer than twenty-six miles. Carmen said he could tell Mr. Werther and hung up. 'Do that, kiddo,' Lasater murmured. He turned again to Lyle, who had her head back, her eyes closed. 'Listen, sweetie, they think I'm Richard Vos, a New York editor. I told them I had your contracts for you. They don't need to know more than that. Got it?'

Her nod was almost imperceptible.

'Okay. He'll probably send the kid over. When he gets here, I'm leaving. I'll be back at the park by the lagoon. You just get some rest now, take it easy for a couple of days. I'll see you later in the week.'

Again she moved her head slightly. 'I won't help you,' she said.

'Okay, just don't worry about it for now. Get well first. And, Lyle, don't tell them anything. You're up to your pink little ears in this and it's classified. You blab, and, honey, they can put you away for a long time.'

She started to take off her coat, and when he touched her in order to help, she flinched involuntarily. He shrugged and moved away again. Her eyes were sunken, her face haggard, but her windburn was clearing up. She was pale as a corpse. 'Honey, you look a hundred years old,' he said softly. 'I wouldn't lie down and stay still very long if I were you. Someone might want to shovel you under.' She opened her eyes and for a moment he was startled. He had not noticed how very green they were before. Or now they looked greener against her pale skin. There was hatred in her gaze; when a woman is on the downhill slide of thirty-five, she doesn't want to be told she looks like hell, he thought maliciously. He regretted his own impulse to make her open her eyes and acknowledge his presence; now she looked more alive. Coolly he said, 'I'm leaving your contracts on the table. I think he's coming. Remember, I'm Richard Vos.'

He had heard steps on the porch, but no automobile noises in the drive-way. It was the kid, come over to check first. He nodded, it was as he had expected. He opened the door and admitted Carmen who was carrying a paper sack.

'Mrs. Taney, how are you?' Carmen hurried to her and took her hand in both of his, studying her face. Lasater noticed that his fingers went to her pulse. Medical school dropout? Paramedic? He made a mental note to check it out.

'Don't try to talk,' Carmen said, rising then. 'I brought some soup. I'll just heat it up for you. Have you eaten anything at all since you left?'

'A little,' she whispered in her hoarse voice.

'Soup is what you need,' Carmen said and went to the kitchen where he shrugged off his coat and tossed it over a chair, and then rummaged for a pan.

'If you think you can manage,' Lasater said, 'I'll be going. I'm susceptible to viruses and bacteria and things like that. Get a sore throat if anyone within a mile coughs, you know. I tried to get a doctor, there isn't any in Salmon Key. I'll be going back to the Lagoon Park.' He was keeping his distance from Lyle, watching her as if afraid she might sneeze in his direction without warning. He snatched up his coat and tossed it over his shoulders and opened the door. 'If you need me, you know. But I can't do anything. I don't know a thing about how to care for sick people.'

Inside the motor home he snapped to Follett, 'Let's go. Back to the park.'

'What the hell's going on?'

'Never mind. We're leaving. At the first turn, I'm going to stop and you get out, go back up here and keep an eye on things. Werther's got to come over. The kid will either call him or go collect him when he thinks the coast is clear. She's really sick.'

He drove slowly, unable to see more than two feet ahead through the fog. Grumbling, Follett left the motor home when he stopped, and Lasater continued down to the highway. Visibility was so poor it would take him nearly an hour to get back to the park. If Taney could drive in it in her shape, he thought, so could he. He reached the bottom of the drive and stopped, trying to remember if the road had the white line on the side all the way, or only on curves, trying to remember if the road curved between here and the bridge.

'This is silly,' Lyle said, as Carmen held out a spoonful of the clear, strong broth he had brought from the other house. 'I can feed myself.'

'I know,' he said, smiling. 'Open up. This is fun.'

'Carmen, wait a second. I have to tell you something. That man who was here, he's an agent of some kind. He's after Saul. You have to warn him.'

'We already know,' Carmen said. 'Open up, you're almost done.'

She swallowed, then shook her head when he offered another spoonful. 'You know?'

'Not who he's working for. But it's been pretty obvious that there are people watching us.'

Lyle felt childishly disappointed, as if she had run a mile to warn of robbers only to find them already safely locked up.

Carmen looked at his watch, then said, 'Now a hot bath for you, and then bed. Hold up your foot.'

He pulled her boots off, as he had done another night, she remembered. She had forgotten that night. Again it alarmed her that she was not more fearful of the lapse, not at all fearful about it, in fact. He met her gaze and his face was somber.

'You'll gradually remember it all now. By morning when you wake up, it will all be there waiting for you to examine. You're not afraid?'

She shook her head.

'Good. I'll go fix the bath for you.'

A few minutes later, at her bedroom door, he said, 'Yell when you get in bed. I'll tuck you in.' His grin was back; he looked like a precocious child enjoying enormously this reversal of roles.

She didn't dare remain in the tub more than a few minutes; she had become so relaxed that she feared falling asleep and sinking forever under the water. Regretfully she got out, toweled herself, rubbed her hair briskly, and pulled on her gown. She was as eager now to be in bed as she had been to be in the tub. When she called Carmen, her eyes were too heavy to keep them open. She was in a time-distorting presleep state that made it seem to take him a very long time to get to the bed, but when he was there, his voice close to her, she was startled that he had arrived so quickly.

'You're going to sleep like a baby,' he murmured, and touched her shoulder lightly, drew the cover up closer to her neck. 'You won't hear anything at all until morning. I'll be here tonight, no one will come in to bother you. Goodnight, Lyle.' He kissed her forehead. She slept.

Driving the motor home at any time was difficult for Lasater, who had never driven anything like it before this trip. He had trouble getting used to the rearview mirrors, which more often than not seemed focused on the sides of the monster itself instead of the road. And he did not like the feel of it on the highway; it was too high, the weight was in the wrong place, it felt skittery if there was a glaze of ice or a slick of water on the road, and that night fog was freezing to form black ice. He feared black ice more than an ice storm, because it was invisible; it formed in one place but not another that was equally exposed. The road surface of the bridge was already covered, and he skidded alarmingly. He shifted gears and slowed down even more, wondering if he would be able to pull the grade up to the top of the hill between here and the lagoon.

He had passed Werther's driveway and was starting up the hill, when he heard a car engine roaring somewhere in the fog. His first thought was that it was an idiot speeding on the coast road, driving blind. Then he heard a crash, and he knew someone had gone off the cliffs behind him. He yanked on the brake and got out, ran back on the white line at the edge of the road.

'Turk?' he called. 'What the hell's going on?'

'Mr. Lasater? Where are you?'

The fog scrambled directional signals; it was impossible to say where any sound originated. Only the surf remained constant, and it was everywhere.

'Hey!' Turk yelled then. 'Stop! Where you think you're going?'

'Get out of the way! I'm going down to find him.' Carmen's voice.

Lasater crossed the road; he could hear scuffling sounds now, then a sharp exclamation followed by harsh cursing.

'Turk, what's happening?' he called again.

'The old guy came down like a bat outta hell, picking up speed all the way, didn't even try to stop, but straight through and over the cliff. The kid's just gone down the trail. Must have radar.'

'Call Follett. Tell him to meet you at Werther's house and give it a good dusting. Give me your flashlight. I'm going down there.'

Turk began to signal to Milton Follett, then said softly, 'Jesus H. Christ! Look!'

Up the hillside the fog was lighted from within as if by volcanic fires. There was a glow in the form of a mammoth aureole.

'That bastard! That goddamned fucking bastard,' Lasater muttered. 'Get up there with Follett, see if anything's left.' He snatched the flashlight from Turk and looked for the trail down to the beach.

10

By midnight the fire had burned itself out; the woods had not ignited; they were too wet and the moist fog had acted as a damper. The house had burned thoroughly, down to the foundation stones. Carmen sat huddled in a blanket near the stove in Lyle's house, his clothes drying on chairs. Lasater sat on the couch staring moodily at the exhausted boy, who had tried to find the car for over an hour until, retching and gagging, he had staggered from the pounding surf into Lasater's arms. The police had come and gone; they would be back at daybreak to look for the car and the body. Accidental death, they said.

Except, Lasater thought coldly, no one was dead yet. He did not believe Werther had been in the car when it went over the cliff, no matter what Turk thought he saw. Werther had to be somewhere nearby, freezing his balls off in the woods, waiting for the coast to clear enough to show up here at this house. Taney wasn't out of it yet. Werther must be planning to use her to get him out of here.

Lasater slept on the couch that night; Carmen rolled up in the blanket and slept on the floor. At dawn he was up cleaning Taney's car with Lasater watching every movement, thinking she was more of a pig than he had realized. Carmen made coffee then, and presently said he was going shopping and would be happy to drop Lasater off at the park. When they went out, the trunk lid was still raised, airing out, and the back doors were open. Lasater felt a cold fury when the thought came to him that the boy was playing games with him, demonstrating that he was not hauling Werther out of the woods that morning.

Lyle awakened slowly, first semi-aware that she was in her own bed again, that she was warm and dry and comfortable, and hungry; and slowly she began to remember the two evenings she had spent at Saul's house. She sat upright and pulled the blanket around her.

All those questions! He had examined her as thoroughly as any medical doctor had ever done. And she had permitted it! She closed her eyes hard, remembering. He had said she was to feel no fear or embarrassment, and she had felt neither; it had seemed the most natural thing in the world. She was startled by the memory of telling him all about Lasater, her involvement with him. Saul had known since that first night, and still had treated her with kindness and even love. The second night swam up in her consciousness and she shook her head almost in disbelief. He had injected her with something, and the rest of the night he had monitored her closely, her temperature, her pulse, her heart … She looked at her finger; he had taken a blood sample. Except for the physical examination, which had taken place in the bedroom, Carmen had watched it all, had participated.

As she remembered both evenings, snatches of conversations came back to her; they had talked seriously of so many things. She had been lucid, not doped or hypnotized, or unnatural in any way that she could recall now. But she had allowed it all to happen, and then she had forgotten, and had accepted not remembering. He had told her about that part of it: a drug in the sweet wine, suggestion. He had even said that if she truly objected to anything, she would refuse the suggestion. And she had refused nothing. Except, she amended, she had left the next morning although he had told her to wait for Carmen.

Slowly she got up and went to the bathroom. As she showered, more and more of that last evening came back to her. Just before telling her to wake up he had asked if she wanted to sleep there, in his house, and she had said no. She remembered thinking at the time that there was something she had to do the next morning, something she would not be able to do from his house. She had already made up her mind to leave so that Lasater could not use her to get to Saul. And she had to be home in order to carry out her intention. If he had asked even one question about her reasons, she would have told him, she knew, but he had not asked. He had suggested that she wait for Carmen to come for her.

It was nine o'clock when she finished with her shower, dressed, and was ready to face Carmen. She was still weak, but she felt now that it was due to hunger, not illness. The house was empty. Coffee was on the hot plate. She poured herself a cup of it and sat down to read a note from Carmen on the table. He had gone shopping for breakfast. Back soon.

She was still sipping the strong coffee when he returned. He looked her over swiftly. 'I'd say the patient is recovering,' he announced. 'What is prescribed for this morning is one of the biggest steaks you've ever tackled. Bet you finish it all.'

'I've never had steak for breakfast in my life. Toast sounds like plenty.' She wanted to challenge him, demand an explanation, but she was too hungry. After breakfast she would have her confrontation with Saul, not with Carmen, who was simply a tool.

'Wait and see.' He was unloading grocery bags and putting things away. When he unwrapped the steak, she almost laughed. Big enough for a party. While the steak was broiling, he opened a package of frozen peaches and sliced a banana into a bowl with them. She eyed it hungrily. He laughed and moved it out of reach. 'Dessert,' he said.

Then he brought two plates out of the oven where they had been warming, and they ate.

Lyle was on her second cup of coffee when Lasater arrived. He scowled at the table. 'Surprised you can eat on a morning like this.'

'What does that mean?' Lyle asked. She had a dim memory that he was pretending to be someone from her publisher's office, and Carmen was pretending to believe that.

'They're searching up and down the beach for Werther's body,' he said bluntly. 'No luck so far.'

She dropped her cup; it hit the saucer and toppled over, spilling coffee on the table. She turned to Carmen, who nodded.

'He had an accident last night. He drove his car over the cliff.'

Lyle did not move. She was trying to remove herself so far that she could see the house, the cliffs, the road, beach, forests, everything as she had seen it all in a dream once. So far back that nothing could touch her ever again. Faintly she could hear Lasater talking about a blood-stained car, one shoe, the wool-knit, navy blue cap that Saul always wore. The distance seemed even greater when Lasater said something about leaving that afternoon. She was brought back when Carmen covered her hand with his.

'He's gone, Lyle. Are you okay?'

She nodded. He began to wipe up the spilled coffee.

'Why didn't you tell me?'

'You had to eat something. I knew you wouldn't afterward.'

'What happened? Was it something I did?'

'No. There was a fire at the house and he went out in the car and the car went over the cliff. That's all they know about it.'

'Is he really leaving?'

'I don't know. Maybe.'

She nodded. They needed the body to make their identification. She started to speak again, but Carmen put his finger on her lips, silencing her.

Late in the afternoon she felt so restless that she could no longer stand the house and the waiting for something, anything, to happen.

'Let's go for a short walk,' Carmen said. 'Are you up to it?'

She said yes. All day she had felt stronger and stronger until by now she felt almost normal. Her recovery was proceeding as rapidly as the illness had done. Carmen drove to the beach they had walked on before; he went closer to the black rocks to park this time.

Today the sky was gray and low, pressing on the tops of the coast range mountains, making the world seem very small, confined to this winter beach. The water was a shade darker gray, undulating with long swells, breaking up into white water where the wind waves rushed to shore. They walked slowly, not speaking.

That was where they had investigated the tide pools, exclaiming over the multicolored life forms there, the starfish, urchins, crabs ... And over there she had found the blue float after its journey of many decades. And there they had eaten their lunch, and Saul had put the Styrofoam cup in his pocket to throw away later. And Saul had talked about the way the ocean savaged the winter beach when so few people were around to witness its maniacal fury.

'It seems lonesome,' she had said, looking both ways on the deserted beach.

'It has presentiment of endings now,' Saul had said. 'Endings of life, of pleasure, of laughter in the sand. The winter beach is lonesome, but it fights back. Each grain of sand wrested from it is fought for, yielded finally, but never easily. And in the summer, very peacefully it all comes back, scoured clean by the mother ocean. But in the winter, that's always forgotten.'

Gray, black, white; the winter beach was a charcoal drawing today, chiaroscuro colors that reflected her guiit, Lyle thought suddenly. And her guilt lay over every corner of her soul, every phase of her life. Her child, her ruined marriage, her failure as a teacher, her loss of faith both religious and secular ... Her helplessness even. Had she told Saul why she had lost faith in history as it was taught? She could not remember. She hoped she had.

One day it had occurred to her that every great change brought about historically had been the result of a very few people, men usually, who were driven by the basest impulses: greed, the urge to ever more power, vengeance ... The great majority of people had always been content to work their land, to mold their pots, weave cloth, do the life-sustaining things that were also soul fulfilling; and the great majority of the people had always been manipulable by those few, ten percent or less, whose needs were so far removed from simple survival and personal salvation.

That day she had realized that she was living during one of those turning points of history, and like countless millions before her, she was doing nothing, could do nothing. Prometheus brought fire and civilization, she had jotted in her notebook that day. The new Prometheuses bring another kind of fire and threaten to put us all back in the caves, those of us who survive for a short time. Who could control them, the politicians, the scientists, the military? Day by day they grew closer to unleashing that new fire, now by inches, now by giant steps, but always closer. Trained to see the patterns, educated to see the recurring patterns through the ages, she had seen this pattern emerging, and she had withdrawn, helpless. The marches, the demonstrations, the petitions, the letters to congressmen, the president, none of it caused a missed step, none of it caused even a hesitation as inch by inch, giant step by giant step the world advanced toward that new fire, drawn along by a minority in power who could see no other way. She had lost faith.

Saul had understood that, even if she had not explained. He had been interested in the other people, the ones with great ideas, the ones who created beauty, the ones who had tried to comprehend the mysteries.

Saul had been her natural ally, she thought dully, and by silence and inaction she had failed him, she had betrayed him; she had allowed herself to be used by Lasater, who was a member of that minority.

And that was how they always succeeded, she went on, taking it to its conclusion, allowing herself no excuse, no possibility of deliverance from guilt. True in the large political arena, it was also true in the private, personal confrontations. They found people who were too weak to resist, who were too afraid, too apathetic, too ignorant of their methods, and they wielded them like swords to strike down or capture the opposition. She had recognized Lasater immediately, had known his goals were not hers, were not even human, and she had done nothing. She had tried to ignore evil, deny its ability to influence her, and now Saul was dead and she would always know that she might have saved him if she had spoken early, before the trap was too tight, before Lasater and the blond man came. Just a few words in the beginning might have been enough. She had done nothing.

And if Saul had been crazy, if he had killed people? She could not resolve the confusion in her mind about him, about how she had responded to him, about the grief and sense of loss she now suffered.

'You're crying,' Carmen said, his hand on her arm.

She bowed her head and wept, and he held her for a long time, until finally she tried to free herself. 'I'm sorry,' she said. 'It's so pointless, isn't it? I didn't even know him. And he must have been very sick, he must have suffered terribly. No one like that can go around killing people and not suffer. He almost killed me. I know he almost killed me and yet, I can't help it, I'm crying for a madman who would have been put away if he hadn't killed himself, and I know he wanted it this way ...' There was no way out of the contradictions and finally she stopped. When she looked at Carmen's face, she realized he was laughing silently.

Stiffly she drew away and started to walk toward the car. 'You can't deny that he tried to kill me and almost succeeded. That injection of his, you were there, you know about it.'

'It was a gamble,' Carmen said, still smiling slightly. 'But you were dying anyway.'

'That's a lie. There wasn't a thing wrong with me before that shot. I had a life expectancy of at least thirty years.'

'Exactly,' Carmen said. 'This walk has probably been too much for you so soon after your illness. Let's go home and have dinner.'

She opened her mouth to respond, then clamped it shut again and got inside the car where she sat staring out the window all the way home. He was as crazy as Saul, she reminded herself.

11

Lyle saw a speck in the distance and knew the eagle was coming home finally. Every day there had been fresh evidence of the arrival of at least one of the pair, and now it was coming. She watched the speck gain definition, become separate parts. A wing dipped and the bird made a great sweeping curve, and she could see the tail feathers spread like a fan, rippling now and then as it made adjustments in its flight. She could see the white head, gleaming in the sun; it was looking at something below, turning its head slightly; it abandoned whatever had attracted it and looked ahead again. She was watching it through the view finder of her camera, snapping pictures as it came nearer. It cupped its wings, its feet reached out before it, and then it was on the spur, settling its wings down along its sides, stretching its neck. She snapped a few more shots of it as it preened, and then she sat back with her camera at her side and simply watched it. If the eagle was aware of her presence, it gave no indication of it. She was certain those sharp eyes had studied her blind, that they had seen her that day. There was a touch of majesty in its indifference to her.

Throughout the afternoon the eagle toiled at refurbishing the nest. It brought long strands of seaweed, and mosses, and sticks up to four feet long to expand the sides, and it worked the materials into place with an intentness and fastidiousness that was awesome.

Under the tree was a circle of litter; the eagle had picked out materials that had been good enough last year, but no longer pleased it. Old moss, old fern fronds, sticks. With an almost reckless abandon it tossed them over the side. When the light began to fade, Lyle picked her way back down the hillside, around the ruins of Saul's house, through the creek and to her own house, where Carmen was waiting for her.

She had not asked Carmen to stay, but neither had she asked him to leave; it was as if they both accepted that he would remain with her for now. The matter had come up only indirectly when she had said she couldn't pay him, and he had shrugged. For eight days he had been with her in the same relationship apparently that he had had with Saul. He did the shopping, a little cleaning, cooking; he prowled the beaches and brought home clams or scallops or crabs, sometimes a fish. Best of all they talked for hours in the evening, never about Saul, or Carmen's past, but of history, current affairs, art, music … Lyle knew that one day he would get restless and drift on, but she refused to think about it and the hollow in her life that would result.

When she entered the house that day, the odors of food cooking and wood smoke and the elusive scent of another person greeted her. She felt nearly overcome by contentment.

'Carmen! He's home. He's beautiful! A wing span over eight feet. All day he's been fixing up the nest, getting ready for his lady love to join him. Tomorrow you have to come up with me and see for yourself.' She was pulling off her outer wear as she talked, unable to restrain the excitement she seemed filled to overflowing with. 'I can't wait to see the pictures.'

She stopped at the look on Carmen's face, a look of such tenderness and love it made her knees weak.

'I'll come up tomorrow. Maybe I can help you in the darkroom after dinner.'

She nodded. And still they looked at one another and she wondered when she had stopped seeing him as a boy, when he had stopped looking at her as if she were untouchable.

Then she said, 'I'm filthy. I'd better get washed up and change these muddy clothes.' She fled. She was afraid he was laughing at her confusion.

They had dinner and worked in the darkroom for two hours. She felt like purring over the proof sheets; at least half a dozen of the pictures would go in, maybe more. Throughout the evening she avoided his gaze, and spoke only of eagles, her day in the blind, the dinner itself. She began to make notes to go with the pictures, and found herself writing a poem instead. When she finished, she felt almost exalted.

'May I read it?' Carmen asked.

She handed it to him silently.

He read it twice, then said, 'I like it very much. It would make a good introduction to the book. I didn't know you wrote poetry.'

'I don't. I mean I haven't before, not since college days.' She took the sheet of paper back and reread her poem.

The dead tree flies an eagle on the wind,
Then steadily reels it in,
Dip, sway, soar, rise,
All the time closer.
To the left, to the right,
Now too low, now too high,
But closer.
From nothing, to a speck
That could be a cloud,
To a being coming home,
It takes shape;
Sun on snow, the head,
Great wings without a waver,
White fan as graceful
And delicate as a black one
In a pale practiced hand.
From the tree's highest crotch,
From a nest of branches, sticks, twigs, moss,
Elaborate skyscraper room,
A silent summons was sent.
Now the dead tree reels the eagle home.

Abruptly she stood up. 'I guess I'd better get to bed. I want to be up there early. I expect the other one will come in tomorrow or the next day.'

In a scruffy camper in Lagoon Park Hugh Lasater played the tape over again, listening to their voices intently, following them through dinner, into the darkroom where their voices were almost too low to catch, back to the living room. He wished one of them had read the poem aloud. He heard their goodnights, her door closing, Carmen's movements in the living room for another fifteen minutes; then the long silence of the night started. He turned off the tape player. Something, he kept thinking. There was something he should be catching. He rewound it and started over.

What he did not hear, because the device was activated by sounds and this was done in silence, was the opening of Lyle's door at one-thirty. She stepped into the living room to look at Carmen sleeping on the couch, and when she saw him instead at the window that overlooked the sea, she did not retreat. Instead, after a slight hesitation, he came to her, barefoot, visible in the red glow from the glass door of the wood stove. He reached out his hand and she, after a slight hesitation, took it, and together they went back to her bedroom and softly closed the door.

Hugh Lasater listened again, and in the middle of the tape, he suddenly slapped the tabletop hard, waking up Milton Follett on the bunk bed.

'Son of a bitch!' Lasater said. 'The camera bag. Where was it when the house burned down?'

Follett regarded him with hatred, rolled over and went back to sleep.

Lasater had not been asking him; he already knew about the camera bag. Follett was good at certain jobs; he could watch and report movements down to a casual scratching of the head. And Follett had said that Carmen showed up with the bag at Taney's house when she was gone, and he had left with it. He had not been seen with it again. So Werther considerately put it on a stump out of danger before he set the house afire?

Lasater mused about the boy for a long time that night. He knew photography enough to help Taney in the darkroom. He remembered that sure way he had taken her pulse when she returned from her little jaunt. They had only his word that he had been hired by Werther in Los Angeles; if that was true, what had made him jump into that crazy surf in an effort to find the old man? No one risked death for someone he had known only a couple of months, and that surf was a killer. Someone had to make sure that the car door had not jammed shut, Lasater said to himself. That would have screwed it up royally, if there had been no way Werther could have been thrown out. They had waited for the right kind of night with a pea-soup fog for their little charade; maybe the kid even had a rope guide to take him to where he had figured the car would land. No one paid much attention to him; he was always on the beach prowling around.

Lasater knew his foremost problem now was to convince Mr. Forbisher that his theory was right, that Werther had not been in that car, and that the boy would lead them back to him sooner or later. Turk was convinced that he had seen Werther go over the cliff; Follett believed him, but Follett would have bought anything to get him off this job. He hated the rain and wind and cold weather, and he hated the isolation here. He wanted a woman. When they got back to civilization, Follett would vanish for a day or two. There would then be a news item about a woman's body being found ... It was one of those things with Follett, a little weakness of his. Lasater could sympathize with his frustration even while his own frustration mounted to a dangerous level. Even Lasater had to admit that he no longer believed Werther was hiding out in the woods now. Not for eight days. In another day, August Ranier would show up, listen to the arguments for continuing the hunt, make his evaluation, report to Forbisher by phone, and then render the decision. Lasater's mouth tightened as he repeated the phrases to himself, all so legal sounding, so proper and genteel.

He was certain they would not continue to pay the small army Lasater had brought to the coast to watch the old man and the kid. Maybe one operator, or two at the most. They might go for that. He would bring in someone who could get in close to Carmen, and stay close to him. A girl, he thought then, remembering Carmen's body as he had stripped in Taney's house. Even blue with cold and shaking almost uncontrollably, he had been good-looking, so young and unmarked it had been like a stab to Lasater. Hell, he thought, the kid was human, he must be almost as horny by now as Follett. If he could produce a girl who looked even younger, who looked hurt and vulnerable, who asked for nothing and apparently expected nothing, a runaway with a car of her own, a little money, Carmen would figure he could use her to get him to where he had to go. And where he had to go, Lasater had convinced himself, was home to Saul Werther.

'Look,' Lyle said softly. 'She's pretending she hates it. That's stuff he just brought in yesterday.' The female eagle was discarding seaweed vigorously; the male sat on a nearby tree watching her.

Carmen laughed. There was mist beyond the blind; it was too fine and too gentle to call rain, it was rather as if a cloud were being lowered very slowly to earth. Carmen had joined Lyle only minutes earlier; there were mist beads on his hair.

She had been afraid the morning might be awkward, but he had been up when she awakened, and when she had gone into the living room he had kissed her gently on the nose and had continued to make breakfast.

The female eagle reared up and half opened her wings threateningly when the male approached the nest. He veered away and returned to his perch. 'All in the genes,' Carmen said in a hushed voice. 'She's doing what nature programmed her to do.'

Why this pretense of free will? Lyle wondered. She knew the female might pretend to become too disgusted with the nest, with the male; she might pretend to leave, might even go through some motions of starting a new nest. And in the end they would mate here and the fledglings would hatch out and learn to fly from that dead spur.

She found herself wondering about her own attempts to escape Lasater's plans, to free herself from the burden of betraying Saul, her own mock flight to freedom. From any distance at all, it now seemed as programmed as the eagles' behavior, at least her actions and Lasater's. Only Saul and Carmen had been unpredictable. Suddenly she felt that they had been from the start as alien to her as the eagles were, as strange and unknowable. And it had not mattered, she thought, and did not matter now.

'Why are you smiling like that?' Carmen asked.

'I was thinking that you and Saul came to Earth from a distant planet, that you're aliens. They won't find his body because he changed himself at the last moment into a great snowy owl and sailed away in the fog. He could come back as a butterfly, or an eagle, or whatever he chooses.'

'I hope Lasater doesn't start believing that,' Carmen said, laughing. 'He might get the Marines out.'

'Oh no. He thinks that Saul was a Jewish student in Hitler's Germany and that he discovered something tremendous ...'

She stopped at the change that came over Carmen's features. He leaned toward her and suddenly there was nothing boyish about him, nothing soft or tender.

'Tell me what he said.'

'That last morning he stopped me as I was leaving, when I was ill ...' She told him all of it. He did not move, but she felt more alone than she had felt in her life, as if a barrier that could never be scaled had come up between them.

'It's true, isn't it?' she whispered.

'Essentially. Some details are wrong. David's two younger brothers died from Tay-Sachs disease when they were children, and it nearly killed his mother. David and his older brother Daniel swore they would find a cure for it. But Daniel just couldn't make it in school. He dropped out, David went on. The professor was already into genetic research, and he allowed David to pursue his own studies because he saw that the two would come together at a later date. When the two lines did converge they realized they had something they had not counted on. The professor was terrified that the German government would get it, he was vehemently anti-Fascist, and of course there was the danger that David would be picked up and forced to work in a government lab somewhere. So they kept it very secret, kept the papers on the farm the professor's family had owned for two centuries. David's brother knew what he was doing. When David was called up for registration, fingerprinting, the works, Daniel went. No one noticed. All those Jew boys looked alike, after all. So David never was on file actually. David's parents and Daniel were hauled away one day. He found out – they always found out rather quickly – and he returned to the laboratory that night to destroy certain cultures. A Hitler Youth gang caught him there carrying a culture dish across the laboratory. The culture had to be maintained at blood heat or it perished. All he had planned to do actually was to put it in the refrigerator, because there was a danger of incriminating the professor if he actually destroyed anything in a way that could be proven. When the gang burst in on him, he dropped the dish. They threw him down on the mess and rubbed his face in it. Glass, culture, dirt ... Then they took him outside the building and beat him to a pulp, and they dragged him back to the professor's house, and left him on the steps.' He paused. 'The rest of it is pretty much as Lasater suggested, except that the professor wasn't dead. They escaped with the paperwork.'

'If his fingerprints aren't on file, why did it matter if Lasater got a set? It would have ended there when they didn't match up.'

'David's prints aren't in anyone's file,' he said slowly, gazing at the eagles' nest. 'But the professor's are. We simply couldn't be certain they wouldn't be available for comparison.'

'You're saying that Saul is that professor. What about David?' Her voice sounded harsh and unfamiliar to her; she had to make a great effort to speak at all. She was caught up in a battle against disbelief and despair: Carmen was mad, as mad as Saul had been.

'You know I'm David,' he said gently, as if only now becoming aware of her distress. 'Don't look so scared. You really did know already. Watch the eagles this afternoon. I'm going down to the beach. See you for dinner.' He leaned forward and kissed her lips lightly, and then was gone.

Dry eyed, she stared at the eagles' nest. Crazy. Paranoid delusions. It had to be that. Gradually she found that she was accepting that he was mad and that she didn't care, it didn't matter. He had to be insane, or she had to accept something that had kept him twenty for all those years, that had stopped Saul at sixty-four and held him there. Something that had made them both immortal. And she could not accept immortality.

The female eagle returned with fresh seaweed to replace that which she had discarded; her token resistance was ended. The male followed with a long scrap of white material he had found somewhere. Together they rearranged the interior of their nest.

The sun came out and steam rose throughout the forest; the air was heavy with spring fragrances and fertile earth and unnameable sea smells.

And still Lyle sat staring, not taking pictures, trying to think of nothing at all. She would not think about tomorrow or the next day. She would do her job and if Carmen stayed, she would love him; when he left, she would miss him. Each day was its own beginning and ending. That was enough.

But she knew it was not enough. Carmen had pointed out the listening device on the underside of the table in her house. Lasater was still out there, listening, spying. Maybe he thought Carmen would lead him to the papers he so desperately wanted. Maybe Carmen could go to them. And, she thought suddenly, she was still here for Lasater to use. He had put her here, he thought of her as his instrument, his property to use when he got ready, to discard afterward, and so far she had not worked for him. The next time he might use her without trying to force cooperation, without her awareness or consent. When he started moving pieces again, he would turn to her and make use of her, she felt certain. Like the winter beach, she felt buffeted by forces she could not comprehend or thwart or dodge, and like the winter beach, she felt a presentiment of endings, a loss of laughter in the sand.

12

August Ranier had come and gone and Lasater had been stripped of his army with a single word spoken very quietly. 'Do I continue?' he had asked. 'No.'

Ranier had handed Milton Follett and Lasater their termination checks – they had been hired as consultants – and he had left in his dawn gray Seville.

'Let's get out of here,' Follett said.

'Aren't you willing to wait to pick up your bug up in the house?'

'Yeah. I'm driving the camper up there. That little baby cost me sixty-three bucks. Let's go.'

'Milt, hold it a minute. Listen, I know that old man's alive and well some-where and the kid's going home to him one of these days. I know it just like I know the back of my hand. Now that Forbisher's out of it, we could double the price when we get the stuff. You and I, Milt, just the two of us. A million, two million ...'

Milt turned the key and jerked the camper away from its parking spot. He did not even bother to look at Lasater.

'Milt!' Lasater said softly. 'Remember Karen?'

The camper shuddered to a stop and Milton Follett started up from behind the driver's seat. His hands were clenched.

'Would you like another Karen?' Lasater asked, whispering the words.

Follett was pale and his fists opened, the fingers spread wide, then clenched again. 'What do you mean?'

'I'll let you have Taney.'

Follett sat down on the bunk bed. 'Tell me,' he said.

'What if the cops find her messed up, dead, her money, jewelry, car, all gone? What do you suppose they'll think, especially since the old guy disappeared so mysteriously such a short time ago? They'll wonder why a good-looking kid like Carmen was hanging around an old dame like her. But you can have her first, as long as you want, whatever you want.'

'Why?'

'I want that kid to run home to papa. He'll run when he finds her. He'll know they'll be after him, he's not a dope. He'll run and we'll be there. Who's the best team in the business, Milt? Not Turk and that bunch of amateurs. You think there's any way in the world the kid can shake us? I think he'll take us home with him.'

'When?'

'We need a car. One of us has to go up to Coos Bay and get a car, and then we're all set.'

'You,' Follett said. 'Too many people recognize me. You paying?'

'Yep. All the way. I pick up all expenses.'

Milton Follett continued to study the idea. Lasater could tell when he stopped considering it and let his mind drift to Lyle Taney; a film of perspiration put a shine on his forehead.

Outside, the rain started again. It was like a drumbeat on the metal roof.

Lasater was not even certain he had heard a knock on the door until he opened it to see Lyle Taney there with rain running off her. She was dressed in her down jacket and jeans, boots; her hood was pulled low on her forehead. She looked like a commercial for a hikers' club. He grinned at her and stepped aside to allow her to enter. She pushed the hood back and stood dripping on the rug.

'My God,' Lasater said. 'You look great! I've never seen you look better!' Her lips were soft without any trace of chapping now; her eyes were clear and bright, as green as seawater; her face glowed, the windburn totally gone. She had swept Follett with one quick glance, and now was looking at Lasater steadily.

'I think the lady wants to talk to me in private,' he said to Follett.

'Raining too hard,' Follett said, not shifting his gaze from Lyle Taney.

'What can I do?' Lasater asked helplessly. 'He's bigger than both of us. You want a cup of coffee? Let's get that jacket off, dry out a little.' He made no motion, but continued to study her, the changes in her. Always before she had kept herself way back where she thought she was safe, but now she was right out front, not hiding at all. Her eyes blazed at him, straight on. Then he thought, She's sleeping with the kid! He was fascinated and disgusted by the idea.

'Why are you still here?' she asked. 'What else do you want? You drove Saul Werther to his death. What more can you do?'

'He isn't dead, Lyle. Let's not pretend. Werther, the kid, you, me, we're all in this together. We've come too far to try to kid each other.'

'I'm warning you,' she said, 'if you don't get out of here and leave Carmen alone, and leave me alone, I'm going to call the sheriff's office and the nearest FBI office and anyone else I can think of and make a loud noise about an ex-agent and an ex-football player who keep threatening and harassing me.'

'Baby, I'm on their side. National security takes precedence over local affairs every time.'

'You're a liar, Mr. Lasater. I intend to make those calls if you don't get out of here and leave us alone.'

Lasater laughed and reached past her to lean against the door. 'Honey, what makes you think you'll be going anywhere to do any complaining?'

She did not move. 'I asked everyone in the park which camper you and the football player were in,' she said evenly. 'Two tents, a motor home, two campers, and a trailer. Some of the boys thought it was neat to be camping out next to Milton Follett. They might even ask for an autograph.'

Follett made a sound deep in his chest, a grunt, or a groan. Lyle continued to watch Lasater. 'Just so there wouldn't be any excuse to delay,' she said, 'I brought you this.' She took her hand from her pocket and tossed the bug onto the bunk bed.

'She's lying,' Lasater said to Follett then. 'She doesn't want cops asking that kid questions any more than we do.'

'Let her go,' Follett said. He had stopped watching her and now was looking at Lasater murderously. 'She's been using my name around here. Let her go.'

He was infuriated because the plum had been yanked out of reach, Lasater knew. There would be no way of getting him to cooperate again soon if she walked out the door. 'Let's take off, go down to the beach a ways and decide how to handle this.'

'You'll have to move my car,' Lyle said. 'It's blocking you. One of you will have to go out and move it, and some of the people I talked to will be curious enough to be watching.' Now she looked at Follett, as if she knew he was the one to work on. 'I left a note for Carmen, telling him I was coming here. If he comes down, and he will, and finds all of us gone, he'll call the police fast.'

'He put you up to this, didn't he?' Lasater demanded.

'You win because no one really opposes you,' she said, and there was a new intensity in her voice. 'I tried to close my eyes to what you were, what you were doing, trying to make me do. But I'm not afraid anymore, Mr. Lasater.'

She was telling the truth; she was not afraid. He knew it, and he realized that Milton Follett knew it. For a moment the tableau held. Then, as if from a great distance, Lasater heard himself mutter, 'Oh, my God!' and suddenly he knew what it was the old man had found. 'It wasn't a cancer cure, was it?' he whispered. Wildly he turned from her toward Follett. 'I know what it was! Look at her!'

Follett was moving the few steps that separated him from the other two. Savagely he jerked Lasater away from the door. 'Get the hell out of here,' he said to Lyle.

She left. She had not yet reached her car door when the camper shook as if a heavy weight had been slammed against the side of it. She did not look back, but got inside her car and put the key in the ignition.

She started the car, left the camping area, climbed the steep gravel driveway.

He used it on me, she thought clearly, and it seemed as if the rain had come inside the car, was blurring her vision. She saw Carmen on the road and stopped for him. He examined her face quickly.

'You could have been hurt!'

'But not killed?'

For a moment he was silent. She started the car again and drove south, toward the beach where they had walked with Saul.

'You could be killed,' he said then. 'But you could be hurt and hurt and hurt for a long time first.'

She nodded. 'Why did you do it to me?'

'We need help. We have to stay together in case one of us gets hurt. The other has to take care of him. No hospitals. No doctors. There a few others, but they all have work to do, and some of us have to be able to travel here and there.'

'To attend conferences, see who is getting too close.'

'Yes. Lyle, who would you hand it over to? Our government? A church leader? Who should be given it? A billion Chinese? Two and a half billion Asians? Four and a half billion of all of us? A scientific elite? The military? Who, Lyle?'

She shook her head. 'You're as bad as Lasater. Judge, jury, executioner.'

'We know we are,' he said very quietly.

She thought of the immensity of the sadness she had detected in Saul.

'Four people so far have followed that line of research,' he said. 'One of them was already spending his Nobel Prize money. I killed him and buried him.'

They had reached the wide beach. Today the water was almost black under the low clouds and pounding rain. It was low tide, the waves were feeble. Lyle parked and they sat staring out at the endless sea. She thought of the story of the fisherman and his three wishes. This was her third trip to this winter beach. I wish ... I wish ... There was nothing to follow the words. Golden wings, she thought. She could wish for golden wings. Why me? she had wanted to demand of Lasater. Why me?

The windows were fogging up. 'Let's walk,' he said. They pulled up their hoods, left the car, walked in the rain to the edge of the water.

'I don't want it,' she said. 'I didn't ask for it. You didn't ask me if I agreed.'

'I know. If you had wanted it, we wouldn't have chosen you.'

'You can't make that decision for the rest of humanity. No one can make such a decision for everyone.'

'I know. We can't, but we have to, because if we don't someone else will. Who? That night, in Germany, Saul took me to his country house to bury me. When I didn't die immediately, he almost killed me himself because he knew that the Nazis would use me for forced labor, or in an experiment, or kill me outright, or something. He was opposed to the Nazis, but he didn't leave the country as many other scientists did. Instead he immersed himself in work, tried to pretend he didn't know what was happening all around him. There was a lot of that going on. He'd had a heart attack a year or two before. He really thought he'd be out of all of it very soon. But I didn't die. I started to run a fever, like yours, and after a couple of days, the fever subsided, and my cuts started to heal. He had wanted to kill me not only because he knew what the government would do, but because he could see that I'd be disfigured, maybe lose sight in one eye. My recovery was complete,' he said simply.

Lyle stood with her hands thrust deep into her pockets, her shoulders hunched, although she was not really cold. As he spoke, she saw the incident again, saw the beaten, bleeding boy.

'We talked about it, and talked,' he went on. 'We had to get out of the country, not let our work end up in Hitler's hands. Think what it would have meant to him if he had been able to immunize his troops. We had no idea yet of the limitations of the stuff. It just seemed that it would cure anything, wounds, disease, whatever. And we knew that we didn't dare let Hitler get it. But Saul couldn't have left with me. He couldn't have walked all night, hidden wherever he could find shelter, go without food, be out in the winter cold. He was old and he was sick. Thinking about how I had been inoculated decided it for us. The serum entered through cuts and scratches, broken skin was all it needed. We became blood brothers. There wasn't any more of the serum and he didn't dare go back to the lab, put in months refining more of it. Any day his heart might have given out. We didn't know that it could kill half of those who tried it, either. We might not have gone through with it if we had known. I think we became really frightened when it took with him and we realized how easily it could spread. Transfusions, sexual contact, anything that allowed lymph secretions to enter another human body would do it. We began having nightmares about it, afraid we might spread it unwittingly, unknowingly. We got to Switzerland and hid there for the duration of the war. *Lebensraum.* In Germany, in Japan, that's what they said the war was all about. Living space. And we thought we had a secret that would make everyone immortal. We visualized the population doubling, doubling again and again, and everyone living on and on until they all died of starvation.'

'But you said it kills half of those who use it. It almost killed me.'

'We found out later. We had both been lucky. The next two people weren't.'

He started to walk and she fell into step by him. The waves hissed at their feet, made patterns in the dark, wet sand.

'We had taken money out, jewels, we had enough to set up a small lab and we went to work. We happened to come across a scientist from Poland. He and his family had fled the terror, and he was the only survivor. We took him in, included him, and he died.' He stopped and looked out at the gray ocean. 'The other one was my fault. A girl. A refugee, alone, without money, without papers, friends. She ... I fell in love with her. She died.'

Love me and die, she thought bleakly. She remembered the look on Follett's face back in the camper. She had recognized that look, cruelly possessive, hungry. Sexual contact. And the Folletts and the Lasaters would be the ones to get it. The others might all die, but not the Folletts and the Lasaters of the world. Although Lasater knew, it did not matter. No one believed him, and soon he would grow old and die. She gazed at the sea, wishing for a sign, for a rainbow, a streak of gold at the horizon, anything. There was only the gray water rising and falling in slow swells, and the steady rain.

'We watched it all. The Holocaust, the V-Two attacks on England, the fire bombings, the start of nuclear warfare. It ended and we knew we needed a bigger, better-equipped laboratory. We had made no progress at all. We came to the United States, the only civilized place, it seemed, that hadn't been devastated, where we could get supplies, a building, whatever we needed. And the madness went on – the cold war, the McCarthy years, the buildup of nuclear arsenals. The Soviet satellite states. Korea and Vietnam. It was all going to happen again. War was inevitable again, and what we were going through was no more than a pause, a time for regrouping, for rearming. It was like the interstadial of the glacial period we're in. We think the ice ages are over, but the records show that this is a pause among many pauses, a retreat of the ice for a period that is an eye blink, geologically speaking. The ice will come back. War will come back. And it gets worse each time, as if each time it's a new dress rehearsal for the final war. We think, all of us, that the next war will be the final one. And the serum we discovered could be the trigger to start that war.'

A harbor seal barked and was answered by another and both became silent. A seagull screeched once, wheeled away. 'Just the two of you,' Lyle said in a low voice, 'deciding the fate of the entire world?'

'For almost twenty years, just the two of us. Think, Lyle. We believed then that a woman would live on and on, as we seemed capable of doing. Her childbearing years stretching out indefinitely, and her children's and their children's, procreating, limitless babies, limitless new adults to procreate. The population explosion is real now, but it isn't the fertility of the human race that has made the world crowded today. It's altering the death rate. Every time we increase the life span, every time we invent a new device to save those who would have died without it, every time we find new ways to purify water, dispose of wastes ... These are the things that have given us the population explosion. But it's a feeble explosion compared with what we could have handed out, or so we thought.'

'You learned something new,' she said dully. 'What else?'

'In the fifties we began to recruit others. And we found out the real limitations of the serum. Sexual contact with a woman inoculates her, immunizes her, or kills her. And if she's immunized, there is no pregnancy. It's a total immunological system.'

They both stopped. 'But then ...'

He shook his head. 'We thought so at first. There were six of us. We wanted to run in the streets, celebrate, have a party ... Publish. We were drunk with excitement. When we sobered up, we knew this was even worse. Half the people dead, the survivors all sterile. A static world, a dying world with no hope.'

She remembered what he had said to her earlier: 'You could be killed.' Of course – accidents, murders, suicides. God, yes, suicides! A long, slow death of the human species.

'There has to be an answer to that problem,' she said at last. 'If enough people work on it, with government support, a big project ...'

He was shaking his head. 'We thought of that, too. We've recruited some of the best biologists in the world. We've got one of the best laboratories in the world. And we're all as motivated as human beings can get, believe me. We've been searching for even a clue about this part of it for thirty years, following every lead, searching the literature for something we might have missed.' His voice was flat, without hope. 'We haven't dared reveal the secret. What if there really isn't an answer? Sometimes there aren't any.'

Living like pariahs all those years, she thought, walking, seeing the lace edges of waves crumple, fade, vanish. Pariahs, outcasts. Turning others into pariahs, or killing them. Turning her into a pariah.

'Why did you do it to me? I can't help you. I don't know anything about science. What do you expect of me?'

She realized with surprise that they were approaching the car again. She did not know when they had retraced their steps.

'First write your eagle book. We'll stay here and go on just as we've been doing. You'll become rich and reclusive. Saul and I were both happy to meet you because of your book. Others will be happy to meet you, too. They'll be attracted by the same things that attracted us: your honesty and courage, your compassion, understanding, your gentleness and your strength. You'll travel around the world, taking pictures, talking to people, moving on. And now and then you'll meet someone who would work out. We need others, Lyle. We need help in finding them, and recruiting them, and we need someone who can help them accept what it means. No friends beyond our own group, no lovers, no children ...'

Friends, lovers, children, all the relationships that made them human, those were the things they would be told they would have to give up.

'Others for what purpose? To do what?'

'At first we thought no one could ever have it, no one at all. It doesn't change you. You don't gain wisdom, or courage, or anything else. You just keep living, exactly the way you are. But we've decided that if the world could change, if enough people could change ... I don't know if it will work. Sometimes I know it can't. But we have to try. We can't keep waiting for answers we may never find. We have to try something else. A few people here and there, people like you who don't want power or glory, who don't want to drive others to do their bidding. Unwilling recruits every one, the most reluctant elite the world has ever seen. Lyle, if we don't try to do something, this world is going to blow itself to hell. You know that. You ran away from it once.'

'And you've dragged me back into it.'

'Yes.'

They reached the car; she walked to the driver's side and opened the door, looked at him over the top of the car. 'What if I said no? What if I run away again?'

'You won't.'

She felt a flash of anger that they had taken her so much for granted, that they were so certain of her. She looked past him at the ocean. It was starting to get dark; the clouds pressed closer to the sea, as if waiting for darkness to hide their possession of it. Lyle got in the car and turned on the ignition. Carmen sat watching her, waiting.

'Why are you here, at this place?'

There was a long pause before he answered. 'Sometimes we have to go somewhere far away from people, where there are things that haven't changed much, where no one talks to us very much. There are a few mountains, places in the desert, upper Maine, here. We need a place where we can just live without having to think for a while.'

Lyle nodded. When the pain gets too great to bear, you try to escape, she thought – the bottle, pills, sex; and when none of them gives more than a momentary surcease, you go to the woods, or to the winter beach.

'Saul is well, then. It was a trick to get him out of here.'

'Yes. We waited until we knew you had made it. If you had died, it would have been much the same plan. I would have hung around for a day or two, then drifted on.'

How casually he said it, if she had died. She turned on the windshield wipers.

'I kept waiting for you to remember everything,' Carmen said, still watching her. 'Tomorrow I'll send a message to the *Times* personal column to let him know you're okay, you're one of us.'

Now she shifted gears and started to back up. 'I know what the message should say. "Blue float is safely ashore."'

'Welcome home,' Carmen said in his most gentle voice.

She thought of the eagles, beyond good and evil, the winter beach entering a transition now, going into spring, and then summer when the ocean would bring back the scrubbed sand, make amends. All ordered, necessary, unavoidable. She started the drive home.

13

A phrase kept repeating in Lyle's mind: the glow of the beech, the flame of the maple. The cemetery, outside Lancaster, Pennsylvania, ended at a wide, brown field, and bordering that were woods with beeches and maples turning color. This part of the cemetery, the new part, held no mausoleums, no tall columns decorated with sweet angels; here the headstones were low, simple. The path was gravel, stark white against the grass that showed no sign of the drought that had devastated the fields beyond. She could hear the grating of her feet on the stones, keeping time to the phrase: the glow of the beech, the flame of the maple. By a student perhaps. Something she had come across in one of the student magazines or newspapers. The cemetery would soon be out of space, what would they do then? It worried her that she did not know what they would do when they used up the available space. She was slowing; as soon as the realization came to her, she walked faster.

'Do you want to stop to buy flowers?' Carmen had asked.

'No. I just go there and look, sit down for a minute or two, think ...'

No flowers. No ritual to appease her conscience. She regretted that rituals had fused with orthodoxy, with dogma, with rigidity. But was this annual visit a ritual in itself? A set way of behaving, go there and look, sit down for a minute or two, think, remember ... She had reached the Taney plot. She paused and read the first headstone, as she always did: Louise Weber Taney ... Gregory's mother.

Louise Taney had climbed a ladder to pick cherries from their back-yard tree; the ladder had slipped, she had fallen. Gregory had arrived home from school, assumed his mother had gone out somewhere, and had left again to play ball. His father had found her when he got home from work. She had died at midnight. First Gregory's mother, then his son. If only he had done something. Always that same desolate cry, if only I had known, if only I had done something.

She moved past the grave and stopped at the next one. It was indistinguishable from the others, the grass the same, the neat little headstone of red schist, more tan than red, no matter what they called it. The day of his birth had been so hot, over a hundred, stifling, with dead air and the oppressive feeling of a thunderstorm that had not yet shaped itself, but hovered just out of consciousness. Strange how she could remember with such clarity the ride to the hospital that day, how frightened Gregory had been, afraid to drive fast, afraid not to.

She stood at the graveside for a moment, then walked a few feet away and sat on the grass, looking toward the woods across the field, seeing the baby, the boy, seeing the past that remained undimmed. When she began to see the beeches and the maples once more, she stood up, feeling as if she had been gone a long time to a very distant place. She whispered goodbye to her son, and turned to retrace her way.

'Hello, Lyle.' Gregory stood in the shadow of a pine tree.

She stopped. 'Hello, Gregory.' The only surprise was that she felt so little.

'Do you come here every year?'

'Yes.'

'I saw you in town, driving through. I thought you must be coming up here. It's good to see you.'

She started to move again; as she drew closer to him she could see how he had aged, how tired he was. He always had looked older than his years, but it was a shock to see him now like an old man, like his father.

'Congratulations on your book. I meant to write to you, say that.'

'Thanks.'

When she reached him, he turned to walk by her side. The path was so narrow that their arms brushed lightly.

'You look wonderful,' he said.

'And you look terrible. What's wrong?'

'Not much. Just everything. Dad's dying. That's why I'm back here. I'm separated from my wife. The world opened up a crack and I blundered into it.' His jaw was clenched in the way she remembered.

'I'm sorry about your father. Is it his heart?'

'Another attack last week. Intensive care, but the doctor says he won't make it.'

Cry, she thought at him fiercely. Weep, scream, show something! 'I'm sorry about your marriage,' she said.

'Don't be. It was pretty bad from day one.'

His arm brushed hers, and he stopped walking, caught her wrist. 'Lyle, when I saw you in town all I could think of was to find you, talk to you again. Can we go somewhere to have coffee, a drink?'

She shook her head. 'I'm sorry. It wouldn't help.' He had the look she remembered too well, vulnerable, somehow hurt, somehow betrayed that his body demanded a reaffirmation of life at a time when his brain was numbed; it was the look of desperate need.

'Help me,' he said harshly, as if he resented the thought, resented the need.

'Not me. Someone, but not me.'

'You! We never should have drifted apart! I always loved you.'

'Don't do this! Just don't do this,' she said in a low voice. 'It's over and done with. We have different lives now.'

'Just for one evening, one night. Please, Lyle. Can't you give me that much?'

She started to walk, he remained unmoving.

'Lyle, I'm really scared. I need you so much. Just one night let me hold you, someone warm and alive. Just one night. If you ever cared for me at all, please, just one night!'

She ran.

Carmen drove, she gazed out the window at the Pennsylvania landscape, static, yet moving inexorably from summer to fall.

'Are you all right now?' Carmen asked.

'Yes.'

'Can you talk about it?'

He had asked nothing when she had run to the car, crying for him to take her away from there. Her eyes hurt from weeping, and she wanted a drink of water. 'Gregory was there,' she said finally. 'It was bad. He ... he wanted to go to bed with me.'

Carmen let out a long breath. 'I'm sorry.'

'He doesn't really want me, not me, Lyle. He wants the past, back where we were before everything went to hell for us. That's what he wanted for just a few hours. Something no one else can give him, no one but me. And I couldn't.'

'No, you couldn't. No one can give the past to anyone else.'

'You don't understand,' she said wearily.

Carmen reached for her hand and held it. 'I understand exactly, Lyle.'

Looking at him, she knew that he did. She thought of the high north country of Maine where they went occasionally, the Oregon coast, the desert ... Sometimes when it gets too bad, you have to go away from people, she thought, and knew with a pang what that meant. Carmen's face was set in a way that made him strange, like a child wearing an old man's face. She lifted his hand and kissed it; for a long time neither spoke as he drove northward toward the mountains.

Everything had gone as Carmen had said it should. They had stayed at the coast; she had written her book, all she could do away from a good library; then they had moved into a New York apartment, where she had finished the work. To her question about when would she visit Saul, he had answered that first they had to establish her lifestyle. Five months had passed, long enough to show that she was a well-off middle-aged woman with a live-in young assistant. If anyone had been watching her during that time, that was all that could have been learned.

'He's really dead, isn't he?' she had asked one night.

Carmen looked up in puzzlement. 'Who?'

'Saul. Just tell me if he's dead.'

'No, of course not.'

'Then why can't I go see him? I have to talk to him.'

'Soon.'

October had come and her annual visit to her son's graveside.

'Let's take some time, go through the Pocono Mountains. The foliage will be beautiful this time of year,' Carmen had said.

This was part of their plan, too, she thought. Now she would start traveling, establish that she would come and go freely so that when they needed her to go somewhere for them, it would not appear unusual to anyone who might notice.

The countryside flowed by: brown fields, flaming sumac, scarlet maples, yellow poplars. Most of the barns had hex signs on them, all slightly different, all maintained with fresh paint, clearly delineated. The land became hillier and they were in the Delaware River district. Carmen stopped at the water gap, the passage through the mountains the river had made for itself, and they walked to the summit to look out over the farms, the lovely river. Everywhere there were the signs of an early autumn.

'It's because of the drought,' Lyle said, when they started to drive again. 'A drought brings fall, as if the trees have decided they might as well go dormant until spring.'

'I always liked autumn better than any other season,' Carmen said. 'I'm glad we're back east for it.'

'I am too. Where are we going now?'

'A place called Hawley, in the Poconos. Not in Hawley, actually, but near it. There's a pharmaceutical company up there—'

'Saul!'

He turned to grin at her, nodded.

'Why didn't you tell me?'

'I thought it would be better to tell you after you stopped at the cemetery. Maybe that was wrong.'

She shook her head. 'No. I'm glad.' She knew that if he looked at her now, he would see her cheeks flushed, see the excitement she could not hide. And yet, and yet … She glanced at him, away. How many times had she played through this scenario where she had to tell him that it was Saul she loved? Sometimes she played it through to an end, other times she faltered, or she denied it … There were many variations, all difficult, impossible even.

'The place we're going is actually a private residence with a laboratory, the production plant and main lab are near Philadelphia.'

'What's the company name?'

'M and S Pharmaceuticals.'

Lyle exclaimed in disbelief, 'But that's a real company! I use their stuff. My doctor used to prescribe some of their sleeping pills.'

He laughed. 'It's real. We pay taxes and everything. And we do real research.'

'You too?'

'Most of the time.'

'This must have been a hard year for you then.'

'Sabbatical. I was due time off.'

She turned her gaze to the countryside again, trying to assimilate this new information. A real company, real drugs, real identities. 'How old is the company?'

'Twenty-five years now. Saul – Dr. Hermann Franck, that is – is also Clive Markham, the M part, and I'm Joseph Steilburg, Jr., the S!'

'Do other people work there?'

'You mean outsiders? No, not at Hawley. Right now there are four researchers, you'll meet them. Others come and go. They are mostly outsiders at the main lab.'

'How many altogether?' She heard sharpness in her voice.

He looked at her. 'What is it? What did I say?'

'How many insiders? And are they all scientists?'

'Oh. I see. You're the first nonscientist. There are a couple dozen, twenty-six actually, altogether, and you make twenty-seven.'

'Maybe I can keep their computers oiled, or sharpen their pencils for them now and then.'

'Lyle, if we hadn't wanted you, needed you, we wouldn't have included you. We do need you.'

'So you keep telling me. How many women are there?'

'You're the eighth.'

'Do you draw lots for them?'

Carmen snorted with laughter and did not answer.

She had not asked questions before, had been reluctant to talk about any of it when Carmen brought it up. For hours at a time she had managed not to think of a group at all. A small band of lonely men, she had thought once, frustrated in their work, frustrated sexually, forced to maintain isolation from other human contact, how had they survived? She had endured celibacy for several years, but that was different. She had been dead emotionally. She had shied away from the answer she found in her mind. They had endured the same way prisoners do, the same way men at sea for long periods had endured through the centuries, the same way human beings always find to endure. Anyone who could not tolerate celibacy found sexual relief with other human beings, she had concluded, and had thought of it no more. Carmen never had spoken of any women in the group, but she must have known there were some. How else could they have tested the theory that no pregnancy could take place? She had known, had put it out of her mind so thoroughly that it had become almost a taboo, something that was no longer forbidden because it had dropped totally from consciousness.

In her mind the configuration had been with herself between Carmen and Saul; no other pattern would form now. She had been like a child, she realized, refusing to think of something in the hope that it would go away. If she did not think about it today, maybe she would not have to tomorrow and the next day.

After a few minutes of silence, Carmen said, 'Let me tell you about the building. It's rather pretty. Used to be a mill, abandoned years ago, but the water wheel is still there. We generate our own electricity with it. The building is made of stone, as if they meant it to last for all eternity, and the water is so pure, so cold all summer you can't even wade in it without having your feet go numb. A few hundred feet down from the building there's a waterfall with a drop of seventy-five feet. That's the background noise. We set up a bird refuge years ago; people come from all over to bird watch, take photographs. You'll like it.'

'You let other people in?'

'Sure. We have regular maintenance people, a little parking area for the tourists, picnic tables. They don't get inside the main house, of course.'

'And the maintenance people ...?'

He answered slowly, 'They're all local people, outsiders.'

And from time to time you have to get away, go to Maine, or to the Oregon coast, or a desert somewhere ... She sighed. 'Is Saul going to tell me what I'm supposed to do now?'

'I think so. Remember, I haven't seen him either for a long time. And talked to him only briefly a few times. I know as little about this meeting as you.'

It was dark by the time they arrived at the company house. When Lyle got out of the car she heard the waterfall like a noisy grumble in the distance. Then Saul was hurrying to her, his arms out, and the waterfall entered her, thundered inside her head.

'Lyle, my dear! My dearest Lyle!' He held her tightly against his chest and rubbed his cheek on her hair. 'Welcome home, Lyle. Welcome home.'

Several other people had come out were helping Carmen with the bags, embracing him.

'Let's get inside,' Saul said. 'Introductions, hot coffee, a drink, a hot bath, food, whatever you want. Inside, come on now.'

There was a woman's soft laughter at his peremptory tone, and a deep chuckle from a man; as a group, they all moved up the walk and into the building. Saul kept his arm about Lyle's shoulders.

They entered an anteroom with a desk and a few chairs, passed through it into a wide corridor. At first Lyle felt selfconscious with Saul's arm around her, but Carmen was being held by the woman and one of the men, and she had the feeling that touching, hugging, open displays of love, friendship, whatever it was, was the norm here. The corridor was paneled in pale golden wood; there were silk prayer rugs on both sides, and a plush red Persian carpet on the floor. At the end of the corridor there was a circular room, or continuation of the corridor, with a center post that was eight feet or more in diameter; it had a circular staircase leading to the upper floor. Here there were many large potted plants, some nearly full sized trees, all lush and healthy looking.

'I'll show you around properly tomorrow,' Saul said. 'Surprisingly big, isn't it? They used to drive their wagons right inside the building to unload the corn, wheat, whatever they wanted ground. We had to do some extensive remodeling, of course, but as soon as we saw this place we knew it was just what we wanted.'

He guided her through another doorway into a very large room with several groupings of comfortable chairs and a pair of matching couches at right angles to a mammoth fireplace. It was a green and brown room with touches of brilliant red in cushions, picked up in a bowl of chrysanthemums. There were modern paintings here – Kandinsky, Miro … One entire wall was made up of windows.

'It's rather pretty in daylight,' Saul said.

'It's beautiful right now,' Lyle protested. It was beautiful, but more, it was comfortable, with books on tables, magazines here and there, a bowl of nuts with some shells in an amber dish …

'Now, let's see, where will we start? Dora Lewis, Lyle Taney.'

'Hello, Lyle,' Dora said, moving in to shake her hand. Dora was tall and very slender, almost thin. She had the same look of good health that Saul and Carmen had, that Lyle herself now had. And she had the same hint of underlying sadness. Dora was very young, she thought, then corrected herself. There was no way of telling how old she really was. She was striking, but not pretty; her eyes were a bit too deepset, her nose a bit too prominent, her mouth a little too large. When she smiled, Lyle forgot her instant assessment. Her smile was lovely.

She met the others: Hilary Nast, whose accent betrayed his British origins, portly, middle-aged, ruddy complexion with startlingly blue eyes. Steve Trumbull, as young as Carmen, but heavier, with broad shoulders, big hands, and very thick and long red-brown hair. His eyebrows were like woolly bear caterpillars; she bit her cheek to suppress the giggle that followed the thought. The last one was McDermott Evans, Mutt, Saul said gravely. She knew why: his brown eyes were very large and soulful. He was suntanned a deep mahogany color, his hair was wiry and almost kinky curly.

'Do you play bridge?' he asked, still holding her hand.

'Yes.'

'Well?'

'Not very, I'm afraid.'

He let out a whoop of pleasure. 'Wonderful! Confidentially, two of the people present in this room at this very moment are nothing less than card sharks. They must never be allowed to play partners. Now if one of them has you, and I have the other one, we may be able to get a decent game.'

Dora threw a pillow at him, and Saul took Lyle's hand and steered her to a buffet table. 'We didn't know if you'd stop to eat a full meal, or just snack along the way. Anyway, we're prepared. It wasn't easy to keep Steve from gobbling it all up while we waited, I want you to know.'

There were chafing dishes with hot roast beef, mushrooms simmering in a wine sauce, an icy, crisp salad, and tiny pickled carrots. Steve filled a plate alongside Lyle and Carmen.

'Lesson I learned real young,' he said cheerfully. 'Eat when food's available or you might not eat at all.'

Their talk was good-natured, bantering, a little teasing. Anyone looking at them would think what a nice group of people, how pleasant and civilized they all were. Lyle wondered if they fought, if they became angry with each other, jealous of each other. Did they become too depressed to stay and work? She knew the answer to that one. Saul and Carmen had left for almost a year. She tried to imagine how the others would pair up to go away for a few months, a year, two years. They never went alone. Carmen had said they did not dare go out too far alone. What if one of them got hit by a car, was taken to a hospital? 'What would show?' she had demanded. 'How are we different?' He had hesitated, then said, 'If you're really battered and start to heal all by yourself, they might notice. If they give you an anesthetic and it doesn't take, they might notice. Sleeping pills, drugs, they won't work for you anymore, Lyle. Yesterday you scratched your leg, where's the scratch now?' It was gone, no scratch lasted more than a few hours. Her face never got windburned anymore. Her lips did not chap.

We're not quite human any longer, she thought suddenly. None of us here is really quite human. She had sensed a difference in Saul at her first meeting with him, and a bit later she had known that Carmen shared it, even though she had had no idea then what the *it* represented. They all looked radiantly healthy, and tonight the gaiety was unfeigned, was deeply felt, she was certain, but it was the kind of gaiety that comes with a programmed holiday, and when the holiday ends, the gaiety departs with it. Underlying the holiday spirit that Carmen's return had generated, there was a bitter sadness, the same relentless sadness she had detected in Saul. The same despair. They were like prisoners in a common room celebrating Christmas, knowing that as soon as curfew comes, they would once more be prisoners. It made them look haunted in a curious way.

Carmen was in a deep discussion with Dora and Hilary, a technical discussion that Lyle had not tried to follow. Steve was eating cookies. Mutt had gone to the window and was standing with his back to the room. He beckoned to Lyle.

'Look, two does and a buck. They come every night.'

The deer were across the stream, just visible in the light from the building. The buck finished drinking, raised his head. For a moment his eyes glowed orange, he looked downstream and the light was gone. The does drank and they all walked away sedately.

'Hasn't anyone ever taught them about guns?'

'This is a refuge, forty thousand acres. Even so, they'll vanish during hunting season,' Saul said. He stood up and held out his hand for Lyle. 'Would you like to see your room now? You've had a long day.'

She glanced at Carmen in confusion. He blew her a kiss.

'Goodnight, Lyle. See you in the morning.' He returned to his conversation with Dora and Hilary.

Everyone was saying goodnight, sleep well, see you in the morning, and she walked from the room with her hand in Saul's.

14

'I'm afraid your room isn't quite as large as some of them in this part of the building. There are bigger ones in the new addition. If you want to move tomorrow ...' He led her back the way they had entered the building, stopped at the first door in the main corridor. 'Here we are.'

The room was spacious, with a sitting area curtained off from the bed.

There were easy chairs, tables, a coffee table with a bowl of fruit, and there was a wide window that overlooked the stream. Her suitcase was on the floor by the bed.

'It's a lovely room,' she said faintly.

'Your bath is through that door,' he said pointing. 'Are you very tired? Can we sit and talk for a few minutes?'

They went to the chairs, which were in shadows. Light from the bedside lamp was filtered through the curtains. Lyle stood looking out over the water, aware that Saul was watching her.

'You were very upset when you found out, weren't you?'

She moistened her lips. 'Yes. Did you think I wouldn't be?'

'I knew you would be. I'm only sorry I wasn't there. Are you still unhappy?'

She turned to face him. 'Yes. You didn't ask me. You didn't warn me. You just went ahead and did it. What I might have wanted never came into it. I feel ... used. Lasater used me. You used me. It's degrading.'

'I'm sorry,' he said. 'Please sit down.' She sank down into a soft chair and he sat opposite her, across the coffee table. 'Have you remembered that night yet? Remembered it all?'

'Yes. You examined me, took my medical history, gave me an injection ...'

'That was the second night. Have you remembered anything of the first night?'

Her lips had gone dry again. She felt strange, disconnected, apart from herself. She closed her eyes, and saw the fire in the hearth, heard the rain beating on the roof, saw Carmen on the floor, Saul in the chair opposite, speaking.

'*Do you believe that we all have a duty to humankind?*'

'*Yes, but it's too hard to know what it is.*'

'*If you could perform such a duty, at great personal cost, do you think you would?*'

'*I don't know. I think I would, but what does that mean? I think I would be generous, and kind, and good, but I'm not always, not even very often.*'

'*I'm going to tell you a story, Lyle, and then I'll ask you a question. I'll ask you to decide.*'

Her eyes jerked open. 'You told me that night! Before you included me!'

'Yes, Lyle. You decided that night.'

'But I was hypnotized!'

'No. I hypnotized you before that and then woke you up. When we talked you were perfectly normal. Later I hypnotized you again and told you to forget the conversation until you were ready to deal with it. I don't know why you didn't remember it before now.'

She remembered her disbelief, then confusion, and finally acceptance of what they had told her.

'It should be a wonderful, joyful gift!' she had cried. 'Not a burden laden with guilt.'

'Half the people who try to use it die,' Saul had answered soberly. 'Those who can use it successfully are sterile. That is not a gift we can give to the world, not yet.'

And then she had forgotten it all. Why? She looked at Saul who was watching her quietly. When she was with him she believed that she might have a role to play, she might be able to do something for the world, she was not simply another failure. But only with him. As soon as they were parted, she knew herself again. 'Most people who are basically decent really want to serve their fellow human beings,' she had said that night. 'I'm no exception. Only there's usually no way we can find to do it. March in demonstrations. Donate to causes. Serve on committees. And all the time feel futile, feel that we're spinning our wheels, accomplishing nothing. I want to help you, if I can.' And then she had forgotten it again. She was such a glib backslider.

Saul stood up and came to her, holding out both hands.

She shook her head. 'I have to tell you about Carmen and me.'

'I know about you and Carmen. Come, Lyle, I want very much to make love to you, if you'll have me.'

She reached out and he took her hands and drew her up from the chair. They stood apart and she knew he was waiting for her decision.

'I love you,' she said faintly. 'I've loved you from the start. Even when I thought you hadn't been fair.'

'We've had to wait an awfully long time. I've envisioned this night many, many times during these past months.' He stroked her hair gently, then traced her eyebrow with one finger. 'You are so lovely.'

She awakened alone and could not stop smiling. Supporting herself on one elbow she looked at the pillow where his head had rested all night. Several times she had come awake and had reached out to touch him, just to make certain.

'Good morning,' he called from somewhere not in her room.

There was another door that she had not noticed last night. Now she got up and looked inside the other room; it was his study. He was near the window, rising from a deep leather chair. He crossed the room quickly, his smile wide and infectious.

'I left the door open so I could hear you when you began to move. Did you sleep well? Are you hungry?'

'Yes, yes. Good morning.' He kissed her and she left to shower. When she came back, he had coffee and toast waiting, an orange peeled.

'This is why I wanted you in the little room,' he said. 'Next door to me. What I thought we would do first is go inspect the geese. They began arriving two days ago. Did you hear them last night?'

She shook her head.

'And then we'll look at the waterfall, there's a nice path we can take on the other side. I want to show you our refuge. The colors are magnificent right now. Nothing as wild as the Oregon coast was, but still nice in its own way. I think you'll like it.'

'How long can I stay here?'

He poured more coffee for both of them before answering. 'A week, maybe a bit more.'

'When can I come back?'

'Next month.'

She put down her toast and pushed her plate away. 'Isn't there any way I can work here, stay with you?'

'I'm looking for a property to buy, somewhere not far from here. It will be yours, in your name, your retreat. I have two that I want you to inspect this week. Then I can be your house guest.'

'I'll take one! The first one I see! I don't care what it is.'

He laughed. 'No you won't. This is a lifetime investment. You want a house with suitable facilities for a darkroom, for guests, something you'll be comfortable in.'

She laughed too then. 'I'll find something fast. I promise.'

The days were golden, one after another. Each day Saul kept her out for hours to look at geese, to admire the waterfall, to walk in the woods where the leaves were knee deep. She talked with the other scientists from time to time and came to like them all. She got to know the housekeeper, Mrs. Lanier, and her grown daughter, Alice, who was retarded. Saul took her to inspect the two properties that he had mentioned.

The first house they looked at was a derelict, vacant for six years, mistreated for many years before that. They did not even bother to go inside. The second one was too small, a two-bedroom A-frame summer house.

'Why do I have to have a big house?' she asked, back in his study afterward. A freezing mist was painting everything beyond the window with fairy silver. Lyle was on a pillow on the floor, her head on his knees; he was stroking her hair.

'Where were you during the Cuban missile crisis?' he asked.

She glanced at him in surprise. 'I was a student.'

A rueful smile crossed his face. 'I keep forgetting. Of course you were. We were here, Carmen, I, a few others. For several days it appeared that the war we all dreaded was in the making. And we had not done anything to plan for it, nothing. When the crisis passed, we did begin to make plans. We were all still certain we could find answers to the two major questions about the serum, why it kills so many, and how to achieve pregnancy. Just a few more years, we all thought. That's all we needed, just a few more years. But what if another crisis developed? What if the next one was not averted? We had to have something planned just in case. And we needed more help. Our group was too small. So many died,' he said softly. His hand tightened on her hair, then he resumed stroking. 'We built up our staff gradually over a long period, and we were as far as ever from our answers. Two years ago we decided to expand again, this time to bring in people who aren't scientists, but are clear-sighted, intelligent, knowledgeable about the world. People like you. You're the first one we've found. Carmen and I both knew at once that you would fit in, that you would be a valuable asset. If you can help us find others, help them go through the period of adjustment ... You'll need a large house for that.'

The period of adjustment, she thought and nodded. 'What do you want with your larger community when you get it?'

'We need to make decisions. What if we finally have to admit there are no solutions to the problems with the serum? Will we abandon it utterly? Will we break up our group and go back among the public at large, start spreading it through human contacts? Go to the government, start a massive project? Publish? If we decide none of those will be appropriate, will we then try to infiltrate governments? Try to perfect the institutions, the people? Each of these is a possibility. Each has been discussed for many hours, and we have no final decisions about any of them. We decided to postpone all decisions until we had found a few other people to bring in, people not from science, but from the humanities, from history, literature, the arts, maybe psychology ...'

She was shaking her head. 'What you'll get is a mess.'

Now he laughed. 'We talked about that, too. Lyle, I can't tell you how happy I am that you're here. That first night when you came to the house on the cliff you talked about the Titans, Prometheus and his brother Epimetheus, and I could hardly contain my happiness. I doubt that a single one of our brilliant scientists here even knows that Prometheus had a brother, much less what his name was. You made me realize how desperately lonely I had become, and become used to being.'

Later, reading in the living room, she remembered that she had meant to return to what he had said about making plans following the Cuban crisis. There would be time, she thought, and looked up as Dora joined her.

'Find a house?' Dora asked, sprawling ungracefully on the couch.

'No. The search is on though.'

'I hope it's soon. It'll be nice to have someplace close by where we can go when the pressure here gets too high.'

Lyle felt a mild surprise that Dora should have mentioned what she herself had not detected. They appeared loose, easy, comfortable with each other. But there had to be times when they snapped at each other, times when the sight of one of the others would drive any one of them out of the house, away altogether.

'How long have you been here?'

'This time? About sixteen months now.'

'Working on the serum all the time?'

'No way. None of us could take that. We get an idea, run it into the ground and then work on something else until there's a new idea. We've come up with some pretty nifty things for the company over the years. Whenever we get a new idea about the serum, we drop everything and go back to it. I stayed with it for seven years once before it nose-dived.' She looked disgusted.

'How were you brought into the group?' Lyle asked, and quickly added, 'I hope you don't mind my questions. It sounds like prying, doesn't it?'

Dora laughed and waved her hand, as if clearing the air of the objection. She had been one of those child prodigies, she said, with heavy self-mockery. In college by fourteen, a doctorate by twenty-one. 'The great white hope of the University of Wisconsin,' she said, laughing. When she was twenty-four, she had read a paper at an international symposium of biologists in Denmark; she had met Carmen, and through him Saul, under different names, of course.

'They told me where my work would lead, and I didn't believe them. They showed me proof, their notes, diagrams, figures. It was all there. And the conclusions were obvious. If I continued with the work, at the university, others would be involved, they would know. At that point I was pretty much alone and the implications certainly were not apparent. But there aren't any secrets in a university laboratory. The funding comes from the government, work has to be approved, reports written, verified, approved. When I published, others would be free to replicate my work, carry it on even if I dropped out. I had to leave it, Saul told me quite firmly. The only way I could continue that line was by joining the group here, and I could work for the rest of my life on whatever I chose in complete freedom, privacy, with more than adequate funding. Only I would never publish or be famous.' She laughed quietly. 'That's what he said to me, I could work the rest of my life on whatever I chose.'

She seemed to be looking back into the past with a glint of amusement now as she continued.

'I didn't know what to do. I was twenty-four! What did I know? I screamed and had a tantrum and called them names! As a child prodigy I had been allowed to use language. I had been allowed to do anything I damn well pleased. Everyone was scared to death of me because I was so bright.'

'Did they tell you about the sterility? About the mortality rate? I mean, before they gave it to you.'

'Oh yes. Everything. They talked to my brain and my answer came from my guts.'

'But you agreed.'

'The next day. That night I cried and screamed at them for hours, then I did a flip-flop and became all cerebral on them. I went over the work again, point by point, pretended not to believe their conclusions. They knew I was lying. The funny thing is that from the start I knew they both loved me. You don't know what that means to the kind of kid I was. Precocious, funny-looking all my life, afraid of boys, more afraid of men when I grew up. No friends. No social life at all. Hated my family, my pretty sister, handsome dumb brother. I lived in a vacuum. Just me and work. Anyway, they looked through what other people saw and they found something different and showed that they approved of it. I don't know why or how, I don't even know what I mean by that, but it's true.'

'I know it is,' Lyle said. 'That's how it was with me. They loved me, accepted me just the way I was. It was the first time that had happened to me, too.'

'Well, that was in nineteen sixty-eight. I pretended illness and left the conference, went with them, and later resigned from my position, claimed bad health, a breakdown. No one doubted it. Too busy saying "I told you she was crazy." I'm not officially dead, not like some of them around here, but I'm officially through, a has-been.'

The morning before Lyle and Carmen were to leave, Saul got a phone call from Seymour Oliver. Lyle was with him.

'You probably don't know of him,' Saul said, after hanging up, staring out the window at the stream. 'He's the head of the biology department at Harvard. One of us. He thinks the Russians have discovered the serum.'

Watching his face, Lyle felt a chill that raised goosebumps on her arms. She never had seen him like this, distant, hard, cold, ruthless even. For a long time he continued to stare out the window. Then he sighed and looked at her. 'My dear, can you occupy yourself today? I'm afraid Carmen and I have a lot of work to take care of.'

She nodded. He already was lifting the house phone to call Carmen when she left him. In her room she sat before her own window and tried to think what it would mean if the Russians really did have the serum. A new phase, she thought. Something was ending, something else beginning.

That afternoon, too restless to stay inside, she took her camera and tripod to the pond half a mile from the house, and for hours she photographed the geese. There were about a hundred of them by now. Adjacent to the pond was a field with standing millet, food for them, for the deer, for field mice, whatever came along for a free meal. The sun went behind the hill and the air became cold fast. Reluctantly she returned to the residence.

No one was in the living room, or in the room they called the nursery, where there was a pool table, a television, the card table, another table with a chessboard inlaid with mother-of-pearl and black marble. She wandered around the circular corridor and then went up the steps to the second floor. Dora and Mutt were at the far end of the laboratory talking in low voices. There were stone-topped benches and work tables, refrigerators, sinks, burners, shelves of glassware that Lyle could not identify, and several desks. Across the hall from the lab there were two offices, both with the doors standing open.

In the first one there were two desks, a couch, two leather chairs, files, and a library of reference books. The second office had a computer that had made her catch her breath when she first saw it. In here there was a printer, a very large screen, the terminal keyboard, and again, files. No one was in either office.

She went downstairs. This was what she had feared; they all had skills, things they could do, work they wanted to do. She was like a third elbow. She caught a glimpse of Alice Lanier, but that young woman smiled and fled, as she always did. She had said no more than a dozen words in Lyle's presence. Lyle continued to her own room.

Had they discussed this possibility also? It was bound to happen eventually, if not now, that the Russians, or the Chinese, or some other group would find the secret, a group they could not monitor, could not restrict, could not recruit. She remembered the hard, set mask that had come over Saul's face and she knew they had discussed this, had planned for it somehow, and she shivered hard.

Unaccountably, her thoughts turned to the geese stuffing themselves on the millet, preparing for the next leg of their long flight. Responding to signals they could not perceive, they left their nesting grounds, their feeding grounds, and started the hazardous journey to a place many of them had never even seen. Oblivious of the hunters, the traps, the destruction of their resting places where ponds had been filled in, houses built, roads built, they carried out the imperative of their genes. It mattered little that many of them would not arrive, the species was preserving itself the only way it could.

What if the Russians did have it? she thought then. What would that mean? Troubled, and suddenly afraid, she sat down to consider what it might mean to them here at the residence, to the rest of the world.

15

Seymour Oliver and Daniel Malone arrived at ten that night. Lyle had read many of Daniel Malone's science articles in the *New York Times* and the *New Yorker.* Seymour Oliver was white-haired, benign-looking, with pink cheeks and pale blue eyes. Daniel Malone was almost preternaturally tall and thin, like a latter day Ichabod Crane, gangly, awkward in his movements, so slow speaking that she expected him to stammer at any moment.

Lyle had known that someone would accompany Oliver, and after a momentary feeling of surprise to find that it was someone as famous as Malone, she thought, how appropriate. He could go places where none of the others would be admitted. He traveled throughout the world. His credentials were very good; he had been a physicist or something like that. She caught Carmen's gaze and shrugged. If the president or the chief of staff or a senator arrived, she would accept that, too.

As soon as everyone had been introduced and they were all comfortable, Seymour Oliver spoke.

'Let me fill you in on background,' he said. 'Four years ago the International Biology Congress was held at Vienna. At that time I met a number of Russian scientists, including Boris Lepov, whose paper was disturbingly close. I found the opportunity to talk to him before we adjourned. We agreed that there are some things in science that should never be controlled by any government. It was oblique, of course, but I thought at the time and think now we both understood exactly what was being said. We talked a little about the feasibility of forming an international group of people dedicated to the principle of keeping some discoveries out of the hands of governments. Again, I am convinced our understanding was mutual. I told him that if ever he, or any of his people, wanted help of any kind, to please write to me directly and include the phrase "we would appreciate your personal assistance" and finish the sentence any way that would be appropriate. This morning I received such a letter from Boris Lepov.'

There was a long silence that Hilary Nast finally broke. 'Do you think he wants you to help him get out?'

'Not him. He was scheduled to read a paper at the Congress in Amsterdam at the end of the month. He has withdrawn his own paper and presence. One of his assistants, Yuri Korolenko, will appear instead. Lepov has asked for our assistance for Korolenko.'

'Have you met him?' Carmen asked.

He shook his head.

'I have,' Malone said in his halting manner. 'When I was in Moscow three years ago I met Lepov and his assistants, five in all. Yuri Korolenko and his wife, Fanya Shchastny, both worked with him at that time.'

'It could be meaningless,' Steve Trumbull said. 'Political. It could be unrelated.'

'The paper submitted for Yuri Korolenko to read is titled: "Spontaneous Mutations as a Result of Specific Variations in the Gaseous Elements."'

Lyle looked from one to another of them, and when no one spoke she said, 'I don't understand the significance of that.'

'It's a five-year-old work,' Saul said. 'Not even Lepov's work.'

Lyle sighed in exasperation. 'If you all know that, won't it seem suspicious to other people for them to change it at this late date? What was the title of Lepov's paper?'

'He hadn't submitted it yet. Sometimes it works that way,' Seymour Oliver said. 'I'm on the committee, you see. If Lepov said he would appear and read a paper, I'd know it was going to be important enough to allot him program time, and I would hope to get the paper in enough time to have it translated, distributed, and so on. The fact that they have submitted this title tells me that nothing of any consequence is to be presented by them. They'll probably tie this work in with their space program and no one will give it another thought. But when I talked with Lepov we both agreed that the really important work was going on here on Earth, not in space. I read the title as a message, as much as the key phrase is.'

Lyle sat back and for the next half-hour listened to them discuss it, arguing for and against the idea that Lepov wanted them to get his assistant out of Russia. She was startled when Saul looked at her and said, 'Lyle, exactly what would it mean if Russia had this secret?'

'Why me?' she asked. 'You all know more about this than I do.'

'Not more about history, about the odds of one action as opposed to another. What do you think it would mean?'

She thought for a moment about the notes she had made that afternoon. Then she asked Seymour Oliver, 'Has there been another international meeting since the one when you talked to Lepov?'

'No. About every four years more or less is common.'

'Then I would assume that in the intervening four years they came up with the same method you have. And if they did, I would assume that their government knows about it. Depending on when that happened, probably the government has already started testing it on human subjects – prisoners no doubt. That's what this government would do. And the scientific team more than likely is under some kind of restraint if not actually in prison.' She paused, thinking. 'They'll want to find out exactly the same things you do: why the fifty-percent mortality rate, and how to predict it; and why the

477

sterility and how to overcome it. If they have the answer to either question, or both, they will start using it on their top leaders, military personnel, key industrial figures, and so on, in something like that order. And they will probably start thinking seriously of launching a first-strike attack as soon as they know their people are protected from radiation, and before the other side has a chance to develop it for themselves. I also think,' she said deliberately, 'that this is the scenario that either side will follow if that side believes it alone possesses the secret.'

'Why?' Saul asked quietly. 'It isn't a new weapon system.'

'But it is. Civil defense is also a weapon in the war that's going on now. And this can be seen as a civil defense system that is invulnerable to attack with the weapons that are set to be fired. Radiation no longer will be a necessary deterrent to war. If A and B are at parity more or less and either side develops a new system that cannot be equaled instantly, that could be the trigger. We have to leak secrets, and so do they. We are afraid not to. Because paranoia is so rampant, either side will have to assume the other is learning of this secret, and will be tempted to strike before the other gains access and deploys the new system also, or else fear being hit before they can deploy it fully themselves. They call it a preemptive defensive strike,' she finished bitterly. 'Why are you doing this? You must have gone over it again and again.'

Saul nodded. 'We have. I hoped you would see something different. There was the possibility that our own thinking had become paranoid.'

'Remember how the flu and meningitis spread around the world in nineteen eighteen?' Dora said. 'This will spread even faster. The world will go screw crazy!'

'That's why I think there would be very little time between using it and striking,' Lyle said. 'Assuming the Russians have solved the problems with the serum, they will feel most vulnerable during the time it takes to start using it and before it spreads around the world. They know, just as we do, that a small group like this one, dedicated and committed, can contain it, but not the military, not the party functionaries, whoever else they select to receive it. Its only real value as a weapon lies in their being the only ones who have it when radiation covers the world, otherwise it's simply parity all over again on a higher level. We have to keep in mind that our military and theirs are equally crazy. To talk about a preemptive defensive strike is insane and yet both sides do it. They could see this as the deciding factor, just as our government could see it that way, and they could be planning to distribute it and strike very quickly afterward.'

'That's where we kept ending up no matter where we began,' Malone said, studying her with interest. 'But we've lived with the problem for a number of years.'

'And I've read history for a number of years. There's nothing in all the history I've ever studied to make me believe this crop of political leaders is any different from the others that have gone into the history books starting more than four thousand years ago. Smith and Jones have fought over that shrinking water hole from the dawn of civilization.'

'You said we leak secrets,' Mutt Evans said thoughtfully. 'Of course we do, they do. We're scared to death they may think we have the edge, and so are they. But what if this leaked? There could be a new Manhattan Project-type research group set up with orders to discover the secret overnight. It can be found, you know. Dan found it, others can.'

Malone said to Lyle, 'I caught on to their little secret. Lost my greatest book, I'm afraid. They drafted me.' His voice was rueful. 'But that's right, it is out there to be found. It's just that no one really believes in it.'

'Hugh Lasater does,' Lyle said.

'And no one believed him,' Carmen said.

'Not then. But if they suspect there's anything to it, if they suspect the Russians have it ... They'll believe him enough to follow up on what he told them,' Lyle said with certainty.

We should have killed him, she thought, and felt a deep chill at the ease with which the thought formed, wrapped itself in words. She looked at the others, Saul with his eyes that had gone so hard and cold; Carmen intent, frowning in concentration; Mutt, Dora, Steve, all thoughtful, all capable of killing. Hilary Nast could do it without a qualm, coolly, neatly, expeditiously, and then go back to his newspaper or novel without another thought of the deed. And Daniel Malone? Could he? Could Oliver? Judges and juries, all of them. Deciding the fate of the world. She closed her eyes hard. They were keeping the world safe for death.

'To get back to the question,' Oliver said then, 'I'm afraid a leak is the last thing we want right now. There's the time element,' he said apologetically to Mutt. 'If they've had it a number of years or even months, they've had time to start producing it, if that's their plan, if they've decided it's safe enough to use. They'll be watching so closely there's not a chance of duplicating that kind of work without their catching on to it. I'd say every biologist in the country must be under surveillance at this point, if that's what they're up to. Any sudden activity in that area might be the signal for them to make their move.'

'And if this government finds out and realizes that they're that far ahead, possibly ready to start mass distribution, *that* could be the opening move,' Malone added.

'We have to know,' Carmen said suddenly. 'What are we going to do about Yuri Korolenko?'

'What does he look like?' Saul asked Malone.

He gazed at the ceiling thinking. 'About five ten, slender, almost delicate looking. Dark brown, rather thin hair, sallow complexion, brown eyes. Twenty-five to thirty, I'd say.'

'Why would they send him, a nobody?' Dora asked.

'Oh, I expect because they think he'll go back. He and his wife were newly-weds when I met them.'

'Why let anyone go to the meeting?' Lyle asked. 'You'd think if they really had it, the government would forbid any of them to go anywhere.'

'It would look too suspicious for no one to show up from that team. They are the foremost biologists in Russia. It might make other people go back through their past papers to see what they were onto.'

'We don't know for certain that he'll want to leave,' Saul said then. 'Maybe he just wants to talk to Oliver, tell him what they're doing, ask his advice. We don't know. But if he does want to leave, we have to have a plan. Any ideas?'

'Wouldn't they turn to the CIA for something like that?' Lyle said. 'You certainly don't have the manpower for such a maneuver.'

'Remember, they may want to keep it out of the government's hands,' Saul said. 'They may have the same scenarios in mind that you outlined for us. If this government knows what they have, it could be disastrous.'

'We'd have to do it before the conference gets started,' Carmen said thoughtfully. 'Away from the conference center. It'll be swarming with CIA, KGB, God knows who all.'

'He'll be watched closely, at the center or away from it.'

'Franz can help. That makes three of you who will be there,' Carmen went on. He looked at Malone. 'You could be interviewing Franz while on a sight-seeing tour. Franz already asked Yuri to go along, so he's there, too. You probably would be a little annoyed that Franz is making it a party, taking Oliver along, taking Yuri. Anyone else going to be there?'

Oliver nodded. 'Luis Betancourt.'

'He's part of the group too. That's enough. You go to Anne Frank's refuge, take a ride on the canal, end up at the Van Gogh Museum and that's where we make the switch.'

'What do you mean?' Lyle asked sharply. 'Who? What switch?'

'Didn't you hear the description he gave? He described me to a T.'

'*No!*' She looked from Carmen to Saul. He was nodding slowly. 'You can't let him do it! It won't work! They'll just end up with Carmen and their own man!'

No one paid any attention. Each of them seemed to be considering the plan, each of them willing to risk him. She stood up and went to the buffet where the coffee was on a heating unit. Her hands shook when she poured it. Capable of killing, capable of losing Carmen. Inhuman, all of them.

She stood with her back to them, not listening to their talk any longer. They were trying to come up with a workable plan to get Carmen out. What if this Russian scientist told them his group really had it? What would they do? What could they do? She remembered her notes, her conclusions, and asked herself if she believed them, and had to answer yes. Either government was capable of starting the next war over a misunderstanding, over a series of incidents that might escalate, over a third country, over a secret as world-changing as this one was. And the next war was destined to be a war of extinction – except for anyone immune to radiation, she corrected herself. Even they, though, even they would be doomed, eventually, when the food ran out, when a poisoned earth could no longer support crops, when the animals and birds died. They had to know that, the governments had to know that. They knew it now, and pretended it was not true. They acted as if they believed their own statements that a nuclear war could be won; if either side had immunity from radiation, that side would certainly believe the war could be won. Did they have it? Did the Russians have it? They had to find out, she admitted to herself. They had to know.

She stared at the coffee cup that she had put down when her hand shook too hard to hold it steady, and now she lifted it again, and returned to her chair. Her hands were no longer trembling. She had stepped back, had become an observer, very distant from everyone in the room.

'... pass as a waiter. Your Dutch is still fluent, isn't it?'

'Sure. And be sure a bike is waiting for me to use. That sounds pretty good.'

Pedal away from all the spies in Europe on a bicycle, Lyle thought in disbelief. She shook her head slightly. 'I'll have to bring Yuri Korolenko home. Do I bring him straight back here, or to my apartment?'

Carmen looked at her sharply, but again Saul was nodding.

16

Hugh Lasater never slept past six o'clock. He had tried blackout shades, and plugged in a white-noise machine, but it made no difference. Six in the morning and there he was back in the world, no matter what time he had gone to bed the night before, no matter how many nights in a row he had stayed up late. This morning he looked at the woman on the other side of the bed with dislike. At six in the morning none of them looked good. Suddenly he realized that he should not be able to see her and could only because the bedroom door was ajar, the light on in the hallway.

Noiselessly he slid out of bed and removed a .38 from the nightstand drawer. He did not bother with his robe or slippers. Let the dude see him naked, he'd never tell what he saw, he thought grimly, and went to the door, keeping flat against the wall. No one was in the hallway. He listened. The kitchen. Water running!

Now he went back for his robe and slippers. He put the gun in his pocket, keeping his hand on it, and went out into the hallway, down the length of it to the kitchen, listened. Making coffee! He pushed the door with his foot.

'Morning, Hugh.' A man standing at the sink, running water into the coffeepot, turned and grinned at him. 'Don't shoot.'

'Alex, what the hell are you doing in here? How'd you get in?'

Alex Radek, he thought coldly, could get in wherever he chose. Whenever he chose. They had worked together often enough for him to know locks did not exist for Alex.

'Now, Hugh, that'd be telling. You always liked it pretty strong, didn't you? We both will need it strong this morning.'

'What do you want?'

'Just some talk for openers, but not until the lady friend is gone.'

Hugh turned and went back to the bedroom, shook Marcie awake. 'Up and at 'em, tiger,' he said. 'Business. Come on, time to be up and out.'

'My God! It's the middle of the night! What's wrong, honey?'

'Told you, business. Five minutes, sweetie. Give you five minutes.'

She was groaning as she staggered toward the bathroom. He went back to the kitchen. 'She's on her way.'

Alex shook his head admiringly. 'You can really pick them. Toss her out at six in the morning and she doesn't even holler. I couldn't get away with that. I didn't even dare wake up Lori.' She was his wife.

When Marcie was dressed, Lasater hurried her to the door.

'Don't I even get a cup of coffee?'

'All-night place half a block away, sweetie. Call you later.'

Her look was venomous. 'Don't bother.'

He closed and locked the door after her, and went back to the kitchen where Alex was pouring coffee for them both.

'Okay, give.'

Alex Radek was forty-seven. He had served in the Navy, then Naval Intelligence, and finally CIA, where he still worked. Lasater had known him for at least twenty years, and it didn't mean a damn thing, he thought, watching Alex. On either side, he added.

'They want you in Virginia,' Alex said. 'You think you have it rough, this early-morning stuff. They called me at five. It's the difference in time, you know. They never remember that three-hour difference. Rawleigh was bright and cheerful, already had his shower, his breakfast, shaved. Called from home. Would have been better if he'd waited to get to the office, at least. Would have given me another hour of sleep. We have a plane to catch at eight-twenty. Drink up.'

Lasater grinned and sat down at the kitchen table, sipped his coffee. 'Hot. There's just one little hitch, Alex, old pal. I don't work there anymore, remember? They can call you and tell you to get your ass to Virginia, but not me. Not anymore.'

'Maybe they want you to come back, after all.'

'Nope. Tried that back in April. No dice.'

Alex sat down and leaned back. 'It's like old times, isn't it, Hugh? You and me sparring when we both know exactly what we'll be doing at eight-twenty.'

'Rawleigh say what he wants?'

'You know better than that. Does he ever say more than six words at a time on a long-distance call? Rawleigh the miser, remember?' He glanced at his watch, then said, 'Almost forgot. Stopped for some Danish on the way over. Don't like to fly on an empty stomach.' He went to the counter and picked up a paper bag, brought it to the table, and sat down again.

Lasater helped himself. The rolls were still warm. Again Alex looked at his watch. The phone rang and Alex nodded in satisfaction. 'Right on the button,' he said. 'It's for you. Rawleigh.'

Lasater pushed his chair back, reached up, and took the wall phone. 'Yes?'

'I was hasty last April,' Rawleigh said, sounding just as he always had, like a prissy schoolteacher. 'I want to talk to you about that material you have. We may want to purchase some of it. Alex will bring you to the farm.' He hung up.

'Bastard!' Lasater snapped and replaced the phone.

Alex grinned in commiseration. 'Don't forget to pack some warm clothes. It's already getting cold back east.'

Flying across the country, Lasater tried to fix a scenario that would play. Rawleigh had turned him down flat in April, not interested in anything Lasater had dug up about anybody.

'It's our budget cuts,' he had said. 'Can't do anything with the money they're giving us this year. Sorry.'

Lasater no longer wanted them to take him back. Now he wanted cash for what he had. Cash deposited in a Zurich bank, with a secret number and everything. But how little could he tell and still have a product they would buy? He would not tell them about Taney, he had decided already. Probably not about Carmen. Just the old man. He'd give them the old man, let them play games with him. He had confidence that Werther would not be found, not after being on the run for all those years. He had tricks he hadn't even thought of pulling out of the hat yet, he was certain. Crafty old bastard. They could chase their tails for a long time looking for him, and he, Lasater, with money to back him, would get on with it. How much should he ask for, how much should he settle for? That was the hard part. Rawleigh talked like a man with his mouth full of marshmallows, but he was shrewd, and he was miserly.

In April Lasater had asked to be taken back, had told enough of what he knew to tantalize them, and they had treated him as if he had lice. Now they could screw, he thought coldly. Demand half a million, and accept half of it. No less. He closed his eyes and napped until they were ready to land at Dulles.

Grover Rawleigh liked to tell people that he was a simple farmer; his family had been farmers back four hundred years or more. The real satisfactions came from growing things in the good land, the good earth. His farm had been in the family for six generations, his father born in the upstairs bedroom, his grandfather before him born in the same room, laid out in the living room when he died ... He entertained congressmen, visiting dignitaries, the president even, not this particular one, but others before him, and no doubt there would be others after him that would make their way to his farm. Hollywell, it was called. Everyone who worked on it, the house staff down to the stable hands, were all ex-spies.

Lasater and Alex were greeted by Aunt Jane, the housekeeper, who had appeared one day without a past, or a past known only to Rawleigh. She was forty-five, handsome, and had an accent that might have been Slavic. *He* was due at nine or a little after, she said, serving them roast chicken and mashed potatoes in the kitchen. Home-grown chicken, garden potatoes.

'You'll have the same room as usual,' she told Alex. 'And I'll show you yours as soon as you finish eating,' she added to Lasater. 'You two boys are the only guests we have right now. Do you want apple pie for dessert?'

Grover Rawleigh liked simple food, good country food.

It was after ten when Rawleigh sent for Lasater. Rawleigh was sixty years old, six feet five, just starting to show a paunch, deeply sunburned, with pale brown hair that was thick and lustrous. All those home-grown turnip greens, Lasater thought sourly, greeting him.

'Hugh, you look fit. Keeping busy? Alex, you've had a busy day, why don't you turn in?'

Alex waved at them and vanished, closing the library door after him. The books in the library were all leather-bound, behind glass doors.

'Sit down, Hugh. That's a comfortable chair. My father had it made. He was a big man, bigger than I am. Needed specially made furniture.'

Lasater sat down and waited. Rawleigh chose an even larger leather chair and grunted when he sprawled out in it. 'Getting old,' he said. 'Too much running around, too much traffic, can't take it anymore.' He stretched out his legs, reached high with both hands to stretch his arms, then relaxed.

'Well, Hugh, you gave us a little problem last spring. Did you bring your material with you?'

Lasater shook his head. 'I don't keep stuff like that in the house. And there wasn't any time for a side trip.'

'Too bad. Should have thought of that. Oh well. Tell me about it again, just to make sure I haven't forgotten anything.'

'Business first,' Lasater said pleasantly. 'I made an offer and you turned it down. Your turn.'

Rawleigh laughed. 'Pissed you, didn't I? Can't blame you. You wouldn't believe the budget they expect us to operate with! It's incredible! We can offer you an independent contractor's stipend, the usual thing. Can't hire anyone full-time, just can't do it.'

'How much?'

'Ten thousand.'

Lasater stood up. 'I've had a busy day, too, come to think of it. Maybe I should turn in.'

'If it's good, I can go to twenty-five, but that's it, Hugh. Believe me, if the money was there, I wouldn't hesitate, but ...'

'Oh, I believe you,' Lasater said. 'Really. But I'm not in a hurry. I've been sitting on this stuff for a long time, it's not going anywhere. Things will get better. Light at the end of the tunnel, all that stuff. I believe in it. Things will pick up again.'

'Hugh, not too fast. Whatever happened to Milt Follett?'

'You've got me. What?'

'The LA police department's asking questions still, I understand. You ever tell them you were with him just before he disappeared?'

'Did he disappear? I hadn't heard.'

'Yes, right after you abandoned the siege of Mrs. Taney and her assistant. Never did show up again.'

Lasater waited.

'Did you report that little transaction to IRS, Hugh? The cashier's check, or was it more than one?'

He sat down again, waiting, watching.

'You can have twenty-five thousand, although it's going to mess up our cash flow, you understand. If what you have is good enough to warrant it.'

The next day when Lasater woke up it was nine o'clock, East Coast time. He grinned. The only way to beat the six-in-the-morning routine was to go east. When he got down to the kitchen for breakfast, Aunt Jane told him that Mr. Rawleigh was at work, and Mr. Alex had left very early. He could ride one of the horses, or take a walk, or read, whatever he wanted that day. Mr. Rawleigh would join him for dinner.

Hugh Lasater detested horses, except at races, where, he had to admit, they looked damned good running their hearts out.

'Pretty dreary out there,' he said glancing out the window. Everything that wasn't growing was painted white, fences, barns, sheds, the stable. The trees were bare but no leaves were on the ground. It was a *neat* farm, also an isolated one, miles from anything.

'You should have been here last week before the leaves were knocked off. It was so gaudy, like a postcard. Then we had a rainstorm, and that was the end of them.'

He wandered around the house after breakfast, almost decided to take a walk, and thought better of it. He did not mind walking when he had to get somewhere, but to walk for the sake of moving his feet and legs never struck him as necessary. There was a smaller library off the one that obviously was for show. The smaller one had books that people actually read: paperback mysteries, half a dozen biographies, even Taney's book about hawks. He looked at it thoughtfully; a page was dog-eared two thirds of the way through. He sat down and picked up a mystery and opened it, and thought about last night.

He did not know how much Rawleigh believed. He had told him the same story he had told Taney, had drawn the same conclusion that Werther was the kid from Germany, getting old, and very crazy now. A man with a secret cure for cancer. That was the sticking point. Now when he said it, when he considered it, he wondered why anyone had ever bought it. Why he had bought it. It was so patently ridiculous. Say Rawleigh did not believe it, then why was he sending Alex back to California to get the evidence Lasater had stashed away? Why was he shelling out twenty-five thousand dollars? His mouth tightened when he thought of the amount. It would be enough, he had decided last night. That and his own money, and Milt's money. It would be enough.

But they were holding out on him. Something had made Rawleigh hot for him now after all this time. Something had made him dig around to find a lever to use if Lasater came on stubborn. Something was going on and no one was going to tell him shit about it. He turned a page, just in case anyone was watching, give him something to report. Subject sat in red upholstered chair for two hours and turned pages now and then.

It was fair that they were holding out on him, he thought, and flipped several pages, as if bored with the story. Tit for tat, that was fair enough.

'Hugh, it really isn't sporting to charge us for the tip that you got from our own files,' Rawleigh chided that night.

'I reported to Cushman. He said to forget it, not interested.'

'Yes, Cushman. Too bad he's dead now. He's seen the error of his ways, I'm afraid.'

'Yeah, too bad.'

'It certainly does appear circumstantial, doesn't it? There he is time and again at the scene of the crime, you might say.'

He looked through the pictures once more, sighing. 'You're certain he didn't die in that car crash?'

'It was the oldest trick in the book. A real setup. They waited for the foggiest night of the year to pull it, burned down the house and everything, just like from a script.'

'But your erstwhile, ah, employers believed he died.'

'What do they know? Naive, all of them.'

'Yes, of course. Now tell me again about Mrs. Taney, and the young man, Carmen? Is that a man's name?'

'Damned if I know. Look, why again? We've been over it three times. You know everything I do. I'm a good agent, I don't forget details and plug them in later. Let's get some sleep.'

'You say she cried, carried on when she found out that the old man was presumed dead? Was it an act?'

'No. She's a schoolteacher, not an actress. She turned white as a ghost, dropped her cup. I thought she might pass out. I told you she'd been sick, good and sick. Nearly died. It was a shock to her.'

'Strange, isn't it, how she formed such an attachment to him in such a short time. She's a mature, intelligent woman, educated, experienced. I wonder how that happened. I mean, if your neighbor dies a violent death, you're shocked, but you don't act personally grieved, now do you? Most people, I mean.'

'I told you I think it's because she was still weak and sick. She wasn't normal yet. It hit her harder than it would have if she'd been well.'

'Yes, you did say that. And then the young man stayed on with her. Isn't that strange?'

'I don't know. She liked him, they were sleeping together. Maybe he thought she was a soft touch.'

'Yes. Opportunistic young people like that don't really care much about appearances, do they? Are they still together?'

'I told you that, too. I don't know. I paid the grocery store clerk to tell me when they left the area. It was in July. I lost them after that.'

'Of course. It's good that you didn't hang around and keep them under surveillance, after all, now isn't it? All those months! You say she came to you and threatened to call the local police, the FBI, news media, and so on if you didn't leave her alone. That suggests that she still believed Werther was dead, that there was nothing for her to hide, doesn't it? Was she sincere?'

'Milt thought so. So did I. We pulled out.' He looked at his watch and yawned.

'Hugh, I don't understand. West Coast time it's only eleven. I thought you were a night person.'

'It must be the country air. Look, let's knock it off. You pay me, and I go to bed, and tomorrow I go home. Okay?'

'Oh dear, I'm afraid I did forget a detail. We'll want you to stay on the East Coast for just a few days, to identify someone for us next Tuesday. Can we help you get a hotel room in New York?'

'You paying expenses?'

'Of course.'

'I'll get a room. Who is it?'

Rawleigh smiled gently. 'We'll want you tell us that.'

Lasater stood up. 'You want me to call, give you my address, room number, all that?'

'Yes. Just tell anyone who answers the phone. Aunt Jane, probably. Alex will be in touch on Tuesday morning. Be certain to keep the day free.'

'You bet.' He paused as Rawleigh picked up the pictures once more. 'You were going to pay me my independent contractor's stipend, remember?'

'Sorry. Let's see.' He reached inside his desk drawer and pulled out a large manila envelope. 'Twenty thousand now, and Alex will pay the other five on Tuesday. Is that agreeable with you?'

'You know damn well it's not!'

'Of course, I know,' Rawleigh admitted with a sigh. 'It's just that we're so used to doing business this way, it's hard to break the habit. I'm afraid I didn't bring more than twenty thousand out with me.' He pushed the envelope across the desk. 'An assortment of used bills, nothing over one hundred. It'll take you a while to count it, I'm afraid.' He began to examine the pictures.

17

Tuesday was a mystery to him. He knew about the international conference coming up in Amsterdam, due to start Tuesday evening with opening ceremonies, a cocktail hour, whatever they did to break the ice. But Tuesday in New York? Taney and the kid, maybe. That shouldn't be a deal for them. They knew as well as he did that they were still living together in a posh New York apartment. Or they could know it if they were interested.

He flew to JFK, made a phone call there, took a limo to Manhattan, and checked in at the Victory, where they found a room for him when he produced a twenty.

Later he walked the few blocks to Fiftieth, turned left and went another half block. The street was packed curb to curb with traffic; the sidewalk packed with transients, down and outers, call girls, pimps, spaced-out cases, nuts, all pushing, all in a hurry. It was ugly and it stank. He found the address he sought and looked at the building with disgust. It was crumbling, the sidewalk before it was broken, the curb worn down to nothing. This was why he had moved to the West Coast; New York was on the skids, no doubt about it.

He paused before the jewelry in the window of the ground-floor shop, but he knew no one was following him. Not yet. After today he would not come here this directly, but for a short while it was safe enough. He left the shop window and entered the building through the business door into a dusty short foyer with a ten-watt bulb over an elevator door. There was a directory that he ignored. When the elevator wheezed to a stop and the door opened, two young men in jeans and leather jackets got out talking Arabic or something. He stepped in and pushed eleven, praying the elevator would make it.

Herb Balinski was a licensed private investigator; his sign on the door admitted it in chipped and fading letters. He had been trained in the FBI but had run afoul of Hoover himself over, it was rumored, his fondness for adolescent boys. Balinski never said. His office had good upholstered furniture, good paintings on the walls, and he was dressed conservatively in a three-piece suit as if due to make a presentation to the chairman of the board at any minute.

His polished desk was bare, except for a white ornate telephone, but his secretary's desk had the usual clutter of in and out baskets, typewriter, a couple of notebooks.

'Lasater, good to see you. You get a room at the Victory? Settled in okay?'

'Yeah, it's okay. Thanks for the tip.'

Lasater had known him for eight, ten years. Balinski was good, he delivered, but he never looked as if he knew his way around the block. He looked dumb. Big open face, blond hair, an ingratiating smile.

'Well, as you see, I let my secretary go early, while I stayed put this afternoon, waiting for you. Didn't know you were east again.'

'I'm not. Short visit. Too damn cold here, and too ugly.'

'It's what you get used to. I can't take those waving palm trees myself. What can I do for you? You said on the phone you wanted me personally. That was a nice thing to say, but I have several top-notch people working for me these days. Business is pretty good.'

Lasater had called him from the airport, and he was getting the impression now that Balinski no longer worked cheap. He sighed. 'There's a woman, Lyle Taney, and a kid she's living with I want watched.' He wrote her name and Carmen's, and their address in his notebook, tore the page out, and handed it to Balinski.

'How close?'

'Real close. I have a feeling that she's going to bolt and run in the next few days and I want to know where to. That's all. We'll play it by ear.'

Balinski pursed his lips. 'Close means three people around the clock. Doesn't come easy, Lasater. You know? My people like to eat too well. Not like the old days, not anymore.'

Lasater sighed again. 'When she runs, I don't want it to be one of your people who follows her. I want it to be you.'

'That's real flattering, you know. Okay. Five grand in advance, and we'll see how long that lasts at five hundred a day.'

They settled the details, Lasater counted out five thousand dollars in cash, got a receipt, and then said, 'I'll call you every day. If you want me, leave a message about insurance. I'll call back.'

For the first time Balinski looked interested.

Lasater called the farm and talked briefly with Aunt Jane. He went to a movie, had dinner at a delicatessen, and finally at eleven returned to his hotel. There was a message from an insurance agent waiting for him.

He got Balinski at home.

'You're off the hook with your money for a while,' Balinski said. 'The woman and the kid are out of the country. In Europe somewhere. Won't be home until Tuesday.'

'Jesus Christ!' he muttered. 'Okay. I'll see you on Monday. Not at the office. I'll call.'

Europe! The Netherlands, he thought coldly. Amsterdam. And that son of a bitch Rawleigh knew it. Something had happened recently, since they left, and now all at once he wanted a look at the kid. It had to be that. Her picture was on her book, had been in the papers; she was too easy, but the kid ... That's who they wanted him to finger for them. Carmen. When they returned on Tuesday. But why Tuesday? The conference started Tuesday night and they'd be home by then. Unless they were delayed? Something would come up to keep them for another day or two? Must be.

He left the pay phone, took the elevator to the twenty-third floor to his room, and there sat at the open window looking at the lights, the traffic far below, too distant for the noise to intrude enough to interrupt his thoughts. He should have asked Balinski how long they had been gone, he thought, but decided it really didn't matter. Not long, or that faggot editor would have told him. He thought briefly of the people he had manipulated in order to get to Taney in the first place: her department head, the magazine editor, the book editor, the clerk at the grocery store ... Everyone had had a handle he had found, everyone had a soft spot for him to poke. They all delivered. And then Taney had balked at playing. He could almost admire her for not caving in, almost.

So she was in Werther's camp now, taking orders from him, doing his dirty work, although she had looked at him, Lasater, like some kind of low-life because of the job he had tried to do. And what difference did it make in the long run, who had the secret? They were the selfish ones, the Fascists, trying to keep it to themselves, even killing to keep it. His people would have made a buck with it, sure, but they would have made it available for a price, and there wasn't any price too high. Not any.

His room was stifling, the way New York rooms were summer and winter. It did no good to turn the heat down; the controls accomplished nothing. He opened the window wider. Wasteful. No wonder his room cost eight-five a night.

When he finally went to bed and closed his eyes, he saw Taney walking toward him, handing something to him. The same image he had carried from the beginning, the image of Taney coming through finally. And she would, he said softly to himself. She would.

18

London had been rainy, cold, gloomy, and exciting down to their last day. They had met her editor near Fitzroy Square and, after lunch, she and Carmen had walked through the neighborhood, stopping to point now and then: 'Look, Virginia Woolf lived there!' and again, 'H.G. Wells!'

It was strange to walk the same streets that Virginia Woolf had walked, to see the same houses, the same park, the same trees even. Had Mr. Wells paused here for a carriage, at a corner where a kiosk now sold newspapers, flowers, cigarettes, and candy? Had he walked through that small park deep in thought about his Martian invaders? Deep in thought about his men in the moon? Had Virginia Woolf looked at the trees across from her house only to see the lighthouse that beckoned, ever beckoned? Listening to the wind through the window had she heard the mysterious rhythms of the waves?

They had viewed the crown jewels, had visited the Tower of London, the majestic buildings that contain the Houses of Parliament, and they seemed contrived now that she had seen the house where Virginia Woolf had lived and thought and written, the house where H.G. Wells had dreamed his fantastic stories. Money could buy a magnificent building, could buy gems of inestimable value, but no money could buy one exquisite phrase of an inspired writer, she thought. No money could order the sensibilities of a Woolf, the linkages of a mind like that of H.G. Wells, who combined and recombined the familiar to invent the new and wondrous.

Dreamily she permitted Carmen to guide her to the bus stand, and dreamily she boarded it when it came, and took an upper-level seat. Neither spoke now. The London skyline was another of those things that could never be ordered, planned, bought. Against the chimney pots, here a gargoyle, there a lion rearing like horse. There a pair of angels ...

The bus filled as they drew nearer Piccadilly, but suddenly it swayed to a too-fast halt in the middle of a block.

'All out! Out here now!' the conductor began to call.

'Why? What happened?' Lyle asked, bewildered.

'Riots in Piccadilly,' someone muttered as the upper-level passengers began to leave their seats, file down the narrow, curving steps.

When Lyle got to the front of the bus, she could see through the wide windows a mass of people a few blocks ahead, but not until they were on the sidewalks could she hear the dull roar that surged, ebbed, surged.

'Come on!' Carmen said, clasping her arm, nearly dragging her in the opposite direction. A few blocks later they were able to find a taxi that took them to their hotel.

'If I were you, being Americans, I mean, I think I would stay inside this evening,' the driver said kindly. 'By tomorrow it will be quiet again, I'm sure.'

They watched the riot on television in their room. It had started in Covent Garden, a rally against American rearmament, but had erupted explosively until it had filled Piccadilly Circus, where cars were overturned, buses set afire, store windows smashed. Late that night there were still fires smoldering in a cold drizzle that held the smoke low, made the area look like a scene from Dante.

They went to Sloane Square to a pub for a light supper and even here where they had had meals nearly every day since their arrival, they were met with hostile looks and open snubs. They ate quickly and went back to their room.

The next morning they flew to Paris.

When you're playing a role, Carmen had said, you have to be it every minute of the day and night. No lapses. They played it well, she thought, watching him the day they arrived in Paris.

He carried her camera gear and hung back a step or two at the hotel desk, probably flirted with the young woman who was at work there. Her gaze kept drifting to him as Lyle signed the register.

He had been like this when she first met him, she remembered. She had believed then that he was Saul's handyman or something. Not subservient, but neither was he an equal, that was apparent in his every movement, his every look. When she walked to the elevator, he was slightly behind her. Lyle glanced back at the reception desk and caught an amused look on the face of the clerk. It was clear what she thought, at any rate.

They had a two-room suite, and if the rooms had been joined to make one, it would have considered small by American hotel standards. A porter followed them into the room and put down the bags.

'No!' Lyle said sharply. She walked out stiffly, back to the elevator, not looking to see if Carmen or the porter followed. She returned to the desk and made a scene with the receptionist. She had reserved bigger rooms, she insisted, a suite of large rooms. It was robbery to charge a fortune for broom closets.

'But, madam,' the woman said in flawless English, 'we have no other suites.'

'Then we will go elsewhere.' She glanced at her watch. 'I have an interview in one half hour. I have no time now to inspect other rooms. Carmen, take care of it.' She swept from the lobby. End act one, she thought, and wondered if they had noticed the shaking of her hands, believed it was from anger.

She returned three hours later, tired, from a magazine interview, a session with a fussy photographer who spoke no English but smiled a lot, and from a difficult television interview. She had not expected that one. Her publisher had arranged it, had been jubilant that he could work her in on such short notice.

At first she did not recognize Carmen when he crossed the lobby to join her near the entrance to the hotel. On this trip he was wearing a wig that was exactly what his own hair would be like if he ever allowed it to grow too long: thick black curls like a bush. And now he was wearing a pale gray cowboy hat with a spray of feathers, and a red and gold band.

'Where on earth did that come from?'

'Shop around the corner. Isn't it neat! They love cowboys here.'

'It's ridiculous. Did you change our rooms?'

'Yes, ma'am. A really nice suite overlooking the garden in back. You'll like them.'

'Tomorrow we have a luncheon with my editor and his publicity people. And on Friday there is another luncheon. We'll have Thursday and Saturday free.' Still talking, she entered the elevator and waited for him to press the button for their floor.

As soon as they were moving, she slumped against the wall, and looked at him miserably. He winked.

'When I was a little girl, eight or nine,' Lyle said, looking at the stained-glass windows in Notre Dame, 'my father brought me here, and I burst out crying. I never did understand why exactly.'

'Not even now?'

'Not exactly. I think I was simply overwhelmed by it all.'

She turned from the *Rose Ouest* and glanced back through the cathedral. People were everywhere, walking up and down the aisles, looking at the engravings, the candleholders, all the magnificent art that adorned the walls, every niche. Off to one side there was a mass being said, the faithful on their knees, oblivious of the tourists coming and going. Somewhere in a clump of people a loud German woman was talking, talking.

Out there, among the tourists, the faithful, was there someone watching her and Carmen, noting their actions, where they went, whom they saw, what they did, how they treated each other? She said abruptly, 'Let's get out of here.' Carmen looked like an ugly American in his grotesque cowboy hat, carrying her camera everywhere they went, ogling the women. She looked like a rich bitch with a pet on an invisible leash.

The next day they went to the Jeu de Paume. The Louvre would take a full week, she had said, choosing the smaller museum.

'Besides,' she said, standing below Monet's water lilies, 'this is what I wanted to see again.' She had had a fantasy once in which she had glided in and out among the lilies, never touching them, but feeling them with some other sense that she could not locate. She could not recall what form she had had in the fantasy; no form, probably, just a spirit weaving in and out of the flowers. She backed far enough away so that she no longer could see the brush strokes, and for an instant she almost achieved the same feeling she had had that other time. The moment passed and she was outside looking at them again. She wished she could talk to Carmen about the feeling, what it meant to her to be able to slip inside the painting even for an instant. She felt tears form and turned away, not wanting to see anything else now.

Their last real talk had been on the day they had left Pennsylvania when they had walked to the pond.

'Why did you volunteer?' he had asked.

'Not because I think it will work. I don't. But it has a slightly better chance this way than any other.'

'Is that all?'

'No. I want to be with you as long as possible. I'm afraid for you, afraid I'll never see you again.'

'I'll be back within a week of your return,' he said.

She had stared at the pond, at the geese floating easily in the cold water that looked like liquid steel, hardly rippling it with their movements. He touched her shoulder and when she turned toward him, he took her into his arms and kissed her. She wept.

'I think I must be crazy,' she had said. 'I love you. I love him, too. I don't want you to go. I don't want to lose you.'

'I'll be back,' he had said again. 'I don't want to lose you either, Lyle. I'll be back.'

In the car returning to New York, he had outlined their plan for the trip, had gone over the details thoroughly, and they had not talked of anything else. And then they had stepped into their roles for the next act, and they would not leave them until they met again at the laboratory, if they met at the laboratory.

She left the museum, trusting him to follow. A fine mist was settling on the pavement, on their clothes when they walked toward the corner to hail a taxi.

That night they had dinner in a small restaurant not far from their hotel. 'Our last night in Paris,' Carmen said. 'Let's hit a night spot or two.'

At the next table several Englishmen were talking in loud voices, complaining about the sandwiches in Paris. 'Thick pieces of bread with a crust no one could bite, no one. And buried somewhere a transparent piece of ham, if you can find it. I told them, more ham, and cheese for God's sake, enough to see without a post mortem. I told them.'

Lyle looked at them with distaste, then glanced at Carmen. 'I'd rather not. I'm a bit tired.'

'You've been tired ever since we got here!'

The Englishmen stopped talking, watched them with interest.

'That's not true. But tonight I'm tired. I've had an exhausting week with interviews, luncheons, too much sightseeing. It was your idea to walk for miles today.'

'I may never to get to Paris again. I want to see some nightlife!'

'I don't.'

'And it's your money, isn't that the rest of it? Isn't that the next line? You bought me and paid my way, I'm to behave myself right? Wrong! I'm going out tonight!'

He stood up, picked up the cowboy hat and jammed it onto his bush of curls and stalked from the restaurant. Lyle signaled to the hovering waiter for the check. She could feel her cheeks burn as she began to count the unfamiliar money. Finally she pushed too much across the table, gathered her purse and coat, and walked out, looking straight ahead. At the door Carmen fell into step a few feet behind her, and they returned to the hotel not speaking, not looking at each other. When she entered the elevator, he remained in the lobby, his hands jammed into his pockets, scowling.

The next morning when she paid their hotel bill, she was cool and distant with him, treated him exactly the same way she treated the porter who carried their bags out to a waiting taxi. She did not speak to either of them.

At the airport she checked them both in, then left him to change the remaining French money for Dutch guilders, again without speaking. It was as if he had become a necessary shadow, a robot that carried her camera bag, nothing more than that.

In Amsterdam at the hotel she changed their room reservation. 'I'm sorry,' she told the man at the desk, 'there's been a mistake. We need two rooms, obviously.'

'But madam, your wire, here it is, it says a large room.'

'Two.'

She got the large room overlooking the canal, and Carmen was to be put in a back room that the manager moaned over as inadequate, but all they had. If only he had known … It was fine, Lyle said, cutting him short.

'As soon as you're settled,' she said to Carmen, looking past him at the wall, 'I want to take the boat ride, and walk over to to Dam Square to see the Royal Palace.' She did not wait for a reply, but went to the staircase and up the one flight to her room.

It was comfortable, with antiques; the view was lovely even if the canal looked frigid, and the naked trees were all shivering in a steady wind that had come straight down from the North Pole.

Lyle had a heavy, fur-lined raincoat, and Carmen wore a shapeless black mackintosh that came down to his calves. There was a light, icy rain, the wind was piercing. They walked the three blocks to Dam Square, but they took a taxi to the boat loading area several blocks beyond. There were few people out that Sunday afternoon. Last week there had been demonstrations, but now it was quiet. When they looked at the glassed-in launch with its few passengers, they changed their minds and walked to a sandwich shop instead.

'The idea,' Carmen had said, 'is to let anyone who might be watching see that we're together, what we're wearing, see that we're not speaking, hardly even bothering with each other by now. That's going to be important, our attitudes toward each other.'

The sandwiches were delicious, inches high with delectable ham, topped with cheese, the crusty rolls meltingly soft inside, liberally slathered with butter that made Lyle close her eyes with pleasure. Why weren't they all obese, she wondered, glancing at the other people in the warm, cheerful shop. She did not let her gaze falter as she recognized a man near the door, ordering something. She had seen him at the airport, buying a newspaper. It had to be coincidence, she told herself, it was too clumsy otherwise. Even she would not let herself be seen twice if she were following someone. Unless they wanted her to know, wanted her and Carmen aware that they were being watched, that they would not be able to get away with anything.

'Are you finished?' she asked sharply then. 'It's stifling in here.'

The man's order had not arrived yet. Would he leave? Would he remain there, prove her wrong? Carmen picked up the camera bag and they walked out. The wind-driven mist was sharp and penetrating; she pulled her coat tightly around her, glanced both ways down the street for a taxi.

'We'll have to go to the taxi rank at the corner,' Carmen said, starting to walk ahead of her.

She caught up with him, keeping her head ducked against the wind.

'Don't look back,' Carmen said in a low voice. 'He's there.'

They got a taxi at the corner and returned to the hotel and did not leave again that day. There was a small restaurant off the lobby where they ate Indonesian food for dinner, and then went to their rooms.

Lyle sat at her window looking at the canal with the play of lights on it for hours that night. Here the streets were too narrow for more than one car at a time, and sometimes the cars were lined up from corner to corner waiting for someone to park, or leave a parking space. One day they would close in their canals in the name of progress, she thought, trying to follow a ripple of light from its source to its demise. That would be the end of Amsterdam. Maybe they would reject the notion when it was seriously suggested. She almost wished they had taken the boat trip, even though the glass had been fogged, visibility terrible. To glide over the canals would be nice. Too bad they were not yet frozen, or did they still let them freeze solid? Stories of Hans Brinker and his magic skates stirred in her mind. To skate the canals would be lovely.

Van Gogh had walked these narrow streets. Rembrandt. Just a few blocks away was the house where the child Anne Frank had been hidden for two years, had left a childhood hardly even lived, had become an adolescent, and then had died. Had been killed. Intrigues, deaths, wars, always they intruded on the beautiful, the peaceful, the human.

Where would a watcher post himself out there? In one of the parked cars? Shivering, wishing he were in a warm bed, wishing someone else had drawn this assignment.

One more full day to get through, meet her Dutch editor, see the cover art he had commissioned for her book, meet the artist, have dinner with them, pretend Carmen was invisible ...

She closed her eyes, wishing they had had this one last night together, wishing they were back in New York, back on the Oregon coast, anywhere but here.

When this was over, she would leave them both, she decided. She had to leave them both. All the others acted as if they were on an ocean cruise, loving each other, leaving each other, but she could not live that way, not with the confusion that made her thoughts spin and curl around themselves and refuse to come to an end that she could accept. She would walk away from them, until, perhaps in some future, she had found a way out of her dilemma and could return easily, as easily as the others did.

Out there in the cold rain someone was watching, someone who believed that she and Carmen had come here to murder a scientist. And in other circumstances, another time, that was what they might have to do. Cold-bloodedly, mercilessly, as deliberately as the Nazis had taken the girl Anne Frank out of her refuge and killed her. Where was the difference? Saul could make it sound reasonable, plausible, acceptable. Carmen could also. But here in the dark, staring at the canal, knowing someone was watching and waiting for murder, she knew she could not accept it. As soon as she knew Carmen was safe, if he ever would be safe again, she would leave them both, leave them to their deaths, their intrigues.

The pain she felt already at the thought of leaving them both was intense and real, and again she wished Carmen was with her, in this room, in that bed that she was so reluctant to get into. He would understand that she was afraid, she admitted then. His danger was greater than hers, but she could be caught, seized, imprisoned, interrogated ... Now that she had shaped her fears with words she started to shiver. If she had to be caught, please, she thought at the silent canal, don't let it be the Russians. She was most afraid of them. But it would be bad, she knew, if any secret agency caught her or Carmen. They all had learned from the same teachers, used the same great weapon of terror against their victims. Her shivering increased until she was forced to crawl into the bed, under the down comforter, where she huddled staring at the ceiling until a pale light filtered through the curtains.

19

Monday was as bad as Lyle had anticipated. She met people she could not remember an hour later, pretended interest she did not feel, ate food she could not taste, and when night came and she was alone in her room, she stared again at the canal until the lights across it went out one by one, and until she started to shiver violently and was forced into bed, where she could not sleep.

Tuesday morning they ate a leisurely breakfast and then went to the reception desk together.

'We're checking out,' Lyle said to the clerk on duty. 'Is it possible to hire a taxi for the entire morning? We have a plane to catch and have to be at the airport by one, but I want to see your museums before we leave.'

'Indeed it is possible,' the clerk assured her. 'When will you want the car?'

'Half an hour. That should give me time to finish my packing and settle our bill, I think.'

It was nearly eleven when they reached the Rijksmuseum, and it was raining again. They left their suitcases in the taxi and Carmen carried the camera bag over his shoulder. Inside, he had to check it, as they had known he would. They went straight to the painting *The Night Watch*.

Lyle caught her breath sharply. She had only seen this one in copies that she realized had all been bad. The flesh in the painting was alive, glowing; the clothes were fabric, woolens so real she felt that if she were to touch them her hand would sink into the material. Each face was expressive, with living lights behind the eyes ... She did not know how long she had been standing there; she had entered the painting, just as she had entered the water lilies painting before. She had been there, had seen those people, had felt them, had known them. She had seen them with Rembrandt's eyes, sensed them with his senses ...

'We have to leave,' Carmen said, pulling her arm.

She blinked dazedly and followed him to the check stand where he retrieved the camera bag. They left the museum, and, she felt, entered a world confounded by time. Slowly she shook off the disorientation. This is what linked all people, she wanted to say, in spite of time and space; this joined them in a timelessness, a spacelessness, in a collective mind that transcended all boundaries. This is what endured forever and ever, as long as the painting was preserved, as long as the written word endured. Sappho's few words, Plato's, Homer's ... The works of a great artist entered that other kind of reality, the words of a great poet lived there; this is what human history is all about, our efforts to transcend our limitations, our petty wars, our fears. We build cathedrals, paint pictures, write our poetry, our music, all in the same effort to transcend ourselves. They fill the history books with trash about conquests, wars, treaties, and they are transitory. The human spirit sails high above them, yearning for that other reality, finding it in moments through great art ...

The taxi had stopped again, this time at the Van Gogh Museum. The driver looked at his watch and said, 'If you have to be at the airport by one, we should be on our way there in half an hour. It is not much time for a museum.'

It was raining somewhat harder now; they ran to the entrance, Carmen's hat pulled low, Lyle's hood down to her eyes. Again Carmen had to check the camera bag. They wandered through the lower level for a few minutes, then went upstairs to the van Gogh collection that started with his early, more conventional work and progressed to his last paintings where the brush strokes were inches long and, at close range, the paintings merely blobs of color. Backing away from them, Lyle could almost see the colors merge, blend, magically fuse to make coherent houses, trees, flowers. At what point did the change occur? One moment there was the incoherence, the work of a madman, and then it was orderly, sublime. She could not find the one point where the change happened.

'I'm going to the john,' Carmen said at her shoulder.

She froze. Now it would begin. 'Give me the check for the camera,' she said, amazed that her voice worked. 'It's nearly time to go. I'll get the bag.'

He handed her the check and walked away, the ugly American in his wet cowboy hat, his shapeless raincoat. She forced herself to turn again to the painting, but she no longer could see it.

Wait one minute, then go down to get the camera.

Halfway down the stairs she saw the group of men heading for the lavatory. There was Seymour Oliver, talking, joking with a strange man; there was Daniel Malone talking more earnestly with someone else, including now and then in his comments the young Russian who kept his head lowered. Two of the men had heavy coats. The other three, including the Russian, wore raincoats. She had gone down steadily; when she reached the ground level she no longer could see the Russian. Two of the other men were taller, broader than he was; only from the higher vantage point of the stairs had it been possible for her to pick him out. From up there the plan suddenly had become ridiculous, doomed. No one would be fooled.

The men disappeared into the lavatory and she went to the check stand for the camera, took it to the outside door to wait. She looked out through the rain for their taxi. The driver waved urgently to her, pointing to his watch. She nodded and looked back inside impatiently.

It was going wrong, she thought in despair. Something had happened; they both had been caught in the restroom ... Then she saw the cowboy hat and the black raincoat, and she opened the door, held out the camera bag for him to take. As soon as his hand took the strap, she ran ahead of him to the taxi, did not look back. The driver had got out, was holding the door open. She hurried to get in, the Russian right behind her.

'We must hurry, madam. I was afraid half an hour was not enough time ...' The driver closed the door, rushed to get in behind the wheel.

'Now we can go,' Lyle said. 'There surely isn't much traffic at this time of day?'

'No. We will make it. Don't worry.'

He turned on the windshield wipers, and they moved away from the museum, away from the other taxis, the other waiting cars. Lyle did not dare look at the man beside her. She kept her gaze out her side window. The driver had accepted him. No one in the museum had looked at them suspiciously, she was certain. She did not look behind to see if anyone was following. Someone would be, of course, someone who did not believe they intended to fly out of Holland this afternoon without even attempting to kill a scientist, or kidnap one. Her hands were clenched; slowly she relaxed her fingers. They were very stiff.

The landscape spread out flat, was lost in rain and clouds in the distance; the canals were like gray ribbons holding the sodden fields in place. Traffic was light; the driver concentrated on the road that held a skim of water; now and then he muttered about the windshield wipers. They were hardly able to keep the rain off enough for visibility.

'There it is,' he said finally, nodding off toward their right. 'Not quite one right now. You have plenty of time.'

It was nearly ten minutes before they came to a stop. The driver found someone to help with their suitcases, and wished them a pleasant trip when Lyle paid him and tipped him generously.

Again she did not look directly at the man with her, but went ahead, following the porter to the check-in counter where there was a line. Near the head of the line was Hilary Nast. He was dressed in a heavy tweed overcoat and was chewing reflectively on a pencil stub. When he got to the ticket agent, he said in a voice that carried to the end of the line, 'I say, you don't think our flight will be delayed because of the weather, now do you?'

He was assured that there would be no delay, his bags were checked through, and he sauntered off a few feet, stopped suddenly, and drew a folded newspaper from his pocket. He looked at it intently, filled in a section of a crosswood puzzle, and walked on. In front of Lyle a man and woman watched him, smiling.

'The English are crazy,' the woman said. The man nodded.

Was the watcher still there? Still watching? Would he board with them, sit in the first-class section with them, go to New York with them? Lyle's fingers were clenched again; she felt as if a heavy weight were on her chest restricting her breathing. They should have warned her about the fear, prepared her for this, rehearsed her. At the counter, she pushed her ticket across silently, watched her companion load the suitcases onto the scale, and saw that his hands were trembling. At once she felt removed from the scene, distant from him, from the line, the man behind the counter, as if she were watching everything from a safe place.

'Nonsmoking,' she said calmly, almost coldly. 'Will there be time for a coffee before we depart?' She picked up the tickets he was returning to her. Her fingers were quite steady.

'Yes, madam. There is a first-class waiting room where they serve coffee, wines, cocktails, whatever you wish.'

He directed her, then looked past her at the next person, and she walked away with her companion a step behind her, carrying the camera bag, the cowboy hat low on his head, the shapeless coat hiding his body.

'I would like a cup of coffee,' she said, hoping to ease his tension, hoping the trembling of his fingers would not yet betray them both. 'You must want something also. It's been a long time since breakfast. Of course, we'll have dinner on the plane, but that will be quite a while ...'

In the waiting room, seated in comfortable chairs with a tiny table between them, their coffee in delft cups, Lyle looked directly at Yuri Korolenko for the first time, and she could not conceal her start of recognition. He seemed to glow with good health, as Carmen did, and Saul, and as she did also. She averted her gaze, but not before he acknowledged her recognition with a very slight nod. When he picked up his coffee, his hands were no longer trembling.

Their flight was announced and the first-class passengers were escorted aboard before anyone else. Yuri took a window seat, let the back down all the way and stretched out, the cowboy hat over his face. The steward smiled at Lyle. 'If he falls asleep before takeoff, will you see that he is upright, please?'

She nodded. 'Yes. We're both very tired. He'll probably sleep all the way.' The steward took her coat to hang up, offered to take Yuri's. 'Perhaps later. We were chilled by the rain.'

Three seats in front of her, Hilary Nast was settling himself. Other people on both sides were arranging their carryon bags, finding books, surrendering coats and hats to the steward ...

Which one, she wondered. Which one would watch her every movement, Yuri's movements, ready to pounce if either of them made a mistake? She leaned back and closed her eyes. It was futile to guess. A spy who looked like a spy would be a failure.

As soon as the plane was off the ground and the FASTEN SEATBELTS sign had been turned off, she went to the lavatory, locked the door, and leaned against it taking deep breaths. They had done it! Now she felt weak, faint almost, and, curiously, she wanted to weep. She found herself wishing that alcohol still had an effect on her; she wanted to drink a very large brandy, to get lightheaded from it, to celebrate the success of her part of the plan. She looked at herself in the mirror, clear skin, clear eyes, unlined face, a youthful woman going into middle age, who had given up drinking. She sighed. She would settle for a very good wine, glass after glass of it all the way home, and let them wonder how she had managed to build up such a tolerance.

And, she knew, she would try to follow the thread of tortuous reasoning that now presented itself. She had recognized Yuri exactly the way Lasater had recognized her on the Oregon coast. It was unmistakable – the glow of health, the clear eyes, the lovely smooth skin ... Soviet science, like all Soviet institutions, was closely supervised by the government, and that meant the serum was controlled by the Soviet Union. How to use it would be a state decision, a political decision. They must have felt secure in their belief that no one had penetrated the secret, that no one even suspected there was a secret. Their first thought now would be that the CIA was involved, that the United States government had learned about the serum, or had learned enough to seize the scientist. No doubt they would also assume that he would tell everything eventually. She found herself going over the scenarios they had talked about that last night in Pennsylvania and she knew that all at once the world had become an extremely dangerous place for every living creature, more so than at any previous time in its history.

20

Right up to the time that Alex Radek collected him to go to Kennedy, Lasater believed that their jaunt would be cancelled. Lyle Taney would come down sick, he had reasoned, or the kid would, or they would be delayed and miss their flight, or something. They were not likely to leave Amsterdam before the biologists even got started on their meeting, he was certain. He was surprised when Alex entered the coffee shop promptly at one.

To his relief they took a cab out to the airport. That made him believe that Rawleigh had been leveling with him, that they only wanted an identification; they did not want to pick up anyone. He knew this routine. He would make the identification; someone would be around with a camera taking pictures, and they would all fade away, job done. Then they would run the pictures through and come up with zilch.

The driver talked about the damn Puerto Ricans, damn voodoo economics, damn kids standing on bridges throwing rocks at cars passing below. Alex blew his nose a lot and ate throat lozenges and talked about the damn cold weather when he could get in a word. Lasater felt no urge to say anything. He hoped he would not catch a cold from Alex; he did not even want to breathe the same air Alex was breathing.

They entered the terminal and Alex looked about discontentedly. 'God, I hate airports. I remember how I used to love them, all of them, no matter how ratty. Flying was still exciting.'

'Yeah, back when the dinosaurs roamed. I know.'

'You too?' Alex glanced at him and sighed. 'I guess we're both getting on, a little long in the tooth. Takes a hell of a lot more than a plane in the sky to fire us up these days. Sad, ain't it?'

'If I had a violin, I'd play. Honest. You going to tell me anything yet?'

'Soon. Let's go look at the board.'

The terminal was as crowded as usual. People were sleeping sprawled out on the floor, in chairs. Little children were running, laughing, screaming. Teenagers were trying to look bored. Young couples looked forlorn, or elated, or stoned, or all three. Nothing was out of the ordinary. Lasater did not spot Herb Balinski, and had not expected to. He did not know Balinski's associate, did not even try to find him in the crowd, nor did he try to find Alex Radek's camera man. Let them do their thing, he thought, following Alex to the arrivals and departures board. He did spot the plane from Amsterdam: three-ten, on time.

'Nearly half an hour to wait,' Alex said. 'You want a beer, or something? Let's go to the bar and I'll fill you in.'

Lasater shrugged. He drank very little; ulcers ten years ago had put him on the wagon for over a year and afterward he had not found it necessary to pick up old habits.

The bar was dark and there were empty tables although men were standing hip to hip at the bar itself. 'What do you want?' Alex asked. 'I'll get it. Never get waited on over here.' Lasater told him a beer and watched him ease his way between two men at the bar. He came back with the beer and a screwdriver for himself. 'For the orange juice,' he said.

They drank in silence until Lasater said, 'You were going to tell me a story, remember?'

'Yeah. It's your girlfriend, Taney, and lover boy. We want to know if she's still playing house with the same kid who was on the coast.'

'You couldn't just wait outside their house, apartment, whatever? Had to drag me down here for this?'

'They've been on this trip for a couple of weeks,' Alex said in a tone that was almost conciliatory. 'They'll get home and go inside and maybe not come out again for days, tired of traveling, tired of restaurants. You know how that goes. It seemed easier this way.'

'Yeah, yeah. When do they come in?'

'Oh, I thought you saw on the board.'

'Pal, you haven't even told me where they're coming from,' Lasater said. It was like old times, he thought, sparring with Alex. He had been right about that. Testing each other, always testing, that's how it had been with them.

'Right. Amsterdam. Due in at ten after three. Our man in Amsterdam sees them off. We see them in. It's a miracle, isn't it? They leave Amsterdam at two and get in at three.'

Lasater looked at his watch. 'Christ! They'll be an hour in customs. You want another one of those? I'm getting another beer.'

At four they made their way to the corridor where international travelers entered the terminal. There was a mob there.

'This is the pits,' Lasater said with disgust. 'I can't get close enough for her to get a glimpse of me. What am I supposed to do, turn on my x-ray vision and look through the jerks?'

'Take it easy,' Alex said, but he looked worried now. 'Come on, if we stay back near the wall, she'll go past and you'll get a look at her and the kid, right? That's all we want. No chat or renewing old acquaintances, anything like that. Just a good look at the kid.'

People were coming through the corridor, being met, hugging, kissing, vanishing with their loved ones, or their creditors, or whoever it was who met planes.

The crowd did not thin out; if anything it seemed to increase moment by moment. Suddenly a shrill voice cried: 'There she is! She's coming!' Now the crowd surged forward, and Lasater saw that the parcels many of the people had been holding were being unwrapped, bags opened, satchels unstrapped; they were carrying Lyle Taney's book on hawks. A goddam fan club, he thought savagely.

'What the hell ...?' Alex muttered.

'Yeah, you and your bright idea, get them before they lock themselves away ...'

He saw her then and instantly she was surrounded by a couple dozen fans thrusting books at her for her autograph, all talking, pushing, shutting her up in a people wall. Briefly he had seen a cowboy hat, curly hair sticking out, but too briefly. A tall, broad man in a tweed coat, enveloped in the mob, was in the way. His voice carried over the others.

'Oh, I say, are you a cinema star? If only I had known on the flight! Dear me, don't push, please, you'll crush her ...'

The mob surged past, headed toward the door where the sign said TAXIS, the tweed man talking all the way, completely blocking the view of Lyle and the boy in the cowboy hat.

'Shit!' Alex said.

'That says it. I'm going home. You have something for me, right?'

'Yeah. I'll call the farm and be in touch with you in a couple of days. You hanging around?'

'Do I have a choice?'

'Hugh! What a thing to say. Here you are, the envelope. I hope you don't want to count it in here.'

'I'll trust you for it, until I get to my hotel room anyway. You going back to town now?'

'Might as well. Can you wait just a minute? I want to speak to someone first.'

'I'll be at the door over there. You paying the taxi back?'

'Yeah. What a bust. And me with a sore throat and a cold. Shit!' He looked at Lasater hopefully. 'Did you see enough to say one way or the other?'

'Are you kidding?'

'Yeah. Goddam!'

Lasater waited while Alex went to find his camera man, who could not have had any better luck than they had. No way could anyone have got a picture of them. A perfect setup, he thought suddenly, right down to the dude in the tweed coat, surrounding the kid. Why him? What was so special about Carmen all at once? He never had tried to keep a low profile before. Why start now? Suddenly he started to laugh. They had pulled it off! Hot damn! That wasn't Carmen; he must still be back in Amsterdam, or in a rowboat heading for England, or in a wet suit swimming one of the canals. They had lifted someone and brought him home in Carmen's place!

Alex returned and looked at him sourly.

'Foiled by the Bird Watchers of America,' Lasater said, still laughing.

He nodded toward a small group of young women who had been in the mob around Taney. One was showing her autographed book to the others. 'She'll actually come out and talk to us,' she was saying. 'And bring the pictures they couldn't use in the book! Wasn't she wonderful!'

Lasater glanced at Alex, who seemed to qualify for sick leave, and he started to laugh again. 'Wonderful!' he said. 'She was just too wonderful!'

'Just shut up, will you?'

'Ninety-eighth and Riverside Drive,' Lyle said. She leaned back in the taxi and closed her eyes. Beside her Yuri Korolenko was taking deep breaths.

'You someone famous or something?' the driver asked.

'Not at all. I just wrote a book about birds and they liked it.'

'Yeah, you never know what'll turn people on. I thought I saw you on Carson's show few weeks ago. Some homecoming.'

'Overwhelming,' she admitted.

'Picked up Bette Davis once, just like I picked you up now. Kept wondering where I'd seen her, you know? Never expected to have *her* in my hack ...'

He talked about the famous people he had driven, and Lyle slowly relaxed. Yuri's breathing returned to normal. He began to stare out the window intently. The driver talked on and on.

'Worst possible time of day, you know? Look at them cars! Lined up five miles already!'

The traffic increased until they were barely moving; the trip to Manhattan took over two hours, and then they were at the corner near where her car was parked.

Don't go near your apartment. Get your car and head for the Tappan Zee. Traffic will be bad, but that can't be helped.

She waited until the taxi was lost in the swarm of cars, and then crossed the street with Yuri. They carried the suitcases halfway down the block where she said, 'Wait here until I get the car. Do you understand me?'

'Yes,' he said.

'You speak English?'

'Very little, and bad.' His accent was thick.

'I'll try to be fast,' she said, 'but it will take a few minutes.'

He nodded and she hurried to the attendant of the garage. It took them ten minutes to move enough cars to get to hers and then bring it to her with brakes squealing at every turn on the ramp.

Finally, they were in the stream of traffic heading for the Tappan Zee Bridge.

'I think I am afraid before,' Yuri said, sitting straight upright, his hands balled on his thighs. 'But I am wrong. Now I am afraid. And in taxi I am afraid very much.'

'I don't blame you,' she muttered, gripping the wheel hard. 'I hate this kind of driving. It scares me too.'

'I wish you don't tell me this,' he said. 'For you who are so brave to say this makes me close my eyes.'

She glanced at him and he managed a weak smile, but he obviously was frightened by the traffic. 'It's all right,' she said. 'Really, we're all used to this. I don't like it, but I'm used to it.'

They crossed the wide bridge and headed north on Interstate 87. The traffic thinned out now as car after car overtook them and passed. Lyle held a steady fifty-five miles an hour. No ticket, no trouble, just a steady drive to the next turnoff. She was getting very tired. There was a tightness in her shoulders, and she was hungry now. It had been hours since they had eaten on the plane. Too much excitement, too much tension, always made her hungry. Yuri had hardly touched his food; he must be even hungrier than she. She turned on the radio and switched the stations hunting for news, and realized she was trying to find out if Carmen had made his escape, if Yuri's disappearance had made the evening news.

At last she found a news station and they listened intently. War in South America, as usual. Talk about the new Congress. They had held an election without her. A new biological control for the Med fly. A kidnapping in Rome, and one in San Salvador. Blizzard in Wisconsin. Russians blame CIA for the disappearance of brilliant young scientist ...

'... Yuri Korolenko, one of the Russian scientists at the International Biology Congress in Amsterdam vanished without a trace from the hotel where the conference was being staged late this evening. The American government has denied any knowledge of the incident.'

'It worked!' Yuri said in astonishment.

'It worked,' Lyle repeated, wondering where Carmen was, how he was. 'Do you want to keep listening?'

'Please,' he said, gazing at the radio with rapt attention. He listened to it all up to the sports news, and then leaned back.

Lyle was watching the highway signs now. Her turnoff onto 17 was coming up soon. One mile. She eased up on the accelerator, made the turn, and drove more slowly. It was not very far to Monroe, where they would stop. The headlights behind her could be Hilary, or police, or CIA, or anyone. They did not get any closer, and, watching them in the rearview mirror, she realized that they had been there for a long time, exactly that far away. Other cars had come between them and had passed her, but one pair of lights had remained, never wavering.

Hilary, she prayed. Please let it be Hilary.

She reached out and turned off the radio. 'I have to tell you the next part of the plan,' she said. 'We'll stop soon at a roadhouse, a restaurant. Friends will meet us there. You will go with one of them who will take you the rest of the way. Do you understand?'

'Yes. But you? What do you do now?'

'I'll come along with someone else a little later. That's not important. We have to be certain no one follows you.'

'Yes, is important. I have many thank yous to give to you. Is important.'

'We'll meet again very soon, Yuri. I promise you. Then we'll talk, if you like.'

'Yes. I like.'

She slowed to forty-five; the lights behind her maintained the same distance. Another car sped around her follower, accelerated and passed her; its taillights dwindled to nothing very quickly. She neared the turn and visualized the streets leading to the restaurant. She and Carmen had driven to it, had looked at the parking lot together, had checked the hours. She made her turn, made another sharper right turn and cut off her headlights for the next two blocks; she went through an alley to the roadhouse and pulled into the parking lot from the back.

The Volvo was there! It had not been Hilary following, after all. Even before she got her door open, Hilary appeared at it. 'Quickly,' he said. 'Yuri, come, get on the back seat and lie down. Hurry!'

The Volvo door opened, Yuri darted toward it and flung himself inside, vanished down onto the seat. The door closed. Hilary said to Lyle, 'Go inside and order for two as if he's still with you. Come out in half an hour.'

She hurried inside the restaurant. The door was closing behind her when another car pulled into the lot. She found a booth and sat down facing the door. When the waitress came, she said, 'Two coffees, please. My husband is fixing something on the car. We'll both have roast beef sandwiches.'

A young black man entered, glanced down the length of the restaurant on his way to the restroom. He could not tell if anyone was across the booth from her, she knew; the backs were too high. He reappeared in seconds and stood at the bar, not ostensibly looking her way, but including her in his range of vision. He watched the waitress deliver two cups of coffee to the booth. He was still there ten minutes later when the sandwiches were ready.

'He's taking his time out there,' the waitress said. 'The sandwich's going to get cold.'

'I know. He won't mind.'

'Won't even notice, if he's like most of them.' She went away.

The black man was eating pie, drinking coffee. Lyle picked up her sandwich, then began to eat it hungrily. It was good, hot, with a spicy mustard. She drank her coffee, then the other cupful, and it was nearly time to go outside again. The waitress came back shaking her head.

'I'll take it out to him,' Lyle said, getting out her wallet. The waitress left, came back with a white paper bag, and took the money and the bill. When Lyle left, carrying the bag, she did not look at the black man.

Hilary was at the wheel of her car. She got in the passenger side, locked the door.

'Now we lose them,' Hilary said happily. 'I was afraid they would catch on and go after Steve, but they didn't. You've been splendid, Lyle, really splendid!'

He pulled out of the parking lot and drove to 17 again. 'Ah, there they are, faithful dogs.' He hummed as he drove. The countryside was very dark, deserted looking. 'What we will do,' Hilary said a little later, 'is turn onto Interstate 84 and make them think we have some serious traveling to do tonight. Won't be long now. I may accelerate sharply, Lyle dear, so do brace yourself, won't you?'

The turn was very sharp. He made no signal, hardly slowed for it, and they screeched on the ramp terrifyingly. As soon as the car was straightened out on the interstate, he accelerated and passed two other cars that were cruising more sedately; then he turned off his lights, hit the brakes, and they were turning again, leaving the interstate, heading back to 17. Now he stopped and waited. Two cars passed, a third, another one. He began to hum again, and put the car into first, started to drive.

'I do believe we've lost them,' he said, after a few miles. 'Now we can go home. I say, is that a sandwich you've brought me?'

Lasater had been waiting in Herb Balinski's office for hours. Balinski's secretary was sleeping on a couch, snoring gently. She was heavy-breasted, blonde, and could even type. He had seen her typing a long time ago, hours ago. A natural blonde, with pale blue eyes, fair skin, she had a twangy Kansas accent. She was meant to reassure clients; Balinski had no use for her. 'You going to wait all night?' she had asked earlier.

'If I have to.'

'Okay by me, but I'm getting some sleep. See you in the morning, honey.' And just like that she had stretched out on the couch, closed her eyes and started to snore. For this he was paying her overtime, he thought bitterly, glaring at her.

She hardly even twitched when the phone rang finally at fifteen minutes after twelve.

'Yes!'

'Listen, I'm afraid we lost them.'

'Where the hell are you?'

'Monroe, New York.'

'Just tell me for Christ's sake!'

'Yeah, I'm trying. It was sledding on a twelve-foot snowpack all the way to Monroe. She was driving nice and slow, not paying any attention to anything but the road in front of her. A real Sunday driver. Then she pulled a fast one in Monroe, doused her lights, did the back alleys, and ended up at a restaurant. She was just going inside when we pulled up. My associate went in and I checked the car, made sure no one was hiding in it, you know? Anyway, my associate spotted her, and thought the guy was with her in the booth. He would've had to go look in directly to tell otherwise, you know? High back, dim light. Anyway, he thought the guy was there. I stayed outside. A white Volvo pulled out right after we got there, but what the hell? Duck soup up to then, we weren't expecting anything fancy. Then that English guy from the airport comes from nowhere and gets in her car, and a minute later she comes out alone, gets in and they take off. He knows a trick or two and lost us on Interstate Eighty-four. Probably pulled off at Seventeen and doubled back, but no way to be sure. We cruised around some looking for them, no dice.'

Lasater stared at the blonde malevolently, wishing she would choke on the next snore. He remembered the white Volvo, the one Werther had run off the cliff in Oregon. It made him feel weird – Werther raised from the dead, the car reassembled.

'Hugh, you there?'

'You son of a bitch, where'd you think I'd be? What else?'

'Not much. But if it helps, the Volvo that pulled out had a Pennsylvania license. It was out of sight before we got more than that.'

'You know how fucking big Pennsylvania is?' He smashed the phone down and stalked from the office, slammed the door as hard as he could. 'Wake up, you bitch!'

21

'Someone followed me to Monroe,' Lyle told Saul before he had time to embrace her.

He swept her into his arms and kissed her, cutting off her words. When he released her, he said, 'You were wonderful all the way. Come inside where it's warm. Everyone wants to congratulate you.'

'Have you heard from Carmen yet?'

'We don't expect to until he's in Canada. Don't worry about him. He's too wily to be caught.'

The night was clear and still, very cold, nearly down to zero. Saul hurried her into the house. Hilary had already entered the living room; the others rushed to her as soon as she appeared in the doorway.

'Here she is, the hero of the day,' Hilary called out; he was warming himself at the fire.

There were hugs and kisses, as if she had been part of them for years and they seriously had worried about her. Yuri was standing near the fire also, smiling at her. He had taken off the wig; his own hair was brown and straight, cut short.

'A hot drink first, and then talk. We would not allow Yuri to say much of anything until you two got here.' Saul made two Irish coffees and handed one to Lyle, one to Hilary, and then sat down on a couch near the fire. The others arranged themselves; Steve and Dora chose cushions on the floor, Mutt sat next to Saul, and Lyle and Yuri sat opposite on the other couch. Hilary dragged another chair close to the group. The room glowed; Lyle realized it was because the gold drapes on the wall of windows were drawn.

'Actually,' Hilary said, 'Dr. Korolenko and I haven't really met even though we do keep bumping into each other. Hilary Nast,' he added.

They shook hands and Yuri turned to Lyle. 'We have not met too.'

She felt her cheeks go hot. 'Good heavens! I never did tell you who I am. Lyle Taney. I'm sorry.'

He kissed her hand and sat down once more. 'She is very brave woman. Very smart and brave.'

Saul nodded. 'I know. She doesn't know it yet, but we all do.'

Lyle looked at the whipped cream on her Irish coffee and waited for them to change the subject. Brave? She had been baby-sat all the way, with Carmen or Hilary or someone always within reach. Even so, she had been terrified. Smart? She had led someone almost all the way to the door. She looked at Saul when he spoke again.

He was being very courteous, radiating warmth and charm, and more, friendliness. He looked at the young Russian as if he had known him for a long time, and liked him very much. There was compassion in his look, perhaps even pity.

'Are you too tired tonight, Yuri, to tell us about your group? If so we can put it off until tomorrow. There really isn't any rush.'

'Now,' Yuri said quickly. 'Is all right to speak French? I speak too bad English, have to stop to think too much.'

His teacher, the director of the biology department in the University of Leningrad, he said in rapid and perfect French, was Boris Lepov, a genius. He had been studying molecular biology for many years, even before Watson and Crick made their fantastic discovery of the structure of DNA. Dr. Lepov had been pleased with their announcement because he had been certain it would stimulate other scientists to look into the matter of the ability of the cells on some occasions to heal themselves quickly, almost as quickly as they were damaged. He had been dismayed by the start-and-stop progress in an area first broached fifty years ago. Boris Lepov had studied the articles written in the thirties by a German biologist, Hermann Franck, he went on, and stopped in confusion when Hilary laughed softly.

'Meet Herr Doktor Professor Franck,' Hilary said, pointing at Saul.

Yuri leaped to his feet. 'You? Is true?'.

Saul nodded. 'Boris Lepov came across my old articles? How curious. I didn't know they were extant anywhere.'

'Yes, we have your articles! If only Boris could be here instead of me! He would be happy! He said you made the same discovery of the DNA structure, twenty years earlier!'

'Not quite, but close. But go on, please.'

Yuri sat down once more, but he kept his gaze on Saul; his attitude had changed, as if now he knew he was addressing an angel, or a god, perhaps.

Seven years ago Boris Lepov had discovered that the tissue samples they were using in their lab had been contaminated with the curiously long-lived HeLa strain of uterine tissues that had traveled around the world masquerading as everything from brain tissue to epidermis tissue. The samples were good for nothing, had to be discarded, the laboratories decontaminated. But then he began to wonder why those tissues had the ability to contaminate everything in the same building with them, in the same city even, it seemed. Why did they keep on living?

Hilary explained it to Lyle the next day. In 1951, a woman named Helen

Lane (hence HeLa) had donated her body to science when she knew she was dying of uterine cancer, and after her death, the uterine tissue had been kept alive for experimentation. If even one cell of that tissue found its way to samples of any other tissues, it overwhelmed them; the HeLa cells divided, multiplied, overcame everything else until the entire sample was HeLa, the original completely gone. Quite a few years later it was learned that most tissues from a number of laboratories that supplied others throughout the world had been contaminated with the HeLa cells, had become HeLa tissues, no matter how they had started. The life work of many scientists had to be done over, was being done over even now, because the findings suddenly had been invalidated.

'That's the very line I was following at Stanford,' Steve said. 'I'll be damned! I wonder how many others are poking into those tissues with this in mind.'

'Too many, no doubt,' Hilary said. He looked at Yuri. 'Boris Lepov found what he was looking for and didn't publish a word of it.'

'We were forbidden,' Yuri said simply. Although Steve and Hilary had lapsed into English, his response was in fluent French. 'When I went to work for Boris Lepov, six years ago, he was already well into the research. I became one of his assistants; during my first year with him, it became clear. He found what he was looking for.'

'Not DNA,' Saul said quietly.

'No, not that. RNA, ribonucleic acid, the messenger of the gods.'

Saul glanced at Lyle who was following the conversation with little comprehension. She met his gaze and shrugged helplessly. 'Bear with us,' he said, then turned again to Yuri. 'And you found that although you could isolate the factor, you could not test it on living organisms, only on tissues. Is that correct?'

'Exactly so. It does not work with animals, not even chimps.'

Hilary laughed. 'Ninety-nine percent is too far away,' he said to Lyle. 'Chimps share ninety-nine percent of the same chromosomes as humans. That one percent is a terribly big gap, though.'

'Yes. Too much difference. We had to test it on a human. Boris wanted it to be himself, and we panicked, all of us. We would not permit it. Instead we drew lots. There were eleven of us then. We did not allow him to gamble with us. One of the women was our first test subject. She became very ill and nearly died, but then recovered completely. This was four years ago. Boris went to the conference knowing what he had discovered, but not enough about it yet to dream of publishing, even if it had been permitted. But he was frightened. The paper he read was sufficient for anyone who knew enough to guess the significance. Your professor Mr. Oliver guessed and that was when he told Boris to get in touch with him if he wanted help. Boris was even more frightened at the thought that the Americans had the same secret. Only very slowly did he come to believe that your government did not have it, that it was in the hands of a small group of people who were keeping it a secret.'

'Were you testing it yet?'

'Not yet. The woman was being observed very closely, of course. Gradually the extent of her immunity became evident, and also, she infected her lover, and he became like her.' He was looking at Saul fixedly, speaking to him as if the others were not in the room.

'Then we knew we could not contain it. There were eleven of us in the laboratory, working on this research. Some of them were party members; there were also administration people, supervisors; few of the others knew exactly what it meant, but we all did, all eleven of us. We were all treated early. Five of our team died. Some of the others used it, many of them died. And the government took it over.' He became silent.

Mutt Evans got up and put another log on the fire. Dora went to the buffet and poured herself more coffee, no one spoke.

'When the government took control,' Yuri went on, 'they isolated all of us, the scientists, the secretaries, the administration, the supervisors, everyone who possibly could have had any contact with it, their wives and husbands and lovers. But some of the officials used it. Would they report themselves, lock themselves up? I think not. They began to test in a massive way, with prisoners. That was when we discovered that no woman who survived the treatment became pregnant.'

'Oh damn!' Hilary said. 'The same stone walls! We hoped you would have something different to tell us.'

Yuri nodded. 'Yes, I understand. We too were dismayed for three years. Then we learned that my wife, the first one of us to be given the serum and survive, she was pregnant. There is an answer to that problem. Within a week to ten days she will bear our child.'

'That's why they sent you,' Steve said softly, with great sympathy. 'Those bastards! Is she all right?' Again he spoke in English and Yuri answered in French.

'Perfect. And the baby, a boy, is also perfect. They did an amniocentesis. He is one of us, naturally.'

'Do you know why she was able to become pregnant? Are there others?' Saul asked.

'Fanya, when she was only a girl of thirteen, became enchanted with mysticism. She became a follower of yoga, and she became an adept over the years. She never gave it up, not even when her university studies became difficult and demanding and there was little time. She learned to control her autonomic system, control pain, do all the things an adept is able to do. We think she controlled her own immunological response to the sperm.'

'I'll be damned,' Dora said in awe. '*Are* there any others?'

'Two others have become pregnant. However, there are very few adepts who are young women.'

Dora began to laugh. She put her head down on her knees and laughed until her voice became faint. 'God, it's finally happened! It's in the hands of the women! Finally!'

'It's in the hands of the Soviet government,' Mutt said bluntly.

'For now. As Yuri said, it can't be contained. Not forever. All girls, all women can be trained to meditate. With biofeedback methods anyone can be taught!'

'I'm really more concerned with the near future than with forever,' Mutt said. 'What's going to happen over there?'

'They are still testing with prisoners, trying to find why it kills so many. We are housed in a prison, something like a prison. No one tells us the plans, but we think they will start a massive inoculation this year, this winter, and call it flu shots or something of that sort.'

Saul closed his eyes, frowning, as if in great pain.

'Dear God!' Lyle whispered. 'They wouldn't do that to their own citizens! Half of them will die!'

'They know that,' Yuri said. 'But the half who do not die will be protected from radiation. They will start with the Politburo, officials, party members, the army ...'

Mutt was staring at him fixedly. 'How many of the original survivors knew about Seymour Oliver's offer to help Boris Lepov?'

Yuri nodded at him, as if he had been thinking the same thing. 'Four besides Boris. One of them is too political, a party member. One is crazy. We didn't tell them our plan. If the government had chosen Ilya to attend the conference, we would have had to kill him. One of the four had to come, had to speak with you. It had to be Fanya or me.'

'But the others will tell eventually. One of them will,' Mutt said, still looking hard at Yuri.

'Of course. Perhaps even Fanya. There is the baby, a tool they can use against her very soon.'

Mutt stood up. 'I'll go call Seymour, tell him his brother is dying, he has to come home on the first flight.'

Saul nodded. 'They will assume he's with the CIA, and in turn the CIA will become interested in him. I'm afraid his career has just come to an end. A pity. He liked his work.'

Yuri looked strained and tired now. 'For us too the careers are over. Already the government has taken the laboratories, moved them, moved all of us to this secret place where we were not allowed to leave, to make phone calls, send out uncensored mail. Now the others will be locked up, away from the work. There are many new people in the laboratories, none of the old will be there again.'

'Oh, damn!' Hilary said then. 'It's two in the morning, and I must say I feel as if I've had a rather full day. Yuri, let me show you to your room. There's an assortment of clothes, I just hope something in there will fit you all right. Let's do totter off to bed.'

Lyle had not admitted how tired she was until she let herself relax in a hot bath. The tensions melted, flowed away, dissolved in the fragrant water, scented with a mixture that Saul had given her, herbs, flowers, seeds that he had collected, dried, ground, blended. Everything had changed, she reflected, lying back. What about her plans to walk away from it all? What about the confusion she still felt about Saul and Carmen? Neither seemed very important any longer. Everything had changed. She could smell wood sorrel, and a hint of the spiciness of carnations, and something else too elusive to identify. The water was silky, spring water, incredibly pure and soft. Billows of suds had filled the tub enclosure the first time she had washed her hair with this good water. She wanted to think of Yuri and the new problems he had given them, the new worries, but her mind kept skittering away, locking onto things of no consequence like the softness of the water, the fragrance of the sachet...

Resolutely she got out of the tub and dried herself, put on her robe, and went to the study door. She could hear nothing from the other side, but she knew he was not yet asleep. He would be sitting in his deep chair by the window in the dark study, looking out over the silvery world that was so quiet and cold that night.

She tapped on the door softly before she opened it enough to see in. He was at the window, as she had known he would be.

She went to him and put a pillow on the floor, sat down on it and rested her cheek on his leg.

'Listen,' he said in a near whisper.

She could hear it now, distant honking of geese.

'They've had their rest, now they're on their way again,' he said, still speaking very low. 'How I envy them. No hard choices to make. Just listen to the blood, or the nerves, or the sound of moonlight on cold waters, or a strange god we can't even conceive of, and obey. That's an enviable freedom.'

She shook her head. 'No. Freedom is knowing you have to choose and being able to do it.'

'What a rationalist,' he said with a touch of laughter in his voice.

'Whoever followed me must have been waiting at the airport,' she said. 'I can't imagine anyone would have been keeping a parking garage under surveillance.'

'I think you're right.'

'Yes. And that means they knew when I would be back, the flight number, time, everything. Do you know who it could have been?'

'I don't think so.'

'Me neither. Anyway, if I go back to New York, I'll have to remain there. I can't risk coming here again. Next time they might be more clever, and they surely would be more careful.'

'I don't want you to be exposed, as you would be in New York,' he said. 'And we can't spare Carmen now.'

'I know. Or I could run somewhere and hole up, hide. There are a lot of cities to hide in.'

This time he did laugh. 'And you know so much about how to hide!'

'I know. I'm an amateur, but I probably would learn very fast.'

'Yes, no doubt. But there's another choice, isn't there?'

'Yes. I could simply stay here.'

She became silent, looking out the window at the gleaming water, the still woods beyond. 'Does the brook freeze in the middle of the winter?'

'Not all the way. The waterfall becomes very lovely with ice sculptures that no artist would ever attempt.'

'Do you ice-skate? The pond must be wonderful.'

'I used to, many years ago. My wife and I used to go out to a pond behind our house and skate there. She was a very good skater; I'm mediocre at best.'

'I didn't know you had been married.'

'No, I suppose not. I was thinking of her earlier, before you came in. She died when she was forty. A senseless, pointless death, useless death. There were skirmishes between the Communists and Fascists, sometimes they turned into outright war on a limited scale. Germany could have gone in either direction, I think. It just took someone with enough power, enough charisma to say this way. You know about the bad times in the late twenties, early thirties; you had them in the States here, but not as bad as we did. We, my family, were not hurt too much; we did not go hungry, or have to beg or steal. There was land, and a house that was like a miniature castle, four hundred years old, with turrets, gray stonework ... There were fields of wheat turning golden in the fall, livestock ... We were living well even if our money was worthless. There were no debts to pay off, just taxes, and we managed. Then, in the village near us, between our property and Berlin, there was a skirmish. Fifty men fought for causes none of them could explain. She had taken a wagonload of wheat, apples, eggs ... I don't know what all she had gathered together. She was delivering it herself to the village church, for distribution, when the fighting started. Someone shot her.'

Lyle pressed her face hard against his leg.

'Even the village is gone,' he said. 'It's become a suburb of Berlin. And my house is a historical landmark of some kind. They permit tourists to wander through to see how life used to be.'

'That was a long time ago,' Lyle said gently.

'Yes. A long time. Only sometimes it seems such a recent past. Listening to the geese brought it to mind, I guess. We used to sit on cold nights like this and listen to the geese fly overhead. We never could see them, just hear them.'

'Your house, the turrets, that's where the logo came from that you use for the company name?' The M of M and S Pharmaceuticals was ornate, with two turrets, or crowns, on the points. The S looked like a winding path leading away from massive doors.

'I know I should have resisted, but I liked it. I liked the old house very much.'

'I think seeing Yuri, knowing he has left his wife and unborn child behind has made you go back,' Lyle said. 'Everything is changed now, isn't it?'

'I'm afraid so.'

'May I stay here with you?'

'Are you sure you want to?'

'Yes. But will you please never ask me to kill anyone?'

Saul's hand on her hair, the warmth of his body, the distant geese saying their farewells, the brilliant moon-lighted, crystalline world where only the brook moved, was all dreamlike, almost surreal. Her question could have been asked only in such a surreal setting; his answer, when it came, could not have been said anywhere else, under any other conditions.

'So much death,' he said in a voice so low she could hardly hear it. 'So much dying. Senseless deaths, brutal deaths. If I could go back to that night when Carmen lay close to death, would I do the same thing? I don't know any longer. I filled a syringe with a lethal dose of morphine. I held it against his skin, and I withdrew it. How different it would all be now. How different. I wept over him as a father weeps over a dying son, bitter tears, filled with rage and despair and helplessness. As I had wept over my wife. Over so many others. And now ... I can promise nothing, my dear.' His hand had stopped moving over her hair. She covered it with her own hand. 'Lyle, I would not keep you here. You know that. You are free, not a prisoner.'

'You've made plans for something like this, haven't you?' she asked, not moving, her hand still on his.

'Yes. We have always known that one side must not have it exclusively. Boris Lepov and Yuri understand this also, that's why Yuri risked everything to come here. Their government has had this for years without divulging anything. Now that the pregnancy problem seems to be solved, they probably will start administering it, and if they do, we must also.'

She shut her eyes so hard they hurt. So much death, she thought, hearing his words once more in her head. So much dying.

'Let's go to bed now,' he said gently. 'Not to make love. Not tonight. Let me hold you. You are so tired.'

She was. Two sleepless nights, the long exhausting day. Certain she would not be able to sleep, she fell asleep in his arms, listening to the voices of the geese. Later, when she woke up before the morning light, he was not beside her and she knew he had stayed only long enough to comfort her, to permit her to sleep. The geese were still crying their farewells in the cold distance.

22

'You read the story?' Rawleigh asked, tossing a newspaper across his desk to Lasater.

'What story's that?'

'About the scientist who vanished at the Amsterdam meeting.'

'I saw it.'

Rawleigh sighed and leaned back in his chair. It had high, carved posts supporting a leather backrest. His great-grand-daddy had made it, no doubt, Lasater thought bitterly.

'Look,' he said. 'I'm getting fed up with Alex popping in and telling me I have to take a trip. I'm not on the payroll, remember?'

'I do regret all this, Hugh. Really. It's a damn nuisance to all of us, believe me.'

When he had gone down to the coffee shop at ten, Alex had been there, finishing his own breakfast.

'Milking time on the farm,' he had said pleasantly.

'So what is it this time?' Lasater was seated across the desk from Rawleigh, but his chair was not comfortable, did not have a leather back, and he was tired. He had been up nearly all night.

'It's that damn conference in Amsterdam. And your friend Taney and her child lover.'

This time Lasater sighed. 'I hope Alex told you all about the airport mob. No way could I get a glimpse of the kid.'

Rawleigh waved it away. 'We'll catch up with him sooner or later. They didn't go back to the apartment, you know.'

'I didn't know,' Lasater said evenly.

'Oh, right. You see, we're all in a bit of a dither today. The Russians seem to really believe we have their man. He's like the man who walked around the horse. You know that one, Hugh?' When Lasater shook his head, he went on, 'It's a famous disappearance. This chap gets out of his carriage and just walks around the horse, or horses, I forget if it was one or two ... Anyway, he walks around them, and is never seen again. Ever.'

'They never used to have horses in Amsterdam.'

'Not just like it, but enough, is what I meant,' Rawleigh said with a touch of impatience. 'Don't be difficult, Hugh. It's been a really bad morning. I think I have a headache coming along. Let's see, where was I? Oh, yes. The young Russian. He left a group of people, to wash his hands, or whatever, and was never seen again. That's what I meant.'

Lasater listened with interest. The paper had given no details, only that he was gone. He still did not know how Taney and Carmen had pulled it off.

'That's not quite the same thing,' he objected, when Rawleigh seemed to want him to say something. 'A conference hotel is full of people, mostly men. He got lost in the crowd.'

'I suppose. But who helped him? He never had been out of Russia before. He speaks very little English, some German, very good French, and positively no Dutch. I think even the Dutch will have to give it up soon, don't you? I mean only eight million people speak the language! And they all speak English. They could do worse than simply adopt English as their national language.'

Lasater sighed again, louder, and looked at his watch.

'Sorry. But you see the problem. He had to have help. No money, Russian clothes, no language except French that was passable, besides his own Russian, I mean. Where could he have gone? And really the big one, why? Who would want to take a Russian scientist, not even a physicist, you understand, but a biologist? We didn't lay a hand on him. The English? Why? And how? He walked into a restroom and never came out. People saw him walk in. Good people, honest people, people with no reason for lying about it. I mean not just Americans. If they had just been Americans, God help us all! But they weren't. There was a German, a Cuban, a Peruvian ... I don't understand it, Hugh, and that's God's truth.'

'Well, I sure wish I could help, Mr. Rawleigh,' Lasater said.

'Now, Hugh, don't get sarcastic.'

'He had to have made contacts earlier in the day,' Lasater said, going along with it since Rawleigh seemed to want to play the inane gambit to some sort of finish.

'That's what we thought. We've been checking. He spent the day in the company of a group of biologists, and the writer Daniel Malone. They went sightseeing.'

'Well, there you have it. He goes out in a crowd, slips off for a few minutes, and returns with no one ever the wiser.'

'I'm afraid not. It was a group of five. They were together all the time.'

'Then there has to be a conspiracy.'

Rawleigh shifted in his chair, making it creak. He laughed, but not a very good laugh, and Lasater felt chilled throughout.

'Well, that one's not your problem, is it, Hugh? And not ours, either, since we never laid a hand on him. What I'd really like to ask you to do is go through some more pictures for us.'

'He won't be there,' Lasater said in resignation. The game was over. Who scored? He did not know.

'I suppose not,' Rawleigh said broodingly. 'There aren't many, though. One other thing, before you leave again, would you mind just running through the other disappearances once more? I asked Edgar Bushnell to come over and take it down, if you don't mind.'

'I do mind, Rawleigh. You know damn well how Edgar operates. In real time, minute for minute, that's how. He wants you to remember one hour out of your life and it takes him days to get to it, get through it. No dice. You've got what I found out, all hearsay. I wasn't investigating, had no standing, asked no questions. Go ask the local cops, or the FBI. Either one can tell you more than I can.'

'What is it? More money? We probably could scrape together a few more thousand, but not much more than that. It has to come out of petty cash as it is.'

Hugh Lasataer had seen too many people in trouble not to recognize the symptoms, even if Rawleigh was one of the higher echelon untouchables in the CIA. He had stood up, but now he sat down again, looking intently at Rawleigh. 'I'll be damned,' he said softly. 'Well now, I'll just be damned! I do believe you're flying solo, Mr. Rawleigh. Why are you having Alex, a West Coast kid if there ever was one, hanging out here back east? Why are you seeing me here at the farm instead of the office? Why petty cash? You could have covered the airport like a blanket if you'd wanted to, but you didn't. Why not?'

'If I were you, Hugh, I'd be very careful,' Rawleigh said, without a trace of the southern gentleman in his voice.

'Oh sure. And if I were you, Rawleigh, I'd be very polite. I seem to have something you want. Why not just come right out and say what it is and be done with it. Not money,' he added. 'Just an exchange of ideas. A frank discussion. Isn't that how the TV people put it when both sides are out in the open, each hoping the other will drop dead before dinner?'

'Hugh, do you think I'm not being open with you? What have I left out?'

'Where was the KGB spook when the scientist took a piss?'

'Didn't I mention them? Two of them. They'd been with him all day, through the museums, watching the group eat *rijsttafel*, back to the hotel. They saw him go into the washroom. I expect they're feeling rather chagrined right now.'

'Two on one? Really?'

'You know, we should have talked you out of leaving us. We really should have. You pick up on the right things each and every time. Two of them. He must have been important to them.'

'Then why'd they let him go in the first place?'

'He's the least important member of the team and he has a pregnant wife. Someone had to show. I guess they thought he was the likeliest to return.' He spread his hands helplessly. 'I don't know why they do anything. They seldom say. Now, Hugh, I've been frank. Just look at the pictures, and go over the other disappearing acts again, with Edgar listening. Not his usual session, I promise you. I want to be there, and I certainly couldn't stand to watch him nibble away like he does.'

Lasater shrugged. 'Why not? It's all in my report.'

It took six hours; Alex joined them, Rawleigh sat in, and Edgar led Lasater through each disappearance he had mentioned in his notes. Who, where, under what circumstances, how the investigation had proceeded. He was thorough, but obviously not happy with being limited in time. He was a small mouselike man with a thin mustache, pale, lank hair that fell over his forehead repeatedly. Absently he brushed it upward, it fell again, over and over. Also he put his glasses on when he read or wrote anything, and took them off when he listened. By the end of the first hour Lasater wanted to kill him.

There was nothing helpful, as he had known from the start. Each case was different. One man had walked away from a Mexico City restaurant and was never seen again. Another had gone to bed at midnight in Paris, and vanished. Another had left for the airport in San Francisco to meet colleagues from Harvard, and failed to show up. And so on. There were scant details about any of them, but no one had been watching any of them. They had had it easy. The Russian was different.

The pictures proved hopeless also. Twenty men, young, dark-haired, not Carmen.

Aunt Jane served them dinner, pork chops, mashed potatoes, green beans – good wholesome American food, Rawleigh said with satisfaction. Edgar was sent to bed early, and Alex and Rawleigh remained with Lasater.

'When you went to the drug companies for backing, what did you tell them?' Rawleigh asked.

'What I told you. I thought the old man had a cancer cure.'

'But they saw the published articles, the papers that had been read at conferences, all that. What did they say about it?'

'Not a damn thing.'

'They didn't believe in the cancer cure, though, did they?'

'I told you, they didn't say. I thought they did.'

'Yes. Well, I doubt it.'

'Take the stuff to Lawrence Truly and ask what he thinks,' Lasater said. Lawrence Truly was their man; he was also a very good biologist, one of the experts they relied on for germ warfare advice.

'He's on sabbatical,' Rawleigh said. 'And Hanford Wilkes is out of reach, making a tour, or something.' He was the other biologist who could be trusted.

Lasater considered this, his eyes narrowed, alert now to a difference in the air, a difference in the way Rawleigh was watching him, the way Alex was watching both of them. Now it was coming, he thought coolly, and waited for it, whatever it was.

'Strange that they both should be gone, isn't it? Not even a forwarding address,' Rawleigh said.

'Off in Afghanistan or somewhere checking out germ warfare,' he suggested.

'Yes, probably that's it. Hugh, the files on those disappearances are gone. What do you think of that?'

'Gone, or reclassified?'

'Well, reclassified, actually. I can't see them. I don't know anyone who can.'

'You mean the local police files too?'

'Everything.'

Lasater stood up. Very carefully he said, 'I don't think I want to know anything else about any of this, Mr. Rawleigh. If you don't mind, I think it's past my bedtime.'

Alex laughed, a sharp barking noise that turned into a cough.

Rawleigh looked at him morosely. 'And he's coming down with a bad cold.' He stood up also. 'Yes, it is late. I'm sorry to keep you at it so long. I just have the feeling that you have something that hasn't come out yet. You know the feeling? Intuition, of course, nothing to back it up. Probably you don't even know what it is yourself.'

Lasater almost felt pity for him. He was getting old, this was his life, and suddenly he had had the rug pulled out from under him. He didn't know how, or why, only that it was very big, likely the biggest thing to come his way, and he was being cut out. Also, Lasater thought, Rawleigh knew he was holding out something; he could not have a suspicion of what it was, just something. And he was afraid.

Rawleigh went to the door with him. 'Look, I hate to ask, but could you hang around on the East Coast for the next week or so? I know you and Alex love California, but if something comes along that I want to talk to you about, it does make it easier if you're handy.'

'I can't afford to live in a hotel, or even a Manhattan apartment,' Lasater said. 'And I hate Washington.'

'Yes, of course. I understand. New York's where the action is. Isn't that what they say? Can't see it myself, but I do understand how others feel. We'll pick up the tab. One thousand a week living expenses? Surely that would cover it.'

'Two grand comes closer.'

Rawleigh shut his eyes hard and nodded. 'Agreed. It won't be for long. A week, ten days, probably not more than that. As soon as Taney and her lover show up, Alex will be in touch again. Sooner if anything else comes up that we should discuss. All right?'

'Whatever you say.'

Lasater was awake for a long time that night. What did Rawleigh want from him? What did he expect to get? Why had he told him as much as he had? He worried each question over and over, poking at it, posing it differently, feeding it answer after answer, each one more unsatisfying than the last. Suppose, he mused, Rawleigh had figured out that he, Lasater, was still on this case, on his own now, without any client. Suppose he expected Lasater to find Taney, the old man, Carmen, and the Russian scientist, just to make it a jolly foursome. That meant that he would be having Lasater followed, his phone tapped, the works. Crude. Too crude? He was not certain it could be too crude for Rawleigh. The real reason he did not like it was that it made Rawleigh think that he, Lasater, was a dummy, and he did not believe Rawleigh thought that. But what then? To identify Carmen when he surfaced again? Probably no one else could, but that seemed too little a payoff for the cash Rawleigh was shelling out. Because he had linked the various disappearances? Now that the files were closed, no one else could make the connections he had made. No one besides Rawleigh and his few trusted people knew the connections had been made already by someone on the outside of the agency. He felt a prickling on his arms, scalp, down his back at that thought. He remembered the way Rawleigh had reacted when he had suggested a conspiracy among the group of scientists who had been with the Russian in Amsterdam. He cursed under his breath. Of course Rawleigh believed that. It had to have been a conspiracy, but Holy Mother of God, he breathed, what exactly did that mean?

He backed up. Rawleigh believed the group in the hotel had been in on it, not the group out touring all day. Lasater knew better. Carmen and the Russian had switched places early enough for the Russian to fly home with

Taney, and they had left Amsterdam at two. All day Carmen had pretended to be the Russian and no one had caught on, not the KGB anyway, following at a distance, watching outside the restaurant where the group gorged on *rijsttafel*, probably never closer than fifty yards. Heavy coats, the group being careful to keep Carmen shielded, it could have worked. All of them had to have been in on it. Then back to the hotel where Carmen vanished into the john. Probably put on an apron, took off a wig, or added one, and carried trays of food right in front of the KGB, jibbering away in Dutch. Who had been in that group? Rawleigh had said simply a group of biologists, and a writer, Daniel Malone, five in all. Daniel Malone! Rawleigh would not have given away a name if he believed that was the group of conspirators. He thought the conspiracy was during the vanishing act later, at the hotel. But the Russian had been halfway to the States by then. Daniel Malone! One of them? He had to be. Who else would risk his neck in a crazy scheme to help a defecting scientist? And Daniel Malone, he thought with satisfaction, could be reached, could be contacted. Rawleigh had given him a piece after all.

Daniel Malone and four others, he thought with a chill. An international group? It had to be. Some of the people who had vanished over the years had been French, there had been two Englishmen, an East Indian ... For a long time he had thought each and every one of them had been killed. He had been wrong. How big was the group?

This was what Rawleigh had come up with, he realized, and this was why he was frightened. Someone had gone over his head to reclassify the files he wanted, no one was telling him anything, he suspected that something bigger than a cancer cure was at stake, and an international conspiracy was afoot. No wonder he looked bewildered and no wonder he wanted Hugh Lasater at hand to talk to from time to time.

He realized too that his own safety now depended upon Rawleigh's cupidity, his ambition, his fury at being excluded from something as big as this was turning into. Just keep the lid on, he thought, beaming the message to another bedroom where Rawleigh was more than likely also awake, staring at the ceiling. Keep wondering how the Russian managed to vanish from the hotel, he thought at Rawleigh. As long as he concentrated on that, Taney was relatively safe, she was still his to find.

The fact that Carmen had pulled the vanishing act under the noses of the KGB and a dozen other witnesses did not surprise him, or even interest him very much, except as a technical maneuver. Carmen and Saul Werther, he thought darkly, had been around long enough to learn a lot of useful tricks. No doubt they could teach the best agent a thing or two.

Finally he turned his thoughts to his own plans for the next few days. Herb Balinski, in spite of himself, had told him several useful things. One was that the man who had driven Taney away, and lost the following car, had been the same man who had hovered around her and her companion at the airport, the Englishman. It had all fallen into a neat pattern with that bit of information. But Balinski had had more. Taney had known the town where she had met the Englishman. She had been able to drive to the restaurant through alleyways, with her lights off. That was a good bit. The Englishman had known the area also, enough to know exactly where the turnoff from the interstate highway was, just four miles from where he had entered. And the other car had had Pennsylvania license plates.

It was not a lot, but it was something, and it was more than anyone else had. And he knew about Daniel Malone, he thought, and now he yawned. Surprisingly the day had turned out all right after such a lousy start. Not bad at all. He yawned again, turned to his side and fell asleep.

23

Yuri and Lyle stood at the pond regarding the ice. It was frozen across, but how deep? That was the question they had come to answer.

'Do you have a way to tell?' she asked. 'My father used to go out on a pond near our house carrying a light hammer and a stake. As long as he could still drive the stake through the ice, he kept us all off it. We used to hold our breath waiting for the day he couldn't get the stake in; then he stamped on it, and finally jumped up and down. Of course, we already had skates on.'

Yuri laughed. 'Is good way.' He looked at her anxiously and corrected himself. 'A good way.' He tentatively stepped onto the ice. 'How we find out,' he said. He put his other foot out and stood there for a moment, listening. He took a step, listened again. Then he stepped off. 'Not yet.'

'What did you hear?'

'I don't know exactly. Water? A cracking noise? Is not clear, but something. Soon.'

They walked back to the big building companionably. He was practicing his English with her; for technical discussions with the other scientists, he still preferred French. He talked about his wife, about his childhood growing up in a small village, working on a collective farm. His mother had lived in Paris for over ten years, had spoken French at home, taught it in secondary school. He had met his wife at the University of Stalingrad. Although he did not say so, it was evident that he was homesick already, that he desperately missed his wife, that he was worried about her, the repercussions she might suffer because of him.

'Are you political?' Lyle asked. It was a gray, still day with a threat of snow in the air, and it was very cold.

He shook his head. 'I did good work in mathematics and in science, that is all. Later there was no time.'

'You left out languages,' Lyle reminded him.

'Yes. Language, and mythology. I read mythology very much.'

'You covered more ground than I ever did. I never could grasp math, and science seemed too ... finished. Or something. If they already had the answers, why should I interest myself in it? That was my attitude.'

'Covered more ground? What does this mean?'

'You learned things in many different areas. You did not limit yourself to your own field.'

'Yes. But no political courses, except what was required. What do you mean when you say science seems finished? I do not understand this.'

'Oh. I know that I was mistaken, but when I was still in school they seemed to teach science as if they had solved all the problems. They understood physics, and they understood the Darwinian theory, and astronomy and chemistry, and everything. I thought from what they said that great scientists had discovered all the secrets, that from now on it was just a matter of applied science turning the discoveries into the appropriate technologies. Do you understand what I mean?'

'Yes. But it is wrong.'

'I know that now. But because I believed it at the time, I didn't bother with science. I think a lot of people are like me in that.'

'In Russia all students study science and math. It is required. All mothers can boast that their daughters married engineers, or are engineers themselves. Do you know this passage: "And God shall wipe away all tears from their eyes, and there shall be no more death, neither sorrow, nor crying, neither shall there be any more pain; for the former things are passed away"?'

'It's from the Bible.'

'Yes. Boris Lepov told us that. We memorized it because we were afraid of what we had done, what we were continuing to do. We were afraid of what our government would do, what your government would do. Knowing science cannot protect anyone from the consequences of great discoveries. I say to Fanya I wish I still worked on farm, still drove tractor, mowed hay. Fanya say to me this passage from Bible, and she say to me: "Former things will pass away and world will be open now for all things. There will be time to mow hay, and do science, and learn scuba diving, and study brain, and learn everything. Everything!" He laughed self-deprecatingly. 'Not that I can do so many things, but some people will do all. There will be time to learn science and mathematics and politics and history and poetry …'

They were walking on the gravel driveway that led to the building hidden by firs and spruces and rhododendrons. Only the little drive hinted that something was there, something not seen. Lyle looked back at the pond, the driveway that wound out to the road, barred now with a chain, closed for the season. A new world, she thought. They were entering a new world where time was no longer the limiting factor. It seemed to her that the world she examined was different, more fragile perhaps, and the responsibility for the earth belonged to those who used it, not their descendants. No longer could the living claim there was not enough time to undo what their carelessness did. There was time to plant a tree and watch it grow to maturity, time to rake its leaves, pluck its fruits, time to watch it become gnarled and tired … Time to study, to learn, time to explore the world below, the universe above … Time enough, or no time at all.

Yuri touched her arm. 'You are troubled. Is it political?'

'Time enough,' she said. 'Or no time for anything except annihilation. Those are the alternatives now.'

'Yes. We know this also. For all my life there has always been the threat of war, and your life also. So many brave people go die for what? Ideas. Idea of religion, or idea of politics, or economics. They think perhaps life is so short, causes are important enough to die for. But now, if annihilation does not come, if war does not come first, and people know life is not so short, will they die for ideas? I think they will not. There will be time to try ideas first, test ideas, no reason to fight and die for them.'

'If war doesn't come too soon,' she said and he nodded. 'Let's go inside. I'm getting chilled.' Soon it would be dark; nights came early and stayed long at this time of year. They were all terribly frightened that war would break out first, she knew, and knew that was the reason for the chill that had seized her. Smith and Jones, she thought, and now Jones was erecting a new shield, immunity from radiation poisoning. Would he shoot before Smith could do the same? Would Smith shoot before Jones had it fully in place? If Smith and Jones were sane, the question would never even arise, but over the years, she thought bleakly, Smith and Jones had both become terrifyingly insane.

Lasater stopped in a diner in Stroudsburg, Pennsylvania. He had covered the town thoroughly, up and down every street, up into the hills around the town, nothing. For the first time he began to believe his plan was foolish. He was not even sure what he was looking for. A sign. What kind of sign? He did not know. He would spot the white Volvo with the Pennsylvania license if he saw it, and he would spot Taney's black Renault if he came across it, but neither situation seemed as likely now as it had when he left New York earlier. After studying the map of this section of Pennsylvania he had been certain no one could hide here. If they had wanted to go to Philadelphia, they would have flown, he had reasoned. If they had wanted Scranton, or Pittsburgh, same thing, airplane. They had chosen to drive, had been met by someone who knew Monroe, New York. Taney knew Monroe. That meant they were not heading for anywhere too far from the New York border; he had been certain yesterday, the night before, and this morning. Now, in a steamy diner that smelled of doughnuts and bacon, he no longer felt so certain.

He drank coffee and went over his own reasoning. Not Stroudsburg, he had decided. Interstate 80 came straight to it from New York City. They would not have kept so far north if they had wanted this dump. He had decided to use this place as the outside boundary of the area he would drive through, search, look for a sign in. He felt reassured now; if they had wanted to rendezvous outside Stroudsburg, they would have chosen one of the little towns across the river in New Jersey, not Monroe, New York.

It was going to get dark soon. He would get a motel, find a decent restaurant, turn in, and start his search first thing in the morning. All he needed was a sign. He could not anticipate what the sign would be, but he knew he would recognize it when he saw it. A feeling he had, like Rawleigh's feeling that he was holding out. Intuition, that was it. He was following his intuition. Rawleigh would be pleased to know that.

'Let me tell you,' Seymour Oliver said to Lyle. He had rejoined them that evening. 'We spotted you instantly in the museum, of course. We were all a bit nervous, but you were so poised, so calm that it made me, for one, feel like a schoolboy. Anyway, we worked on Carmen and Yuri as fast as we could to make the transformation, while Franz stood at the door, holding it closed just in case. Full house, he was going to sing out, if he had to. He didn't.' He was grinning broadly as he retold the adventure. 'After the museum, always keeping Carmen covered as best we could, we went to a restaurant, and took as long as possible. More wine, more coffee, more everything! We waddled out, believe me. Carmen had on a janitorial outfit under that awful raincoat, of course, so it was nothing at all for him to get into a disguise. All he had to do was take off the raincoat, take off the wig, and he was a simple janitor mopping the men's lavatory. He stuffed the raincoat and cap down in the mop bucket – one of those great tubs on wheels with a roller mechanism on top. And he flushed the wig down a toilet. When someone asked him if he'd seen a man enter, he answered in Dutch, then in good, but accented, English. No one gave him another look.'

'But how did he plan to get out of Holland?' Lyle asked, unable to laugh with the others.

'Train to Rotterdam, boat to England. He was going to play the part all the way, even waiting for a standby flight to save money.'

'And the bicycle? He said he wanted a bicycle.'

'To ride to the train station,' Seymour said, as if she should have known that. 'All the Dutch workers ride bikes everywhere.'

She leaned back on the couch and took a deep breath. It sounded so simple, but she knew from her own escapade that it had been difficult, terrifying, and very dangerous.

'Of course, when they exhaust the possibilities of vanishing from the men's room, they will start to backtrack,' Mutt said, his face furrowed in thought. 'The Holmes method will assert itself eventually. I think everyone with Yuri and Carmen that day should run to cover.'

'Dan will balk,' Steve said.

'I sent a message out today,' Saul said quietly. 'I didn't tell anyone that we have to move now, but I warned them that it may happen very soon. Dan will go along.'

There was a long silence in the living room. Lyle finally broke it. 'Is anyone going to tell me what that means?'

'Yes, of course,' Saul said. 'We've known for a long time that the day might come when we would have to disperse the serum ourselves. We have several different plans for doing that. But first, before any plan is initiated, our people around the world have to be warned to take cover, to get ready. The fact that someone followed you makes me think that it is time now for them all to take the first step. The next step will wait for Carmen's return. Meanwhile, Seymour and Mutt will start for California tomorrow, and Dora will return to the Philadelphia plant and resume her job there.'

'Have you decided to try the lotion?' Dora asked.

'Yes. We have to know. I gave a sample to Alice this afternoon.'

Lyle turned away from him, tried not to react; she felt frozen. Alice Lanier, the thirty-year-old retarded daughter of the housekeeper, worked hard and cheerfully all day, dusting, mopping, changing linens, doing laundry ... She never spoke, but always smiled at anyone she came across, and then fled. Poor Alice, she kept thinking, poor Alice. If she survived, doomed to clean after others forever? Or would her damaged brain be mended, as Saul's heart had been? If she died, killed by something she could not have understood, she would be the first totally innocent victim ... She got up, walked to the window to look for the deer that still came for a drink every night, looked beyond the room, out to a clean world, a world of ice and stillness, a world waiting, holding its breath, waiting.

She sat in her dark room gazing out the window at the rushing brook. It was snowing lightly. Not a serious snow, but a forerunner of what the winter would be like here in the Pocono Mountains in a few weeks. She had left the door open to the study; Saul and the others were still talking in the living room. Their talk concerned the details of distribution, if the lotion they were testing on Alice worked. A simple lotion, mineral oil, perfumes, cocoa butter, emulsifiers, a solvent that would carry it all through the skin to the lymphatic system, and a minute quantity of a new, nameless substance, a messenger of the gods. She remembered the phrase Yuri had used: messenger of the gods.

She thought again of the Bible quotation: '… and there shall be no more death, neither sorrow, nor crying, neither shall there be any more pain; for the former things are passed away.'

But there would be pain and sorrow, suffering as there never had been on earth. The lamentations would echo and reecho. Families sundered. Mother from child, lover from loved one, brother from sister …

Saul had told her they would make an effort to see the president, to try to persuade him that the Russians did not pose a threat by having it if the United States began a mass distribution immediately, if they made it available worldwide. He had said it and neither of them had believed the effort was worth making, but it had to be tried. And it could not be tried until they had the samples ready, until they had literature ready, directions for isolating the serum, directions for the care of the ill, information about what it was, how it was transmitted … The biggest fear was that the United States government would find out the Russians had it before the samples could be readied. Time, it circled around itself, came to a dead end, or it extended into an indefinite future, and no one could say for certain which was the correct perspective of it.

She thought of Alice. None of them had any doubt that it would work. Had there been enough time for her to start feeling headaches, start shivering with fever chills, start dreaming fever dreams? What did a woman like Alice dream?

Less than fifty miles away Hugh Lasater was watching his television, unaware that it had started to snow. On one of the beds was an open map; he had gone over his route with a yellow highlighter. He should be able to cover it all in a single day, he felt reasonably certain, but if it took more, he would put in the time. He hoped Alex did not call while he was out of New York. No point in alarming Rawleigh any more than he had done to himself. He watched the television with the sound turned too low to catch, the picture too fuzzy to try to follow; it was company, no more than that. He went over one more time the final conversation he had had with Rawleigh that morning at breakfast. It had been a puzzling talk, disturbing, and snatches of it that had come back to him off and on during the day now flooded back, as if it were a conversation he had to report to someone, remembered with clear details, down to the hesitations, the nuances.

'Hugh, try some of the ham. Finest damn smoked ham in the world. Virginia ham.'

He already had eggs and homemade sausage on his plate, two biscuits, honey on the side, raspberry jam, sweet butter, churned every Tuesday ...

Aunt Jane glanced over the table, then left. Alex was ignoring food, trying to drown himself in orange juice. His eyes were red, his nose red and runny; he looked miserable.

Rawleigh ate heartily, jam on one biscuit, honey on another, ham and sausages ... He looked at Hugh and shook his head. 'Nobody eats right anymore, you know that? All those health faddists have people afraid of good food. Look at me, do I look like a man dying of high blood pressure or too much cholesterol?' He laughed and cut his ham. 'People believe too easily these days. Whatever comes along, they believe.'

Alex sneezed. Rawleigh said emphatically, 'I haven't had a cold in fifteen years, maybe more. Good food, that's what keeps a man healthy.' He poured more coffee for them all. 'Hugh, there's one other little thing I wanted to bring up last night, but we all got too busy and I forgot. You know how the department always braces when there's a change of administration? Remember? I've been with the department for twenty-two years, and it's always been like that, always will be. Nothing really changes, but still, we're ready for it if it should ever happen. You know?'

Lasater nodded. He knew.

'A new man comes in at the top, new names on a few doors, memos fly, meetings are held, and then things settle down and the old experienced hands run things just as they always have. It has to be like that, you know? It really does have to be like that.'

Lasater waited, done with eating, done with drinking coffee, wanting only to be on his way, out to Pennsylvania, to get on with it.

'We see a Republican president after working under the Democrats for years, and we think, this time things will really change, a clean sweep, out with the old, in with the new. We are braced, but it doesn't work out like that. Then a Democrat returns to power and it's the same kind of trepidation. Back and forth, nothing really changes, not at the level where things really get done. Only the names on the doors change, the top half-dozen people who come and go, glory in power for a few years, feel in on the secrets of government, go back home and itch to write books about what they've learned. You know how that goes. You remember all that.'

He made the same point a few more times before he was willing to leave it. Alex yawned and sneezed.

'But we never expect things to change much after an administration has been in as long as this one has.'

Lasater was careful not to glance at Alex, to avoid Rawleigh's gaze. He studied the way his remaining egg yolk ran, how it edged around the sausage grease ...

'You remember Carl Ely, don't you? Best damn Soviet man that ever worked.'

'I remember Ely.'

'Yes. Funny how you brought up Lawrence Truly last night, made me think of Ely. I wanted him for a little matter and he's out of touch. Nothing in the files, nothing anywhere, just out of touch.'

'Truly, Wilkes, and Ely? That's a curious combination,' Lasater muttered. 'Are there more?'

'As a matter of fact, several more. Most of the team that worked out of Denver a few years back when there was that ridiculous sheep death panic. Remember? Nerve gas escaped, something like that. They put every biologist they could find to work on that one. I keep wondering,' Rawleigh went on, offhandedly. 'You know, you can't help wondering in this business. You begin to make connections without noticing. But I wonder. What if Ely had found out something important? He reports back to Lightfoot, you know. And then he vanishes. Nothing in the files. Lightfoot reports to Scanlon, one of the new people, and Lightfoot is off on a year's R and R all at once. Curious, that's the word for it.'

'Do they know you're poking your nose into any of this?' Lasater heard the harshness in his voice but did not try to soften it even a little.

'Hugh! I have my own show to run, keeps me plenty busy, too busy to mind anyone else's business, I can assure you.'

'But you do have to wonder,' Lasater said.

'Exactly. Scanlon, Ballinger, that whole crowd, they sometimes worry me. They don't know how the game is played, you see. They don't understand the balancing act we've come to accept and even anticipate. They tend to link communism with Satanism, or something like that, and they are too frightened to trust with important decisions. Frightened men are likely to become very dangerous men. You understand what I'm saying?'

'How much of this did you know back in April when I came to you?' Lasater asked coldly. 'You had your chance then to get a hand in.'

'I knew some of it,' Rawleigh admitted. 'Not enough. And I couldn't quite believe that whatever file I wanted was unavailable. I thought it was a temporary matter. But, Hugh, if I had known, I still would have turned you down. No matter what you have, no matter how much you know, or suspect, I would turn you down. I would not like to think that you suddenly had found a tremendous need for a year's sabbatical, or rest and recreation out of touch with anyone who ever knew you. If you returned to the payroll, and if I had to report your fantastic story, why ... Who knows? Your file could even vanish overnight.'

On the television a man had broken into an apartment and was shooting everyone in it. It took them a long time to realize that he was slaughtering them all.

Rawleigh was frightened. With cause. It was scary to think of the new people and the president getting together and discussing how to handle immortality. If the Russians had it and Truly and Wilkes could not come up with it, then obviously the government would have to stop the Russians before they had a chance to use it on their people in any significant way.

Lasater realized that the screen was gray and wavery and did not know how long the movie had been over, how long he had sat looking at the blank screen.

If the government decided they had to stop the Russians before they could use the stuff, he had concluded, all hell was going to break out, and soon. Better no one should have it than for the satanic powers to have it alone. Better to take your chances with a preemptive nuclear war, which they maintained was winnable, than to risk having them bomb the hell out of this country after they had spread the stuff around over there.

He thought of the dogged insistence of the government spokesmen that a war was winnable, in spite of the protests overseas, in spite of the protests in this country, in spite of the articles, the books, the television specials, in spite of everything to the contrary. The statements had become more persuasive, more widespread, more insidious, more sloganlike during the past year, during the period that they had had Wilkes and Truly and Ely and others stuck away somewhere looking for something.

And if the new Manhattan Project, Son of Manhattan Project, he thought darkly, came up with the secret, what then? Would they see that the balance had been restored, equilibrium again achieved? Slowly he shook his head. The Russians had had it too long. They could have been using it for years, depending on when they got started. Rawleigh was right about the new people, he went on, in that they seemed genuinely to believe their own rhetoric. They believed that the Russians were satanic, that the world was engaged in the opening moves of the final war between good and evil. They would assume now that the Russians would strike just as soon as enough of their own people were protected. They still believed that we blew it with the bomb, that we had the chance of a lifetime to dominate the entire world, make it safe for capitalism, apple pie, and Christianity, and we were too chicken to take the advantage that was clearly ours. They would assume now that the Russians had that kind of advantage, and, being satanic, they would not be chicken. They would use the advantage. They would strike, knock down the opposition, and go on from there.

And our good old boys, he thought then, certain of all this, would be compelled, justified even, in hitting back first.

But did they know what it was they were looking for? That was the tough one. Did Truly and Wilkes have enough to go on to find it? He stared straight ahead and knew he would have to find out. But first he would find Taney.

The agency had come to it from the Russian angle and had no reason to link Taney and her gang with any of it. Only Rawleigh had that connection and he was not telling anyone anything. He was thoroughly frightened; he knew the ones calling the play were dangerous men even if he did not know what it was they had, or were looking for. He had told Lasater enough for him to plow through this, to come up with the conclusions he obviously had made also. Lasater knew that Rawleigh was smart, but not how smart. He could not decide if Rawleigh had given him what he had with the idea in mind that Lasater would find Taney for him, haul her in, let him in on the secret. Or had he counted on his going away to mull it over, and coming back frightened, eager to divulge everything? Or had it all been a lie? Maybe they had a dozen people on him, watching his movements, wiring his rooms, tapping phones ...

He shook his head. He knew no one had followed him that day. And tomorrow he would spend as many hours as it took searching for the sign he knew was out there waiting for him. Taney was near, the old man not far from her, probably, and Carmen on his way back to them both, he felt certain. Like old times, he sighed, and turned off the television, glanced again at the open map, and then went to bed.

24

They all prepared their own breakfasts and ate in the kitchen, or the dining room, or even in the laboratories upstairs. Mrs. Lanier and Alice arrived daily at noon and made lunch for one o'clock, and dinner for seven. This morning Lyle sat in the kitchen alone sipping coffee, not hungry, thinking about Alice, waiting for the phone to ring.

Yuri and Mutt entered, nodded to her, but did not interrupt their conversation.

'Scientists don't want to rule the world,' Yuri was saying firmly. 'Scientists want to do science. Painters want to paint. Doctors want to heal. Dancers to dance. Only a few people want to run the world and they must be prevented from doing it ever again.'

'How the hell will you make other people take on the problems of government?' Mutt demanded. He foraged for eggs and bacon in the refrigerator. Yuri poured two cups of coffee, took one to the table where Lyle was sitting.

'You make them, that's all,' he said.

'Christ! Make them! What, with guns held to their heads?'

'No! Never again! Obligations, duties, respect ... Why do men volunteer to save flooded peoples? Climb mountains to save someone unable to save himself? Put out dangerous fires? People do things they don't want to do all the time, this would be another such thing.'

'Maybe. Maybe.'

'People don't do it now because they don't think they have enough time. Their careers, their families, everything they love will be gone too soon, no time for other things. When they have time ... You make them.'

They had leaped ahead, to afterward, Lyle thought, twisting her empty cup around and around, envying them the ability to do that. They were creating utopia out of the chaos that would envelop the world, and she was fixated on the creation of the chaos. Once, she had been able to look ahead, see herself ten years in the future, fifteen years, all the way to the end, but now her gaze could not penetrate the rest of any single day; tomorrow was too uncertain to consider, next week a fairy tale, next month a nightmare ...

The phone rang and all three stopped, watching it on the wall, not moving, hardly breathing. Saul would take all incoming calls today, he had said. They waited. On the third ring it stopped. It was nine-fifteen.

Five minutes later Saul came into the kitchen. No conversation had been resumed, although Mutt had turned to the task of frying bacon and scrambling eggs. Yuri had sat staring out the window, as had Lyle.

'Mrs. Lanier won't be coming in today,' Saul said quietly. 'Her daughter is ill with a high fever.' He turned and walked out again.

Yuri took a deep breath. The smell of burning bacon began to fill the room; Lyle got up and left the kitchen.

Lasater had seen a lot of summer camps, boy scout camps, school camps, lodges, summer homes, most of them closed up for the winter. There were hunting camps just opening, and signs directing him to ski areas, open starting December 1, if weather permitted. Did they all make snow? Surely there would not be enough snow in a couple of weeks. The light flurry of the night before had vanished soon after daylight; he saw traces in sheltered spots here and there. He had driven a scenic route, and the business route, and dirt roads. He had seen townships so small that it appeared any group of three buildings could qualify for a name just as long as there was a gas station and space for a mail drop. He had seen enough waterfalls and rustic, quaint bridges and sparkling brooks to last him a lifetime, two lifetimes. He had driven half a dozen dirt roads that he had had to back out of when he reached a chain with the now familiar sign: CLOSED FOR THE SEASON. Summer playground for New York City, winter playground for the same, and right now was in between time. No one was playing, no one was out at all, except high school kids who drove like truckers on bennies.

He had seen deer, too, and he did not like that. Some of them were grazing along with cattle in one field, passing. Several had been on the side of the road, dead. He had heard about deer at twilight, after dark, the worst menace there was in this part of the country. Three different people had told him that today and he believed them. At twilight he would pack it in, he had decided, get a motel room in Milford, or Matamoras, and study the map a little more.

Highway 6 wound upward out of the Delaware valley, blacktop here and wide enough to pass, but there was no one else on it. The traffic was on the interstate a few miles back. He would go to Hawley, twenty-five miles up the road, turn around there and go back to Milford for the night and consider his next move. If Hawley was anything like Dingman's Ferry, or any of the other little towns he had passed, it would take no more than a minute or two to check it out. Why people lived in places like this was a mystery to him. Nothing here but trees and deer, nothing to do but get in the car and go for a drive, no one but hicks. When the summer people were around it must be okay, lively. Probably some gambling if you knew where to look for it, parties ...

Saul and Lyle walked by the pond late that afternoon. 'Carmen may arrive tonight,' he said. 'I hope so.'

'So do I!'

He stopped. 'Are you still confused?'

'Of course. I don't see how a woman can love two men equally and not be confused.'

He laughed and started to walk again. 'Look, the ice is nearly white all the way across. It's thickening fast.'

'I have to have something to do,' Lyle said. 'Everyone else is off at work on various things, but I have nothing. I've been thinking about it. I should write the history of this group, yours and Carmen's, Dora's, Steve's, everyone's. It should be preserved, in case ... It should be preserved.'

'I agree. You remember that idea I was working on back in Oregon? It's been a project of mine for many years, but I always get sidetracked from it. I am seriously interested in writing a thorough study of the idea of immortality through the ages. I have reams of notes; my problem is too many reams of notes. If you're at all interested in including any of that material, it's yours.'

'It should be included. Why don't you mind that I sleep with Carmen, that I love him?'

'Maybe because I've had more time to think about it than you've had. I don't believe love is something that comes in discrete packages that can't be divided, that it can be used up, like a battery that steadily grows weaker until it is exhausted. You would think nothing of it if for so many years you loved one man, and then stopped loving him and started to love another.

Sequential love is all right, but simultaneous love is a sign of moral turpitude, isn't that what bothers you?'

'You know it is. And don't laugh at me again.'

He was gazing thoughtfully at the ice. 'I never thought of it before, but can you use *turpitude* without moral? I never saw it used alone, did you?'

She sighed. 'You never really tell me anything, do you? I ask a question, raise a doubt that's bothering me, and you manage to sidestep it and make me find my way every time.' They walked on silently for a minute and she said, 'I envy Mutt and Yuri. They seem able to put things out of mind, just go on to the next stage.'

'Remember that Yuri has lived with the testing for a long time. And he knows that his government plans to disperse it. It isn't a new idea for him to adapt to. He's forcing Mutt not to dwell on the near future since it can't be avoided.'

They were almost directly across the pond from the building now. Soon it would be dark. Soon Carmen would be home.

Lasater drove very slowly, studying driveways, dirt roads that left the highway, planning a more thorough investigation of the area on the following day. He passed a bird sanctuary with the usual CLOSED sign and drove on, then suddenly braked, and belatedly looked in the rearview mirror to make certain he would not be clipped from behind. Nothing was in sight. He backed up and pulled off the road at the sign. There was a chain across the gravel driveway. It was locked with a padlock. From here he could see the driveway wind and lose itself among the trees. Nothing was different from the many other closed camps, parks, lodges he had already seen that day, but something had caught his eye as he drove past. Now he studied the wooden sign that was on a stout post. Bird sanctuary, with the dates it was open – April through October, like most places around here, eight in the morning until dusk, day use only. Welcome. He gnawed his lip, staring at the sign. An insignia of some sort in the lower lefthand corner, M and S, done in fancy letters. The M had turrets on the tops, the S looked like a path, or a river ... He had seen that logo somewhere, he felt certain, but where? M and S. The M looked like a castle almost. He knew he had seen that same design ...

Alex sneezing, Alex popping another throat lozenge ... Closing the small box ... He blinked and suddenly felt almost faint. The drug company! He had found them! There was no doubt, no uncertainty. He had found them! It almost frightened him that he had been looking for a sign, that was how he had thought of it from the start. Looking for a sign.

Slowly he took out the keys, left the car, locked it up, and then stepped over the chain, started to walk on the gravel driveway. He felt as if he were dreaming. He remembered his heavy coat only when he began to feel chilled, but he did not go back for it. He came to a fork; one side had the sanctuary sign, the other a no admittance sign. Everything was very still, no breeze stirred, nothing moved, and he heard faint voices off to his right. He went that way, walking on the side of the drive, ready to step into the underbrush if he had to. Then he was at the end of the drive; before him was a pond, a field beyond that, and coming around the pond, walking toward him were Lyle Taney and Saul Werther, arm in arm.

He wished he had brought a gun with him, something. What if Werther had a bodyguard with a gun? What if he carried one himself? What if Taney had taken up weapons? He almost smiled at that thought, but he did not move out from under the trees yet. He could hear the sound of her voice, but not the words.

'I can't imagine why I'm so excited at the thought of ice skates,' she said. 'It's so silly. I skated in high school and through college, but not since then. Yet, I can hardly wait for the skates to get here.'

'Maybe you've grown so used to activities that you are finding this sedentary life a strain,' he suggested.

'Maybe. For years all I did was walk to my car and back, and pace a little before my classes. And then I hit Oregon. Up and down mountains like a goat. And, of course, in New York you walk all the time ...' She stopped, staring, her fingers digging into Saul's arm.

'You!'

'Hello, Lyle. You look absolutely smashing! And Mr. Werther, your recovery is complete, I see.' He stood near the trees, his hands in his pockets, smiling at them.

'What do you want now?' Lyle cried. 'How did you get here?'

'Carmen get back from Amsterdam all right?' he asked. Neither of them moved. 'I didn't blow the whistle on you and the Russky at the airport, Lyle. I could have, and there were CIA swarming everywhere, but I didn't. It's only a matter of time until they begin checking on the other passengers, the English gentleman, for instance. One thing will lead to another ...'

'What do you want?' Saul asked calmly.

'In. That simple. I just want in.'

Saul shook his head.

'I know. I know. But, you see, I can help you, and you're going to need help. Have you got a pencil, pen? Something to write on? I have a number for you to call when it's time to shuffle and redeal.'

Lyle was staring at him incredulously. Saul shook his head again. 'I don't have anything to write with.'

'I'll do it.' He fished a pen from his pocket, and his notebook, wrote down Herb Balinski's number, and put the paper on the ground, weighted it with a stone. 'I'm calling the shots now, Professor Hermann Franck. This mess is going to blow up right in your face. It's out of control, getting awfully near critical mass. Three things can happen. They can find you and haul you and your friends away for a vacation. They can find the formula and use the stuff themselves. They can push the panic button. I'm in a position to keep an eye on what they're up to. I can get word to you, and at that time I want in. Understand? I want in!'

'How will you get a message to me?'

'You'll get a phone call and one hour later, exactly one hour later you call that number. Is that a good number out on the sign?'

Saul nodded.

'Be seeing you, Lyle, Professor. Take care of yourselves.'

He turned and strode away quickly, was lost to sight within seconds.

'He's lying! Can't we stop him before he gets away?'

Saul walked slowly toward the paper Lasater had left on the ground. Lyle followed.

'You can't trust him! He's treacherous! I don't believe anything he says. I don't think he can tell the truth.'

'I know, but ...' He stopped, listening. They could hear a car engine start, then the squeal of tires, the roar of acceleration, and finally nothing.

Lyle drew a long breath. He was gone. They had simply let him go. She watched Saul retrieve the telephone number, glance at it, place it in his pocket. Silently they started back toward the building. They could not have stopped him, she knew. They might have thrown rocks at him, or raced him to his car, but they would not have caught up, they had been too distant. She looked at the ground as they walked, despising herself for leading him here, for not being smart enough, aware enough to know he had been following. She had brought him to Saul and Carmen, had nearly worked with him once, had put the only two men she had ever loved in danger because she had been weak and foolish, and now she had done it again.

At the door Saul stopped and touched her cheek gently. 'He would have found us sooner or later,' he said. 'He's so afraid, you know. Nothing would have stopped his finding us eventually. Now's the best time, after all, because already we have started to move. Don't blame yourself so much, my dear. Please.' He looked at the driveway thoughtfully. 'He's a rather extraordinary man. He leaped to the correct conclusion back on the coast, identified me, found us here. I don't believe there was a thing you could have done to prevent any of it. He's really a remarkable man.'

'And a dangerous man.'

'Undoubtedly. But he may be useful to us, after all. If he is in a position to learn something he can use for barter, that could be very important.'

25

Carmen arrived at ten that night. He was dirty and hungry; he had hitched a ride from Scranton with a trucker, and they had had engine trouble.

'How on earth did you get to Scranton?' Lyle asked.

'Actually I hitched from Canada, and I was sort of compelled to go where my various rides would take me, as long as it was in the right direction. I figured Scranton was as far west as I wanted to get.'

They were in the kitchen where Saul was broiling a steak for him, and Lyle was making a salad. He looked wonderful, even if he was grimy and thinner than she remembered. Yuri was beaming as if his own brother had appeared. The two had embraced each other like old friends. Steve had a wide grin that he was not even trying to control, and she knew her happiness at his return was just as open as everyone else's. How strange, she thought, tossing the salad, that she never had been part of a group in her life, never had had this kind of love for others who were not related, never had felt so uninhibited about displaying her love for others. She had been the first one to reach him, to hold and kiss him. She found herself wishing that Dora had not had to leave before now, and she felt her confusion rush back over her.

While Carmen ate, Saul gave him all the current news. He ended up saying, 'Of course, Lasater saw the crest, my little display of childish egocentricity, and he put two and two together without any difficulty. A drug company, two initials, the two of us.' He turned to Lyle. 'He warned me years ago that it was a mistake to use that logo; I refused to pay heed. I liked it.'

'It took both of us,' Lyle said. 'I led him here, you invited him in. Two of us.'

He came to her and kissed her lightly. 'This man is in desperate need of a bath and clean clothes. Why don't you go tell each other your adventures while Steve and Yuri and I plot. I'm afraid I'm going to have to send him and Steve away in a few hours.'

So soon? But, of course. Lasater knew where they were; Carmen had to be safeguarded, the plans had to go forward. She looked from Saul to Carmen, back, and then nodded. She reached for Carmen's hand, and they left the other three in the kitchen, went down the long corridor to his room and closed the door softly.

'I'm too dirty to touch you,' he said. 'I'm so proud of you, Lyle. I love you very much. I was so afraid for you.'

'I was the one who was afraid, for you. It was so dangerous.' She remembered how beautiful she had thought him when they first met. 'You are beautiful,' she said faintly. 'As dirty as you are, you are still beautiful.'

Now he laughed and took her into his arms. 'You've stolen my lines, witch. For that you get greasy and smelly and wet, just like me.' He pulled her along with him to the bathroom and they undressed each other and got under the shower together laughing.

For a long time they debated if Yuri should go with Carmen and Steve, until he settled it himself.

'I stay here,' he said firmly, looking at Saul, 'with you. I know no manufacture processes, have too bad English ...' He switched to French. 'I would be a burden for them, someone to look out for. Here, I can try to think how we can get samples into Russia, into Poland, Hungary. It is not enough to tell the world how to do it if in some countries it is not allowed, the process is controlled by the state. There must be a way. If there is, we two will think of it, will think how to implement it. This I can do without burdening others. If they come here and catch me, I say I kidnapped Lyle with a gun, forced her to bring me with her, that I have held you both captive for all the time I have been here. They may think I am crazy, but—' he finished in English '—what the hell?' His thick accent made it sound even more incongruous.

They all laughed; as soon as it was quiet again, Lyle said, 'Why don't we just close this place down and go somewhere else? You must know dozens of safer places than this.'

'You forget Lasater,' Saul said. 'If he can find out anything that he thinks we'll value, he'll tell us. He's desperately afraid.'

'You can't trust him! You can't believe anything he says. I don't think he can help himself, he has to lie.'

'I know. But if there's even a slight chance that he can tell us anything useful, I have to accept the risks. You don't, obviously. You could go with them, even be of help to them.'

'You know I won't. I'm going to write a history book, remember?'

At two in the morning Carmen and Steve left. No one said where they were going. From now on, the less any one of them knew about the activities and whereabouts of the others, the safer they would all be. Only Saul and Carmen knew all the details of the plan that had evolved over the years.

Lyle knew there were drug manufacturing companies in the country that were already at work packaging the samples containing the serum, samples of after-shave lotion, hand lotion, bath soap. She did not know how many plants there were, or what their names were; she knew that Saul and Carmen had bought them over the years. And she knew the Philadelphia plant would not be involved in producing the samples, even though it was geared for the work; now that Saul's identity had been discovered, that plant was suspect. They regretted not being able to use it because of its capacity for turning out a sample a second, but it was not worth the risk. She knew there were plants in foreign countries, but not which countries, or how many plants.

Yuri insisted on cleaning up the kitchen, and refused Lyle's halfhearted offer to help. She sat before the fire with Saul and felt the emptiness of the big building, like a resort hotel after all the seasonal guests are gone.

'You should go away now,' Saul said after a lengthy silence. 'It will be hard to participate, to know what is happening. It will be very hard, Lyle. It isn't fair to let you get involved. You haven't had all the years we've had to think it through and accept it. It will be very hard.'

She nodded. 'On all of us.'

The next day she learned how hard it would be. Mrs. Lanier called to tell them that her daughter had died.

'She's going to her sister in Georgia for the winter,' Saul said, facing the window, away from Lyle and Yuri. 'Alice was her only reason for staying here, she was frightened by travel, frightened by strangers ...'

Yuri murmured something in Russian, turned, and left the room. Lyle went to stand by Saul at the window. Snow was falling in large drifting flakes that settled gently on the shrubbery, the trees, everything. She saw through the snow, back to the cemetery outside Lancaster, the small, neat headstone of red schist, the field and woods ... They were running out of space at the cemetery, and what would they do then?

Lyle studied the frozen waterfall. Where the flow of water was greater, ice masses had built up like chalcedony in a thunder-egg, rounded, gleaming, with deep blue shadows captured inside. Where the water flow was less, where it seeped, grotesque shapes were forming, some jutting straight outward, some curved and recurved, flower shapes, alien flowers. An ice shelf was trying to grow from side to side of the stream, but always it fell before the linkage could be made; each successive start thickened the ice, the shelf was a foot thick at the banks of the stream, and the strata were clearly defined, narrowing to nothing finally. The edges farthest from the banks were as thin and delicate as the finest crystal goblet. The sunlight sparkled on them.

The brook never had frozen completely since Saul had been here, he had told her. It was spring fed, and the shallow water flowed too fast. Below the waterfall it was too deep to freeze solid. There was a cover of ice and snow on the brook, hiding it, making it treacherous. Under the insulation, secretively, it raced to the waterfall, rushed to create ice sculptures.

The sun held no heat, radiated no warmth. Now that the weather had cleared it was even colder than it had been during the three days of falling snow.

She had not planned to come so far, had not dressed warmly enough to stay out more than a few minutes. She walked back in the trail she had made through the snow, picked up her bucket of birdseed, and went inside. They were feeding cardinals and juncoes, and sparrows, the ever-present sparrows; last night she had heard the plaintive call of an owl, the first time she had heard one. And there were grosbeaks that came at dusk every day. It was good that they had an abundant store of seed; it was going to be a long winter for the birds.

Life had settled very quickly into a routine that burdened no one, left out no one. Yuri had attempted to take over all household chores, and together Lyle and Saul had forbidden him to do their share. For hours Yuri and Saul played chess, using it as a focus, she felt, for their attention, because at any point in the games, one or the other of them might suddenly make a suggestion about getting samples inside one of the Soviet states, and the game was forgotten until they talked it out thoroughly. They had come up with no idea that they both agreed would work.

She was writing the history, as she had promised, using the word processor in the upstairs office. Her material was scattered, not organized in any coherent form yet. As she thought of bits of dialogues she had overheard, or participated in, she included them.

Yuri: 'I read that after the Black Death in Europe, the terrible plague years, there was abundance such as the world had never seen before. Is true?'

Lyle: 'Yes. There are theories that it led to the renaissance in art, commerce, exploration, everything. For at least a generation, people had their basic needs and a surplus without having to work from sunlight to dark. In many places we think the mortality rate could have exceeded fifty percent. Then, of course, the population pressures caught up with them again and it was a scramble to find another piece of arable ground, another method of preserving foods, shipping them ...'

'This time it will be different,' Yuri said matter-of-factly.

'Women will learn the meditation techniques necessary to control their immunological systems,' Lyle agreed. 'It will take time. Is it true everyone can learn to do this?'

'Oh yes. Already people are learning to control their blood pressure, to lower it when it rises. They are learning to control their sugar metabolism, no longer needing daily insulin injections. They can control other organs, other systems. They will learn this one also. A few years. It will not take very long when the necessity is understood. And the world will have time to plan, to think. The women will control it. It will become a strange, perhaps wonderful, world, when the first period has ended.'

Lyle reread those words on her video display screen and then touched the print button. A strange world. Perhaps a wonderful world. She wanted to weep. If only they could just *be* there, not have to get there. Resolutely she continued to work.

She left the office door open, and they left the door open to the lab in an effort to dispel the feeling of desolation the big building had acquired. They all shoveled snow, and they all used the tractor with the snow blade and worked at keeping the drive open to the highway. Saul was firm about that; it had to be kept clear at all times.

He was in touch with others of the group daily through his computer hookup; they were busy, working long hours, shipping samples here and there, getting ready for distribution. Dan Malone had finished several papers, one instructing scientists in the methods of isolating the RNA factor, ways of storing it, using it. One paper he had worked on even harder, he said, was for nonscientists, trying to explain what the factor was, how it worked, to reassure people that pregnancy could be achieved. He had done articles for newspapers, television, radio, and the popular magazines, each slightly different from the others, writing for each particular audience. The final one would be for the science journals; he was not finished with that one yet. As he completed them, he transmitted copies through the computer for Saul's approval, editorial changes, whatever he felt he should contribute. Lyle put them through the printer, stuffed them into envelopes, affixed address labels on some, typed some, wrote out some, stamped and boxed them. Ready.

Somewhere else Dan Malone was doing the same thing, duplicating her work. Perhaps even a third person was also preparing copies, she did not ask.

Dan Malone had not returned to New York. Balinski could find no trace of him anywhere he tried. Lasater chewed a fingernail, caught himself doing it, and spat it out in disgust. He had not bitten his nails since what, thirteen, fourteen? His old man had painted them red and promised to do it again every time he found them chewed up.

He had not thought of his father or mother for a long time. They were both alive, in a retirement community in Florida, playing golf, fishing, sunning themselves, drinking gin and tonic all day.

'Think of all the money you're saving,' Balinski had said. 'You want them watched, and they're already out of sight. Costs nothing to watch someone you can't even see. You got another one for me?'

'Not now. Maybe later. I'll have to find someone who's on a cruise first.'

'Yeah, another grand saved. See you later.'

He had to find out the names of the others who had made the museum circuit with the Russian in Amsterdam. Five of them altogether, Rawleigh had said. Dan Malone had dropped out of sight. Seymour Oliver was gone. Two to go. He knew where the Russian had gone. He'd have to go to the farm, he thought angrily. Rawleigh had not sent for him, might never send for him, just one day tell him the spigot had been turned off, no more dough coming through. Get lost. He would have to give him something. Not Taney. She was his.

He had to have something to trade, he knew. And right now he had nothing that Werther didn't already know, or suspect. He began to feel panicky again and he forced himself to go back over his reasoning. Werther would stay put, hoping to learn something from Lasater that was worth a dose of his magic elixir. Rawleigh would turn to Lasater again, hoping for an inside track also. Werther believed he had an in with the agency, and Rawleigh believed he was onto Taney and Werther, or something equally important. He was not certain what it was that Rawleigh expected of him at this point. The only thing he felt certain about was that if Rawleigh found the hideout first, or if the agency found it, he was out on his ass. But he had done the right thing, he reassured himself once more; he had found them, made his offer and left, before they could consider shooting him, having him run off the road, anything dirty like that. He knew they would be capable of any dirty trick that occurred to them; he had been lucky in making his pitch and hightailing it away from them. They must be as worried now as he was, wondering what the others were up to, how close they were, when the knock on the door would come.

He knew that other people were moving, doing things, only he was at a standstill, and it was lousing up his eating and sleeping. He had thought Rawleigh would want him before now, had been certain of it. It had been ten days since he had located Taney and the old man. Ten fucking days! He saw them again coming around the pond arm in arm. And, by God, she had looked smashing. Not a day over thirty-seven, he added derisively. Any woman over thirty was too far gone to suit him. Any woman. Even if she did look as good as Taney, with her cheeks fired up by the cold, her curly hair blowing around her face like a kid's.

Again he thought of his parents, arm in arm on a beach. They liked to walk on the beach every evening. He thought of them as they had been fourteen years ago, the last time he had seen them, the time his father had called him dirty, filthy, underhanded, cheating, lying, reprehensible ... The list had gone on. All good clean words, all razor sharp, not a one had missed or failed to cut deeply.

'I thought you were the patriot,' he had answered. 'I'm in the service of the country.'

'You're a spy. You can't be a spy and keep your hands clean. No one can. Your country! You're doing it because it's a game with you, a dangerous game, exciting, makes you feel superior. Do you think I don't know you?'

'Old man, you don't know nothing! Nothing!'

'Thank God, I don't know what you know! Thank God!'

And he had left, just like that. No goodbyes, no last-minute kisses, nothing. Fourteen years. Suddenly he realized that they weren't the way he had seen them then. They were old. They could even be dead. Who would have told him? The state would have notified him, he thought quickly. One of them could have died, but not both. The state would have told him. He did not try to understand the relief that rushed through him.

He had paced his hotel room for nearly an hour. It was cold and gray outside, with too many people everywhere, too many crazies, nowhere to go and not be surrounded by them. He had come to hate New York. They had warned him at the desk about the gangs of teenagers who picked out victims randomly, pursued them, and beat the shit out of them, money or no money. There wasn't enough money in the world to buy them off, it was the beating up they were after, the act of beating someone. He had almost hoped someone would try to mug him, pull a knife, a gun, anything. Nothing had happened yet. But he did not like the noise of the streets, or the smell of exhaust mixed with dirt and the acrid cold air.

He had gone to movies, to shows, and even had walked quickly through the Metropolitan Museum. He had had women, had played cards and won, had done everything he wanted to do in the city for the rest of his life. Now he wanted action, any action.

Two more days, and if Rawleigh did not get in touch, he would make the call himself. The next morning when he went down to the coffee shop and saw Alex, he could have hugged him.

'Milking time,' Alex said cheerfully.

'Your cold all gone?'

'Yep. Fit as a fiddle again. But I'll tell you in strict confidence, I think the East Coast is the pits. I even lived here for a couple of years, and now ... The pits.'

'Too bad. It's the first vacation I've had in ten years. Real vacation, nothing to do except play.'

'Rub it in, pal. You going to eat, or leave?'

'When's the flight?'

'Noon.'

'I'll eat.'

Rawleigh was not in a good mood. He mentioned he was burning apple wood, that was why the house smelled so good, but he did not really boast about it, or repeat it more than a couple of times. He led Alex and Lasater to the small study and closed the door firmly, then stood with his hands behind his back at the window. 'Snow again before night. Won't last, never does here, but still, it's a mess. Can't keep denying it, those damn weathermen, it is changing. Anyone who's lived here more than a year or two knows it, why don't they?'

He wheeled about and said brusquely, 'Hugh, this affair is too important for you to try to play it alone. I want you to come clean with me.'

'I know. You think I have something I'm not telling.'

'Yes. That's exactly what I think. Alex, get those pictures.'

Alex left the room and returned quickly carrying an artist's portfolio.

'Stand them up against the bookcase,' Rawleigh directed, watching Lasater.

They were the pictures of Saul taken at various conferences, the same pictures Lasater had shown Lyle nearly a year ago, but now Saul's face was blown up to sixteen by twenty size.

'Examine them closely,' Rawleigh said, scowling at the pictures.

Lasater examined them and found nothing he had not seen before.

'Taken over a ten-year period? Isn't that what you told me?'

'About that.'

'Look at his face! Makeup, hair color, all that can do wonders, but it can't really age a man, can it? Look at the lines around his eyes, just look at them. They're exactly the same in every picture! Exactly the same!'

Lasater kept his face turned toward the pictures, cursing silently.

'You know what causes wrinkles, Hugh? I asked an expert. What he said was mainly solar radiation; it dries out the skin, makes it lose elasticity. Exposure to the elements does it, not aging in itself. Radiation. He's discovered an immunity to radiation! That's why Scanlon had the Russian grabbed in Amsterdam! They think the Russians have it already.'

Weakly Lasater sat down and pretended to continue to study the pictures. Too close. It was far too close, but not a home run yet.

'You think Scanlon has the Russian?'

'What else? Who else could have pulled it off like that? Not in the hotel, in the restaurant! And that means everyone in that little party was mixed up in it. Malone, Oliver, Franz Leiberman, Luis Betancourt, every one of them! Working for Scanlon, all of them!'

Rawleigh leaned forward and jabbed toward Lasater with his forefinger. 'They've all vanished. Every man jack of them! Like Ely and Lightfoot, Wilkes and Truly. Gone, every one. Nothing in the files, no forwarding addresses, just gone!'

Rawleigh had opened the door a crack and glimpsed an international conspiracy, and promptly had slammed the door on it. It was easier for him to suspect the people he knew, the methods he knew, than to accept that a group of amateurs could be operating, and doing it better than his own people. Accordingly, he had to believe they were all part and parcel of an inner circle at the CIA. Let him, Lasater thought, and frowned as if trying to follow Rawleigh's reasoning.

'You could be right,' he said finally. 'But where do I fit in? What do you want from me?'

'I don't want you to vanish out from under us, Hugh, my boy. That's what I don't want. I want you to know everything I've been able to learn, Hugh. Everything. Soon after the first of the year this government is going to start a mass inoculation. Remember the swine flu shots a few years ago? The fiasco, the lawsuits that followed? This time it's to be a secret. They don't want a public outcry again. The first round will go to a very select group. The Joint Chiefs, the Cabinet, certain members of Congress, the president and vice president, the armed forces, or part of them ... All very secret, discreet. There won't be time for a second round.'

'And you're not on that list.'

'That's right. I'm not. You're not. Alex, Aunt Jane. Most people aren't on that list, Hugh. Hardly anyone you know is on that list.'

'If they've got something like that, why not just hand it out wholesale, to everyone?'

'There's not enough time. And there would be a leak. It would be disastrous if the Russians knew we have it, too. If they get a couple thousand doses of whatever the damn stuff is, they'll be lucky. But the word is that in a few weeks, they'll be ready to start giving it out. And the Russians have had it a couple of years! You know what that means? God knows how many of their people are protected already. The way our side figures it, our only chance now is a very massive and secret launch with everything we have. As soon as enough of them have the goddam stuff!' He took a deep breath. 'They're praying that they'll have time for that much, because the idiots know that the Russians plan exactly the same thing. Hugh, if both sides are that sure the other is planning the first strike, one of them's going to do it, and it won't make very much difference which one it is. Not to you, not to me, not to most people.'

'That's crazy,' Lasater said, but he knew they would do it. Rawleigh knew they would do it.

'Crazy. Exactly. What do you think I've been telling you about this bunch of new people? They're amateurs, and they're crazy. Push the button, that's their solution to everything, always has been. But they'll be protected before it starts.'

'Christ! Look, if I can remember anything at all, I'll let you in on it, but it's a blank up here.' He touched his head. 'I think I've given you everything I ever had. I never put the pieces together in this way, I have to think about it. Give me a few days.'

'Take as many days as you want, Hugh. Just keep in mind that the new year starts in Washington with shots for certain people and not others. I'm sure your imagination will carry it on from there.'

'Keep it in mind. Right. As if I could forget.' He stood up. 'I've got to go walk and think.'

'No way, Hugh. I can't risk you out there. Think of Dan Malone, gone. Or Seymour Oliver, gone. Ely, Lightfoot, all of them. Everyone who's been near this is gone. I want you safe, Hugh. You're safe here on the farm. No one suspects that I have even a finger in this. I don't know anywhere else you could be as safe as you are right here.'

26

Lyle had set up a darkroom in the laundry, and for weeks before Christmas she worked on presents for Yuri and Saul. For Yuri she did a group of portraits of Saul, and for Saul she worked on finishing a study of the waterfall, the frozen sculpture. Day after day she was disappointed in her results and doggedly went back to photograph again, from another angle, from another perspective.

They exchanged presents on Christmas Eve. Yuri had carved an elongated, stylized bird for her; it was poised for flight, and very lovely. Saul gave her a necklace with a cluster of garnets around a pearl. It had been his mother's. Yuri was moved to weeping when she gave him his present, and Saul looked at the pictures of ice for so long that at first she feared he did not like them, or see them as she did, but then he sighed and kissed her.

'I'm afraid you're really an artist, not a historian, or writer, or anything of the sort.'

'And why is it so sad if I'm an artist?' she demanded, again studying her pictures. They had not worked as well as she had hoped, but they did capture the waiting feeling, the time-frozen feeling that she had been after.

'Because you're probably destined to starve in a garret.'

'It's same in Russia,' Yuri said gravely. 'Unless you are honored by state, it is best not to be artist. Except in spare time.'

The clock above the mantel chimed midnight softly.

'Merry Christmas, my dears,' Saul said.

They raised their glasses in a toast of champagne.

'If you can't come up with a workable plan to get the samples inside Russia and the Soviet states,' Lyle said later, 'what you can do is have ready a broadcast in the different languages telling the people that the government has it, where the plants are, who developed it and so on. Would the people demand it then? Would they demonstrate the way they do here?'

Yuri laughed derisively. 'For longevity or even immortality? I think they might demonstrate. But government probably would deny it, call it

American ploy to disrupt society. Who knows if anyone would believe?'

'The scientists would,' Lyle said. 'If you gave the particulars, they would believe, and they would try to isolate it to see for themselves, surely. They wouldn't believe a government statement to the contrary. And if your government does start using it and the death rate continues, it would be hard to hide, wouldn't it?'

'Government is able to hide many things in closed society,' Yuri said somberly. 'You don't understand how closed society functions, I'm afraid.'

'I think I do, but usually most people are able to say that whatever is happening doesn't have anything to do with them. They can't do anything about foreign policy, or trade problems, or allocation problems, and they deny their responsibility about all of it, because it's too complex. But think how fads sweep the world, even your world. People are determined to hear the same music, read some of the same books, eat the same kinds of food, wear jeans ... Many governments try to keep out the American influence, but to what avail? Can they really keep them out?'

He was gazing at her thoughtfully.

'Besides,' Lyle went on, 'if your government believed it's being distributed widely, among civilians as well as armed forces, as it will be, they will want to hand it out, won't they? Once it's known they possess it, once it's known that others are getting it, they would have to yield to the pressure.'

Every day Lasater walked around the farm; every day he had company, sometimes at a slight distance, sometimes by his side. Alex hated his walks. The others who kept an eye on him were the regular employees of the farm, a stablehand, a groundskeeper, Aunt Jane, others whose functions he did not know. They would shoot if he tried to get away, Alex had warned the first day, and he believed that. He had eyed Aunt Jane, then had given up the idea of trying to get anywhere near her. She might shoot even if he did not try to get away.

He had written a letter to Balinski, and carried it with him all the time, stamped, ready to go. Down the road there were several mailboxes, rural delivery, but he never had a chance to get near them. The nearest town was fifteen miles away.

Two weeks before Christmas he wandered into the kitchen where Aunt Jane was at the table addressing cards, jotting a note in some, just signing others, consulting an address book, preoccupied by the ritual.

'I'm not allowed calls,' Lasater said morosely. 'First Christmas in years I won't be calling my parents. They're getting on, expect things like that, you know? Seventy-eight, seventy-six, they get set in their ways.'

Aunt Jane made a noise and went on writing her note.

'Maybe I could send them a card, no message or anything, just my signature. Wouldn't be the same, but ... Could I have one of your cards to send them?'

She seemed annoyed with his interruption. 'Help yourself. I'll have to look it over.'

'Sure, sure. I know that.' He sat down and began to sort through the cards, examining the pictures, the verses. They were all sickly sentimental, and expensive, with gilt and silver and red plush, cute angels and reindeer.

'Pretty neat,' he said, picking up one then another. Finally he stood up, holding one. 'Address is in my room. Be right back.'

He walked out studying the card, and in his room he looked at an envelope he had pocketed, addressed in her heavy, bold script. Also he had a spare envelope. When he readdressed Balinski's letter it would have taken an expert to tell that Aunt Jane had not written it. He addressed his parents' card, and returned to the kitchen with all three envelopes. He did not try to replace her card yet, or to slip Balinski's into the stack. One thing at a time, he told himself, handing over the legitimate one. She looked at it carefully, sealed it herself, added it to the pile. He went to the sink for water.

'Mind if I put on some coffee?'

'You drink too much coffee.'

'Yeah, I guess so, but still, it helps me think.'

He splashed water around on the shiny-clean counter, and spilled a few beans on the just-as-shiny-clean floor, and whistled as he waited for the automatic machine to grind the coffee, then brew it. When it was done, he spilled a little as he filled his cup. He stepped in the spilled coffee and left prints.

'Want some?'

'No. I never drink coffee after four in the afternoon. You shouldn't either.'

'Yeah, yeah.' He went to the windows near the table and stood sipping his coffee. She was methodical. She wrote her notes, read them over, put the cards into the envelopes, sealed and stamped them, one by one. The stack must have had thirty-five cards or more. She had maybe a dozen to go. He sipped coffee and waited.

It was getting dark already. Everything outside was mushy and gray, sodden. It was lonely as hell out here in the country; he could not fathom why anyone stayed, no matter what Rawleigh was willing to pay. Maybe he had something on each and every one of them; that would account for it.

One of the workers came in with a load of firewood in a leather carrier. Aunt Jane looked at him sharply. 'Did you take off your boots?' He was in his socks, his boots left out on the back porch. Aunt Jane saw the coffee on her floor, the footprints in it, through it, tracking it nearly to the window.

'Damn you, Lasater! Look at that mess you made!' She jumped up and went to the other side of the kitchen and cursed when she stepped on a coffee bean, crushed it.

The worker grinned at Lasater and hurried on through with his wood, heading for the living room where he would make a fire before Rawleigh arrived, have the house fragrant with apple smoke for him. Lasater moved closer to the table shaking his head over the mess he had made.

'I didn't even notice,' he said. 'Sorry. Want me to clean it up? Where's a broom and dustpan?'

'Just stay out of it! Don't set a foot in it again!' She went to the utility room and returned with the broom, dustpan, a mop, and a pail.

Lasater sauntered to the hall door and stood watching her. 'Guess I'm just in the way here.' He was carrying his empty cup. When she glared at him, he reached out and put it on the table, as if he was afraid to move into the room again. Then he left, the two cards safely buried in the stack she had finished with. Now, if only she did not go through them one more time, if she did not notice a strange name among them, if she mailed them promptly, if the post office actually delivered them, if Balinski opened his and read it, if he believed Lasater would pay him for going to an obscure village in Virginia and holing up for an indeterminate time ... He took a deep breath. It was a try. The first step of what he knew would be his only attempt to get the hell out of here.

At dinner that night Rawleigh said, 'Aunt Jane tells me you sent your parents a card. Where are they?'

'Down in Fort Myers, Florida. Why?'

'You had to go upstairs to get the address. I'm surprised you don't know it.'

Lasater shrugged.

'Where's your address book?'

'On the bureau. What are you getting at, Rawleigh?'

'You just never struck me as much of a family man. Go get the address book, Alex.'

Lasater glowered at him and drank his wine. Alex went out and came back quickly and handed the black book to Rawleigh who leafed through it, stopped when he came to the address. Lasater had written it in that day. A post office number. It was a good address, as was the telephone number. He hoped Rawleigh would tell Alex to call it just to make sure. Instead, Rawleigh turned pages, stopped now and then, remarked: 'Janet. Marcie. Liz. Betty.'

Betty was his code name for Balinski. Soon he would get to Tess, Taney's code. He was glad he had not added an area code to any of the phone numbers. Let him think they were New York, or LA.

Rawleigh tossed the address book down and picked up his fork, resumed eating, dismissing the incident. After Aunt Jane had served cherry pie and coffee, Rawleigh said, 'Tomorrow Edgar's coming to spend a little time with you. I want everything, from the beginning.'

'You've got everything,' Lasater snapped. 'I won't play with Edgar. He drives me crazy.'

'You don't have a choice, I'm afraid,' Rawleigh said. 'Time's running out, Hugh. Cooperate, or we use some harsher methods. If you've told us everything, you have nothing to worry about. If you've forgotten anything, Edgar may help you remember. I've seen a lot of his debriefings come up with useful stuff that had been forgotten, sometimes for years.'

Lasater tossed down his napkin and stalked from the room, went up to his bedroom and paced angrily. Rawleigh had been right about one thing, time was running out. How long until the damn letter got delivered? Five days? Maybe. He had said he would meet Balinski the day after Christmas, but now he did not know if he could stand this that long. That night he got his first ulcer attack. Two hours after dinner he pounded at Rawleigh's door and told him he was sick. Aunt Jane's food was getting to him. He knew all about ulcer attacks, knew exactly what symptoms to complain about, what would relieve them. Aunt Jane was furious with him.

Edgar was concentrating on Taney, everything he could dredge up about her, every minute he had spent with her, how she had looked at the airport coming home. Had he seen the man with her, could it have been Carmen, or someone else? Would Carmen's hair be that long, that curly, enough to stick out from under a cowboy hat? On and on and on. He became ill rather quickly and they had to stop.

Rawleigh, damn him, he thought, again in his room. If he was onto Taney, that must mean he no longer believed the CIA had snatched the Russian, and he had ruled out the restaurant as a possible place for the switch. If he had backtracked that much, the others must have also. Once they got their collective noses on Taney's scent, they would run her down. It was too easy to make the connection, if that's what they were looking for.

He knew Rawleigh, his kind, too well to believe he was acting out of anything more noble than self-preservation, as he was doing himself. If Rawleigh could deliver Taney, Werther, Carmen, the Russian in any combination, they would have to deal him in, that was how his mind worked. In his situation, Lasater would be acting the same way. But he did not believe they would deal in anyone at this point. They might put Rawleigh away for safekeeping, and all others connected with him, but they would not include him. They were playing too close for that; this crew was taking care of its own, preparing for the worst. He thought Rawleigh was an idiot for pretending to trust them with his catch, if he made a catch. They had dealt him out, they were not likely to deal him back in, no matter what he came up with. He'd wake up behind a locked door, if he woke up at all. And Lasater would not be at his side, no matter what.

They found that Lasater could work with Edgar no more than an hour or two a day. He was too ill to continue after that. Almost every night he had an acute attack, usually one and a half hours after dinner, sometimes during the night. Ten days after his first attack he vomited blood.

'I need a doctor,' he said weakly. 'X-rays. That's what they do. They x-ray the stomach. Rawleigh, I could bleed to death without a doctor.'

Rawleigh nodded, almost as if he wished he would do just that. 'I consulted a doctor a few days ago. What we're doing is what he recommends – diet, rest, no coffee, no alcohol, bland foods ...'

'Sometimes that's not enough. I know, Rawleigh. I've been here before, remember? It's killing me.'

'He said if the medicine didn't help, he would give you something else. They have all kinds of new medications these days for ulcers, Hugh. We'll get the other prescripion filled for you.'

Lasater spent Christmas Eve in his room, too sick, he said, to join the festivities. He was starving, he thought darkly. He had forced himself to stay out of the kitchen, not to snitch at night, to keep the hell away from the goodies that Aunt Jane had spread around the house this week – cookies, fruit, nuts, candies. He had not gone outside since his first attack: he was pale, thin, as well he should be since he has starving to death.

He passed Christmas day in bed. When anyone came in to see him, he drew up his legs in pain and moaned. Rawleigh sat by the bed and watched him for a minute or two.

'If you're shamming us, Hugh, I'll skin you for it. You hear me? Tomorrow I'm having Alex take you to town for x-rays. The doctor agrees that you need them. Hugh, if this is an act, I'll have your head, but first we'll empty it of everything you ever put in it. You hear what I'm telling you?'

He dressed carefully the next morning, feeling shaky and nervous now that it was act two. He was careful not to have anything suspicious on him, no knives, no lead weights, no rocks ... When Alex searched him at the front door, he carefully did not smile. He knew the routine as well as they did. A follow-up car, he was thinking, when Rawleigh said:

'Teddy and Ray will be right behind you all the way in, all the way back. Don't try anything fancy, Hugh. Don't let's have any more trouble than we already have. Seven or eight days, Hugh, will you keep that in mind? That's all the time we have left.'

'Sure,' he said. 'I know.'

It was very cold outside; he started to shiver when the wind hit him. It looked good, he thought, made it all more authentic. Poor sick, weak Hugh shivering in the cold, shivering from weakness ... He was so hungry he wanted to cry.

'The story,' Alex said, driving, 'is that you're a house guest from New York. Rawleigh has agreed to take care of your bill, so there shouldn't be any questions about insurance, stuff like that. If you have to sign a release, your name is Tony Mudd.'

'You're kidding.'

'Nope, that's it. They're expecting a Mr. Mudd at eleven.' He was being careful, watchful, but he had accepted that Lasater really was sick, that was apparent. When he turned too sharply, he murmured, 'Sorry. Does motion bother it?'

'Yeah. Everything bothers me.'

Alex slowed down a little.

'Even if I had something, what would Rawleigh do with it?' Lasater asked. 'It's crazy. What could he do except take it in and make them add his name to that list? Where does that leave you?'

'Right at his side,' Alex said cheerfully. 'We go together. And you do have it, Hugh. We agree about that. You give and we all three go.'

'You just wish I had something for you. You've got nothing to bargain with. It's wishful thinking.' He leaned back and closed his eyes, visualizing the town, where the motel was, where the clinic was. He did not know where the clinic was. 'If this is a quack doctor, he doesn't touch me,' he muttered. 'And he sure to God doesn't cut.'

'Hugh! Really! Would we trust you to a quack? He's Rawleigh's own doctor, runs this little clinic out in the boonies two days a week, cuts in Roanoke at a real hospital. Don't worry about him.'

They crossed the highway where there were two motels; three blocks down they slowed, turned into the clinic parking lot. When they left the car, Lasater saw the follow-up car with the two farm workers in it. He staggered and leaned against the hood for support, taking in the layout of the clinic, parking lot, street, then walked up the steps and into the anteroom.

'Mr. Mudd? Dr. Casterman is expecting you. This way, please.' The nurse was competent, efficient, in her forties. She took his arm and started to lead him past the reception desk.

'I'll come too,' Alex said, following.

'You wait out here,' she said without glancing at him. 'We'll take good care of him. Have a seat, please.'

'Mr. Rawleigh asked me to stay with him,' Alex insisted.

'Will you please take a seat! Mr. Rawleigh knows Dr. Casterman will take care of his friend. Only patients are allowed in the examination rooms.'

'After the examination, when the doctor is explaining what's wrong, maybe he could join us then?' Lasater said.

'Of course, if you wish him to. This way.' She led him through a doorway, turned left into a hall lined with open doors to tiny cubicles. 'We don't usually open until one,' she said. 'But Mr. Rawleigh asked Dr. Casterman if he could see you early, before anyone else arrives. Have you had this much pain very long?'

There were no windows in the cubicles. A back door? He hoped so, otherwise he would have to face the goons in front of the building, and he was not ready for that, not today.

'Over a week,' he said. 'Could I use the bathroom before the doctor sees me?'

'Of course. Back down the hall, first door on the right. I'll be in room number three. That's where the doctor will examine you.'

No window in the bathroom. He left quietly and went down the corridor away from the examination rooms. There was the x-ray room, no window. Next to it was a small empty office, and across from it the doctor's office, the door slightly ajar. He glimpsed a man in a white coat at the desk, and tiptoed past. The last door opened out onto the back of the parking lot, which was empty. Satisfied, he went back up the corridor to room three.

'Good, there you are. If you'll just take off your outer coat, I'll weigh you and take your temperature and then let you get undressed for the ... What are you doing?'

He had glanced around the room quickly. There was a tiny sink, with several towels on a rack near it. Before the nurse could say anything else, he clipped her once on her neck and caught her as she fell. As gently as he could, he bound her wrists and ankles, hesitated over taping her mouth, and settled for one of the towels instead. He liked the way she had put Alex in his place.

He went to the doctor's office and entered. Dr. Casterman rose from behind his desk and came around it, his hand outstretched. 'Mr. Mudd? How do ...'

Lasater hit him before he realized it was happening, and he fell heavily. Lasater used the doctor's belt and tie to bind him, and he taped his mouth. Any doctor who would treat Rawleigh deserved it.

There was a window in the office. He looked out and stepped away instantly. The follow-up car was there. Alex must have sent them around. He cursed briefly. He looked around the office for a weapon, anything, and his gaze stopped on bookends on the desk. Onyx, in the shape of whales. He lifted one, hefted it once or twice and decided it would do, had to do. Now what? He stopped and thought, then took off his overcoat and jumbled it on one arm and hand, the one holding the bookend. He pulled his tie off, stuffed it in his pocket, pulled his shirt tail half out as if he had dressed hurriedly, and then strode down the hall to the door to the waiting room.

He opened the door, nearly doubled over, one hand clutching his stomach, the other under his coat. 'Told you,' he mumbled. 'Told you no quack can touch me ...'

'What the hell?' Alex said. 'He's not ...' He came to Lasater who was reeling, nearly falling, and reached for him. Lasater brought out the hand clutching the bookend and smashed it against his head, right behind his ear. He was breathing heavily by the time he had dragged Alex to one of the cubicles and taped his wrists, ankles, and mouth. 'Sorry, old pal,' he muttered, and went out and closed the door. He arranged his clothes, put on his coat and walked out the front door, walked to the motel, and asked for Herb Balinski.

'North,' he snapped to Balinski when they were in his car. 'And the first hamburger place you see, stop and get me half a dozen, and a malted. Then back to New York. As fast as you can get there.'

27

He had six hundred dollars, more or less, on him, the rest was in the hotel safe. Rawleigh had sent Alex back to check him out, bring his clothes to the farm; no one had asked about the money and he had not volunteered. But the hotel was not a good place to go to now. There really was no good place, he added to himself.

'You don't look too hot,' Balinski said when Lasater was finishing the hamburgers.

'Yeah. I've been sick.'

The car swerved slightly, straightened out again. 'You haven't had the flu, have you?'

'No, why?'

'You hear any of those rumors going around? About this new kind of flu? It's in Washington, maybe in Europe. No one's saying much about it officially, but it's a killer, from the rumors. Don't want any part of it.'

'Rumors,' Lasater muttered.

'Yeah, but this time it's a little different. We had this job last week, tailing a woman up in New York from Washington, can't mention names, you understand, but there she was having herself a little holiday fling while hubby's on the job in the higher circles, paying to have her watched, phone tagged, the works. One of the calls was from her housekeeper, dragging her back because her husband was sick as hell with flu. Not a word about it in the paper, and with him being who he is, you'd think there would be something at least. Could have died by now for all I know. The housekeeper was scared, and so was she. Didn't even want to go near the town for fear she'd get it. That's not your garden variety rumor, Lasater, you have to admit that.'

He shrugged. There was always a new killer flu in the works. He remembered Rawleigh's mention of the fear of swine flu a few years back, and there was Hong Kong flu, Asian flu ... The list went on and on. All the more reason for them to start the bogus flu shots the next week or so. He stopped listening.

He had to have a car, with snow tires, or studded tires, or something. He wished he had his maps, but was glad that he had gotten rid of them before Alex cleaned out his room. Good training, get rid of everything that might lead someone to where you didn't want him to go. But he might need a map. He had gone out on the route Taney had taken, but there were other ways, shorter ways. He needed some clothes, a toothbrush, razor ... Most of all he needed to ditch Balinski as soon as they hit the city.

Balinski turned on the radio and Lasater turned it off again. 'If you don't mind,' he muttered. 'Still headachy, can't stand the noise.' No way did he want Balinski to get word of a crazed drug addict who had mugged a doctor and nurse for dope. That was the story they would put out, he felt certain. A good enough story, enough to keep the doctor and nurse quiet without telling anyone anything real. Eventually they would get around to the motels and they would find Balinski. Hours? A couple of days? He did not care now. As long as he got to the city, got to a car rental agency, he did not care about Balinski, who had been around long enough to know how to cover his own ass. He owed Lasater nothing, and would throw him overboard without a blink when they got to him, but what could he tell? Damn all. Nothing that Rawleigh did not already have, or almost have. And by then he would have got to the little hideout in the mountains; they would all be gone somewhere else.

It sounded okay to him, but he was worried. Things were happening that he could not control, could not anticipate, plan for. He wanted it over, his part done with. He wanted away from all of them, Taney, Werther, Rawleigh, all of them.

They had just cleared Washington when he realized that he had been a fool. He really had been weakened by his ten-day fast. What if Rawleigh's people got to the motel sooner rather than later? They would find out the car make, model, year, license, everything right there on the registration card. Any second a siren could sound ...

'Take the next turnoff and head back into Washington,' he said curtly.
'What now?'
'I have to do something in the city, that's all.'

'Jesus, Lasater, make up your mind. You know it's going to snow before evening? I don't want to be dragging my ass through snow all night.'

'You drop me in Washington and take off,' he said. 'You got any of that deposit left?' He had paid a grand in advance, just in case he needed someone at a funny time.

'Damn little. Today will just about eat it up.'

'Okay, okay. We're square as of right now. Just turn around and head back to Washington, anywhere downtown.'

He would rent a car, get a map, and get off the damn interstate, and then pay a call on Taney and her pals. He would go by way of Philadelphia where he knew a place to buy a gun.

Midmorning Christmas day Carmen called. Dan Malone had been picked up, everything in his house confiscated.

'Carmen, are you all right? Are you secure?' Saul asked.

'For the moment. But I'm clearing out. Call me after seven in the morning Wednesday. From a safe phone. I can't get to the computer terminal any longer. I go to Seymour now, all right?'

'Yes. Seymour has to try. Get out now. Take care.'

He hung up and frowned at the phone for a long time. Lyle watched him, waiting. 'The government has seized Dan,' he said finally. 'Carmen and Seymour are both in Washington. Carmen will try to get to Steve in California. We'll have to distribute our information from this end, after all, I'm afraid.'

Lyle moistened her lips. 'Can they make him tell them anything?'

'Yes. They can always make people talk if they have time enough,' Yuri answered brusquely.

Saul shook his head. 'We just don't know. We have to assume he'll talk finally. You always assume that much.'

'How will Seymour try to get in to see the president?' Lyle asked.

'They went to Harvard together, they've been friends for many years. I have to stay here, Lyle, and wait for whatever develops, but you can still leave. You and Yuri ...'

'He'll believe Seymour! He has to believe him! I'm sticking, Saul!'

He rubbed his eyes. 'For now we have to wait. Carmen will get in touch with Seymour, tell him it's time, and then we have to wait for twenty-four hours. We have to give them time to consider our plan.'

Yuri nodded. 'You can trust them not to talk for twenty-four hours, for a week perhaps, but after that every hour is suspect.'

'The problem,' Saul said, 'is that now they know what our plans are. They know what Dan had, the information he was going to mail out. Perhaps they will assume that was all of it, perhaps not. And we have to assume that they have linked Dan to your disappearance, Yuri, and that means they could have backtracked all the way to Lyle. If that man Lasater could find us here, so can they. He may even lead them to us.'

'I should take all that stuff and go somewhere else with it,' Lyle said.

He shook his head. 'You daren't. With this snow we may lose our telephone. You can't put anything in the mail until we're certain the president isn't going to act. We won't know for another twenty-four hours. We have to sit here and wait and watch the television for an announcement. If we haven't heard by seven tomorrow evening, we'll assume the worst.'

Their lights would not go out since they generated their own power, but the phone ... Lyle had not thought of it before. Of course, here in the country in a snow area it must happen often. She was glad they had had their Christmas celebration the night before.

'If Seymour can't persuade the president to make an announcement about the serum,' she said, not believing that was possible, 'we'll know by tomorrow evening. Then, why can't the three of us leave? You won't have to stay here. What's the point?'

'He'll tell them everything except where we are. But I don't think that will be a problem very long for them. They'll come sooner or later. If it's right away, they had better find me here, and Yuri. They'll think they have the ringleaders, and perhaps give you time to mail the envelopes. If I'm gone, they may put up roadblocks everywhere instantly. You have to remain free through the night and morning, no matter what. You must call Carmen! He'll wait for that call, thinking, if it's delayed, that we're dealing with the government. Stay out of their hands, Lyle, until you have made the call, until you know the envelopes have been delivered. Stay out of their hands altogether, if you can, but do whatever you have to at least that long.' He was studying her as he spoke.

It was strange, she thought, how she could look at them, including herself, as if she were high above them all. They had not taken off their boots and now the snow had melted, leaving puddles here and there on the kitchen floor. Her own face looked frozen, although she was not cold, was sweating in fact, dressed as she was in a heavy jacket and snow pants, heavy boots. You really won't have to do it, that other self seemed to say without words, without a voice. Something would happen, she thought, something that would make it no longer necessary. Something. At the last minute. No one can make such a decision and stay human. Something would happen. Something, at the last minute.

The day stretched out interminably. The snow piled up under the windows, crept over the sills. They took turns working with the tractor to clear the driveway, keep it clear enough for a car to leave. It seemed hopeless. By dark fourteen inches of new snow had fallen and another foot was forecast for the night and early morning.

Nothing of any consequence was on the late news, and during the night the telephone lines went down. At times throughout the night Lyle could hear the road maintenance people trying to keep Highway 6 open. She kept closing her eyes, willing herself to sleep but finally admitted that it was futile and left the bed.

'Lyle?'

'I'm sorry. Did I wake you up?'

'No. Are you all right?'

'Restless. I'll read for a while.' But she could not read. She turned on the television, switched stations from movie to movie to talk show to ... She did not even know what she was seeing and turned it off again, and went to stand before the window to watch the snow.

She was not thinking, not wishing, not anything, she realized later. Just watching the snow, her mind not functioning at all. She found that she was weeping and did not try to stop. When Saul came to her even later and led her back to bed gently, she did not resist and finally fell asleep with his arms about her.

In the morning when they went out to start work on the driveway again, they saw that the road crews had failed; the highway was impassable.

The world was a wonderland that morning: the spruce branches touched the ground under their sparkling white mantle; the hedges had vanished under mounds of glistening snow; the brook was buried. It was there, running, hidden away, pursuing its own destiny that would carry its water finally to the sea, take the sea a message from the mountains of Pennsylvania.

How different this storm had been from the Pacific gales of a year ago, how silent, how deceptively beautiful the world it had created, how cruel to the wildlife that had to forage for seeds, roots, anything edible ... Lyle filled the birdfeeders before she took off her heavy outer wear. It was bitterly cold outside although now the sun was shining.

They all had hot chocolate while the radio played in the background. They would keep it on all day, in case there should be word of an announcement. The storm had swept into upper New York State, was creating blizzard conditions there; a new snowstorm was predicted for tomorrow in Pennsylvania. The road crews finally had been able to open Highway 6, but they were advising everyone to stay home.

'I'll finish the driveway,' Saul was saying over the radio background noise. 'You and Yuri should load up the van, have it ready to move as soon as you can get out, if you have to go. And put in extra blankets, and a sleeping bag, just in case you get stranded somewhere. You must be prepared to stay warm. Take the thermos of coffee. Maybe the camp stove would be better, and soup. I'm really concerned about letting you go out at all, my dear.'

'You're coming on like a Jewish mother.'

He laughed. 'So I am. Well, back to work. Don't either of you stay out too long in the cold ...' He caught himself, laughed again, and pulled on his coat and gloves, left them.

Rawleigh hung up the telephone and stared murderously at Teddy and Ray. No cars had been reported stolen that day, no hitchhiker had been noticed. No one had seen anything.

'You sat on your thumbs and let him beat up Alex, a doctor, and a nurse. It didn't even occur to either of you that an hour and a half was too long for a simple examination. You gave him an hour and a half head start. He could be in New York by now. Get out of here!'

As soon as they were out, he dialed again, this time to his superior. 'Mr. Scanlon, please, this is Rawleigh. I have to talk to him immediately.'

He listened, protested, listened, and hung up. Mr. Scanlon would return his call. He was still sitting there a few minutes later when his phone rang, the sheriff's department on the line.

'We just got a call from a private investigator in New York,' the sheriff said. 'Heard the news release. Says he's clean, but he picked up a man at the motel in town today, different name, but still, it could be ...'

This time when Rawleigh hung up, he did not waste any time; he called his office, told his secretary whom to have waiting for him, gathered up what material he thought he might need, and left his house, not even telling Aunt Jane where he was going or when he would be back.

A line of traffic snaked up the valley by the side of the Delaware River with enough room on the road for two cars to pass in opposite directions only if they were moving very slowly, very carefully. Trucks were not permitted on the highways yet, not until more snow had been removed. Lasater inched along, cursing now and then, but absently, not with any enthusiasm. There had been a news item about the mugging at the doctor's office; they were looking for him, for Tony Mudd anyway. The doctor and nurse were okay, but Alex was hospitalized with a possible skull fracture. His condition was called guarded.

Since it was already on the air, Balinski probably had heard it too. He would have hightailed it to the cops, come out smelling like roses. The cops would have called Rawleigh by now, keeping him informed, and if Rawleigh got his hands on Balinski ... He would know everything Lasater had found out. Taney, Werther, the Russian, the Monroe connection ... Rawleigh could add just as well as Lasater could, and he would have access to computers with lists of drug companies and their locations. It was enough, Lasater knew, for him to take to Scanlon, get himself back in the game.

He had not counted on being this long, had not counted on snow up to his eyebrows, had not counted on being paced by a state trooper through the boondocks of Pennsylvania. If one driver had a flat, or ran out of gas, or lost courage, everyone had to stop and wait for a truck to make it through the line, tow out the stalled car, and then they would creep forward again. It would slow *them* down just as much, he kept telling himself. They did not have a magic wand; they could not make the snow vanish. But his fear was deep and the chill he felt was not caused by the weather.

Lyle and Yuri put snow tires on the van and carried out the boxes of envelopes to be mailed. She kept thinking that at any time the radio would interrupt the music and someone would say the president had an announcement to make ...

He had to believe Seymour, she told herself firmly, positioning boxes, tucking a sleeping bag and blanket near the front seat where they would be available easily. He would trust Seymour, his old friend, a knowledgeable scientist, a responsible teacher, in touch with other responsible scientists all over the world. Seymour would make him understand that since one of the terrible drawbacks had been removed, they had to give it out, let people choose. The president would have to believe him. No doubt they would call in their own scientists who would confirm what Seymour said ... And the president would go on television, radio, make a world-shaking announcement, offer this gift to the entire world ... The Russians would have to do the same thing. They would explain the risk, no one would be allowed to choose for anyone else, each individual would be responsible for accepting or not. But available to everyone who chose to take that risk. A new world tomorrow ... He had to believe. She kept coming back to that until it set up a rhythm in her head, until it lost all meaning.

It was dark when they finished with the van, and the drive way was cleared, the mountain of snow at the road entrance removed. If the road crews came back, they might pile it up again, and if that happened, one of them would go out and clear it again.

No one spoke as Yuri prepared their dinner. They were in the kitchen watching the evening news, silent. Weather stories predominated. And war stories. War in the Middle East, war in the south Atlantic, war in the Far East. Toward the end of the broadcast there was an item about influenza in Russia, a particularly virulent strain, it was said, that was killing many people.

'They have started,' Yuri said soberly. 'It is started.' His face looked pinched, he was pale.

Saul nodded. He turned the volume down, but left the set turned on. He looked at Lyle. 'First we eat.'

Although she tried to eat, she could taste nothing, forgot to take one bite after another, and found herself staring at the food on her plate with no recognition. She had not believed it would happen, that they would be forced to go through with it. She had not allowed herself to believe it. Something would happen. Something. She remembered her plea to Saul: 'Promise you won't ask me to kill anyone.' And he had refused to make that promise. Not any*one*, but thousands, hundreds of thousands, millions.

She watched Saul incuriously when he got up to make sandwiches with thick fillings of ham and cheese.

'We'll erase all signs of your presence here for the past months, try to convince them you have been somewhere else, if they come. They must not even suspect that you have duplicate mailings. We can't have them looking for you on the roads. Take any route that's open, Lyle. Forget the plans, head south out of the snow zone. And tomorrow morning at ten call here. If the lines are still down, or if I don't answer, hang up and call Carmen, tell him to go ahead. You have to do that, Lyle. No one is going to move until there is a signal from here. Carmen won't know if we're secure or not and he won't call long distance for fear of being traced. He has to be free to contact everyone else. You'll be the link; we can't get in touch with anyone else with the phone lines down.'

Slowly she found herself concentrating on his words even though they had been through it all before. He was speaking calmly, matter-of-factly, reviewing everything, giving her time to accept that it was going to happen.

'If I answer and don't mention ... what, Lyle? What should our signal be that I have been forced to answer the telephone? Or that it is I on the phone, not an imposter.'

'Welcome, chaos,' she said. 'If you don't say welcome, chaos, I'll know, and hang up.'

He nodded.

'If the lines are still down, if I can't get through to you?'

'Call Carmen. He'll have to decide alone. It's all we can do.'

She felt numb. When she dressed again in her heavy coat, boots, gloves, she moved like an automaton. The outside air made her blink, she had forgotten how cold it was. Saul put a package inside the van on the passenger seat, then held her tightly.

'Be careful, Lyle. I love you very, very much.'

Then Yuri kissed her and she got behind the wheel, locked the doors, and turned on the ignition, eased out of the garage. She had one more chance to look at them, to look at Saul, his face like marble; she made the turn onto the driveway. She drove slowly and carefully on the winding driveway out to the road, where she had to stop and wait for a motorist to let her take a place in the line of traffic that was following a snow plow to the cloverleaf of the interstate, twenty-five miles away. The plow was widening the lane, going ten miles an hour.

Halfway down the hill she saw helicopters that followed the road in the opposite direction. Checking traffic? Police? Government agents? There was no way to know.

Lasater listened to the radio as he drove, stopping and starting automatically in the jerky traffic. Nothing but weather stories and static was on the air. Bored, he turned it off; more bored, he turned it on again, over and over.

He heard the helicopters before he saw them. They swept up the hill, hovered, then descended. And when they had gone, he found himself looking at the approaching traffic dully; he had lost after all. Then he saw her, Taney, pass by so slowly that walking would have been faster. The other line was like his, stopping, starting, creeping when it did move. He spotted a partially cleared driveway ahead, drew abreast of it and twisted the wheel hard, rammed into the snow and became stuck. He jumped from his car, started to run after her in between the two lines of traffic. Horns blared, cars stopped in his line, some of them skidding, and he ran.

When the other line stopped, he caught up to her van and pounded on the window. He averted his head so she could not see him fully; when she rolled down the window, he reached in, unlocked the door and yanked it open.

'Slide over, baby. Move!'

She looked past him, looked behind the van.

'You don't want cops any more than I do, Lyle, honey. But that's what you'll get if you make a scene. Now move over!'

She moved over to the passenger seat, staring ahead. He got in behind the wheel, slammed the door and locked it, and edged forward with the traffic that had started to roll again.

28

After talking to Herb Balinski, Rawleigh had turned him over to Edgar Bushnell for further questioning. Half an hour later he had demanded to see Scanlon. It had been a shock to Rawleigh to realize that his superiors in the agency had not kidnapped the Russian. With over twenty years of agency training in his past, nothing of this feeling had shown, he knew, but during the few seconds that he had to assimilate the information, he had leaped to the only other possible conclusion: there really was an international conspiracy, and the group that had gone sightseeing in Amsterdam was made up of its members. The man who had come home with the Taney woman had been the Russian. That was what Lasater had been holding out.

He now studied Lee Scanlon thoughtfully. How much did he know?

Scanlon was military in appearance, had been a light colonel or something in Vietnam, and had no government experience behind him. He had come out of a business school, had done some research for the president-elect, and had been rewarded handsomely. In his fifties, handsome, smooth, he was so erect that he made Rawleigh feel tired with his own effort to keep his developing paunch sucked in. They were in Scanlon's office, richly decorated with sleek Danish furniture, and American Indian rugs.

'You have some pieces of a great puzzle,' Rawleigh said, 'and I have other pieces. Neither of us can finish without the other. I think it's time to talk.'

'And I told you we're not interested in the Russian. The British probably picked him up for something they have going.'

Rawleigh shook his head. 'What if I told you I know about an American-led group that has both the Russian and the solution to radiation sickness?'

Scanlon leaned forward, both hands flat on his desk.

'*What do you know?*'

Now Rawleigh sat down. He had not been invited to before. He had been told he could have one minute, no more than that, Scanlon was busy today, would be busy tomorrow, next week ...

'Ely learned that the Russians have come up with a new health treatment,' he said slowly, watching Scanlon. Business school had not taught him how to hide. He went on. 'You put a team of scientists on it, not really believing, but not daring not to follow it up. The Russians pulled their heavy gun out of the conference in Amsterdam and sent a relatively unknown member of their team instead. He vanished. Not from the hotel, but from a sightseeing tour earlier.' Scanlon twitched and tried to cover it with a cough. 'The other four in the group were all in on it. Dan Malone, Seymour Oliver, Luis Betancourt, Franz Leiberman. But I know who brought him home, and I know approximately where he is now. Or at least where he was taken.'

Scanlon nodded, almost in relief; he took a deep breath. 'You're right, Rawleigh. I said you should be included from the start. Old experienced hand like you, we should have let you in on what was happening. But, goddam it, no one believed there was anything in it, not for months, almost a year! Where is the Russian? Who got him out?'

Rawleigh shook his head soberly. 'Not so fast, Mr. Scanlon. I've given you a lot. It's your turn.'

'Of course. Of course. Ely got wind of it a little over a year ago. They had moved the team of scientists down to a prison complex on the Gulf of Taganrog, twelve, fifteen miles south of Rostov. And half the team had died. That was what alerted him. Then prisoners began to die, a lot of them, but others didn't die. And they didn't get sick again, ever. He flew home with it and we called in Lawrence Truly and Hanford Wilkes for a conference. They went back through the papers the Russian scientist has published in the past dozen years, and when they put it all together, they came up with an immunological system that seems impervious to everything. Everything!'

Rawleigh was rigid now, while Scanlon was talking eagerly, as if he had been corked so long he could not contain the flow once it started.

'We really thought the British were onto it,' he said. 'We thought they got the Russian, and only gradually realized they were completely in the dark, not a suspicion of anything at all. We ruled out the hotel, too, of course. No way could he have vanished there. And we ended up with the same group you did. But they were all out of sight by then. Every last man of that group, gone. Fortunately Malone was one of them, and he's been under a rather loose surveillance for years, ever since he wrote those articles about nerve gas, and Agent Orange even before that. You know him, negative, all the way, every time he does an article about the military, the government, any authority at all, it's always negative. Anyway, we staked out the places where he showed up now and then, and he did indeed appear.'

Rawleigh felt a great heaviness pressing on him. If they had Malone, they would not need him, what little he had left. He remained impassive, listening.

'They have it, all right,' Scanlon said darkly. 'And they're terrorists, murderers! They plan to hand it out! Do you have any idea what the death rate is for it? Half! They're willing to kill millions of people! Terrorists, conspirators, collaborators, anarchists, satanists, communists … I can't tell you how I feel about them! They're guilty of treason, every last one of them! They'll hang. One by one, they'll hang!'

'But you don't have them yet,' Rawleigh murmured. Of course, he thought, Malone would not talk, not this soon anyway.

'No! We'll get them, naturally, but not soon enough. We have to stop them before they hand out so much as a sample! And they're ready. Malone had tons of material ready to mail out. Radio, television, magazines, newspapers, universities … They're ready to move and we have to stop them!'

'It's just a matter of time before Malone talks,' Rawleigh said when Scanlon finally stopped.

'And we don't have time! They've issued an ultimatum! They're giving the president orders! They plan to start distribution if the president doesn't make a public announcement telling the world what has been discovered, promising distribution to everyone who chooses to take the chance on it!'

Rawleigh tried to make sense of it. Why would they do it now, when they had not given it out before? They had the Russian; they knew whatever the Russian knew, and that had to mean the Russians were using it, or planned to use it soon. The flu epidemic? Of course, the flu epidemic. Fifty-percent mortality!

'What was the time limit for the ultimatum?' he asked briskly.

'Right away. Oliver came to the president himself, told him they were going to move in twenty-four hours if the announcement is not made.'

Would that be so bad? Hand it out to the world, let the pieces fall? He thought suddenly of the secretary of defense who had died, whose death had not yet been made public. Flu?

'Have you had a treatment yet, Mr. Scanlon?'

'Don't you understand? Half of those who try it die! Half! A couple of our own people have died. We aren't going to use it again until we find out why and fix it. And we're not going to let the Russians keep on handing it out either!'

'Today the president is going away for a vacation. And the vice president is out of town, Congress adjourned ... When, Mr. Scanlon? When are you going away for a short vacation?'

Scanlon looked gray and haggard. 'Tomorrow. I'm leaving in the morning.'

'We don't have much time, do we? You were right about that. If they plan distribution, they have the means to make the stuff. A pharmaceutical company, chemical plant, something of the sort.'

'Yes, yes! We're looking into them right now.'

'But in the right place? Let me tell you where I think we should be looking.' Concisely and thoroughly he reported everything that Lasater had told him, everything that the private detective, Balinski, had told Lasater.

Two hours later they decided that the firm M and S Pharmaceuticals was the company they were after. Because of the recent blizzard in the area, they chose to use helicopters to pay a call on Mr. Markham. Grover Rawleigh elected to go along with the fourteen men who would make up the party.

Rawleigh sipped coffee and watched the old man. It had been almost too easy, dropping out of the sky, walking into this place that could have been a fortress. Markham, Werther, whatever he called himself, and the Russian had been in the kitchen finishing dinner; now the three of them were in the living room while the place was being searched. But no one else was here, obviously. Just as obviously it was headquarters of their group.

'It's over,' Rawleigh said. 'Your friends have told us everything, you might as well confirm it and save us all a lot of trouble.'

'Am I under arrest? Are you taking us away in your helicopters? I should turn some things off if that is the case.'

'Soon,' Rawleigh said. 'There's no rush any longer. Our agents are picking up your people around the country at the moment. Mr. Oliver was very helpful.'

Now Werther/Markham smiled at him, and he had the feeling that the man was laughing inside. He knew Oliver would say nothing that had not been long planned. Rawleigh finished the coffee and waited for the search to be concluded, waited for Doerring to report. They would find nothing, he was certain. No trace of anyone else, nothing incriminating, nothing to haul back as evidence.

'How long have the phones been out?' Rawleigh asked.

'Since the storm hit, I imagine. I really don't know. I haven't been trying to call, you see.'

'Probably they'll be back in service soon now. The roads are passable, crews are out working. I have to admire those men working out in such weather. I'm surprised that you stay up here through the winter.'

Someone would call, Rawleigh reasoned. They had to get a signal to him, or he had to get one out to them. For all they knew Oliver was still waiting to see the president. None of his people could know the house was occupied; someone would call. They all waited for Doerring to report.

This would be as good a place as any to wait it out, he decided. Plenty of hills between here and New York City, no targets nearby, plenty of food in the freezer. He would send back one of the helicopters, most of the men, and he would wait it out with Markham/Werther, wait for the call, wait for whatever came next. His gaze was bleak as he stared at the fire. Whoever launched first would win, he knew. But he also knew that there would be retaliatory strikes. The only question was how many and how big? That was the question no one could answer. He hoped the strike was so massive that no Russian would be left with a finger to push down on a button.

Doerring finally reported in, and Rawleigh left Rusty Wagner with the two men in the living room.

'There's a fancy computer hookup in an office on the second floor. And I don't think the woman's been gone very long. Her bed's stripped, but the sheets are still in the washer in the laundry room. No papers of any account, but it will take time to go through everything. We need a computer man here.'

'Are we in radio touch?'

'Yes, it's hooked up now with the scrambler.'

'I'll talk to Scanlon.'

By the time he finished the conversation with his chief it was close to midnight, and he was tired. His bedtime was usually earlier than this.

'Dr. Korolenko, we are sending you to Washington to talk to our people there. The helicopter will be leaving in a few minutes. You'd better dress warmly.'

Neither the Russian nor the old man spoke as Yuri rose and walked from the room with Rusty Wagner at his side. When he was gone, Rawleigh said, 'You're a cold-blooded son of a bitch, aren't you? You know he's due for an interrogation tonight.'

'He took his chances, as we all do.'

'Yes. Well, he lost. You've lost. You might as well make it easy for all of us,

Mr. Markham, and tell us where the others are. Where is Lyle Taney?'

The old man's gaze on him was steady, thoughtful. It made little difference if he talked tonight or tomorrow, or never, Rawleigh knew. A team of electronic experts was on the way; they would rig up the telephone, tackle the computer, find out everything that had gone into it. If anyone called, they would trace the call, dispatch another team. Everyone was ready to move very fast. They would find out what kind of car Taney had left in and put out a bulletin on it; the first of a series of announcements about espionage, Russian spies, germ warfare, God knew what, would be on the air as soon as the Russian was in a safe place. Everyone was ready to move, the first moves had been made, the rest was a matter of inevitability.

'We know she left after the storm,' he said easily. 'That isn't much of a lead for her, is it? Where are your insurance papers, by the way?'

Werther/Markham shrugged. 'I never try to keep track of that sort of thing and my secretary quit some time ago. I'm afraid I can't help you.'

'We'll find them. Doerring, take him to one of the offices and see if he can remember anything that will be of help. I'm going to bed.' If no papers turned up, the state licensing department would track down the car for them.

He was glad that he no longer had to be involved in all-night interrogations; he no longer had to go through drawers, shelves, boxes of junk looking for the one item that would complete a picture. He had done all that, too many years, he thought sourly. Now he could go to bed, let others take care of it, hand him reports when the job was done. Seniority had its advantages in government service. Doerring was young and eager; let him earn his right to climb the ladder just as everyone else did over the years. Doerring was only forty, perhaps a bit too eager, too pushy, but on the other hand, he did not have a clue about what was at stake in this game, not really. He thought they were after spies, simple as that. He thought the world was made up of our agents and theirs, simple as that, and their guys deserved little consideration, no matter what their ages, their affluence, anything else. As he watched them leave the living room he was not sure which of the two men he pitied more. Werther/Markham would talk the minute he decided he wanted to and Doerring did not know that yet. His forty years had not been long enough for him to know people like Werther/Markham, to know that he was going to be under as much pressure as the old man for the rest of the night, through tomorrow, however long he kept at it. Rawleigh was convinced that all-night stints like this one exacted a terrible toll, but in this case only Doerring would have to pay, and he especially did not know that.

Sighing, he wandered down the hallway to choose one of the empty bedrooms for his own use that night. All were spacious and warm, all equipped with towels, soap, shave lotions, body lotions, toothpaste, and brushes in pristine plastic cases. He told Jules Blakeley which room he had chosen, in the annex, glanced in at the two men going through the papers in Werther's study, and at others going through books, riffling through them page by page, and again was glad he was not part of that end of it any longer. He went on to his room. A hot soaking bath, then bed, that was all he wanted now. Everything was under control here, everything being done that could be, should be done. A hot soaking bath, a bit of lotion on his hands, chapped from the frigid wind, maybe a few minutes for reading, then sleep. The distant highway noise was inaudible in the annex. There were even robes in the bedrooms, he noticed with pleasure. He would still be awake when the helicopter brought in the team of experts, see that they got started; let them envy him his comfort of a robe, a waiting bed. He began to hum under his breath as he drew the water. Maybe he would even drop in on Doerring for a moment, see how he was making out.

He heard the helicopter arrive as he was luxuriating in the oversized tub, almost falling asleep. He shook himself, got out and toweled down briskly and put on the borrowed robe. A touch short, but comfortable enough. He examined the lotions, selected one and rubbed some on his hands, and then went looking for slippers. None fitted him. His feet were slender, elegant, he liked to think. Regretfully he put his own shoes back on and went out to greet the newcomers. Blakeley had already taken them to the office with the computer setup. He did not like computers very much, did not trust them, did not understand them. He stood back watching for a moment as the computer men conferred. His attention wandered to an open closet door, and he walked over and looked inside. Shelves of supplies, reams of paper, boxes of envelopes in different sizes. A lot of empty space where supplies had been; dust still outlined box shapes. He stared at the boxes, blinked several times, stared. Why would they need so much of this kind of stuff here? The main office was in Philadelphia, that's what Doerring had said. This was a personal computer, a laboratory computer, with a printer, and a screen ... a telephone connection. Postage scales.

Abruptly he turned and left the office, walked down the circular stairs that wound about the center post in the building, and went to the kitchen where the radio was. The operator was dozing in a tilted chair.

'Get Scanlon!' Rawleigh said, and the man jerked awake, nearly fell. 'And then get out.'

They had made copies of everything Malone had done, he thought viciously, and someone had the stuff out there now, copied, printed, addressed, stamped, ready to mail.

29

Mentally Lyle had made an inventory of the contents of the van: the boxes of envelopes to be mailed, sleeping bag, blanket, thermos of coffee, sandwiches … her purse, a handful of clothes in an overnight case. There was a tire jack, of course, but under a panel, under the boxes. In the glove compartment were maps, a flashlight. No weapons, nothing that could even serve as a weapon. The flashlight? Too small, lightweight. In her purse was a nailfile, too small, too flimsy.

'Which way you headed?' Lasater asked.

'South, out of the snow.'

He looked at her sharply when she spoke. 'Just take it easy, Lyle,' he murmured. The trouble was, she was taking it too easy; she was too cool, too remote, too much in control. Planning something, that was it, preoccupied with her plans. The traffic stopped again and he twisted in the seat, reached behind him and pulled one of the boxes within reach, opened it. Envelopes. He pulled one out and felt it, then tore it open. He could not read it in the dim light.

'What's all that stuff?'

She did not answer.

'Listen, Lyle baby. You're in such trouble, you wouldn't believe it. And so am I, sweetheart. So am I. Those choppers landed back at your little retreat. By now your sugar daddy and the Russky are in the hands of the government. How many others have been picked up already is anyone's guess. Don't hold out on me, Lyle. Not now.'

She continued to gaze out the windshield with that same absent expression. He put the typed message on the floor between them and eased the van forward with the traffic that was moving once more.

The thermos, she had decided. It was heavy enough. Not here, not with so many people trapped by the snow, witnesses who could watch any little drama they might have to play out. Later, after they left the packed cars, when the highway was clear and they were not under constant observation, then she would get the thermos from the back, hit him with it enough to stun him, enough to kill him if she had to. Push him out of the car, and speed away from him. She concentrated on the problem of swinging the thermos in the confines of the front of the van.

'Were you clear of the driveway before those choppers showed up?'

'Yes.'

'Good. They'll know you're gone, but not when. Listen, Lyle, I'm taking the interstate east. We'll leave it as soon as the snow lessens. I don't think anyone's stopping traffic here yet, but if they are, don't you even peep.' He reached into his coat pocket and withdrew the gun he had bought in Philadelphia, not much of a gun, but sufficient. He showed it to her and pushed it back into the pocket. 'I take it you have a chore to do tonight, somewhere you have to go, something you have to do, and believe me, honey, you won't be doing it with a hole in you, no matter what kind of immunity you have now. So be good, okay?'

They were almost to the cloverleaf entrance to the interstate when they had to stop again. Now he turned on the dome light and picked up the paper, started to read it. 'Jesus!' he whispered. 'Jesus Christ! Is this what's in all those boxes?'

She looked straight ahead. He pulled out a few more envelopes, opened one, then another, tossed them all back into the box. No wonder she had made no attempt to get out of the van, no wonder she was sticking, had not even checked to see if her door was unlocked. He was gripping the wheel so hard his hands ached. They started to move forward.

He would not turn her in around here, she reasoned. He would try to take her back to Washington with him, take the evidence to the proper authorities, his bosses, not hand it over to local police. Washington was an all-night drive; there would be time during the night …

They turned onto the interstate, and here the crews had opened a lane in each direction, with mounds of snow between them. Traffic picked up speed, still single file, but definitely moving now. They headed east.

Lasater felt numbed by what was in the envelopes. They were handing it out! Just like that, they were giving it away! All the fighting he had done, all the conniving, the cheating, the money he had spent, the worry, all for nothing. Now everyone would have it. For free! There was a catch, there had to be a catch. He had read only the opening paragraph, scanned the rest. As soon as they got to the open road, with a safe place to turn out, he would read the whole thing. There had to be a catch.

The Russians had it, were using it! Scanlon and his crew were aware of it. He could not seem to keep his thoughts going forward; they kept skittering away as if what they approached was too terrifying to deal with. Grimly he started over. Scanlon and his gang knew the Russians had it and were using it. They had Werther; they were not making any announcements about what it was, what it would do. They must believe the Russians were too far ahead. He forced himself to follow the line of thought. They had to believe the Russians were secretly immunizing their own people, and when enough of them had it, the Russians would launch a strike.

He shivered. Rawleigh must have hightailed it to Scanlon; they were dealing each other in. They probably got Balinski without too much trouble, traced the Russian, just as he had done, to Monroe, New York, and from then on, it was child's play to find Werther's hideout. So they had a lot of pieces now. Did they know what Taney had in her car? Probably not, not unless someone had talked, and he did not believe any of them would talk, no matter what kind of persuasion was used.

'Where are the samples the letter talked about?' he demanded.

She remained silent.

'Damn you, Taney! Tell me! Do you have them in the van?'

'Of course not! You saw what I have.'

He believed her, but he would look anyway, as soon as they could stop somewhere. Were others out in another van, many other vans, stuffing samples in mailboxes, hand delivering them to households like samples of a new toothpaste, or catsup? Pills? Sugar cubes? How was it being given?

She was thinking hard, also. He would read the information sheets, understand finally that it was transmitted sexually, and then ... She felt such a pervasive chill that it seemed the arctic air had penetrated the van in spite of the excellent heater. No matter what happened, she had to stay alive, able to act, and out of the hands of the government until ten in the morning when she would phone Saul, and then Carmen. She knew the call to the laboratory was futile. But maybe Saul would give the signal and tell her to come home, tell her it was being done in a more orderly way, the government was going to make it available ...

'Fill me in,' Lasater said, his voice grim and hard. 'I'm going to read the stuff anyway, so tell me. What's the catch with it?'

'What do you mean?'

'Why hasn't your pal handed it out before? Why now?'

She took a deep breath and suddenly saw a way to prevent his reading the papers. 'I might as well,' she said. 'It's all on the information sheets. It kills half of those who use it. A high fever develops and they die; others recover completely. You saw me when I was sick, when I recovered. That's how it reacts in the human body. Until the Russians discovered a way around it, it left sterility. They learned how to overcome that, but it will take years of training for most women to be able to conceive. Saul and Carmen couldn't turn it over with those two drawbacks. It would have been the death of the race. Half the people, never any children ... It would have been a hopeless, static society. But now that the Russians have it and they are distributing it, Saul knew we had to use it too.'

'You're willing to kill half the population!'

'If they start a war it will be *all* the population before it's over,' she said quietly. 'Those who don't die in the first week, will die during the weeks that follow. You know that.'

He did know it. He was gripping the wheel too hard again. He wanted to hit her, to hit anyone. He wanted to cry. Fifty-fifty! It wasn't fair! To have come this far, to have learned this much, to have found her, and then find it was only fifty-fifty!

'Who dies? What's the critical factor?'

'No one knows.'

'Damn you! You're lying!'

'I'm not lying. They don't know. There are warnings on the samples, explanations, warnings not to let children use them, or pregnant women, or seriously ill people ...'

'You said *use them*. What does that mean? How do you take the stuff?'

She bit her lip, then went on. It didn't really matter if he knew; as soon as the samples were distributed, everyone would know. She told him.

He cursed. 'Hand lotion! For Christ's sake! Soap!' He cursed again. They had reached the end of the snowfall. He had not been noticing, but now the road was clear, with slight accumulations beyond the shoulders. The speed of the traffic had increased until it was normal.

He estimated the time it would take to drive to Washington, directly to Scanlon, directly to the top, bypass Rawleigh altogether. They would have to cut him in if he delivered Taney and her printed material. Without that her group was done for. They wanted to give the world information as well as the samples. Scanlon had the old man – his doing. He would have Taney – his doing again. It would just be a matter of time before they picked up the others, one by one. He would be on the inside then, not out in the cold with his nose mashed on the glass. And then?

They would bomb the hell out of Russia, stop the stuff in its tracks, and then take their own sweet time to find the glitch that made the stuff kill half the people.

He knew that was a lie. There would be no one left to do the research, there would be no place in which to do it. Besides, they were already trying to cover their own asses by using it ... He remembered what Balinski had told him about the vicious flu that was loose in Washington. Like the flu that Lyle Taney had had back in Oregon last year! But would they drop bombs while this group was out threatening to start distribution? That was the tough one.

'What were you supposed to do tonight?'

When she did not answer, he glared at her. 'You're to mail that stuff, aren't you?'

She nodded.

'And other people are mailing the samples, or handing them out somewhere, aren't they?'

Again she nodded.

He drove fast, overtook other cars, then slowed down. No tickets, for

Christ's sake! Not now. He had thinking to do. He was cursing under his breath. 'Why did they send you? You're so green you're sure to get picked up!'

'Anyone can mail a letter.'

'And they can stop the mail deliveries! You bunch of idiots! You have no idea of what you're up against! The whole fucking federal government! The post office department! CIA, FBI, everyone!'

'Then I'll have to deliver them to the addresses.'

'Christ!'

She was stunned by his words: they could stop the mail deliveries! She had not thought of that. No one had thought of that. Or had Saul? Some of the letters had the M&S logo for the return address; many had no return addresses; some had false addresses. Some of them were in script, others in type, some printed ... Surely they wouldn't open every single piece of mail. They would pick out the M&S ones, they were easy to spot. She would have to mail them from many different post offices, mail drops ... A few here, a few there, through the night, into the morning ...

Meanwhile they were speeding toward Washington.

'There's a rest area ahead a mile or so,' he said after a short silence. 'I'm stopping to see what other little goodies you have stashed away in the back. Don't try anything, Lyle baby. Or I might take off without you.'

'You said you didn't want police any more than I do. Why?'

'I nearly killed a man today. Maybe he's dead by now. I think you'll make up for him, though. I think it'll be a fair exchange.' He grinned at her. 'And if I have to take off without you, I've got the real payload in back, don't I?'

'Lasater, if you take me in, take that material in, you know what it will mean. If they can suppress this long enough, there will be war, and no one will win, no one will survive to use the samples, or even suspect what might have been.'

'Just shut up, baby. I know everything you do and then some, so just shut up.'

They pulled into the rest area, stopped at the end of the parking lane, and then he motioned to her to go into the back of the van before him. She slid from her seat, eased herself over the gear shift, and went to the rear in a semicrouch. He followed. There were no windows; there was a curtain that he drew between the cargo space and the front. Then he turned on the dome light.

'You saw the message,' she said, kneeling on the floor. 'It's basically the same, some more technical than others, depending on who is to receive them.'

He opened the boxes, poked in among the letters in each one shaking his head. No samples. 'You don't have a chance. They'll stop the mails.'

'Why would they? They don't know I'm going to mail anything tonight. No one knows.'

'If the stuff is at the building back there to print up all these, postage scales, supplies, they'll suspect. Will they find that stuff back there?'

She nodded.

Lasater sighed. He picked up one of the envelopes he had opened earlier and started to extract the sheet of paper from it.

'Look,' Lyle said, holding up several other ones. 'If I mail all of them with the M&S return address together, from the same post office, they'll assume they have them all. Won't they?'

'Maybe. Then what?'

'Then we keep driving and stop now and then and mail the rest a few at a time, some in post offices, some in mail drops, in shopping centers, wherever we can.'

He shook his head. 'Not we, baby. No way.'

'Yes, we! You won't get it from them in Washington! They'll pretend no one is going to get it until they find out why it kills so many, and meanwhile they'll be trying it on themselves, or the army officers, or officials ... But you won't get it. They don't trust you enough!' She watched him, went on. 'They might even decide to kill you outright just so you won't talk, won't be a nuisance later when the war starts. You know too much.'

He was holding the envelope with the letter halfway out. Now he slid it in again and tossed it down.

She reached for the thermos. 'I have coffee, sandwiches. They're in that bag by your elbow.'

He did not move yet. 'What's the difference if a million people die from bombs, or die from your damn secret ingredient? What's the difference? Dead is dead.'

'The survivors are the difference! They get to choose for themselves to use it or not. Who chooses to get killed in a war? And there's no end to the dying in that kind of war, not until we're all dead, not until every bomb has been exploded, every warhead used, every missile ...' She was handling the thermos, watching him, tensing her muscles, getting ready.

He was looking at the boxes again, all open now, all revealing only letters, hundreds of letters, and no samples. She didn't have the stuff with her, and her time was nearly over. They would track down the van, find her, haul her in, and where would that leave him? Hauled in with her? His only chance lay with Scanlon, the agency ... He wished suddenly that he had just stayed with his own car, driven the hell away from it all. Washington would go, New York would go, the whole fucking East Coast would go ... and the West Coast, and the interior ... He reached for the bag of sandwiches just as she raised the thermos and struck.

If he had not moved forward, leaned, it would have caught him in the head, but it glanced off his shoulder and he dived, avoiding the full brunt. Reflexively he jerked out the gun and rolled so that it was pointing at her. She was very pale and there were beads of sweat on her forehead.

She should try to talk him out of shooting; she thought it very distantly, almost coldly, as if she were thinking about someone else, someone not real. His face was without expression, masked, his eyes looked dead, as if he too had to withdraw first, watch himself from a safe place.

He saw her jerk, saw her drop over, twitch a little, stop moving. He saw it flashingly, and, as he saw it, he knew if he did it his last chance was gone. If she had moved, if she had spoken during that instant, his finger would have squeezed the trigger, she would have been dead. The moment passed; he began to think again, regained control over his hand, and now he felt sweat on his back. No way could she ever know how close that had been for her. No way. He pulled himself up to a sitting position, still leveling the gun at her. 'Listen, Lyle baby, and listen good. You've got a little job to do and, honey, there ain't no way on God's little green earth that you can get it done alone. You called the play, now we're going to run with it. And you do as I say. I know every trick they know. They trained me, remember? We do it my way. And now, if there's any coffee left, if the thermos isn't broken, we'd better have some. It's going to be a long night, sweetheart.'

She stared at him, not moving.

A long night, he repeated to himself. And more than likely they would not make it. Scanlon, the rest of them, they'd pull out all the stops now, and they had the manpower, the organization, the need to find her, have themselves a little bonfire with the stuff in the boxes. But they'd work for it, he thought grimly. They'd have to work their asses off for it. Taney was his, had been his from the start, would be his at the finish. He had some unfinished business with Lyle Taney, he thought, watching her, and he was going to keep her until it was settled.

As he looked at her he suddenly remembered a statue he had seen in India, in Calcutta, years ago. One of their crazy-looking gods. A female with a great figure, breasts like apples ready to be plucked, narrow waist, and spreading, flaring hips. From her belly there was a torrent of goodies – flowers, fruits, even animals, for Christ's sake! And in her hand there was a sword. Like Taney, he thought, or Taney was like her. Take off his head with that sword in a flash if she had to. And she would try again, and again, unless they had an understanding.

Slowly he reached out with the gun and laid it on the floor between them. 'After we have coffee, while I'm driving, you can sort out the stuff with the M&S addresses.'

30

For many seconds neither of them moved. Finally Lyle said, 'I don't believe you.'

'I don't believe me either. Talk me out of it. It wouldn't take much.'

Still she did not move. It was a trap, another one of his tricks. He shrugged and again reached for the sandwiches, took one out and unwrapped it, started to eat. He continued to watch her, now with a glint of amusement.

'You've certainly come a long way, honey. Last year you couldn't have hit me with a cream puff, you know?'

'I'll kill you if I have to.'

'I know. That's why I'm offering you the gun. Symbol of a truce, or something like that. Don't like the idea of you lurking behind me with blunt objects in your hands.'

She snatched up the gun and held it, not pointing it. 'Is it loaded?'

'You kidding? Most dangerous thing in the world is an unloaded gun. Sure it's loaded. Probably a lousy sight. I just paid forty bucks for it. Still, at this range ...' He finished the sandwich, picked up the thermos and shook it. 'Don't hear glass. We'll see.' He opened it carefully and looked inside. 'Think it survived. If you'd got me in the head, you'd have to go without coffee all night.'

'You're afraid too, aren't you?'

He sipped the coffee, watching her over the edge of the plastic cup. 'Honey, I'm just scared shitless, that's all. You want some of this? Is there another cup?'

She shook her head and now she put the gun in her coat pocket. 'I think I should mail all the M&S ones from Philadelphia where the main plant is. They might not suspect there are more.'

He nodded. 'Are there maps? I want to stay on the interstates until we get out of the snow range, and then get the hell off them onto state roads.'

'In the glove compartment.' She watched him crawl forward, her hand on the gun in her pocket. Driving toward Philadelphia was also driving toward Washington, she reminded herself.

She should kill him now and be done with it, not have to worry about him any longer. They should have killed him a year ago. But he was afraid, she reminded herself. He knew what was at stake and he was afraid. Also, he wanted to keep away from the police. She believed that, no matter if what he had told her was true or not. If he delivered her to anyone, it would have to be his bosses in Washington, not state police, or local police. And he knew about roadblocks, how to avoid them. If they got through to Philadelphia, if they actually mailed any of the envelopes, he would be as committed as she was ... She shook her head. No. He could tell them where the envelopes had been mailed, they could still pick them up. Why had he given her the gun? Why had he told her they could stop the mail deliveries? She took out the gun and looked at it.

'Lasater, I want to see the bullets in the gun. How do I open it?'

He groaned. 'Christ! Don't point it in my direction, okay?' From the front seat he told her to point it at the rear of the van, then told her how to see the bullets, where the safety catch was, how to tell if it was on or off. Satisfied, she put the safety on and replaced the gun in her pocket. He had gone back to studying the maps. She would use the gun if she had to, she told herself, and knew it was true, but as long as he was helping her get south, if he actually stopped for her to mail the envelopes, the gun would stay in her pocket. If she could use him now, that seemed only fair.

When they started again, she was in the back of the van, the curtain closed, the dome light on. She began to sort the envelopes. About a third of them had the M&S imprint.

In a little while she heard him cursing, and their speed was cut, cut again. She finished, and joined him in the front of the van. It was snowing.

The snow blew against the windshield, piled up under the wipers. It was sticking to the road, accumulating fast on the shoulders.

'What kind of tires does this thing have?' he asked.

'They're good, heavy-duty snow tires. We should be all right.'

'Yeah. Is it licensed in Pennsylvania?'

'No. Ohio.'

'That's good. They won't be looking for an Ohio car for a while, let's hope.'

A truck passed them and he cursed more audibly. 'Bastards! One of them will jackknife and then we'll all have to stick it out waiting for cops, tow trucks, God knows what.'

She turned on the radio and fiddled with it until she found a station not choked out by static. Weather news, nothing but weather news. The storm was a full-fledged blizzard in upper New York state; snow was falling in New York City, down the Jersey coast. Philadelphia had escaped it so far.

The radio cackled, garble won out, and Lyle turned it off. The snow was not getting heavier, but the accumulation was continuing.

'We'll have to stop eventually,' Lasater said. He was concentrating on the road, holding the wheel in a tight grip. The road was getting slick; it would be treacherous before long. 'Anyone asks, we're from Toledo. Spent Christmas with my folks in Scranton, and now we're on our way to Florida for a vacation. Snowbirds, that's us. Mr. and Mrs. Hugh Lasater on our way south for a couple of weeks.'

She nodded. No one would ask, but it was best to have something ready, in case, something they both knew in advance.

He was thinking about his mother and father in Florida, arm in arm, strolling the beaches, sipping gin and tonic in the shade, fishing now and then. His father had been okay, strict, but okay. Just grew up in different times, that's all that was wrong with him, and he was not responsible for that, for Christ's sake. What if they took the stuff and made it? Walking arm in arm for the next ten years, fifty years, forever? Too old to work, not ready to die. Who'd support them, for Christ's sake? He chewed his lip. Maybe the old man could get a job again, he'd been a crack accountant. Maybe he could be again. Would they take it? He did not know. Would they feel they'd had theirs together, no point in going on longer? There was no answer. Married more than fifty years now, how had they managed not to kill each other? They even seemed to like each other in exactly the same way they always had. He shook his head, not understanding them a bit. Never had, he realized. Never had.

'Isn't your bleeding conscience going to bother you?' he asked harshly to turn off his own thoughts about his parents.

'Yes,' she said in a low voice. It was an impossible choice, she knew. No human should have to make such a choice. No saint, no angel, no god should ever have to make such a choice. She remembered how startled she had been, and how outraged, at the concept of triage when the first came across it. In battle, if you're a doctor, you don't help those who need extensive care, who might not survive; you don't help those who will survive without your help, no matter how painful their injuries are; you help only those who will survive with help. Each person to be judged in a flash, each injury assessed in a flash, then on to the next, and the next, and the next. The doctors would come out inhuman, she had thought. Their humanity could not survive, their souls would be killed by being forced to choose like that.

They turned onto Interstate 87, and soon the snow became intermittent, then stopped again. They sped south.

She remembered lying in bed with Saul, neither of them sleepy yet, just talking in the dark of the room.

'Afterward,' he had said, 'if you feel differently about us, will you come back and talk about it?'

'You're not serious!'

His arm tightened about her, he drew her closer. 'Carmen and I have had so much time to think about this, to talk about it, what it will mean. You know about the great discontinuities of the past? The establishment of the Christian religion was one. It changed the way people thought of themselves and their relationship with their god. The Copernican theory was another. It changed the way people thought about themselves and their relationship in space with space. Then came the proof that the world was really round. Finally we knew pretty well what our world was, where it was in the universe. From the center of it all we slipped into an insignificant position in a nondescript galaxy, on the fringe of that even. Each great change was tumultuous; each one changed our ability to perceive. Perhaps our synapses are changed with each discontinuity. First only a few people believe, then a few more, and after a *very* long time the rest of them follow. Many of them are still rebelling against the last two great discontinuities: the Darwinian theory and Freud's theory of the subconscious. It takes a very long time for such things to be accepted, for the adjustments to be made.'

Lyle's mouth felt dry. She swallowed. 'And there won't be time for this change. Not the next generation, or the one after, but this one has to adapt.'

'Yes. Can they? My dear, I'm sorry. You're shivering.'

They clung to each other in the dark and neither answered his question. When he and Carmen had talked, she realized, they had understood what they would do to the entire world, and, more, they had understood what this would do to the ones responsible. It was a long time before her shivering stopped.

Occasional snow flurries were driven by a brisk wind as they drove into Philadelphia. The streets were nearly empty of traffic. Lasater drove past the M&S plant out of curiosity. It would be occupied, but what would show? Nothing showed. It was a modern building with lots of glass, set back, landscaped, prosperous-looking, deserted-looking. He did not slow down.

They had decided to go to a post office substation a few miles from the plant to mail the first batch of envelopes. When he stopped the van, pulled in to the curb to park, she hesitated.

'Now what?' he asked in annoyance. It had occurred to him that they might be watching post offices. Not likely, but possible, he thought, studying the cars up and down the street.

'Let me take the key with me,' she said.

He laughed harshly, yanked out the ignition key and handed it to her, and watched her leave with a box of envelopes, watched her deposit them a few at a time in the mailbox. It was done. He was committed.

He had told her the truth that he was scared shitless. He knew that her outfit had no idea of the odds they were bucking, how slim their chances of success actually were. They were a bunch of starry-eyed innocents, and they were his only hope. Taney didn't have the stuff with her, but she sure as hell would lead him to it. And then he would decide about taking it, if they got that far.

She came back, handed him the key silently, put the empty box in the back of the van and looked straight ahead as he started, left the curb, got back into traffic, and headed south. She looked like someone in shock.

They were still heading toward Washington, now on Highway 1. He could still change his mind; this might still be a trap, she kept thinking, but she no longer believed that. He was too frightened. He had got her into it all, a year ago, and now he was her ally … She had hesitated at the mailbox. She had watched her hand as if she never had seen it before, doubted its function. It had refused to move for what had seemed a long time. Her ally … as long as she had the gun in her pocket, her hand close to it. Then she had willed her hand to move, to drop in the first of the envelopes, forced her fingers to release them … She would kill him if she had to, if this was a trap. Then the next batch had slid down, vanished without a sound to indicate when they hit. How many other letters had been in the box? Nearly full? Almost empty? How long to sort through them? To separate them by zip codes, start them on their way? To sort through them and pull out the ones with the M&S logo on them? To open them, in a secret room somewhere, burn them? File them? What would they do with them? Her hand had acted as if it no longer had been connected with her mind, her will, her nervous system. It had not wanted to release the envelopes.

'Taney, pay attention. I asked you if you want to mail any of them in Washington.'

'No.'

'Okay. We stay on One until we go through Baltimore. We'll make as many stops as you want there, and then we get on Interstate Ninety-five and head south, bypass Washington, and back to One. Okay?'

It was easier in Baltimore. Resolutely she held the envelopes over the chute, dropped them, and went back to the van. At the next stop, he got out and mailed a batch; he took the key with him. Soon after that they stopped for gas, to use the rest rooms. When she left, she took the key with her; when he left, he carried it. Partners, she thought soberly.

They skirted Washington, headed for Richmond. Lasater was getting very tired, but when she offered to drive, he refused. He did not like being driven by a woman. It was three in the morning, and it had been a very busy day for him, he thought. That morning and the trip to the clinic now seemed another lifetime, a distant past. Edging his way toward the Pennsylvania mountains seemed a dream fantasy, nothing directly connected to him. The road before him wavered, and he jerked upright.

'I came looking for a sign,' he said, to keep himself from falling asleep. 'Funny, that's how I thought of it, looking for a sign, and then I saw that fancy sign to the bird refuge and I knew that was it. You believe in coincidence? Fate?'

'I don't know. Sometimes.'

'Look, Lyle, I'm falling asleep. Talk to me, sing, tell jokes. Something. Or listen to me talk, and now and then agree with me, or argue with me.'

'Let me drive.'

'I'm not that sleepy yet.'

'Why did you almost kill someone?'

He told her about Rawleigh, about Alex, about working with Alex for twenty years, give or take a little. She asked questions and he answered them. No point in lying to her, he thought, no point in hiding anything from her. He told her the truth, and he grinned as he realized that she probably believed none of it. For the first time since he had met her, he was telling her the straight truth, and she doubted every word.

'Why are you staying with me?'

'Maybe I can keep you out of Rawleigh's hands, away from Scanlon, and if I do, and if the kid stays in the clear, eventually you'll head for him, and I'll tag along. He has the samples, doesn't he?' She made no response. He did not blame her. As far as she was concerned, he was still an unknown factor, not someone to hire to guard her life savings.

She was thinking that she understood him in a way she never had been able to understand Saul and Carmen. She knew Lasater's motives, his fears. He was harsh and cruel and selfish; he had nothing but contempt for anyone who got in his way, anyone he used. It was evident that nearly killing his onetime friend meant nothing to him, and yet, she understood him. He was like a child in his amoral unconcern for anyone else. He was with her now simply because he thought he had a better chance with her to get the serum than he would have had with his own agency. But now, for the first time, she felt some doubt that it was quite that simple, that he was quite that simple. He had been genuinely afraid of war, as afraid of it as she was, as Saul was, or Carmen. And he had been compelled to choose her because of that fear, not because of the serum. As far as he knew there was no chance of getting it through her, not for any foreseeable future.

'How'd you manage the switch in Amsterdam?' he asked suddenly, his voice too loud, making an obvious effort to fight his fatigue.

She told him and he laughed. 'Do you want more coffee?' she asked then. 'There's another sandwich, I think, if you want that.'

'Yeah. Anything. The coffee's cold, but what the hell, it's still full of caffeine.'

They mailed the last of the envelopes in a small town north of Raleigh, south of Richmond. Neither knew where it was. It was six-thirty in the morning. The sky was lightening, but there were thick clouds, the light was bleak and cold.

Lasater sat with his hands on the steering wheel, so tired he felt he could not lift his foot to the accelerator, could not push it on the clutch, shift gears.

'You did it, sweetheart,' he said when she took her seat, locked her door. 'Job's well done. Let's find someplace in the hills to hide and get some sleep.'

She shook her head. 'I can't. There's something else I have to do first, but not yet. Let's have some breakfast and then drive on to Raleigh and I'll finish there. You can do anything you want after that.'

'When will you be finished?'

'Right after ten.'

He sighed. 'I'll find a cafe or something. You know, they serve grits with breakfast in this part of the country. Pretty good, too. Can't stand them anywhere else, but down here, they're pretty good. Must be the way they cook them.'

'After we eat,' she said, 'I'll drive. You might kill us both, you're so sleepy.'

'Kill you? Not a chance.'

'You could kill me,' she said. 'It isn't a magic cure-all.' But it was, he knew. She looked mildly tired, nothing drastic, nothing to make anyone feel concern over her, while he, on the other hand, must be looking like death on the prowl. Breakfast would help, but not enough. 'Okay, okay,' he said. 'I'll catch a nap and you take us on to Raleigh. Get there about nine-thirty or so, and you can do your last little chore.'

It had to be a phone call, there was nothing left to mail, and she had had no set destination, no meeting with anyone in mind. Call the old man and report the job was done? Why not now, why at ten? Check to see if the mail actually got delivered? Not so soon; no one would expect delivery until another day, two days even. More if it was heading for the West Coast ... West Coast! That was it. Ten here, seven there. A call to the lover boy? To other accomplices? Tell them this part was done, go ahead with the next step? He did not ask; he knew she would not tell him. Again, he did not blame her.

They had breakfast in a small roadside restaurant and, on the way out, he picked up an Atlanta paper. She was an okay driver, but he could not sleep, as he had known. After trying for a while, he gave it up and started to read the paper. Nothing about the flu in Washington. Nothing about the president, the vice president. Nothing about anything in particular. He flipped pages and then stopped.

The Russians had announced a major flu epidemic in the USSR. The strain had not yet been isolated and meanwhile they were curtailing travel to limit the spread of the disease, said to be the most virulent ever to surface.

He read the scant item again, then read it aloud and watched her knuckles go white as she gripped the steering wheel harder.

'That's it, isn't it?'

She nodded. 'Yuri thinks so. We all think so. They can't hide the fact of death on that scale, they had to announce something.'

'How much time will it take them?'

'I don't know. How many have they inoculated? How long ago? We don't know. Fever starts within hours, but it takes twenty-four hours for the illness to become really bad, and then two or three days before recovery even begins. People can die any time after the inoculation, a few hours, two days, three days ...'

He folded the paper carefully and put it on the floor in the back of the van. Neither spoke again until they came to a stop at a mall in Raleigh.

She started to get out and he caught her wrist. 'You know they have Werther under wraps. If you call him, they'll trace the call. You know that.'

She nodded. 'How long does it take?'

'Not as long as you think. They'll be ready, waiting.'

'I have to call him,' she whispered. There was still a chance that he had convinced the government people that they had to distribute it themselves, that it was the only way to avert war. She had to try.

'If anyone stalls you, says he's in the john or something, asks you to wait, hang up. You can try again in a few minutes. But don't wait on the line.'

'Yes, I know.'

'Do you have a signal arranged? Something that will be quick?'

'No more than a second or two.'

He chewed his lip, hating it, not trusting it. Finally he released her wrist and watched her walk to the pay telephone.

She dialed the number, deposited coins, and waited. For what seemed a long time it did not even ring and the line was filled with noise. Maybe the phones were still out. Then it rang. She counted and knew they were tracing it. Saul would have answered instantly, expecting her call now, ready for it. She closed her eyes, eight ... nine ...

'Hello.'

'Saul, it's Lyle. Are you all right?'

'My dear! How good to hear your voice. We've had the most terrible storm—'

'Welcome, chaos,' she whispered, her eyes closed hard, and she hung up.

'Come on, let's get the hell out of here!' Lasater started to pull her away from the booth.

'Not yet. I have to make one more call.'

'From another phone. Down the road somewhere. Come on!'

This time he drove. He stopped at a gas station that had a phone booth. 'I'll fill it up while you call. It isn't that number again, is it?' She shook her head. 'Good. I'm going in that little store over there and buy some stuff to eat. No more restaurants for us, no more public appearances. Come on over there when you're finished.'

It was five minutes before ten. She listened to the distant phone ringing, ringing, and then stop ringing.

'Yes?' Carmen's voice.

She took a deep breath, heard a waver in her voice when she said, 'Carmen, they have Saul and Yuri. I mailed the envelopes. Saul said you have to carry through.'

'Oh God. Are you all right?'

'Yes. But they may have traced a call I just made to Pennsylvania.'

'Okay. Hide, Lyle. Stay out of their hands if you can. I'll see you when it's over. I love you, Lyle.'

'I love you!' she cried. 'Be careful. Carmen, be careful!'

Everyone kept telling her to stay out of their hands. They thought she might tell everything if they caught her, and she was not certain she would not talk. If they said, watch us do this to Saul, watch him sweat, writhe ... Lasater would tell them everything, she thought suddenly. He would have to just to save himself, get a promise from them that he could have the in-oculation. He might know they would lie to him about it, but he would have to try one last time. She understood that. He had worked with her through the night, but if they failed, if they were picked up, he would have to think first of himself, pretend to believe any promise they made to him. Would he remember which post offices they had stopped at? She was afraid he might.

She found him in the store, at the check-out counter, and shook her head when he asked if she wanted anything. They were going out the door when they heard a siren, not far away, and then another more distant one.

Abruptly he turned and nearly pushed her inside the store again. 'We forgot cookies for the kids. You go pick them out.' Thank God she wasn't stupid, he thought, when she glanced outside and then turned quickly and went to the back of the store. A police cruiser was passing slowly, the cop in the passenger seat studying the cars parked in the small lot.

Okay, he thought darkly. They didn't know the make of the car yet; that was a plus. But they would have her description, and that was most defi-nitely not a plus. At least Werther had had enough sense to have Ohio plates on the van, another plus. The fact that local cops were already searching was bad, very bad. The state police would cover highways leading from town; the county sheriff's department probably would take care of the country roads. That could be very bad indeed. To them an out-of-state license plate might be cause enough to stop the van. So he would switch, he decided.

He was grim when they got inside the van again. 'You'll have to stay in the back,' he said brusquely. 'I'll get a few tools, and road maps for this county, anything I can find for south of here. You keep out of sight.'

'You think they're already putting up roadblocks?'

'You bet your sweet ass. It's been over twenty minutes, plenty of time if they were ready to start the machine. And they were.'

She went to the rear of the van and closed the curtain between them and made no comment at his next stops. He removed a license plate from a car parked at the edge of the vast lot at a shopping mall, the area where the employees had to park. With any luck, he thought, no one would notice until the next day; it would be dark, he hoped, by the time the clerk, or whoever, knocked off, came out to get in the old buggy, head for the stable. He backed into a parking space bordered by hedges, and there put on the stolen plate. Now he felt better.

His other purchases included a compass and a dozen county maps. He studied one carefully and when he left town he went by way of city streets to county lanes, to a dirt road that wound westward. Once he glimpsed a police car parked behind a sign. In the distance there were sirens now and then for a short while. Pulling some poor sucker over, he thought and grinned. He pitied anyone from Pennsylvania heading south that day.

He stopped finally in a deep wood, hidden under a canopy of pine branches. She slipped into her own seat again.

'I could drive now,' she said.

He shook his head. 'We'll go on this afternoon. Do most of our driving at night from now on. But first some sleep. I want to give you the address of my parents, a place you can go if we get separated and you're still able to go anywhere. Tell my old man the truth. He likes the truth.' He wrote out the address, handed the slip of paper to her.

'You think they're going to catch us, don't you?'

'Yeah, I think so. They've done everything but call out the Marines, and they'll probably get around to that too. I'm counting on your ignorance, honey. They know you're dumb. You don't know shit about hiding; that may save us. They won't look for you on dirt roads out in the boonies. I hope that's how they figure you. If we do see a roadblock and can't avoid it, we split. I stick with the car, you hoof it to the nearest place you can find to dig in. They'll go after the car. I'll tell them you ran out on me in Raleigh.'

'What will they do to you?'

He yawned. 'You must be kidding. They really hate it if their own people give them trouble. They'll look on me as one of them, one who went bad. Eventually I'll probably talk, and then I'll join the list of the missing. Simple.'

'You think they'll kill you?'

He was eyeing the back of the van dubiously. The floor was carpeted; it would have to do. His coat would help some, and the blanket. He worked his way over the gear shift, to the rear.

'No, they won't kill me. They'll ask questions, day after day after day. I can imagine the scenario: year after year getting a little grayer, more stooped, more tired, while they come in fresh-cheeked and shiny-eyed and rub it in.'

'You've decided you would use it?'

'Yeah, I'd try it.'

And he would tell them everything, sooner rather than later, she thought distantly. His last chance at getting it, he would think, and he would make a deal with them. And then they would renege. In her mind some lines of T. S. Eliot's repeated over and over: *I grow old ... I grow old ... I shall wear the bottoms of my trousers rolled.*

She thought of the gun in her pocket and rejected it. Not now. Not after he had helped her. He was rearranging the bags of food, the empty boxes they had not got rid of. She swung around and joined him, sat back on her heels.

'Lasater, I have it. I can give it to you.'

31

At ten-thirty Rawleigh was ordered to bring most of his men back to Washington, along with Werther/Markham. Only the computer specialists were left behind, still trying to unravel the program. In the CIA building Saul was locked in a room along with two fresh interrogators. Down the corridor Seymour Oliver was undergoing interrogation; farther down Dan Malone was still being questioned.

Scanlon and Rawleigh attended a three-hour conference with various secretaries, generals, admirals, and congressmen. It became a shouting match very quickly.

At one, Seymour Oliver was taken away to confer with the president at a secret location.

Rawleigh sat in his office at four and cursed silently. He had got up with a headache; minute by minute it had grown worse. The woman was still missing; none of the others had been located. No one knew if the letters they had found in Philadelphia were the end of that. No one knew if other letters had been mailed. None had been mailed from Raleigh, where she had stopped to make her phone call. The reports from Russia indicated that the flu epidemic was rampant in Moscow, in Leningrad, in several other major cities, that it had spread to the armed forces. Here, the vice president was seriously ill, running a high fever; the secretary of the treasury was ill; two generals had become ill ... The Joint Chiefs were in chaotic disorder, screaming at each other like madmen. If they caught the rest of the gang of terrorists, they would go forward with their plan, but not until then, not until they found the samples the letters talked about. No announcements, no leaks ... And the reporters were like piranhas, aware that something was happening, schooling hungrily, pressing everyone, offering rewards ...

He turned on the closed-circuit television and studied Werther/Markham who was sitting upright in a straight chair, calm, at ease, only slightly tired from his all-night ordeal. Doerring was in bed somewhere, exhausted, feverish, the two new men were already showing twitches of weariness. The old man was serene.

He flipped to the other room where Dan Malone was being questioned. His style was different; he had been talkative from the start, only he never said anything. He bantered with his interrogators, kidded them, told them jokes, told them of his various travels throughout the world. And said nothing.

He too looked as if he had been sleeping regularly, eating regularly, got in his daily nap ... There were slight circles under his eyes, and he was not quite as quick as he had been, had begun to stammer now and then, but it was an insignificant change.

Rawleigh turned the set off and drummed his fingers on his desk. Fifty-fifty, he thought. Not good odds, not good enough, but, by God, those two men had gambled. Others had gambled. And when the gamble paid off, it paid big, very, very big. But not for Ralph Wilders, who had been the secretary of defense. For him it had not paid off.

Scanlon was ready to bolt, he knew. This was turning out to be too much for him. He would snatch himself some of the stuff and run, stare at it until he got up his nerve to give it a go. Who else would leave, or yield to the irresistible promise of the serum? He began to sort them out, and when he finished, he knew the government would fall apart. It was too big, no one could handle this. With the president hiding, the vice president maybe dying, maybe not, who would take over? His fingers were no longer tapping, had become very quiet as he stared at the far wall thinking. The military would seize the government, he thought with incredulity. It would come to that.

The wall was moving toward him, back again. He blinked and shook his head, making it ache unbearably. His mouth was dry, his eyes burned. He had a fever, he thought fretfully, now of all times, he was coming down with something. Probably the same cold that Alex Radek had been suffering from. He closed his eyes for a minute or two, but when he opened them again, he found that he was having trouble focusing. It was time to go home, he thought distinctly. Let them bomb each other to hell and be gone, he wanted to go home. He had not been ill for years, fifteen years, twenty? He could not remember the last cold he had caught, the last time he had run a fever. Damn Alex Radek, he thought, damn his eyes; he almost hoped he had died during the day. He stood up shakily, went to his washroom and drank down a glass of water, then another.

Go home, he thought again. Aunt Jane would know what to do. If he had to die, he wanted to die at home, where his father had died, his grandfather had died, where all his family went to die, to be born, to live ... He pulled on his coat and walked from his private office into the anteroom where Mathew

Sedgehorn was speaking on the phone. Mathew looked at him in surprise.

'Going home,' he said, walking across the room.

'But sir, Mr. Scanlon has called for another meeting in an hour.'

'Tell him I'm going home.' He walked out, let the door close itself after him.

Mathew was already dialing Mr. Scanlon's number.

At six the rumor went around that nearly every man who had gone to the Pennsylvania hideout had come down with a mysterious disease. They were taken to the communicable disease wing of Walter Reed Hospital and put under top secret security. Those who were still well began a debriefing that was to go on through the night.

The rumor started life no bigger than a whisper of air, but soon swirled to hurricane size and strength; no one in official Washington failed to hear several versions of it every fifteen minutes or so.

The first leaks made the eleven o'clock newscasts. The Russian flu was devastating Washington, the report went, and there were hints of biological warfare.

At twelve the attorney general announced to staff that the president was returning within three to four hours. His major speech writers were to prepare texts for several alternate announcements. It was not known yet which one he would decide to deliver.

Belatedly the interrogators were pulled out of Saul's room and he was left alone for the first time. Immediately he stretched out on the narrow sofa in the office and went to sleep.

The computer men were taken out of the Pennsylvania laboratory and the building was quarantined until a team of experts could be assembled to track down the source of the disease.

The radio stations had been off the air for hours. There had been no follow-up story about the flu that was raging in Washington. Lyle turned the knob back and forth, finally gave it up. Lasater was sleeping in the back of the van while she drove; now and then she could hear him groan or whisper or make an incoherent sound. His fever was very high; he was having fever dreams. She hoped they were not as frightening as hers had been, but from the sounds he made she suspected they were, or even more so.

She was desperately tired, but dared not stop now. They were so close to his parents' home, another two hours, three at the most, and she could hand him over to their care, and go someplace and sleep and sleep. She jerked her eyes wide open and turned on the radio again, welcoming even the static as a diversion. If it had not been for him, she would not have made it, she knew. He was wise about roadblocks, about back roads, county roads, dirt roads, when to get back on a real highway. He was mumbling again. He needed a bed, cool water, his face wiped off with a cool cloth ... She drove on, forcing herself to concentrate on the road, on staying on her side, on approaching lights that came very rarely now. Today the envelopes would be delivered, the samples would be delivered, people would start using it. Today was the end of the world. The beginning of a new world. Long live the world, she whispered to herself.

She stopped at the condominium at six in the morning. The air was cold and still, the sky clear with stars shining although the sun was rising also. Pelicans flew toward the gulf; a heron lifted from the lawn before the massive building; no person was in sight anywhere.

When she got out of the van the earth seemed to continue to move under her. She was uncertain in her walk, steadied herself with a railing that had been designed for just that purpose. There was a sleepy-eyed security man who watched her suspiciously as she called the Lasater apartment, waited for an answer.

He was even more suspicious when she went back out and brought in Lasater, virtually holding him upright, supporting his weight, guiding him.

'He's been very ill,' she said. 'He's still weak from it.'

He did not offer to help; rather, he backed away from Lasater and watched closely until they were inside the elevator, the door closed. Lasater clutched the rail in the elevator, weaving back and forth.

'I dreamed you cut your hair all the way off,' he said, in a surprisingly clear voice. 'I cried. It's so soft. I thought it would be, back at the coast, I thought it would be so soft.' He closed his eyes and leaned his head against the wall.

Mr. and Mrs. Lasater were in their nightclothes. His hair was tousled from sleep, but she had run a comb through hers. They were white-headed, suntanned to a deep rich brown, and frightened-looking.

'Is he running from someone?' Mr. Lasater asked, helping her get him inside. 'This way. There's an extra room.'

'Yes, he's wanted. He's very ill. He needs care ...'

'We'll take care of him until he's well,' Mrs. Lasater said, following closely, her gaze on her son, worry and fear creasing her face. 'Is he dying? He needs a doctor, the hospital.'

'That won't help him. Please, just put him to bed, try to ease his pain, his fever.'

When they got him to the bed, and she no longer had to support him, she swayed, and found herself being guided to the other bedroom, their room. Mr. Lasater was firm in his insistence that she sleep for a bit. She sank down to their bed gratefully and did not remember stretching out, closing her eyes.

Jeremy Troy sat at his desk in the Oval Office and scowled at Seymour Oliver, whom he had known for nearly all his life. They had gone to the same summer camps, the same prep school, had gone on to Harvard together. Hell, they had rowed on the same team. He had believed a man could trust someone he had known that long, someone who had rowed with him. The Oval Office was crowded, but he ignored most of them and concentrated on Seymour Oliver, and on Werther/Markham, whatever he was called, when he arrived. They were the only ones in the room who were not threatening to go out with a stroke any minute.

Werther bowed respectfully and waited in silence as President Troy studied him. They had brought his clothes, had allowed him a shower and shave that morning. He looked rested, and he looked calm, as if he was the one in charge, and he already knew the outcome.

'Seymour suggested I ask you directly how you infected those men in your place. And how you intend to distribute samples of your serum to the entire country.'

General Strand coughed and Yancy moved in closer; otherwise everyone was quiet for the moment. Werther/Markham glanced at his watch. It was going on nine.

'If your mail has been delivered yet, you'll discover our delivery system,' Werther/Markham said. 'I believe the White House was on the list.'

Clarendon raced to the door, left. No one else moved.

'As to how I infected your people who invaded my property, I didn't. If they stole my soap, or lotions, or shaving creams, anything of the sort and used them, they infected themselves, I'm afraid. I did not invite them to use my personal toilet articles.'

'My God,' someone across the room said. He moved away from the window where he had been standing, came around the attorney general. It was Hanford Wilkes. 'You mixed it with a solvent? Something to carry it into the lymphatic system?'

'Exactly,' Werther/Markham said. 'Hanford Wilkes? How do you do.'

'I thought soap was antibacterial,' someone objected.

'This isn't bacterial, it's RNA, and our soap is exquisitely pure, completely organic, a perfect medium for it.'

Scanlon and Senator Fullerton were whispering together. The senator said, 'We think we can stop the mail deliveries today, if we act immediately, Mr. President. It will take an executive order ...'

Werther/Markham said gently, 'The mail has been delivered up and down the entire East Coast, in most of the interior. It's much too late, I'm certain, to stop enough to matter.'

'Issue a warning, then. Say it's germ warfare, terrorists have sent it out to kill the American people. You can stop this right here, Jeremy! But you have to do it now!'

Werther/Markham was eyeing him curiously. 'You'd rather go to war?'

'Nobody wants war! But this may be the last chance we'll have in this generation to beat them down to their knees!'

Others were talking now, some were shouting. Wilkes was talking to Oliver; Werther was standing before the wide desk, partly facing the room, watching, listening. He turned back to the president.

'It's too late,' he repeated firmly. 'It's out and it can't be put back in. You can either disown the whole thing, or you can announce it for what it is, offer this country's help to all people to make it available worldwide.'

Clarendon rushed back in then, carrying a small box containing samples of the soaps and lotions, each individually wrapped, the size that hotels issue to guests. He dumped the box out on the president's desk.

'It's out,' Werther said once more. 'There are explicit warnings on the back of each package, but I doubt that many people will pay very much attention to them.'

There was a scramble for the packets. Senator Fullerton read part of the warning aloud: 'This product will cause a serious reaction in the human body. There will be fever and chills that will last for a period of one to three days. Those who recover will find they are immune to bacterial and viral diseases, to diseases of aging. Approximately half of those who use this product will die of the fever.' He looked at Werther venomously. 'You're killing them! You're an insane mass murderer!'

'Would it be more sane to kill them with bombs?'

'You'll hang for this! Hanging's too good for you—'

'Harry!' President Troy's voice was sharp. 'Knock it off, will you? How many of those samples did your people put in the mail?'

'We were aiming for five million in the States, and of course there are mailings in Europe, Asia, South America ... Nearly ten million altogether, I think. I haven't received any figures yet.'

'Five million!' President Troy repeated. He was ashen-faced. 'And half of them will die?'

'They won't all use the products,' Saul said. 'From our previous mailings of samples, our own studies, we think that one out of five may use them right away, perhaps one out of six. People put them down, forget them, toss them out. Of course, articles will start appearing simultaneously, and they may cause more usage, or perhaps less. We had no way of knowing in advance.'

'One out of five. A million. And half of them ... God help us! And this, this immunity is passed sexually? Isn't that what your information sheets claim?'

He nodded.

'We can isolate all those who use the stuff,' Fullerton said fiercely. 'We can find them and put them in camps, for their own protection—'

He leaned on the president's desk, pushed the samples aside. 'You can't back out now, Jeremy! For God's sake, don't go chicken on us now!'

'Fuck off, Harry! Don't you understand it's a whole new game! Everything's changed!'

'Why? Last week you were with us one hundred percent! Now you're waving a white flag. Why?'

'Last week I didn't think there was an alternative. They were going to push the button, or we were. Now, no one's going to push it. That's what's different!'

'Right now we've got a window! They're vulnerable, they're helpless with so many of their people sick. Twenty-four hours, that's all it would take! Jesus Christ, Jeremy! Twenty-four hours!'

'Get the fuck out of here!'

Fullerton stamped to the door, paused to yell at Werther, 'You're not free yet, old man! I want you, and I'm going to get you! Just you wait and see!'

Before the door was closed behind him, President Troy began to give orders. 'Wilkes, take these two with you, prepare a detailed statement of effects, what to do for those stricken, what to expect, the works. Brief the Surgeon General, NIH. General Strand, report back to the Joint Chiefs and tell them we're preparing a mass inoculation of our armed forces just as fast as the stuff can be prepared and shipped. You're going to need more doctors for the duration of the illness. It will have to be done in sections, figure out the optimum method. God, I have to call the Premier! I wonder if that son of a bitch has already had his.'

When the office was clear, except for his aide, Clarendon, he counted the samples on his desk.

'How many were there originally?'

'Twenty. Are some missing?'

He laughed and tossed a sample of shaving lotion to Clarendon. 'We have nine now, counting that one.' He examined them briefly, then slipped a bar of soap into his pocket. 'Well, let's get on with it.'

32

In Denver, Mavis Oblatney heard the mail hit the floor in the hall and shuffled out in her robe and slippers to collect it. Bills. A slick advertising pamphlet. A sample of something. She carried them back to the kitchen where Mike, finished with breakfast, was tying his boots, ready to go to work.

'Anything?'

'Nope. The usual.' She glanced at the advertising pamphlet. Expensive furniture, tableware … Nothing for them. The bills could wait for payday. She knew the amount of each one without opening them. She unwrapped the soap sample. It smelled nice. As soon as Mike left she would have her shower, get to work at ten … She yawned and put the soap down, gathered up the ad, and the soap wrapper, and tossed them into the trash can.

At ten minutes past ten, in the department store where she worked, she heard that the soap samples were all poison, or an immortality treatment, or part of a conspiracy …

In Buffalo, Stuart Poulson hooted with laughter when he read the warning on the hand lotion sample. 'Hey, listen to this! You'll be immune to all kinds of disease if you use this junk!'

Ann Sneed took the sample from his hand and read it for herself. She squeezed some of the lotion from the tube and, laughing, chased him through the apartment to the bedroom where she smeared it on his cheeks, his neck, his stomach, his penis. Laughing, they tumbled back into bed together.

In Los Angeles, Terry Grimes put the lotion on her dining room table and considered it. She had heard the president's message that morning, and here was one of the samples he had talked about. She was sixty, lived alone, and wondered if she cared one way or the other. If Nicky were here with her, now that would be different. Eight years too late for Nicky. The president had warned people not to use the stuff, to turn it in if they received it. The FDA had not approved it. She laughed at that one. The FDA! All morning the sample remained on the dining room table that had not been used for eight years. In midafternoon, holding a glass of gin with one ice cube in it, she considered it yet again. Hand lotion with a nice fragrance. There was no one here to take care of her when she became ill, she thought, and shrugged that away. She could take care of herself. But was there any point in it? That was the hard one. She wandered out, sipping her gin. It was midnight when she finally rubbed the lotion on both hands, over her elbows.

In Detroit, Eugene Jones skipped first period, U.S. History, to break into old man Henson's apartment. Everyone knew the old fool kept money there, he never went to the bank, and always had cash. Eugene searched rapidly and found nothing. There were only two rooms, the search did not take long. He looked over the few pieces of mail, pocketed the sample of after-shave junk, and fled with nothing more than that to show for his trouble. His old lady would give him hell for skipping again, he'd have to forge an excuse … That night when he cleaned up to go out, he used the after-shave lotion, decided he didn't like the smell, and washed it off again. He kept smelling it right up until his fever tumbled into nightmares.

In Lexington, Susan Kreschner put the sample down in the middle of the table and said dramatically, 'There is our salvation!'

Her sisters, Leigh and Nancy, looked bored; her brother, Walter, did not look up at all. He was reading the paper. Their parents had left them alone for the first time ever; Susan, the youngest, was sixteen.

'It's what they were talking about on television,' Susan said confidently. 'Really. Look at the warning on it. It's the hand lotion they warned everyone not to use.'

Walter snatched it up and examined it, read the label. 'Where'd it come from?'

'It was in the mail. Just like the president said. Addressed to Occupant. That's us, or at least me.'

'You crazy or something? You're not going to touch this stuff!'

'I knew you would take that attitude,' she said and held up both hands. 'I already used it. My plan is to be the first girl in the area to have it, and then go into business. I can sell a fuck for ten, twenty dollars ...'

Walter knocked his chair over rising, coming at her, his face dark with anger. She ran away laughing at him.

'I will, though! Just you wait and see!'

In Atlanta, Bob and Martha Alward examined the soap without touching it, then pushed it into a plastic bag, using the wrapper, being careful not to get any on their fingers.

'What will we do with it?' Martha asked.

'Throw it away, say nothing to anyone. If we turn it in like they said on television, they'll ask questions, pry, come back again and again. Toss it out.'

'Maybe we should just put it away until they tell us more about it ...'

'You crazy or something? No more questions! Ever!' The ghost of his first wife drifted between them, invisible, silent, but there. He picked up the plastic bag and threw it into the garbage can. Later, when he went out for his walk, she pulled it out again, washed it off, and put the package away carefully in her jewelry drawer.

In Missoula, Sylvia Loos looked at the soap, studied her face in the mirror, and, sighing, threw the soap away and never gave it another thought. Her cleaning lady found it the next morning, recognized it for what it was, and took it home where her boyfriend melted it down along with half a dozen bars of regular soap and sold them all for five dollars each. He made fifty bars of soap altogether. They had not read the article that claimed that any temperature above one hundred seven degrees F. would destroy the RNA.

In San Francisco, Jimmie Lee and his girlfriend, Doris, tossed a coin to see which one would use the lotion first. The other would be nurse, and in turn be nursed. If she died, Jimmie Lee promised, he would kill himself. Gently he helped her smooth it over her skin.

In Boston, Joseph Gartman slapped his wife Hilda when she suggested they turn it in, as the president had asked people to do. Turn in a gold mine? Turn in eternity? Turn in pills, medicines, hospitals, doctors? Turn in their whole goddamn future? The problem was when, he brooded. Not this week. He had that deal with Horstt. Not next week either. Contracts would be back from the lawyers, there was the luncheon meeting to celebrate the new acquisition ...

In Paris, in Rome, in London, Buenos Aires, Rio, La Paz, Mexico City, Beirut, Johannesburg, Madras ... The same scenes played over and over, the same decisions were being made, the gamble accepted ...

The next day the dying began.

33

Lyle drove aimlessly. Mr. and Mrs. Lasater had asked her to stay with them until their son recovered, but there had been no conviction in their voices. A friend of his, they had implied, could be no friend of theirs. They had asked no questions; she had volunteered nothing, but they had watched television, read the papers; they knew. She had left after one glance at Lasater, who had been delirious.

Now she was driving nowhere in particular. They hoped he would die, she knew, and pitied them and he. Once she stopped on the beach road, parked, and walked for several hours. The sun was shining, but a bitter wind blew and it was very cold; no one else was walking.

She listened to the radio most of the first day. They were hashing it out over and over, repeating themselves endlessly. Late in the day they began to have panels of experts. Economists, doctors, educators, politicans ... When she turned off the radio she could not remember what she had heard.

That night when it became dark, she was in northern Florida, near no town. She found a parking spot away from the highway and crawled into the sleeping bag in the rear of the van and slept. At dawn she was driving again, her mind still blank, yesterday a blank. Sleep had been fitful, dream-ridden.

She would need food, she thought suddenly, and realized she could not remember when she had eaten. At the Lasaters' she had had something; she could not remember what.

Food. And a stove to cook on, a pan or two, dishes. Blue jeans and boots. Warm jacket. She might as well spend the paper money; everything was going to smash, very soon no one would want it. She shook her head at the idea, but could not deny that she believed it. She turned on the radio again, and this time she listened.

'... orderly sequence. Hospitals, police stations, schools will all be used to dispense the serum. An effort will be made to ensure that no more than one family member at a time receive the inoculation—' She switched the station.

'... riots. In Rome the crowd has continued to swell, but it is an orderly crowd, not a mob. The Pope will speak in two hours—'

'... martial law. The fires are still out of control, but the National Guard has manned the fire-fighting equipment now—'

'... repeat, not. Do not allow any child under eight to touch the lotions or the soap. Seriously ill people should not use the material until they are recovered. If you develop a fever, go to bed, rest, take fluids. During the first days of the illness aspirins should be used to fight the fever—'

She turned it off. She was on an interstate highway. The sun was behind her now; she was driving west. It was as good a direction as any.

She stopped in Tallahassee for gas and found a supermarket. There had not been a run on food yet, but there would be. When people began to re- alize that truckers would be ill and dying, airlines not functioning, trains stalled because the crews were feverish ... She stocked up on everything she could think of for the next month. She bought a camp stove and fuel, and an icebox and ice. At a shopping center she bought jeans and shirts, a sweater, jacket, warm socks ... Her last purchase was a coffeepot that plugged into the cigarette lighter. It was on sale, half price, after-Christmas clearance. The clerk was flushed-looking. Lyle nearly ran from the store, shoved the coffeepot back with the clutter of boxes and bags, and began driving again. Now she knew why she had purchased the kinds of things she had. She would not enter another city if she could avoid it. By tomorrow it would be chaotic.

'... special prosecutor. The investigation will proceed along the lines sug- gested earlier by Senator Fullerton. To date there has been no agreement about who the special prosecutor should be. We switch now to Stanley Wyman in Washington for more on this development—'

'... toll continues to rise. The official count is now nine hundred forty- seven. In Topeka the entire family of Jackson Merrick—'

In Pensacola she found a stereo shop that was open, and bought a tape deck and many tapes.

Tristan and Isolde got her across Louisiana.

'... regret this inconvenience, and we all hope our disruption will be of short duration. Meanwhile, all you guys and gals out there, you take care, you hear?—'

There was no open gas station in Beaumont. She waited all night, and when someone appeared, he was a policeman. He gave her directions to a station that would be open from ten until two that afternoon. He advised her to get a couple of five-gallon cans and fill them, also.

She was charged four dollars a gallon for the gas they pumped into her car, and five dollars a gallon for the gas they put in the two five-gallon cans. It had started.

Under the carpet in the back of the van, under the metal floor, there was a box with twenty thousand dollars in gold and silver coins. Saul had insisted that everyone have a stake in gold and silver. Spend the paper first, as long as people will take it, and then use the real money, he had said. Right again, she thought, and realized how little she had thought about him, about Carmen, the others. Maybe they had all been picked up, had given themselves up. She had an address in San Francisco where she could go, to await Carmen, or orders, or something. She would not go there.

Stabat Mater and the *Pachelbel Canon* got her to San Antonio.

'... and Adam lived a hundred and thirty years, and he begat a son in his own likeness ... And the days of Adam after he had begotten Seth were eight hundred. All the days of Seth were nine hundred and twelve. All the days of Enos were nine hundred and five; Mahalaleel, eight hundred ninety-five; Jared, nine hundred sixty-two! I say to you that the Lord gave man those long years in the beginning and He took them away in His wrath! Now He has given them back to us! Praise the Lord, brothers and sisters! Praise—'

Would they all be imprisoned for life? Would they be executed?

'... toll now stands at sixteen thousand—'

'... this insanity. There will be a return to order rather quickly when the government begins distribution. The plan that is evolving is designed to space out the inoculations over the next ten years, you see, and that will prevent another—'

That day she saw the first bumper sticker: FUCK THE FLU! Later she saw another: GIVE A FUCK! PASS IT ON!

'... say how sorry I am for being late. I was busy at the office, trying to sell my stock in the Dispos-A-Diaper Company—'

'... of course, doctors won't be put out of business. There will always be accidents, broken bones, the like. The people I'm concerned about are the children's furniture producers, baby food companies, infant and children's clothing. And elementary school teachers, on up to the college level. We anticipate a lot of new entrants to the universities—'

The Tales of Hoffman saw her through to El Paso.

'... forty thousand. In Boston today the police arrested nine men and women for what was called public prostitution. All nine had recovered from the fever and were engaging in the act of prostitution for amounts in the five hundred dollar range and up—'

In Albuquerque the toll jumped. Two hundred thousand or more.

'… explain it. Many people waited a day or two to hear what was happening before they used the stuff. Some of it was late in getting delivered, no doubt. If it is true that five million samples were distributed, and if it is true that the mortality rate is one half, it will get much, much worse. In every state the National Guard is being put on the alert to help with this crisis, but, of course, many of those men also received samples. The government urges you, if you have those samples on hand, do not use them! The crisis is worldwide—'

What would they do when they ran out of space at the cemetery? She had to pull off the road to wait for her vision to clear. For the next three days she remained in New Mexico, away from any radio station, away from people. Then she started to drive again.

She yearned for a night of unbroken sleep. Every night was the same: she could fall asleep, but she could not stay asleep more than a few hours. She jerked wide awake again and again, with no memory of dreams or nightmares. She wished she could take a pill, sink into oblivion for twenty-four hours, not think, not hear the wind in the window, the radio voices that echoed in her head after the radio was turned off, not hear her own body noises. Simple oblivion. She did not feel especially tired; she felt virtually nothing. She had withdrawn so far that she could not find herself again. She was out there watching, waiting. Maybe she never would come back. Maybe that was the only safe way.

Beethoven's symphonies got her to Phoenix. She did not turn on the radio, listened instead to the Mormon Tabernacle Choir singing Bach cantatas.

In Phoenix many businesses were closed, people looked like zombies. They were in shock, she thought, and drove on.

Las Vegas, Reno, Alturas. She stopped in Alturas and called John Donleavy to ask if his house on the coast was available. It was. He would turn on the electricity, get some wood stacked, leave the key under the loose board on the bottom step.

Now her movements all seemed to have been planned although she had not thought about a destination, had not used a map. She did not even know how long she had been driving.

For the past few days, ever since Phoenix, she had been using the silver for her purchases. In Alturas no one had received a sample, but they had been cut off from the world effectively by the failure of the truckers to keep them supplied. She had to pay ten dollars a gallon for gas. When the attendant saw that she had silver, he gave her a different figure: four dollars eight cents, total. She had not seen a paper, had no idea what the current price of silver was. She paid, and that night when she stopped, she got out some of the gold coins and a hundred dollars in silver.

She would need a poncho, rain pants, rain boots … Now that she knew where she was going, she wanted to be there, perhaps never to leave again. She would want her own bedding, towels ... She drove and made her list and then she listened to Debussy.

Klamath Falls, Chemult, Eugene.

'... open again in a week or ten days. The Emergency Mortgage Act survived its first hurdle today when the spokesman for the Savings and Loan Associations conceded that the organization would not challenge it. And today the New York State Supreme Court ruled that the victims of the serum are not accidental death cases, but suicides. The attorney for the class action suit has already announced that the decision will be appealed immediately to the Supreme Court, as soon as that body reconvenes. In other financial—'

'... thirty million people have died in wars since nineteen forty-five, and twenty million Russians—'

'... hospitals. They cannot accept any more patients. Go to bed—'

'... town of Andrea where the mass burial—'

'... estimated that in the Soviet Union that figure is approaching five mil—'

She shopped in Eugene where the department store was open half days only. She consulted the silver announcement board before she paid for her purchases. When the clerk asked where she was going, she said she was going home.

Nothing had changed in the house, or outside it. Hard rain pounded the roof, the surf sounded close by and loud, the wood stove emitted billows of smoke before it settled down, everything felt clammy and cold.

It was nearly eleven at night before the house was heated enough to open the door to the bedroom, let some of the warmth enter. She had unpacked the van in the rain, and had her clothes draped on chairs drying. She had bought a warm robe and slippers, and now sat near the stove sipping coffee. The world seemed very far away.

Now she surrendered herself to timelessness. Every day she walked the beaches, or climbed the hills until she was exhausted, until her muscles throbbed, until she was certain that this night she would be able to sleep through.

The eagles returned; she watched them briefly, turned and walked away. After that she avoided that section of the hills. She avoided the charred spot where the other house had burned down. If she saw people on the beach, she always turned and walked in the opposite direction.

When her food ran out, she shopped in the village. It was like attending a funeral; she bought enough to last a long time. There were few choices, many of the shelves were empty; she did not care what she ate. At the check-out counter she saw stacks of news magazines. She picked up one of each, and bought a newspaper also.

'You need stamps for the milk and the coffee,' the checker said.

'I'll put them back. I don't have stamps.'

'You better sign up pretty fast. It'll be everything by next month. Gas rationing starts Monday, you know.'

The checker was a survivor; she had the bright eyes, the vivid coloring of those who survived. Eddy, the middle-aged man in an apron who swept up, helped load groceries, he was another survivor. Lyle drove off thinking of Eddy. Would he be sweeping up in ten years, twenty years, a hundred years? She felt her muscles tense with anger at the thought.

The storms came with the frequency she remembered; sometimes she stood on her cliff and watched, sometimes she was inside, sometimes on the beach, or on one of the hills.

It took her many days to read all the magazines and the newspaper. The government was not sending out checks; there was a moratorium on credit collection, on the use of paper money. People had to sign each week for ration coupons and scrip, entire families had to be present in order to be issued both. Deserters who reported back to their units within thirty days would not be prosecuted. The list of senators and representatives who had died was long, and growing; there was no government, only executive orders. The vice president had died; the president had promised not to use the serum during the crisis. Daniel Malone had been named the president's press secretary, and Seymour Oliver his science advisor ...

There were pleas for volunteer survivors to come forward, to assist in caring for the ill, to perform police duties, to form day-care centers ...

She stopped reading midway through an article that described the worldwide chaos that had paralyzed nation after nation, caused governments to fall, threatened new horrors if the nuclear facilities were not maintained ...

She began to take her notebook with her on her walks; she wrote in it on the beach, or under a tree, on the cliffs. One day she saw a group of young people playing on the beach, flying kites, throwing sand at each other. Survivors, unmistakably so. A second group, larger, chased them with sticks and even a rifle. That had started. Saul had predicted that the survivors would be at terrible risk for a time. Those who had not yet used the serum, those who feared it, might try to stop its use, might try to harm, even kill, those who had survived.

The next time she went to the village, the store was closed. The gas station was closed. She found two old men in the tackle shop. They glared at her.

'They're all leaving,' one of them said. 'Won't be no tourists for a long time, no way to make a living here.'

'If I was you, lady,' the other one said brusquely, 'I'd get out too. Your kind ain't too popular around here.'

She drove away slowly. It was time to go, but where? To do what? Start a day-care center? She shook her head angrily. That would simply be another dodge, she knew, and the time had come for her to stop refusing her responsibility. She thought longingly of tramping through the woods with her camera, turning her back on the world again until it had become sane once more. She had reached the campsite overlooking the lagoon and abruptly turned into the drive. She parked and walked to the rail and stood looking at the water far below. A new storm was blowing in, driving the surf high up on the beach, howling through the rocks, but the storm lacked the fury of the winter storms; it was an imitation storm, a feeble attempt after all. Spring had come.

In her mind's eye there came a glimpse of her New York apartment, empty, waiting for her return. She could finish the history of Saul's group. She rejected that also. Another year, another decade even.

All her adult life had revolved around history, and then art, humanity's two attempts to conquer time. We used art, she thought, to carry our present into the future. And we used history to try to give order to what was always chaos. Always. We used history in an attempt to unite memory, to make our collective memory tangible, give it permanence, bestow it with authority, as if the act of writing, the magic of print was enough to make human memory in all its frailty somehow real, to make our existence now somehow more real. We always forget, or refuse to believe, that our history is little more than the nuggets that fall through our psychic filters. And the nuggets themselves are reshaped in the passage, made larger or smaller, prettier or uglier than the experiences they represent. We draw a bold line to separate myth from history, and pretend we no longer know that the line marches through time with us.

And yet, she thought reluctantly, there was a use for history. There was a very real need to be anchored, to know where we have been. She thought of her own survival, the help she had needed, the confusion she had felt. It had taken her more than a year to accept this new reality. Suddenly the rain started, but she did not move yet. She remembered Yuri's reponse to the question: How do you get people who don't want power to take command, lead? 'You make them, that's all.' A world traumatized, dazed, in shock, and a few people who had had enough time to accept the changes. You make them, she repeated to herself. *Something* makes them. She returned to the van and started to drive.

That afternoon she went to see the eagles. She stopped short of where her blind had been last year. They would be too startled, she knew, if she got that close now. Rain was falling, as silent as snow here in the woods where the lichen and mosses glowed and the ferns were high and freshly green. She could not see either of the eagles until suddenly one of them cried, flew into sight, carrying a fish in its talons, and she realized the eggs had hatched.

The sea was restoring the beach now, bringing back the scrubbed sand, rearranging it, a cycle completed. And high in the spur of the dead tree another cycle was completing itself. Suddenly Lyle felt as if she were being overwhelmed, invaded almost, and she knew that her other self that had remained so distant, so untouchable had come back. She no longer could see herself as someone apart, alone, meaningless. She was back. The eagle rose on the side of the nest and stretched his wide wings, lifted into the air, circled, and flew away with such ease and grace that Lyle felt tears start in her eyes. She lifted her face to the rain. It was time to go home.

She began to hurry back down the hillside, running by the time she reached the spot where Saul's house had burned. She had to find him, call him, tell him she was coming home. She splashed through, the creek, clambered up the bank, and stopped. Saul was there, hurrying toward her. She flew the rest of the distance. He held her in the rain and there was the sound of the white water hissing over rocks, and the rhythmic booming of the surf and, high above it all, the cry of the eagle as it flew to its nest. All ordered, necessary, unavoidable.

If you've enjoyed these books and would like to read more, you'll find literally thousands of classic Science Fiction & Fantasy titles through the **SF Gateway**

✳

For the new home of
Science Fiction & Fantasy . . .

✳

For the most comprehensive collection
of classic SF on the internet . . .

✳

Visit the SF Gateway

www.sfgateway.com

Kate Wilhelm (1928–)

Working name of the US writer Katie Gertrude Meridith Wilhelm Knight, born in Ohio in 1928. She started publishing SF in 1956 with 'The Pint-Sized Genie' for *Fantastic*, and continued for some time with relatively straightforward genre stories; it was not until the late 1960s that she began to release the mature stories which have made her reputation as one of the 20th century's finest SF writers. She was married to noted author and critic Damon Knight and together they have had a profound influence beyond their writing, through the Milford Science Fiction Writers' Conference and its offshoot, in which she was directly involved, the Clarion Science Fiction Writers' Workshop. She won the Hugo Award for Best Novel with *Where Late the Sweet Birds Sang*, and has won the Nebula Award three times. Kate Wilhelm lives in Oregon, USA, and still hosts writing workshops.